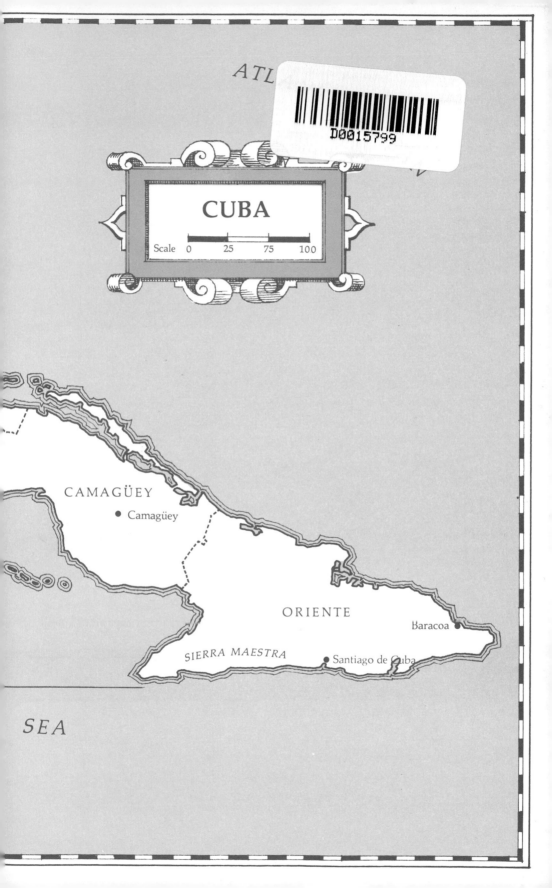

ATL...

CUBA

Scale 0   25   75   100

CAMAGÜEY

● Camagüey

ORIENTE

Baracoa ●

SIERRA MAESTRA   ● Santiago de Cuba

SEA

by Peter Bart
and Denne Bart Petitclerc

SIMON AND SCHUSTER *New York*

DESTINIES

Published by Simon and Schuster
A Division of Gulf & Western Corporation
Simon & Schuster Building
Rockefeller Center
1230 Avenue of the Americas
New York, New York 10020

Designed by Irving Perkins
Manufactured in the United States of America
Printed and bound by The Book Press
1 2 3 4 5 6 7 8 9 10

Library of Congress Cataloging in Publication Data

Bart, Peter.
   Destinies.

   I.   Petitclerc, Denne Bart, joint author.   II.   Title.
PZ4.B2836De 1979   [PS3552.A746]   813'.5'4   79-11701
ISBN 0-671-24677-1

BOOK I

CHAPTER ONE

*I*t seemed she heard her son scream a long time before she could react. *Camilo was caught in a mountainous wave that had come from nowhere, glistening as it rose from the flat horizon of water. She saw his body lifting slowly in the transparent green wall of water, his thin arms and legs spread-eagled, his head thrown back, his hair flared like sea grass just below the boiling crest. For a moment it looked as though he were entombed in crystal.*

Camilo shrieked, and she watched him drifting away, his head just above the surface that reflected the brilliance of the sun like a great blinding mirror. The next thing she knew she was swimming wildly, in panic, through the choking salt water, swimming toward him and reaching out her hand.

Less than five feet away, she saw his face, eyes panicky, arms thrashing. She reached for him, but he moved steadily out with the undertow. Again she reached and touched his hand, then it was gone. His head went under. The next wave lifted him, and she saw his pale shape reappear. His blue eyes stared at her and he opened his mouth: "MOTHER!"

Darkness. One foot entangled in the sheet, which felt damp from the humidity. She reached for the comfort of the man beside her, touching instead the wrinkled sheet, the soft linen of the pillow. The musky male smell of him, cigar tobacco, cologne, permeated the bedclothes. She sat up. Her skin was moist.

"Gustavo? Where are you?"

"Over here . . ." The voice husky, deep.

Now she could feel the cool air on her bare shoulders and breasts. The French doors were open, so when he turned, Gustavo's face showed pale in the moonlight.

"What's the matter, Elizabeth?"

It was so quiet in the room she could hear the clock on the nightstand ticking. She listened to the whisper of cloth and the sound of his bare feet on the tile floor and looked up again to see his face above her.

"Did I wake you?"

"No. I was dreaming . . ."

"You're trembling." He put his hands on her hair. "What is it?"

She paused for a moment to get her voice under control. "I dreamt about Camilo." She pressed her face against the furry warmth of his chest. "What time is it?"

"A little after three. Go back to sleep now."

"It was a terrible dream." She lifted her face and looked at him in the darkness. She tried to tell herself that she was here, in this house, in Miami, beside her husband, and that it was three in the morning and she was safe. But she had a picture in her mind of Camilo's hair slicked to his head, the whites of his eyes showing wide in his dark face, the little swirls in the water as the wave sucked him under. A sick, hollow feeling pulsed in her stomach.

He caressed her hair. "It's gone. Don't be afraid. It's gone."

But it wasn't gone. She awakened at seven o'clock and found that her husband had showered and gone out. The moist steamy smell lingered in the room. Sliding out of bed, she went to the French doors, which opened onto a narrow balcony. The sunlight slanted through the screens and made bright rectangular patterns on the red floor tiles. The tiles felt warm under her bare feet. Even though it was early January in Miami, she knew the day would be muggy and hot. There was not the slightest breath of wind. The tops of the palm trees in the yard hung limp and motionless. Below, she saw Pepín, one of the houseboys, sweeping the flagstones around the swimming pool. The water in the pool caught the morning light and mirrored it up at her so brightly she averted her eyes. There were no clouds on the horizon, only the clear blue radiance of the sky rising above the sea. To her right she saw the flat shape of Virginia

Key with the Australian casuarina trees showing silver-green along the edge of the water.

The sound of her husband's voice caused her to look down. She saw him walk around the corner from the veranda toward his office on the far side of the pool. He had a rolling walk, heavy-shouldered. He was a middle-aged and really handsome man, with thick black hair silvered at the temples. His coat, which she had bought for him in Havana on his birthday three years ago, was of green tropical material and flopped open as he walked. He turned partly around to look up at her.

"Ah, good morning, Elizabeth," he said. "Would you like me to have some coffee sent up?"

"No, thank you, darling. I'm going to take my shower and then come down. I've a lot of things to do today. Any word yet?"

He lifted his right hand to shade his eyes against the sun. "All seems to be going well," he said. "I'll know more this afternoon. Tipton's coming back from Havana. This could be a very interesting week for us, eh? How are you feeling? Did you get some sleep? No more bad dreams?"

"Yes, I'm fine," she lied.

"Good. I'll be gone most of the day. What are your plans for this evening?"

"To have supper with my husband."

"Nine-thirty?"

"You've a date, Dr. Carta."

He blew her a kiss and turned aside, disappearing into the gloom of the office. Elizabeth hesitated, staring at the empty space on the patio where he had stood. Despite the warmth of the sun, she felt herself tremble. She looked out at Biscayne Bay. A sailboat glided silently past the tip of the key. It seemed foolish to have one's flesh crawling from a nightmare in the brilliant sun of a January morning. How stupid and silly of you, she thought to herself.

The boy finished sweeping the patio. She saw him hoist the broom over his shoulder. He started to whistle sweetly as he walked out of sight around the back of the house. Elizabeth felt suspended. She heard the timer click and the pool filter hum mechanically to life, and saw the air bubbles break the slick surface. But the chill gripped her, and for a long moment she stood immobilized, unable to take her mind off it.

To break her mood, she turned from the window and let her gaze sweep the bedroom. She drew comfort from this room. The ceiling was high, with baroque swirls in the white plaster. The French doors gave it light and air. There was an unused fireplace, a mantel, a row of framed family photographs, and a large gold-edged mirror. From where she was standing she could see the mirrored reflection of the palms outside.

It had been the bedroom which prompted her to buy this old mansion. Though the place had not been lived in for years when she first saw it, she felt it would be a perfectly suitable residence in which she and Gustavo could wait out their exile. With a roof of Spanish tile, it stood on Brickell Point between downtown Miami and the Key Biscayne Causeway, surrounded by nearly an acre of lawn, garden and trees, all behind a coral rock wall higher than a man's head. There was a sea wall on the east end, with a dock for small boats. The only other house visible was at the south end of the yard, where the white stucco of their neighbors' mansion peeked through the leaves of the banyan trees.

When she had first arrived from Havana last May, she'd been shown many contemporary houses—squat stucco structures that reminded her of motels. They had depressed her thoroughly. But this old mansion, decaying and mildewed, had kindled vague memories of their big *finca* house outside Havana where she and Gustavo had spent most of their married life. The large rooms, the pool and the patio suited their needs, and some coats of paint had helped. But it had been this bedroom that intrigued her and somehow helped assuage her sense of dislocation.

At first it had surprised her how much she missed Havana. Her first years there, as the American bride of a wealthy Cuban, had been trying ones. But time had blurred the social snubs and awkwardnesses, and all she remembered now were the lovely things. She knew she was being foolishly sentimental about all of it, but she didn't care. She permitted herself that luxury. Sunlit mornings in the garden, the sound of birds singing in the big ceiba trees, the lazy afternoon lunches with Gustavo, the frantic shopping expeditions amid the narrow, teeming cobblestone streets of old Havana, the long warm nights in the master bedroom with the windows opened, the fragrance of the night-blooming jasmine; the dinner guests laughing and chattering endlessly over cigars and coffee, their raucous voices ringing through the house, the aroma of rum and cedar and tobacco; all the parties in the courtyard, with the gay music, the women in their flowered dresses and the men with their white *guayabera* shirts and shiny black hair.

She missed it all. Missed it terribly. She disliked Miami. The city to her seemed to be a mercantile void bathed in tropical sun and almost unbearable humidity—a formless, spiritless place—but it was the place where she had to live as the wife of a Cuban leader in exile. And there were, at least, some side benefits. Miami meant living near her firstborn son, David, who worked at the marine laboratory on Virginia Key. The house David shared with his wife, Robin, was only a twenty-minute drive away. They had not spent much time together since his early teenage years before he left Havana for prep school. Their relations had become awkward—"distanced" was perhaps the better word. She realized, with a nagging sense of regret, that she hardly knew David. He was so quiet really that he appeared self-consciously composed; like a person who had learned to live a long time in an empty house. Elizabeth felt there was a chance, with time, to become closer with her first son. It would never be the sort of almost mystical bond that she felt with her younger, Camilo. Tall, darkly handsome, and blue-eyed, fiercely passionate in his every mood, Camilo took on an unreal quality in her mind. There was something mysterious behind his eyes, she felt, something wild and unpredictable. From his birth Camilo had captured her fancy. But then Camilo too had become estranged.

Their final breach had been so painful it made her ill to think about it even now after so many months. She blamed herself. She should have exercised greater restraint. She should have used her guile to reason with him, even if it meant begging him to let her take Elena, their granddaughter, to Miami with them. If, in his youthful fervor, Camilo was permitting politics to form a wedge between himself and his family, Elizabeth should have been more understanding. But she had overreacted and she was afraid she had lost him.

Now she found herself longing for Camilo desperately. It had been eight months ago. She had been in the garden cutting flowers for the house when he drove into the yard in a jeep. There were two rebel soldiers in the back. They had rifles in their hands and looked very young. She remembered how tall Camilo looked as he stepped out of the jeep, and how thin, and the way his eyes looked at her, and how unfamiliar he seemed with his hair so long and his face bearded. He had come at noon when he knew his father would be in Havana. He told her that she and Gustavo should leave the country as soon as possible, for their own safety. The tone of his voice was urgent, but coldly impersonal. He would take Elena with him, he said, and she sent one of the servants for the child. When she asked him if he would be bringing Elena back, he merely shook his head. Gustavo Carta was persona non grata with the revolutionary government. He had no place in the new society they were building. He must leave Cuba or be eliminated. It was all said with military finality.

His words sent a shock through her. Persona non grata? How? Not only had he fought for the overthrow of Batista, he had risked everything, including his life. How could they do such a thing to him? He was devoting all of his energies to the new government. Wasn't he Castro's Minister of Finance? How dare they? Her son had stood there in his pressed khaki fatigues, his weight on one leg, and looked at her. Because we must, he told her. It was the *we! We?* What did he mean by *we?* Was he part of this decision? He was, he said. There were no alternatives. Carta was finished in Cuba.

"But you?" she had demanded, incredulously. "How can you? He's your father!"

"It is my duty," he told her.

Now, standing in the quiet of her bedroom, her mind breaching the months as though it were a moment ago, Elizabeth saw the hurt expression in her son's eyes, his lips, oddly naked amid the hairy mask of his beard, parting to protest as her words lashed at him. His treachery! His disloyalty! His damn revolution! Duty? What about duty to his family?

Camilo had said, "I do love you, Mother."

Love? Did he know the meaning of the word?

Elizabeth, in the humid warmth of a Miami morning, her silk nightgown clinging damply to her skin, now wondered what might have happened had she taken the hand he reached out to her. What if she had quelled her anger, appealed to the child in him? She should have taken him into the house, away from the suspicious eyes of his soldiers, walked him into the living room where they had spent so many hours together, and kissed him and begged for his help.

But instead what she had done was to explode in a fury at him, accuse and humiliate him, and then, quite viciously, slap his face as though he had been an unruly child instead of a twenty-four-year-old man who had risen to a position of power and authority in the new revolutionary government of Cuba.

It was all madness, she thought now. Sheer, utter madness.

Slipping out of her nightgown, she turned aside and went through the door into the tiled bathroom, flicking on the light. She turned the knobs that started the shower, and picked up the plastic cap. It isn't unusual that mothers fall in love with their sons, she thought.

Stepping into the shower, she shut the glass door and let the warmth of the water splash over her. But then she started to cry, foolishly, stupidly, yet unable to stop. I must stop this, she thought. I must!

Yet she could not arrest the feeling she had, the fluttering, emotional, uncontrolled, wild impulse: "Maybe," she said aloud. "Maybe he's coming home . . ."

CHAPTER TWO

*C*uba *cuts across the Caribbean like a scimitar. The northwest point of Pinar del Río thrusts at Mexico's Yucatán peninsula; the southeast at Oriente juts against the Windward Passage above the big island of Hispaniola, which is now Haiti and the Dominican Republic.*

This 745-mile strip of green is the largest and most westerly of the Caribbean island chain, which may in some past geological age have been a string of mountains, ranging from the Bahamas to the Lesser Antilles. The Cuban coastline is approximately 2,500 miles in length, serrated with hundreds of bays and inlets. The harbors at Havana, Nipe, Guantánamo, Cienfuegos and Bahía Honda are among the best in the world. Only 112.5 miles divide the north coast of Cuba from the southern tip of Florida. Through this gap flows one of the great ocean currents of the world, which moves out of the Gulf of Mexico, north along the east coast of America and out into the cold waters of the North Sea. The island of Cuba is tropical, but the trade winds and the surrounding seas make its climate one of the most pleasant on earth except during the hot months of July and August, the hurricane season.

Nature was generous to Cuba. More than half the island is flat or rolling terrain with fertile green valleys; the rest is hilly, with mountains rising to more than six thousand feet in the Escambray of Las Villas Province and to above eight thousand feet in the Sierra Maestra in Oriente. The rich red soil and tropical sun provide perfect growing conditions for sugarcane; and in the Vuelta Abajo mountains of Pinar del Río are the best velvety green tobacco plants in the world. Fish abound from the cobalt blue of the Atlantic to the clear green water and white sands of the Caribbean: porpoises, sharks, marlin, swordfish, mackerel, tuna, pompano, dolphinfish, sardines, snappers, barracuda. In the earth is manganese, nickel, iron, copper and chromium. Cuba's rivers are generally shallow, narrow and navigable for only short distances, yet they flow through every province.

The original inhabitants were the Ciboney and Taino Indians, who established a primitive but prosperous culture, with stone age tools. Their only enemies were hurricanes and the more warlike Caribs, who occasionally raided the island and ate their captives. The Cuban Indians were a happy, friendly people, good-looking, with light-brown skin. They called their island Cubanacan. Except for the sharks, there were no dangerous or venomous animals.

13

Then one fall morning in 1492 three small sailing ships appeared off the island's east coast.

Christopher Columbus was a tall, blue-eyed Genoese seaman who understood how to turn imperial aspirations to his own ends. The Spanish monarchs, having expelled the Moors from most of the Iberian Peninsula and achieved unity in their country, looked with envy at Portugal's growing imperial supremacy. The Portuguese were busy exploring the western coast of Africa; their ultimate dream was to penetrate the mysteries of the Far East. Hence it was Columbus' proposition that the Spanish monarchs focus their own exploration on the New World. On their behalf, Columbus would find vast new continents and bring back the gold of the Indies. It was surely a plan worthy of the investment of three ships and ninety men.

Columbus, whose proposition had earlier been turned down by the Portuguese, found a predictably receptive audience in Spain. He was, after all, more than an explorer; he was a mythmaker. His promises and expectations were positively grandiose. Unfortunately, his achievements as an explorer never matched his myths. One of Columbus' notions was that "the hidden empire of the Great Khan" lay somewhere on the southern coast of Cuba. It was a mythical empire that was positively resplendent in gold. And Columbus would find it, and deliver its riches to his patrons and benefactors.

On the morning of October 7, Columbus was startled by the crack of a cannon. He looked west to the Niña, which was off his bow, and saw white smoke thinning over the water. A flag was being run up. The signal for land ahead. On the horizon lay a thick cloud. And in the air he smelled land.

After that every crewman was awake, alert, watching the horizon. On Monday, the eighth of October, they saw flocks of parrots. On Tuesday, they could hear birds passing overhead all through the night. On Wednesday, the tension became unbearable. They saw a reed on the surface. Next a green plant floated past their bow; then a water-soaked piece of timber. But the horizon showed only the unbroken line of the sea against the sky.

Columbus promised those on watch "a silken doublet" for the first to sight land. Queen Isabella had offered a reward of ten thousand maravedis. Columbus failed to mention it.

All Thursday night he kept watch from the sterncastle of the Santa María, smelling the land breeze. Once he thought he saw a light. But he kept silent.

At two in the morning, Rodrigo de Triana, the lookout on the forecastle of the Pinta, thought he saw a dark smudge on the horizon. He strained his eyes. Yes! It was there, land! He was the first to see a new world. He shouted. Land! Land! On all three of the ships men poured from the forecastles. Sails were lowered and furled.

14

In the silence on deck, the ninety men waited in the morning breeze for the first light. As the eastern sky brightened, the air grew radiant, the sea began to change from black to indigo blue. There before their eyes lay the New World.

On the sterncastle of the Santa María, Christopher Columbus, who until then had maintained his posture of serene, steadfast calm, went mad with joy. His theory had been proved: You could sail west and reach the east! He began the dawning of October 12, 1492, with a prophetic stroke. He bilked young Rodrigo de Triana out of his ten thousand maravedis.

"The reward went to the Admiral," Columbus' son wrote years later, "for it was he who first saw the light in the darkness of the night, which was symbolic of the spiritual light he was bringing to the darkness."

CHAPTER THREE

HAVANA, FEBRUARY 4, 1934

It took eight days aboard the New York and Cuba Mail Steamship Company freighter to reach Cuba. The morning they were to arrive in Havana, Elizabeth was awake before dawn. She dressed quickly in the dark of their stifling cabin, leaving Gustavo asleep in the bunk, and went up on deck into the cool fresh-smelling sea air. Standing on the bow, she could feel the vibrations of the engines in the deck beneath her feet and hear the hissing of the keel as it sliced through the water. Bracing herself against the gentle pitching of the ship, she looked off into the darkness around her. A single morning star glittered in the sky which was gathering light to the east. There was a gentle warm breeze coming off the land and she could smell earth and trees in the salt air. The breeze blew against her, soft as silk. As it grew light, she saw birds circling over the water and then, for the first time in her life, she saw flying fish bursting in clusters from the surface, soaring and splattering little spastic splashes twenty and thirty yards beyond. From the height of the bow, they looked like dragonflies.

As the light grew more intense, filling the expanse of sea with a luminous glow, she strained her eyes on the horizon to catch her first glimpse of land. She had been married ten weeks to Gustavo. They had spent their honeymoon in Paris, in a suite at the Ritz overlooking the courtyard. It was wonderfully romantic, except for the fact that it rained

15

every day and they both caught colds. On the trip home the Atlantic had been stormy and they had walked the deck in the freezing rain to ease their seasickness. They were hugely relieved to catch sight of the brass-green Statue of Liberty through the mist coming into New York harbor.

And now she longed for sunlight and tropical warmth. She had traveled extensively in Europe as a child, but had never been south of Palm Beach. The idea of living in Cuba filled her with excitement, mixed with a certain apprehension. Gustavo, she sensed, felt much the same way. He had lived mainly in Washington and New York after his forced departure from Havana five years ago. But now his father was dead, his family's affairs were in confusion and he had made the commitment to live in Cuba once again and to make his peace with whatever regime might come to power.

Standing on the undulating bow of the freighter, she could not wait for the full light so that she could see Cuba on the horizon. Something splashed in the sea to her left, and she caught a glimpse of some triangular-shaped fish that gleamed in the air and splashed down hard on the surface. She watched its dark, batlike shape, gliding along just below the surface, and then it vanished. When she looked back to the horizon, she saw green hills rising above the haze, the first rays of the sun etching their shapes against the sky. Cuba! My God, she thought, it is beautiful!

Less than an hour later they were moored at the United Fruit docks and descended into a chaotic jumble of humanity that swirled around the pier: Orientals and blacks, Cubans and an occasional American, nuns in black habits and naked children, all shouting and screaming at once in a wild cacophony of voices. Lottery vendors, dozens of them; shabby, thin men and boys, holding packets of brightly numbered sheets, all shouting and waving; taxi drivers in their sleeveless shirts tugging at them; shoeshine boys with filthy imploring faces, black longshoremen with bulging biceps lounging on crates, half asleep in the sun.

Gustavo took her hand firmly, leaning close to her ear so that he could be heard above the din. "Stay close to me, I don't want you stolen."

"What about the luggage?"

"I gave the customs officer five dollars to have his porters deliver it to the house. Don't worry. It'll be taken care of."

"You gave money to the customs officer?"

"It's his *chivo.*"

"*Chivo?* What's that?"

Gustavo smiled at her. "His payoff." *Chivo* was a word she was soon to learn for herself. She followed Gustavo, linked to his hand, as he pushed through the mob, gesturing, shouting, waving them aside.

16

"This place is like a Chinese fire drill," she shouted at Gustavo. "Everybody is moving and nobody is doing anything!"

His reply was a nod. He looked annoyed as he searched out the faces around him. "Where the devil is Juan?"

Everywhere Elizabeth looked she saw gaudy advertising signs. LOTERÍA! CERVEZA! HOJAS! BACARDI RON! Along the edge of the wharf was a line of Negro boys, naked except for their ragged swimming trunks. Occasionally, one would dive as a coin was tossed from the deck of the white ocean liner that was docked beyond the freighter. The noise of the traffic out on the street was deafening, a constant blaring of horns and roaring of motors. Cars flashed past. A little yellow streetcar careened around the tracks, jangling its bell to scatter the pedestrians who flowed across its path in a constant wave.

"Ah!" she heard Gustavo exclaim and felt him tugging her hand. He led the way to a short, thick-chested black man in gray livery and cap who came pushing through the crowd. When he saw Carta, his brown face brightened into a grin.

"Juan, where the hell have you been? You knew we were arriving at noon!"

"I'm sorry, señor, the traffic. Jammed all the way into town. They're working on the road."

When he looked over at her, Elizabeth saw that Juan's eyes were bloodshot. She could smell the rum on him as he led them to the shiny new Packard convertible.

"He's drunk," she said to Gustavo as they pulled out of the dock into the maddening traffic, horns bleating at them.

"Don't worry, he's a great driver," Gustavo said. "Very fast reflexes."

In the next ten minutes Elizabeth came to appreciate Juan's reflexes. The traffic moved fast on the narrow streets. No one used brakes, only horns. Pedestrians leaped out of their path, fenders and hoods flashed within inches. Every moment seemed to present a new crisis, an imminent collision which somehow Juan managed to avoid with great skill and no little luck. The big car weaved at unbelievable, unslackening speed, through spaces she didn't think it could fit. Juan never touched the brakes.

"Do people always drive like this?" Elizabeth's voice sounded small and tremulous.

Gustavo held her hand in his lap and squeezed it. "You'll get used to it," he said.

"Never," she replied breathlessly. "Never."

17

Half an hour later they were out of downtown Havana on the broad stone-paved central highway, moving up the hill, past the open shops that lined the dusty road. The Packard passed a horse and cart along the side of the road. Elizabeth had never seen a horse so skinny. It moved slowly, on gaunt legs. The cart was heavily laden with boxes. The driver, a young man in a green shirt, held a whip poised above its flanks, snapping it, as the old horse staggered to pull the load up the grade.

"That poor animal," she said when they passed the cart. "Are all the horses like that here?"

"No," Gustavo said. "We have good horses in Cuba. That man is very poor."

She did not look at him, but he saw her lips stiffen. She wore a white dress and she held her floppy hat on her head with a gloved hand. Her hair blew around her face from under the hat. There was a glisten of perspiration on her upper lip. She looked suddenly very tired.

"It won't be much longer," he told her and gestured. "Just to the top of the hill. Are you all right?"

"I'm fine." She turned her eyes to him. They were so blue they had a quality of being shot with light like crystal. He could not read the expression, but her manner worried him. He yearned for her to like Havana, yet he had forgotten how it would look to a stranger. During his long exile, Gustavo had remembered only how beautiful the city was. His mind had conveniently erased the squalor and the filthy children begging in rags, the blaring noise of the traffic, the crumbling, shabby look of the buildings, the shacks, the flies and the heat.

Now he was trying to see it through her eyes. She must hate it, he thought, why wouldn't she?

He felt suddenly defeated. He looked over at her profile. Her skin seemed so delicate it was translucent. He knew that the brilliance of the tropical sun was unkind to delicate skin. "Shall I have Juan stop and put up the top?" he said to her. "I'm afraid you'll burn."

"I may burn, but I won't wilt." She flashed a resolute smile at him. "Besides, I want to get a tan. I might as well start now."

They moved through a cloud of dust that the wind blew up from the roadside, and she wrinkled her nose against the smell of raw sewage. "Didn't you tell me Havana smelled like a perfumed woman, Gustavo?"

"It's ugly," he said. "I'd forgotten." He gestured at the tattered shacks they were passing, the naked children in the yards, the ragged women who stood staring at them. "I feel like a fool, asking you to give up living in Georgetown for this!"

She touched his arm quickly. "Don't be offended. I was only making a joke. Remember, it's all still new. I never fall in love at first sight."

18

But Gustavo still sat there, glowering. She leaned over and kissed him impulsively. He turned toward her in surprise and she kissed him again, her hat blowing off and flying into the dust, landing on a pig that stood in the yard of a palm shack. The pig squealed and bolted away in terror. Juan slowed the car, but Gustavo laughed and so did Elizabeth and she waved for him to go on. "Don't stop!"

"But your hat!"

"It will look better on the pig."

She looked at Carta now and saw that his black mood had been broken.

"Señora Carta, I love you very much," he said.

"I hate only those days that I have lived without you," she replied.

They were laughing together as Juan turned off onto the narrow road that led to the house.

It stood on the hill. The red tiles of the weathered roof showed above the big laurel trees as they drove through the gate, then one-eighth of a mile to the house. The road was narrow and paved with stones and climbed gradually through the trees.

"Oh, it's beautiful," she exclaimed. "What is that lovely tree?"

"Spanish laurel," Gustavo told her. "Very old."

"And that one? The big one with the pods?"

"It is called a ceiba."

"It's gorgeous." She squeezed his hand. Her sudden animation pleased him. "How much land is there?"

"Around the house? Ten hectares."

She looked at him, puzzled.

"It's metric. About twenty-five acres, more or less."

"Can I have a horse?"

"You can have a regiment of cavalry, if you wish it."

"One horse will be fine," she said. "And perhaps a pony for David when he gets older."

He had, in the excitement of returning to his home, forgotten about the child. Her child. The chubby blond boy with his thoughtful blue eyes and his pouting mouth. He felt a twinge of discomfort. Something about the child troubled him. The thought of her naked, giving herself to another man, made him ache. He tried to put it out of his mind.

When they drove onto the courtyard, René was standing on the steps, tall, skinny, in his white coat and black trousers, looking older and bent in the shoulders. His curly black hair was flecked with gray. The house loomed behind him, massive in its Spanish Colonial architecture, the palms shading the roof, the tropical flowers red and yellow and white. The fountain in the circle of stone in front of the house, with its Greek statue of a woman naked from the waist, should have been spewing water. But it was dry. The car stopped.

"Oh, Gustavo, it's magnificent."

"You like it?"

"I'm overwhelmed."

"My grandfather built it."

"Your grandfather had taste."

"He had many things. His name was Camilo."

"I'd like to have known him." She sat staring at the vaulted windows and arched promenades and the slanting roof of heavy red earth tile.

René opened the door and greeted Gustavo in Spanish. Gustavo stepped out. The black man's gaunt, mournful face broke into a wide grin, showing yellow teeth and pale red gums.

Gustavo took her hand and helped her out of the big car. She looked up at René and brushed a wisp of hair away from her forehead.

"René," Gustavo said in Spanish, "may I present to you my wife, Isabel."

René bowed, never taking his eyes off her. *"Qué linda! Hoy su padre estaba orgulloso . . ."*

"What does he say?"

Gustavo smiled. "He thinks you are a great beauty."

Elizabeth smiled at René. "Tell him I think he's just made a new friend."

Eyebrows were raised in Havana society by the young American woman Gustavo Carta had brought home with him. That she was a great beauty no one disputed, but it was an enigmatic beauty. Though she was small-boned and slender to the point of appearing delicate, there was about her a hearty exuberance that suggested an inner toughness. Her lovely blue eyes could brighten with merriment as she struggled with the unfamiliarities of the Spanish language, wildly mixing tenses and conjugations; but when she felt that someone was speaking to her condescendingly, those same eyes acquired a dangerous glint of defiance. Gentle and genteel, clearly the thoroughbred product of Southern aristocracy, she could also lacerate with her tongue anyone who offended her sense of self-dignity. Her boldness intrigued and disconcerted the Cuban gentlemen and absolutely shocked their plump, staid wives. Her skirts were too short, too revealing of those long legs which she was in the habit of crossing and recrossing as she spoke to someone, usually with great enthusiasm and many quick, charming smiles. The wives chattered about her endlessly.

"She is a woman who is fast."

20

"She smokes cigarillos, like a man!"

"She has no respect."

"The gardener says he saw her swimming in the nude in her pool."

"They say her first husband died very young."

"But she had a child."

"I have seen him. A boy, with blond hair. He lives with them now."

"How old?"

"Two."

"She is very extravagant, and Gustavo's father left his affairs in very bad condition when he died."

"He'll send her home within a year. It will never last."

Elizabeth was aware of this furtive hectoring, and thought it amusing. Carta, engrossed in his own affairs, and deeply in love with his wife, was oblivious. Friends noticed that he too had changed a great deal from the young man who fled Cuba years earlier. His body had filled out. He had lost his youthful propensity for rash judgments and impulsive anger. He spoke quietly and slowly and rarely smiled. He had matured. When one spoke to him he seemed to pause, considering his words before he answered. Despite his many acquired Yankee mannerisms, he was what his friends called in Spanish *simpático*. And since he had a law degree from Georgetown University, they always respectfully called him "Dr. Carta."

The boy appeared two weeks after the Cartas returned to Havana. He came on the ferry from Key West in the company of a man who looked to everyone to be a professional wrestler, he was so big and wide; yet his clothes were those of a rich man. The man had an ugly face that was strangely pleasant in its ugliness, and he spoke with a deep, hoarse voice in very good Spanish. He was called Señor Amato and stayed only two days and then disappeared. For a child barely over one year old, David seemed equally strange. He was quiet, withdrawn and shy. He never cried. In society it was noticed that Carta treated the child with distant affection, as though out of courtesy to his wife rather than real affinity for the boy.

The Cartas led a lively social life and were welcomed into the loftiest social circles. Many evenings, however, they kept to themselves, dining alone at the best restaurants and taking in the night life. They loved riding their horses through the countryside and relished picnics at secluded beaches.

The only pall over their life in the first several months following their return was Carta's alarm over the disintegration of the family fortune. Though aware of his father's infirmities and tendency toward vacillation, Carta had greatly respected the old man and had been so en-

21

meshed in his own youthful activities that he never really thought about the family business. Like many rich young men, however, he had assumed that the family's great wealth was somehow inviolate. Now he realized the foolishness of those assumptions. Carta became more and more absorbed in business affairs. His father's sudden death revealed the extent to which the family fortunes had fallen. The Cartas had lived for three generations in Cuba. When young Gustavo left the island, the family owned eight thousand hectares (twenty thousand acres) of sugarcane fields in Oriente, 402 hectares (one thousand acres) of tobacco land in the rich Vuelta Abajo of Pinar del Río province, west of Havana; a house and ten hectares of land (twenty-five acres) in the suburb of San Francisco de Paula, near the village of Cotorro; two sugar mills in Oriente, a cigar factory in Havana; lots and two buildings in the city; a large isolated summer home on the beach near Boca de Jaruco; stocks and bonds in American, Cuban, British and Spanish corporations. They were estimated to be worth twenty-two million dollars.

On his return, young Carta found that most of the stock was not worth the gilt-edged paper it was printed on. The collapse of 1929 had taken care of that. Both sugar mills were closed. High tariffs and the price of sugar on the world market had forced his father to cease operations. Only the tobacco interests were barely holding their own. Don Andrés had sold off the lots he owned in Miramar in 1931 and then the downtown Havana buildings the following year. There had been some graft and no little embezzlement by key employees and government officials. Assets, Carta found, amounted to three million American dollars. Debts totaled ten million.

"To survive," he said to Elizabeth in the candlelight at the dinner table that night, "I must dedicate my life to it . . . my time, all of my energy."

"You can sell it all," she told him. "Didn't you say United Fruit had made an offer?"

"If I do that . . . what is left? It won't take care of the debts."

"We have the money my daddy left me. We can live on that comfortably."

He smiled and took her hand across the table. "No."

"Why not? I am a very wealthy young woman, you know."

"Get thee behind me, Satan." He grinned at her and kissed the tips of her fingers.

"Macho," she said to him.

He wagged a finger at her. "No. No! There is a difference. 'Macho' is bragging in a bar. But 'machísmo'—that is being a man and doing what a man must do. You see the difference?"

"Barely."

"A man has value only in the risks he is willing to take, in the challenges he accepts."

"Quote, *que?*"

"Don Camilo, my grandfather."

"Then I'll probably never see you again, if you're going to bury yourself in your father's business affairs. I suppose I should take a lover to while away my lonely hours."

"I have just the right man in mind. An outstanding candidate. You'll adore him."

"How exciting. What's he like?"

"Well, he's handsome. Charming. Good manners. He loves music, literature, poetry, art, horses, shooting, fishing, and beautiful women."

"Is he rich?"

"He used to be."

She paused and looked at him. "He will be again. I'm certain."

Carta set about energetically opening new offices in Havana and Santiago de Cuba, putting his father's affairs in order, taking the reins of his various businesses. His energy, astute business acumen, and absolute honesty (a point of honor with him in a system that thrived on corruption) gained for him respect in every quarter. Several of his father's key employees who proved to be dishonest or corrupt were summarily discharged and replaced by younger men, friends of Carta's who were absolutely loyal to him and who shared his zeal for a fresh approach to business. "If we cannot change the system," he said to them, "we can make changes within our own affairs and let the rest of them go to hell."

Several of his father's old friends, aware of his financial difficulties, came to him with business propositions which they guaranteed would solve his problems. Thick, heavyset Antonio Ugalde, whose pale-skinned face always reminded Carta of an aging boar, came to him one Sunday afternoon at the club, Los Cazadores, where they were shooting pigeons. Two sugar mills were to be built with government financing, he said. If Gustavo would put up $200,000, Don Antonio's friends in the government would grant the financing, four million. Batista's cut off the top was thirty-five percent. His friends would take ten. For himself, five percent. Additional financing from the government would be forthcoming for cost overruns. He laughed. He slapped Gustavo's shoulder. In the end Gustavo could realize several million. It would be wise to take ten or twenty years to complete the factories. Meanwhile, they could obtain government loans indefinitely. Perhaps, in the end, they could sell the mills to the Yankees and force them to pay a big price for them, too! What did he say, eh? His father's friends never forget! Don't worry. It is as they say a sure thing, huh?

23

Gustavo went home that night sick at heart. He dreaded becoming a part of this sort of thievery, yet the offer could not be refused out of hand. Don Antonio and his friends were very powerful men in Cuba. He explained the situation to Elizabeth, who listened intently. Her prompt response was, "Tell him frankly, darling, to get fucked!"

The rambling old-fashioned Spanish house in San Francisco de Paula had been the Carta family home since 1867. It had fallen into a state of disrepair from his father's disinterest and neglect.

"Make it ours," he said to her that first day they drove out from Havana to see it. "I want to feel us in every room. Something of the old, the past, and something brand new, which is us, you and me."

Elizabeth set about the task with an energy that amazed him. Potted plants appeared in the vast entry; the tile floors took on a polished sheen, the heavy dark furniture with its frayed velvet cushions was replaced with fine old Louis XIV pieces, shipped from Paris; Oriental throw rugs appeared here and there on the shiny tiled floors; pieces of primitive Caribbean and South American art went up on newly plastered walls and on the side tables; the heavy old drapes were taken down from the windows, and rooms that had not seen sunlight in twenty years turned radiant; plumbing was torn out and replaced; tiles were reset in the bathrooms and in the big open kitchen, and a modern stove was added; a refrigeration locker was built out of the old pantry; workmen swarmed through the house carrying ladders and paint. Hammering echoed through the halls, and through the noise and confusion Elizabeth was like an avenging angel; her hair, which she was letting grow long again, wrapped in a flowered print scarf, her dresses discarded for worn khaki trousers and an old white shirt of Gustavo's, spotted with paint. The Cuban workmen, who were not used to seeing a woman in trousers, were amused by her. But they realized she knew what she was doing and she did it with a cheerful good humor, even in her bad Spanish. She intrigued and motivated them. They called her "La Señora" and carried out her wishes with pride.

"Shouldn't you slow down a bit?" Carta said to her one night in June. "All this effort and energy you are spending worries me—you look tired."

"How long did you work today?" she replied, squinting her blue eyes at him. "Hmmm?"

"Oh, ten hours, maybe."

"More like fifteen. How many hours did you work yesterday? The day before?"

24

He laughed. "All right, all right—I just do not wish you to wear yourself out, is all."

"Did I seem worn out a moment ago?"

"No."

"Did you enjoy yourself properly?"

"Wonderfully."

"Then kindly discontinue all worry in my behalf. When I'm tired, I will complain to you in the appropriate manner, sir."

Crates of books began arriving at docks in Havana, and she supervised their unloading in the big main room, directing where each volume should be placed in the library shelves that reached floor to ceiling. She wrote to her cousin, Charles Danforth, and had him take her father's library, which had been stored after his death, and some of the family furniture, from the warehouses in Charleston, and ship them to Havana.

". . . You sound as though you're having a grand time down there," he wrote her. "Wish I could join you all, but have just been granted a professorship here at Cambridge and am up to my neck. Perhaps this summer . . . How is David? . . . Give Gustavo my regards. . . . And is there another heir in the wind?"

She laughed, reading the last sentence, seated crosslegged on the floor in the library, thousands of books stacked around her in broken piles.

One night in October, Carta came home to find her seated alone in the vast space of the living room, reading. As he marveled at the transformation of his house, at its austere splendor and beauty, she took him by the hand and led him up to the master bedroom, stopping at the tall carved double doors. Looking at him with a mysterious smile, her blue eyes brightened with delight. She told him to close his eyes. He heard the door unlatch and then open. He gazed across the bedroom to where an enormous fourposter bed stood, the biggest bed he had ever seen. It required a broad stool to climb up to it. He walked to it amazed, pleased. Where had she gotten it? She laughed at his reaction, clapping her hands together like a child. My granddaddy's bed from Stargrove, she said. Stargrove? Yes, their place in the country. My father was born there. Don't you just love it, Gustavo? He took her in his arms, kissed her gently, and then lifted her from her feet, while she squirmed and laughed in protest, and he tossed her onto the surface of that great bed, lunging at her with a warm and affectionate lust, and when he lifted her skirt and touched her, resting his hands between the fleshy warmth of her thighs, she gazed at him very solemnly and told him that she was pregnant. They would have a child in May.

He kissed her lips, gently, tears coming to his eyes in the surge of

25

warmth and tenderness he felt. A child! The mystery of it overwhelmed him. A child from their love, their bodies! A living being that would embody both of them and all that had been before them, through all the generations that had been theirs. The joy of it was almost too much to bear.

It must have been three in the morning that same night when she was awakened by the sound of guitars coming from the veranda. It startled her at first.

Gustavo was not in bed beside her. Lying there in the dark trying to orient herself, she heard a guitar again, then another and another and yet another. There must have been twenty!

Groggily climbing out of bed and gathering up her robe, she went to the balcony and peered down. Arrayed beneath her was a yardful of men, some of them holding their guitars, others holding tiny candles that glittered in the dark. The guitars were being played in total disharmony. Some of the men were unshaven, some in rags, several were swaying from drunkenness.

Gustavo now appeared behind her.

"How do you like it?" he asked.

Elizabeth was trying to suppress her laughter. "It's wonderfully romantic, darling," she said. "But they're all drunk."

"Every one." Gustavo shrugged. "Try to find thirty sober musicians in Cuba at three o'clock in the morning and see what you come up with!"

"Aaaaaa-vay . . . Mariii-aaa," the voices sang.

She started laughing and crying at the same time.

"The operation is very simple," Dr. Herrera told him as they walked along the corridor. "A matter of tying off the fallopian tubes. You understand?"

Carta nodded.

The doctor was a short man with solid shoulders and a rounded chest. He wore a surgical cap and gown. "I wish I had better news for you, Dr. Carta. But one must face the facts. If she were to become pregnant again, it would be very bad. Very bad."

"I see."

"I have discussed this matter with her. She understands. Disappointed, of course. She said you both wanted a large family . . ."

"I want my wife alive and well, señor."

"Of course. Clearly. She wishes to see you before we proceed."

"When will you do it?"

"At once."

26

"Is she strong enough?"

"I would not suggest the operation if I thought she was not."

"Yes. Of course."

"Have you seen your son?"

The image of the red-faced child wrapped in the white hospital blanket came to Gustavo Carta's mind. The nurse had opened the blanket revealing the wrinkled miniature face, the thin red arms, the white diaper, the bent red legs with their tiny toes. He looked so small, so ugly and vulnerable, Carta loved him on sight. He looked at the doctor and nodded. "A moment ago."

"Eight pounds, four ounces. A good, healthy male. Congratulations."

"Yes. Thank you."

He opened the door to her room. She was in the high hospital bed with the lamp on over her head. She looked very pale and tired. He went to the side of the bed and kissed her. She smelled of ether.

"Did you see him?"

"Yes."

She smiled faintly. "I am so sorry . . ."

"About what? We have a son. What more could we ask?"

"Did you speak with Dr. Herrera?"

"Yes, I did speak with him."

"Did he tell you what he wanted to do?"

"He told me."

She took his hand and pressed it. Her lips quivered. "You're disappointed in me . . ."

"The hell I am." He kissed her. "Like hell."

"Is he really beautiful?"

"No! No, he's ugly."

She smiled at him again. "I've given him a name, without asking you."

"What?"

"Camilo. Does it please you, Gustavo?"

"Immensely! How could it not? Camilo. Camilo! My son, Camilo! It sounds marvelous, doesn't it?"

"I wonder who he is."

"He's our son, who else?"

"No. I mean, who will he be when he grows up? What kind of a person?"

"What thoughts you have!"

"I felt very strange having our son, Gustavo. . . . I just saw a glimpse of him when Dr. Herrera held him up. Such a feeling from him . . . as though I had never loved anything in my life so much. . . . Aren't you pleased he was a boy?"

27

"I cannot tell you what it means to me."

"Oh, Gustavo, you make me feel so happy."

They held each other for a long time without speaking until the doctor came in.

CHAPTER FOUR

PUERTO ESCANDIDO, CUBA, JANUARY 13, 1961

Before it was really light he could see the squall clouds above the open sea, gray and massive in the gradually brightening sky. The air was muggy for this time of year in Cuba. The *comandante* stepped out of the hatchway onto the metal deck of the cutter. He was tall, his bearded face weathered by the sun. He wore olive-green fatigues and paratrooper boots. His tired blue eyes peered out wearily from under the billed khaki hat.

He turned to the *militiano* who followed him. "Bring him up now."

"And the others, Comandante?"

"Yes. The crew too. I want this terminated."

The *militiano* saluted and went back into the hatchway. For a moment, the *comandante* looked up into the sky and let his breath escape from his lungs, relieved to be out of the confined quarters below deck. Overhead, the Cuban flag snapped in the wind. High above him, a man-of-war bird circled in the wind, a tiny cross, the wings like miniature sabers. He was a great fisherman, that bird, and the *comandante* felt elation at seeing him. It was a good omen.

One of the two militiamen under the forward gun turned. He came walking quickly in a strange, disjointed gait up to the *comandante*. He did not salute. He was an old man the *comandante* had known for years.

"How does it go?" the old man called.

"Good. We are almost finished."

The old man grinned. *"Van, van, van!"*

"Yes," replied the Comandante. "We'll make it, *viejo.*"

The *comandante* turned away and clasped his hands behind his back. He was tired and very thirsty. He also had the beginning of a bad headache, a dull throb at the base of his skull. He had taken three aspirin before coming from below. He now hoped the fresh air would dispel it. He was pleased with the results of the operation this morning, but he was also worried.

His plan had been executed perfectly. At midnight, Raúl Menéndez, the cook's assistant, had returned to the Coast Guard station at Puerto Escondido from his leave in Havana. He brought with him a case of Bacardi rum. He seemed very drunk and very happy. The rum was a gift from his father, he told the others. Everybody was to enjoy. After all, the days ahead would be filled with danger. There was a chance the men would never see their homeland again. He made a joke out of an old Spanish proverb, *"Los dineros del sacristán cantando se vienen y cantando se van!"* Translated loosely, it meant, "Easy come, easy go!"

They were all quite drunk by 3 A.M. The radioman fell asleep on his radio. Captain Roberto Escalante had a few drinks with the men, yawned and retired to his quarters to sleep. The duty officer, Ramón Silvia, sat trying to play dominoes in the wardroom with two of the gunner's mates. Menéndez took a bottle out to José Samoza and Lupe Valle, who were on guard at the gate. They had all been on duty without leave for three months.

At five-thirty a jeep and two personnel carriers rumbled along the road and turned into the gate, headlights blazing. Two militiamen, dressed in black berets and blue denim shirts, stepped off the jeep.

The drunken Guardsmen were sitting with their backs to the sentry shack. Sensing betrayal, they groped for their rifles. Samoza stood up, holding the Garand rifle in his hands, and stepped forward. Lupe Valle never got to his feet. He was on his knees looking scared sick when they shot him. When they fired the second volley he was sitting on the ground with his head between his knees. Samoza was face down in the grass.

Moving with silent, swift efficiency, the young *comandante* directed his men to fan out through the buildings. Others ran toward the dock. Only the crunching of their boots on the gravel broke the silence. There was no further gunfire. The groggy captain and his crew were taken in complete surprise and without a struggle. Less than ten minutes had elapsed since the militiamen arrived at the gate and shot the guards.

Unfolding his hands, the *comandante* placed one against the steel bulkhead and listened to the noise of the men being routed out belowdecks. The steel was cold and wet with dew under his hand. He wiped it dry on his trouser leg and then scratched his jaw, as was his habit when troubled.

He had an unreal feeling about all this now. It had started in the sour-smelling confinement of the captain's quarters. The cramped little

29

room smelled of diesel oil, disinfectant, dirty clothes and, oddly, some oppressive citrus-scented shaving lotion the captain had used. For a fleeting moment down there he had been gripped by a claustrophobic panic. The walls of that room seemed to close in on him, encasing him in a metal coffin.

Captain Escalante, seated at the edge of his bunk in his underwear, still disoriented with sleep, his eyes furtive, sweat glistening on his stubbled jaw in the hard glare of the metal-caged lamp overhead, had kept answering stubbornly to each question, *"No sé nada! No sé nada, Comandante, no sé nada!"*

The *comandante* could smell the sour rum breath the captain had as he leaned down and took his stubbled chin in his hand and lifted it so that their eyes met solidly. "You will tell me, Captain, everything I wish to know."

"I'll tell you shit," Escalante said to him. He was tough and very brave.

Yet now the *comandante* was on deck knowing all that he needed and more. The counterrevolutionary plot was extensive, involving far more than this Coast Guardsman and his crew.

"Gustavo Carta would have been aboard this ship by tomorrow night," Escalante had said, almost spitting his words. "He would have been the commander. My men would have been his."

"Where were you to take him?"

Escalante had looked up, squinting against the glare of the overhead light. "The Isle of Pines."

"The Isle of Pines is heavily fortified. You're lying!"

"No, Comandante. For the lives of my wife and my daughter, I am telling you the truth. I was to take him to the Isle of Pines. That's all I know."

"How was all this organized?"

"Through contacts in Havana."

"Havana? The names? You will give me the names?"

"I know no names, Comandante. I only saw their faces and then only once."

"There were several?"

"Perhaps four—no, five."

"Men?"

"Men and women . . . one a boy . . ."

The *comandante* could not look at him. He stood and rubbed the back of his neck, sighing wearily. He heard Escalante cough.

"My wife and daughter, Comandante?"

"As I promised, they will be released this morning. No harm will come to them."

30

Now the crew was assembled on deck. They had not been allowed to dress. Most of them stood at the storm rail in their white shorts and T-shirts, gaping down at the dock with awe and fear in their faces. Captain Escalante was forced to his knees, facing out to sea.

Standing five yards behind the captain, the *comandante* unhooked the flap of his holster. His hand closed around the butt of the Colt .45 automatic. For a moment he studied the back of the captain's head, watching the black hair fluttering in the wind. Escalante's shoulders bent forward slightly, shivering in his white underwear, his head inclined in prayer. There was a hole in the heel of his right sock.

"Captain Hernando Escalante," the *comandante* shouted into the wind so that they could all hear him on the deck of the patrol boat, "has been found guilty of treason against the revolution and against the people of Cuba who are fighting without respite for a country free of imperialism, despotism and misery. The treachery of this counterrevolutionary was intended to destroy us, as a worm would destroy from within. He and all worms like him are to be dug out and eliminated!"

The *comandante* felt a cold fleck of rain against his forehead. As he drew close to the captain, he heard his voice praying quietly: ". . . heartily sorry for having offended Thee . . . I detest my sins . . . above every other evil. . . ."

The *comandante* placed the muzzle of his pistol against the base of Escalante's skull. The captain's spine and shoulders twitched as he felt the touch. "I am proud to die," he said in a hushed voice, his words slow and deliberate. "I am proud to die for freedom! For Cuba!" His voice rose in the wind. "Viva Cuba! Viva la libertad! Viva Gustavo Carta and all who are with him! *Venceremos!*"

The *comandante* felt the weight of the pistol in his hand, and squeezed the trigger. The automatic made a quick, heavy jolt in his hand and thumped in the air. He saw the captain's head jerk and the splatter of bone and blood on the dock and then the tiny splashes on the slick surface below. He saw the quicksilver glint of the barracuda striking at the pieces as they sank in the clear water.

"*Bueno,* Comandante."

He turned to see the old militiaman, his chin gray-stubbled like the chin of an old dog, the rheumy eyes watching him affectionately. The ancient lips parted in a smile. "Well done, Camilo . . ."

CHAPTER FIVE

David Carta could see the northeast chop building up on Biscayne Bay, a speedboat jolting along like some mechanical skipjack in the distance, a burst of white and then a pause, a burst of white. He suddenly envied whoever it was out there. Removing his glasses, he wiped the salt haze from the lenses with a handkerchief, squinting off at the blur that had been the horizon a moment ago. From old habit, he closed his right eye and tried to see through the smudge that was the vision of his damaged left eye. Only around the edges could he discern shapes and colors. The rest, as the result of an auto accident in Havana as a child, remained a blur. He replaced his glasses and adjusted them to his ears and looked out to see the speedboat flash white again on the horizon.

The sound of the crane made him turn quickly to see the white boom, with its winches and steel-twist cables, hoist the decompression chamber from its resting place on the flatbed truck and swing it slowly and heavily through space toward the squat gray ship that was to take it to sea. For several painful seconds it dangled helplessly. He glanced at the operator, whose gloved fists shifted slightly, and the boom swung its burden across the space between the dock and the ship, halting with a metallic squeak over the aft deck. David saw the shadow sliding back and forth across the steel cradle where it was to alight, and he turned aside, lit a cigaret and inhaled. He could not blot the image in his mind of the whole rig crashing to the deck. He waited for the sound of it. The crane engine revved. Maybe, he thought, if I don't look, my luck will change. Normally he was not given to fits of anxiety, but today was somehow different. Since his moment of awakening, he had felt a sense of disquiet, an uneasy feeling that everything was a beat off.

First, it was Robin, his wife. She almost always slept later than he. He was accustomed to feeling her warmth at his side as he lay collecting his first thoughts in the morning, usually languishing there in the humid coolness until the urgent need for coffee drove him to the kitchen. Yet today she had been gone. He had awakened to hear the car going out the drive. He swung out of bed and stumbled to the screen porch that looked down onto the paved drive, and saw the rust-stained top of her white Chevrolet sputter onto South Bayshore Drive. He was left staring at the space where the car had been. Where the hell had she gone? What was going on?

Although their marriage, now into its fifth year, had produced certain upsets and spats, David felt that things this last year were improving. The pressures of his work and her studies kept them apart a great deal, but lately both seemed less defensive and demanding; less sensitive to minor slights.

Now he found himself wondering, after her sudden early-morning flight, whether she was trying to reject him with neglect.

His reverie was shaken by a clanking thud. He lifted his eyes to see the steel decompression chamber cradled in its platform on the aft deck of the converted minesweeper that was to be its home as well as David's until sometime in mid-June. He flexed his arms, feeling, as he hadn't in a long time, a healthy male pleasure in his strength. All right! He had work to do. Let's get at it. The hell with her!

He flipped his cigaret into the water and took a deep breath. His gaze swept the horizon where an oil tanker, low in the water, its superstructure showing white against the blue sky, was gliding into view beyond the wooded tip of Key Biscayne. Four more weeks and he would be out there. He'd be at sea where the water was so blue it seemed almost purple, with prisms of sunlight filtering in long streaks down into the depths, and dolphins splashing around the bow. Ten fucking days. He felt, with sudden realization, the depth of his desperation to get away. He longed for the freedom of being on a ship in the open sea. He wanted to bury himself in his work, be absorbed by it every waking moment, think of nothing else.

The fact that the voyage was now reality seemed in itself miraculous. Grants were always difficult to obtain for scientific research in the sea; but they had finally hit pay dirt. Starting in mid-February, a team of marine biologists from the University of Miami would explore the phenomenon of the upwelling of the Humboldt Current off the coast of Peru. The studies were to aid Peru's fishing industry. The plan was that each of the seven marine biologists aboard would overlap and coordinate with the others on the primary project, while at the same time conducting research in their own special fields. For two years now, David's study of dangerous sea creatures had led him to the field of giant cephalopods. Locked in his desk at home were two hundred and eighteen pages of his doctoral thesis, on which he had been laboring since completing his master's at the University of Miami in 1958.

The giant squid, center of his current scientific interest, was known to inhabit the plankton-rich depths of the Humboldt Current, where the upwelling of the deep water to the surface spawned some five hundred species of fish, all on the monstrous cephalopods' menu. Little was known about the great squid. He was a scientific mystery. The thought of observing one of those huge predators filled him with awe.

"She's secured, Mr. Carta," one of the crewmen shouted at him. He waved his hand.

"Good job, Charlie, thanks!" David turned, walked up the dock to the door of the marine lab and entered. Momentarily, Robin flashed across his mind—no, he told himself, he would not allow it. It was time to work, not to brood.

CHAPTER SIX

HAVANA, APRIL 20, 1941

Camilo came out of the swimming pool and hit him. He knocked David's glasses onto the deck stones. "Come on, now, fight!"

Camilo was only six. He stood there pushing out his jaw, his fists raised. David picked up his glasses. Without saying anything he started up the path to the house.

Miguel, the gardener, was standing at the far end of the pool lifting leaves out of the water with a screen net at the end of a long pole. He looked at David as he limped past.

"What's the matter, David, afraid?" Camilo's voice taunted from behind him. He didn't feel like answering.

He walked up the path under the ceiba trees. Overhead, he could hear some birds quarreling in the higher limbs. His mouth stung where Camilo had hit him. He looked up at the sunlight filtering down through the thick leaves. He saw the two birds fluttering and then a leaf falling, and he watched the birds fly away. He could not make out what kind they were. He wiped his eyes, sniffed and took a deep, shuddering breath. He did not want to let his stepfather see he had been crying.

When he came in the door, Carta was just walking out of the library. He was in his shirt sleeves and had a black ledger in his hand. The stub of a cigar protruded from under his black moustache.

"What's the matter, David?"

34

"Nothing. I had a fight with Camilo, is all."

"What was it about?"

"Nothing."

"How can you argue about nothing?"

Elizabeth came into the entry hall from the living room. He heard his mother's voice before she appeared. "Gustavo, I was just thinking . . ." She stopped and fixed him with her blue eyes. "David? What's wrong? Have you been crying?"

"I wasn't crying," David said. "Can I go to my room now?"

"He had a row with Camilo," Gustavo told her. They stood staring at him.

"May I?" he said.

His mother frowned and came over to him. "Tell me what the trouble is," she said. "What were you two fighting about?"

"Nothing. It was nothing, Mother, honest."

"You don't want to tell me?"

"It was really nothing." He looked away from her because he felt that hot flush of tears coming again. He would not let them see him crying. "Please, let me go to my room. I'm wet and cold."

Gustavo took the cigar from his mouth and cleared his throat. "Let him go," he said softly.

"But he's upset," his mother said. "I'd like to know why. Tell me, David. What's the trouble between you two?"

"It's just something that was said, is all. It's nothing. I'm all right." He had control of it now. He looked down at the sunlight patterns on the shiny floor tiles. He felt his stepfather's hand on his arm.

"David, answer your mother. What was said?"

"He called me a bastard . . ."

"What?"

David felt the sting of tears again. He looked up into his stepfather's dark eyes, saw the pained look in them. His lips trembled against his will, he lowered his gaze and shook his head. "Not the swearing kind of bastard," he said. "The kind that doesn't have a father."

"I'll speak to him," he heard Gustavo's deep voice say. It was the tone he used before punishment. "I'll go down to the pool and speak with him."

"Is it true?" David looked up at them, one then the other. "Is it?"

He saw his mother's furtive, troubled glance at her husband.

"Is it?" David demanded.

Gustavo clapped shut the ledger in his hands. "David, come into my office. I think we should talk."

"No, Gustavo, I—"

Carta silenced her with his look. "This is a matter for David and me to discuss," he said. "David . . ."

David followed him into the library. The ceiling was high and the four walls were covered with shelves of leatherbound books. Across the room was Gustavo's big desk with its shiny wood surface piled high with ledgers and manila envelopes. Gustavo closed the doors.

"Sit down," Gustavo told him, gesturing toward chairs opposite the desk. Gustavo sat down next to him, took a fresh cigar from his shirt pocket and lit it. He cleared his throat, then turned his eyes to David. "Look at me, son."

David looked at him.

"You love your mother?"

"Yes."

"So do I. Very much. To me, she is one of the very special people in the world. I would have wished my mother loved me the way your mother feels for you, David." David blinked at him and swallowed hard. "Oh, yes," Gustavo continued. "My mother went mad at the end, did you know that?"

"No, sir."

"Yes. Insane. She tried one night to kill both my father and myself with a butcher knife from the kitchen. I was only four at the time. My father was rather seriously injured attempting to stop her. She spent the last five years of her life locked in a padded room at the Mazorra Asylum. Totally homicidal."

Carta lowered his eyes. He tapped the little gray ash from the end of his cigar. Then he looked up and smiled tenderly. "You wonder why I tell you this?"

"Yes, sir." David's voice cracked.

Carta leaned forward and gestured with the cigar between his fingers. "For many, many years I was ashamed of my mother. It was a great family scandal. Her madness caused my father untold grief. Yes. He never left this house. He conducted all of his business affairs from this room. We both felt that her insanity had somehow tainted us. I lived with that from the time I was this high." He gestured again. "A very sad business."

For the first time since he had come to Havana as a a small boy, from his earliest memories of Gustavo, David felt a warmth in his presence, a closeness. "How did she die, sir?"

Gustavo's brows lifted. "She hung herself. I believe it was a light cord." He sighed and replaced the cigar in his mouth. "Poor wretched woman. I suppose she just couldn't stand things. I tell you these secrets, David, so that you will know that we share certain griefs between us. You see?"

David felt a rush of emotion. "It is true?"

Gustavo's tone was measured, precise. "Yes. Your mother and father were not married before you were born. He was, unfortunately, killed in an auto accident before their wedding day. Technically, it makes what Camilo so foolishly told you correct. Actually, in fact, since I have legally adopted you and given you my name, it is incorrect. For I am, in every way, your father. Do you understand?"

"Yes, sir." David looked away. He saw the play of sunlight and shadow on the white ceiling.

"You can imagine how distressing and painful this was to your mother at the time, can't you?"

"Yes, sir . . ."

"I would not like for that pain to be rekindled, David, in any way. You see?"

David looked at him quickly, holding his stepfather's eyes.

"It isn't Camilo's fault, sir. I mean, he didn't know what he was saying." He paused. "I don't want you to punish him."

Carta nodded. "I think I shall speak with him, in any event." He lifted his hand. "Not a punishment, David. A talk. All right?"

"Thank you, sir."

David went out. He did not see his mother in the hall. He went up to his room and shut the door, feeling strangely alone. He lay on the bed for a long time thinking. He wondered what his father had really been like. He missed him now, terribly. Why did he have to die?

Someone had been knocking on his door for several moments before he realized it. "What?"

"*Oye,* David, it's me—Camilo. Let me in."

"Go away, huh?"

"Come on, please?"

David got up from the bed and unlocked the door. He opened it a crack.

Camilo peered up at him contritely. "May I come in?" he said unsteadily.

"Did your father send you up here?"

"No. This was my idea."

David opened the door and walked to the window and looked out. It was getting dark outside.

Camilo stood behind him without saying anything for a long time. Finally David turned and saw him standing in the center of the room, hands at his side, head down. He was crying without making any sound.

"Hey, Cam, come on." He put his arm around his brother's slender shoulders. "Come on, it's all right. I'm not sore at you."

Camilo lifted his chin. His glistening blue eyes looked at David. "I'm sorry I hit you."

"You had a right. I called you a liar."

"I won't ever hurt you again, David. I promise. Just say it's all right between us, huh?"

"It's plenty all right between us, Cam. Plenty all right."

"I don't ever want to fight with you, OK?"

"OK."

"*Hermanos?*"

"*Hermanos.*"

"Always and always?"

"You bet."

CHAPTER SEVEN

MIAMI, JANUARY 14, 1961

It was past three o'clock in the afternoon when Ian Tipton climbed out of the taxi and hurried through the entrance of the Key Biscayne Yacht Club. He felt heavy with fatigue, having gone all night without sleep before catching the plane from Havana. Tipton hated being the bearer of bad news; it made him physically ill to think about it.

Tipton nodded to the two men standing sentrylike on either side of the entrance to the dining room. One was a thick Cuban with an Indian face, named Salazar, whom he knew only slightly. The other, swarthy, heavy-shouldered, with a thick moustache and dark glasses, he knew very well. His name was Alfaro. He had been Gustavo Carta's bodyguard for several years now. Standing in his summer-weight gray suit, hands clasped behind his back, Alfaro presented himself as the big, lazy-faced bystander. But behind the sunglasses the alert insolence of his eyes marked him for what he was, a tough, brave man of fierce loyalties. Tipton had great respect for him.

"We've been expecting you," Alfaro said without turning to look at him. His eyes, behind the sunglasses, kept sweeping the crowded dining room and the bar. "He wants you to meet him at the pool afterward."

Tipton offered him a cigar. He took it and thanked him, opening the little metal tube and sniffing the tobacco carefully. He glanced at Tipton, without smiling. "Smells like home." He replaced the cap and put the tube into the pocket of his coat. There was a bulge in the left side from the .357 magnum revolver he carried in a shoulder holster, and Tipton saw the butt showing against the white shirt when Alfaro put away the cigar. All the time, he kept watching, his face placid, expressionless.

Tipton, following Alfaro's lead, took in the dining room in a glance. Cigar smoke tarnished the air. Every face was turned away from him, watching the speaker, whose familiar voice Tipton had heard as he entered. Glancing around at the intensity with which the audience was listening, Tipton smiled to himself; the tone of that voice—Gustavo Carta's voice—carried a fervent quality, enthusiastic and affectionate, that arrested your attention.

Gustavo stood at the head table across the room, his figure seeming to radiate energy as he spoke; his right hand was suspended a moment in the air, and then suddenly and sharply it smacked into the palm of his left as the words burst from his lips. "It was not the first mistake I have made in my life, *caballeros*—not the first, but probably the most painful to me as a man, as a Cuban!" His head jerked slightly in emphasis. He lowered his eyes. In the pause, Tipton heard someone cough, a spoon tink against a cup. When Carta's eyes lifted again, they swept the faces before him with a fervent energy. "I, like many of you here, come from a generation of Cubans who fought the tyrant Machado in the thirties and was exiled. After we finally drove that tyrant from our beloved and long-suffering homeland, I, like many of you, returned to Havana, turned my back on politics and buried myself in my family and my work. Let the politicians bicker among themselves, let them fight over their graft, I said. Yes, I had done my fighting. I had paid my debt to Cuba. Now I had mouths to feed and bills to pay. To hell with politics! Yes, to hell with it." He lowered his head again, with a look of anguish shaping his expression. "To hell with it," he said softly.

Someone beside Tipton exhaled in a sigh of self-recognition.

"I am," Carta's voice rose again, "essentially a stupid man. I stand before you condemned by my own failing. Exiled by my own culpability." He turned aside and looked to his right, slowly letting his eyes sweep the intent faces before him. "Aren't we all?"

A soft murmur of assent wafted like a wind through the room. Heads nodded.

Watching him, Tipton felt a swell of pride at being associated so closely with this man. Look at the bloody bastards, he thought. He's got them eating out of his hand.

Carta's hand swept in a wide gesture through the cigar haze.

"Let us not fool ourselves, *caballeros*—where were we when Batista overthrew our constitutional government in 1952, eh? How many of us here in this room shrugged our shoulders and said to ourselves, Well, that's how it is, I can't change it. Eh? How many of us buried our heads in the sands of our lives and pretended it didn't matter? I, for one, confess: that's what I did. Not until four years later did I decide to fight —four years! Four precious years! I stand before you a man ashamed. Oh, yes, I fought again. Yes. I joined the underground in Havana. Many of you here recall. Many of you here were my comrades in arms in those terrible days. And again we threw the tyrant out! This time, I said, it will be different! This time we are free men, and free men must be ready to give their fortunes, their energies, their lives if necessary, for their country—just to go on calling themselves free! It is our God-given duty!"

Carta thrust his big head forward, eyes blazing. "I believed! I believed in the revolution we had made! I believed in the new democracy we were making! I believed in the Cuba we foresaw, a country free of imperialism and foreign domination—yes, free of Yankee domination —a country in which justice prevailed for all men. All! I believed in that future in which every Cuban had a home, food to eat, medical care, and work for his hands! I believed in land reform! I believed in eradicating illiteracy! I believed in education for all Cuban children!" Then a long pause, and Carta swung his gaze slowly over the crowd of faces in the room. "I still believe!"

Tipton waited for the applause. It had to come. And did. It started, like a wave, gathering force. But Carta didn't wait for it to break. His fist came down onto the table with a thud as his voice slammed against the gathering roar: "And I am still fighting for it!"

They were standing on their feet now, shouting and applauding.

Good, bloody Christ, Tipton thought, he'll have me cheering him in a moment.

Carta waited for the tumult to subside. "Without breach of security, I am here today to tell you that very soon I shall return to Cuba, to Cuban soil, to fight—against the new tyrant who has seized our country: Fidel Castro!"

Again they were on their feet, applauding, cheering.

Carta waited again, head bowed, until the noise died down, and then he looked up at his audience. "I shall restore our revolution. I shall return Cuba to social democracy in the traditions and concepts José Martí gave to us! To do that, I need your help. I need your money. I need your loyalty. I need your lives. With them, I shall destroy Fidel Castro and his Communist dictatorship. So . . . help . . . me . . . God!"

Ian Tipton found himself pounding his hands together, shouting into the roar of the crowd. "Bravo! Bravo! Bravo!" he yelled. He glanced at Alfaro. The thick Negroid lips spread into a smile.

For nearly six months Tipton had been Carta's military adjutant and adviser.

A Sandhurst man, a career military officer who had served under Wingate in Israel, in the Ethiopian campaign and in Burma, Tipton retired after the war at the rank of major, an expert in guerrilla warfare, totally fed up with military life. He wanted to get as far from the United Kingdom and its army as was possible. He had visited Cuba on holiday in 1939, just before the outbreak of the war, and had remembered it fondly. When it came time to retire, Tipton was surprised by the strangely instinctual urge he felt guiding him back to Havana. He hadn't planned it that way; it happened almost against his conscious will.

When he returned to Havana, the city's charms seduced him once again. He had never considered himself a romantic—quite the contrary —but after the first few months he realized, reluctantly, that a romantic was what he had become. He felt more Cuban than the Cubans. Even his clipped, military British accent began to take on a quiet lilt as he mastered the rapid-fire Cuban Spanish. After dabbling at several jobs, he finally invested in a small shop, off Parque Central, with a Cuban partner, Tomás Estrada, selling men's wear. The shop was quite successful. His partner, a jovial, vivacious man in his fifties, proved to be an astute businessman, and he gave Tipton an entree into Cuban society. Through Tomás, he was introduced not only to Gustavo Carta but to a petite brown-eyed artist named Teresa Mella. She was a vivid girl with raven-black hair and an energetic nature, who embodied in Tipton's mind all of Havana's sensuousness. She was twenty, he had just turned forty-five. Six months after their meeting at a small party in Estrada's Vedado apartment, Tipton asked Tete to marry him and she accepted.

To an English bachelor who had spent most of his life in the rigid discipline of the military, the intrusion of a lively and intelligent Cuban woman made a major change in his austere ways. They bought a house in the Marianao suburb, which Teresa redecorated. She was a painter, and Tipton found himself surrounded by huge modernistic paintings in vivid colors that bewildered his intellect and pleased his eye; flowers and plants flourished everywhere in the white stucco interior; music that ranged from Bach to the Latino nuances of Villa Lobos came drifting into his life with the same wonderful air of excitement his bride brought to his marriage bed. During those years of what seemed pure joy, Tipton had never even considered what would happen to him if he lost her.

41

It had been a frightful incident. How could he forget that day? He had caught a rather nasty cold and decided not to go into the shop that morning. Teresa took the little Austin-Healey into town to visit a friend, a young artist named Raúl, who lived in an apartment on Calle Villegas, near the shop. When she hadn't returned by ten o'clock, Tipton became worried and telephoned. The voice that answered was not Raúl's. Twenty minutes later, he found himself being ushered under guard into the green-walled G-2 headquarters downtown, on Fifth Avenue. He found himself in a cell for the next three days with Major William Morgan, the young American who had distinguished himself in Castro's rebel army, and who had been arrested for trying to carry a carload of weapons to anti-Castro guerrillas in Santa Clara. (He was later executed at La Cabaña prison). The lights in the cell were kept burning day and night; sleep was impossible. Guards kept announcing their arrival by banging on the doors. Finally, on the third afternoon, Tipton was brought in for questioning.

Teresa, he was told, had been in Raúl's apartment with three counter-revolutionaries, when G-2 agents burst in the door, guns drawn. One of the youths pulled a revolver, and seconds later, in a blaze of automatic-weapon fire, Teresa and the four young men were dead. Stunned, Tipton had gone through the hours of questioning in a trance. He was finally released, with the aid of the British Embassy, that same evening.

It took several days for the shock to curdle into rage. For two days he sat alone in his bedroom, staring at the wall. He'd been all for Fidel at the outset. But this smacked of a police state, and Tipton detested it. On May 7, 1960, he booked passage on the 5:30 P.M. Pan American flight to Miami, locked the shop, and, without even bothering to go back to the house in Marianao to pack his things, took a taxi to Rancho Boyeros airport and went into exile. It was the day after he had buried Teresa in Havana's Colón Cemetery.

Nearly bankrupt (he had his army pension and a small business account in London he had used for the shop), Tipton moved into a cheap hotel in downtown Miami and began inquiring into the newly formed anti-Castro groups; he wanted to settle his personal score with Castro.

It seemed to Tipton that every Cuban in Miami of any significance had organized some kind of movement for liberation. What struck him immediately was the prevalence of people who wanted to talk a great deal and yet were obviously disinclined to fight. He also felt that self-interest dominated most of the political organizations that had sprung up—petty politicos trying to put themselves in power.

Then, in June, through some of his exile friends, he heard about Gustavo Carta. He had done a bit of duck shooting on the Isle of Pines with Carta, back in the 1950s, and knew him socially. They had occasionally played dominoes and chess together at the American Club. He had found him a delightful companion, very Americanized and apparently very nonpolitical. Any discussion of Cuban politics brought a look of contempt from Carta, who seemed to have a healthy skepticism about all politicians and all political dogma, particularly Cuban. It shocked Tipton when he learned that during the last days of Batista's rule Carta had spent vast sums supporting Castro's guerrilla operations in Oriente, that his son, Camilo, had actually gone to join the guerrillas—and, finally, that Carta himself joined the Castro regime.

It wasn't until after the revolution had triumphed and Castro had taken power in Havana, appointing Carta as Minister of Finance, that Tipton began to hear stories about his friend's previous incarnation. As a young man in the revolt against the Machado dictatorship in the 1930s, Carta had been implicated in the assassination of one of Machado's henchmen, a secret-police captain named Hernando Casáliz; as a result, Carta had been forced to flee Cuba. Again Tipton had found himself both surprised and amused. It was so typically Cuban. The fiery young student retires after the overthrow of a dictator, devotes his life to a wife, children and the family business; then suddenly, on the brink of middle age, he catches fire again and plunges wholeheartedly back into a rebellion to overthrow still another dictator. He had misjudged Carta. The man had a deceiving American veneer; scratched, he was all Cuban.

He had seen Carta only once in Havana after the Castro regime took over, walking down the Prado with his wife, Elizabeth, and their son, Camilo, a tall, handsome lad who, with his beard and olive-green fatigues, cut a rather popular and romantic figure among the Castro entourage; at times, it was said, too popular. "Everybody loves Camilo," Teresa told him. "I hear that even Fidel is jealous of him."

"Why is that?" Tipton had asked.

"Oh, the usual thing, I suppose, women."

That June, Tipton heard that Carta had resigned from the Castro government, and there were rumors of a clash with his son. He felt genuinely sorry. He knew Carta was an honorable man who had held out until the last, trying to sway the revolutionary government away from the Communists and back to the democratic ideals everyone thought the whole bloody mess had been fought for originally.

What intrigued him, as July came around, were reports of the formation of the Partido Revolucionario Cubano (PRC) with Carta at its head. The PRC, Tipton learned, was composed of once-devoted Castro supporters in the rebel army and the government who had decided that the revolution could no longer be salvaged. They had now allied themselves

43

in an underground organization aimed at restoring the revolutionary goals under a democratic government. This to Tipton sounded like the first reasonable political program for his adopted country that he had encountered since going into exile.

Four days after Carta fled Cuba and surfaced in Miami, Tipton unceremoniously turned up on his doorstep. His manner was as breezy as ever, but his eyes were angry.

"Hello, old chap," Tipton had said. "I think perhaps we have some matters of common interest to discuss."

By then, Carta's underground had created an atmosphere of open rebellion against Castro. Carta was an unpleasant thorn in Castro's side. Tipton intended to help make it a fatal sword. He trusted Carta the moment they shook hands. But it was what he had said at that first meeting that captured Tipton's fancy completely.

"We don't need large forces," Carta told Tipton. "We beat Batista and his fifty thousand men with fewer than three thousand at the peak of the revolution. No, my friend, we want them to *think* we have large forces. A successful revolution happens in the mind of your enemy. I remember once in 1958 telling my friend Raúl Masetti that we would one day capture the Columbia barracks without firing a shot. He laughed at me. Batista had ten thousand men in that camp. A fortress! Artillery, tanks, machine guns—enormous military forces! You know, Tipton, a year later we walked into the Columbia barracks without firing a shot. All of those thousands of soldiers, that formidable military power —they gave us their weapons. Why? Because we had touched their minds. We had convinced them that we were right. They truly believed it. We did it to Batista, and that is what we shall do to Fidel. You see? It is not bullets that make victories. Fidel does not fear our guns. He fears our ideals—our dedication to freedom!"

Feeling tense and impatient, Tipton paced along the edge of the swimming pool. He glanced over his shoulder at the glass wall of the club. Inside he could see Carta struggling through the crowd, trying to reach the outside door, but several men had stopped him. Carta was shaking the outstretched hands and nodding his head in greeting, trying to maintain a polite veneer while moving through the maze of well-wishers. Tipton knew how important this appearance was to them all. Those men inside represented Miami's affluent, progressive exiles. They were Carta's chief source of financial support. Tipton regretted intruding. He regretted even more having to break the terrible news he had learned that morning in Havana.

He took a deep breath. Get it over with, old man, he thought. He glanced about. A few children were splashing at the far end of the pool under the watchful eyes of their mothers, but the area was otherwise deserted. They could talk here.

Carta came toward him smiling and held out his hand, which Tipton clasped warmly. "How was Havana?"

"Masetti sends his regards," Tipton replied. "I'm afraid I have some rather unpleasant news."

Carta's smile grew more tentative. "Oh? Very well, my friend—let me have it."

"They've taken Escalante," Tipton said, his voice flat and emotionless.

Carta stared at him. "When?"

"Yesterday morning. We just got word. We think he might have been compromised by a boy in his command. His name is Menéndez, a cook's assistant—"

"And the Coast Guard station?"

Tipton shook his head ruefully, his eyes moving from Carta back to the pool. "They took the entire station. They shot Escalante in front of his men."

Tipton saw Carta turn his head as his teeth bit hard on his lower lip. "*Coño!*" he swore under his breath. He looked as though a dead weight had suddenly clamped itself to his shoulders. "How did this happen?"

"The boy, Menéndez, was on leave in Havana. He told his father. The old man took him to see Fidel."

"And the boy?"

"Masetti has plans to deal with him."

"What about the naval units at Baracoa?"

"Castro suspects them. This morning he ordered their fuel rations cut to nothing. They can't move a single torpedo boat at the moment."

"*Mal suerte,*" Carta mumbled. He lifted his chin and looked out at the boat harbor. The breeze off the water stirred the gray hairs at his temple. Tipton saw his nostrils flare as he breathed deeply, his chest expanding slightly and then easing. His eyes were moist. "*Mal suerte,*" he whispered.

"It's a nasty bit of luck, all right," Tipton agreed. "But as I see it, it rather depends on whether Escalante talked, doesn't it? If he did, we could be in for it. But if he didn't . . ."

"It isn't so bad . . ."

"Right. We may have to shore up a few things here and there, but the operation can proceed pretty much as planned, eh?"

"It would be nice to think so." Carta smiled thinly. "Will you tell Rodríguez?"

"Certainly. But I don't think we ought to say anything to the men at the camp just yet. Bad for morale, y'know? Let's hold off until we get Masetti's evaluation. He'll be reporting to us in a few days on just how badly our security's been breached."

"Yes, I agree," Carta told him. He noticed how Tipton kept avoiding his gaze. "Is there something else?"

"Sure."

"What?"

"It was Camilo that led the raid. Camilo executed Escalante."

"I see."

"I debated not telling you . . ."

"You're certain, are you?"

"Yes."

"I see," Carta said softly. He looked, suddenly, very tired.

Tipton glanced at Carta, then shrugged helplessly. "I am sorry, Gustavo."

But Carta had already looked away, lost in his own private thoughts.

★

Gustavo scrambled over the tile roof in the dark and he saw the lights of Havana all the way to the Malecón and the arc-light glow in the street below, where the cars were parked. The sharp, muffled reports of the gunfire behind them scared him. "Come on," he said to Raúl Masetti, and they went down the fire escape to the street. It was a hot night, *June 1, 1929,* and he was soaked with sweat, but he felt cold inside and trembled all the time. They were still shooting in the apartment upstairs. Benítez was making a hell of a fight of it. He was a tough kid. Gustavo felt rotten about leaving him like that. They had been friends since the first day at the university. "I'll cover you! Go!" he yelled at them from the staircase. Go. It made Gustavo feel bad now that he hadn't stayed.

The shutters on the shops along both sides of the narrow street were closed. Up the street they could see four motorcars parked under the street light. The police were crouched behind the cars, shooting up at the building. They could see the little flashes the guns made, like sparks, and hear the *bop! bop-bop!* as the sound reached them an instant later.

Breathless, they waited and watched in the doorway, a block away, afraid to move. They saw a cluster of men on the street, like a soccer face-off, then they saw them bringing out Benítez. His shirt was torn off his shoulders, and his face looked puffy and yellow in the light. His hair kept bouncing as he was shoved along between two policemen who were holding his arms. A man in a Panama hat hit him with something as they shoved him into the sedan. He went down on his knees just inside the door and held his head in his hands. The Panama hat kicked him twice in the spine. They saw Benítez jerk every time the Panama hat kicked him.

"Bastards!" said Raúl Masetti under his breath. It made him sick to watch it.

After a while, the four cars started up and went off down the street and turned the corner.

At one-thirty in the morning, the big Graham-Paige stopped in front of the apartment on Eleventh in Vedado. The son of a bitch was still wearing the white Panama when he got out. They could see him in the street light. He was shorter than the two soldiers with him. He wore a light suit, and his stomach bulged where he had his coat buttoned. One of the soldiers got back into the car and slammed the door. The taller one stood on the narrow sidewalk in front of the house, holding his rifle at his side. He looked to Gustavo to be several inches over six feet tall. The Panama hat stood waiting. For some reason he seemed reluctant to go inside. It was Mama Pérez' place. She had told them Captain Casáliz came there every night. "He's a pig," she said.

"All right," said Raúl Masetti, "let's go!"

Miguel was driving. He started the car. They were all scared. Gustavo sat in the back next to the open window and felt the ribs on the wooden handle of the big Smith & Wesson revolver, excited about what was to happen. A truck went past, headlights bright. Miguel turned in behind the truck.

"Keep it slow," Raúl said. "Keep it slow." He ducked down under the dashboard, sitting there with the Thompson submachine gun between his knees. From the back seat Gustavo heard him cock it.

Miguel said, "Now!"

Gustavo sat up from the back seat and saw Casáliz in the Panama hat standing on the steps. He had stopped and was looking back over his shoulder at them. His hair was gray and he was short and fat. Gustavo brought the gun up and pulled the trigger. It flashed and bolted like something alive in his hand. He saw the look on Casáliz' face just as he fired. Gray splatters burst on the wall as Raúl let go with the Thompson. A window crashed. The police inspector went down hard on the steps. Raúl was shooting from the front. Gustavo heard the windows of the car breaking. *Splat! Splat! Splat!* Out of the corner of his eye he saw the tall soldier go down against the wall. Raúl was firing in short bursts. Gustavo remembered to cock the revolver. They were past the sedan now. He had to lean out of the window. Casáliz was below the steps. The bastard had fallen face down on the sidewalk. Gustavo let him have another one. He heard it hit solid and saw the body flop. Raúl shot out the windshield in the touring car. The driver had his face against the steering wheel, and the impact threw his body back against the seat. The tall soldier was trying to sit up against the wall. Raúl gave him a short blast. He slumped over and went down on his face.

"Let's get out of here!" Raúl said. Miguel gave it the gas. Raúl looked back at him and raised his fist in a salute. "We killed the *maricón* police bastard!" he said between his teeth. "We killed him good!"

But in the back Gustavo kept looking over his shoulder at the street behind them. He kept expecting headlights any minute. It wasn't until they turned the corner that he realized there was something warm and wet between his legs. "Oh, Jesus . . ." he said aloud.

Raúl Masetti turned from the front seat to look at him, alarmed. "What's the matter—you hit?"

"No," Gustavo told him. "I think I've pissed my pants."

It was dangerous in Havana those next two days. The assassination of Police Captain Hernando Casáliz-Ruíz on June 2, 1929, touched off a series of reprisals by President Machado's secret police. The university was closed. The whole city was scared. The secret police in their white suits and broad Panama hats were out in cars, cruising the streets. They were using loudspeakers to tell people to stay in their houses until the criminals were caught. Nearly two hundred suspects had already been arrested. Chino told them the police had picked up Miguel last night.

He saw the crowd around the sea wall above the dock. They pushed through and looked down into the water. Everyone was looking at what the two boatmen were fishing out. He saw a yellow grapefruit rind floating in the debris between the heavy boats. The canvas canopy over the back of one of the boats had a hole in it, and a streak of sunlight fell on the body in the thwart. The other body was face down in the water. One of the boatmen had its leg in his two hands and was shouting for someone to help him drag it onto the dock. Gustavo recognized the one in the boat. He was a fellow student. He was quite small and thin and his face was blue. He saw the gaping slash in his throat where someone had cut it and then he noticed that the boy's penis and testicles were burned black and swollen huge between his pale legs. They had a sickening barbecued look.

When they got the body of the second boy onto the dock, he saw that he was naked, too, and there was only a raw fleshy gap where his genitals had been. The bastards! It made him want to vomit.

Gustavo turned away. Raúl took his arm.

"I wonder what they'll do to Miguel," Raúl whispered.

48

"You better get out of Havana," Gustavo told him.

"Yes," said Raúl. "Where will you go?"

"Out to the *finca*. My father's there."

Chino came up even with them as they crossed the street. He had an Oriental face and shaggy black hair. He looked awfully worried. "You think Miguel will talk?" he asked them. "What will you do if they come to get you, Gustavo? What can you do?"

"I'll fight them," Gustavo told them. "I'll fight the bastards until I die!"

Gustavo saw Raúl off on the train to Santiago de Cuba at four o'clock that afternoon, then drove his Ford to his father's house in San Francisco de Paula. At six-thirty that evening, René informed him that his father was in the library and wished to speak to him immediately. Gustavo put on a clean shirt, tie and coat, combed his hair, and went down to the library. Although he was outwardly calm, the events of the last few days had unnerved him. He felt afraid. Outside the library door, he took a deep breath and knocked.

Don Andrés was seated behind his desk. The shades were drawn and the metal lamp on his desk illuminated his dark suit and clean white shirt, which he had buttoned at the throat without a tie. The collar seemed too large for him. His wrinkled neck rose from the collar to his gaunt face, which bore a stern expression. He sat erect in the leather chair with his thin hand placed in front of him on the green felt blotter. Behind him was the oil portrait of Gustavo's grandfather, Don Camilo. He looked at it, waiting for his father to speak.

"I am pleased to see," his father's voice said, with surprising vigor, "they have not yet killed you."

Gustavo smiled at him.

"You were responsible for the death of this policeman, were you not?"

"He killed my friend, Manolo Benítez."

Don Andrés looked at him blankly and then said, as though he had seen too much of death in one lifetime, "Ah, yes, I read about it in the papers. He was shot while trying to escape arrest, wasn't he?"

"No. They tortured Manolo before they killed him. Casáliz tore out his eyes with a screwdriver. Shall I tell you what I saw them fish out of the harbor this morning?"

The old man raised his hand, cords of blue veins showing through the almost transparent flesh. His long fingers trembled. "I know these men." He spoke softly. "They have been with us for a long time. Like you, I am outraged at the cruelty. But I have seen much, Gustavo. Too much. It doesn't change. Only their faces change. Only their names. They are always with us. You kill them, others take their place, just as bad. I have

49

seen it." He lifted his chin so that the light reflected off his pupils. "One of your comrades was arrested. A boy whose name is Miguel Fuentes. Do you know him?"

"Yes. He drove the car . . ."

"He was persuaded to talk."

Gustavo felt a thickness in his throat. "I see."

"They will come to arrest you at nine o'clock."

"Are you sure?"

"Quite sure. I have a friend . . ." Don Andrés' voice trailed off. He lowered his eyes and then lifted them again; again catching the luminosity of the lamp in the pupils, so that it seemed his eyes glowed. "I have made arrangements for you to leave Cuba—immediately."

"Leave Cuba?"

"René will drive you to Cojimar. There is a boat waiting—it will take you to Key West."

"I wish to stay and fight, Father."

"Fight?" His father's voice rose. "Fight? You are my only son! You are the last of us on earth! Fight?" His whole thin body was trembling. He leaned forward in his chair, gripping the edge of the desk so that his knuckles stood out on his hands, white as bone. "Gustavo, these beasts will always be with us! Kill them and they will be replaced by others, just as bad. It has been so through all history—but you are the only male left in this family! I am too old to remarry, to have children. There is only you! As your father, I make this decision for you. If there is dishonor in it, let it be on my shoulders."

"Machado is—"

"I know Machado!" his father interrupted. "You don't have to tell me about Machado. Was Gómez better? Was Estrada Palma with all his fervor able to keep us from greed and brutality? When I was your age I fought the Spaniards. I saw my brothers blown to pieces! And for what! We are no better now than we were then."

"It will all change when we have won," Gustavo broke in, his voice fervent. "We will make a better place, where men are free!"

"How many times have I heard that word spoken in Cuba? With the same ardor. Who knows what it means anymore? It is a word that we have worn out shouting at each other. It seems each of our generations takes it for their own, beats it to death, and leaves it in the gutter for the next to find. Don't speak to me of freedom. We don't even have a definition any longer."

"We have José Martí's definition, Father—"

"Martí—ha! I remember Martí. His words once burned in my soul! 'When one dies in the arms of a grateful fatherland—with death, life

50

begins.' They were only words, Gustavo. Only words. Let me give you more words by the Apóstol that perhaps you have forgotten: 'There is a limit to the tears we can shed at the tombs of the dead.' You remember? Where is Martí now, eh? Does he sit in his house, with his land, his children? No. He is rotten bones in a grave, without children—nothing. The Spanish killed him!"

"Martí is an idea . . ."

His father looked at him intently, his eyes narrowing. "An idea? You would let your family end—now! For an idea? And what of us? What of the name of Carta? Eh? What did our lives mean if you do that? All the generations of Cartas who have lived. What of them, eh?" He shook his head. "No. I will not let you have this madness. I am your father and you must obey. You will go now—at once—to the United States."

"You talk like a man who wants his son to be a coward!"

"No, I talk like someone who wants his son to have the chance to grow old! Part of becoming a man is learning to accept. Perhaps it is the hardest part. You must learn which things can be changed and which must simply be accepted."

"You mean you want me to believe in nothing? Fight for nothing?"

His father almost rose from his chair, his lips trembling to get out the words. "I want you to believe in your family! To fight for your family! There is nothing else worth dying for, but your family! There is no other purpose to life than having children, having them to carry on your family name!"

Don Andrés leaned back in his chair, his chest heaving with exertion. He closed his eyes. After a moment he opened them, fixing his gaze on Gustavo. "You understand me?"

Gustavo lowered his head and nodded. His voice came as almost a whisper. "What will I do in the United States?"

"Bishop Zaragoza has written me about a university—Georgetown, a Jesuit school. I have written you a letter of introduction." Don Andrés' hand fumbled with the three envelopes on his desk. "You will go there until I write you that it is safe to return to La Habana."

Gustavo took the envelopes and stuffed them into the pocket of his jacket.

His father said, "One of those contains a thousand American dollars —that will keep you until you reach Washington. The other is a check drawn on the bank in New York. If you need more, write me. I will see it is sent."

Gustavo looked down at his hands. "I am sorry, Father."

"Sorry? For what? I am proud you are my son. This murder, it is between you and God—you will answer to Him, and to Him alone."

51

Gustavo looked at his father's face in the glow of the lamp. It seemed some of his old vigor and strength had come back into it. Don Andrés rose stiffly, slowly, drawing himself erect. He held out his arms. Gustavo moved around the desk and embraced him in silence. There was a smell of tobacco and clean linen about his father, and his face was prickly with the stubble of his beard. It surprised Gustavo how thin his body felt. But the old arms held him strongly, as though he wished to never let go.

When Gustavo moved from his embrace, he saw the tears glistening in his father's eyes. Don Andrés' lips quivered.

"It is . . . not a good life," the old man said in a quavering voice filled with emotion. "I do not know how people survive this life without God."

CHAPTER EIGHT

Kirby Pelham sat watching Charles Danforth's face attentively. The only expression he could detect in it was annoyance. Looking lean and patrician in a navy-blue pinstripe suit, Danforth was seated behind an antique oak desk which was littered with papers and black-bound folders. Occasionally, as he listened, he glanced out the window at the gray afternoon. The view from his office looked onto Pennsylvania Avenue, where the midday traffic glided between the bare trees in a steady, slow-moving flow. As President-elect Kennedy's newly designated special assistant, Danforth was charged with coordinating the tangled affairs of what was euphemistically called "the transition period."

Abruptly, Danforth turned in his chair, the swivel squeaking, and tossed a pencil sharply onto a stack of papers. "I don't want to seem rude, gentlemen, but you're telling me more than I need to know at this time. The President-elect was briefed on the Cuban situation seven weeks ago, right after the election. I don't see that developments warrant another briefing."

"In his memo," Richard Vermillion said, "the President specifically suggested that the best plan for the Cuban operation had not been presented. Events are breaking rapidly. We wish to keep you closely informed."

"Yes, but I also have to be closely informed about the twelve hundred appointments we have to make before the Inauguration, the recession, the balance-of-payments crisis and the goddamn Peace Corps, which is the President's pet." Danforth was not letting good breeding disguise the magnitude of his harassment. "The Inauguration is only six days away, gentlemen, and we don't even have a speech yet. Instead what we have is a mess in Laos and this goddamn Lumumba running around the Congo."

"We have an army of men prepared to invade Cuba," Vermillion cut in. "With due respect, do we have armies in the Congo or in Laos?"

There was an urgency in Richard Vermillion's normally languid voice that gave Danforth pause. Tall, bespectacled, professorial in manner, Vermillion was the Central Intelligence Agency's deputy director for plans. Danforth had known him casually for many years. Both were Groton men and both had gone to Harvard. During World War II both had been in the Office of Strategic Services, before Danforth entered the Foreign Service and Vermillion the CIA. He sat now across the desk, wearing a gray glen-plaid suit, white shirt and tie, looking at Danforth with shrewd, ironic eyes.

Danforth switched his gaze to the man seated beside Vermillion. He had seen him before, too, years ago, but he could not recall where or under what circumstances. He was in his mid-forties, Danforth judged, medium height, compact and, from the expression on his rather featureless face, severe in manner. He leaned forward in his chair as though he was about to leap up and pace around the room to wear off some of his excess energy. From their conversation Danforth gathered that he was running Vermillion's Cuban operation in Miami.

Danforth did not welcome their visit. The interregnum between the Eisenhower Administration and the New Frontier had proved to be frantic. Demands for position papers were relentless. Communication between Kennedy, who spent much of his time in Palm Beach, and his close advisers in Washington and Cambridge, Massachusetts, was frustrating, sporadic and incomplete. New problems, domestic and international, seemed to keep breaking around him, and yet Danforth was now worried about the basics—firming up plans for the Inaugural ceremonies, organizing a smooth continuity with outgoing Administration officials, nailing down the Cabinet appointments. He felt like a rock sitting in the midst of a rushing stream. He did not want to tumble into the current. And he did not feel, at this moment, like listening to tales of Latin intrigues stemming from Eisenhower's inept handling of Cuba.

The broad outlines of the Cuban mess had long since been known to Danforth. It was eminently clear to him that Fidel Castro, having liberated Cuba from the right-wing dictatorship of Batista, was now intent on establishing a Communist dictatorship of his own. On November 17, shortly after Kennedy defeated Richard Nixon in the presidential election, the CIA formally briefed the President-elect on its plan to frustrate Castro's objectives. The CIA said it had started training small bands of anti-Communist exiles in the mountains of Guatemala. These units would be infiltrated into Cuba, hopefully to provide the nucleus of an anti-Castro resistance. The plan sounded reasonable enough to Kennedy and to Danforth—the prospect of a Communist toehold in the Caribbean was unthinkable—but there had been disquieting indications lately that the CIA's plan, which had seemed so neat and self-contained, was somehow beginning to get out of control. Isolated reports were appearing in the press suggesting links between the guerrillas and the CIA. And Fidel Castro was displaying a relentless determination to exploit these rumors to the fullest and, if possible, to escalate the situation into an international *cause célèbre*. On New Year's Day, Castro, amid a fusillade of press agentry, filed a formal complaint with the United Nations Security Council charging that U.S.-backed mercenaries were preparing aggression against his country. On cue, Nikita Khrushchev condemned the U.S. actions. A day later Castro further escalated events: he issued sudden orders that the State Department immediately withdraw all but eleven of its three-hundred-man staff from the embassy in Havana. On January 4, President Eisenhower angrily broke off diplomatic relations with Cuba. All this struck Danforth as bizarre; the break in relations seemed to be an absurd climax to these tit-for-tat machinations, which were more suitable to small boys fighting in a schoolyard than to the delicate processes of international diplomacy. It seemed to Danforth that effective communications between the United States and Cuba had broken down back in 1959, when Castro took power, and that the two governments replaced it with a kind of hopeless, self-fulfilling prophecy in which each side predicted an eventual confrontation and then set about dealing economic and diplomatic blows to bring it about. Somewhere down the road a coherent Cuba policy would have to be hammered out, but not now in the midst of a turbulent interregnum.

"Our short-term objective must be to keep this thing contained," Danforth said, unfastening the top button of his shirt and loosening his tie. "Let's just keep the decibel level down. Even Khrushchev can't foment a diplomatic crisis out of a few guerrillas training in the mountains."

"Yes, but you see, Danforth, it is no longer question of a few guerrillas," Vermillion replied. "The plan is now known as Operation Trinidad. It calls for a full-scale amphibious invasion of Cuba. There will be an air strike first, then the landing by a major assault force."

Danforth felt as if he had just been kicked in the stomach. "When did all this develop?"

"Over the course of the last few weeks," said Vermillion. "You will recall, Danforth, when we last briefed you people on the Cuban matter we mentioned this more orthodox military solution as a possibility."

"It was a contingency!" Danforth exclaimed. "A contingency plan, you said. How the hell did a contingency plan become operational, without anyone knowing it?"

"Our plans for guerrilla operations simply didn't work—so we abandoned them."

"Why?"

Pelham leaned forward and put his hand on the edge of the desk, looking straight at Danforth with his cool gray eyes, his lips compressed. "There were a whole range of difficulties, Mr. Danforth. You understand, when you have a clandestine underground organization in a hostile country, your main problems are supply and communications—"

"Yes, yes," Danforth said with an impatient wave of his hand. "I've heard that lecture, too."

"All our attempts at supplying the underground in Cuba, the countryside particularly, proved inadequate, you see? Communications were impossible, even to people in Havana."

"Are you serious?" Danforth uncrossed his legs and leaned forward, looking from Vermillion to Kirby Whatshisname and back. "I can pick up a phone now and call Havana! You can take a plane from New York, Miami—hell, even Key West. How can you sit there and tell me communications with Havana were and are impossible?"

Vermillion's voice broke in, speaking as though he were an old actor reciting his lines. "We're not saying you can't communicate with Cuba, Danforth. It's a matter of who down there is answering the phone. Castro's agents managed to penetrate the various underground organizations in Cuba, all of them! We could not rely on them, or trust their people. And without the support of an internal network, the whole guerrilla operation became untenable."

"Mr. Pelham, did you people make any attempt to rebuild the Cuban underground organizations? Form new ones? Train new people? Anything?"

Pelham looked to Vermillion. The older man lifted one leg and crossed it over the other, smoothing out his gray pants leg with his left hand. "We made some attempt, yes. Unsuccessful, I'm afraid. Quite impossible, given the nature of the Cubans. 'Security' is hardly a word in their vernacular." Vermillion's creased face broke into a faint sardonic smile. It was evident he did not like the Cubans, and his expression underlined it.

Danforth was still trying to recover from his surprise. "This Operation —Trinidad, is it?—how far along are you?"

"It is fully operational," Vermillion said, in his same dry, matter-of-fact cadence, as if he were talking about census data instead of fighting men. "We are presently increasing the size of the force training in Guatemala from two hundred and fifty men to fifteen hundred. Pilots are being recruited for an exile air force. We have already supplied them with B-26 propeller aircraft of World War Two vintage. American 'advisers' have been flown in to supervise training. The invasion will be launched in early March."

Danforth listened to this recitation with mounting alarm. "President Kennedy is under the impression that we are dealing with plans for a small, low-profile guerrilla operation," he said sharply. "You gentlemen are suddenly talking about air attacks, a major invasion. These are decisions that will ultimately be up to the President. I would remind you that he is the Commander in Chief. He may not choose to go along with this military adventure."

"It's his decision, of course," replied Vermillion. "However, as I said earlier, we are talking about a large force of men here. Even if you would want to, you can't simply disband an army. You would be left with what one could call a 'disposal problem,' if you get my drift. Once you have an army of men they're going to attack someone—if not the other fellow, then you."

Pelham leaned forward. "Our alternative, of course, is to return them to Miami, under, say, a Marine guard. But we'd be forced to release them to the streets, you see? Can you imagine the problems that would create?"

It was too unbelievable. Danforth felt he was being ensnarled in a web of bureacratic thinking that was all but indestructible. It had a curious beauty and power to its very structure, as he viewed it for the first time, which awed and at the same time appalled him. How can this happen? he kept asking himself. How can I cut through it?

He turned and looked out the window to collect his thoughts. The January afternoon was growing dark rapidly. The cars passing under the window had begun to turn on their headlights. Now and then the cacophony of horns drifted up to him in the smoke-colored twilight. He spoke without looking at them.

"Your point is clear. But we must keep our options open. At the appropriate time after the new Administration takes office there will be a full-scale review of the whole situation."

Pelham, watching Danforth's handsome face now, smiled to himself. It pleased him to see Danforth flustered, his cool façade penetrated, trying to maintain a certain superiority even now. Well, old boy, Pelham thought, you've got a few more surprises coming to you.

Vermillion's hand smoothed out his pants leg as he spoke, eyes lowered, watching his fingers. "On the other hand, you must understand that we're confronted with very considerable time pressures. Castro's been scouring Europe to buy small arms and ammunition. The Russians are pouring supplies into Cuba. Our agents tell us they've already started delivery of MIG jets—they're sending the parts in big shipping crates to avoid detection. And Cuban pilots are in training in Czechoslovakia."

"What are you trying to say, for Christ's sake? Say it directly, Richard."

"Simply that Castro is just a little Caribbean Communist at the moment. He will be a world power by spring."

The intercom buzzed. The secretary's voice carried an edge of panic. Eight officials had been waiting outside for the meeting on Cabinet appointments. How much longer would they be waiting? Danforth put down the phone and looked at his two visitors, who sat there calmly, almost taciturn, like two diplomats who had just made a routine call on a newly appointed ambassador. A flurry of questions and doubts raced through Danforth's mind. There was something odd about the tone and the timing of this meeting. The earlier presidential briefing had obviously been deliberately vague and incomplete. And this session was not so much a briefing as a formal notification: the CIA was serving notice on the new Administration that it had diagnosed the Cuban crisis and was bent on implementing its own plans for resolving it.

Danforth wished he had known during the campaign what he knew now. Kennedy had blasted the Republicans in speech after speech for allowing Cuba to become "Communism's first Caribbean base." He had come on strong—even stronger than Nixon. Perhaps the CIA was now shrewdly exploiting Kennedy's campaign rhetoric as a wedge to advance its own strategy. The President had already committed himself, in a sense; it would be awkward to back down.

There was nothing more to be said at this time, that was clear. Danforth rose and shook hands with Vermillion and Pelham, but he had the strong suspicion that he would be seeing a great deal more of them.

Danforth stared at the phone. The President was in Palm Beach. Perhaps he should be forewarned that the Cuban mess loomed as something more ominous than the minor irritant he now thought it to be. It was such an obscure little country. Yet it was a tinder box. What was needed desperately, he realized, was a cool assessment. But that was the problem. The President-elect had no one in his immediate entourage who knew anything about Cuba, let alone Latin America.

Whom could he trust? His thoughts suddenly fastened on Elizabeth, his cousin, and her husband, Gustavo Carta.

Danforth now realized that his office was filling up with visitors who were coming up to him, their hands extended, their faces visibly perplexed by Danforth's own look of preoccupation. Danforth forced a smile. He greeted them absently and shook their hands. He stared at the phone again. This was not the time for a call. But soon. He must make it soon.

Vermillion and Pelham decided to walk for two blocks and enjoy the crisp January twilight. They were striding briskly, their limousine following slowly behind them.

"I want you to go back to Miami and pull it all together, Pel," Vermillion said. "I want you to tell your people they have a job to do."

"I understand."

"It is vital that the invasion appear to the world to embody the unified will of the Cuban exile community. This 'front' that you spoke about at the last meeting . . ."

"The 'Frente.' "

"Frente, yes. It must be broadened to reflect a more liberal element, the younger Cubans. The Kennedy people will look at things like that."

"But not Communists, Richard."

"Certainly not Communists or radicals. But people like this fellow Carta . . ."

"He's very headstrong. A difficult man."

"Bring him in, Pel. I want to stop all this political infighting among the Cubans. It's going to hurt us. I want you to run this operation with an absolutely firm hand, but I want it all to look like the will of the Cuban people—one voice, one movement."

"Carta has a rather extensive guerrilla operation—in Cuba itself. We've been withholding logistical support."

"By all means, don't go too far, Pel. We want cosmetics, not a guerrilla leader on our hands who'll be a problem later."

"Understood."

Pelham nodded thoughtfully, and they walked in silence for a few moments, each man lost in his own thoughts.

"Fait accompli," Vermillion mumbled as though his thought process had not been interrupted by the silence.

"What, sir?"

"Fait accompli, Pel. I want this all wrapped up in a neat package for

58

young Mr. Kennedy by the time he steps into office. A neat package, Pel."

"Do you think the Kennedy people will go along with all this?" Pelham asked at last. "Do you think they'll see it through?"

Vermillion glanced at him and kept walking. "I don't really see that they have any other options. Do you?"

Pelham thought about that briefly. "No, I suppose I don't."

"Besides, they have all sorts of convenient alibis. They can say they inherited the operation from Eisenhower. They can say they didn't know, it's just a Cuban show. You will learn, Pel, that Administrations and Presidents become much more courageous if you give them the chance to deny everything. Plausible deniability, it's called. Set it all up so they can claim the credit if things go well and deny everything if things go wrong. That's Vermillion's First Law of Bureaucratic Procedure."

Vermillion gave his companion a wry smile and then signaled for the limousine, which accelerated and came to a halt at the curb beside them. Vermillion climbed in, Pelham on his heels, and the automobile moved into the flow of Washington traffic.

CHAPTER NINE

HAVANA, 1946

The pigeons broke from the cages with a flutter of wings and exploded into the air. Gustavo Carta lifted the double-barreled shotgun and fired. One bird folded up in a puff of feathers and fell in an arc to the ground. The other guns were firing now. They sounded to David like sledgehammers against his eardrums. *Thump! Thump! Thump!* "Why didn't you shoot, David?" Gustavo asked him. But he hadn't seen them very well. Only the flickering of the light on their wings. They moved too fast. He couldn't get his good eye focused on them in time. Would he try again? Yes, he wanted to. He was just fourteen and he wanted to please his stepfather; he wanted the man to love him. Gustavo signaled with his hand, and the birds broke again. David lifted the shotgun and tried to see them over the barrel, swinging with their trajectory as he'd been taught. He fired twice. The kick of the gun hurt his shoulder, but he tried to ignore it. Carta smiled and said he was afraid David would never make much of a marksman. But that was all right. The other shooters were standing in line with their shotguns. They were making jokes under their breath and grinning. David ignored them. He wanted to try again. Someone in the crowd said he should try eagles, perhaps he could see them better. The others laughed. Camilo, who stood behind David at the gun rack, glowered at them. In a quiet voice he told them to shut their stupid mouths. Let his brother shoot without being molested. He kept looking at them squarely with his angry blue eyes. One or two laughed, but the others avoided his stare, embarrassed. Carta watched this and said nothing at all. He nodded to David, who set himself, the gun at his shoulder as he had been taught. He strained to see. He had to show them. He just had to. The birds broke with a fluttering whisper of wings and climbed rapidly into the sky. He saw them pass through the blur on his blind side, saw them take shape, white in the sun; swung the barrel smoothly in line to give them a proper lead and fired. The shotgun banged loudly, too loudly, he thought. He fired again. He saw the sudden burst of feathers, the second bird arcing downward behind the first, the little puff of white feathers lingering in the air above them. He felt elated. When he turned he saw Camilo putting the pump gun into the rack. "Did you shoot, Cam?" Camilo put his arm around David's shoulder. "No, I just backed you up. You got both of them. You dusted them!" His voice rose louder. "Great shooting!" Carta laughed and put his arms around both his boys. He looked over at the other shooters now, his eyes filled with pride. "Next time we'll let him shoot sparrows," he said in a boisterous voice. "Hell," said Camilo, "let him try hummingbirds!" They went to the clubhouse like that, arm in arm, laughing and joking. The other shooters standing in line with their guns watched them go. "Gustavo really has his sons with him, doesn't he?" said one man. The other nodded. "Yes, yes, he certainly does. He's a lucky man."

In the morning they fished east of Havana along the coast and caught two small tuna. David caught both of them, and it excited him. He kept opening the bait box to look at the fish. He wanted to study them. When he had brought them alongside, they were blue and silver in the water. Now they were dull, almost black, lifeless. "Isn't it funny how the color fades?" he said to Camilo. "I wonder why." Gustavo came down from the bridge and told them he would put in at Bacuaranao so that Mother could swim and they would have lunch. But when they came into the narrow cove around the reef they saw that the water was cloudy. There were trucks and a steam shovel on the beach, digging sand. Gustavo was

60

angry. He said the Batista officers were stealing the sand to sell to cement contractors in Havana. It was their graft. He took the *Tiburón* back out, and they drifted in the current while they ate. Gustavo sat eating sullenly. Elizabeth kept saying it was not important. She hadn't wanted to swim all that much anyway. Not the point, he said. Standing on the bridge after lunch, Camilo saw the small boat. He yelled at David to put out the flag. The boat came alongside with two black Coast Guardsmen in denims and white hats. They were very polite, looked at the papers and got back into the boat. All the time Camilo waited tensely on the bridge. After they'd gone, David climbed up to join him. He saw the white wake the motorboat made on the blue water. Camilo watched it. "It's a good thing they didn't make trouble," he said. "I could have blasted them easy." He took Gustavo's revolver from under his shirt where he had secreted it and showed it to David. Then he aimed it at the speck the boat made on the water. "Easy," he said. "Very easy." David just stared at him.

★

It had begun to grow dark when they reached Las Yaguas. The hovels of the shantytown, arrayed along narrow alleyways, seemed to sprawl endlessly up the sides of the low hills and past the line of the horizon. The decrepit huts, pieced together from scraps of tin and wood and other debris, leaned against each other as if for support.

Sal Amato looked apprehensively at the two boys as they began to walk along the alley. Camilo, gangly, almost reedlike, with his unruly mop of black hair, was wide-eyed with fascination as he stared at this totally alien setting. David, husky and sandy-haired, walked tentatively, clearly repelled by what he saw. He halted in his tracks now and flicked a quick glance at Amato as the stench of an open sewage pit assaulted them.

Amato had not wanted to take them here, and he regretted now that he'd given in to Camilo's nagging. The day had been planned in quite a different way. The three of them had gone fishing early that morning. It had been sunny and warm, and the fish were running. Amato had conceived of the day as Camilo's birthday present, though he had actually turned eleven the day before. David had just come home from prep school for the Easter holidays, and they all felt good to be back together again.

After the fishing, Amato had intended to drive the boys home and return to town to see his aged uncle, Rafael. The old man had been a great fisherman in his day, and Amato had often regaled the boys with tales of his feats. Just as Amato had initiated David and Camilo to the sea, so Rafael had taught Amato when he was a boy. They had been close, almost as father and son, until Amato, then fourteen years of age, migrated with his family from Las Yaguas to Youngstown, Ohio. Years later, as an adult, Amato returned to Havana to find Rafael sick and penniless, living in a hut in the shantytown. It had been a shock for Amato to revisit Las Yaguas. As a child he had somehow shut out the unrelenting squalor of the place, the filth and the stench. But now, as old Rafael lay on his deathbed, the horror and hopelessness overwhelmed him and he realized with gratitude why his father had snatched at the chance to escape.

Amato had made the mistake of mentioning his uncle's illness to the boys, and that had started it. The old man had accompanied them on two or three fishing trips a few years earlier, and Camilo in particular now peppered Amato with questions about him. Why was he ill? Would he get better? Why couldn't they visit him too?

Camilo had heard stories in school about the shantytown—about its whores and criminals and marijuana peddlers—and his curiosity had been aroused. He wanted to be able to tell his classmates that he had had the courage to go into the most notorious slum in Cuba.

At first Amato had been adamant, but Camilo persisted. "What difference will it make?" Camilo had said again and again.

"I promised to get you home by suppertime," Amato had replied lamely.

"We can tell Mother we were late getting in from fishing," Camilo persisted. "I've never seen Las Yaguas, Sal. I want to see. I've never been in one of their houses. Please?"

"Maybe some other time."

Camilo set his jaw, his eyes stubborn. "Then I'll go alone. I want to see it."

David was less enthusiastic about the adventure. "Rafael is an old man," he said. "We may disturb him." It was typical of David, Amato thought, that he would be so filled with curiosity about the sea, hungry to know about every fish and sea creature, yet was oddly oblivious to people around him.

Camilo had grown petulant now. "I want to go," he shouted at his fourteen-year-old brother. "If you're afraid to go you can stay on the boat."

"Who's afraid?" David shouted back, shoving his brother away from him. Camilo flapped his arms and made a plucking sound, like a chicken. David flushed with anger. "Take that back, Cam!"

"Make me!"

David started to take off his glasses. Amato watched them, aware that

62

despite his handicaps David was bigger and stronger than Camilo; yet the little one stood his ground, ready to fight, his fists clenched to swing, his chin jutting out toward David in challenge. Amato stepped between them.

"That's enough, boys," he said. Then, looking at Camilo with amusement, he added, "You get in a fight with your chin stuck out like that, you'll get knocked on your can, kid. Tuck it in behind your shoulder, like this." He demonstrated. Camilo watched him carefully and imitated him. Amato laughed and scrubbed the boy's head with his big hands. "Come on, let's go home!"

"Please take us to Las Yaguas!" Camilo cried. "Rafael will be so happy to see us. We'll cheer him up. Please?"

Amato looked down at Camilo's pleading face, a face that was almost pretty at this stage of his development, yet was already betraying signals of approaching adolescence. Camilo was right, of course. Rafael would be delighted to see them. It would make his day.

And so he took them, and now he regretted it as they walked along the narrow dirt path between the shacks, catching glimpses inside the open doorways of gaunt, dark faces, and hungry eyes staring out at them, as though in a stupor. They passed a group of children who watched them in silence, their faces smeared with grime. A baby sat shrieking in an open doorway, his eyes black with flies.

"Why doesn't somebody help that baby?" Camilo said angrily.

"Maybe he doesn't have anybody to help him," Amato said. "Come on."

"But look at the flies on his eyes!"

"You'll see a lot worse than that around here." Amato took his arm. "Come on."

They came to a wooden building with a palm-thatched roof, where five young girls, all budding in their adolescence, their cotton dresses tattered and dirty, stared out of the door at them, giggling. Their arms and legs were skinny; their dark hair was matted, oily. They all had bad teeth that showed in their grinning faces. One girl, who was the oldest, put her leg out and lifted her dress above her brown thigh, revealing her dirty gray underwear. The others all broke into giggles, putting their hands to their mouths. But the girl stared at David and Camilo without blinking.

"*Un peso, hombre . . . todo por ustedes. Un peso, por favor.*" She held out a dirty hand and lifted the hem above her waist. "*Un peso, por favor?*" When they walked past, trying to avoid her eyes, she screamed obscenities at them in a shrill, fierce voice until they turned the corner onto a narrow dirt street.

The street was crowded. They passed open shops where flies buzzed around pieces of raw meat that hung on hooks, the yellow fat streaked in the red flesh, peppered with flies. The stench was appalling. Raggedly dressed women, their heads covered with black shawls, moved in and out of the shops. Here and there drunks lay sleeping on the ground. A stream of black water flowed down the middle of the narrow street. The overpowering smell of raw sewage filled the air and made both David and Camilo gag. A woman in a black dress stepped out of a doorway, a tin can in her hand, and tossed the contents splashing onto the street.

"It stinks like shit," David said, covering his nose and mouth with his hand.

"Is that how they go to the bathroom?" Camilo asked, watching the woman disappear back into the gloom of the shack.

"That's it," Amato said.

"How do people live like this?" Camilo said, looking around him in awe and disgust. "Did you really grow up here, Uncle Sal?"

"Sure."

"Did you eat that meat in the shop?"

"That's horsemeat," Amato said. "When I was a boy here, it was a luxury. We ate mostly rice and beans, when my father made a little money. Now and then, we got some fatback bacon, or a piece of pork he managed to steal from the garbage at the slaughterhouse."

"Look in these shacks," David said, pointing. "They all have dirt floors. It's awful."

"No one cares, *chico*" Amato said. "You wanted to see poverty—well, take a good look and remember. Work hard all your life and appreciate what you have. Think how lucky you are not to be one of these here."

They came to a broad ditch filled with greenish water on which rusted tin cans and bits of moldy garbage floated like grotesque flowers.

"We used to swim there," Amato told them. He smiled. "We'd be swimming there naked while the women did their wash. No one cared. It wasn't until I grew up that I discovered the ditch was actually the drain for the tuberculosis hospital on the hill up there."

"Didn't you get sick?"

"Many did. But we never knew why."

They walked past a yellow sign nailed to a post, which read "INFECTIOUS ZONE." Amato pointed up at it. "That's a brilliant new idea of the Ministry of Health to scare people away from settling here. It's ridiculous—people have been living here for years. The land costs nothing, and so do the houses. The people who live here have always been squatters."

Four small black kids dressed in rags suddenly appeared in front of David and Camilo now, staring at them with dark, hostile eyes, their hands outstretched. Amato brushed them aside, and they started walking again.

"They say at school this place is filled with crooks. They say they sell dope. Is it true?"

"Come on, Camilo," David said. "Quit asking questions. Let's go see Uncle Rafael and get out of here."

"I want to know. Is it true, Uncle Sal?"

"It's true. There are all sorts of criminals here. In the old days some of the police would have deals with a few of the kids. They would give us a little marijuana which we would peddle to tourists. Of course, we'd give the cops back most of the money."

"Did you do it?"

"Only once or twice. I worked mostly as a shoeshine boy. We'd hang around the docks because American sailors were our best customers. They'd give us forty centavos sometimes. We'd also wait outside the movie theaters and sometimes the hotels. You'd have to be careful about the hotels and fancy restaurants. Some of the headwaiters and doormen would come after us with a big bull whip. They'd beat the shit out of us for laughs."

"The bastards," Camilo said.

"Some of it was all right," Amato said. "Sometimes when I wouldn't make any money shining shoes I would be afraid to go home. I would spread cardboard on the floor of an old warehouse and sleep there. My friends and I would take turns fighting off the rats. Then we'd look for customers again in the morning. Believe me, it's nice to know you have a bed to sleep in."

Weary of the questions now, Amato was relieved to see they had arrived in front of the hut where Rafael lived. It was a small one-room shack, with walls made of cardboard nailed to tree limbs. The roof was palm fronds weathered with age. He had tried to get the old man to move, but he had politely refused. "This is my home," he said. They moved through the doorway. It took a moment for their eyes to adjust to the darkness. The air was fetid in the small room, and there were flies everywhere. He could see the old man lying in his shorts on an old mattress, staring up at the ceiling.

"It's Sal, Uncle Rafael," Amato said. "I have brought a surprise. Two surprises. David and Camilo."

The old man turned his wrinkled face and stared at the boys. His toothless mouth curved into something that resembled a smile. "I remember—we used to go fishing . . ." the old man whispered.

Both boys greeted Rafael now. He held his yellow withered hand toward them and they each clasped it.

"We came to tell you we want you to get well," David said earnestly.

"Thank you," Rafael said. "It is so nice that you would come to see me. That you would come to this place."

"The boys are pestering me with questions about Las Yaguas," Amato said. "They want to know all about it."

"It is not a place as good as yours—that's all you have to know," Uncle Rafael said, his face becoming more animated now, as he propped himself up on an elbow.

"That's what I tried to tell them."

"I was a boy here and now I am an old man here. That's too long. Too much of this place."

"My Uncle Rafael was quite a man with the ladies in his day," Amato said.

Rafael smiled and nodded his head. "When I was your age, boys, I used to lie when the girls asked me where I lived. If I said I lived in Las Yaguas it was all over for me. The girls would never let me stick in my machete if they knew I was from this place. They were afraid of getting some dread disease from Las Yaguas, right, Sal? You remember how it was?"

"Why are you sick?" Camilo asked. "Is there a doctor treating you?"

Rafael frowned. "No doctor. There is a *santero*."

Puzzled, Camilo glanced at Amato.

"*Santería* cures are different from doctor's cures," Amato explained. "People here believe in them."

"They don't even know about cures?" Rafael rasped. "How do they stay well?"

"What does he mean?"

"There is a saint for every part of the body," Rafael said. "Obatala controls the head. Saint Lucia controls eyesight. Saint Lazarus is the saint of the feet. Osain can cure impotence—it is important you boys learn someday about Osain. The *santero* knows how to deal with all the saints to make you well."

David looked at Amato and shook his head. "It's no wonder the old man is sick," David whispered. "We should get him to a doctor."

"He would not see a doctor. He would sooner sip his *aguardiente* and rely on the saints."

"The boys need to know about these things," Rafael said wearily. "You must teach them, Sal." Several bedbugs were visible scampering across the old mattress.

66

They talked a few minutes longer, but then the old man grew weaker and sagged back against his mattress.

The boys shook his hand and Amato bent down and kissed him, and then they left him lying there in the dark. The air outside smelled foul, but they all breathed deeply after the stale air of Rafael's hut. Then they started walking. They walked silently for a long while.

ORIENTE, 1948

The rattling, jarring motion of the train awakened him; he felt the warmth of his mother's breast against his cheek. He was nestled under her arm in the wicker seat of the first-class section. The seat trembled slightly, shaken by the vibrations of the fast-moving car, which was plummeting down a grade, the steel wheels beneath click-clacking in a steady metallic beat. He sat up and rubbed the sleep from his eyes and yawned. There was only a single light burning in the car, at the far end, and he saw the heads of the sleeping passengers lolling with the swaying motion.

His mother's handsome face smiled at him as she stirred herself, straightening her skirt, brushing back wisps of hair with her hands. "Did you have a good sleep, Cam?" Then she said in Spanish, "You've been asleep since below San Luis junction. Look outside. See the moonlight?"

Drowsily, Camilo pressed his face against the cool vibrating glass of the big window. He saw an immense basin filled with clusters of bamboo, the dark pillars of royal palms along the crests of the hills, with masses of dark foliage, all shimmering in the moonlight. The train was speeding downward, snaking through the hills. They were rushing into the trough of a deep railway cut, rumbling across a viaduct that seemed to lift the tops of the royal palms to his eye level. Suddenly they plunged into a tunnel of vegetation, trees and leaves shiny in the pale light, flashing past. Then they were in a vast rolling plain, the fields of sugarcane stretching to the hills.

"Are we close to Santiago?" he asked.

"Almost there, darling."

"Will Papa be there to meet us—at the train station?"

"I'm not sure. He's very busy with the contractor who is clearing our forests. But someone will be there, I'm certain."

"I hope Papa is there to meet us," he said, looking again out the window.

67

The train began to slow gradually as the grade lessened, the hills diminishing and sliding away into the distance behind them. Five minutes later he saw the lights of Santiago de Cuba spreading out around them. I hope Papa meets us at the station, he thought. He had not seen Gustavo since November. He missed him terribly. It was now mid-January, and he was excited about being let out of school as well as being with his father in Oriente through the whole next year. He had never really been out of Havana, and the thought of being in the mountains, the wild country, as Gustavo called it, with horses to ride and woods to explore, made him tremble with anticipation. His thirteenth birthday was less than four months away and he looked forward to it with special pleasure, for it was on that day he would be considered a man, worthy of taking on a man's worries as well as a man's pleasures. That and the fact he would not have to enter a schoolroom for a whole year filled him with delight.

They had argued about his missing school, his mother quite adamantly opposed, but his father had prevailed. "He shall learn more in a year in those mountains than they could teach him in ten years at school," he said.

When they stepped off the train, they were greeted by a tall man in denims who wore a broad, high-crowned hat made of palm fronds. His face was wide and his eyes slanted, like an Oriental, the skin dark and smooth. He bore himself erect, with an air of dignity and confidence that impressed Camilo immediately. Although he never seemed to smile, his eyes, which were brown and quick, often brightened with amusement. He said his name was Lupe, that he worked for Señor Carta and he had been sent to carry them to the *finca*. His voice, deep and rich, made Camilo think of a cello. He at once determined to pitch his voice at that tone and to speak slowly, choosing his words carefully, the way Lupe did. He must have been a man of fifty years, but Camilo watched him loading the luggage onto the back of the open Chevrolet truck, marveling at the way the big cords of muscle in his forearms bulged when he closed his large hands around the handles and swung them easily onto the truck bed. He tied down the collection of steamer trunks and leather valises with rope, working smoothly and expertly at the knots, without wasted motion.

"Are we to stay at the hotel here tonight?" Elizabeth asked him as they climbed into the cab of the truck, Camilo scampering first to sit beside Lupe at the wheel.

The big workman shook his head and said politely, "No, señora, my orders are to bring you to the hacienda at once."

"Isn't it a long trip?"

"Not bad," he replied. "We shall be there sometime tomorrow morning."

Sitting wide awake with excitement, Camilo watched through the windshield as they drove along the narrow streets of Santiago. The streets climbed steeply into the hills. Houses were built on either side of the slopes, with their great wall foundations and uptilted tile roofs. Now and then he glimpsed a family at dinner, behind an iron-grated window; and when they reached the crest and looked below, they could see the landlocked bay, bright in the moonlight, the cluster of houses terraced up the hill to the spire of the cathedral on top, bright in the full moon's glare. "Isn't it lovely?" exclaimed Elizabeth. "I had no idea this was such a beautiful city."

The rows of old Spanish houses gave way gradually to tightly packed hovels with palm-thatched roofs, the streets crowded with people walking in the dark, oil lamps outlining their figures with a yellow glow. They passed bodegas where Camilo saw shabbily dressed men standing at the bars, or clustered together outside on the corners, watching the flow of traffic. It gradually grew darker and darker, the shacks giving way to trees and open fields, tall gray palms and an occasional yellow glimmer of a house in the distance, and then he felt the sudden jarring as they drove off the paved road onto a dirt path that climbed into the darkness, Lupe gearing down the truck until its engine growled and whined with the strain of the grade. Camilo yawned, suddenly unable to keep his eyes open. He leaned against the warmth of his mother and felt her arm slip around his shoulders.

In the morning he woke and realized the truck was motionless. He sat up and looked out. They had stopped in a clearing at the edge of a broad, fast-flowing river. A crane was lifting a peeled log toward a half-finished bridge. Across the river, the trees had been cleared in a straight, broad path that stretched off as far as he could see to the vanishing point. A barge on the river moved slowly toward him. To his right, a dozen horses had been loaded with their luggage; four or five *guajiros* in their straw hats moving in and out among them.

"Camilo!" His mother's voice was calling him, and he turned his head to the palm-thatched shack at the edge of the river and saw her waving to him. She was dressed in a man's shirt and riding breeches and boots. Men in straw hats were standing around the shack, looking out at the slow-moving barge. There were stacks of boxes on the pier below the shack. "Camilo! Come on, come on!"

He got out of the truck into the cool smell of the morning air. He looked around for Lupe as he walked toward her, but he couldn't find him in the crowd of workmen. "What are they building the bridge for?" he asked her.

"Isn't it beautiful? It's ours. Papa's building it for the railroad spur. You remember him talking about it? That's why we're clearing the forest. Five thousand acres. All of it will be sugarcane. The railroad line is to go right to the *finca*."

"You mean we're going to have our own railroad?"

"Absolutely. Twenty miles of it."

"I wish David were here. Wouldn't he be excited?"

"He'll see it, maybe this summer when it's finished. Come on, now, we're taking the barge across the river."

Lupe emerged from the mass of faces on the riverbank, leading the pack horses clattering onto the barge. He spoke occasionally to the other men. Camilo liked the way the other men all looked at Lupe with respect in their eyes. When his mother stepped on board, they all removed their straw hats and nodded to her politely. It was a whole new world to Camilo, and he loved it.

As they moved slowly across the river he went up to Lupe, who was retying one of the packs. "Why are we going to ride horses, Lupe?"

The big man ducked his head, adjusting the bellyband on the brown horse, so that Camilo looked at the top of his weathered straw hat. "You see those hills across there?"

"Yes."

"There's no road yet. It won't be terminated until September. In September you can drive from the *finca* to the *batey*. Now we use horses." He stood up and looked down at Camilo with his slanted eyes. "You ever ride a horse?"

"Yes, lots of times. My father taught me."

"Good."

"What's a *batey?*"

"Headquarters. You know, the headquarters of the *central.* The *ingenio* is there."

"The what?"

"*Ingenio,* the mill."

Once across the river, they mounted the horses amid a great deal of confusion and shouting. Camilo rode a bay mare whose ribs stuck out through the hide. His mother was on a spirited big gray that pranced like a parade horse as she rode off. The workmen were all laughing and they waved their hats as the column got under way.

It was a long ride, and the sun was hot. Swarms of flies attacked them unmercifully, blanketing the flanks of the sweating pack animals. When they crossed the little valley and climbed the path through the thick forest, deep in shade, the air still and stifling, Camilo could look back and see the path cut through the forest for the railroad, like a new wound in the blanket of trees. They rode across the crest, coming suddenly into the hot bright sun and then plunging into a tunnel of foliage again. It was just at the end of the dry season, and red dust drifted up from the horses' hoofs and choked his throat and nose, covering them all with a powdered film. Lupe's faded blue shirt bore wide dark patches of sweat under his arms, and the flies buzzed about his face, but he seemed to ignore them, as though he never felt their irritating touch. He rode at the head of the little column, followed by Elizabeth, then Camilo, the dozen pack horses, and two other riders bringing up the rear, the mottled sunlight flickering over their figures as they moved under the trees.

The sun was directly overhead when they came out into the clearing and saw the low palm-thatched roof of the *finca* house. It stood in a copse of big green ceiba trees, shaded and cool-looking in the blazing noon sun. Smoke drifted lazily from the treetops. It was Camilo's first look at the hacienda that was to be his home for a year. The house was a single story, sprawling out to the bottom of a hill, with a thatched barn and a courtyard of red brick and a wide shaded veranda. It had been built by his great-great-grandfather, Don Camilo, his namesake, and as he saw it for the first time he had a strange sensation of recognition, as though he were coming home. Four servants were standing on the veranda as they came clattering onto the brick courtyard. Camilo saw weeds growing between the bricks, and at the far end of the yard, near the barn, he saw the old grinder with its big worn gray stone, where the sugarcane had once been ground by oxen. There were horses out in the shaded corral and cattle grazing in the pasture, which was punctuated here and there by the stately gray royal palms.

His mother dismounted with the help of Lupe, her face powdered with dust, the unruly strands of her hair pasted to her skin.

"Is Gustavo here?" she asked the majordomo, whose name they learned was Rodolfo. He was short, stocky, with gray hair and gentle brown eyes, his manner brusk, yet polite.

"No, señora, he is in the woods with the contractor. The crews are ready to begin work tomorrow. He will probably arrive home late."

Camilo was disappointed. Rodolfo showed him his room, a large, high-ceilinged bedroom with thick whitewashed walls and a single window that looked out to the barn and the corral, where he could see the horses. It was furnished with a low bed, a heavy chest of drawers and a mirror. There were kerosene lanterns on the stands by the bed. A small door led to a bathroom which had no sink, only an old-fashioned tub with iron claw feet.

"Is there no faucet?" he asked Rodolfo.

The majordomo smiled and replied that water had to be carried from the cistern to fill the tub. He showed him the porcelain basin for washing, and the soap and towels. "I will bring you a pitcher of water, if you wish, Patrón."

After he had gone out, Camilo lay on the bed, cupped his head in his hands, and looked out at the horses. The room, in fact the whole house, smelled of cedar and wood smoke. The horses were standing in the shade under the ceiba trees. He decided he would like it here, if he could have a horse of his own.

The afternoon meal was served on the long harvest table that stood on the veranda. Camilo found he was very hungry. Platters of meat, chicken and pork, and yellow rice were served him, with a metal pitcher of cold milk and one of cold white wine, which Rodolfo poured into a glass for his mother. She had appeared looking fresh and clean from her bath, wearing a print shirt and faded Levi's and tennis shoes. Her hair was covered by a white scarf. Camilo thought she looked beautiful.

The view from the table was spectacular. They looked across the pasture to the thick forest. The hills were low and rolling and broke the seemingly endless vista of thickly packed trees. His mother told him that by the end of summer all that he saw would be cleared and cane planted. As they sat eating, Camilo looked out across the green pasture where a dozen cows were grazing and saw riders appear out of the dark line of the woods.

"Someone's coming!" he shouted. "Look! Do you think it might be Papa?"

He saw his mother stiffen as she looked out at the tiny figures of the two horsemen. "Maybe," she said.

As they watched, the horsemen grew larger and larger. There was one black horse and one buckskin with a blaze on its nose; on it he saw his father's erect figure, his face tanned, his white shirt fluttering as he spurred his horse, pulling away from the man with him. His mother pushed back her chair, scraping on the paving stone. For a moment she stood motionless and tense, and then with a little cry she was running out into the sun toward his father. He saw his father rein his horse and swing down from the saddle in time to catch her in his arms. Her white bandana fell from her head and he lifted her off her feet, whirling her in the air, their happy voices drifting across to Camilo on the veranda. Standing there, watching them kissing, their bodies and faces merged, Camilo felt a pang of jealousy. It was as though they had forgotten he existed.

They embraced like that for a long moment, until the rider on the black horse reined up beside them. Camilo watched the man dismount. He was a short, heavy man, with bowlegs and a face the color of tanned leather. He saw the man nod and bow to his mother. His father said something to him that Camilo could not make out, then turned, his arm around his mother, and came striding toward the veranda, laughing and talking, his head turned to look at Elizabeth, who kept her eyes riveted on him. The short man led the horses away to the corral. Camilo waited, feeling strangely unhappy, until his father came into the shade of the veranda and reached down, fixing his dark eyes on him, holding out his hand.

"My son, how are you?"

"Very good, Papa."

"Well," said his father, looking from one to the other. "Well . . ."

Camilo held his father's moist hand in his, aching to embrace him. But the hand went away, encircling his mother's slender shoulders. She kept looking at his father with that odd expression in her eyes, as though something had melted in her, draining all her strength and resistance, all her dignity.

"Have you finished your lunch, Camilo?"

"No . . ."

"Why don't you sit down and finish. Your mother and I want to be alone to talk, eh?" He patted Camilo's shoulder with his free hand. "That's a good boy."

He watched them enter the gloom of the big house, dissolving through the wide doors, their footsteps on the tile floor echoing, going away. He heard his mother's laugh, not a laugh, really, but an odd girlish giggle, and then a squeal of protest, the door slamming somewhere in the bowels of the house.

Camilo felt humiliated. He turned and ran the length of the veranda and out into the sun, running as fast as he could toward the corral. When he reached the fence he stopped, breathless and sweating, and plopped down beside the trunk of a ceiba tree. A little wind stirred the leaves and the pods overhead, and he saw the patterns of light and shadow move on the dirt. A horse neighed. His eyes moved over the rumps and the legs of the horses he could see through the fence. It pained him to think of what had happened. He hated the image in his mind of their embrace, their faces and lips tight together. He hated it.

All through the spring the woods rang with the sounds of axes and machetes and the voices of the workmen calling to each other, the crack of trees being felled, the rushing roar of flames blazing through the branches, sending a lurid tower of reddish-brown smoke billowing into the sky, until the sun turned bronze through the haze, and the night sky glowed red and orange. Each day Camilo, mounted on the little black mare his father gave him, rode with Gustavo out to the virgin forest, where the crews were at work. His father had contracted with Fernando, the short, heavy man he'd seen the first day, to replace the forest with cane for a fixed sum. Bands of workmen had erected *baracones* in the clearings at the edge of the forest, roughly fashioned structures of poles and palm-thatched roofs, the sides open, so that he saw the hammocks strung one after the other under the long roofs. There were rows upon rows of the rough sheds where the woodsmen slept and ate. Smoke drifted from the cookfires. The cooks stood sweating in the heat, making great pots of rice and frying meats. The smell of frying meat in the open air delighted him. Camilo liked the laborers. They were good-humored, smiling men, who took off their straw hats to him and called him "Patrón," and who looked upon his father with a kind of awe that Camilo found annoying.

Each morning, they would wrap their possessions in the hammocks, then head in ragged ranks toward the forest, carrying their crude axes and machetes. By the time the first rays of the sun touched the tops of the trees, the hammering din of the axes could be heard. The underbrush and the saplings fell first under the glittering slash of the machetes. Then the big trees, the cedars with their red trunks, were felled and denuded of limbs, left to burn in the widening path of cleared land. Camilo spent as much of his time in the woods as he could, often working with a machete alongside the laborers, who joked and laughed with him. He loved the feeling of working, of sweating and whacking at the living wood, the fresh smells of wood chips and crushed leaves; the sense of power and the joy of accomplishment he felt in his fatigue after the sun melted over the hills and they paraded back through the cleared land. His father joked at him one night at dinner, telling his mother that her son had turned into a woodsman. "You will probably never see him in Havana again," he laughed.

Day by day the immense, seemingly inpenetrable wall of green steadily diminished, the lines of workers in their straw hats advancing by quarter-mile sections. Everything fell before the relentless line of ten thousand men, cedars and ceiba trees, royal palms, the immense and iron-wooded caquaran trees, the wide-spreading lacy algarroba with its thorn limbs. Camilo loved watching the torches being touched to the dry leaves, tinderlike now in the final days of the dry season, blazing brightly in a sudden *whooosh!* that swept upward through the limbs and the leaves, spewing smoke into the sky, until it seemed the whole horizon was on fire.

On his birthday, his father presented a Winchester rifle to him. He was thrilled. They rode east into the untouched forest, Camilo, his father and Lupe's stoic figure, working their way through the trees until Lupe held up his hand, reined his horse and cautiously slipped from the saddle.

"What is it?" Camilo whispered.

"Pigs," his father whispered. "See, there, where they've been rooting the dirt?"

They climbed down from their horses. Lupe gestured to them, his attention arrested by something in the thick underbrush. Camilo trembled with excitement as he cocked the Winchester and moved alongside his father toward where Lupe stood, motionless, poised, his face lost in shadow. "They're in the clearing, Patrón," he whispered. "Be cautious."

"Stay behind me, Camilo," Gustavo said to him. Camilo saw his father draw the big revolver from the worn leather holster on his hip. "Remember, these are wild pigs. They're dangerous."

Camilo's mouth went dry and he felt a hot thirst as he worked his way forward through the brush beside his father. Gustavo crouched now, crawling under the heavy tangle of leaves. They emerged into a grassy clearing. The wind rippled the high grass, making it shine in the sun. Camilo couldn't see anything. But his father motioned for him to stay where he was. He watched his father in his khaki shirt, black trousers and boots moving cautiously out into the hip-deep grass. Something caught Camilo's eye. To the left of his father, a faint movement in the grass. His thumb eased back the hammer until he felt it click. Then he saw its head, the squinting eye, the hairy mass of its back.

"There!" Camilo shouted, and then he was running toward it, bounding in the heavy grass. He heard a snort and saw the hairy shape turn. He leaped forward, landed on his two feet, brought the rifle to his shoulder, fitted the sight in the V, saw the brown shape running, the grass parting before it. He fired. The pig shrieked and tumbled, knocking the grass down ahead of it. The whole field seemed to explode. It was like the scurrying of field mice, but mice the size of dogs. Camilo caught a movement, jacked a new shell into the rifle, aimed and fired—

75

seeing the flesh pop, the hairy shape tumble in the grass; saw two more, side by side, running straight at him. He dropped the first one ten yards away and the second right at his feet. He had only a moment to glimpse the bristles swarming with vermin on the limp broken pig that lay kicking at his boot tips; a loud snort to his left, and he wheeled to see the big boar, tusks gleaming, foam frothing at its lips, the mean little eyes red and glittering, as it came charging at him, fast as a cat. Camilo swung the rifle easily and fired. The boar let out a wild shriek, swung in a wide swath, recovered and stood glaring at Camilo. With a grunt, he charged again. Camilo felt a rush of joy. He jacked the shell into the chamber and fired again and again, each time seeing the huge pig, the size of a calf, lurch and stagger. His last shot blew half the head away, and the beast, carried by its weight and momentum, plunged against him, knocking him backward. But Camilo regained his balance quickly, and, drawing his machete, he lunged after it, swinging with all his strength, chopping, chopping, blood spurting and wetting him with its sticky, raw-smelling, hot touch. "Bastard! Bastard! Bastard!" he shouted with each blow.

Finally he stood, dizzy with exertion, his chest heaving. He lifted his eyes from the mutilated remains of the boar and found his father and Lupe standing ten feet away, staring at him. The ground seemed to be spinning. He looked from their faces to the blood on his hands, and wiped his cheek, then looked at his father again. Gustavo's face had gone pale. Lupe's was a mask, his eyes intent on Camilo.

"Did you see?" Camilo said, struggling for breath. "Did you see that bastard knock me? He almost got me."

Carta saw that his son's eyes looked glazed.

"Are you all . . . right?" his father asked.

"I've never . . . never had anything so exciting . . . ever!"

Camilo felt elated. He saw his father and Lupe exchange a look. His father came over and took his arm.

"Come, Camilo, there's a stream over here. You can wash off the blood. Your mother would be upset, seeing you like this."

"What about the pigs?"

"Lupe will take care of them."

"How many did you get, Papa?"

"I didn't shoot." His father seemed to be speaking out of a stupor.

"I got five," Camilo told him. "Are they good to eat?"

In late August, David arrived to spend two weeks with the family. Camilo was overjoyed to see him. His half brother was sixteen, tall, slender, still suffering from the injuries sustained in the automobile

76

accident five years earlier. He wore thick glasses and walked with a decided limp from his stiff right knee. His manner was shy, withdrawn, unsure. He carried two suitcases and a book bag and spent his evenings reading by the kerosene lamp in his room. During the day, the two brothers were inseparable.

Camilo was lean, tanned, muscular for a thirteen-year-old and bursting with energy. On horseback, he took his brother to the open savannas where the swarming army of woodcutters had cleared the land, leaving blackened stumps here and there. Hundreds of workmen were hoeing away the grass, piling debris and brush into bonfires, or moving in long ranks down the proposed rows, carrying stalks of cane and machetes.

"They're planting the cane," Camilo told him. "See, they take the sugarcane in one hand, the machete in the other—watch now . . ."

The nearest workman poked the cane into the ground and chopped off the unburied end, then moved three feet forward to repeat the process.

"How long will it take to grow?" David asked.

"About eighteen months."

David looked at his tanned brother and shook his head. "Sounds like you're going to make a career of sugarcane, Cam."

"It's a good life," Camilo replied gravely.

He took David on long walks in the dense forest, following the narrow trails to his secret places in the gloomy woods. Beside a stream one afternoon he showed him a strange-looking tree with thick bark. "Don't touch it," he said. "It's a manzanillo. The sap is poison. You swallow a single drop—you die! I've seen men who've hit it a careless blow with an ax and get splashed with sap. They swell up like an elephant. It's true, David."

"You're pulling my leg."

"Watch, I'll prove it to you." Camilo drew his machete and sawed into the bark until it oozed sap onto the blade. "Come on, let's go."

"Where?"

"I'll prove it to you."

David followed his brother's swift figure along the trail until they emerged into a clearing where there were cattle grazing. "See that bull, the brown one? Watch."

"Hey, Cam, come on . . ." David started to protest, but his brother was already running into the pasture, shouting and waving his arms. The herd of cattle spooked, trotting off, except for the bull, which turned, lowered his head and snorted. "Cam, for Christ's sake! Come back here, he'll charge!"

Cam danced in the air, yelled, waved his machete. The heavy-necked bull lifted its head and came lumbering at him, looking huge, gaining speed as it closed the gap between itself and Camilo. Frightened now, David started to yell, but it was too late. The bull flashed toward Camilo, who was shouting like a bullfighter now, "Hey, *toro*, hey, hey, *toro!*" An instant before the long sharp-pointed horns struck him, he leaped aside, the machete flashing. David saw a thin red gash on the bull's heavy neck as it turned in a cloud of dust and prepared to charge again. The massive head lowered, Camilo still waving his arms, taunting him, and the bull started forward slowly again; but then David saw him slow, stagger, as the head wavered back and forth. A frothy foam bubbled from its mouth and dribbled onto the grass. Then, slowly, heavily, the bull slumped to its forward knees, its flank raised in the air, poised. Then it toppled sideways, the legs flying up, dust rising. Camilo raised his arms and shouted triumphantly.

He came running back to David, grinning. "Well, didn't I tell you?"

"Jesus, Cam, you killed him!"

"Sure. What did you think I was going to do, pet him?"

"But . . . doesn't he belong to somebody?"

"He belongs to God now," Camilo said, and laughed. "Some poison, huh?"

In September David left to return to school in New England. For days at a time, Camilo would be gone from the *finca*, taking only his machete and his horse, saying he was going into the woods. Elizabeth worried about him constantly. "What do you do all this time by yourself?" she would ask when he returned.

Camilo shrugged his shoulders, picked at the callus on his hands and mumbled, "Explore, just explore, that's all."

"Do you like to be alone so much?"

"Sure. It's nice in the woods. No one to bother you, you see? It's quiet. I like that."

Camilo felt her skeptical gaze upon him. He sensed that she knew he was hiding something from her. But he didn't want to tell her. This had to be his secret. His alone.

He had met her on the trail one hot afternoon. He was sprawled out in the shade to nap, when he saw her coming along the gap in the trees, carrying a white chicken. She was tall, black-skinned, with short-cut kinky hair like a boy's. Her eyes were large and expressive and her teeth were as white as shells. She wore a tattered green cotton dress and swung her hips as she walked, her longish, pendulous breasts jiggling beneath the cloth.

78

Camilo sat up as she approached him, barefoot; he flicked his machete. It stuck in the ground just where she was about to plant her bare toes. She did not miss a stride. With a toss of her head, she told him haughtily, in her musical English, "Mon, if you can't handle your blade any better than that, you aren't worth stopping for!"

Camilo lunged at her, throwing his arms around her thighs, sending them both plunging into the brush. The chicken exploded from the girl's arms, fluttered in the air, and settled back on the trail, clucking in muted outrage, while her mistress thrashed in the brush with the thirteen-year-old Cuban boy.

"What in the hell are you trying to do, mon?" the girl kept shouting at him, as she struggled to gain control of the furiously thrashing arms and legs and hands that seemed to be all over her at once. Grabbing his wrists, she managed to swing her body on top of him and, straddling him with her strong legs, pinned him to the ground. She glared furiously into his startled blue eyes. "Now we see who's in charge here," she said, breathing between clenched teeth. "Let's find out what's going on. Who are you and what are you trying to do, child?"

"Rape you," Camilo replied, his face drenched in sweat, his teeth clenched with his effort to free himself.

"Rape?" The black girl broke into laughter. She rolled off him and clutched her stomach, kicking her legs, as she contorted with laughter.

Camilo sat up and watched her with his intense gaze, his mouth set angrily. But her laughter, like music, infected him, and he too began to giggle. Every time she started to regain herself, she would look at him, meet his eyes, and start again.

It took some time to regain her composure. She sat up, straightened her skirt over her knees and appraised him casually. "What's your name, boy?"

"Camilo."

"How old are you?"

"Sixteen."

"Sixteen? No, mon, you're more like ten."

"I'm thirteen!"

"That's more right. You go around these woods raping girls all the time, Camilo?"

"When I feel like it."

She chuckled. "You know how old I am? I am nineteen years. How come you speak such good English?"

"My mother's *norteamericana*. Yours?"

"We're from Jamaica. Your daddy Cuban?"

"Mmmm-huh. Are you going to let me see your tits, or what?"

She threw back her head and laughed again, and then looked at him out of the corner of her eyes. "Why you want to see my tits, little boy?"

"Come on, let me see them."

She hesitated, started to get up, then looked at him again, sharply. "Say please!"

"Please."

"I don't know. You're young. You ever had a woman before, Camilo?"

"Sure, lots."

"Yes, like you are sixteen years old lots?"

She sat in the broken sunlight, patches of shadow across her lap, her long, angular legs stretched out on the grass, tightly together, the toes dipping forward and back, forward and back, while she contemplated them. Her arms were behind her, bracing her body upright, thrusting her breasts against the faded cotton cloth of the green dress. Her eyes flashed to him and then back to her toes, which she wiggled. "No, Mr. Thirteen Years Old, I don't think I shall."

"Why not?"

Again the eyes slid to his serious face, appraising the stare of his blue eyes. "You are a virgin, aren't you?"

"Yes."

She pressed her lips together. "You seen a woman with her clothes off, ever?"

"Once."

"Who?"

"My mother."

The girl laughed, her whole body shaking.

"Don't laugh at me!" His tone was menacing.

She looked at him and widened her eyes in mock fear. "What will you do, Mr. Mon, beat me up?"

"I'll cut your throat."

Again the flash of white teeth in her shiny black face. "I honestly think you would. You're a little firebox, aren't you? Tell me, when did you see your mommy naked?"

"What do you want to know for?"

"Because it is a secret." She tossed her head and looked up into the trees. "You show me your secret, Mr. Thirteen-Year-Old, and I'll show you mine. You understand me?"

Camilo pulled a twig from the ground and made a circle in the dust. "One time . . ."

"One what?"

"One time I saw her. I looked in the window and saw her."

"And she was naked?"

"Yes. She was on the bed and she was naked."

"What was she doing?"

"Nothing. She was on the bed and she got up and walked to the bathroom . . ."

"What were her tits like?"

Camilo's handsome brown face turned to her, the eyes bright. "Big . . ." He made a gesture with his hands.

"What else did you see?"

"Her ass. And . . . the other thing."

"What other thing?"

"The thing between her legs, the hairy thing."

The girl laughed in her light, airy way, and then fastened her eyes on his again. "You want to rape her?"

"Mmmm-huh."

Her hand with its slender dark fingers reached out and touched him. "Make you get stiff down here?"

Camilo nodded and smiled. It felt good, her fingers touching him, kneading him, an aching sensation from the pit of his stomach that filtered down between his legs; pleasant, so pleasant it almost hurt. No one had ever touched him before. He looked at her shiny brown eyes, her long, tapered neck, wide shoulders and bulging breasts, the cloth clinging wetly to the skin so that her nipples protruded in the green cloth.

"You a mon yet?" she said, her voice growing husky. "You pop the weasel yet?"

"I don't know. What is it?"

"If you had popped the weasel," she grinned, "you surely would know it, mon."

"Can you do it?"

"Certainly," she said, lifting her chin, looking down her nose at him. "I can pop it anytime I please to."

"How?"

"With my fingers, the same as I am doing to you, right now . . ."

"Let's do it?"

"Mon child, you are going to do it." She grinned at him and moved her body, leaning on her elbow, her free hand kneading him softly. "In a short time, you are no longer a virgin." Her eyes looked up at him mischievously, her lips parting over her teeth. She leaned so close he could smell her. "You take off your trousers, Mr. Mon, and your shirt —and I'll show you something."

Camilo stood and unbuttoned his shirt, tossing it onto the leaves of

81

the tree. He pulled off his boots and unbuckled his belt, and slipped out of his pants. He stood before her naked, his belly, chest, arms, neck and face brown from the sun, his groin and legs as pale as a child's. Her brown eyes swept him from head to toe and settled in a long stare at his erect penis. "Oh," she said, puckering her lips, "you are as pretty . . . and as hairless as a baby!" She laughed.

He felt a flash of embarrassment in his nakedness. He had seen naked men, their chests and loins hairy, their balls hanging like a bull's. His own smallness made him cringe and want to cover himself. He yearned to be strong and hairy and to possess an organ that looked formidable.

But now he stood transfixed as he watched her uncoil her body and stand, towering over him. She was a full seven or eight inches taller. She stretched her arms toward the treetops and sighed, sucking in her breath. Her fingers touched the hem of the dress and she lifted it in a single motion over her head. She wore a tattered pair of white knickers, but her breasts were bare. Camilo thought they looked like some exotic black fruit, the ebony nipples fully erect. Camilo stared at them, at their mystery, and felt himself quiver.

"You are a delight," she said, her fingers rolling the knickers down to her knees, one foot and then the other stepping out of them. She stood erect, raised her arms, and turned her body slowly in the sunlight. Her dark skin gleamed. Camilo felt as though his penis would become so taut it would break the skin. He stared at the kinky triangle of hair between her thighs, black wiry hair that glistened when the rays of the sun touched it. "I see what it is you're staring at, Mr. Thirteen-Year-Old," she said. "You come over and sit down beside me. We've a lesson to learn today."

She took his hand and pulled him down beside her in the grass. The patches of sunlight on his bare shoulders were warm. There was a sweet acid scent to her skin. "Go ahead, touch them," she said to him, "go on, now."

He touched her breasts, jiggled them, weighed them in his hands; the texture of her skin was smooth and oily. All the time her eyes were fastened on his face.

"Want to really see something, do you?"

"Yes."

"Look here. Look."

He saw her brown thighs part, the kinky tuft of hair spreading. Her fingers glided over her belly and sank in the hair, and he saw her open the two dark lips beneath, revealing a pink smile. "See? That, my dear child, is a woman. You may touch me, if you like." He sank his fingers

82

into the moist pink flesh, feeling the slimy softness, the warmth. "Delightful, isn't it?"

"Incredible . . ." he said weakly, and coughed to clear his throat. "Like a flower . . ."

"It is a flower, mon."

And she fell back, grasping his shoulders in her strong fingers, pulling him onto her body, yielding beneath him. He felt her fingers fumbling with him down there. His eyes looked into hers. The light seemed to sink into the brown irises, like prisms. He felt his penis penetrate something soft and moist, like warm honey, and the muscled flesh closed around him, engulfing him, holding him. He felt her hips move, and heard a sharp hiss as she sucked in breath between her teeth, her eyes closing, the lids and dark lashes falling, blotting out the mystery of her dark eyes. The ache spread throughout his loins. The heat and movement of her body sent waves tingling along his spine. She groaned and sighed, her head falling back, mouth agape.

"You will come to me again, here . . ."

"Yes."

"Tomorrow?"

"Yes, tomorrow."

"Ohhhh, Camilo, mon . . . how sweet you are, like a baby, like a baby . . . so sweet."

He saw her only three times after that, although he went each day into the forest and waited along the path where he had first seen her. Once, they spent the night together, huddled in the warmth of each other's arms. The forest grew totally black at night. Under the tree, it was so dark he could not see her face when he was so close he could feel the warmth of her breath. "Where are you?" he said to her. He felt her hand touch him, drawing him to her body, the moist warmth of her skin touching against his, the wiry feel of her hair against his face, then the touch of her hand on him there, the rustle of leaves as she moved. "I'm here, Camilo. Come on, baby . . . And he felt the scalding heat as he entered her flesh, the wet sticky yielding of her body as he penetrated deeper—the aching in his loins changing suddenly, uncontrollably, to an intense pressure that seemed to swell inside him, urgently, straining to be relieved, every muscle in his body taut and quivering; and he felt something like a spasm, a release, a hot rush that was unbearably pleasurable. It left him dazed and exhausted in her arms. He felt himself withering inside her. He couldn't believe how good he felt.

Later, as they lay, looking up at the stars through the interlacing black leaves of the trees, she turned, resting on her elbows, her face barely visible in the dark.

"The weasel popped, Mr. Camilo. You are a mon, a mon who can make babies. Perhaps, we shall make a baby." She laughed and kissed his belly. "A fine mon child, hmmmm? Perhaps his eyes will be blue, like yours."

Once after they had made love in the hot humid afternoon on a hillside, she told him she had come from Kingston with her father and mother two years earlier to work the cane fields. She lived in a palm-thatched hut on the far side of the hill, near the river. She had seven brothers and six sisters. "This time, the dead season, we are hungry . . . all hungry."

"Hungry? Why?"

"There is no work. None. Not until the cutting starts in October. No work, no money. Nothing to eat."

"I'll get you money," he told her, kissing her lips.

"No. You give me love. I don't want your money."

He last saw her walking off through the trees, swinging her hips in the green dress, glancing back over her shoulder at him occasionally until he could not see her for the foliage.

When he rode into the yard of the *finca* that night, his father was standing on the veranda. There were trucks by the barn. Men were carrying luggage out of the house and loading it on trucks. "I am happy you decided to come home," he said. "I was just about to send Lupe out to look for you."

"What is this?" Camilo asked.

"We are moving tonight—to the mill. Thursday we start cutting the cane in the lowlands.

Camilo felt his heart sink.

The sugar mill stood smokeless and silent, its towering chimneys looming high against the horizon. Seated beside Lupe in the truck that brought them down the new road from the *finca,* Camilo looked out at the unbroken landscape of cane-green and longed to return to the mountains. The cane stood higher than the truck along both sides of the road, which was made of packed red earth. Dust billowed behind the trucks ahead. The little caravan of three trucks and a Ford station wagon, which carried his father and mother, moved along the cleared path in the cane fields until one by one they turned off into the *batey* compound at the mill.

The *batey* was headquarters for the entire *central,* as the sugar estate was called. Ceiba trees shaded the company houses, all painted gray.

"Lupe, why do they paint everything gray?" Camilo asked.

"To save money."

84

"Does my father own all this?"

"*Sí*, Patrón. All you see belongs now to your father."

"When it is mine, I'll paint the houses all different colors. The mill too."

Lupe smiled at him. It was the first time he had ever seen Lupe smile.

They drove through a plaza with flowering trees and bougainvillea in reds and oranges and whites. They pulled up in front of a large gray house. A screen porch dominated all four sides of the one-story building. Workmen were already carrying luggage and boxes from the trucks up the walk and through the screen door.

Two days after they were settled in the house, the cutting season started. Almost from the moment they arrived, Gustavo was in a frenzy of activity. Men came and went from their house as though it were a train station. In his hurried business activities Gustavo tried to include his son as much as possible. "I want you to learn everything you can about this, Camilo," he said. "Someday, all this will be yours."

Camilo went from the house to the mill with his father, watching the mechanics at work on the machinery, and to the office, where the walls were covered with large maps of the region, each outlined in sections designated by different colors. He learned that the sugar estate was divided into seven *colonias,* as they were called, each under the direction of a *colono,* who operated independently until the cutting season started. "Now, you see here, in each colony it is marked month by month the condition of the soil, the age of the cane, and whether it has been burned over. It is very bad for us when the cane burns."

Camilo learned that his father employed two hundred inspectors, who rode day by day through the various fields connected with the mill, offering advice to the *colonos,* or ordering methods changed when a planter deviated from the company's policies. Fire, he was told, was the chief fear of sugar growers, next to hurricanes. All the fields were cut up in sections, divided by broad open lanes called *guardarrayas,* some more than fifty feet wide, which served not only as roads but as firebreaks. In all the Carta fields there were watchtowers where men stood guard night and day to give warning the instant a fire broke out. During the drier months, regular patrols were mounted to watch over the fields. "It goes hard with a man who is caught in a field where a fire has started," his father told him. "The penalties are severe under our laws."

Ten days into October Camilo woke in the morning to hear the hum of machinery. When he came outside he saw smoke rushing from the tall stacks above the mill. The cutting had started two days before. He rode in the station wagon with his father, moving from field to field, where skirmish lines of workmen were chopping with machetes at the tall slender stalks. Others were loading the cane into wooden carts pulled by oxen and into the trucks from the mill. The whole countryside was alive with activity. Trains belching smoke pulled into the railroad yard beside the mill, their open cars loaded with the shaggy piles of cane. The mill machinery hummed through the nights. There was no escape from the sound. Camilo woke to it, ate to it, spent the days with it, and went to sleep at night with the low-pitched hum of the machines and the splashing sound of water.

Camilo spent many hours wandering through the huge mill. He saw the cane unloaded into chutes, where it was washed by streams of water as it moved along the conveyor. Tons of juice splashed from beneath the steel rollers that crushed the cane. The juice cascaded into the steaming, boiling vats. Giant centrifuges, tended by sweating blacks, whirled the thick molasses into brown grains, which were then poured into great jute bags. The sacks weighed thirteen arrobas, or 325 pounds. In the docking area, the bags were loaded end up on the shoulders of burly Haitians, who were forced to run with them to the railroad car.

"Why do you have to run?" Camilo asked one of the black men.

The sweating Haitian grinned at him, wiping his brow. "Because of the weight, you see? You stop, the bag will topple. We are paid by the number of bags we carry."

"Why don't they use smaller bags?"

"Because the bags are made in India. No one wants to change it, here or there!"

One night, outside the high fence that surrounded the mill, Camilo came upon a crowd of workmen who had formed a circle around a tall young Cuban dressed in a white shirt and slacks. There was a young woman with him. The workmen stood with grave faces, listening to him speak. Some smoked thoughtfully, all standing motionless as the young man's ardent voice shouted to them. Camilo pushed through the crowd until he could see the man's face. He looked like a student, his black hair falling over his sweaty forehead, his eyes intense, his voice straining to be heard. The young woman stood behind him, holding a package of leaflets, which she handed to the workmen who would take them.

"Cuba is being more thoroughly exploited now than in the days of slavery!" the young man shouted, waving his arm. "Our national wealth goes not to Cubans, but to *norteamericano* masters who have never set foot on Cuban soil! They own our industry. They own you and me! Are there none among you here who do not remember when they paid us only five cents an hour? Less than it took us to live. We abandon to the *norteamericano* masters all of our country with good grace. Our politicians grow fat in Havana on the riches they steal from us. Our politics are monuments to greed and corruption!"

The crowd murmured in response.

The young man licked his lips, glancing around at the faces of the men. He brushed back his hair and raised his hand. "Yet how do these Yankee masters look upon us, upon Cuba? They profoundly despise us! We are dirt beneath their feet. We are called 'spicks' and exploited like slaves! This is true, comrades. We gnaw at the bone, while the Yankee exploiters, who are not Cubans, eat the meat. If we show our teeth, what do they do? They complain to our government, and our police kick our teeth out! If we growl, our police beat our throats. The matter is thus settled. Yes!"

Again the assenting murmur came from the workmen. Camilo edged closer.

The young man wiped his face with a white handkerchief. "Sugar is king in Cuba. Yes. We have only one national crop—sugar! We all slave for it. We cut the cane. We grind it. We produce it, but do not share in its profits, and as a nation we are then at the mercy of the *capitalistas* in the world market. The *capitalistas* are the ones who sit in their offices and smoke their fat cigars and drink their fat liquor and tell us what they will pay for sugar so they can continue to grow fat, while we, the workers, the ones who sweat to produce the sugar, are left lean and hungry and, yes, comrades, angry!"

The workmen cheered. Camilo, strangely moved, joined the cheering.

"How many," shouted the young man, his voice now growing hoarse, "how many of you live through the dead season when there is no cane to cut without seeing your children go hungry? How many have not great debt at the Carta company store? How many do not spend all your wages right here on Carta property?"

There was a stir among the men as Camilo saw the headlights of two cars approaching. "*Policía,*" someone whispered. There was a sudden movement in the crowd. The men started drifting off into the darkness.

The young man glanced at the girl. "Comrades, don't be afraid. See? I am not afraid. My wife is not afraid. Come back. Show courage. Show your *cojones.* Stand up to the oppressors!"

The headlights silhouetted the young man and the woman suddenly. In the glare, Camilo, who had not moved, watched the car doors open and four men in army uniforms emerge. The young man straightened his shoulders, took the woman's hand, and turned to face the oncoming policemen. "Comrades," he shouted, "I forgive you!"

Camilo saw a rifle butt flash and the young man's head jolt backward. He dropped to his knees. The woman began screaming and crying, trying to get to the young man, who knelt on the ground, his head in his hands. Two policemen dragged the woman away, shrieking and kicking. Camilo saw the other two men in uniform standing over the young man. One raised his rifle, but the other stopped him with a gesture, staring over at Camilo.

"*Oye! Niño,* who are you?"

"My father owns this mill."

He saw the young man's face, blood streaked on his sunken cheeks, staring at him.

One of the policemen walked over to him and took his arm gently. "Come, *chico,* I will take you back to your father."

"What are you going to do to him?" Camilo asked, trying to see back over his shoulder.

"Don't worry, we'll take care of him. Come." The policeman's grip was firm on his arm. "Come, *chico.*"

"Take your hand off my arm," Camilo told him. "I can walk myself." And he strode off, leaving the policeman staring after him.

When he saw his father that night, he told him all that had happened and what had been said by the young man. "Is it true, Papa?" He expected Carta to be angry, but instead he answered patiently, thoughtfully.

"Some of it," his father said. "We are not owned by *norteamericanos,* as he said, Camilo. But we do have stockholders."

"Yankees?"

"Like your mother."

"Do our workmen all spend their wages at our store?"

"Usually, yes. It is unjust, but it is the system."

"Can't it be changed?"

"Once, I thought so."

"But you no longer think so?"

"Camilo, it is very complex. You must understand that. Very complex. What is so difficult is that, once you change one thing, you must change it all." He looked distressed.

Camilo went to bed that night troubled. All that he had heard and seen disturbed him. He kept seeing the young man with blood on his face and hearing the screams of the woman. What was it all about? he wondered. It seemed beyond him, frighteningly beyond his powers to comprehend.

The whistles at the mill began to blow in steady, regular blasts. Smoke belched in a broad tower on the horizon, spreading out in the upper air to a yellow haze. Workmen poured out of the fields, some climbing onto trucks, others running along the road. Men on horses, in cars, in trucks and on foot streamed toward the fire. By now the immense column of smoke could be seen over half of the district. Gustavo Carta heard the whistle while driving the station wagon along one of the cane roads. He wheeled the car about and drove toward the smoke, bouncing and jarring along the cane roads at sixty miles an hour. All around him men were running, carrying machetes, clubs, the tops of banana plants, wet gunny sacks, clumps of brush. When he turned onto the field where the fire was burning, Carta saw the bright-red flames licking above the tops of the cane, the smoke black and oily. The sun burned yellow through the haze.

Horsemen were riding up and down the road, shouting orders. As he stepped from the car, Carta felt the blast of heat from the flames that soared in the air like tearing sheets of parchment. The crackling changed to a whooshing roar when the wind it generated caught it, sending forth great sheets of luminous fire. Bits of black cane leaves drifted thick around him.

"Take the car, get it out of here! Leave me your horse!" Carta shouted to one of the men.

"*Sí*, Patrón," the man replied, sliding from the saddle.

Carta mounted quickly and spurred the horse down the road, which was filling more and more with firefighters.

The entire village was on the fireline, stabbing at the flames with whatever they could get their hands on. The wind blew hot and sent the burned bits of leaves skittering in horizontal patterns in the bronze light. Carta rode the fireline, shouting orders to cut a fresh *guardarraya* here, start a backfire there. The company's two bulldozers growled into the fray, cutting away wide swaths in the cane for fire lanes. Sweat streamed on Carta's face. His voice grew hoarse. The wind freshened suddenly and sent sparks glittering to the next field. Carta kicked his sweating horse into action, drawing a crowd of men with him to attack the new flames that were starting to eat into the fresh green wall of cane. Looking back over his shoulder, he saw a whirlwind, generated by the intense heat of the fire, send sparks dancing hundreds of feet into the air. For a moment it seemed to be hopeless. The fire was out of control and there seemed little possibility of stopping it. All around him, men were falling back from the flames, staggering onto the road, gagging from the smoke. He wheeled his horse and rode among them, shouting and gesturing until he thought his lungs would burst. But the firefighters, their faces streaked with sweat and soot, eyes red and watering, turned about and went to thrashing at the flames again. The pungent smell of burnt crude sugar filled the air, mingled with the choking smoke.

Riding down one of the firelines, Carta saw a small figure stagger out of the smoke onto the road, where he stood gasping for air. His face was blackened with soot, his hair singed. Carta reined up beside him.

"Camilo!" Carta dismounted. "You shouldn't be here! It's dangerous."

Camilo lifted his machete into view. "It's fun, Father. Don't worry, we'll stop it."

He turned and ran back to take his place in the line of men hacking at the flames. Carta watched him a long moment, feeling proud.

Bit by bit the towering flames began to succumb under the relentless efforts of the thousands of men. The firebreaks held as the wind died. The roar of the fire lost its ominous sound, the voices of the men rising more clearly above it. In the twilight, the red glare died out as black particles still fluttered in the air. Leading his exhausted horse, Gustavo walked with the throngs of weary firefighters, smeared, smudged, sweat-stained, along the open lane. A figure standing in front of him startled him out of his stupor.

"Lupe. Are you all right?"

"Yes, Patrón. I wish to speak to you, alone."

There was a hard, stern cast to Carta's face that night at the dinner table. Camilo, seated to his right, ate in silence. Elizabeth was agitated by the day's event.

"Does it mean you'll lose all that cane?" she asked.

"No," said Carta. "We must cut it quickly and grind it, or it spoils. I am having extra men assigned to that field tomorrow. We'll save it."

"Is there any idea how it started?"

Carta stared straight at Camilo and replied in a flat voice, "No. Not really. Nothing certain. All we know is that it was deliberately set."

"Why would anyone do such a thing?"

Carta wiped his mouth with his napkin and leaned back in his chair, looking at Camilo. "There were some Marxist agitators at the mill the other night. Camilo heard them. Didn't you, son? Perhaps one of those workers . . . one of their comrades? How can we be certain?"

"With so many men in the fields," Elizabeth said, helping herself to the yellow rice, "it seems strange that no one saw anything, doesn't it?"

"Lupe thinks he saw something."

He saw Camilo stiffen slightly. Elizabeth let the spoon drop into the rice bowl and then set the bowl down in front of Camilo, who gave his father a noncommittal glance and then piled rice on his plate.

Elizabeth asked, "What did he see?"

"He's not sure. He thinks he saw someone on a horse in the field, just before the fire started."

90

"Could he identify him?"

Carta laughed, but there was little humor in his tone. "Well, it's amazing. Truly, very funny. You see, he thinks the person was riding a small black horse. He wasn't sure, but he said it looked like a boy on the horse."

"Lots of people have small black mares," Camilo said, his voice husky.

"Including Camilo," Elizabeth added. "Surely, you're not suggesting . . ."

"As I said, no one knows who started the fire," Carta said.

Elizabeth slapped her fork down on the table. "I know you must be exhausted, darling," she said to her husband. "But I don't think you realized that you implicated—"

"He said he didn't know, Mother," Camilo interrupted.

Carta's eyes burrowed into Camilo's, then shifted to Elizabeth. "As you said, I am very tired," he murmured. He cleared his throat. "May I have some more pork?"

Her cheeks flushed, Elizabeth passed him the platter of pork in silence. Carta again cleared his throat. "Tell me, Camilo, did you think any of the men in that crowd the other night were affected by the agitator?"

"Agitator, Papa?"

"That boy you mentioned. The one who spoke."

"He said some interesting things, as I told you. Many of the workmen seemed to agree with him, Papa."

"And you? Did you agree with what he said?"

Camilo carefully set his fork down beside his plate, wiped his mouth with his napkin and then looked squarely at his father.

Elizabeth said heatedly, "Gustavo, I've had enough of this!"

"Enough of what, my darling?"

"You're not being very subtle. You are practically accusing your son of being an arsonist! I won't stand for it!"

"I am merely questioning him about the Marxist. He was present. Perhaps he saw something, overheard something?"

"What do you want me to say, Papa? That I started it? Will that make you happy?" Camilo moved his chair back and stood erect, dropping his napkin onto his plate. He never took his eyes from his father's.

Elizabeth got up and moved around the table to him. "Camilo, tell him. I want you to tell him to his face. Did you have anything to do with that fire?"

Camilo did not look at her. "No," he said between his teeth. Glaring at his father, he turned aside and walked out of the dining room.

Lupe was waiting in the garden when Carta came out of the house. He removed his straw hat as he saw the *patrón* approach in the light from the window.

"Lupe?"

"*Sí*, Patrón."

Carta came up to him. He stood for a moment looking up at the stars. Then he let his breath out in a weary sigh. "I spoke to the boy."

"Yes, Patrón."

"It was not he, Lupe."

Lupe lowered his head and nodded. "That's good to hear, Patrón. Very good to hear. I was sick thinking perhaps . . ."

"I know. I know." Carta touched his arm in the dark, reassuringly. "You were right to come to me."

HAVANA, 1949

Several days after David arrived home from school for his Christmas holiday, the family began to notice the difference. David was seventeen that year, a methodical, serious boy who never spent time just hanging around like other boys his age. He always seemed to have a project of some sort; that year he was building up a collection of microscopic sea organisms, and he spent hours peering at them and studying their behavior.

Living away from home at prep school seemed to heighten David's pleasure in being home for Christmas. He bought gifts for everyone, including the housekeeper and the gardeners, and helped decorate the huge tree. He seemed less inhibited about displays of affection. The distance between David and Gustavo had been substantially bridged now. Carta was proud of David for doing well at Exeter. He was proud of him and he loved him. The boy who seemed so unreachable at thirteen had now acquired a new sense of himself, a new equanimity.

It was at Christmas dinner that the family began to notice another change. The house was filled with holiday decorations, and the table was laden with turkey, ham, sweet potatoes and fruits and vegetables. David seemed delighted to be there, but between his sudden bursts of conversation he looked distracted, staring off dreamily into space. After dessert, he quickly excused himself, saying he wanted to take a walk outside.

"Is there something wrong with him, or is it my imagination?" Elizabeth asked.

92

"I think I know what's wrong with him," Camilo said, an edge of adolescent scorn in his voice. "It's disgusting."

"Who is she?" Carta said, grinning.

"It's that girl Constancia. He met her playing tennis at the club."

"The Medina girl—I'll be damned."

"I think she's ugly," Camilo said.

But Constancia Medina was anything but ugly. She was a lovely dark-haired creature with tawny skin and jade eyes and a budding figure. Her father was a wealthy plantation owner, and Constancia had the sort of timorous, refined manner that reflected good Catholic schools and an overprotective Spanish home.

David started seeing Constancia every day now, and his demeanor grew increasingly dreamy and distracted. They went horseback riding, had solitary picnics at the beach, and went for long walks. Though Camilo was cautiously disdainful of his brother's infatuation, he was also fascinated by it. Camilo well understood the meaning of lust, but his brother had fallen victim to something beyond lust, and that baffled him. He yearned to question David about it, but David had grown more remote, and though Camilo used to wander freely into his room at night, David now kept his door locked and made it clear that he didn't want to be disturbed.

One night Camilo caught David coming home; he trailed him into his room and plunked himself down on his bed before he could lock him out. David looked over at him impatiently.

"Where did you take her?"

"Who?" David said, unbuttoning his shirt.

"You know who, come on."

David said nothing as he continued undressing.

"You've really lost your marbles, haven't you?"

David continued to undress in silence.

"What do you say to her all the time? Doesn't it get boring?"

David stared at Camilo peevishly. "What is this, a school quiz?"

"I just want to know."

"What is it you want to know?"

"What it's like. To lose your marbles."

"There are some things I can't explain." David was removing his trousers and Camilo was staring at his protuberance with avid curiosity.

"Does she let you stick your machete in her?"

David had had it now. He leaped toward the bed, grabbing his brother by the legs, trying to yank him toward the door, but Camilo clung to the bedpost.

"Come on, Davy," Camilo pleaded. "I really want to know. What's the big deal?"

David saw he wasn't making any progress, and he relented. "OK, if I answer one question, will you get the hell out of here?"

"One question?"

"Just one."

"Do you fuck her?"

David flushed. "No. Damn you, Camilo, I won't have you saying things like that about her. She's not one of those sluts from the village you chase around the streets at night! Her parents are very strict. If you want to know the truth, all I've done is hold her hand. So take it back!"

Camilo looked properly humble. "I take it back. You don't have to get sore. I just asked." He shook his head. "It must be awful to be in love."

"It's not awful."

"Do you dream about her?"

"All the goddamn time. Oh, Christ, Cam . . ." David snapped out of his reverie and shot an angry glance at his brother. "Get the fuck out of here, OK?"

Camilo reluctantly got to his feet and headed toward the door. "OK, I'm going, I'm going." The moment he had slammed the door, however, he jerked it open again and poked his head in. "Just don't wear out your machete tonight, OK, Davy? You may need it tomorrow."

David slammed the door hard.

David didn't talk to his brother much during the next few days. Once Camilo saw him riding with Constancia in the pasture behind the house. And one morning he walked down to the tennis court after hearing their voices and laughter and the pop of the ball being hit. He stood for a long time at the fence, hidden by the foliage, and watched them play. She was a good player, quick and athletic. She wore a white tennis dress and white shoes and socks and looked to Camilo to be very worthy of his brother's attention. She had a nice rump and slender, pretty legs, and when she drew back to hit the ball with her racket he could see the lumps of her budding breasts. Not bad, he thought. Not bad at all. He waited until they finished the game and watched David hand her a fresh towel, his eyes fastened on her. There was no doubt about it, his brother was in love. They went off the court holding hands.

One night Camilo was just leaving to meet some friends when he was caught in the sudden blaze of automobile headlights. The car came right at him at great speed, and he had to jump into the ferns to avoid being hit. Camilo turned angrily and recognized that it was David's car, which came screeching to a halt in front of the house. "Goddamn it, Davy!"

94

Camilo shouted, but David bolted out of the car and ran into the house without even bothering to close the car door.

Camilo stood there angrily, uncertain what to do, then ran upstairs and hammered on the door to David's room. There was no response. He knocked again, then turned the knob. The door opened. He saw his brother lying on the bed, his face buried in his pillow. He had taken off his glasses. Camilo saw them on the nightstand, glistening in the light.

"Davy, you almost killed me out there. What the hell's going on?"

David did not answer.

"Davy?" Camilo thought he detected a shudder running through his brother's body.

"Go away, I said."

But Camilo could see something was terribly wrong. He stood riveted in the doorway.

"Maybe if I called Papa he could—"

"There's nothing, goddamn it. Can't you understand? There's nothing anyone can do." David had turned his head to him now. The tears were coursing down his cheeks. It was the first time Camilo could remember him crying since they were both small children.

Camilo sat down on the bed beside him and put his hand on his brother's shoulder. "Listen to me, Davy. I am your brother. You can tell me anything. What's wrong? Tell me."

"I can't." David turned his face away, trying to wipe off the tears with the back of his hand.

"Did you break up with your girl?"

"No."

"But something happened between you, huh? Something bad? Did she slap you, what?"

David shook his head. He turned his face to Camilo, his eyes glistening again with tears, his lips quivering. He could not keep from crying. "Oh, God, Cam . . . Jesus . . ."

Camilo put his arm around him. "Hey, *hombre,* don't cry. No girl's worth crying about . . . none of them."

"It isn't that."

"Well, Jesus, Davy, what is it?"

David wiped his nose on his shirt sleeve and looked at Camilo again, trying to blink away the tears. "You won't tell . . . you won't tell anyone, not even Mother?"

"OK. Sure."

"Promise? Promise me, Cam? You won't tell?"

"I promise. On my word of honor, I promise."

"She was raped."

Camilo stared helplessly. "Who raped her? I don't understand."

"The fucking goddamn priest raped her," David sobbed, burying his head in the pillow again.

"The priest? There must be some mistake."

"There was no goddamn mistake. She was taking lessons from her tutor, Father Andrés. Last night during the lessons he told her he had to examine her. It was a special ceremony of the church. He put his hand under her skirt . . ."

"She didn't let that old man do anything—"

David lunged at him now, grabbing onto the collar of his shirt and shaking him. "She was scared to death. She couldn't believe what was happening. He put his fingers into her. He made her bleed—"

"Stop shaking me, David."

"He put his filthy fingers inside her and . . ." David's voice was shrill with near-hysteria.

"Did she tell her parents?"

"She told no one except me. She is too ashamed. But she won't see me again."

David released Camilo and plunged onto his bed, his face on his pillow.

"She'll change her mind, Davy. Wait and see."

David was sobbing softly as Camilo looked on, feeling helpless. Seeing David like this made him realize how much he loved his brother. There had to be something he could do—some way to show him. He felt a sudden anger toward the priest.

"That filthy pig priest," Cam said. "He should be killed."

"She won't let me see her again, Cam. Ever!"

Camilo stood there for a few moments, staring at his brother. Then he turned and left the room, feeling cold anger.

David remained in his room that night and most of the next day. He told his parents that he was sick. Carta and Elizabeth assumed it was a lover's quarrel and left him alone to work it out. And Camilo did not reappear.

That night at about ten o'clock, however, David heard a knock. He opened the door to find Vicente, a friend of Camilo's, standing there nervously.

"What do you want?"

"Camilo sent me. I am to take you with me."

"I don't want to go anywhere."

"He said it was very important that you come."

"I don't feel like pranks."

"Camilo is in grave danger. I think you should come."

David looked at the boy. He was small and wiry. His big eyes looked genuinely frightened.

David followed him downstairs. Vicente led him down the road in the dark for about fifteen minutes, then veered off onto a path. Vicente stopped so suddenly that David almost crashed into him.

"We are here."

"Where?"

"Follow me."

Vicente led the way. It was very dark, and David felt the sting of branches against his skin and the thick brush catching his ankles. They came to a small clearing. It took David several seconds to see the others. There were five boys standing around. One of them was Camilo.

David walked over to his brother. "What's this all about, Cam?"

Camilo put his finger to his lips. He pointed to the center of the clearing.

In the starlight, David could make out the figure of a man tied to the trunk of a royal palm. Camilo tugged at his arm. "Come on, it's your fucking bastard priest."

Camilo led him across to the palm tree. The priest, who was in his late forties, with a pinched, arrogant Spanish face, was blindfolded with a white rag. He lifted his chin as they came up to him. David saw that he wore a black cassock that had been cut away in front. His white belly, bulbous as a soccer ball, bulged from his torso. His skinny legs had been tied by ropes at the ankles. David saw the hairy patch between his legs and the pale length of his uncircumcised penis. He had never seen a man with an organ of such size before.

Camilo grinned at him. "He's hung like a horse, huh?"

"Who's there?" the priest's voice came to them. It sounded high-pitched and frightened, but he was trying to speak with authority. "I demand to be released at once! This is a major crime, kidnapping. A major crime. Whoever is responsible shall pay the full penalty—"

"It's you that's going to pay the penalty, priest," Camilo said to him. "Tell us about the virgins you've ruined in your career, huh?"

"Who said that? What are you accusing me of?"

"Raper of children," Camilo spat at him.

"You are damned to hell!" the priest cried out. "God damn thee for thy sins!"

"It's your sins that we are dealing with tonight, priest. How about the virgin you gave your special benediction to the other night, huh? How about her, priest? How about what you did to her? How did you feel when you made her bleed and cry, priest?"

97

"I don't know what you're talking about," the priest replied, but his voice wavered, without conviction.

"I wonder what the police will do to you when we give them the evidence, huh? What will the Bishop say, huh?"

"It's lies! I have done nothing to anyone—"

"Lying bastard. *Oye!* Alfonso! Bring the calf . . ."

David heard a sound in the brush. He was trying to calm the conflict within him. He hated this priest. But seeing him humiliated publicly frightened him. "What are you going to do to him, Cam?"

"Watch." Camilo pointed off. Following his gesture, David saw two boys leading a calf into the clearing. It must have been no more than two or three days old, for it wavered unsteadily on its long legs as it walked. It bawled loudly. Looking around, David discovered he was surrounded by boys, who stood fascinated in the dark, transfixed by the spectacle they were witnessing.

The calf bawled again. Camilo grinned. "Hear that, priest? He's hungry. You think you can feed him, priest?"

"Dear God . . ." the priest gasped. "What are you doing?"

"He has come to hear your confession," Camilo said. "Are you prepared, Father?"

Camilo took the rope from the two boys and dragged the calf to the palm tree. "There you go, *niño.* There's your supper." David heard the sharp sound as the calf snorted through its nostrils.

"Holy Jesus, save me!" the priest yelled. "Someone, anyone, help me! God, save me! Oh, please, please, don't . . . don't!" His voice grew more and more hysterical.

The calf's tongue licked him. Camilo held the head up. "That's it," he said. "Good . . . good calf, good boy . . ."

David felt himself growing sick and weak as he saw the calf suddenly fasten its mouth onto the priest's organ. The man tried to squirm away, his voice gasping, "Oh . . . oh . . . oh, no, don't, don't . . ." The calf butted him as it began to suck, a steady slurping sound that made David cringe. He butted again and the priest cried out in pain, "*Ay . . . ay . . . ay!*" The calf was sucking him fully now, the thick penis disappearing into its mouth. "Oh, Lord . . . Lord . . ." the priest gasped. "Oh, no . . . no, no . . . please stop, stop . . . stop!"

Camilo turned suddenly and laughed. "Look, look!" he cried, pointing. He pulled the straining calf back from the priest and pointed. David saw the swollen penis jutting from beneath the priest's round belly. It looked like a cauliflower, white in the starlight, jiggling as the calf was pulled away. The calf bawled and Camilo released it, letting it get a hold

98

with its mouth again. The penis was so large and strongly erect now it slipped twice from the calf's mouth. The third time, the calf butted the priest with his muzzle, and the man screamed; but the whole length of the penis had slipped into the eager mouth. Camilo dropped the rope and stepped back.

The calf kept nudging and sucking and the priest groaned and cried out in wordless anguish. The boys were all laughing in the dark. David felt cold and clammy.

Camilo came up to him. "We got him, Davy. When that calf is through with him, he'll think twice before he touches a girl again."

"Look, look at him!" someone cried. "He's coming!"

The priest was straining against the ropes, his belly bouncing, his gasps growing stronger and stronger. "Oh, God, forgive me!" he pleaded. "Oh, no . . . no . . . no." And they saw his body spasm, and heard his moan.

"He came," one of the boys shouted. "The son of a bitch came!"

But the calf seemed oblivious, nudging, sucking, butting. The priest began to squirm violently, trying to extricate himself from the calf. He began to moan in pain. "I'll bet that hurts," one of the boys said.

Camilo looked at the calf and said, "Let him suck that bastard until his cock falls off."

"Let's go," someone said.

"Maybe he'll come again?" someone else said.

"How long will that calf keep it up?"

"As long as he has that priest in his mouth."

"Will he ever stop?"

"After he gets tired."

David heard the priest praying breathlessly in Spanish. He was delirious and hysterical. Suddenly, David tasted vomit in his mouth. His stomach lurched. He bit down hard to keep it down. This was his fault. The man was suffering because of what he had said to Camilo.

His brother came up beside him. "Hey, Davy, you all right? What's the matter?"

"Nothing," David gagged.

"We got him good, huh? The bastard."

Sickened, David turned away. He knelt in the grass, gagging. Then he began to run, feeling the vines and the brush biting against him. A nightmare. The whole thing. He kept running faster until his chest ached. But he still heard Father Andrés' shrill voice, choked with panic, screaming!

The next day David packed his bags and left for school early. He explained that he had a report to get in. His parents saw him off at the airport. Camilo smiled as he said goodbye. David shook his hand gravely and did not smile back.

MATANZAS, 1953

Camilo first saw her on a horse. A black Arabian mare. She wore a man's shirt and faded jeans, her thick raven hair caught in a ponytail behind her delicate head, bouncing as she rode in that smooth gliding motion of a real rider completely at one with his mount.

Her sudden appearance out of the trees startled him. They had been expecting to see doves. His father, standing with his double-barrel Purdy, laughed and waved to her. "Alicia! Hello!" he shouted. Then he turned to Camilo grinning. "Now, there's a dove for you to shoot, Cam."

She rode toward them in the failing sunlight that slanted into the trees. There was something expressive and sensual about the cast of her mouth. Her skin was flushed from the sun and the fresh air. Wisps of black hair floated about her head as she reined the mare and smiled down at his father. The angle of the sunlight made shadows of her breasts under her white cotton shirt. She did not look at him at first, but when she glanced over at him finally, Camilo saw that her eyes were an odd amber color.

His father gestured for him to come over and made the introductions. He felt shy and uncomfortable in her presence. Even her casual glance made him feel restive and uneasy. He thought she was the most beautiful girl he had ever seen. She was the daughter of a business acquaintance of his father's. They had a summer house not two miles from the Carta house at the beach. She had just completed secondary school and was enrolling at the university in Havana for the fall semester. She wanted to be an architect, she said. Gustavo had reacted with a mild expression of surprise.

"What will you build? Houses or skyscrapers?" he asked her, laughing good-naturedly.

But Alicia replied very seriously that she wished to build houses—attractive, low-cost houses for people who now had to suffer the slums. She had given Camilo a shy look when she said it, but she knew she had his interest.

He saw her quite often during the two weeks they spent at the beach that summer. His reputation at the university was well known to her and she took pride in his company. Camilo was in his third year and he planned to graduate as a law student only to satisfy his mother's desire that he have a profession.

His real passion was the overthrow of the Batista government, not the study of law. They spent long hours together sitting on the veranda while their parents played bridge in the house, and discussed Marx and Engels and Mao and the rising aspirations of colonial nations throughout the world. Her awareness surprised him. He found she was a voracious reader. Despite her Catholic training, she was sharply critical of the Church in Cuba. Her hostility bordered on obsession. "What have they done for Cuba? They only tender their services to the upper and middle classes and ignore the poor! Their priests are all Spaniards. As far as the Church is concerned, we're still a colony of Spain! Have you ever seen any of the rural churches, Camilo? They're painted like circus tents, and half the services are a mixture of Catholic saints and voodoo rites." When he laughed at her, she touched his arm urgently, leaning toward him. "No, don't laugh at me, it's true. The revolution must destroy the Church, it must!" He was stunned at her fervor. She was so young, and a woman!

By Christmas, they were engaged. He had gone to her father, following all the rules of politeness and protocol so dear to the older generation. Alicia's father was a banker, a staid, quiet-spoken man, who listened to him with respect and then said to him in a very calm voice, "But you understand, Camilo, she is only sixteen."

"Her mother was fifteen when she married," Camilo replied sharply. "Why should it be different in this generation?"

Camilo stubbornly refused to accept a negative reply, countering every argument with his own cool logic and single-minded adamance. Her mother appealed to Camilo with emotion, tears and finally anger. He told them that he would, if they refused, kidnap Alicia and marry her without their permission. Did they wish to be deprived of witnessing their daughter's marriage ceremony? When they realized that this tall, hot-eyed young man was sincere, they relented.

Alicia, meanwhile, had been forced to remain in her room, with only her sister, Pepita, who was two years younger, to console her. She was so terrified when she heard them coming out of the library downstairs, she locked herself in the bathroom and refused to come out. Finally her father pounded on the door and asked if she was going to keep her *novio* waiting downstairs all night. Camilo was standing at the bottom of the stairs when he heard her shriek of delight and saw her appear abruptly above him, tears glistening in her eyes, looking down at him with a devotion and love he could never hope to see again in his life.

After his engagement was formally announced, Camilo, by custom, was allowed easier access to the house of Aljendro Chavero, his future father-in-law. It was a great Spanish mansion built after the turn of the century in the Vedado section of Havana. He visited almost nightly, sitting in the big high-ceilinged drawing room. He tried to avoid discussing politics with Aljendro, who was a Batista supporter. Señora Teresa, his wife, a thick, graying woman, adored her future son-in-law, as did in fact the rest of the Chavero family, which included Pepita, the youngest, and Arturo, her older brother, a stocky, thick-chested youth, two years older than Camilo, who had graduated as a lawyer from the university in 1952.

There were times in which Camilo and Alicia were left in comparative privacy and he uttered his formal expressions of love in flowery Castilian, as was the old custom, rolling his eyes and trying to keep them both from laughing as he urged his fiancée to command him to do whatsoever she pleased and he would obey. "Make of me your doormat," he told her, "and I shall bless your feet."

"If that's all you do, Camilo Carta, I'll not think you worthy to be my husband."

"You don't want your feet blessed?"

"It's elsewhere I want to be blessed, you fool!"

There were squeals of laughter and protests as Camilo lunged at her, shouting, "Prepare for your blessing, woman!"

Her screams brought Señora Teresa running into the room, her face red with alarm, only to find the two lovers crumpled on the floor, convulsed with laughter.

Once when they were taking a stroll in the garden, Alicia turned to him with a serious expression and asked, "Camilo, do you like your father?"

He was startled. "Of course. Why do you ask?"

"You rarely speak of him. You always tell me about your mother, or your brother, David, or this family friend, Amato. He seems to be more of a father to you than your father!"

"Not really," Camilo said. He stopped by the fountain and picked up a handful of small stones to toss in at the goldfish swimming beneath the broad ear-shaped green leaves that floated on the surface. "My father is busy a lot, you know? He has much responsibility with the sugar fields and the tobacco business. He does not really understand . . ." She detected a certain defensiveness in his tone.

"It's all right. I didn't mean to—"

"No, you have a right to ask. My father has great expectations for me. He wants me to take over the family businesses. To perpetuate the Carta tradition and domain. But these are things that do not interest me. He doesn't understand that. He thinks that ultimately I will slide into his world and his way of doing things."

"And will you?"

Camilo regarded her sharply. "Never."

They fell silent a moment. Then Camilo looked at her out of the corners of his eyes. "Something's troubling you. What is it? Something about my father and me?"

She looked pensive. "I don't know, really. It's a feeling I get when I see you together. It's as though maybe he's a little frightened by you. Does that make sense, Camilo?"

Camilo laughed, taking her arm. "My father has never known the meaning of fear. He doesn't have a fearful bone in his body!"

HAVANA, 1954

They were married the following June in ancient La Santa Iglesia de la Virgen María de la Inmaculada Concepción in old Havana. Limousines with black chauffeurs in white liveries swept up to the edge of the lovely old square in a continual procession. Women in long gowns and men in dark suits dotted with orchids and carnations filled the square. Musicians in their tuxedos were stationed in front of the Havana Club Rum Company facing the square, playing Mozart and Bach. The guests jammed into the club's glorious old patio, which was dominated by two royal palms that soared above the tile roof in the hot sun. Waiters hired from the elegant Restaurant Paris circulated through the plaza carrying trays that gleamed like mirrors, laden with frozen daiquiris or decorative clusters of fresh fruit.

At precisely one o'clock the first sections of the wedding party pulled up, causing a stir among the four hundred wedding guests in the plaza. Camilo, in morning coat and tails, appeared with his ushers and Ángel Maceo, flushed and nervous in his best man's attire, moving across the ancient cobbles in a black phalanx, while the guests applauded, smiling and cheering. They were followed by Gustavo and then Elizabeth, who wore an elegant gown of lapis blue, with delicate sequins about her shoulders, and carried a bouquet of white star jasmine. Delayed by traffic, Alicia's party arrived seven minutes later, a dazzling tableau of young maidens in identical pink gowns and veils, their heads crowned with white flowers, their faces shiny and smiling. Alicia was hidden in a sweeping white veil and white satin wedding gown that required four

103

pairs of hands to keep it off the cobbles. She moved up the broad cathedral steps like a white cloud, brilliant in the sun.

Among the many anxieties that had beset the Cartas that morning was the fact that David had missed his plane connection in Miami, due to a weather delay out of New York, and wouldn't be able to get to Havana until the following afternoon. Camilo and Alicia had earlier decided to take the morning plane to Paris, and it meant they would not see David before they left. Camilo was heartsick. He wanted his brother as his best man. Ángel Maceo had to be persuaded to stand in his place at the last minute, since he had performed the function during all the rehearsals and was Camilo's closest friend. Elizabeth was beside herself, and Gustavo had spent the entire morning shouting into the telephone at airline representatives. He had even tried to charter a plane to fly David from Miami, but none was available in time.

Camilo had spoken with David on the phone, his clean-shaven face flushed and glistening with moisture, saying how terribly disappointed he was David couldn't be there, laughing nervously and telling David they had spent the last four days with lawyers making up the marriage contracts. "You can't believe how complicated it is to be married in Spanish," he joked. "You'd think we were merging two business corporations! Come the revolution, all you're going to have to do is say yes!" When he hung up, Camilo quickly abandoned his façade and stood looking at his mother and father sadly. They all felt the void.. They wished David were there.

He stood in silence beside Maceo, who fidgeted with his hands, and waited for his first glimpse of Alicia. Camilo had not seen her since the morning before, and the anticipation was building to a keen pang of desire. Their courtship had involved certain intimacies of touch and tender kisses, stolen in the intervals allowed under the stern code of Spanish morality. But he had never seen her undressed, only in her modest bathing suit. And though he had ached for her almost from the moment he first saw her on horseback, he had had less physical contact with her than with his mother. When he let his mind touch on their wedding night, on the idea of possessing her, he found himself uneasy. He sensed the same uneasiness in Alicia, though they didn't discuss it. The whole thing struck him as bizarre. He and Alicia, the two young rebels, had so zealously followed the rigid code laid down by her parents that the notion of sexuality somehow seemed foreign and impure. It was as if they had found themselves trapped by their own blind obedience to custom. He felt this strongly now as he gazed up the long aisle of the church, past the rows of faces, and heard the voices of the children's choir lifting in the echoing and re-echoing vastness of the vaulted chamber. He saw them appear in ranks of two, girl after girl in their flowing pink gowns, their crowns of flowers like snow in the gloomy light. He saw Pepita, her younger sister, and smiled at her. The child blushed. The crowd stirred, heads turning, voices murmuring, for there, suddenly poised in the big arched doorway, her father at her arm, was Alicia, like an angel in white, her face lost in the gauzy haze of her veil, walking toward him so lightly and so erect. There was a grace and a mystery in her attitude and he longed suddenly to run to her and catch her by the hand and race out of the church, away from all these people; yet he stood frozen, watching her approach, a cloud of white. He wondered if there was indeed a girl inside all of that flowing cloth, or whether she was merely some evanescent spirit, a ghost who would vanish in a blaze of light the moment he touched her.

All during the long mass, he kept stealing furtive glances at her, at the diffused profile of her face. The impulse of tender joy and excitement made his throat tighten, so that when he spoke his vows his voice sounded thin and choked; not his own. When he lifted the veil for their marriage kiss, and saw her radiant face, her eyes brilliant with love for him, her skin blushed as though by windburn or a fever, he felt they had escaped their mortality, that nothing could touch them, now or ever. He touched her lips with his as gently as if he had been kissing the petals of a delicate flower, and she pressed warm and lovingly against him, the barrier of her thick gown and his heavy clothes all that separated what had already been consummated and joined as one being.

All night the marriage fiesta went on. They escaped to their room in the big family house and locked the door behind, and stood for a long moment, she still in her flowing mass of white wedding dress, he in his Prince Albert coat and tie. He was sweating from the dancing. Outside, the music blared into the lighted trees. Voices shouted. Her amber eyes beneath the long, curved lashes stared at him, as though she were seeing him for the first time, a bit frightened of him. She stood with her hands at her sides, motionless as a deer in the trees. He touched her cheek with his fingertips and felt her moist skin. I love you, Alicia, he told her. Don't be afraid. She did not speak, but shook her head in reply. Show yourself to me, he said. Please? She nodded. Wait. She crossed the carpet and went into the bathroom, her gown rustling as she moved. She glanced back over her shoulder at him, then she shut the door. He stood for a long time listening to the music and the clatter of voices coming from the garden below. Then, quietly, he removed his coat and tie. The room was furnished with a couch and chairs and an enormous bed with a flowered canopy. The lamps on either side of the bed were lit, throw-

105

ing pools of light onto the ornate ceiling. He crossed and turned them out, throwing the room into a twilight. He heard the orchestra strike up a lively cha-cha-cha and the crowd cheer. He opened a bottle of champagne that had been set in a silver bucket at their bedside, letting the cork pop. It flashed up to the ceiling, hit and bounded to the floor. The champagne spilled cold over his fingers, foaming. He raised the bottle to his lips and drank. He went to the window and looked down into the garden. Directly below, he saw Pepita on the walk. He heard the snick of the bathroom lock and heard the door open behind him. He turned slowly to look at her. She stood in shadow, a vague image of white in the dark shape of the door. She still wore her wedding dress, but she had removed her veil and let her hair down. It fell in a dark halo over her shoulders to below her waist. Close the shutter, Camilo, she said in a voice that trembled. He closed and latched the wooden shutter. The lamp clicked on. The glow gave shape to her. She stared at him, and then began to unfasten her waist. It seemed to take forever for her to unhook the back of her dress. Suddenly it slackened. Do you want to do the rest? she said. Or shall I? You, he replied. You do it. Her hands fluttered about her breasts, and with an easy motion of her body she stepped out of it, standing in a cloud of white petticoats. One by one she let them drop. There were four. He saw her hands tremble as she reached across to slide the chemise strap from her shoulder. He walked to her and set the champagne bottle on the table beneath the lamp. He could see her bare shoulders, smooth and delicate to his touch. His fingers moved the lace strap until it crumpled from her shoulder. He stared at the crease the flesh of her breasts made above the lace border of the chemise. His fingers slid from her shoulder, to her cheek, skimming gently, barely touching her warm skin, to her left shoulder, where he nudged the lacy strap to the edge, then slid it off slowly with his whole hand. He looked down and saw her breasts as two circles of protruding flesh, the nipples erect and pale brown. Then he looked into her eyes. I love you, Camilo, she whispered. Take it all away. I want to be naked with you. Take it. Now!

CHAPTER TEN

Camilo walked out of the deserted Club Palermo into the cool night air. He was very drunk and knew it. He looked up Calle San Miguel and saw the street lights on the buildings. A horse and cart were coming down the cobbled street. The driver was whistling in time with the clop-clopping of the skinny horse. Camilo straightened his shoulders. He saw two young militiamen standing at the corner, their automatic weapons slung over their shoulders. They were smoking, and both had turned their heads to look at him.

"*Buenas noches,* Comandante. May we be of service to you?"

"No, *chico,* I'm getting drunk." He waved and walked across the street. I am getting drunk, he repeated to himself. Not getting. Am! Though a little unsteady, he walked erect, with a certain dignity. He went down the street and turned the corner, crossing the street again, and then he saw a café and went toward it. As he walked, his footsteps echoing in the arcade, he found himself thinking of Alicia, of how lonely he was without her, of how much he missed her. There was only a hollow emptiness in his life where she had been, and nothing could fill it now. She was gone. The absolute finality of it made him ache when he thought about it. He went into the bar. The lights in the bar were so bright they hurt his eyes. He was the only customer. The lights shone on the mahogany.

The barman was black, with a wrinkled face and bulging eyes. "May I serve you, Comandante?"

"Bacardi, dark. You have some limes?"

"Of course, señor." He placed the bottle on the bar, then a small clean glass and a white porcelain plate with cut limes, and another with meats and cheese.

The bartender went back to washing and drying the glasses. Camilo poured himself half a glass of dark rum and drank it, squeezing a lime between his teeth. He shuddered and poured another. He ate a piece of the cheese and sipped the rum that warmed him through.

He was pouring his third when he felt a hand touch his arm and turned to see Paco. The enormous black man had skin so dark it seemed to absorb the light. His broad nose and thick lips showed shiny.

"Camilo, you should go home now."

"Drink with me, Paco, I am lonely tonight."

"One," said Paco. He gestured to the bartender for a glass, then poured out half a glass of rum. "I heard you were drinking," he said. "I just missed you at the Palermo."

"Did they tell you I was drunk?"

"It is not good for you to be out on the street alone, Camilo. It is dangerous."

"I don't think I have disgraced myself, Paco. Do I look sloppy drunk?"

"You look fine, except for your eyes."

"What's wrong with my eyes?" Camilo tried to see himself in the mirror across the bar, but it was an old mirror, tarnished and broken, and he could not focus on his face. He scratched his beard and looked sideways at the black man. "Are my eyes drunk?"

"Your eyes look drunk, Camilo."

"By God, they should be. I have put away a great deal of rum, my friend. Maybe a whole quart by now. Yes, my eyes look drunk, all right. It is a sin?"

The black man's thick lips formed into a smile, showing his gold teeth. "If it is, we are all damned."

They laughed.

"I have the jeep outside, let me take you home."

Camilo shrugged, leaning his elbows on the bar, lowering his head. He took a deep breath. "Where is home?" He looked at Paco quickly. "Vedado? Miramar? Cojimar? I have places to sleep in all those, but do I have a home?"

"Where did you sleep last?"

"Miramar. No, Vedado. The apartment. That was . . . I don't know, three, four days ago? Maybe yesterday. Does it matter?"

"I shall take you to the convent. The sisters can care for you."

"Convent? I don't want to go to the damn convent."

"It's safe, Camilo. I think it's best for you tonight. Have you eaten anything?"

Camilo picked up one of the cut limes in his long fingers and examined it carefully. "Limes . . . you like limes?"

"Come on, Camilo, let's go."

The black man put a bill on the bar, waved to the bartender and then followed Camilo's swaying figure out to the street and helped him into the jeep.

There were few cars on the broad street. Here and there people were walking. The shops and the restaurants were all closed and shuttered for the night. As Paco started toward the convent, he saw that Camilo had fallen asleep, his bearded chin on his chest, his head lolling. Paco drove slowly so he would not fall out of the jeep.

There was a light in the room. Camilo opened his eyes and saw the soft glow on the ceiling and realized it was the moon.

The bed was back from the windows and he heard someone open one and looked over to see the nun in her black robes and hood. She turned and looked at him, a delicate pale face, framed by the white starched inner hood. She had gentle eyes and a pouted mouth and she looked very calm and clean.

"I thought you'd need some air," she said, her voice as delicate as her face. "How do you feel?"

"I'm drunk, Pepita, my sister. Very drunk."

"Yes, Paco brought you. He had to carry you up the stairs on his shoulders."

"Good old Paco," Camilo sighed.

She started for the door with a swishing of starched cloth. "Sleep now."

"One request, my sister. One?"

"What?"

Camilo gestured and she came to the edge of the bed. He looked up at her in the moonlight. "Give me your hand."

He felt her hand slide into his. He closed his eyes and sighed again. He felt very strange. Nothing mattered, really. Nothing at all, he could do anything he wanted now. The room swirled around and he opened his eyes. "Come to me tonight."

She withdrew her hand quickly. She looked flustered. "Camilo, don't . . ."

"Be my whore, Pepita, I want no other."

"Camilo, please . . ."

"You want a man?"

"No. Please don't, not now, not this way . . ."

"All right, but will you someday?"

"You are drunk, Camilo. Don't be disgusting."

"I would like it to be tonight."

"Stop it."

"You are right, Pepita. I am drunk and I am disgusting. I am sorry. Forgive me?"

She looked down at him, then hurried to the door, shutting it softly behind her.

Camilo groaned. Perhaps he could sleep.

But it was still there. When he closed his eyes, he felt it again. It was

109

still there, as it had been this morning sitting in the café drinking coffee with Ángel Maceo, while the waiters were putting out the chairs around the tables on the sidewalk. He couldn't keep away from it. Every time he let down, he started thinking about his father. He should have let them have him. After he sent his mother to Miami, he should have let them do it, instead of protecting him. The others had been right—his father was too stubborn for his own good. So were his followers. There were too many people in Cuba who if they had a choice would follow Gustavo Carta and not Fidel Castro—too many people. It was like a cancer, and it had to be cut away. There had been plenty of chances.

During the mass trials, who would have noticed? It would have all been over now and she would never have known who had done it, only that Gustavo had been executed. His mother would get over the grief. She was still a good-looking woman, and she had money. Someone would marry her and take her back to South Carolina, or Washington, where she belonged.

"What good is all this? You can't blame yourself, Camilo," Maceo told him. "Who knew it would turn out the way it did? Hell, none of us thought . . ."

"Some did. I should have known. I knew what a stubborn bastard he was."

"Listen, my friend, it is no problem. We'll send someone to Miami, if you want. We have people—"

"It is my father, Ángel. My honor."

"Camilo, I can't talk to you about it. That's all."

"You have to talk to me about it. I'm the one who is going to do it."

Maceo leaned forward and stared him in the eye. "You are serious?"

"Would I joke about such a thing?"

"Look, Camilo, I will talk to Fidel. We will take care of it all."

"No need. He has plenty of other things to think about."

"His brother, then."

"I have already spoken with Raúl."

"And . . . ?"

"Look, Ángel. You and I know it is the only solution. For the good of Cuba."

"You can't do this thing, Camilo!"

"Why can't I?"

"Camilo, you're crazy! I always said you were, and now I know it. You're crazy!"

In the dark, remembering, Camilo lay looking up at the patterns of moonlight on the ceiling. His thoughts kept jumping around. But he always came back to it. He had to kill all feeling. Otherwise, he would fail, and failure was out of the question. He had to succeed. Time was running out.

Camilo closed his eyes and turned onto his stomach. He felt the undulating, swirling dizziness. The room moved around him. He felt sick. Too much, you bastard! He sank his head into the blanket, smelling the clean wool. He felt himself slipping off into sleep.

Through his groggy half-consciousness he heard the latch on the door click. He opened his eyes. The moonlight slanted in the open casement window, casting the room in a white glow, and in it he saw her. Not clearly, but as a presence, something black, moving. He rubbed his eyes and looked again. She was standing at the foot of the bed. He saw that she was removing the hood.

It came away with a whisper of cloth against cloth, and he saw it float to one side and vanish beyond the edge of the bed.

He looked at her face, in shadow now. Her arms were raised and brought together behind her neck, her head slightly inclined forward. He shifted to one elbow, blinking his eyes, struggling to clarify his vision. He tried to sit up; but the room reeled around him. A whisper of cloth, and he blinked and saw her holding the black robe in her right hand. The curve of her jaw and one naked shoulder came into the white light. She was looking at him, unsmiling. Her undergarment was of muslin, which, with her small figure, made her appear like a child standing before him. He could hear her moving in the room, her bare feet on the tile floor. He heard the click of the door latch. He lifted his fingers from his face and saw her cross the light, one curved breast showing silhouetted, a pale naked shape, and then, darkness.

He closed his eyes, slipping slowly back into an enveloping torpor. Again, he heard the padding of bare feet and he smelled the clean sweetness of soap, a soothing scent in the humid darkness. He heard her breathing close to him and then felt the gentle touch of her hands on his cheek, and felt her warmth as her breath brushed his face, scented like cloves, and there, in the dark, he felt the tips of her nipples against his chest. She kissed him, a gentle touch of her lips on his. She moved away in the dark.

Now he felt a soft touching. His penis, lying against his thigh, stiffened. He felt soft lips encasing it, wet and warm, sliding down toward its base. Silky hair caressed his stomach, and he discerned the feminine head against his abdomen. The head turned up and two lovely black eyes smiled at him.

". . . you?"

"Do I do it properly? I have only seen photographs . . ."

"You do it beautifully and I love you."

111

"Did my sister do this for you?"

"Yes."

"Do I do it as well?"

"Beautifully, Pepita. Come to me, here, come. I will show you all of it, all that can be done."

"I am small there; I'm afraid it will hurt, Camilo."

"Come now, come to me."

"How shall I do it?"

"Here, put your legs on either side, like this."

He heard the slight squeak of the bedsprings and felt her weight shift as she moved, lifting her body, hovering over him on her knees, straddling him, and he felt her touch, bending his penis toward her, and then the touch of flesh, scalding hot, tightly enclosing him: engulfing him in soft muscle, the heat of her body radiating over the length of his phallus.

He saw her face grimace in the pale light and heard her suck in her breath.

"Is there pain?"

"Oh, dear God, Camilo. What shall I do now? Can I do something?"

"I will guide you with my hands." He touched the soft, smooth flesh of her hips, feeling her body lift with the pressure. He could hear her breathing in the darkness, mingled with faint, short little gasps as she moved.

"Oh, Camilo," she said. "I love you more than my own life, my own soul."

As he drove in the half-liquid gloom of the early morning, Camilo saw a fisherman walking with his head down along the edge of the paved road, a wet gunnysack thrown over his shoulders. There were palm-thatched shacks along the white beach. A woman with a black shawl over her head was squatting in the shiny green palmettos behind one of the shacks. The jeep jolted over the little square holes in the pavement, dug in checkerboard patterns to plant mines against the invaders. They were filling with water. The wipers slashed to clear his view. He passed through the village, where the rain had swept away any signs of life except for a brown dog with a curved tail, trotting, head down, through the downpour. He was sobering now as he drove, the wind clearing his head and his vision.

The rain stopped by the time he reached the gate.

A militiaman came out of the stone house. He was an old man with shrunken cheeks and hollow eyes that squinted at him from under the black beret. His FLN rifle was slung over his back as he splashed through a pool of water in his heavy boots, smiling as he recognized Camilo. Yes,

Comandante? The old house, as you know, has become the property of the people. Confiscated. A rich man once owned it. Yes, surely, Comandante. He scurried to the heavy wooden gate, fishing for the key. He swung it open slowly, turned and saluted.

The narrow road led into a grove of palms. The undergrowth rushed at him as he accelerated the jeep. Through the windshield he could see the ocean, whitecaps frothing on the surface. The gray trunks of the royal palms moved toward him and passed, passed, passed. Ahead, the view of the sea with its foaming crests grew larger and larger. When he stopped the jeep, he saw the beach. White as flour, it curved in either direction for a mile and vanished into the trees.

He stepped out of the jeep and took the path through the brush. Walking along the narrow passage, he saw the tall weeds growing through the cracks in the masonry. Limbs and leaves, pieces of branches flashed and swayed in front of him, scraping against his chest, slapping his legs. Then, suddenly, he looked up and caught a glimpse of the house through the foliage; a patch of gray stone, a collection of mortar and rock.

He stood in the crumbling courtyard. Built on the high ground overlooking the beach and the sea, the stone walls were weathered, moss green from age. His great-grandfather had built the house before the turn of the century, hauling the tiles and the windows from Havana on the backs of mules. There was a veranda with steps leading down to the beach. He could see the wind-blown palms twisting in the air above the roof. The windows were covered with rusted iron storm shutters. The unkept garden had almost overgrown the courtyard in a green mass of wet, dripping vines and leaves.

He thought about that time on the beach in the hot summer sun, his father laughing and carrying him from the house on his shoulders, while David ran ahead and splashed into the water. His mother, tall and suntanned, wearing a yellow swimsuit and carrying the blankets, came out of the doors behind them. Be careful, Gustavo, you might drop him! His father only laughed and set him down in the sand. He was running after David, down the beach and into the surf, and he heard his mother's voice yell from behind him and turned just long enough to see her standing now, with an alarmed look on her face—and then the blow from behind; he was tumbling as salt water choked his nostrils, the sand swirling around him, tiny pieces of shells spinning in his vision; hands lifting him, pulling him out of the suction; he saw his mother's face, her blue eyes frantic with alarm. Are you all right? Her fear frightened him. He buried his face against the warm flesh of her neck and cried, unable not to.

113

He remembered mornings with the sunlight streaming in the big casement windows, the air still and hot; and outside sunlit trees and the sounds of birds. David, his eyes heavy from sleep, lifting his blond head from the pillow and telling him to go away and let him sleep. Now, the breakfast table in the high-ceilinged dining room, scrambled eggs, black beans and rice, fried pork; his father leaning forward from the end of the table, fixing him with his dark eyes in an expression of disapproval. "Eat your breakfast, Camilo."

Walking along the beach with David, looking for the tiny pink seashells that washed ashore from the storm. The gelatinous tentacles and purplish cellophanelike balloons of the Portuguese men-of-war were everywhere along the edge of the white sand, thousands of them.

"David, what are these things?"

"Men-of-war. See?" David stepped on one with his tennis shoe. It popped. "If you're swimming and even brush one of these tentacles you get stung. People have been known to die from the stings."

"Why?"

"Toxins. They don't know what it is exactly. Don't step on them with your bare feet, Cam."

"Will it hurt?"

"You bet."

"Ouch!"

"I told you not to!"

"Look, my foot's all red! Owww!"

David always knew everything about the sea.

But now, as he knew he would, Camilo came back to it.

A wave of loneliness and longing swept over him. He longed for them. His mother's hands, soft and cool. His father's strong fingers grasping his shoulder, the prickly feel of his face, the smell of tobacco and coffee.

He felt the sting of tears in his eyes. He had not cried since he was a boy. He hated it. He turned now, his body shivering, and walked back along the path toward the jeep. His boots splashed in the water. He felt the steady tug of the wind. He would not go into the house.

For the first time in days he felt easy with himself. It was gone. He had killed it inside him. He felt only numb where all the feeling had been. Now he could do it. Now, without thinking further, he would go home to the apartment in Miramar and take a bath and crawl into clean sheets and sleep through the night. For the first time he thought about the nun. He smiled to himself. This time yesterday Pepita was a virgin. He laughed aloud. Hell, he thought, in a way, so was I!

BOOK II

CHAPTER ELEVEN

In 1511, a Spanish soldier, Diego Velásquez de León, sailed from Santo Domingo with three hundred men to establish settlements in Cuba. They landed on the southeastern tip of the island in a small natural harbor they named Baracoa.

At first, the 200,000 native Taino and Ciboney Indians greeted the invaders in their villages with warm smiles and open arms. The men wore no clothes. The women wore only a patch of cloth between their thighs. Like their Hispaniola brothers, they were fond of festivals and singing. The maidens, two and three hundred at a time, would gather around the campfire to sing and dance areytos in honor of the Spaniards. Their songs told of tribal exploits, legends. To the eyes of the Spanish soldiers, fresh from rigidly controlled Catholic Spain, the sight of three hundred naked girls, their bodies shiny with sweat in the firelight, was a mind-boggling experience. "There was considerable sporting between the Spaniards and the Indian girls," wrote one soldier historian. "For the habits of the Tainos were completely promiscuous."

The Spaniards returned the hospitality by raiding the villages. Each raid went

117

deeper and deeper into the interior of Cuba, the Spaniards growing more familiar with the lovely, rolling countryside, its vast virgin forests, its mountains and streams.

The hidalgo expeditions took on the character of boar hunts. Their savage dogs swarmed about the horsemen, sniffing, wagging their tails, barking. The horses pranced. Men laughed, drank their stirrup cups, bidding each other "good hunting." Lances tipped with honed steel gleamed in the tropical sun.

The Indian men were spitted on lances and swords. In the evening for amusement, they would select victims, wrap them in straw and roast them alive over their campfires. Or they would set them to boil in iron kettles to render the human fat, which they used to treat their wounds.

It was their practice to butcher out the females and keep their haunches on hooks to feed the packs of ferocious hunting dogs. On special fiesta days, dozens of men, women and children would be chained together. The Spaniards would watch as the dog packs were unleashed. Swarming on the terrified Indians, the dogs would tear their helpless bodies to shreds and eat the meat. Then, the good friars would bless the fiesta, and the Spaniards would turn to filling their own bellies with fruits and game and red wine.

The Indians grew more hostile. The women, rather than raise their offspring to be enslaved, killed them at birth. Many committed suicide. Rebellions grew more frequent in the fields and mines.

The Indians in Cuba were at war. Their weapons were crude, but they found themselves a leader. A fugitive Indian chieftain named Hatuey, whom Velásquez had defeated in Hispaniola, had now taken refuge in Cuba to organize the natives in resistance to the Spanish onslaught.

"These Europeans worship a very covetous sort of god," Hatuey told his people. "So it is hard to satisfy them. To perform the worship they render to this idol they will exact immense treasure of us and will reduce us to a miserable state of slavery, or else put us to death."

It was the first cry for freedom in Cuba. Hatuey, almost alone, fought a bitter and hopeless struggle in the forests of Cuba. In small bands he attacked the Spaniards, using bow and arrows, crude spears and, when lacking all else, stones. He had few successes.

The Spanish turned out their packs of dogs and horsemen.

The Spanish friar walked past the soldiers and looked up at the man tied to the stake. The heat was beginning to blister his feet. In God's name, my son, the friar called to him, I beg you to accept God and His Son, Jesus Christ, who died for your sins.

Hatuey looked down through the vapors of heat and thick smoke.

"If you accept Jesus Christ as your Savior," the friar's voice called to him, "you

118

will assure for yourself a place in heaven. If you remain an infidel, thou shalt be cast into a hell of flames, worse than these you now suffer!"

The Indian coughed as the smoke billowed around him. Flames were crackling through the faggots around his legs. The heat was so intense the soldiers had to move back. Their iron breastplates felt like ovens.

"Do Spaniards go to heaven?"

"Yes, oh, yes, my son. Heaven is full of Spaniards." The friar's voice lifted. He filled with hope. He would save the Indian's soul for God.

Hatuey, the first Cuban martyr, squirmed and gasped, his whole body enveloped in a sheet of fire. "Then I choose hell!"

CHAPTER TWELVE

MIAMI, JANUARY 16, 1961

"Tell us, Dr. Carta, are the rumors true? Is there really going to be an invasion of Cuba?"

Mrs. Janis Wilson leaned forward so she could see him seated at the head of the table. He was flanked by Travis Wilson, her husband, and Father Francis McGoldrick.

They were eating brunch on the veranda because Elizabeth had insisted that it was such a lovely morning. The air was cool enough in the brilliant sun, and there was a faint breeze off Biscayne Bay that wafted across the terrace, stirring the leaves of the palm trees that shaded the breakfast table. Carlota, the serving maid, appeared with a silver platter laden with freshly cooked scrambled eggs bordered by crisp strips of bacon and link sausages. She leaned over Carta, presenting it to him for inspection. He glanced at it and nodded. She proceeded, in her starched white dress and black apron, to pass the platter to the guests.

"*The New York Times* this morning says the CIA is training men in Guatemala," Travis Wilson said, wiping his mouth with a white linen napkin and lifting his eyes from his half-finished ham steak. "Good Lord, Gustavo, we're going to end up in the middle of a war."

"Fidel seems to think so," Carta replied, lifting a fork on which was speared a small triangle of ham. "He's had his militia on full alert since early this month."

119

He was wearing a vivid white *guayabera* shirt, intricate patterns stitched down its front, its starched collar standing stiffly at his throat. He chewed the ham slowly, as was his habit, his expression one of preoccupation, as though not concerned with his guests this morning, but rather with some problem nagging at his inner thoughts.

There were sixteen seated around the table. An affluent-looking assemblage, the men were tanned, gray-haired, patriarchal, attired in jackets and ties; the women, middle-aged and formidable, were draped in dresses designed to appear lavishly casual, jewelry glistening around their necks and fingers.

The brunch had been Elizabeth's idea. Both she and Carta had become increasingly alarmed about the plight of the Cuban immigrants streaming into Miami. Tens of thousands had already arrived and were struggling desperately to get settled, and still they came, wave after wave, arriving daily on airplanes, rafts, sailboats, oil drums, anything they could find to escape the Cuba of Fidel Castro. Elizabeth had come up with the notion of inviting Miami's civic leaders and socialites—the local establishment—to a series of brunches where they could acquaint them with the problems of the newcomers and solicit their support in relief efforts.

The brunches had been going on for several weeks, and by now their "pitch" was well rehearsed. Carta and Elizabeth spoke informally to their guests, emphasizing that America had been built upon immigration, that the newcomers should be welcomed in the community despite the size and the suddenness of this newest incursion. The exiles were not poor, uneducated peasants who would become a burden to the welfare rolls. Most were skilled, hard-working middle-class people who wanted to resume their careers and keep their families intact. It was simply a matter of guiding them to housing and jobs, helping their children adjust to their new schools, lending them the money to start new businesses. Castro had seen to it that few could smuggle money out of the country, so their immediate problems were often desperate. Elizabeth, who worked four mornings a week on the steering committee of the Cuban Relief Society, was especially eloquent in describing the plight of former surgeons and university professors who had come into her office, hungry and disconnected, not having eaten for two or three days, willing to accept janitorial jobs simply to feed their families.

"It's pathetic," Mrs. Wilson interjected. "Our gardener is a Cuban surgeon. He hasn't a license to practice here. I feel strange asking him to clip my palm trees. Not that he understands me anyway."

"That's my point," said Dr. Fine, one of Miami's prominent educators.

120

"He'll have to learn our language if he's to rise to the level that he enjoyed economically in Cuba."

"One thing I'd always been curious about," said Father Francis McGoldrick, a thickset florid-faced man who sat farther down the table. "Why did you wait so long before you left Havana, Dr. Carta?"

"I was slow to realize, Father, that when Fidel spoke of eliminating poverty and injustice, what he really had in mind was eliminating me."

Wilson, whom Carta knew to be one of Miami's biggest real-estate men, laughed. "Really, now, what did you think the devil was up to? Couldn't you see he was Communist? Everyone else certainly could."

"Some of the things accomplished by the revolution at the beginning were very constructive," Carta replied. "I refer to the new system of education, to the nationalization of the power company. Even the agrarian-reform law was a very just one."

"Even though it cost you all of your property?"

Carta fixed him in a cold gaze. "We must all be prepared to pay the price for social justice."

"If Nixon had won the election, Father, he wouldn't hesitate to crush Castro, not for a minute. Kennedy, now, I'm not so sure you're right—not at all!"

"But how else can they get rid of Castro?" the priest protested. "Remember, too, that a Catholic President can't let a Communist exist just ninety miles from our shores, now, can he? They must be eliminated—and soon."

"I think the whole thing is very exciting," said Herbert Goldman, a squat man on whose shoulders rested an enormous leonine head. "You Cubans have to learn to think like Israel. You have to take what's yours. You can't wait for someone to hand it to you. Free enterprise works in war just like it works in business."

Carta turned to see Alfaro standing beside the chair, a massive presence, tall, broad-shouldered. He wore a heavy, densely black moustache, his kinky hair just beginning to gray at the temples. "The car is waiting. It's one-thirty."

Carta's eyes met Alfaro's and he understood the urgency conveyed by his glance. Alfaro had been an Air Force pilot in Cuba until 1955, when he resigned to manage Carta's sugar plantations. Since leaving Cuba, he had become Carta's aide and bodyguard.

"Yes, of course." Carta pushed his chair from the table and excused himself. "Please, finish your drinks. I must apologize. I'm afraid I have a pressing appointment which can't be postponed."

121

Carta followed Alfaro out of the hot sun into the interior of the big house and across the main room to the library.

Alfaro turned to him. "By the way, Señor Castillo is here again. I asked him to wait in the library."

Carta nodded. Castillo had been his history professor at Havana University. He had appeared at the house two weeks earlier, explaining that he had left Cuba because he no longer could stomach Castro's regime. He said he was securing a position at the University of Miami in Spanish history. The tall, gaunt old man had reappeared two days ago, asking to see Gustavo, but Carta had been too busy to see him.

"Shall I send him away?" Alfaro stopped with his hand on the library door. "He's come about money."

"I know." Carta gave him a glance and Alfaro opened the door.

Señor Castillo was standing at the far end of the room, wearing a dark suit and tie, his mane of white hair long over his collar. He stood, gaunt and solemn, his hands clasped behind his back as Carta remembered him lecturing his classes.

He turned his long, thin face and smiled as he heard the door open. "Gustavo . . ." He held out his arms and they embraced.

"Professor," Carta said to him, beaming. "You look well."

"I am well. Miami seems to agree with me."

"Come, sit down a moment. I am afraid I have an appointment, but there is always time for you. How may I serve you?"

Castillo looked flustered. He smiled wanly. "Perhaps I should come back later, Gustavo. At some more convenient time."

"No, no, tell me directly, my old friend. What can I do to help you?"

"I . . . I . . ." Castillo looked at his trembling hands, swallowing, and then looked at Gustavo. "I have with me now my son, his wife, their three children. . . . I am hard pressed, Gustavo . . . hard pressed."

Carta went to his desk and opened a drawer, taking out the big leatherbound checkbook. "Then I can help with money. Such a simple thing. How much, my friend?"

Castillo straightened in the chair. "Just until this job comes through. There is some difficulty at the university, but I am sure . . ."

"Of course. How much do you need?"

"You will charge interest, I hope?"

"No."

"Please, it is a loan. I am not yet a charity case, Gustavo."

"Of course, señor. Three percent, payable in three years. Acceptable?"

"Yes, thank you. Would a thousand dollars be too much to ask?"

Carta felt his heart sink. He had three checking accounts but was not sure which of them could accommodate a check for a thousand dollars. He had written two big checks that week for supplies and ammunition for the camp in the Everglades. "Of course not," he said. He wrote the check quickly and rang for Alfaro.

The old man looked at the check, folding it carefully, placing it in his worn leather billfold. He stood as Alfaro entered. "I am grateful, Gustavo."

"Come see me again, Professor."

"I shall."

After he had shown the old gentleman out, Alfaro returned to find Carta closing his briefcase. "We're a little late, señor."

"Yes, coming."

Carta glanced at his watch. He was to meet with Tipton and Rodríguez at two. It would be a long, hot drive to the camp in the Everglades. He picked up his briefcase and looked through the windows to the veranda. The guests were getting up from the table. He followed Alfaro through the main room and into the entry hall. Alfaro opened the front door for him.

Carta went down the steps to the car. Just then, he heard what sounded like a car backfiring. He looked at the hole in the windshield, stupefied.

"What . . . ?"

But Alfaro hit him with a football tackle and they both went down on the pavement.

A silence followed. Elizabeth looked at her guests, a frozen smile implanted on her face, which did little to disguise her fear. They had heard shots fired in rapid succession. Mrs. Wilson, standing beside her, gasped and put her hand to her mouth, her eyes wide. The other guests, who the moment before had been chattering to each other, all stopped and looked around in bewildered disbelief. It took a few seconds for them to react, to realize the danger.

Elizabeth struggled to suppress her panic. "I think perhaps we should all move inside the house now . . ." she heard herself saying in a voice that sounded surprisingly calm. As she turned to lead the way through the French doors into the main room, Elizabeth caught sight of Salazar, the short, heavyset bodyguard, running across the lawn from the boat dock. He was coming toward the veranda steps, pistol in hand, hair flying, legs pumping, looking like a sprinter who had forgotten to change his clothes before the race.

"My God, who's that?" It was Wilson's voice, and it carried a hint of hysteria.

"Don't be alarmed," Elizabeth told them in as cool a tone as she could manage, her voice raised half an octave. "It's our man."

"I think we should be calm, ladies and gentlemen," said Goldman. "Follow me inside, please." He looked at Elizabeth, an expression of support and a little terror in his eyes. "Just be calm," he repeated.

Not fifteen seconds had elapsed since they heard the shots.

Just then, Salazar came pounding up the steps to the veranda, taking them three at a time in swift, athletic leaps. His face was distorted and sweating. A woman let out a shriek at the sight of the gun in his hand.

"Get inside!" he shouted as he dashed past them into the house. "Inside!"

Carta saw Alfaro crouched at the edge of the front fender. His big revolver in two hands, he fired toward the gate. He lowered it and searched in his pocket for more shells. He glanced at Carta. "Stay down, stay down—it'll be the second car!"

"Can you see them?"

"Yes, stay down!" He turned, holding the big revolver in both hands again. Carta heard a car pulling away. Alfaro, crouching, lifted himself slowly, so that he could look over the top of the hood. "Now it comes!" he said between his teeth. "Now it comes."

They hurried silently through the open doors out of the sun. One tall, stately matron with gray hair and a blue dress started to sob against her husband's shoulder.

Elizabeth put her hand on her shoulder. "Please, everything's all right now. You're quite safe."

"Look there, will you . . ." The red-faced priest was pointing at the big windows across the main room, which had been shattered, the sharp edges of the glass framing jaggedly the oak tree outside. There was broken glass on the shiny tile floor. The priest turned, eyes wide, mouth agape. His lips trembled as he formed the words. "Everyone get down on the floor. There may be more shooting." He flopped on the Oriental rug behind the couch. Wilson and several others followed his lead.

Elizabeth swung around to look into the faces of Goldman and his blond plump wife. "I think . . ." she started.

But the sudden crack of a gun cut her off.

They dropped together as they heard another window splinter. She lay speechless and terrified, the shots so ear-shattering that for a moment she stopped hearing. She placed her hands against the side of her head.

"My God! My God!" Wilson kept gasping.

Goldman, holding his arm around his wife's shoulder, glanced up into Elizabeth's eyes. "Dear Lord," he half-whispered. "They're trying to kill your husband!"

A pane of glass burst and a vase on the fireplace mantel above their heads shattered. Outside a heavy gun thumped, and she knew it was a shotgun from the sound of it. Then there was silence. Several of the women huddled on the floor were crying now, their broken sobs the only sounds.

The front door banged open. Carta came in, his face ashen, with Alfaro behind him. Then Elizabeth was on her feet, running to him, her heart pounding. She fell into his arms.

"Are you all right?"

"Yes." Carta's voice sounded strained, shaken. "No one was hit."

Alfaro slammed the door. "Shall I call the police?"

"Yes, at once." Carta looked at Elizabeth, his eyes haunted. "We must expect these things now. We always knew there would be a possibility."

Elizabeth let out her breath and leaned against him, holding him with her arms.

★

The dishes were still on the dining table from last night.

Her voice came from the upstairs bedroom: "David, is that you?"

"Yeah." He went up the stairs, skipping every other one.

"What are you doing home so early?" Her voice led him on to the screen porch.

She was seated on the couch, crosslegged, wrapped in his blue robe, scrubbing a towel through her hair. "I just got out of the shower," she said, smiling at him.

David bent and kissed her upturned face. It was amazing how little she had changed in five years—the same lovely green eyes, the same delicate skin. She smelled of talc. He loved the smell of her after a shower. He sat beside her on the bed and watched her scrubbing her hair with the towel. Her eyes glanced at him. Her fine blond-copper-color hair caught the lamplight.

"So where the hell were you this morning?"

"I had an appointment with a professor. He could only make it early."

He put his arm around her and drew her nearer to him, kissing her mouth and neck; she did not respond, but he slipped his hand inside the robe, lifting it off her shoulders.

"Dave, don't . . ."

He looked into her eyes. The irises were green, with flecks of yellow close to the dark pupils, and he saw the expression of disapproval in them. "Why not?" he asked.

"Have you forgotten what you said to me last night?" She moved away, crossing to the dresser.

He remembered the quarrel the night before—a familiar one. Elizabeth had offered them a set of crystal glasses that had been in the family for generations. It seemed a generous gesture. But Robin had refused to accept it. She said they seemed too ornately old-fashioned and, besides, they would break too easily. Elizabeth had seemed hurt. They had quarreled afterward. The Cartas, Robin had said, were always trying to control her, maneuvering her life in keeping with the dictates of the all-powerful Carta tradition. David tried to persuade her that this was not so, but Robin was, as usual, adamant. She wanted to live her own life, not a life the Carta clan had designed for her. Their words had become more and more heated.

"You think I'm a stupid, ungrateful—"

"Come on, Robin."

"That's what you said, didn't you?"

He closed his eyes, breathed deeply again, clenched and unclenched his fists at his side. He heard a car pass on the street below. Then another and another. He felt his tension easing. Most of his life he had conducted this little exercise in self-control. He looked upon his quick, fierce temper as something foreign to him. He was a rational, thinking, mature human being. He did not have to resort to emotional outbursts to obtain his objectives. Reason and logic were the means at his command. Another breath of air. He opened his eyes.

She was standing at the dresser, her back to him. Her head was cocked to one side and she was brushing her hair in long, slow strokes, the copper strands aglow from the light, swaying and rippling as the brush swept through. He felt a pang of tenderness overcome him. He loved to watch her brush her hair. It was an act so gentle, so womanlike, so appealing. He could not subdue the sexual urge that tugged at him.

His hands felt for her under the robe. "Let's not fight, huh? I love you, Rob. Let's just be together, OK?"

She looked in the mirror. His tanned face was handsome, she thought, but somehow his features were almost too regular, too predictably American, except for his glasses. David had always detested wearing glasses, she knew, but Robin liked the scholarly appearance it gave him. She had even picked out some special tortoiseshell frames, but he refused to wear them, preferring his steel-rimmed ones which he deemed more masculine. That was just like David, she thought—not quite daring enough to stand out in a crowd, even when it came to something as

126

simple as glasses. That attitude was in his face too—an expression a bit too friendly, almost self-deprecating, somewhat like that of a boy emerging from the throes of adolescence. She felt his breath on her neck and then the touch of his lips.

"I'm going to fuck you, madam," he whispered.

"Oh, David, can't you be a little romantic? Can't you say 'make love'? Anything?" She felt his fingers massaging her. Nothing. She felt no desire for him.

He lifted her in his arms and carried her to the bed. She said nothing as he lifted the robe from her and she felt the coolness of the air against her flesh. She closed her eyes, breathing softly, unable to feel anything. She heard his belt click and the whisper of cloth as he undressed. She felt his weight on the bed, his hands spreading her legs, then the hard pressure of his penis against her, the heat of it, his tension. He simply entered her. She felt him slide deeper and deeper inside her. She felt detached, outside herself, as though she were floating above and watching. She felt the moisture of his saliva, mingled with the heat of his breath, and then the hard, quickened thrust of his pelvis against her, harder, quicker, harder, like blows, butting, butting, butting . . .

Later, she lay perfectly still beside him, feeling violated, oddly, as though she had been forced into a corruption against her will, against her adamant desire, and it made her feel stubborn and angry. After a long moment, she felt him stir.

He wasn't looking at her, but his voice came very softly: "What's the matter, Rob? What's the matter between us?"

She felt his weight shift and move off the bed. She closed her eyes, listening to him dressing. He sat on the bed to put on his shoes, and then his weight went away. She heard the water running in the bathroom. When he came out again, she opened her eyes and saw him standing at the end of the bed, his expression one of hurt and resentment. It had become, to Robin, a familiar image, the blue eyes blinking behind the glasses, the corners of the mouth drawn so that tight folds formed at the edges of his lips.

She heard him going down the stairs, slamming the screen door. Then she heard the car start. She turned her face into the pillow and wanted to cry, but nothing came.

CHAPTER THIRTEEN

The white Chevrolet sedan had been sitting in the no-parking zone for half an hour, but the airport police seemed oblivious to it as they moved back and forth ticketing other vehicles.

The driver, Dobbs, sat with his elbow cocked in the open window, listening to the music on the radio. He was tall, his knees grazing the dashboard even though he had the seat pushed back as far as it would reach. Strongly built and even-featured, his hair cropped close, Dobbs conveyed the unkempt respectability of a high-school football coach. His eyes were hazel, and so nearsighted he squinted constantly. With his heavy brows, it made him look combative. He had grown tired of waiting and he yawned and tried to stretch.

"What time is it, Enrique?" he asked his companion, a young Cuban who sat beside him, half asleep.

Enrique lifted his wrist and looked at his watch. "Nine after three."

"Plane's due," Dobbs said, turning his head to nod at the airport officer who walked past.

Enrique Navarro sat up and rubbed his eyes. Ten hours ago he had been in Guatemala, picking ticks out of his clothes in front of his tent in a jungle clearing. His flight to Miami had been unexpected, and all the way in the plane he'd been too excited to sleep. He did not know what the emergency was that had brought him from the guerrilla training camp, and Dobbs had not enlightened him, but he knew it had to be something important.

Dobbs stirred from his slouch beside him and reached out his thick hand to turn off the radio. "There's Pelham," he said.

Through the windshield Navarro saw a crowd of people coming out of the terminal doors: a fat Cuban woman with two children eating Eskimo Pies; a tall girl in faded Levi's, carrying a green suitcase tied with rope; two black men in suits and brown floppy hats. And amid them was Pelham, short, erect, his face severe-looking behind rimless glasses. Pelham's bearing was military, and he carried a black attaché case. He wore

128

a blue-striped seersucker suit with the pants legs slightly too short so that his black socks and black shoes flared into view as he walked in his brisk, hurried manner.

Navarro could remember the first time he saw Pelham, standing on the dock in Tampa as he, Navarro, came down the gangway from the Spanish freighter that had smuggled him out of Havana. Navarro had been struck by the contrast between Pelham's professorial appearance and his brisk, tough-minded manner. He'd been impressed by the thoroughness of his interrogation, which had lasted for three days. Pelham had grilled him relentlessly about everything from the politics of his father to his teenage habits of masturbation, so that he felt naked and vulnerable before him, doubly so because of the lie detector that scribbled incessantly after each response. And through all their later encounters, Navarro had continued to be in awe of the confidence and conviction with which Pelham dispatched himself, his precise manner of speech, the brisk authority he radiated to those around him. It was not so much what Pelham said, nor what he did, but rather what he didn't say, what he implied, which disconcerted Navarro and kept him off balance. It was as though with a gesture of his hand he could destroy anyone he wished to. To Enrique Navarro, the seersucker-clad figure of R. Kirby Pelham embodied the power of the United States government, and he never questioned the man's decisions, nor his actions. Pelham was boss. If Navarro followed orders without question, Pelham would lead him on an adventure that would topple Fidel Castro and reshape history.

"Enrique, how are you?" Pelham said, climbing into the front seat. His tone and manner seemed keyed up.

Navarro shut the door and got into the back.

In a quick glance over his shoulder, Pelham took in Navarro, who sat with one leg crossed over the other. He was a handsome young man, with a fine, light-skinned face and intelligent dark eyes. He had a boyish, college-athlete quality about him that Pelham had liked from the first moment he met him. Even his hoarse accented voice, which sounded as though someone had sandpapered his throat, pleased him. Navarro smiled at him now.

Pelham turned his gaze to Dobbs, who kept glancing in the rear-view mirror as he drove off onto a narrow street that ran along the banks of the Miami River. They were passing warehouses and boatyards and lines of shabby frame houses. The gutters of the streets were littered with dead palm fronds and bits of paper and old beer cans. It was a route into town Pelham had not seen before, and he found it vaguely depressing. But he knew of Dobbs's paranoid insistence on never taking the same route more than once if he could help it. It was a bit too theatrical for Pelham, but he saw no point in arguing the matter.

Dobbs looked at him. "What happened with the Kennedy outfit?"

"I think the meeting was quite satisfactory."

"Now, what the fuck does that mean, Pelham—are the bastards for us or against us?"

Pelham felt himself flinch. It seemed incredible to him that a man so lacking in polish could have risen to a position of such responsibility. Perhaps if Dobbs had had Pelham's advantages of an Exeter education and a more socially acceptable background, his manner would have been less grating. But what could you expect from a man from Iowa State? To Pelham this man lacked every quality necessary to perform the delicate tasks the agency had assigned him.

When he had broached the subject to Vermillion three months earlier, his boss had overruled him, pointing out Dobbs's record in Guatemala. "He's rough, Pel," the chief had told him. "But he gets the job done."

Vermillion's words echoed in his mind now as he appraised Dobbs's bent-nose profile. The thick eyelids blinked, and his expression projected contempt.

"Well?" Dobbs said impatiently.

"Well, we still have a green light."

"Kennedy's for us?"

"The feeling around Quarters Eye is that Kennedy and his brother are for us. But several of his advisers have reservations. You can guess who they are."

"The Haw-vard boys?"

"Right."

"Shit. Those professorial assholes haven't got the sense God gave a jackass!"

"I might remind you, Dobbs, I once taught political science at Fordham."

"I try hard not to hold it against you," said Dobbs. "Just how green in this green light?"

"Green. But we're going to do a little reshuffling of the political lineup in the Frente."

Navarro stirred, leaning forward with his elbows on the seat behind Pelham. His face was flushed and wet. "What was that?"

"We're planning to make some adjustments here and there to appease the powers that be, Enrique." Pelham smiled reassuringly. "Don't worry, it's purely cosmetic."

130

Pelham watched an edge of suspicion glimmer in Navarro's dark eyes. He was very fond of Navarro and he was careful to treat him as he would a younger brother, guiding him with a firm but gentle hand. Yet the young Cuban was no fool and he was well aware of the complicated politics within the CIA-backed Frente, which was supposedly the Cuban government in exile. Jesuit-trained, Navarro was resistant to change of any kind in the established order.

"What adjustments are you going to make?" Navarro asked, his voice flat.

"What it means, Enrique," Dobbs said, "is you're about to find yourself in bed with Gustavo Carta."

Pelham felt a tug of irritation and gave Dobbs an angry look in the rear-view mirror.

"Somebody tried to put a few holes in him this morning," Dobbs said.

"They shot him?"

"Somebody shot up his house."

Pelham looked straight at Enrique Navarro. "It wasn't your people?"

Navarro raised his brows. "My people? Hell, I've nothing against Carta, but if it had been my people they wouldn't have missed."

Dobbs pushed open the door that said "International Business Consultants" and led the way into Ellis Kern's office. The outer office was bare except for the secretary, a gray-haired matron in her fifties, who sat at a small gray metal desk. A calendar from an insurance company was the only decoration on the wall.

"Tell Kern Mr. Pelham is here," Pelham instructed the secretary. Ellis Kern appeared a moment later, his hand extended. He was a slight man with a pinched face and a fringe of gray hair on his bald head. His thin lips and small wary eyes suggested the prototypical small-town banker. His attire was chosen to fortify the image of prudence—gray suit, white shirt and black tie. He did not smile as he shook their hands.

Kern's inner office, like the reception room, was spartan. His metal desk was the sort one rented by the week from an office-supply firm. The only personal touch was a small color photograph of Kern and a gray-haired woman, both beaming warmly at two teenage children. Pelham and Dobbs seated themselves on a tan sofa. Navarro cast a quick glance around the bleak room, then sat in a metal folding chair.

"It's time that you two met," Pelham said, glancing from Kern to Navarro. "Now that we're accelerating our schedule you'll be having many dealings."

Navarro nodded in Kern's direction. "I look forward to working with you, sir." Kern acknowledged with a stiff smile.

Though Navarro had not met Kern before, he had heard a lot of gossip about this mystery man. Kern, he knew, had been considered a shrewd operator when he served with the FBI in Havana, but rumor had it that he left the agency under a cloud.

Kern felt Navarro's eyes assessing him. "I think I should tell you something about my operation," Kern said in a high nasal voice. "My business is small but substantial. I work as a business consultant. Among my clients are a number of big American companies whose property in Cuba was expropriated by Castro. These companies, as you can imagine, are anxious to set things straight again."

"I can imagine," Navarro said.

"Is Enrique briefed on my operation?" Kern asked.

Pelham turned toward Navarro. "Enrique, Ellis here has put together a small elite unit whose mission is to secure captured territory for our side. He will brief you on the functioning of this special unit at the appropriate time. As the head of the provisional government, you will, of course, have authority over their actions. In effect, they will be your right arm."

"What is the role of this unit?"

"We want to see that the right people are put in power in the countryside," Kern said. "It's as simple as that."

"And how do you plan to ensure that?"

Kern looked from Navarro to Pelham and did not reply.

"It's a question of enforcement," Pelham interjected. "If Kern's men find the wrong sort of people taking power, they are authorized to deal with them."

"Deal with them?"

"Through whatever actions are necessary," Kern said softly.

"And who are these men under your command?" Navarro asked.

"Good, experienced soldiers," Kern said. "As you may know, I served a few years in Havana. I maintained my contacts. I know the right man to tap for the right job."

"You will meet Kern's unit at the appropriate time," Pelham said. "The thing is, we want to keep them separate from the main body of the brigade until right before D-Day. Then we'll bring them over to Guatemala and they'll hit the beaches right after the first assault force."

"It sounds like you have worked out a complicated plan," Navarro said, his face reflecting a certain bewilderment.

"There's a lot at stake here," Dobbs said. "This ain't no dress rehearsal."

132

"There's the camp," Tipton shouted to him. He looked ahead and saw the cluster of trees, like a dark island above the mangroves, the flat swamp on either side against the lighter darkness of the twilight sky. A light blinked through the cluster of trees. It was a good site. Even in broad daylight, it could not be seen from the road. Once Tipton had taken him over it in a small plane, and from the air the camp was still unrecognizable as a military installation unless one flew very low and took photographs to study later. The trucks were hidden under the trees; the four frame structures used as barracks, mess hall and armory looked from the vantage of five hundred feet like the buildings of a farm. A creek running through the swamp at the south end of the property was deep enough to get motor launches in and out.

Ahead, in the glare of the lights, two men stood guard at either side of the road, their faces showing pale in the light. They wore baggy camouflage fatigues and paratrooper boots. Beyond them, Carta saw the lighted windows of the barracks and the shadows of men moving in the dark around the low tin-roofed buildings.

They had been expecting to move—140 men with their weapons and ammunition. Tipton and Rodríguez had them in superb fighting shape. It would be a blow to their enthusiasm to hear what he had to tell them tonight. They had all been excited at the prospect of actually getting into combat. He would have to speak carefully, overstate nothing, tell them exactly the situation and how he planned to deal with it.

The guard stepped forward, carrying his Garand rifle, and saluted. "*Salud,* Señor Carta," he said, grinning. He obviously thought the operation was about to begin. His spirits were high. "*Buena caza!*"

As they drove toward the command shack, Tipton turned to him, slowing the jeep. "What did that boy say?"

"Good hunting," Carta replied.

Tipton snorted under his breath. "Yes, good hunting, indeed."

Rodríguez appeared out of the darkness. As he came into the jeep lights, Carta saw his round face and cropped head. He was a big man, two inches over six feet. He wore a clean white T-shirt and camouflage fatigue trousers. His face was shiny from sweat and the oily insect repellent they used. They threw their arms around each other in an *abrazo.*

"Are you all right, Gustavo?"

"Fine." Carta smiled. "I had an interesting morning."

They laughed. Rodríguez moved up the steps and opened the screen door. "Did they catch the bastards?"

"Do they ever?" Carta replied.

133

Rodríguez had been Tipton's find. Born in Havana, the son of a typesetter who worked on the *Havana Post,* Rodríguez had been a captain in the rebel army under Fidel until April of 1960, when he became disenchanted with the number of Communists taking over the leadership and went into exile. Now, at twenty-nine, Rodríguez was Tipton's executive officer.

"Let's go inside, where we can talk," Tipton said to them.

Rodríguez looked at both their faces. "Bad news?"

"Inside," Tipton told them.

As he stepped into the shack, Carta smelled the familiar aromas of perking coffee, Cosmoline and gun oil. The command shack was large, twenty by twenty square. Its walls were covered with maps of the Florida Keys, Cuban provinces and coastal areas, as well as detailed maps of Baracoa harbor and southern Oriente. Over the windows were spread the skins of enormous rattlesnakes that had been killed in the palmetto scrub by Carta's men during training exercises. They had had two men bitten in the last month, one seriously enough to put him out of training. Scorpions and mosquitoes in swarms added to the general discomfort. Yet the men, mostly young Cuban students, had withstood the discomfort and the rigorous training, and now were rigidly disciplined into a crack fighting force.

Across the room, Carta saw the rack of Garand rifles, a Thompson submachine gun, and the weapon Tipton favored, a Browning automatic rifle. The well-oiled barrels gleamed in the light. In front of the gun rack was a battered aluminum coffee pot on a hot plate, perking steam into the already humid air.

Rodríguez crossed to the table and picked up a pencil, the light on his heavy, oily face. "Let me have it."

All the time Carta spoke, Rodríguez listened, head lowered, eyes on the pencil that he kept tapping lightly on the table. When it was finished, he looked up at them. "What do you think?" he said. "Are the torpedo boats lost to us as well?"

"Possibly," Tipton said.

"And Major Mahío?"

"We don't know yet. If Escalante talked, he could be compromised."

"Then you're calling off the whole operation?"

"Yes," Carta said.

Rodríguez shrugged his heavy shoulders. "Too bad. It was a good plan. It would have worked."

"It still can," Carta said. "When we have properly assessed the situation, we'll draft a new version."

"Escalante's the key," said Tipton. "If he spilled his guts, we'll be in rather nasty shape. Did he have a cover story, Gustavo?"

"Yes. He was supposed to tell them we intended to attack the Isle of Pines."

Rodríguez' oily brow wrinkled, a look of puzzlement on his face. "I wonder if it could be connected?"

"What?" asked Tipton.

"We monitor the Cuban military frequencies—there was a lot of activity today on the Isle of Pines. Several new units we hadn't heard about before. Also, the Russian and Czech technicians were alerted to be evacuated. It sounded to us like some kind of maneuvers. You think it could be connected?"

"Only if Escalante convinced them that's where we were going to land," said Tipton. His brows raised and a vague smile stretched his lips. "It certainly would be wonderful if he did, eh?"

"We should hear from Masetti in the next few days," said Carta. "Then we'll know. Our immediate problem is to make new plans. I want to be back on the offensive as soon as possible."

Tipton pulled out one of the metal chairs and sat down, stretching out his legs. He looked worn and tired. Rubbing his eyes with his fingertips, he said, "The way I see it, gentlemen, we are probably still pretty much intact—bruised but intact."

"Agreed." Rodríguez remained standing. "Give us what you brought from Havana, Tip."

"We've got to strike before Castro finishes repairs on the Central Highway. Once it's done, he can move troops into Oriente very quickly."

"When do you think it will be finished?" Carta asked him.

"Hard to say. Probably early April, at the rate they're going."

"What about militia strength in southern Oriente?" Carta asked.

"Twelve hundred men, not counting the three hundred Mahío expects to bring over to us. If Castro reinforces his people there, we know he's on to us."

Rodríguez leaned forward and placed his two hands on the table. "How are they armed?"

Tipton smiled wearily. "Well, Fidel must have himself quite a problem there. Supplying ammunition for thirteen different small arms is no easy go, I'd say. In Havana, they've got mostly the NATO assault rifles, the FALs, made in Belgium." He glanced at Carta. "Your old pal, Amato, supplied those, I'm afraid."

Carta made a vague gesture of annoyance.

It took Tipton until a little after seven o'clock to finish his report in

135

detail. It included the latest estimate of Castro's militia and rebel army strength at 200,000 men under arms. There was a segment of discontent, he said, because food was short and many of the militia in Havana had to sleep in the streets. The city itself was an armed camp. "Two militia on every street corner. All roads in the country have been mined, or holes have been dug for mine emplacements. There are troops camped out on the beaches from Havana to Matanzas."

"What about his naval strength? Did you get it?" Rodríguez asked, sitting down now, his professional interest aroused.

"Yes. The main naval force is composed of three American patrol frigates." Tipton droned on with his list of vessels, including three patrol boats mounting three-inch guns, four Coast Guard cutters, including Escalante's, six more of lesser tonnage, the four American-built torpedo boats at Baracoa, "and six new fast patrol boats ordered from Italy—again, your friend, Amato, I'm afraid. They expect delivery within the next two weeks."

Carta smiled. "We must obtain at least two fast boats, Tip. I don't care where, or how. All I care is they do better than forty knots. If we cannot rely on our friends at Baracoa, and Escalante is finished, we must have a naval capability of our own."

"We have to beg, borrow or steal every weapon we get our hands on," said Rodríguez. "One of our people managed to steal a Thompson from Navarro's group yesterday—I promoted him to corporal on the spot." He laughed.

They fell silent a moment. Carta blew out his breath and pushed away from the table. "Very well. We know what we have to deal with—in a few days we'll know how badly we've been hurt. As soon as you get Masetti's report, I want you two to draw up a contingency plan for the taking of Oriente. Understood? Our task is clear. We must rebuild, immediately. When we strike, it must be in several areas at once. What do you hear about the Escambray front?"

Tipton folded his thin hands. "Masetti told me the students in Havana want to move up to the mountains to join Victorio's group within the next week. Masetti's trying to hold them, but things are heating up in Havana. They'll probably go. If they do, they'll have to be supplied."

"And Victorio?"

"Situation's the same. Victorio doesn't want to start a campaign that will only bring quick reprisals from Castro and serve no useful function in the overall. He sent word that when you move, they'll move."

"All right, then we'll go to work," said Carta. "We'll continue all supply missions, as planned. Agreed?"

136

Rodríguez picked up a camouflage shirt from the back of a chair and started to put it on. "Well, shall we go out and break the news to our people?"

"Can't say I relish it," Tipton said drily. "Want me to do it, chief?"

"No," said Carta. "I think that honor lies with me."

★

It was past ten o'clock when Elizabeth went into the library and poured a scotch on ice. Although she rarely drank, she felt the need of something to calm her nerves. She had fed all the guests who had to remain through most of the four hours of police questioning, and at the same time she had called plasterers and painters and glaziers to replace the broken windowpanes. With enormous energy she had supervised all repairs, and by seven o'clock the windows had been replaced, the bullet holes in the stucco filled with new white patches and painted, and the car taken off to the Buick dealer's. She felt satisfied that her house was back in order. She thought about calling her son David, to tell him of the day's extraordinary events, but she was too weary to answer any more questions. She'd call him in the morning.

The scotch tasted like medicine, yet warmed as it settled in her stomach. She was about to put the glass down when she heard the phone ring.

"Hello."

"Lizzie? It's Charles."

Elizabeth felt a surge of excitement.

"Where are you, Charley? I didn't expect—"

"I'm in Washington. I heard about the shooting. You OK?"

"We're all right. It was a bad scare."

"There have been some briefings here, Liz. Does Gustavo really have any idea what he's up against?"

Elizabeth heard the edge in her cousin's voice. She had known Charles Danforth since childhood. She had always thought of him more as a brother than as a first cousin. He was by nature a cool, hardheaded man who did not get nervous without good cause.

"You know how stubborn he is, Charley. He doesn't like getting pushed around."

"There are a lot of forces to contend with here," Danforth said. "The thing that disturbs me is that in this kind of revolutionary situation it's always the man in the middle who gets caught in the squeeze. The decent-minded man in the middle."

"Perhaps you could talk to Gustavo, Charley. He'll listen to you."

"You're still coming up for the Inauguration?"

"We wouldn't miss it for anything. We're so grateful to you for the invitation."

"Maybe I can talk to him then. You'll be staying at our house. We could have a brandy and a long talk."

"We're really excited about it."

"I just want to get through the next couple of weeks, Liz. This experience is turning me into a monarchist. If there's always this much confusion when one President takes over from another, I think we should switch to kings."

Elizabeth laughed. "Are you nominating Jack Kennedy to be King John the First?"

"It sounds a lot better than King Richard the First."

"You have a point there."

"Take care of yourself, Liz. OK?"

"You too. Don't work too hard. I don't want you getting a coronary before you even get to the White House."

"Nobody's getting a coronary, don't worry. See you Thursday. 'Bye, dear."

The connection clicked off. Elizabeth sat for several moments reflecting on the call. Talking to Charles always lifted her spirits. Yet something in his tone had chilled her. It was as if he knew something affecting Gustavo, affecting the entire situation, that he did not feel free to communicate. Perhaps it was a question of security. Perhaps he didn't trust talking on the telephone.

Elizabeth walked up the stairs and entered the bedroom. The bedside lamp was on, but Gustavo was fast asleep already, sleeping on his side, his face turned away from her. She stared at the bulk of his shoulders and back. She wondered again what it was that Charles was trying to tell her. Perhaps during the Inauguration he would be more candid.

She walked around the bed and bent over, kissing her husband on his cheek, which was warm from sleep. He groaned, his facial muscles twitching.

How wonderful it is, she thought, that this man can sleep so soundly. She always wondered about the brave—it seemed to her that much of their courage was simple obliviousness to the dangers that surrounded them. Yet perhaps that, in itself, was admirable. You had to be a little bit oblivious, otherwise you'd never sleep at all.

Elizabeth got into bed and moved beside her husband. She closed her eyes, but sleep did not come to her.

Anxiety for her husband's welfare had always been of primary concern to Elizabeth. She had been aware of his underground activities against Machado when she married him. She had become increasingly wary after the first year in Cuba, when she began to understand the volatile nature of the country's politics. Over the years there had been several incidents; but there had been one singular event. It occurred in June of 1937. That morning they had awakened before daylight, in the master bedroom on the second floor of the big house outside Havana, shaken by the concussion of an explosion.

She remembered vividly the thump of the blast, followed by the tinkle of shattering glass. The chandelier in the bedroom swayed. Startled, Gustavo swung from the bed to the nightstand where he kept two revolvers. She could never get over how vulnerable she felt lying there naked on the bed; fully clothed, one faced these things with less apprehension, she decided.

Gustavo tossed the smaller of the two revolvers, a stubby 32-caliber, nickel-plated with pearl handle, onto the sheet beside her and told her no matter what happened not to leave the bedroom. She stared for a frozen instant at the ugly little weapon. It looked to her like some grotesque silver toy. She remembered thinking how ludicrous it seemed that her husband was rushing from their bed stark naked with a revolver in his hand. He had no sooner vanished than she realized that David and Camilo were alone in the nursery. Clutching the revolver, she went to the hall. It was deserted. A gray luminous glow of morning light came from the vaulted windows at the far end by the stairway. As she took the first tentative step, she was shaken by an ear-splitting blast of gunfire from downstairs. She could not recall how many shots she heard, only that there were several and that for agonizing seconds she stood absolutely paralyzed. Her body would simply not respond to her command to move. All those frozen moments she stood there she could hear Camilo's screams of fright from behind the nursery door, ten feet away. It humiliated her then and to this day when she recalled it. When she finally summoned the strength, she felt as though she were moving her limbs against an invisible and oppressing current, like walking underwater.

It seemed an eternity between the instant she heard the gunshots from the lower floor until she reached the nursery door and opened it.

The scene that greeted her in that room galvanized her fear into anger. A man in a tan suit and a blue shirt squatted on the windowsill. He had an ugly short-barreled shotgun in his right hand. His head was turned away from her. He was looking out the open window into the yard below. That image was still frozen indelibly in her memory. She could recall his curly black hair. How it grew long down the back of his neck, twisting over the edge of his shirt collar. She saw, still, the dirt on his suit coat and the black hairs on his right hand that held the shotgun. He was looking down at a comrade who was scaling the wall behind him.

At the far end of the room, where the boys' beds were, she caught a fleeting glimpse of Camilo, who was then only two, standing in David's bed, clutched in his brother's arms, tears bright in his wide blue eyes; David scared sick and gaping, holding his little brother in his arms like a big doll; and she brought the revolver up and cocked the hammer with her thumb as she had been taught by her father. She saw the man's surprised expression. She saw it against the tip of the forward sight just as she squeezed the trigger. The little revolver roared. Blood spattered on the wall and the windowpanes.

He fell forward onto the tile floor. The shotgun clattered after him. Elizabeth could never reject from her memory the sight of that tan-suited body twitching on the floor, the blood sliding slowly out from the back of his head. What she also recalled, vividly, was that the man wore black-and-white shoes and that his ankles were dirty. She remembered the acrid stench of the gunsmoke and David's sudden scream, mingled with Camilo's shrieks.

They later learned that the attack on the house had been mounted by a fascist terrorist organization. The assault was intended to kill Gustavo, in fact slaughter the entire household, as a means of frightening Gustavo's political associates in Havana. It was a senseless and brutal act.

The threat to his family prompted Gustavo's resolve to withdraw completely from Cuban politics. He swore he would never again lend his name, or support, to any political organization, whatever the compelling motivations. "Putting you in any danger whatsoever makes it not worth it," he told her. "I don't know what I would do if something happened to any of you."

It was a decision he lived with until 1957, when the brutalities of the Batista regime so outraged them both that Gustavo, with Elizabeth's blessing, joined the underground in Havana.

CHAPTER FOURTEEN

MIAMI, JANUARY 19, 1961

Along both sides of the street the poinciana trees were in bloom, the red blossoms showing through the green leaves, bright in the sun. David drove into the south entrance to the Carta driveway. The Volkswagen shuddered as he braked. He shifted to second and swung between the two coral rock gateposts and saw the white façade of the mansion at the end of the circular drive.

He had not seen his parents since the attempt on his stepfather's life, three days earlier. He felt a tingling on the back of his neck as he turned in the drive and realized that the gunmen had used this entrance. He slowed as he saw the heavyset man step out. It was Salazar.

He was a short, broad-shouldered Cuban of thirty. The thick black hair and prominent bones of his Indian face gave him a forbidding expression, but he smiled upon recognizing David and waved him on up the drive.

To David, the Brickell mansion, in its vast, ornate seediness, symbolized the compromise and frustration of his parents' sudden forced dislocation. Its tile roof was crumbling, and its white stucco façade was chipping away from its concrete substratum. The mansion, David supposed, was designed to suggest elegance, but it suggested instead the memory of elegance, and that, too, grimly reflected his parents' present station. Even the landscaping was awry. The palm trees stood tall and stalwart and the lawn was verdant, but, wherever you turned, a menacing, junglelike tangle of banyans and hammock seemed poised to invade everything in its path.

He saw four cars parked in the driveway, two Chevrolets, a dented blue Dodge and a Ford station wagon. There would be several Cubans waiting to speak to Carta in the paneled anteroom outside the library; shabby men in Sears, Roebuck suits, with worried eyes and haggard dark faces, smoking cigars and trying to maintain the façade that they were there to see their old friend Gustavo on business. David knew they were actually there to beg for financial help.

As he got out of the Volkswagen and started up the steps, David noticed the fresh paint patches that showed in the stucco wall around the door. He counted seven. Looking to the right, he saw three more over the big vaulted window that looked out from the living room. Bullet holes, he realized suddenly. He saw also a fresh wound in the bark of the oak tree by the front window. It gave him an uneasy feeling, realizing that it had all really happened, right here, right where he was standing at this moment.

Alfaro answered the door, opening it a few inches to see him, then wider, revealing his full figure, clad in a light tan suit, a clean white shirt, and a black tie pinned to his shirt by a plain gold tie clasp that caught the sun and glinted. Tall, thick-shouldered, Alfaro always seemed a powerful presence in his father's house. The slanting sun lighted up his thick broad nose, his sunburnt cheeks, the thick black moustache, under which his teeth showed white in a smile. "Hello, David, how are you today?"

"I want to see my father," David said abruptly.

"I can't disturb him now," said Alfaro. His voice was lowered, soft, as though he were speaking in church. He was never either rude or deferential. He was always professional.

David adjusted his glasses and looked at Alfaro disconcertedly. His vision, because of the left eye, made it difficult to focus on someone's face. There always seemed to be a flaw, a slight blur, until he adjusted his glasses and concentrated.

Alfaro's dark eyes looked at him with a kindly expression. "Can you wait?" he asked. "You can probably see him before they leave for the airport."

"It's important," David persisted.

"He asked there be no interruptions, no matter how important. It is a meeting with a man I have not seen before."

"Is Mother around?"

"She is by the pool," said Alfaro. "I will call you the moment I can get to him. It won't be too long."

David walked quickly through the darkened living room. The shutters were closed, and splinters of sunlight streaked the polished floor. A musty aroma pervaded the room as well as the rest of the house.

He paused at the French windows and looked out into the garden toward the pool. He saw the slender, tanned figure of his mother gliding across the water. There was something wonderful about his mother taking a leisurely swim at a time like this, David thought. All sorts of bizarre forces had been set loose in their lives: her husband was closeted in urgent conferences that could not be interrupted; her son was receiving telephone calls that threatened to totally disrupt his life and career; they were leaving for the Inauguration in an hour; and amid all that she was swimming. Watching her graceful strokes, David wished that more of her style had rubbed off on him.

When he had received Amato's phone call that morning, it had totally thrown him. He should be dealing with it himself, in the quiet of his office. Yet his first instinct was to run to Elizabeth and Gustavo, to see what their response would be, what they would advise. David felt a little foolish.

The phone call had also made him feel foolish. He had not expected to hear from Amato—especially at the lab.

142

"I've got you booked on the five-o'clock plane tonight to Havana." The hoarse, gruff voice startled him. "Pan Am. Gate Twenty. You be there."

"Who's this?"

"You so tied up with your fish you don't recognize old man Amato?"

"Christ, I'm sorry, Sal." David readjusted the phone to his other hand. "I'm a bit disconnected today. It's the expedition. All this departure bullshit. Melts your brain."

"Sorry to bust in on your plans," Amato said, his voice flat and serious again. "Your brother wants to see you."

"Is this some sort of joke?"

"No, I'm not joking, kid."

"But I haven't heard from Cam for more than a year. What the hell does he want . . . ?"

"He needs you. That's all I can say."

"Hey, come on, Sal, what is this? I got a lot to do around here—I can't go to Havana!"

"Dave, I used to bounce you on my knee and change your diaper; when I say be on the plane, I want you to be on the plane. OK?"

"Yeah. Sure . . ."

The phone went click.

For several moments David watched his mother swim before she noticed him. Reacting with a surprised smile, she pulled herself from the water with a smooth, lithe motion and reached for a towel. David watched her admiringly as she approached him with her long-legged colt's walk. Lanky, slim-hipped, she was still a remarkably handsome woman.

He felt the cool touch of her skin as she kissed him on the cheek. "What a nice surprise."

"I had a call from Amato about an hour ago. He wants me to go with him to Havana this afternoon."

"Really?" She was drying her legs with the towel. "What on earth for?"

"Cam wants to see me."

He saw her reaction, a slight hesitation, a suspension of movement; then, flinging the towel over a chair, she picked up a white terrycloth robe and wrapped it around her shoulders. She did not speak for a moment, but flicked her hand over her wet hair. "Did he say why? Any explanation?"

"None." David shrugged. "It puts me in a hell of a bind, Mother."

"Why would he ask to see you? It's very odd, isn't it?"

"I want to get Gustavo's opinion. Maybe he could suggest something. I mean, I could just phone Cam and ask him what he wants."

"That might be foolish."

"You think I should just drop everything and race off to Havana?"

Elizabeth's blue eyes probed David's. "That's the only thing you can do, don't you agree? Cam is your brother, darling." She stared at him for a moment, then glanced back toward the house. "I would appreciate you not discussing this with Gustavo," she added quickly. "You shouldn't even mention it to him."

"Why?"

"Because he would object. I want you to see Cam. You understand?"

"Christ, Mother, there's so much I don't understand."

"There are a lot of things I don't understand, either." David turned quickly when he heard Carta's familiar gravelly voice, a voice that had always resonated authority and energy. Carta extended his hand and David shook it, feeling awkward, worried about what his stepfather might have overheard. Though David was slightly taller than Carta, he felt nonetheless that Gustavo's thick-chested six-foot frame dwarfed him. David glanced quickly at Elizabeth, who had affected the steely but outwardly serene expression she always assumed during family crises.

"Alfaro told me you had something important to discuss."

"David just came to say goodbye," Elizabeth interjected.

"Yes. I hope it's a nice change for you," David said.

"How's Robin?" Carta asked.

"She's cramming for exams."

"Tell her we expect to see her after we get back."

"You know how she gets when exams are coming . . ." David started to edge away. "I'll tell her."

Elizabeth lifted her face and David kissed her and then he was gone, hurrying along the path that led from the patio around the side of the house, past the big mango tree. Elizabeth and Carta watched his blond head disappear around the side of the house; David had not looked back.

"He's a strange boy," Carta said, turning to Elizabeth. "Tell me, my dear, what secrets are you two keeping from me?"

"Secrets? I'm not aware of any secrets."

"You wouldn't try to fool an old detector of conspiracies?"

"Never." She shook her head and got to her feet. Her eyes fixed on him for a moment, a hint of a smile coming into her steady gaze. She stood before him, the sun slanting across her white swimsuit to shape shadows where it clung tightly to the fleshy places. He saw the indecision

144

in her eyes for an instant, but then she tossed her hair, grasping it behind her neck with one hand.

"Well?" he said flatly.

"Well what?"

"Tell me what it's all about?"

"How do you know there is an *it*?" She turned from him, took two quick, graceful steps, and dived into the pool, her body slicing the water so that the surface barely rippled.

Carta observed her. "You wouldn't mock me, would you?" he said gently.

She twisted in the water and looked back at him. "I wouldn't think of it, my darling. Nor would I dare." She treaded water as he walked wearily toward the doors to his study. The smile she had fixed on her face dissolved as she turned away, swimming for the edge of the pool. It was her son Camilo who filled her thoughts now.

When Gustavo Carta returned to the library he found his guest, R. Kirby Pelham, seated on the leather couch as he had left him, legs crossed, hands folded around his knee, a quizzical expression on his face. He was wearing his usual seersucker suit, white shirt and blue tie.

"Well, Gustavo, what about it?"

"What you've said is very clear to me," Gustavo Carta remarked. "Now I'm trying to analyze what you've chosen to leave unsaid."

"My proposition is very straightforward," Pelham said impatiently. "We are giving you the opportunity to take a leadership position in the Frente. Events are starting to accelerate now. Critical days are ahead. The organization must be strengthened."

Carta gazed intently at his visitor. "In the past it was made very clear that my presence was not welcome in the Frente," he said. "Why would you want to recruit me at this late date?"

"As I explained, it is a question of broadening the political base . . ."

"Stop playing games with me, Pel. We've known each other too long. It's the new Administration you're worried about, isn't it? Some of the Kennedy people have got wind of all the political infighting down here. They have started wondering why the Frente is composed of a bunch of decrepit old right-wingers—the kind of men even Fulgencio Batista would consider reactionaries."

"What's the point of all this rhetoric, Gustavo?" Pelham was squinting at Carta with cold gray eyes, pursing his lips nervously, a habit Carta remembered from college. Indeed, Pelham had changed remarkably little from his undergraduate days at Georgetown, where the two had been classmates. His hair, though thinning, was still light brown. His

145

complexion still retained that schoolboy gloss, accented by a hint of the rosy cheeks which Pelham had always despised in himself as a young man. His small, taut body could still serve him well on the squash court, Carta thought, recalling the many defeats he had sustained at Pelham's hands. In college, Carta had considered his classmate to be harmlessly abrasive, an ambitious young man, obviously a social climber, with a chip on his somewhat pedantic shoulder. Pelham had gone to school at Phillips Exeter, where his father had been an instructor. He had resented the fact that while most of his schoolmates had moved on to the hallowed halls of Harvard and Princeton, Pelham could not afford these schools and instead had accepted a full scholarship at Georgetown. Carta remembered how desperately Pelham seemed to long for the status of the Ivy League colleges, with their exalted clubs and fraternities. With all that, there was much he respected about Pelham—the incisiveness of his intellect, his command of himself, his basic Yankee integrity. Carta realized that the eyes he now looked into were cunning and manipulative.

"Look at it from my standpoint, Pel. The CIA has scorned the requests of my organization for any form of assistance—supplies, weapons, even the use of your short-wave radio. You've done everything you can to isolate us, to make us seem like outlaws. And now suddenly you come here and tell me I am vital to your cause. Suddenly I'm no longer a dangerous outsider?"

"I think I've responded to that, Gustavo. It's purely a matter of expanding the political base."

"And if I join the Frente, will the CIA then look more kindly upon the requirements of my people?"

Pelham pursed his lips again. "Insofar as your men are concerned, the time has come to join forces."

"And what exactly does joining forces mean?"

"Time is short, Gustavo. We no longer have the luxury of waste and duplication. Your organization must now place itself under the control of the brigade. That means the men training at your camp in the Everglades. That means all your agents and detachments inside Cuba. You have some able saboteurs under your command, Gustavo. We will need to integrate these men into our own network."

"What you are asking me to do, Pel, is to abdicate all responsibility for these hundreds of men who have pledged their loyalty to me, who have entrusted their lives to me. You are asking me to surrender them as if they were pawns on a chessboard. It is unthinkable—you realize that, of course."

"I realize the realities of the moment, Gustavo. It is about time you confronted those realities."

146

Carta studied his visitor across the room and pondered the irony of their encounter. Certainly if anyone would have told him thirty years earlier, in his undergraduate days at Georgetown, that his life would ultimately be entangled with that of Kirby Pelham, he would have laughed at the notion.

"You talk about realities, my friend. Your new invasion plan—Operation Trinidad?—do you really think this strategy represents reality? Do you really think that a thousand men, even two thousand, making an amphibious landing in a single location will defeat the armies of Fidel Castro? Do you really think he is that vulnerable?"

"You don't have the complete picture, Gustavo. You do not know about the air strikes, the diversionary forces . . ."

"Doesn't it strike you as extraordinary that Fidel Castro can stand up and deliver a speech in front of fifty thousand people, as he did last weekend, with little or no security—and that no one takes a shot at him? Does that sound like a leader who will roll over and play dead the minute your troops hit the beaches?"

Pelham shook his head impatiently. He fought to control the anger welling within himself. It was the old Carta stubbornness asserting itself, just as it had in college. The rich man's son, pampered since childhood, refusing to face the real world.

"Look, Gustavo, I am not going to sit here and debate military strategy with someone who is ignorant of the facts. I have a lot to do and very little time to do it. I made you a proposition. I want an answer."

"I'm afraid I can't dignify it with an answer."

Pelham's face flushed with anger. "Goddamn it, Gustavo, come off this pose of yours! Who the hell do you think you're kidding?" He was on his feet now, coming over to Carta's desk. "I know where things stand with you. I know about the execution of Captain Escalante. It's obvious Castro has penetrated your network. I know that you are running out of money for your operations. Running out of supplies too. And running out of time. This latest assassination attempt—they almost got you, Gustavo. You can't afford to support your operation and you can't even protect yourself! It is madness!" Pelham rolled his eyes. "Look, Gustavo, you may not approve of our invasion plans, you may find our strategy imperfect, but let me remind you that we're the only game in town. You know that as well as I. If you ever hope to see your homeland again—"

"You know I do, Pel."

"Then you'd better throw in with us."

Carta stiffened. "I'm not going to, Pel. I am not emotionally suited to be your puppet."

"And that is your final answer?"

"It is."

"Very well, Gustavo. Good luck. You'll be needing it." Pelham started toward the door.

Carta rose to see him out. As he reached the door, Pelham suddenly turned to face him again.

"I don't think you realize what you're doing. I think you'll look back on this conversation a few weeks from now with some regret."

"Is that a threat, Pel?"

Pelham looked at him with a detached smile. "Just keep it in mind, old man."

"You wished to see me, señor?"

"Yes, Alfaro, come in. Shut the door, please."

Carta stood up from his desk as Alfaro turned and shut the library door, an expression of curiosity and apprehension in his eyes. Alfaro sat down in one of the big leather chairs before the desk.

"Alfaro, I have a job for you."

"At your orders, señor."

"I want you to join the Frente's air force in Guatemala . . . as a pilot."

Alfaro looked surprised. "Guatemala, señor?"

"This is very important to us, Alfaro. We must have a clear assessment of the brigade. There have been unusual things going on at Trax. Things that indicate unrest among the men. We must know what is happening, understand?"

"Clearly."

"Also, Alfaro, I must have information as to a secret project called Operation Forty-one. It is vital that we know its purpose. Clear?"

"I will do my best."

"When shall I leave?"

"It has been arranged for you to join their organization tomorrow. You will be taken to the base in Guatemala tomorrow night in a B-26 that is to be delivered to Retalhuleu. You will fly as co-pilot."

"How shall I report?"

"By letter to Carlota. As though she were your *novia*." Carta went to the desk and opened a drawer, taking out a handwritten sheet. "I have devised a personal code for us."

Alfaro took the sheet and started to read it.

Carta said, "Memorize it and destroy it."

"Yes."

"That is the number of the post-office box in Coral Gables."

"I am to send all the letters there?"

"Yes."

148

"This Operation Forty-one? What do you know about it?"

"Nothing. Only that it exists."

"But you have suspicions?"

"My suspicions mean nothing. I need facts, Alfaro. Who are these people? Their names? Where are they training? How many? What is their function?"

"And the brigade?"

"Everything you can get. Everything that is concrete fact, not rumor."

"Of course."

After he had gone, Carta returned to his desk and opened the drawer and looked down at the blue metal shape of the 38-caliber Smith & Wesson revolver he kept there. There was a similar weapon upstairs under his pillow. He sighed to himself wearily. What kind of life is it, he thought, where you must fear so urgently for your safety at every minute? He felt a longing for the old days, which now seemed to him, the edges faded in his memory, to have been safe and warm and happy times. He sighed again and closed the drawer. He resolved that he would, now that Alfaro was going, carry a pistol on his person at all times. He would need to practice with it sometime soon. He was an extremely bad shot with any kind of hand gun. A shotgun was his weapon. But what would you look like going around with a shotgun under your jacket? he thought.

*

The Bradley-Westex Electronics Company occupied a square commercial building in Coral Gables. From the outside, it looked like a perfectly ordinary cement-block structure, worthy of no special note. Passersby could perceive a female receptionist sitting inside the front entrance and secretaries working in their small fluorescent-lit offices. Men wearing conservative business suits came and went each day, toting their attaché cases.

The company, which manufactured printed circuits, had actually gone out of business a year earlier, at which time R. Kirby Pelham leased the building to serve as headquarters for the Cuban operation, or Operation Trinidad as it had now been designated. His payroll averaged $115,000 a month. Like any other businessman in the area, Pelham had established a bank account, business cards, and membership in the local Chamber of Commerce. He had even worked out a ready-made dissertation on the problems of the printed circuits industry in case anyone ever asked him "How's business?" It was, after all, vital to keep up appearances. It was more than a question of military secrecy. The very existence of his operation constituted a technical violation of federal law, since the Central Intelligence Agency was expressly forbidden to conduct any of its affairs on United States soil.

Returning to his office from his meeting with Carta, Pelham was in an irritable, fidgety mood. He knew that Gustavo Carta was a stubborn man, but he resented nonetheless the cavalier manner in which his former college classmate had rejected his invitation for him to join the Frente. It was a ridiculous idea to begin with—having Carta in the Frente. Politically, Carta represented a position that was totally untenable. Carta harbored the belief that he could foster "Fidelismo without Fidel," that he could bring about land reform, nationalize certain key industries and create a broader distribution of income—all within the framework of the democratic process. To Pelham, this was folly. Cuba was a primitive, virtually feudal country. It demanded a strongly authoritarian form of government. The only thing that kept Carta from seeing this was his own enormous ego—the same damned ego Pelham remembered in Carta from their college days together. Yes, Carta always seemed to have an exaggerated sense of his own abilities, Pelham told himself. The starry-eyed reformers like Carta would only lead the country down the road to Socialism, and ultimately to Communism.

The more he thought about it, the angrier he got. In a way, Carta represented as big a threat as Castro. Pelham had been startled by recent intelligence reports indicating Carta's sustained popularity among non-Communist Cubans. To the Cuban people, he was still a leader of stature, a man to be respected, even venerated. It was positively unbelievable—the naïveté of the Cuban people.

Pelham was so absorbed in his thoughts he almost bowled over his hefty secretary, Adele, who was standing outside his office holding several file folders full of messages.

"Excuse me, suh," Adele drawled in her annoyingly thick Georgia accent as Pelham recoiled from the near-collision. "There are some messages of impoh-tance for you."

Pelham took the folders, muttered an apology, and sought the refuge of his office. Seating himself behind his desk, he quickly tore open a sealed Telex from headquarters, and started scanning it with keen interest. It read:

ATTN: PELHAM EYES ONLY
ADVISE AGENT MR/CASTLE HE WILL BE ACTIVATED. HIS MISSION
FULLY CLEARED. URGENT YOU GIVE EVERY SUPPORT
POSSIBLE. EXPECT YOUR REPORT RE OTHER CUTOUT ROLES.
VERMILLION

Pelham took a deep breath and started reading the cable a second time, nodding his head thoughtfully as he pondered its import. The weight of annoyance and frustration had suddenly been lifted. He felt like a poker player who had tossed in his mediocre hand and had suddenly been dealt four aces. His mind raced with his sudden surge of exhilaration. He thought now of the heavyweight planners at CIA headquarters, of the brigade training in Guatemala. What none of them knew, Pelham realized, was that the biggest single factor in their success or failure rested not with their intricate stratagems but with the cards that Pelham now held in his hand.

There was a delicious irony in the fact that the destinies and reputations of so many men now resided with him, and yet no one knew it—no one, that is, except Vermillion and the director of the CIA, to whom he reported. And perhaps the President-elect. Pelham pondered that one for a moment. Was there a possibility that the new President did not know? Could an act of this historic significance be perpetuated without the President having given it his personal stamp of approval? No, Pelham concluded, Vermillion and his superiors were too self-protective to allow that to happen. Kennedy must certainly know. And that realization made Pelham feel even better—that the President of the United States knew that a man named Pelham sitting in Miami at this historic time had been entrusted to play the right card at the right moment.

Pelham snapped out of his reveries. There was much to be done, he realized. There was the matter of the cutouts—those operatives who were to be placed strategically between the actual perpetrator and the ultimate target. The purpose of the cutouts was twofold: to throw the enemy off the track, and also to conceal the role of the agency. Pelham had readied a splendid cast of cutouts for this mission, and it was now time to activate them. And then there was the matter of MR/CASTLE. Pelham had been preparing him for a mission such as this for a long time. MR/CASTLE was Pelham's baby, so to speak, and the execution of his assignment spelled success not only for the entire Cuban operation, but also for his sponsor, Pelham. Pelham's mind spun for a moment with the possibilities for his own career. A major promotion within the agency. Perhaps even an ambassadorship. The opportunities were limitless. Pelham buzzed his secretary. It was time to get down to work.

CHAPTER FIFTEEN

They were the perfect couple. Everybody told them so. They even looked alike—two sleekly handsome young colts, both with gracefully chiseled features and mischievous eyes. Both were offshoots of wealthy Southern families, the products of generations of careful genetic selection and meticulous breeding. They both loved good horses and fast cars and bathtub gin and parties that ran till dawn.

Elizabeth had started hearing about Ewing Chapman even before she left for college. Her mother's sister, Aimee, phoned to tell her there was a young man who would be two years ahead of her at Duke whom she would like. He was rich and handsome and spoiled, the aunt said, and he reminded her of Elizabeth. During her first week of college—a blur of parties and receptions, of hands being shaken and names being dropped—she had heard several girls mention Ewing as someone to meet.

No shrinking violet, Elizabeth arranged to be at a party which Ewing was to attend, and when they met she started blurting the names of aunts and cousins as quickly as she could get them out of her mouth. None of it was needed, because he was clearly as struck by her as she was by him. When Ewing asked her out, Elizabeth played her Southern-belle role to the hilt—she batted her eyes coyly and said, "Why, aren't you nice," and then turned him down. She kicked herself for a week. She dreamed about him and almost fainted every time they passed on their way to or from class.

It took two weeks of careful negotiation and the intervention of a distant cousin of Elizabeth's who was a senior at Duke to elicit a second invitation. But once they started seeing each other, it became a nightly affair. Ewing and his unlikely roommate, a burly, roughhewn steelworker's son named Sal Amato, were the most proficient campus manufacturers of bathtub gin. Ewing and Elizabeth would start drinking at eight and start dancing at nine. Usually by ten Ewing was in a fight, and Sal, who was already making a name for himself on the Duke University football team, was dragging Ewing's opponents off him, and Elizabeth

152

was patching his wounds. And the three of them would climb into Ewing's Hudson and drive fast, always at the brink of disaster, in search of a speakeasy that would still be open. And then there would be more drinking and dancing, and usually more fighting as well.

It became Elizabeth's private fantasy that she would have a long and passionate romance with Ewing, which would be consummated on their wedding night, the day after graduation. The timetable got pushed up a bit. Two months after they met they were parked in Ewing's car by a nearby lake. There were other cars parked nearby, but neither of them took notice. It was cold in the car, but Elizabeth remembered the warmth of the gin in her stomach, the smell of the leather seats and the touch of Ewing's fingers enclosing her nipples.

She also remembered that it hurt. She had been told that losing one's virginity would be painful, but Elizabeth hated being a virgin so much that she assumed the experience would be different for her. In any case, she relished the hurt, just as she relished the closeness it brought with Ewing. After it was over there was a certain amount of confusion. Ewing, who was breathing heavily, mumbled some hasty apologies about not lasting longer—he blamed it on the gin. Elizabeth noticed that the couple in the next car had abandoned any pretense of necking and had become full-time onlookers. They buttoned themselves up and dried off the seat with Ewing's scarf and quickly started the car. And then once they were on the road and their tension began to dissolve along with their ardor, they both found themselves laughing. The whole event which had seemed so grave and ceremonial now seemed almost ludicrous in retrospect. They met Sal afterward and Ewing started to tell him about it, then stopped and looked over at Elizabeth, worried about offending her. But she picked up where he left off, except she told it funnier, how the gearshift kept getting in the way, and Sal, who was far more experienced than either she or Ewing, shared their laughter.

That evening drew the three of them together. Their time was spent sharing Sal's exploits and injuries on the football field, Ewing's constant traumas with his grades, which ranged from mediocre to disastrous, and Elizabeth's mercurial moods, which could run the gamut from ecstatic to suicidal within a fifteen-minute interval. The three of them were somehow good for each other. Ewing supplied the energy and the spontaneity, Elizabeth brought style and grace, and Sal was the solid one—as capable as anyone of having a good time but also mindful of when to apply the brakes of caution. Ewing and Elizabeth were making love whenever and wherever possible now, and their technique had begun to match their passion. They also began to realize that they were falling desperately in love.

153

When Elizabeth became pregnant, her reaction was one of total disbelief. Her whole affair with Ewing had seemed so idealized, so otherworldly, that this sudden intrusion caught her off stride. In panic, she tearfully blurted the news to Ewing, who looked ashen-faced and numb. Elizabeth remembered that he had received the news rather like a sullen child whose most prized possession had just been taken away. The possession, Elizabeth later realized, was his innocence. Ewing became very angry, and stared at Elizabeth accusingly, as if she had committed a grave act of betrayal.

And then he simply disappeared. For three days no one—not even Amato—saw him or heard from him.

It was Elizabeth who now felt a keen sense of betrayal. She couldn't eat or sleep or study. Torn between his two friends, Amato was sympathetic but noncommittal. On the third night, Amato appeared at her dormitory, looking somber. He drove her through the countryside for an hour until they reached a small hotel. Ewing was there, unshaven, red-eyed, and still very drunk. Elizabeth found herself wanting to rush to him, but Ewing greeted them both coldly. He was upset with Amato for having brought her there. He didn't want to talk to Elizabeth and he didn't want to talk about the baby. Elizabeth and Amato exchanged looks of helplessness, and they both left Ewing lying there on a sofa, bottle in hand.

Elizabeth curled up against Amato in the car and cried softly as he drove her back. Amato felt humiliated by the meeting; he had brought them together in the naïve belief that their reunion would be warm and loving. He put his arm around her and they drove in silence. Huddled against him, Elizabeth sensed his strength and resiliency.

She persuaded him to stop for a drink on the way home. She clung to Amato like a drowning child clinging to a buoy. They had one drink and then another. And then Elizabeth told him she did not want to go home that night. She didn't want to have to deal with all the other frivolous girls flitting around the dormitory. Amato asked her where she wanted to go and she said she wanted to go back to the rooms he shared with Ewing. Amato resisted the idea, but Elizabeth started to sob again and he took her there and brought her upstairs. Elizabeth asked Amato to stay with her while she went to sleep, and he agreed. He sat with her as she stretched out on Ewing's bed, and held her hand as she closed her eyes.

It was then she felt a sudden impulse she had never experienced before or since. It was a mixture of love and anger, of hurt and lust. She began to slip off her clothes as Amato looked on with disbelief. She took his hand and made him touch her on her shoulders and breasts and

154

then between her legs. And then she started making love to him. She remembered years later the tension in his muscles as he resisted her, then it subsiding as he responded to her need and to his own. They made love slowly and tenderly. And when they paused in their ardor, Elizabeth felt a sudden surge of power—power over herself, power over Amato, power over Ewing. It was as if, having fused love and anger, she had found in that strange fusion a new source of strength. It was then that she kissed Amato, and started to make love to him again.

They had no idea how long Ewing had been in the room. It was Elizabeth who first saw him, backed against the wall as if viewing some nightmare vision he could neither assimilate nor comprehend. She did not pull away from Amato but simply stared at Ewing with defiance. Sensing something, Amato pulled away from her, and when he saw Ewing he almost jumped from the bed. Ewing lurched at him, striking at him with his fists as hard as he could in his drunkenness. Amato made no effort to defend himself, just standing there, absorbing the blows. Then Ewing turned suddenly and ran from the room, racked with hurt and frustration.

Amato and Elizabeth got dressed silently and he drove her home. The next morning she arose late, phoned for a taxi and went to the apartment. Amato was sitting alone in the small living room, his head in his hands. She sat beside him and kissed him on his powerful forearm.

"He's dead," was all Amato said. He looked over at her, an expression of utter desolation on his features. They sat together for a long time.

It was later in the day that she learned the details. Ewing's Hudson had hit the concrete abutment of a small bridge over a nearby brook. He had been killed instantly.

Elizabeth withdrew from college and went home for a while, then took a job in Washington. Seven months later when David was delivered, it was Amato alone who was at the hospital with her. They named the child David, after Ewing's father. They felt it was the least they could do.

MIAMI, JANUARY 19, 1961

His face had aged. David could see that now as he turned his gaze from the window of the plane and looked at Salvador Amato. David had always thought that Amato looked as though he'd spent his life on the deck of a ship rather than in offices in New York, London, Paris and Havana. He would have looked great in a watch cap and a black turtle-

155

neck sweater, David thought. The white shirt and tie, the gray flannel suit, seemed incongruous with that face and those thick-fingered, powerful hands that protruded inelegantly from the white French cuffs.

Amato's cropped hair covered his big head like a layer of gray steel wool. He turned his eyes to David, and his thick, tight lips curled in a faint smile, and there was a gleam of amusement in his oddly triangular eyes. Amato's face looked tough, because of its heavy, squared shape and the bent beak of a nose, but when he smiled, his eyes bright and lively, his expression took on an air of good humor, the easy manner of an observer who had looked at life, all of it, for so many seasons, and from so many different points of view, that he had decided to be amused by it all.

David's earliest memory of Amato was as a spinner of tales. They were tales of intrigue involving Amato's adventures in Latin America, Europe and Asia. And they were also great football tales—stories of how Amato had "worked" his way through college in the Roaring Twenties. Technically, as Amato told it, he was a scholarship student, the son of an unemployed steelworker, but in fact he was a fullback for hire, available to become a "student" at whichever college would pay for his services. Ultimately, Amato spent six years playing for three colleges, and, as he often told David, it was a good life, filled with great games and cheering fans and pretty girls and good booze.

It was Amato who had first taken Camilo and David fishing. He remembered going out to the Havana harbor with the great stone mass of Morro Castle rising out of the rock embankment behind them, standing together on the flying bridge of Amato's boat, looking at the purple-blue line of the Gulf Stream; seeing ahead the birds swirling in the air, like tiny bits of fluttering white paper over the surface, and Camilo pointing excitedly and Amato saying, yes, that meant fish. When he maneuvered the boat into the school, the birds swarming around them, crying in their high-pitched shrieks, they saw the tuna break the surface, silvery, bullet-shaped, leaving little splashes where they vanished in the blue water. David blurted how beautiful they looked and Camilo made a mocking remark, but Amato said quietly, very seriously, "They're lovely." *Lovely.* It was a strange word coming from the mouth of such a strong man. David had been eleven. He'd fallen in love with the sea that day, completely, spirit, mind and body; a passion that was to be expanded later off New England, but was born there, with Amato, that spring day, in the Gulf Stream. Now, looking at Amato's face, he felt a warmth of affection for him, a feeling of confidence; if there was trouble ahead, Amato was a good man to have around.

156

"Don't be nervous," Amato said. "It's just another plane ride."

David inhaled too deeply and strained to stifle a cough. "You're right, Sal, I have nothing to be nervous about. I'm sitting on a plane heading for a country that is practically in a state of siege. I'm a leader of an oceanographic expedition that is leaving for Peru in three weeks, possibly without me. And I haven't the slightest idea what I'm doing. Why should I worry?"

"You think you got troubles, kid. See that guy sitting over there, the one that looks like an Arab?"

David craned his neck. He saw the little man with a dark face looking out the window in the seat across the aisle.

"He's on his way to Havana thinking he just locked up a deal to sell a few million bucks' worth of farm machinery outa Tangiers to the Cubans." Amato shook his head. "What he don't know is about two hours ago somebody bought the stuff out from under him and he's got what the dog left."

"You know him?"

Amato's brows lifted, his eyes bright with amusement. "Never met him. But I'm the bastard who just did him in."

"You're feeling rather pleased with yourself, aren't you?"

"Yeah. I like my business. I'm good at it." Amato smiled. "How things going for you, kid?"

"Pretty good."

"Robin?"

"She's fine."

Amato frowned at the tone in David's voice. He had always worried about their marriage. He felt Robin was too self-centered for a serious boy like David. She needed constant romance in her life, flowers and poetic notes stuffed under her pillow. He'd known her kind of woman many times, enjoyed their company, but never regretted it when they passed on to someone else.

Something in David's manner, his tone of voice, touched off Amato's well-tuned alarm system. "She giving you a bad time?"

David looked surprised. "What makes you ask that?"

"Is she?"

David nodded, blinking his eyes behind the thick lenses of his glasses. He avoided Amato's steady gaze.

"You want to talk about it?"

"She just seems bored with everything, Sal. Especially me."

It was on the tip of Amato's tongue to ask if she had taken a lover, but he thought better of it. "How long is the trip to Peru going to take?"

157

"Three months. Why?"

"What happens to Robin while you're gone?"

"I've thought about all that, Sal. She's working on her doctorate in psychology at the university . . . it takes up all of her time, even if I'm around."

"When you get back you ought to take a little time with her, woo her a little."

"Woo her? Hell, we're married."

"You ever write poetry for her?"

David laughed. "Come on, she doesn't even like poetry! What are you getting at, Sal?"

"You said she was bored. I think you ought to start asking yourself why. You get me?"

"Sure. Hell, don't worry. It's just a phase she's going through."

"I wouldn't take that to the track. Think about it. A girl like Robin, she needs to feel important, know what I mean? You got to work at it, make her feel adequate, needed. Otherwise . . ."

"Otherwise what?"

"You lose her."

David looked away. Amato kept looking at him. He had always had a special feeling for this boy. He'd seen him through the accident in Havana in which he had been partially blinded and left with a stiffened right leg, through the painful pre-teenage years when he became incredibly shy and withdrawn, limping about on his steel-braced leg. When he reached his teens David left Cuba for prep school in New England and began to find himself. Amato admired the way he had gained toughness and confidence and had taught himself, by exercise and hard work, to walk without a limp. He had a strong, stubborn streak in him Amato always admired. David had turned himself into an excellent swimmer and skin diver, and could sail with the best crews in the world. While Camilo had been a star athlete, a superb first baseman, boxer, wing shot and soccer goalie, David had accepted his physical limits and turned to academic pursuits. He had an incisive mind and learned how to use it to his best advantage. Amato knew how shy he had been around girls as a teenager, and even into his college years, seldom dating, his nose always buried in a book. David once confessed to him that Robin was the first girl who had seemed to need him. And he'd married her. This worried Amato, who rarely worried. He worried about David because he loved him and had always, like Camilo, felt a need to protect him.

Feeling his gaze, David turned and looked at Amato again, removing his glasses and massaging the red-imprinted bridge of his nose. "Come on, Sal. You want to tell me now what happens when we land?"

158

"Nothing special. We go through immigration. Take a taxi into town. You check into the Ambos Mundos Hotel. Remember it?"

David nodded.

"You've got the corner room, fifth floor."

"What then?"

"Wait."

"For what?"

"Somebody'll get in touch with you."

"Won't you be there?"

"No."

David looked at Amato. His matter-of-factness was infuriating. "Christ, Sal, where the hell will you be?"

"I don't want to get in the way. I've got some business meetings with government people."

"You mean to say the Castro people trust you?"

"Sure. They find me useful. I have certain business contacts. I manage to get them items they couldn't get otherwise. You know your Uncle Sal, Davy—always has something that somebody wants." Sal smiled and patted David on the knee, reassuringly. "Besides, I go back a long way with Fidel."

"You never told me that."

"You never asked. I've got an apartment in Vedado next to one of the places he stays. See him all the time."

"What kind of a guy is he?"

"Hey, he's got his own country, hasn't he?"

In all the years he had known Amato, David had never been able to figure out exactly how he managed to support himself in such a grand manner—a world of limousines and expensive women and elegant hotel suites. David's mother, whose loyalty to Amato was unstinting, spoke admiringly of his "import-export" business. David's stepfather, who was angered whenever Elizabeth invited Amato to the house, and usually managed not to be there, would never discuss Amato's business at all. David had heard gossip over the years about his supposed connection with gambling interests and even underworld figures, but Amato, when questioned about it by David, had laughed it off. "I'm too smart to get messed up with those bums," he told him.

The stewardess came by with the drinks, and David and Amato each ordered scotches. David looked over at Amato's impassive face.

"Are you going to tell me about Cam or is that part of the suspense?" he asked.

"I'd rather Cam told you himself. He'd want it that way."

"You don't want me to know in case I get interrogated, is that it?"

"You're coming to Havana as a tourist, right? You want a rest. You haven't heard from your brother, know nothing about him. You don't intend to hear from him."

"And Cam's little girl? What's happened to her?"

"Elena is all right," Amato snapped, and then he sipped his scotch and lapsed into silence.

David waited a moment, then: "OK, enough is enough. What the hell am I getting into?"

Amato's massive face seemed to flinch. He turned toward David and looked at him directly, his hooded eyes studying David's face. "Look, Davy, I love you, do you understand that? Your old man was my best pal, my teacher. He taught me about lots of things I never could have known. He even tried to make me into a gentleman—can you imagine that? An Irish-Cuban gorilla like me? How's that for loyalty?"

"I understand," David said quickly.

"You gotta trust me, OK?"

"If I didn't I wouldn't be here."

"Hey," said Amato, "look out the goddamn window."

Spread out in the late sun, Havana's brilliant mosaic of buildings with tile roofs gleamed white from the air. Coming into view below were the tawny shapes of the lighthouse and Morro Castle and then the harbor, narrow as a river, brimming with ships and small boats. To David, each vista bore an aura of nostalgic magic. He could see cars crawling along the Malecón. He saw the Prado and the green of the trees that divided the avenues and the gray Imperial Roman shapes of the Presidential Palace and the other official buildings. He saw the geometric patterns of the streets cutting like paths through the buildings and the slow-moving line of cars appearing like tiny sparks as they emerged from the shadows into the sun. The miniature ranks of houses, with their weathered tiled roofs, looked Moorish in the diffused light, the patterns of tile roofs broken by clusters of trees in the parks and the vast open spaces of the plazas. My God, he thought, Havana!

BOOK III

CHAPTER SIXTEEN

*C*uba's first conquerors led a singular life on the island, ravishing the Indian women, playing cards, fencing on horseback with spears, forming parties to hunt down the remaining free Indians in the bush and on the many smaller islands; holding gay fiestas at their newly built haciendas; flirting with and seducing the Spanish wives who had begun to put in their appearance in the new colony. Most of these men had been deadbeat nobodies in Spain; now they were noble lords on a great adventure, rulers of all they could see. They began to pour into Cuba by the hundreds.

And with them came their African slaves, their blooded Andalusian horses, their dogs, their goats, their pigs, their chickens. The island became the major horse-breeding center in the New World. Slave markets were established. Ships arrived in Santiago from raids on the African coast laden with blacks for the market; hunting parties returned from as far north as the Bahamas with freshly caught Indians. Commerce began to quicken. Many of the new settlers had come from Santo Domingo to escape unpaid debts, or quarrels, or prison. Others had come from the Spanish settlement at Darién, on the western mainland. Fate had a great deal in store for these early Cuban hildagos. *They were to discover the temples and halls of Montezuma.*

Of all the misfits in the Cuban colony, Hernán Cortés seemed the least likely to become the Conquistador of Mexico. He was tall, stoutly built, with a broad chest, a strikingly handsome face, and wore his blond hair long. He was thirty-four. He had been in the islands for fifteen years.

Somehow, no one was quite sure how, he had become an intimate friend of Governor Velásquez, who had appointed him mayor of Baracoa. Cortés, even before leaving Spain as a boy in his teens, had a reputation as a seducer of the ladies. "He had a weakness for women," López de Gomara said of him. "He was a wonderful dice player, skillful and good-natured, fond of eating, could drink most of his companions under the table, and was both strong and stubborn."

In Cuba, he was constantly in trouble. Once the governor himself had Cortés put in the stocks. On another day, he ordered the young scoundrel hanged for dallying with a Spanish lady of pious reputation. But Cortés had a certain air about him, a style. Upon hearing that new lands to the west had been discovered, Cortés approached the governor through friends. He followed this subtle campaign by appearing at Velásquez' hacienda in Santiago. The two men got drunk together and Velásquez appointed Cortés captain general of the new expedition to Mexico.

On November 18, 1518, he set sail from Santiago with ten ships, some six hundred men, sixteen horses, thirteen muskets and four cannon, all paid for by Velásquez. This was the governor's personal expedition. Just before the ships sailed, rumors circulated that Cortés intended to betray his benefactor. Flying into a rage, Velásquez tried to recall him, ordering Cortés' arrest. But too late. Cortés merely sent his frantic chief a derisive farewell.

Putting in at Trinidad and Havana, Cortés stole all the supplies he could find. In a rage, Velásquez rode to Havana to intercept him. He arrived in time to see the ships sail out, the blond head of Cortés shining in the sun on the sterncastle. The great adventure was under way.

Gnashing his gubernatorial teeth, Velásquez dispatched a punitive expedition under Pánfilo de Narváez to Mexico to overtake Cortés and bring him back to Cuba in chains. This too the governor paid for out of his own pocket. It cost him a fortune. Nineteen ships, nine hundred men, cannon, crossbows, muskets, lances, eighty horses, powder, ammunition and bacon.

Cortés, who had by that time conquered the Aztecs and taken their capital, turned the whole affair around by bribing Narváez' men to enlist under his own banner. Velásquez' expeditionary force simply fell apart. The whole affair took Cortés less than an hour. There were fewer than twenty casualties, and when it was over Cortés had Narváez prisoner, nine hundred fresh recruits and tons of supplies. A farewell gift from the governor of Cuba.

Trade winds blowing west out of Africa pile up warm tropical waters in the Gulf of Mexico, raising the level of the water several inches higher than that of the adjacent Atlantic Ocean. This relentless pressure must find an outlet. It does in the 112-mile gap between Florida and Cuba. Through these straits the Gulf Stream flows at three miles an hour, about two thousand feet deep, one of the earth's mighty ocean rivers.

The Spanish found the eastward current a natural route for their heavily laden galleons returning to the motherland from Mexico. Havana's well-protected harbor, situated astride the Gulf Stream on Cuba's north coast, was the port commanding the only passage by which treasure ships could sail from the Gulf of Mexico to Europe.

Havana became vital to Spain's interests. In 1538, the seat of colonial government was moved from Baracoa. Havana grew accordingly, while the rest of the colony in Cuba fell into neglect, a backwater of an empire that had spread to the west. The Spanish governors of Cuba, with few exceptions, were a bad lot of exploiters. Linked with business interests in Cádiz, the governors in Havana set up a system of forcing the Cubans to sell their goods at low prices. The goods were then shipped to Europe and sold at profit. Likewise, high tariffs were imposed on imports bought cheaply in Europe and sold to the colonists at inflated prices. It was a double profit system that benefited a few rich and impoverished the island's inhabitants.

During the 1600s and the 1700s, the island's population dwindled steadily. Living in small villages, surrounded by an unknown environment that often seemed hostile, fearful of foreign attacks, Indians, and black slave rebellion, the hidalgo immigrants developed a society characterized by brutality and corruption. An arm of the state, the Catholic Church dominated their lives, and kept the unruly Indians and blacks in check.

Only Havana flourished. Dirt streets were laid out, shaded with Spanish laurel trees. The baroque masonry of colonial Spain began to rise at the edge of the harbor. An economy developed based on supplying the needs of the galleons, from shipyards to pigs. Spanish soldiers manned the small forts around the harbor entrance. And as the other nations of Europe began to cast envious eyes on Spain's colonies, they looked with interest at Havana first.

In the 1570s and 1580s, England's Queen Elizabeth unleashed her two great corsairs against the Spanish in the Caribbean, John Hawkins and Francis Drake. At twenty-six, handsome, daring, his hair the color of polished copper, Drake possessed military genius, daring, and great skill as a seaman. The Spanish called him "the Dragon." He attacked the Catholic colonies in a series of swift raids that were to stun and terrify the Spaniards and greatly enrich his queen. Offense was his weapon. He struck at the gold-laden galleons, the pearls of Río Hacha, the silver of Potosí, the treasures of Peru, burning and looting with a brilliance and *skill no Spaniard could either match or stop. He sailed around the world in 1577, after leaving Panama in flames. He hit Santo Domingo and Cartagena, off the coast of Venezuela; and he pumped cannon balls into Havana. To Drake, the Spaniards of the Caribbean were not just subjects of Philip II of Spain; they were worse: they were subjects of the Pope, the enemy of the Church of England. The whole confrontation was buoyed by the religious zeal of the combatants—to the Spanish, Drake was not just an Englishman, he was a heretic.*

When the sails of Drake's fleet appeared off Havana, the residents fled in terror. But the Spanish had more than a thousand men-at-arms and hundreds of cannon in the fortifications waiting for him. The English ships sailed in line past the harbor entrance, their wooden hulls blossoming with puffs of white cannon smoke. Masonry chipped; a few Spaniards fell. The Spanish cannon replied, booming. Spouts flashed in the water near the trim English hulls. Then Drake turned his ships back out to sea, sails swelling in the trade wind.

Instead of landing in Cuba, he went on to sack the Spanish fortifications at St. Augustine, Florida. Then he sailed home to England, where he and his cousin Hawkins smashed the Spanish Armada. They returned in 1595 with a great force of twenty-seven warships and 25,000 men. But the Spanish were waiting for them and inflicted heavy losses. Both Hawkins and Drake died of fever and were buried in the Caribbean.

The death of Drake ushered in the era of the buccaneers. They were a race of sea robbers, as tough and ruthless as the world of that time could make them. They were like gypsies, a breed apart, although their native tongues were Spanish, Dutch, Portuguese, English, French and African. Bristling with weapons, the pirates wore trousers dyed with bullock blood. They swathed their heads in gaudy cloths, often braiding their hair in pigtails with colored bits of material to set it off. They pierced their ears to wear gold rings. Before each raid they elected their captains and officers, and drew up articles allotting each man a share of the expected loot.

During this long period of exploitation and weakness, all of Cuba suffered the terror of these stateless pirates.

The Welshman Henry Morgan had no peer for ferocity. Striking out of Port Royal, Jamaica, he made Cuba a frequent target. He sacked and burned Santiago, leaving the hill city in ashes. The church bells were taken to Jamaica. The fortress cannon were placed in the Tower of London on exhibition. And Morgan made off with more than a half-million pounds in gold and silver.

Amid rumors that the governor of Cuba was fitting out a fleet to retaliate, Morgan set out with five hundred men and ten ships to attack Havana. He stopped on the Isle of Pines, off Cuba's west coast, to recruit two hundred more pirates. He learned from an Englishman who had been a prisoner in Havana that the harbor defenses were stronger than he had believed. Realizing that a frontal attack on the city would be senseless, Morgan drew off and hid his ships

166

in Jardines de la Reina— a remote area of rocks and sand. He marched along the undefended coast and fell upon Santa María de Puerto Principe (Camagüey). Before they could give the alarm, the Spanish found the pirates swarming in the streets. Morgan once again took what he wanted and returned home with his riches.

Though the Cubans continued to live in terror of pirate attack, their fear of Morgan was soon to be eliminated. Acting with unorthodox dispatch, the British decided to take Morgan out of the piracy business by knighting him and appointing him deputy governor of Jamaica.

Cuba breathed easier to be rid of Morgan; but they were not to be rid of the British.

In late August of 1761 a flotilla of galleons weighed anchor in Havana harbor and sailed in stately procession along the edge of the city's tree-lined waterfront, Baños de Mar. Walking along the Prado, one would have thought the ships were moving through the city itself. Each galleon was loaded with gold and silver. Nothing seemed out of the ordinary. Nor was it unusual when a month later two more galleons sailed in and sailed out again. Yet of all the factors that converged in the late 1700s to shock Cuba out of its lethargy, these ships and their cargoes were most important.

In Madrid, on the second of November of that year, the British ambassador to Spain announced to his government, "Two ships have arrived with very extraordinary rich cargoes from the West Indies." Spain had been waiting for these riches from their colonies to pay for a war against Great Britain. On the fourth of January, 1762, it was declared. France and Spain faced the English in the Caribbean. It was to be called the Seven Years' War.

Under Admiral George Pocock and Lord Albemarle a British fleet was reinforced off Cape St. Nicholas by units of the West Indies fleet. On the twenty-seventh of May, nineteen ships of the line, plus smaller vessels, with ten thousand British soldiers aboard, set course for Havana. It was already June, and the hurricane season was rapidly approaching. Admiral Pocock took his ships through the old Bahama channel instead of the usual route around the south side of Cuba. This was an extraordinary feat of seamanship in those days of poor surveys.

With good weather the fleet reached Havana in a week.

At the sight of English ships off their homeland, the Cubans brought their guns and powder, their swords and knives, and primed their weapons to fight. To a man, the male population of Havana took up positions in the citadel beside the Spanish soldiers. However much the Cubans hated their own oppressive rulers, they hated still more to be conquered by an alien force.

From the sea, nineteen British ships of the line pounded the thick stone walls incessantly with cannon fire. Ten thousand British soldiers in their scarlet coats

167

and white breeches, bayonets glittering in the sun, formed ranks for the attack. From their positions on shore, the English manhandled heavy artillery into place. Soon the Creoles in the fortress could see the puffs of smoke along the shoreline and then hear the crash of British shells slamming into the fortifications.

On the sixty-seventh day, the exhausted defenders of Morro Castle surrendered. It took the Spanish governor some time to convince his Cuban allies to quit. They had insisted on expending their last ammunition before putting down their arms. Their stubborn resistance, not that of the Spanish soldiery, had held off the British for so long. They hated to give up, even when the red-coated enemy broke through the citadel walls.

Lord Albemarle described their defense of Havana in one word: "Heroic."

Both sides had suffered greatly during the siege, from fever as well as from the battle. The losses of the British were staggering. They had started the siege with 10,000 regulars, 4,000 black machete fighters from Jamaica, 3,000 American colonials and 15,000 sailors. Now only 2,500 serviceable fighting men remained.

By the generous terms of surrender, twenty-eight ships set out from Havana, loaded with nine hundred Spanish soldiers and officers who had survived the defeat and who wished to return to their mother country. The booty was estimated at £736,000. Pocock and Lord Albemarle each took £120,000 back to England. Each of the British foot soldiers, who had done the fighting, received three pounds as his share.

When the British began their rule the Cubans at first offered resistance.

"My lord," pleaded Havana's mayor, "we are Cuban. We cannot be English. Do what you want with our property. Take our lives. But do not demand we swear allegiance to a prince who to us is a foreigner."

The Creole ladies of Havana signed a petition addressed to the Madrid court declaring that the surrender of the city was an act of cowardice on the part of the Spanish governor.

But resistance to the English disappeared as foreign ships sailed into Havana harbor. The Cubans began to know "all the sweets of free trade." During the ten months of British rule, which ended July 6, 1763, nearly a thousand ships sailed past Morro Castle. The Spanish had allowed only six a year.

The Basque trading company which held exclusive rights to Cuba was the first to suffer the inroads of the invaders. In the wreckage of this defunct monopoly, free trade flourished. Havana's shops were full of merchandise. The habaneros found it a delight to stroll to the docks and watch sweating blacks unload the ships. It seemed like a constant fiesta. Crowds wandered the narrow streets, filling the shops. Money circulated. Agriculture on the island came to life. New settlers arrived daily from England. Business boomed as the energetic Cubans took hold of the situation and gleefully watched their efforts produce hard cash and goods.

Cuba might have become, eventually, a dominion of the British Empire, like

Canada, if it had not been for the envy of the planters and the merchants in Barbados and Jamaica. Since the era of Cromwell, they had been fighting to maintain a monopoly in the market for sugar, rum and tobacco. Now they turned green with jealousy watching the Cuban competitor rise on the horizon.

They pressured politicians in England to see that Cuba was returned to Spain once the war ended. When the matter arose in Parliament, William Pitt, the powerful Earl of Chatham, who had advocated the war against Spain, led the opposition. But even his eloquence could not overcome the influence of the Jamaica lobby. England returned Cuba to Spain and took Florida in exchange at the end of the Seven Years' War.

The Cubans watched the British leave with mixed emotions. Although they were alien to the island, the British had ruled wisely in this brief interlude, developing Cuba's trade miraculously. They had put to shame the shabby, corrupt colonial policy of Spain. The Cubans began to look questioningly at the Spanish, as though they too were aliens.

In Madrid, in 1791, Francisco de Arangoy Parreno, one of Cuba's most prominent Creole planters, saw that Cuba was ready to become the sugar bowl of the Caribbean. He went to the Spanish monarchs to plead for the easing of trade restrictions and for the free importation of slaves. He was granted the request. Forests were cleared. Machetes and axes rang incessantly. Fires sent towers of smoke into the clear air. The land, looking oddly naked in the tropical sun, was swarmed over by black slaves planting cane cuttings. Soon the vast sections were covered with cane, rippling silver green in the sun.

Cuba replaced Haiti as the supplier of sugar to Europe and the United States. The island entered upon an era of material advance. Her prosperity further increased as a result of the wars of independence from Spain that were raging elsewhere in Latin America. In the early 1800s, loyalists from the revolting colonies fled to Cuba in the thousands. The abolition of slavery in the British West Indies gave the Cuban planters, for a number of years, an uncontested advantage of a cheap labor supply. Some 400,000 blacks were laboring on the island by 1825.

The great world sugar market now held out almost limitless possibilities to the Cuban planters, and the emergence of "King Sugar" in Cuba brought with it a new class—the hacendados. They were a well-traveled, self-consciously genteel and, by the mid-1800s, extremely prosperous group of planter-aristocrats, who knew they had a good thing going. The world demand for sugar seemed insatiable, and the climate and soil of Cuba was ideally suited to supply it. Their two or three generations of Spanish forebears had paid the price for their wealth. Their lot, by and large, had been a hazardous and miserable one. Now it was time for a flowering of ostentation.

The hacendados were determined to achieve their own Gilded Age. Their

169

estates were princely. The planters assumed elaborate titles like conde *or mar-qués. Great houses were constructed. Courtesans were regularly imported from the United States to provide variety for the local aristocracy. Gambling grew rife.*

One U.S. consul, James Steele, described the emerging upper-class Cuban as "a born dandy . . . Brought up in a slave country, the presumptive, possible or actual heir to a share in some great sugar plantation, the young Cuban imagines that his destiny is to ornament the tropics, to be a thing of beauty, and kill time while he is elegantly occupied."

In many ways Cuba's developing class system took on aspects similar to that of the Confederate States. At the top were the owners, the cattle, sugar and tobacco barons. Together with the lawyers, the merchants and the Spanish bureaucracy in Havana and Santiago, they charted the politics of the island. Next in line were the small landholders, mostly tobacco growers around Havana and Pinar del Río, who managed a meager existence, sharing their profits with a variety of sharecroppers and leaseholders. Then came the overseers and the plantation employees, bookkeepers for the often absent owners. Their peers were the artisans in the towns, carpenters, masons, skilled tradesmen.

To the native-born Cuban, or "Creole," it seemed there was something of himself in this island. He had inherited a homeland, different from his fathers. He liked the mild living, and, left to himself, he had a dislike of fighting. He much preferred to sing, to dance, to eat well, but most of all to laugh. It became a Cuban characteristic to turn away harsh and bitter reality with a joke.

The crimes that occurred were "crimes of passion," and they were few and were usually dealt with by outraged members of the victim's family. In the main, the Creole maintained the strong Spanish characteristic of pundonor—*honor, dignity. Despite the general corruption of Spanish officials, he considered honesty a highly desirable trait, in keeping with his pride of bearing. Inherently optimistic, he loved life and experienced it with an energetic, cheerful outlook.*

But the important thing for Cuba was that the Creoles thought of themselves as Cubans, not Spaniards. The island of Cuba, not Spain, was their homeland. The fuse of independence—albeit the slowest-burning in Latin America—was lit.

CHAPTER SEVENTEEN

HAVANA, JANUARY 19, 1961

In the smoky twilight they came in low over the palm trees and he saw red earth of a farm and green fields with cows grazing and the lights

170

of a truck along Rancho Boyeros Road and then more tall royal palms with their gray trunks glided past and then the lights of the runway coming at him very fast and the plane dipped, swayed, and they landed with a screech of tires. He saw the high fence around the runway as the plane slowed, engines idling, and there were men in their straw hats and women in dresses standing behind the fence watching the plane.

He saw two Cuban soldiers across the runway now, the plane moving toward them, as they stood in their black berets, their blue denim shirts, with the baggy khaki trousers stuffed into their boots, watching the plane approach, their thumbs hooked in the slings of their automatic rifles. They both turned aside, walking slowly and heavily alongside the plane now. One yawned. The other looked up at him as they taxied past. They were both young.

"You'll get used to them," Amato told him.

"Are those Czech guns they're carrying?"

"Some of 'em. That guy's got a NATO rifle. I bought them for 'em."

David looked at Amato quickly. But he was getting up from his seat, picking up his briefcase and raincoat. The other passengers were stirring. They all jolted and grabbed for the seat tops as the plane stopped.

The sleepy-looking militiaman walked up to the passenger ramp as they came out of the hot cabin into the cool evening air. He yawned and removed his thumb from under the leather strap of the gun he wore over his shoulder. He stood watching with heavy eyes as they came down the steps. A few feet away, two guitarists and one playing the maracas, all dressed in bright-orange shirts, were singing in harmony, performing with frantic energy and a robotlike cheerfulness. He followed Amato in the crowd toward the terminal building, the musicians trailing them doggedly. David read the big banner that hung over the door, which translated from Spanish to "WELCOME TO THE FREE TERRITORY OF CUBA."

So now as they drove the asphalt road in the dark, the dim headlights of traffic coming at them, he saw lines of people moving along the dusty shoulder, mostly young men in baggy slacks and dress shirts coming up in the headlights, turning their faces to watch them pass, tan faces, black hair, thin muscular arms protruding from shirt sleeves, a smile here, a wave there. They passed a bony black horse, head down, pulling a cart, slow, lumbering. The driver in an old gray suit coat and wearing a baseball cap sat hunched up on the wagon, leather whip in hand.

To David, it all looked the same as when he had last seen it on a visit to his parents in 1957. They were moving now past rows of two-story stucco houses. Electric lights lit an interior here and there—green walls, a hole in the plaster, a silhouette of a woman leaning on the iron railing of a balcony. He saw men sitting in chairs in narrow doorways. There were crowds of men on the street corners. Children running. The little open bodegas spilled yellow light into the streets. Workingmen sat in the bars talking, holding their bottles of beer. The public buildings were strung with lights like Christmas trees, and everywhere there were banners and posters that proclaimed the slogans of the revolution: "PATRIA O MUERTE!" (Fatherland or Death) and "VENCEREMOS!" (We Shall Overcome) and "MUERTE AL INVASOR!" (Death to the Invader). They drove past a sports arena in heavy traffic, and he saw army trucks in the car park and the caterpillarlike movement of platoons of soldiers marching in close-order drill out on the field. The amber glow of the lights gave the metric motion of the khaki soldiers an unreal quality. Farther on, they passed a carrousel and heard the music and saw children riding on the frozen white horses, and on both sides of the street were the worn stucco buildings he remembered, with men and women sitting on the porches and out on the balconies behind iron railings.

Traffic was heavy. They made slow progress as the streets narrowed. In the dark there was movement all around them, men, women, children, dogs walking along the edges of the streets. Traffic had always been a bit insane in Havana, and this night, to David, it seemed even more so.

They drove through a narrow street built in the era of carriages, dark, deserted, with water glistening on the cobbles, and came out into the broad circular plaza, passing a square green building where two women in black berets and denim shirts, carrying rifles, were standing in the lighted entrance.

Amato turned his head and gestured. "That's G-2 headquarters," he said. "Secret police."

As they emerged with the moving cluster of traffic onto the broad Malecón, as wide as the Champs-Élysées, David saw sandbag emplacements and antiaircraft cannon along the sea wall. Militiamen stood beside the guns watching the traffic pass. Beyond, across the harbor, on the dark bluff where the neon "IRON BEER" sign had once illuminated the night sky, he read in flashing neon letters, "EL AÑO DE EDUCACIÓN," the red glow of the letters reflecting on the shiny black surface of the water. Ahead, along the docks, he could see an enormous Russian freighter, brightly lit, its white funnel, trimmed in red and gold, bearing a red hammer and sickle.

"Jesus Christ," David mumbled.

"Surprise you?"

"I've never seen a Russian ship before."

"Remember, kid, they aren't enemy here. You are."

172

They angled through the traffic now, the driver bluffing his way in front of a big truck, and turned onto Calle Cuba, picking up speed. David read the names of the familiar streets as they passed each corner, Chacón, Tejudillo, Empedrada, O'Reilly, and, looking along the narrow and dimly lighted cross streets, he became excited as though he were coming home.

The taxi eased to a stop in front of the entrance to the Ambos Mundos. Across the street two militiamen who had been sitting in chairs at the entrance of a new building stood up to watch as he got out. "Don't walk around too much at night," Amato told him. "I'll call you in the morning."

David finished his drink at the zinc bar on the roof and went downstairs in the elevator and out into the street. He walked to the harbor and then joined the crowd along the Malecón in promenade. It was a nice night. Ahead he saw waves breaking against the sea wall. There was no wind, but there was a feel of rain in the air and he knew there was a storm somewhere out at sea. The waves came with a rush, bursting over the top of the stone wall, splashing on the concrete walk. Young couples were walking together, holding hands, and short, stocky men in shirt sleeves were strolling with their plump dark-haired wives who spoke in rapid, angry Spanish to their children who scampered about, shouting and laughing.

David could not imagine these people being at war. The whole experience of war seemed ludicrous in Havana. Yet everywhere there were men and women in uniforms carrying weapons. Ahead he saw the anti-aircraft cannon poised with their ugly muzzles pointed to the harbor entrance, looking like giant steel insects.

As he strolled past, two young militiamen, handsome boys in their late teens, stood guard by the sandbagged wall around the guns. They were smoking and chatting with three young girls. The girls were short, pert, black-haired, with thick hips and rumps. They giggled as David walked by. Their faces were fresh and very pretty.

He remembered when the streets had been infested with such girls. Every street corner you passed they stood in pairs, watching you with their dark eyes, making sucking sounds with their lips as you walked by. "You like to fuckie-sucky?" they'd sing at you. And the lean, quick-eyed pimps, who would accost you, ask for a cigarette, and then propose an evening at Mama Pérez' or, if you declined, "You want to see a show— Superman with two girls?" As he walked, he began to remember things that had happened to him here as a boy. He remembered coming from school with Camilo along the Malecón, throwing a baseball back and

173

forth over the cars that zipped by, honking. It was a long throw, and the trick was not to drop the ball. If you dropped it you had to pay the other a dollar. He stopped now, looking across the broad open plaza to the baroque Presidential Palace, which was lit brilliantly with floods. He saw a crowd gathering in front. Soldiers were moving about, setting up the lights. People were coming from the side streets in pairs and groups of four and five, walking toward the crowd. Something was going on. He wondered if he should come back later to find out what. The wind had freshened suddenly and he saw the palm fronds in the little parks across the street stir and flicker in the light.

It was then he realized where he was standing. He glanced at the harbor and then back at the plaza and then out into the center of the wide Malecón. A truck went past. It was there it had happened. Unconsciously, he had walked to it. A jeep and two cars roared past. A horn honked.

He remembered it had happened very quickly, yet it seemed so clear in his memory in a kind of slow motion, the view through the windshield of the old Packard, seeing the rear of the two Fords ahead of them, the flicker of movement out of the corner of his eye, then the sudden shock of the green Ford sedan careening sideways into them, the crunch of metal, the blur as the Packard wheeled around after the impact and then the shocking jolt as the truck slammed into them. He remembered Juan's dark face, mouth open, eyes wide as he struggled with the wheel, and the look in Camilo's eyes; then he was lying on the pavement in the broken glass looking up at the policeman's face and there was blood on his hands and he could not see clearly, as though everything was out of focus. His left eye hurt and he could not feel his right leg. When he touched it, there was no feeling at all. He remembered hearing Camilo crying and screaming that he wanted to see his brother and then they were lifting him and carrying him to the ambulance. He was eleven that year of the accident. He remembered waking up in the hospital frightened because he could not see. After, when they removed the bandages, his right eye was perfect, but there was a blur in the center of what he saw out of his left. It never went away. The heavy cast had remained on his leg for months and itched terribly, and when the doctor cut it off he could not bend the leg from the knee. He remembered that when he looked at his withered leg with the dead yellow skin flaking off and the powdery plaster from the cast covering it, he started to cry. There had been two operations after, and it had been years before he could walk without a limp. He remembered Camilo, looking worried, taking his arm and saying don't worry, he'd get better. He'd look after

174

him. He'd be his arms and legs until he got better. Don't worry. David knew how badly he felt about it, and he loved his younger brother then.

Someone brushed against him. David glanced to the side to see three boys, not more than thirteen or fourteen, wearing black berets of the militia and blue denim shirts, several sizes too large for them. They all carried Czech submachine guns slung over their shoulders. They glanced at David as they passed. He smiled to himself. My God, they're children, he thought. Amato was right. The whole town was armed. But he did not feel threatened by it, nor have any particular apprehension. He felt hungry.

He ate in a little café on the waterfront, sitting at the table near the arched entrance so that he could watch the people promenading. He was the only one in the restaurant. He looked across the empty tables. The place was lit with a single bare electric bulb hanging from the center of the ceiling. A girl of fifteen or sixteen in a cotton dress and a white apron waited on him and took his order back to the old man in the kitchen. A freighter with its running lights ablaze moved into the harbor. The girl brought him the food on white platters, setting it down on the table with the silverware wrapped in a paper napkin. There were beads of sweat on her temples. She avoided looking at him. He finished eating, paid, leaving a peso tip, and started to walk to the Prado, when he heard a series of shouts. He turned to see people gesturing at him. Coming down the street was the old man from the café. He was as thin as a starved horse, gray-haired, with only two yellow teeth showing in his mouth, like fangs. He came running up to David, short of breath, then grinned, showing his yellow teeth.

"Señor," he said, straightening himself as erect as his bent frame would allow. He took David's hand and pointedly, but gently, placed the peso note in his palm. He smiled again, nodded, turned on his heels and walked away.

"What's this?" David asked in Spanish. "I left it for the tip."

The old man turned and gave him a strange look. "No, señor," he replied. "It would be dishonest."

David was tired now, and yet exhilarated. He decided to return to the hotel. Passing through the tunnellike lobby, he was about to go to the elevator when the night clerk gestured to him.

"Señor, a message," he said, handing him a folded slip of paper.

David read the note: "Delighted to hear you're in town. Meet me for a drink at the Floridita bar." It was signed "Raúl Masetti."

David tried to sort through his memory for the name. Masetti had been a friend of his father's in the old days. He could recall some stories.

Perhaps David had met him as a child. He could not place his face, however. He found it strange that Masetti should contact him now.

David pondered his decision. Perhaps he should go to his room. Camilo might contact him at any time. And yet he still felt the nervous excitement of being back in Havana. He remembered the Floridita. It was an easy walk up Obispo Street from here. It would be good to see it again. One drink? Why not?

He went out of the hotel and along the dimly lit street. The Floridita was on a corner. In the old days, it had been open to the street, with tables and the bar in back, but they had rebuilt and made it fancy for the tourists, with a glass door and carpets and leather booths. Inside, he saw only one customer, a man in a blue suit and a white Panama hat, standing at the far end, drinking a daiquiri. The man looked over as David came in. Waiters stood at the entrance to the richly furnished dining room, with its thick green carpet and spotless white linen. A bronze bust of Ernest Hemingway glowered down from a shelf above the end of the bar. David could remember when the place was jammed with tourists and Cubans, four bartenders working rapidly, the blenders humming, the sound of crushing ice. It made him sad to see it deserted.

"I beg your pardon, señor," a voice said beside him.

He turned to see the man in the Panama hat smiling at him with his long angular face. "David Carta?"

"Yes. Señor Masetti?"

"Wonderful. You got my note. May I join you?"

"Certainly."

"Thank you." He settled himself on the stool. He waved his hand. "Two more, Antonio!"

The bartender nodded and began mixing the drinks. David looked at the man, who seemed vaguely familiar.

The angular Spanish face presented an ingratiating smile to him. "You remember me? My name is Raúl. I am an old friend of your stepfather's. We went to the university together . . ."

"Of course. Dr. Masetti."

"You couldn't have been more than thirteen or fourteen when I last saw you. How is Gustavo?"

"I saw him this afternoon. He's fine."

"Excellent. And your mother?"

"The same."

"Such a beautiful woman. I can't tell you how much I miss seeing them."

The blender whirred with the clatter of ice. "When you came in the door, I recognized your face. You look a lot like your mother . . . I

176

mean, your facial structure, the eyes, yes, most of all the eyes. Are you here on business?"

"No, pleasure."

"Ah! There isn't much pleasure in Havana now, as you can see. We are prepared for an invasion. Fidel is sure that Eisenhower will send the Marines before he leaves office. Hence all the guns. It isn't the same city you remember, is it? Such a beautiful city, Havana. They are trying to spread Slavic culture over us like grease." He laughed. "I am afraid the Cuban temperature is too hot for it!"

"And what do you think about what is happening here? Do you think the changes are for the good?"

"The revolution is good, but it's also a pain in the ass, my young friend. Everyone works, that is good, but no one laughs, that's bad. There are no prostitutes on the streets, that's good, but no one has time to fuck, that's bad. Everyone eats, that's good, but what they eat is awful, and that is bad. We live in a complicated world, David."

The bartender, leaning forward and pouring the pale-green drinks into frozen glasses, smiled with them.

"How long will you stay in Havana, David?"

"Only a few days."

"Oh, will you see your brother?"

David stiffened. "No. I don't expect to . . . I've been working rather hard lately. I just wanted to get away for a few days . . ."

Masetti noticed David's discomfort. "You are wondering if I am not the secret police, right? I don't blame you. A virtual stranger comes up to you in a bar, starts asking questions about your family . . ."

David, embarrassed, started to protest.

"No, you're quite right to be suspicious. I am not a policeman, David, let me assure you. I'm in the government, though. I am a director of the Banco Nacional. In the old days—well, you should ask Gustavo about it sometime. We had quite a time, the two of us." Dr. Masetti paused and looked around furtively. Then he leaned toward David and continued softly, "Gustavo and I took care of one of Machado's hatchet men." He made his fist into a gun and imitated the sound of a machine gun. "What a bloodthirsty bastard that one was. He could have given Batista lessons. Come to think of it, he did give Batista lessons."

David relaxed a bit.

"Anyway, my old friend Carta is now in exile in Miami, a rich capitalist; and I am an old revolutionary in Havana. Who can understand these things?"

"Have you seen Camilo?" David asked.

"Yes, as a matter of fact, Camilo told me you were here in Havana,"

Masetti said. "Everybody loves Camilo. He's so full of life. Some of the ones who came out of the Sierra with Fidel have become like stuffed owls with black beards. They take themselves very seriously. Camilo, he still knows how to live. Some of the others are suspicious of him because he still seems to be enjoying himself!"

They sat at the bar and finished the daiquiris and ordered two more.

"You are a scientist, am I right?" Masetti asked.

"Yes," David replied, sipping his new drink. "I'm the one in the family who never was interested in politics."

Masetti smiled. "Even Cuban politics?"

"Especially Cuban politics."

"I was going to take you to hear Fidel speak tonight. But perhaps you would not be interested. It is something to see."

"Tonight?"

"In half an hour," Masetti said. "It is only a short walk from here."

"I'd like to see him," David said.

Masetti smiled. They had been the only customers, but now two men in suits came in, carrying wet umbrellas. They shook them out and told the bartender it was raining. They sat at the far end of the bar and started talking over their drinks.

Masetti watched them for a moment, then changed the subject. He said that his youngest son, Gustavo, named after David's stepfather, had just entered the university. He'd had two other sons, he said. The oldest had been killed by Batista's police in an attack on the Presidential Palace back in 1957. It had been a very foolish assault, he said. They drove up to the palace in a red truck. They rushed the entrance and tried to get up to the top floor, where Batista had his office. They had been sold some bad grenades that failed to go off. They threw the grenades, but they didn't explode. Someone had tipped off the police and the Army. When the kids, his son included, came out of the palace, they had to run across the open plaza and were shot down as they ran. His son was among the first to be killed.

David had been listening intently. "I am sorry," he said.

"Cuban politics," Masetti said, shrugging his shoulders sadly. "You are wise not to be interested."

"I am glad my parents got out," David said.

"You are quite right. Your stepfather believes, as I do, that this should be a Cuban revolution, not a Russian one." Masetti glanced at the two men, then at his watch. "Come, David. It's time for the *concentración* to begin. It's quite an experience to hear Fidel speak."

They finished their drinks and went out. It was drizzling outside, a fine, warm mist. The streets were wet and glistening in the lights. There

178

was no traffic. David felt lightheaded from the alcohol. He became aware of a sound in the air. It could have been the surf, but it had a human quality to it, as though he had parked a long way from the football stadium and could hear the crowd noise in the distance. They turned up their collars and began walking along the narrow streets. There were a lot of people moving in the dark in the same direction. David tried to keep his stride steady. Looking up the street, he could see the dark ranks of the marchers waiting on the corner of the lighted Prado. They held up a banner. Then the head of the column moved out into the street and they all flowed behind into the light so that he could see their heads and faces.

"They're marching down the Prado to the Palace," Dr. Masetti said. "Do you mind the rain?"

"No. Not at all."

He could hear the drums beating and then the bugles and the massed murmur of voices. They were marching out on the side streets and filling the Prado. The laurel trees were wet and shiny in the rain. The arc lights cast shadows on the wet pavement. The mob came with arms linked, filling the broad avenue, moving in a steady stream, chanting and singing and shouting. The massed voices picked up the chant, "*Paredón! Paredón! Paredón!*" as they moved past him, their faces shiny, the rain falling through the street lights in a fine mist.

"You know what they mean?" Masetti said, leaning close to his ear and shouting. "They're saying, 'To the wall!' In Cuba it means to put the traitors against the wall and blow their brains out!" He laughed. "There's been quite a bit of it lately."

The flow of people moved past them, their feet making a strange soft rustle on the pavement. Umbrellas stuck above the heads of the crowd, and David turned to see two women in straw hats dancing, their feet splashing in the water. They started singing, "*Cuba síí . . . Yanqui no! . . . Cuba síí . . . Yanqui, NO!*" Other voices picked up the chant. It had a strange musical quality, hissing and resonating in the rain. They were all chanting now as they walked past. Then David heard a new sound and looked to his left where the flow was coming from, and he saw a double file of young girls carrying a huge Cuban flag. The flag was wet and heavy from the rain. The girls looked very young and wore olive-green uniforms and black berets. They had pretty faces and dark hair. They marched past them singing and chanting in unison, like a girl's choir, "*Muerte al invasor! Muerte al invasor! Muerte al invasor!*" One girl looked at him and smiled and he watched her going off down the street. They had nice voices.

"Come on, hurry!" said Masetti, and they ran across the street to the pedestrian path under the dripping trees. They moved with the crowd. In the street, the *militianos* were marching past. David looked over his shoulder at them. They carried their NATO automatic rifles jutting above their shoulders, strutting in baggy khaki pants and rain-wet blue shirts, long-haired and bearded, their dark faces grim. They moved along the Prado with a *chomp-chomp-chomp,* left-right-left, in rank after rank. They looked tough enough marching in the rain, the broken shadows from the trees fluttering on their faces.

Masetti looked back at him. "All right?"

He nodded and followed.

The street was clogged with people as far as he could see. They were walking very fast now through the crowd.

"They've been coming from the country for the last few days," Masetti said. "Some of them have never seen a city before."

"How do they get here?"

"Buses."

The Palace was brilliant under the floodlights. A speaker's platform had been set up amid the mob that was a solid mass on the steps. In the crowd, David could see only heads and shoulders, stretching out all around him, with more coming from each direction. The rain drifted through the floodlights like fog, falling in faint bright specks, almost in slow motion. Someone bumped him from behind and muttered an apology. They were shoulder to shoulder.

Masetti glanced at him from under his wide-brimmed Panama hat that was dripping water. "He may not show up in this rain," he said. He shrugged. "We're locked in. Sorry."

David craned his neck. He thought of the photographs he'd seen of the disciplined mobs that had turned out in Berlin and the newsreels of Mussolini shaking his fist from a balcony to a sea of faces below him. This crowd cheered and waved banners and sang and chanted; one enormous living mass of humanity spread out over acres of the plaza, with spotlights flashing on their faces, and all the time a fine drizzling rain falling through the lights. He felt their excitement. Each time there was a stir in the crowd, a rush of voices, he lifted his head in response, looking toward the lighted platform expectantly. Their surge of voices chanting, "*Cuba sí! Yanqui NO! Cuba sí! Yanqui NO! CUBA SÍ! YANQUI NO!*" seemed to sweep him away with its raw power.

Despite the rain and the cold, wet feel of his clothes, David felt elated.

There was a stirring down at the platform, and the girl next to him in a dark raincoat stood on her tiptoes, peering over the shoulder of the man in front of her. "Who is it?"

"It's only the President," someone replied.

"The President," he heard echoed through the close-packed humanity around him.

Masetti leaned close to his ear. "Dr. Osvaldo Dorticos. He's brilliant, but not a great orator."

David saw a short, bespectacled, heavy man with a white face and a black moustache on the platform. His voice rang through the loudspeakers, echoing off the buildings. The great crowd applauded his dull speech politely.

"We won't see Fidel," the young girl beside him said. She looked disappointed. "With him speaking, Fidel won't be here. Not when the President is speaking."

Then abruptly, there was an electric stirring in the crowd. They began to cheer. Voices raised the chant: "FIDEL! FIDEL! FIDEL! FIDEL! FIDEL!" It boomed in the night, echoing and reverberating in a roar off the buildings. He could see movement down by the platform. Heads in olive-green caps making their way through the mob. "FIDEL! FIDEL! FIDEL! FIDEL! FIDEL!" roared the great crowd. The young girl beside him jumped and shrieked. Everyone shouted and pushed to get a better view, and then he saw a tall, heavy-shouldered man in a khaki army jacket and a black beret stride into the blinding floodlights on the platform. His face was bearded and he lifted his hand. The mob exploded. Castro's shaggy beard showed very dark in the light. He stood waving and nodding and waving. The crowd howled, the long roar trembling in the half-liquid night air. They were hysterical, David thought. Then he felt a tingling bright rush. There among the half-dozen bearded men in khaki standing behind Fidel was his brother, Camilo. He stood tall and slender in his olive-drab fatigues, his hands folded in front of him, nodding and waving to someone in the crowd below the platform.

"There's Celia Sánchez," said Masetti. "You know about her?"

"No . . ."

Masetti looked at him with a lift of brows. "She was in the Sierra with him . . . he lives with her . . ."

The slight, pretty girl in the uniform of the militia leaned forward beside Fidel Castro and shouted into the microphone, her voice booming sharply through the loudspeakers: "Our maximum leader . . . our beloved FIDEL!"

And again the mob shrieked.

It was a long time before Castro could speak. The roaring of the great crowd kept drowning out his voice as he leaned to the microphone. He smiled and threw back his head and waved, adjusted the microphones, and waved again, and still they roared at the top of their voices, one great massive roaring. The crowd was hysterical. David looked at the girl who was jumping up and down and screaming, tears flooding her eyes, her face lifted in the rain, her mouth opened wide to emit the shriek that was blended with hundreds of thousands like it. His brother was smiling at Celia Sánchez, leaning down to hear what she was saying.

Fidel lifted both hands. David's eardrums ached with the sound that came booming out of the mob, pulsating the air in decibels beyond hearing, like trillions of tiny fluttering blades soaring through the air. "I hope . . ." Fidel's voice came through the loudspeakers. "*Cubanos!* . . ." And the hysteria roared again out of the mob. Castro lifted his bushy brows and stepped back from the microphone and smiled at Camilo, who shrugged and grinned.

"VIVA FIDEL! VIVA FIDEL! VIVA FIDEL!" screamed the mob. Fidel turned back to the microphones, wiped his beard with a quick gesture and leaned down. "I hope this rain won't spoil our celebration," his voice echoed in Spanish through the settling rumble of the crowd.

The crowd roared back: "NOOOOO! We'll stay and be wet! NOOO!"

Fidel smiled. "Then I shall get wet, too!"

He removed his jacket and then tried to speak, but the great crowd roared back at him, "NOOOOO! Put it back on! Put it back on! Put it back on! Put it back on!"

"*Compañeros* . . . I . . ."

But the crowd kept up its chanting roar: "Put it back on! Put it back on! Put it back on!"

Fidel looked around at the men behind him and shrugged. He swung the khaki jacket back over his shoulders.

A great roaring applause. Then a trailing off of voices. Silence. The rain falling heavily now, hissing over the great silent mass of people in the open plaza. The rain dripped from Fidel's beard as he began to speak.

"*Cubanos* . . ." When he warmed up, he began punching his forefingers together frantically. He waved his arms. He shook his fist. He shouted himself hoarse. And still he kept on. His cracking voice boomed out of the loudspeakers and echoed over the heads of the assembled mob, who listened in silence for a long time. Cuba is the new light of the world. A nation once without hope is now the hope of millions of underprivileged people. Our nation is armed and prepared to meet any aggression from the United States. We are ready. We will defend our homeland stone by stone, house by house!

The great mob exploded into a roar.

If there is no attack by the time the new American President takes

182

office, then we will demobilize and return to our creative work. As to Guantánamo, well, we're in no hurry about Guantánamo. It is the United States's headache. Let them worry about it. We will be tranquil and someday we will use that base for a fine university city.

He spoke, sometimes shouting in his hoarse, high-pitched voice, sometimes whispering, but always very emotional, for an hour and a half in the rain, and no one in the crowd moved except to roar approval of what he was saying. And then, abruptly waving, he stepped away from the microphones.

For a moment there was utter silence, only the falling rain. Then the mob shrieked again: "Fidel! Fidel! Fidel!"

Fidel, followed by the young woman and Camilo and the other bearded young men, walked off the platform and went out of sight.

The crowd began to break up.

"Let's get a drink," Masetti said, hunching his shoulders in his coat. "I'm soaked and cold. It is an excellent excuse to drink. Can you think of one better?"

They stood in the shelter of a corner bodega, drinking rum and watching the rain patter down on the cobbles, the lights eddying iridescently across the paving stones and the little pools of water speckled by the rain.

"Well," said Masetti, "what did you think?"

"You were right," David said. "He has magic. Whatever it is that a leader needs, he's got it."

Masetti smiled. "The people love him."

"That's obvious. What's hard for me to take is the hate-Yankees business. You know what I mean?"

Masetti nodded thoughtfully. "Let me put it this way. Fidel knows how to turn a situation to his own ends. He needs a crisis atmosphere. He's tearing down a whole society and rebuilding it. That means a lot of people must work very hard and make great sacrifices. Look at me. Working in the Cuban government used to mean that you came in, got your instructions, collected your bribes and went home. Now it's very hard work, whether you're a bureaucrat or harvesting sugar. So Fidel needs something to keep up the excitement, you understand?"

They finished their drinks. "Can I drop you at the hotel?" asked Masetti.

"No, thanks, I'd rather walk. It's not far."

Masetti paused for a moment. "When you see Gustavo, you will tell him I have not forgotten. That I think of him often."

183

"I will tell him," David said. "I don't know how to thank you. You have been very gracious."

"It was my pleasure."

"I hope there will not be a war," David said. "It would be tragic."

Masetti nodded. "The problem is, there are always many people who benefit from war. Many people. They're not the ones who fight, of course."

David shook his hand.

"Good luck, my young friend. I hope it all goes well for you."

David watched as Masetti disappeared into the darkness.

As Raúl Masetti walked alone on his way home, along Calle Compostela, he was joined by a short man in a dark raincoat.

"Good evening, Señor Ortega," said Dr. Masetti. "Did you attend the *concentración?*"

"No. I've been to the Ambos Mundos," Ortega replied.

"And?"

"Nothing."

At this hour the street was nearly empty. A few cars passed, the tires splashing in the puddles of rainwater. A militiaman stood on the corner ahead, his rifle slung over his shoulder. He was wet from the rain. He watched them as they walked by, his wet hair hanging from under the beret.

When they had crossed the street, Ortega said to him, "What about you? Did he tell you anything?"

"Not directly. But Camilo's up to something."

"Shall I keep an eye on him?"

"On both of them."

"As you wish."

They came to a bodega at the street corner. "I think I shall have a little rum and coffee before I retire. Join me?"

"No," Ortega told him. "I've given up drinking. Bad for the head." He smiled.

They shook hands. Dr. Masetti watched him a moment and then went to the bar.

184

CHAPTER EIGHTEEN

Below were the clouds, white in the sun as far as she could see, and she felt the angle change as the Electra slanted into them, gradually bringing the clouds to eye level, and then they sank into the mist and the sun faded.

Elizabeth's eyes, wide with surprise, were riveted now on the window. "Gustavo, look at this!"

Carta glanced out the window and saw the snowflakes. They looked like billions of tiny feathers swirling across the sky. "That's no little storm," Carta said. "It's a blizzard."

"How do they run a Presidential Inauguration in a snowstorm?" Elizabeth piped, her voice reflecting an edge of nervousness.

"Perhaps they will shift it to Havana."

"That's very funny," Elizabeth said, as the plane lurched again.

The pilot's voice started droning over the intercom.

"Do you think Charles will be at the plane?"

"I'd lay my money on Eden or a driver. Charles is probably still rewriting the Inaugural Address."

For a few moments Elizabeth tried to conjure up the image of her favorite cousin, Charles Danforth, looking, as he always did, tall and tweedy and freshly showered, standing at Jack Kennedy's elbow, exchanging witty aphorisms and position papers on world crises. Even as a child, it had somehow been assumed that it would be Charles, alone among his various brothers and sisters and cousins, who would carry on the family tradition of public service—a tradition that had started with Elizabeth's grandfather. When Charles had left the Foreign Service to teach political science at Harvard, it was assumed in the family that he would return to government in some future, as yet unborn, Administration. And when Jack Kennedy announced Charles's appointment as a special assistant, Elizabeth also recalled how very matter-of-factly the news had been greeted by the elders of her vast family, almost as if it was an obvious and mandatory gesture of the Kennedy clan toward the Danforth clan.

But to Elizabeth, who had always been closest to Charles in the family, the appointment was breathtaking news. She believed in Charles Danforth, and if Jack Kennedy had the wisdom to appoint him, then she also believed in Jack Kennedy. And, given the desperate problems that had overtaken Gustavo Carta, she welcomed some cause for optimism in the new Administration.

When Charles first invited them to be house guests during the Inaugural week, her spirits had soared. To begin with, she always loved a good party; that was her Southern-belle heritage. As a teenager, she had been taken by her father to Hoover's Inauguration, and she still remembered the spirited parties and the charged excitement. Surely the Kennedys, with their propensity for glitter, would try to top whatever went before.

Apart from all that, Elizabeth sensed an almost visceral need to distance herself from the intrigues and harassments that surrounded her life in Miami. She also felt that the Washington trip would bolster Gustavo's flagging spirits. Perhaps he and Charles would have the opportunity to discuss the Cuban mess. Elizabeth had tried to encourage a dialogue of this sort once before, but both had seemed reticent. But Inaugural Week was a great time to break down inhibitions.

As they emerged into the terminal, Elizabeth was startled by the size of the crowd that had come to meet the plane, their bodies pressing in upon the passengers. She and Carta were propelled forward as her eyes searched the hundreds of strange faces for some sign of Charles or his wife, Eden. The reception area was oppressively hot and claustrophobic, and Elizabeth hated the pressure of the bodies behind and around her, the feeling that she was not in control of her movements.

Now it was Eden's voice she heard. "Over here, Elizabeth," Eden called, trying to push her way past a corpulent elderly couple.

Finally she and Elizabeth were together, embracing, and Carta too had joined them. Blond and willowy, Eden managed to look elegant in her black Persian-lamb coat even in the midst of the sweaty throng. She had a thin, fine-boned face, a tall forehead and the regal carriage that bespoke good breeding.

"I won't ask you how the flight was—it must have been a nightmare," Eden said in her high-pitched, melodious voice. "Come along, let's get out of this damn sauna before we melt. I've got a car waiting."

She started walking briskly, Elizabeth and Carta on her heels.

"I've never seen the airport this crowded," Elizabeth said breathlessly as they shoved through the melee.

"We all might as well get used to the crush," Eden said. "That's the way it'll be all week. One big mob scene."

Inside the limousine, Eden sank back and unfastened her coat. As Elizabeth followed suit, she noticed a mist of perspiration on Eden's fine skin as she shook free her blond hair and breathed a sigh of relief. She had always marveled over the fact that Eden, despite her slight build, had such a plump bosom. Charles Danforth, she knew, liked substantial bosoms; she had often kidded him about it. Eden was thirty-two, fifteen years Charles's junior, and had worked as a reporter for the *Washington Post* for several years before her marriage. Like Charles, she was a blue-blood. Her grandmother had been a Boston Cabot, more exalted even than the Danforths. But while Charles enjoyed playing the role of the patrician to the full, Eden's self-appointed role was that of the maverick.

Snow swept past the window, and Elizabeth could see it collecting in patches on the lampposts and on the windows of the passing cars.

"If the snow keeps falling, you might as well forget about getting anywhere unless you want to walk," the chauffeur told them.

"I brought my walking shoes," Elizabeth said. "I had a premonition."

"I don't mind walking, but it's twenty degrees outside," Eden said. "Why don't we stay home and build a big fire and drink brandy and let the Kennedys go to all the parties? There are enough of them in town to fill any ballroom, anyway."

"Can you imagine Elizabeth sitting by a fire while there's a party going on?" Carta said. "She'll hire a helicopter to get through the snow if necessary."

"It's all academic," Eden said. "I have it on good authority that Jack Kennedy and Cardinal Cushing are interceding with the celestial powers to put a stop to the snow at the stroke of midnight. They've got a good sense of drama."

Eden shot a glance over at Carta. "Sorry, Gustavo, I already promised Charley that there would be no religious slurs until after we inaugurate our first Catholic President. It's 'Be Kind to Catholics Week.' "

" 'Only Great Persons are able to do Great Kindnesses,' " Carta said, smiling benignly, but his voice conveying a tinge of sarcasm. "That's Cervantes—*Don Quixote.*"

"And that's one point for your side," Eden replied cheerfully, patting Carta affectionately on the knee.

After arriving at the house, Gustavo and Elizabeth washed and changed their clothes and had just rejoined Eden for cocktails when the telephone rang.

"That's Charles calling to say he's tied up in a meeting," Eden said, picking up the phone.

187

It was indeed Charles' voice on the other end. "I'm sorry, darling, I'm tied up in a meeting. I could be hours. My suggestion is that you go on ahead to the gala. It'll be Frank Sinatra and an all-star cast."

"I hear the traffic is murder," Eden protested. "It'll take us four hours just to get to the hall."

"Maybe you're right," Danforth said. "Look, there are at least two good parties right down the street and you won't have to venture out of Georgetown."

"I won't go to any function unless you can guarantee the presence of at least two Kennedys," Eden said.

There was a pained laugh from Danforth. "OK, Eden, try the Wheelers'. I'll guarantee you two Kennedys at the Wheelers'. Maybe even Jack if you stay late enough. Wheeler went to Choate with Jack. And I can sure as hell guarantee at least two Kennedys at Joe Alsop's, if you want to drop by there. I can also throw in Dean Rusk and John Kenneth Galbraith."

After she had hung up the phone, Eden turned to her guests. "Well, what do you think? The gala or the snobs of Georgetown?"

They all voted for Georgetown.

Elizabeth dressed with leisurely fastidiousness. She emerged in a fitted ivory dress which was draped with a tunic of forest green. Carta looked at her and whistled softly.

"I don't think it looks right," Elizabeth said fretfully, turning to a mirror. "It's all right for Havana, not for Washington."

"You look absolutely ravishing—I don't care whether it's Washington, Havana or Paris.

"I think I should change into something more subdued," she said.

"Don't touch it," Carta protested. Then he clasped the trousers of his tuxedo, bunching up the waistline. "Look at this damn thing," he said. "I've lost weight. It looks like I rented it from a fat uncle."

Elizabeth smiled at him and gave him a hug. "You look fine, Gustavo. Just keep your jacket buttoned." But she grinned at him in such a way that he knew he looked a little ridiculous.

There was a knock on the door and Eden appeared, stunning and impeccable in a gown of black silk that flowed like dark liquid around her as she moved.

"Are we all ready?" she piped.

"Oh, Christ, Eden," Elizabeth said. "Gustavo and I just decided we both looked like hicks from Havana, and now you walk in looking absolutely spectacular."

Eden turned up her nose. "Perhaps it would damage my budding social career to be seen with you."

"No doubt," Carta intoned.

"I'll risk it," Eden said, and led them toward the door. "It's the courage of the New Frontier."

The parties were dazzling. Though Elizabeth at first felt awed by the setting and by the guests, she quickly acclimated herself.

Inside the manicured town houses, their coach lamps and gabled roofs powdered with snow, were the rich and the powerful—the nation's aristocracy, or what passed for it, packed shoulder to shoulder. The hostesses, Elizabeth noted, had planned their guest lists scrupulously. It was as if each party were a gourmet meal, and though the ingredients were dissimilar the recipes were identical. For every four tycoons, mix in a famous academician; for every six congressmen, add one influential columnist; toss in a movie star for every two homely dowagers.

Though it all seemed a bit calculated, Elizabeth found it great fun. She had almost forgotten the mesmerizing vitality projected by Washington's powerful men—that perverse energy of the supremely egotistical. And she had almost forgotten, too, about the smug competitiveness of their expensive women.

Having been away from Washington for several years, she was surprised how many people she still knew, and how many still knew her. There was the garrulous and inebriated old Southern Senator who regaled her with stories about her father. And the sequined wife of an industrialist who had attended one of the more lavish Carta functions in Havana several years earlier, and who spoke glowingly about it. It was as if Elizabeth were swept up in her own party—a party with rich intimations of the past. At each party there were rampant rumors that Jack Kennedy was about to arrive, but he never did, and that Robert Frost or John Steinbeck or even Frank Sinatra was in their midst, but Elizabeth, craning her neck, couldn't spot any of them. She didn't miss them. There were enough recognizable faces around to fill a dozen albums. Every once in a while she would look over to see how Gustavo was faring, but she could rarely find him amid the sea of tuxedos and evening gowns. Once she glimpsed him standing alone by the bar, and that disturbed her, but then she was swept up in another conversation and he disappeared from her view.

It was the New Frontiersmen who bothered him the most. Carta tried to analyze it as he stood by himself near the bar at one of the parties. They came in all shapes and sizes, these Kennedy people, but it was as if each was securely encapsulated in his own thin film of arrogance. He could sense that in the way they addressed each other and especially in

189

their manner toward "outsiders." There was no problem they could not instantly diagnose, no imponderable that would obstruct the onslaught of the New Frontier.

Carta struggled to be sociable and to mask his impatience. But there were so many self-anointed luminaries basking in the glow of their own egos that he found himself put off. A senator would ask him a question about Castro, and Carta would be framing his response when a newly appointed Cabinet member would step into the circle and everyone would be drawn to him as to a magnet, and the Senator's eyes turned away, as if Carta had vanished. Carta noticed, too, that despite the impressive intellectual credentials of the guests it was gossip that dominated the conversation.

Secretary of State Rusk, it was said, had already antagonized most of his senior staff, and JFK was telling aides he should have appointed Senator Fulbright as he originally desired. Adlai Stevenson, the insiders had it, was deemed too softheaded by the Kennedy people and would be emasculated in the new Administration, as would Chester Bowles, who had committed the ridiculous faux pas of espousing recognition of Red China. The Administration hadn't even taken office yet, Carta sensed, and the bodies were already being tossed from the precipice.

And so Carta succumbed to the role of the observer, standing alone near the bar, scrutinizing the beautiful women, examining their cleavages and listening to the fragments of gossip from those clustered nearby. The Kennedy stories were most in demand.

"Did you hear," one society matron confided, "that JFK had an absolute temper tantrum yesterday after taking a final inspection tour of the White House living quarters? First he got mad because all the carpets were chewed up by Ike's golf cleats. Then he shouted at the staff to send Ike's furniture back to Sears, Roebuck because they were all second-rate reproductions."

"He's just scared Jackie will go on one of her buying sprees," another voice put in.

It was a young White House aide who breathlessly told how Mayor Daley of Chicago had been invited by Kennedy to be the first visitor to receive an official tour of the White House. When the young aide complained that Daley was planning to show up with all six of his children, the President-elect snapped, "The sonofabitch delivered Illinois, didn't he? He can bring the whole fucking Boy Scout troop!"

The stories were all faintly amusing to Carta, but he felt strangely distanced from it all. Though he had spent a great deal of time in Washington, he now felt like a foreigner who was observing the "rites of passage" of a country that was not his own and whose customs he no

190

longer understood. Carta tried to shake his mood with an infusion of scotch, but that only served to depress him all the more. He saw Elizabeth glancing over at him now and then, and tried to smile at her and to indicate he was having a good time. He did not want her pity. That would only make it worse. He really wanted to be left alone in the crowd, to remain the outsider looking in. That was all he required for the moment.

It was shortly after 2 A.M. when Elizabeth and Eden threaded their way over to Carta, finally deciding to retire from the social scene. As they trudged the half block to the Danforth house, the snow was still falling and the walks were treacherously slippery. The Danforth house beckoned like a warm cocoon. Elizabeth and Eden leaned on his arms as they made their way toward the glow from the house that outlined the little ridges of slush and ice in their path.

"What did you think of it all, Gustavo?" Eden said as they came into the shelter of the doorway. "Wasn't it fascinating?"

"Yes," Gustavo replied. "Extraordinary, really. One can imagine what London must have been like the night of Queen Victoria's coronation. Or Rome, in the days of the Caesars. It's the center of the known world, and these are the people who will run it. Fascinating."

"What a lovely country we have," said Elizabeth.

"Let's go have a drink," said Eden. "My feet are soaked. Are yours?"

They followed her into the enveloping warmth of the house.

CHAPTER NINETEEN

HAVANA, JANUARY 19, 1961

Lying in his room in the dark, David could hear the rain. He felt depressed. He had never liked being alone in hotel rooms. The shutters in the corner of the room, in front of the bed, were open and he could see the lights of the dark monolith of La Cabaña across the harbor. He yawned. The rain splashed on the balcony. He swung his feet off the bed onto the cold tile floor and walked through the dark into the bathroom, urinated, and pulled the chain. He heard the crash of water cascading from the overhead water closet, and then flopped onto the bed. The image of his brother on the platform kept lingering in his mind. Jesus, when will the bastard call me? he wondered.

Down below on the street he heard the *clop-clop-clop* of a horse and cart, passing on the cobbles. He yawned again. It was as if he were in a different city, and not in Havana. He knew every street, every bodega, every bar for blocks, and yet he felt he was a stranger.

The huge mob at the Presidential Palace in the rain had dispelled the secure feeling he had felt earlier. He had an unpleasant feeling that powerful forces were at work beyond his or anyone's control, they were making changes that would alter Cuba forever; the Cuba he had known and so well loved. The huge provocative posters with their militant messages, the Russian ships in the harbor, the Russian dancers he had seen on the television in the bar upstairs before going out seemed unpleasantly foreign in the tropical night. He remembered how sad he had been when his mother had suggested he leave Havana to enter prep school in New England. They argued about it. She did not want him to lose his heritage, she said. He was becoming too Cuban. He remembered the voyage to New York and how big and strange the skyline of tall buildings seemed to him when the ship came into the harbor. He had been thirteen and he really knew only Cuba, and the contrast made him feel like a foreigner in his own country. He felt that way about Havana now.

He wanted to put these unsettling thoughts out of his mind. He began to think about all that had happened to him since he left Havana that year.

At first he'd been terribly homesick, but then after the first two weeks it began to change. He liked the calm academic atmosphere of Exeter, with its green lawns and maples and elms. He liked speaking English; he even liked the music played on the radios in the dorm. After class, those early-autumn days, he would wander across the campus and along forest paths nearby, absolutely benumbed by the golden-brown glow of the countryside and the windy cold of late October and early November that blew the branches bare, his nostrils tingling with the crispness of the air and the aroma of burning leaves. It was to David like discovering some distant magical kingdom when the curtain of gold suddenly turned brilliant white with the first snow. David loved the seasons and loved winter most of all. And quite without knowing it, he became a part of it all and it was his country.

Rather than bring him back to the humid heat of the Cuban summer, his mother arranged through her cousin, Charles Danforth, for David to remain in New England during the summer to work as a boat boy at the Edgartown Yacht Club in Martha's Vineyard, where Danforth maintained a spacious summer home. David was quickly captivated by the Vineyard's vibrant salty air, the multicolored sailboats tossing in the rough and unpredictable Atlantic currents, the sweeping beaches with their high grassy dunes. And then there were the girls, blond and willowy, whose skin seemed almost translucent in the moonlight as they sat around the bonfire devouring steamed clams and beer, and who later, sated finally with food and drink, tasted fresh and salty as they nestled against David in the late-evening chill. They were so different from the Cuban girls with their dark hair and dark eyes and olive skin and strict Spanish manners. So much more open and free with themselves. He remembered the first time he slipped his hand inside a blouse and felt soft flesh cupped in his fingers, how delicate and strange and exciting it had been. It was the girls he had liked best of all.

David recalled one evening when his mother was visiting the Danforths on Martha's Vineyard and he had come back very late from a party. She was sitting alone on the porch steps as David came up the front path, weaving unsteadily. His mother smiled at him when she saw him, then laughed as she noticed his half-unzipped fly and salt-encrusted jeans, but despite his embarrassment they sat together for a long time and talked with a frankness they had not before experienced. He told her then how happy he was, how curiously at home he felt in New England. He told her that he loved and respected his stepfather but knew that Carta loved his own son, Cam, far more. He had accepted that fact. But now Carta too must learn to accept the fact that David wanted to make his own life and that that life would be in the U.S., not Havana.

Elizabeth listened quietly as David talked, and when he was finished she leaned over and kissed him on the cheek. It was a maternal kiss, and yet it expressed a depth of affection that David had not sensed before. They sat silently for a time, listening to the sound of the crickets and of the water lapping softly against the shore. The evening breeze shifted so that it carried not only the salty smell from the harbor but also the fishy aroma of broiling lobsters from the restaurant down the street. A party was breaking up at the yacht club nearby, and jovial voices could be heard exchanging drunken jokes and goodbyes.

Then suddenly Elizabeth started to talk to David. She talked about the early times in her marriage when she had felt like a prisoner in the Carta kingdom and yearned for the comforting womb of her parents' home in South Carolina. She too had felt like a stranger for many years, and perhaps that feeling had never fully disappeared. Yet she had come to realize that her life in Havana possessed a joy and gaiety and freedom that she had never experienced in the South during her girlhood. Her husband made her feel like a woman as no other man had ever done, she told David, and though three or four times a year she needed to escape the almost suffocating opulence of her life in Havana, she always was thrilled to return—and, indeed, David too would one day feel the same sense of "coming home" to Cuba.

She had been right. Yet each year, David found some other reason to cut short his stay in Havana and return to New England before summer was over. Finally, he stopped going to Cuba entirely. After nearly three full summers at the Danforths', David's fascination with the ocean had taken firm hold. He started working summers at the Woods Hole Oceanographic Institute on Cape Cod. And after Exeter there were the four years at Yale, followed by graduate work, first in San Diego, California, then in France, and finally his master's from the University of Miami. And though he still returned to Havana for holidays once or twice a year, David's life steadily, ineluctably, shifted farther and farther away from Cuba.

The phone had rung three or four times before he realized it. He opened his eyes. Darkness. For a moment he wasn't sure where he was, and then he heard a horn honking. He looked out the open shutters, saw the dimly lit tile roof across the street. There was a light on in one of the windows. He groaned and stretched his body. The phone rang again, a short, sharp *cling!* He got up and went barefoot to the desk and picked up the receiver.

"Señor?"

"Yeah?"

"Your taxi is here, señor."

"I didn't order a taxi."

"It's here."

David yawned and shook his head. "But . . ."

"The driver said he would wait, señor."

Camilo's image flashed through his mind. "Sure, OK. I'll be right down."

When he stepped out of the elevator, the clerk behind the desk gestured toward a tall black man standing just outside the entrance, his back turned to them. He seemed to be watching something up the street. David saw the profile of his flat Negro face, the back of his neck crisscrossed with rolls of muscle, like a weight lifter's.

The head with its kinky black hair turned, and two cold brown eyes appraised him. "Camilo sent me," he said thickly, in a low voice.

"Why didn't he come himself?"

"You're being watched. Come on, we'll lose them." The big black face

194

broke into a line of teeth, the eyes brightened. "Don't look so worried. I'll get you to Camilo. No problem."

As they turned onto the Malecón, swerving through the oncoming headlights, David saw the lights of a car swing in behind them. The black man glanced at the rear-view mirror and picked up speed. They veered around a truck, then cut right, crossing in front of two honking cars. The expression on the driver's face never changed. His fine, fighter's hands made quick, smoothly coordinated movements on the steering wheel, swinging the car easily and expertly through the maze of taillights ahead of them. But when David looked back over his shoulder, he saw the lights of the trailing car behind them.

"I see him," the driver said in his soft accented Negro voice.

He turned the wheel quickly and they swept left, into the path of an oncoming van looming huge, headlights brilliant, and then they were past and hurtling up a narrow street. The walls of the buildings were so close on either side David could have reached out and touched them. Two men on bicycles appeared ahead and both careened into the wall as the car flashed past. They came out on a broader avenue and turned right again into the traffic. Behind them the headlights of the pursuing car appeared. Whoever was in it was one hell of a driver, David thought.

They made an abrupt left turn, tires shrieking, and were speeding up an alley. A man and a woman looked startled in the headlights' glare, and they both went flat against the wall. The car rushed past them. David looked back and saw the headlights of the car turn in behind them. Jesus, he thought, we're in trouble. Again they turned right, with such speed and so quickly David had to grab for the door handle to keep from being thrown into the driver. Ahead he saw a horse and cart, then a blur as they swung hard left and plunged into an alley, moving fast.

When he looked over at the driver, he thought he saw him smile. But, with another abrupt turn, he saw only the wall of a building, the front fender inches from smashing. Then they were moving at high speed down a slanted street, dark doorways flashing by, and at the bottom they squealed dizzyingly left, then right again, the rear end swaying, and stopped.

Before the headlights went out, David saw they were staring into a stone wall. A cat looked up from its toilet, eyes glowing; then darkness. The wall next to his door was so close he could not open it. It had been one hell of a piece of driving.

For a full minute the driver sat silent. Then David heard his voice, speaking in the same mellow tones. "When I back out . . . you get out. Walk down the alley, you will come to a square . . ."

"What was all that about?"

"Secret police. Their cars are falling apart. Never keep up."

"You do that often?"

"No more than I have to. Last time, they blew a tire. They don't know cars, those bastards. No good. They can't drive." He started the engine and backed out of the narrow space. He backed the car around and braked. "OK, you get out here." He gestured. "One block, you come to a park."

"Great, then what?"

"You want to see Camilo, don't you? He told me to drop you off here. You walk to the park, OK? I got to get the hell out of here. OK?"

"What do I owe you?"

David saw the quick smile on the dark face. "All taken care of." His soft Negro voice laughed. "Hell, I should pay you for the fun!"

David got out and watched the big car move off slowly, its headlights out, and turn into the street. He went onto the narrow curb and walked down the hill. The buildings were close and dark on either side. He heard a dog bark. He came out at the little park. A path led off into the darkness. David stopped and sucked in his breath. He felt a catch in his throat and realized he was as scared as hell. His eyes flicked across the park, looking for someone hidden behind a tree. He saw nothing.

He started walking again. It's all right, he told himself. Just keep your nerve. Camilo must be in a lot of hot water, he told himself. Amato hinted at it in the taxi. Just keep calm and don't lose your nerve and we'll follow this out to the end. Cut out the bullshit, he said to himself. You're getting into something way over your head. You ought to turn around and get the hell out of here! Out of this damned stupid country. What the hell are you letting yourself get involved for?

A black hooded shape loomed in front of him. David drew a quick breath. Then he heard a soft woman's voice say, "Señor?" and he saw the nun's habit.

"Sorry to startle you. You are David Carta?"

"Who else would be dumb enough to be here at this time of night?"

"Please follow me," and she glided stealthily toward a parked car.

David tried to catch up with her. The nun opened the rear door. A driver slouching in the front seat straightened himself and started the engine.

"You remember Havana?" the nun asked.

"I guess so."

"We are going to Vedado."

David instinctively checked the rear window. There was nothing behind them. The man at the wheel was driving carefully, avoiding the dramatics of the previous ride. David sat back, waiting for someone to say something to him, but the nun stared ahead impassively.

David looked at her face in the flickering light. Under the white border of the hood he could discern a pert, pale, almost childlike face with a small upturned nose. Her delicate upper lip was drawn upward so that her mouth, poised half open, gave the impression of a charming squirrel. It was, in its imperfection, quite beautiful. She glanced at him sideways, her eyes luminous, their expression quite calm.

"You do this sort of thing often?" he asked.

A quarter of an hour later, the car stopped at the gaping black entrance to an alley. Without a word, she gestured him out and, as the car pulled away, led him into the darkness.

The alleyway was not paved, and David stepped into a puddle. Water sloshed in his shoe as he followed the nun, who walked with a whispering of silk on silk.

"Be careful," she said, without turning to him. "There is a ditch there."

At the end of the alley David could now make out the figure of an enormous black man, who stood silently awaiting them.

"We are here, Paco," the nun said.

The black man turned and walked down the alley toward a truck. The lights from the street shone behind it.

"Get in," the nun said.

David saw a man in a khaki uniform standing at the front of the truck. The truck bed was housed under gray-green canvas. The black man helped the nun into the back.

"May I ask where we are going?" David said.

"To Camilo," the nun said quietly.

"Sure, but where?"

The black man grinned. "La Playa!"

David climbed into the back of the truck. There were wooden benches on either side. The nun looked like a black shadow in the corner. He sat down opposite her. She looked at him, but her face in the dim light showed no expression. The truck backed out of the alley into the street. The nun stood, hunched so that her head would clear the canvas, staggered to the open back of the truck and pulled the canvas flaps down. He heard her coming back and could see a dark shape as she sat opposite him.

"Why all this secrecy?"

"Your brother has enemies."

The wooden bench was uncomfortable. David tried several positions and decided to stretch out and try to sleep. The truck jogged and bounced. He could hear traffic around them. Lifting his head, he could see through the swaying slit in the canvas the headlights of cars passing. He folded his hands behind his head and looked into the darkness.

The sounds of the truck took on a hollow echoing. They were in the tunnel under Havana harbor, heading east. He felt in his shirt pocket for his cigarets, took out the pack and lit one. He saw the nun's pale face and her eyes in the flare of the waxed match. She sat staring at him, the glow flickering on her face. The hollow roaring of the tunnel stopped abruptly and he looked back through the slit in the canvas to see the lighted entrance of the tunnel receding in the dark. They were on a smooth paved road. No traffic. He looked at the green glow of his watch. Two-thirty.

He moved down the bench and lifted the canvas flap and looked out. He could see a lighted villa on the hill behind them. The floodlights cast a glow into the dark sky. He watched it until it went out of sight.

"It is the villa Fidel took," the nun's voice said. "He rarely stays there. He spends most of his time in Vedado at the apartment of Celia Sánchez."

Campfires along the beach winked bright as sparks. They were quite far away. "What are the campfires?"

"Militia. They have dug trenches and places for the big guns all along the beach."

He sat watching the lights appear and flow away behind them. Then darkness. Then another string of campfires. Then darkness. He moved back to the corner by the cab and leaned against it, stretching out his legs on the bench. "You're a friend of my brother's."

"Yes."

"How are you called?"

"My name is Josefina, but I am called Pepita."

"Pepita?"

"Yes."

"How long have you known Camilo?"

"Several years. He was married to my sister, Alicia. Did you know Alicia?"

"I never met her."

"She was very beautiful."

"I've seen photographs."

"And Elena? Do you know Elena?"

"No. I've never seen her. Only photographs our mother has. How old is she now, five?"

"She will be six in April."

"And you're Alicia's sister."

"Yes."

"I was very sorry to hear of her death."

"She was tortured by Batista's police."

"I didn't know. I only heard she had died in the general strike before Batista fell."

"They tortured her two nights and one day before they killed her. Her body was found in the garbage dump. She had been taken by Masferrer and his Tigers . . . he is in Miami now, yes?"

"I don't know."

"I think so. I think he is living in Miami. Someone should kill him. Why do they let a man like that live in the United States?"

"I'm afraid I can't answer that."

"Yes?"

She fell silent. David crushed out his cigaret and leaned back in the jarring of the truck and closed his eyes.

The truck slowed suddenly, and he came out of his stupor and sat up and looked at his watch. It was 4:35 A.M.

"I think we're here," the nun said to him in the darkness. "Did you sleep?"

"I think so."

The truck turned left and stopped. He heard voices in Spanish. The driver put the truck into gear. They began to move again. He went to the canvas flap and opened it. He saw a jeep and the stone caretaker's house. There were four rebel soldiers with rifles standing around the stone house. A fifth soldier was closing the iron gate. Their bearded faces were outlined by the red taillights of the truck. The truck was moving down a stone-paved road. He looked at the gray trunks of the palm trees on either side of the road. They seemed to flow past in the afterglow of the headlights and fade away into the darkness. He could see the radiant haze of the Milky Way above the dark shapes of the palm fronds.

"Wait a minute . . ."

"What is it?"

"I know where we are!"

The truck picked up speed and went very fast, the engine and transmission whining, and then slowed sharply and turned left. David held to the back of the bench to keep from being thrown off. He heard the driver shift gears and the crack and swish of brush and leaves scraping against the canvas. They drove slowly, thumping heavily into ruts,

199

bouncing out and, with a shift of gears, moving slowly ahead. Then stopped.

The nun came back to stand beside him. He could hear the surf. The air smelled of the sea.

The driver stood below them, smiling. "You go in the house." He gestured toward the stone house that showed in the headlights.

David got down and helped the nun. She felt very strong and light.

"Thank you, señor."

They looked around. The stone house stood dark against the night sky. The shutters had been taken off the windows and the doors and were piled in the wild tangle of vines and leaves at the edge of the stone patio.

"You said you knew this place?"

"I used to come here as a boy. My stepfather . . ."

"You go in the house." The driver gestured.

Together they walked across the patio onto the veranda that went around the side of the house. He could hear the tall palms rustling in the breeze. A quarter moon hung over the dark sea, casting a glittering reflection on the surface. The surf glistened into the light and boomed on the sand. It was a big surf. The night air was warm and pleasant and carried the scent of jasmine and the fresh iodine-salt smell of the ocean.

"We used to spend summers here when we were kids."

"It's lovely," she said.

The French doors were open onto the veranda. David stepped into the house. Inside, it smelled musty. He felt for the box of matches in his pocket and lit one, cupping it in his hand against the little breeze. He crossed to the refectory table, lifted the glass chimney on one of the kerosene lamps and lit it.

When he turned with the lantern in his hand, he saw her eyes widen in the yellow glow. She looked across the room. David turned.

"Hello, David . . ."

"Camilo?"

Camilo smiled and bowed. "Forgive the dramatics, but I just arrived myself. I was about to light the fire." He came toward them and took the nun's hand and kissed her cheek. "I am glad you could come, Pepita."

"It's been so long since we were here as kids, Camilo. It's as beautiful as I remembered."

They embraced. David looked at his brother's high-cheekboned, bearded face in the light of the kerosene lantern. The expression in Camilo's pale-blue eyes was one of amusement. He smiled. "It's good to see you, David. You look wonderful."

"So do you."

200

"I have brought supplies. Everything we shall need for a holiday." He turned and gestured at the boxes on the floor. "You still drink vodka?"

"Occasionally."

"I have some good Polish vodka."

He turned and walked toward the boxes. David glanced at the nun, but could not see her face because of the hood. She was looking at Camilo. He heard the truck start up and back out of the yard.

"Why did you bring us way out here?"

Camilo was bending over one of the boxes, selecting a bottle. He stood with the vodka bottle in his hand, and his face broke into a smile. "I wanted to get acquainted with you again. Havana is impossible. I thought it might be fun . . ." He gestured at the room.

David smiled. "How about that drink?"

They sat on the floor in the bare room and David stared into the fire, watching the quick flames dissolving the pile of twigs Camilo had gathered. The heat was intense against his face, and the fire snapped briskly, spitting sparks onto the floor at his feet. The twigs emitted a pungent smoke.

"What kind of wood is that?" he asked his brother. "Smell it?"

"Spanish laurel. It grows out in the back. Smells good, doesn't it?"

They were drinking vodka in white porcelain coffee mugs, and Camilo shook his cup in his hand, clinking the ice he had chipped from the block wrapped in a gunnysack in one of the boxes. He raised the mug, looking at David. "*Salud*, David. It is good to see you."

"Good to see you," said David, and they drank. The fire flared in the twigs that were turning rapidly into ashy coals, and David studied his brother's face in the light. He looked older than he remembered; perhaps it was the beard, David thought. The fire flickered on his forehead, his cheeks and nose, the gleam catching his eyes. His eyes slid slowly sideways and looked at David, his mouth stirring into a smile in the hairy mass of his face. David looked away from his face at his heavy shoulders in the khaki military shirt he wore, at his delicate brown hands, the fingers thin and tapered like a musician's, at his long legs in the baggy khaki trousers and his muddy paratrooper boots, and then back to his bearded face. His face looked grizzled and tired for a man of only twenty-five, but his eyes were alive, like little flashes of blue, the fire twinkling in the corners.

"It's been a very strange day," David said to him. "I saw you during Fidel's speech."

"Ah, then you were there! What did you think of Fidel?"

"Hypnotic."

"Yes, hypnotic is the word, He's a very special man, Fidel. He holds this country together now by the force of his own will. He has vision, that man. If he told me tomorrow we were going to storm hell itself, I'd put on an asbestos suit." The lips stirred again into a slow smile. "Were you surprised to see me?"

"Actually, I felt quite proud."

Camilo laughed and slapped his shoulder. He turned to Pepita, who sat on the other side of him at the edge of the firelight, her face half hidden by the cowl of her hood. "What do you think of him, Pepita?" David saw her shy smile. Camilo looked back at him. "He's no Marxist, but he's a damn good brother. Did I fuck you up, asking you to come over here?"

"Mm-huh. I'm in the process of putting together an expedition to the Humboldt Current."

"I've heard all about it. There are seven of you, right? All marine biologists. The government of Peru has commissioned you to make this study for their fishing industry?"

"How the hell . . . ?"

Camilo raised a slender finger, his thick brows lifting. "In Cuba, we know everything!" His teeth showed in the firelight. "Surprised you, huh?" He drank. "I asked Amato."

David saw that Pepita had fastened her eyes on Camilo. Her expression was one of adoration, and he thought, Good Lord, she's in love with him! She saw him looking at her, smiled, blushed and stared down at her black-robed knees. A nun in love with Camilo? David pictured her vaguely in his mind in the act of intercourse, dimly intertwined with his brother's body, and realized that the tension he felt between them was real. I wonder how they make that work? He heard Camilo's voice and saw his head turned toward her now and he was speaking in rapid Spanish, his voice soft, gentle, almost loving. ". . . we were nearly killed," he was saying to her, and David realized he was telling her about the auto accident on the Malecón, and his mind slid away from Camilo's voice to center on the face of the nun as she listened to Camilo's story; her eyes were amber slivers in the firelight that gleamed along the curve of her nose and forehead and brightened the arc of her spotless white cowl. Her eyes blinked and blinked again, the lashes long, dark, curved upward, and he thought she must have been a lovely child, for she still had about her that innocent, delicate air of a half-grown girl. Sitting on her legs, one arm bracing against the floor, the small white fingers splayed in the shifting light, the other hand a pale spot on her black shapeless lap, she looked to David like an image out of one of those old Flemish masterpieces, existing in the engulfing darkness only because of

202

the uncertain firelight. As he watched, her lips formed a kind of word-less expression of sympathy, and he saw her eyes dart to him and then back to Camilo. He thought of his parents. What would they say if they could see this? The childlike nun in her black robes and cowl; Camilo rough, lanky, bearded, in his khaki soldier's uniform and mud-caked boots, framed by the plaster walls and the vaulted ceiling and the tile floor on which the light eddied and flickered. David was drawn to them, compellingly, with an affection that surprised him.

". . . even judging him as generously as possible, they had to admit he was drunk. He was always drunk." Camilo gave him a look out of the corner of his eye. "Juan? You remember our chauffeur?" He turned his head back to the nun. "You could smell it on him in the mornings—you know, that dead-rum smell drunks have?"

"What happened to him?" she asked, glancing at David.

Looking away, Camilo said, "Oh, our mother made Papa fire him, of course. It was too bad. He was a good man, even drunk, and he had a large family he supported. I suppose it was the reason Papa never got rid of him, but after the accident there was no choice. But I still think he saved our lives. If he hadn't turned just as that car came at us . . ." Camilo made a sound in his throat. "It would have been the end of us, eh, David? How is your eye, by the way?"

"The same."

"Still blind?"

Suddenly self-conscious, David adjusted his glasses and nodded. "I can see around the edge somewhat, but it's blurred." He shut his eye in demonstration. All he saw now through the damaged eye was a dark blotch where Camilo had been and the firelight like a prism on the periphery of his vision. He opened his eye and saw Camilo and the nun studying his face gravely. Camilo said something he didn't hear.

"What?"

"You should have seen him, Pepita. Would you think that he once could not walk without a steel brace and a crutch? At twelve, a cripple. At twenty, he was the swimming champion at Yale! It's true! He did it! Didn't you, *chico?*"

David felt himself blush and he avoided her stare. "He exaggerates."

Camilo leaned close to him, his eyes bright with amusement. "I do not exaggerate! Do I, Pepita?" Turning his head, he looked from one to the other, comically, expectantly; David could smell Camilo now, the per-meating aroma of cigars, cedar, wet wool and sweat that reminded him suddenly of his stepfather's smell. "How?" said Camilo. "How do I ex-aggerate?"

David ignored his exclamation. "I placed second in a couple of hundred-meter races, that's all." He gave them a shy smile and shook his head. "Camilo was the athlete in the family," he said to her. "He did everything better than I did—didn't you?"

Camilo pulled a long cigar from his pocket, lighting it with a match, puffing smoke from the corner of his mouth. He shook out the match and tossed it into the dwindling fire. He adjusted his legs and canted his head to Pepita. "We both exaggerate—a little." As if rationalizing his laugh, Camilo reached for the vodka bottle. He poured into the cup David held out and then into his own.

"What about her? Doesn't she get any?"

"Pepita?" Camilo swung around, holding the bottle out to her. She gave him a wrinkled nose. "No? You don't want to drink with us? Come on, try a little. Can't hurt you. No?" Turning back to David, he shrugged. "She doesn't drink vodka."

"Have you ever tried it?" David asked.

She shook her head. "No."

"It is forecast to rain tomorrow," Camilo said, draining his cup. "Nothing serious. Like today. Good clean rain. We can swim and fish, if you like?"

"I like," said David and he emptied his cup. He felt good.

"Drink to that!" Camilo poured into his cup and then into David's. He saw that the bottle was almost empty. They had drunk a lot.

"Is there more?"

"Plenty. If we run out, I will send to Havana for more."

"We can always get rum in the village."

"True, but you know what's happened to me? Rum makes me mean. No, truly, *chico.* I get ugly. Can't help it. I want to break things. I commence to fight. With anybody. It's like I have this bomb in me that triggers on rum!"

David grinned. "Since when did you start blaming rum?"

"No, *chico,* sincerely. It affects me. The last two years, awful! Rum is a bastard. I am a bastard when I drink it." He laughed. "I must be getting loaded. . . . I want to sing. What shall we sing?"

" '*Lembraste mina . . . nenia,*' " sang David.

"Ah ha!" Camilo continued in his bass voice: " '*. . . de aquela noite de vran?*' "

" '*Ti contabas as estrelas!*' "

" '*Tieu . . . as herbinas do chan!*' "

They continued together in harmony:

> "Do you remember, my lass. . . .
> That night in . . . summer?

You . . . counted the stars . . .
And I the blades of grass!"

Pepita looked at them, puzzled. "What a strange language."

"Very old," Camilo said. "My grandfather's song. Papa taught it to us." He looked quickly at David. "Remember, *chico?*" He looked back at Pepita. "I think it is Spanish."

"Yes, and Portuguese," she said. "Maybe Catalonian."

"What it is," said David, "is basic dirty."

They fell to laughing. The nun looked from one to the other, suppressing a smile. "You are brothers," she said. "You do not look alike, but you are brothers."

"Yes," said Camilo, his eyes growing warm as he looked at David. "Yes . . ."

"That's true," said David. He held out his cup, and Camilo emptied the bottle into it.

"Brother sacrificing self for brother . . ." Camilo held the bottle upside down and shook it. A couple of drops sparkled and fell into his cup.

"We need another bottle." David stood. He felt unsteady. He wanted to act practical. He did not wish to show how drunk he was before Camilo did. "Which box contains the good ones?"

"Over there . . . see?"

"I see it." David made his way unsteadily to the box and took out a bottle and opened it.

Camilo held out his cup, and David poured. "You want to take a swim?"

David blinked his eyes. The vodka and the failing firelight inhibited his vision, and he saw his brother's face dimly, distorted. He glanced at the nun and back to his brother and realized that Camilo was going about it cautiously. He was going to ask something of David, but he was too Cuban, too polite, to come right out with it. First he had to know that his brother was still with him. David closed his eyes. He remembered how Camilo, as a boy, could be so marvelously ingratiating when he wanted something, so studied in his methods of persuasion. And also how harsh and even cruel he could be when he felt you had let him down—how violently he could lash out.

Camilo was leaning toward him, studying his face. He said, "Are you all right?"

"I feel great. You really want to swim?"

"Why not?"

"Aren't there sharks out there at night?"

"Sure."

"Sharks can eat you, you know?"

"Sure."

"I don't give a damn. If you want to swim in shark-infested waters at night, who am I to spoil the fun?" David knew he was drunk. He didn't care.

Pepita stirred. "I don't think you should go, either of you."

"Don't worry. Sharks are not attracted by the smell of alcohol."

"See. He's the expert. He knows about the feeding habits of every variety of shark in the ocean. If he says it is safe to swim, it is safe to swim. Right, *chico?*"

"That's right."

"You are both drunk."

"It would be a shame if we were not."

Camilo stood up. He pulled his khaki shirt out of his trousers. "Naked we came from the sea . . . naked we shall return to it."

"That's right."

Pepita followed as they went out onto the veranda. The moon poised above the surface of the sea on the horizon. A pattern of clouds shaped its lower edge. In the light, she saw the brothers as silver limbs and torsos, laughing and shouting at each other as they went off down the steps. She was frightened for them. Looking at the low moon, she knew it would soon be totally dark out there.

In the silvery light, she saw their naked figures running across the sand and David, then Camilo dive into the cresting surf that curled and boomed on the beach. Their heads bobbed to the surface in the glitter of the moon. Someone yelled, Camilo or David, she couldn't tell. She saw them swimming, their heads and shoulders lifting as the wave came, and disappearing behind it. Then they were swimming again. She lost sight of them. She was too frightened to watch. The vodka bottle was standing on the veranda wall, David's glasses beside it. She picked them up and went back into the house. As she went through the door she heard one of them whoop, and she looked back but could not see them in the dark water. She did not want to look.

Camilo had stacked wood against the corner of the coral rock fireplace. She felt cold and sleepy. She threw the dried twigs onto the fire. The flames licked through the tangled pile, snapping brightly. She sat crosslegged in front of the fire, feeling its heat on her face. Her back felt cold. She yawned and turned her back to the fire.

After what seemed an endless wait, she heard their voices, shouting at each other. Then laughter. She heard them running. They were racing up the beach. Then she looked up from the embers of the fire to see that the gray light of dawn had given the open doors shape, the shaggy palmettos and tangled vines around the veranda were dissolving out of the darkness. A mockingbird was singing in the top of a palm tree. She felt a sense of relief. She had hardly realized how tightly she had been holding herself since she saw them go into the water. A little morning breeze rustled in the palms. She got up stiffly from the hearth as Camilo, his tall, muscular body shiny-wet, burst through the open French doors.

He wheeled, dripping onto the floor, pointed, shouting, "Ahhhhh! Beat you!"

David burst in the door, breathless and laughing. She looked from one to the other. They seemed to have forgotten her. Camilo was two inches taller, but David was heavier of build, more solid in chest and shoulders and legs. In the firelight their naked skin glistened. They were both short of breath and in high spirits, laughing.

"You lose . . . you get towels!" Camilo roared.

"Where?"

"That box!"

David bent down. She looked at the curve of his naked buttocks, the dark glob of his genitals appearing suddenly between his spread thighs; she watched amazed—the image of him, phantom-like, ghostly, yet solid flesh in the ashen light, enchanted her. She felt her face flush. A hand flashed, the towel appearing, unfolding white in the air. Camilo's arm leaped and the towel dangled from his hand. In one fluid motion he snapped it at David. It cracked against his bare flesh. David straightened quickly, a look of pain and surprise on his face that broke into a mischievous grin, comical as he lifted his brows high, nearsighted eyes squinting, his mouth screwed up in a menacing grimace.

"You son of a bitch!" He swung around and snapped his towel at Camilo.

"Ahhhhh . . . sport!" Camilo circled him, winding his towel slowly, menacingly. "I'll clip thy *testículos*," he said.

"Not if I get yours first, bastard."

The towels flashed, snapping viciously. The two men leaped in opposite directions, laughing. They circled each other warily, passing from the gray light to darkness and back into the light again. Their naked bodies seemed terrible and beautiful to her. Camilo's skin was darker. David's pale flesh was marked with suntan from the throat to his face and from his white biceps to his wrists. Camilo's body was all smooth olive-tan. Her gaze took in their intense faces, Camilo's bearded, David's clean-shaven, squarer of chin and jaw. His chest was hairless. Camilo's was a black fur that tapered to his navel and spread in a fuzzy black mass to where his penis jiggled dark and thick between his muscular thighs. She looked at David's groin and saw the little cloud of pale-blond hair and the stubby phallus bouncing loosely as he moved. Water dripped from their bodies, and they left wet footprints on the tile.

"Would anyone care for a drink?"

As though aware of her for the first time, both men turned to look at her. She stood by the orange coals of the fire in her dark robes. She looked at Camilo and lifted her brows, holding the bottle out to him. "Not that you need it, either of you."

Camilo took the bottle, his hand encircling it, and buried it in his mouth, his neck muscles and Adam's apple working as he drank, bubbles rising in the bottle. He lowered it with a sigh, wiped his mouth and handed it to David, who had been standing watching him with his mouth pursed as though he was going to blow a bubble. "Goddamn, you're going to feel that!"

Camilo couldn't speak, his head arched forward, his fist at his lips, eyes watering. Finally he smiled. "I can keep going forever!" Turning quickly, he gestured.

David slipped the bottle into his lips, but kept the liquid from flowing by the pressure of his tongue and teeth. He gulped as though swallowing and then lowered it with a sigh. Camilo watched him suspiciously.

"Yankee bastard, you faked it!"

"What do you mean, Yankee bastard?"

"Drink! God damn it, *chico,* drink!"

David drank, holding the bottle tipped above his head, the liquor heating his belly rapidly. He felt his gut lurch, suppressed it, and took the bottle away.

Camilo's face was satisfied. The thin morning light played along the left side of his hairy face, his eyes peering out of the dark hollows as David held it out to him. "Better," he said. He swayed as he brought the bottle up to his mouth, steadied himself, and drank until the clear liquid disappeared from the bottle.

Tears sprang into his eyes, and he looked at Pepita now with a bleary gaze. He held out the bottle. She took it from him gently.

"Are you all right, Camilo?"

"Absolutely," he said, and coughed. He cocked his head, looking at David askance. "You know I hate Yankee bastards, but I love you, you *chico* fucker!" Camilo threw his arm around David's shoulder, hugging him. "Look at him, Pepita—my brother! My flesh and blood! I send for him, he drops everything, drops his life and comes to me! Only a brother will do that for you, eh? Only my brother." He scrubbed David's head

208

with the knuckles of his closed fist. He looked unsteadily around at Pepita and grinned. "I'm drunk. Forget it, *chico,* I love you . . . the hell with all the rest of them! What do you say, eh?"

Gazing beyond him, David caught Pepita's eye. She moved to Camilo and took his arm. Her face crinkled into a benign expression of devotion. "Time to sleep, Comandante. Enough for one night. Shall we?"

"Pepita," he grunted. "Sweet, sweet Pepita. God bless you, woman. Yes, yes, I am drunk, time to sleep it off." He hugged both of them. David was nestled in the wet, male warmth of his brother's arm. "My apology, *chico.* I am drunk. You see? Very drunk. Stupid when I get drunk. Very stupid. Hey, Davy, you love me, still?"

"Sure I love you, Cam."

Camilo stared slowly around to Pepita. "She loves me, too. What do you think? Lightning going to strike us? Huh?" He grinned sheepishly, a little boy suddenly, shy and repentant. "You think it's dangerous to take God's bride away from him, *chico?*"

"Forget it, go to bed."

"Yes, come," said Pepita. She urged him toward the stairs. They passed from the light streaming in the door to the darkness at the foot of the stairway. Camilo made soft noises as she led him, his arm engulfing her. Only her hood showed above his thick biceps. David watched them mounting the stairs, swaying unsteadily, moving up one step at a time. He had grown cold and wanted to crawl into some warmth somewhere and sleep.

Halfway up, Camilo lurched around. Supporting his weight on the banister, he peered down at David, gesturing with his free hand. "Your old room . . . you remember, David?"

"Yes, I remember, Cam."

Cam's face slackened. He made a sound in his throat. He turned back and let Pepita lead him on up into the darkness, her robes sliding softly over each step.

David yawned. The sky was glowing with the morning radiance. The sun would be coming soon. He would have liked to stay up and see it rise, as he had done so often here as a child, but his weariness was out of control. He could hardly keep his eyes open. He picked up his glasses from the hearth and put them on.

As he went up the stairs, holding the railing, he found himself too drunk and tried to think about the night's events. He decided, as he went down the blackness of the hallway, his hand sliding along the wall for guidance, he would worry about it in the morning.

At eight-thirty the next morning Gustavo and Elizabeth emerged from the Danforth house to find the air frosty but the skies clear. "Eden was right about Cardinal Cushing fixing the weather," Elizabeth remarked as they climbed into their limousine. The Danforths' maid appeared at the door with a thermos full of hot coffee which she handed to Elizabeth, who thanked her profusely.

It had been five years since Elizabeth and Gustavo had been to Washington and some twenty-seven years since they had met there, Carta as a young student and Elizabeth as a congressional assistant and eligible postdebutante. Sipping coffee and steeped in their own reveries and reminiscences, they rode mainly in silence as the limousine drifted through the cold, still-empty streets. Occasionally, one would tap the other's arm and point out a restaurant or bookstore or art gallery that evoked a memory. Elizabeth asked the chauffeur to make a short detour to ride by an obscure little French restaurant, Le Cellier, where Gustavo had taken her for their first dinner together, the night after Charles Danforth had introduced them.

The morning was dazzling with winter sun, patches of snow here and there on the streets, and the skeletons of trees throwing intricate shadows on the walks. Elizabeth had forgotten how attached she was to this city, how much she missed not being a part of it all. Moments of her life here as a girl flashed on her memory. She missed the tolling of the bells of the Washington Cathedral, the imposing broad boulevards with their great shade trees, the sweeping vistas in the hazy summer heat from L'Enfant's splendid circles, the quiet backways around Georgetown, the terraced lawns and rose gardens of the big ivy-covered mansions near Dumbarton Oaks, the dogwood and honeysuckle along the hills in Rock Creek Park, the great public edifices of government—those monumental and vaguely forbidding nests of bureaucracy. It all still held a magic for her. She looked over to Carta, who was lost in his own ruminations. She wondered what he was thinking, whether he too was remembering their early times together, much simpler they were, how wondrously playful and uninvolved. She wondered if he too felt the burden of sadness—an undefinable weight. No, it wasn't all that undefinable, she thought. She feared for her sons—feared for David, who was somewhere in the unfamiliar maelstrom of Havana, enmeshed in a situation he was unequipped to deal with; feared for Camilo, whose plans and emotions were cloaked in mystery, inaccessible even to those he loved and who loved him. No, she would say nothing about all this to Gustavo.

He had burdens of his own. She would not weigh him down with her own apprehensions.

As the limousine moved closer to the site of the Inaugural festivities, rolling past the columned public buildings, Elizabeth and Carta could feel a heightened stir of activity. Snow plows rumbled along the streets, clearing away the slush. Workers were hooking their tow trucks to automobiles that had been stranded or abandoned during the massive traffic jam of the previous night. At the Lincoln Memorial, a diligent crew of workers were washing away the mud and slush while others appeared to be spraying something on the lawn. Carta asked the driver to slow the car so they could see.

"It's green dye," Elizabeth said, her tone incredulous. "Can you believe that, Gustavo? They're actually painting the lawn green."

"They want it to look like spring," Gustavo replied, watching the workmen. "It's more befitting the dawning of a New Frontier, you see?"

Elizabeth shook her head. "I wonder who thought that one up."

"I am beginning to be impressed," said Gustavo, with a cynical smile. "These Kennedy people think of everything."

Everywhere they drove, special precautions were in evidence. Secret Service men were battening down manhole covers to forestall any would-be prankster or terrorist. An occasional police officer could be seen staring from a rooftop, ever vigilant. Helicopters hovered overhead, looking for potential troublemakers. Workers were even splashing the trees with a repellant to keep the noisy starlings away.

"Would you admit to the feeling that the people in charge don't want anything to go wrong?" Carta said with a grin as he drained the last of his coffee.

"I would say that should be recorded as one of the first great understatements of the new Administration," Elizabeth responded.

The limousine got back to the house just in time for them to change and set forth again, this time with Charles and Eden Danforth. Charles, looking buoyant and handsome in his dark suit and heavy overcoat, his freshly shaved face puffy with weariness, eagerly related all the horror stories of the night before. Half of the National Symphony had gotten stuck in snowdrifts and never made it to the Inaugural concert. Not even soloist Mischa Elman managed to penetrate the traffic jam. As for Frank Sinatra's star-studded gala, the Democrats were happy that they had collected the ticket money in advance, because, though the concert started two hours late, two thousand of the six thousand people who had bought tickets never got to the hall.

"Did Jackie show?" Eden asked.

"Resplendent in a white gown of silk ottoman," Danforth reported.

211

"You don't have to be so damned admiring," she said, pouting.

The traffic had slowed now, barely moving, bumper to bumper along the street, so they decided to walk the last several blocks. The broad sidewalks were packed with people bundled up in fur coats and carrying blankets, steam puffing from their ruddy faces, all of them walking briskly toward the Inauguration stands. It was like a crowd heading for a sporting event, except for the crackling tension in the air. The faces of the crowd were extraordinarily variegated. Silver-haired, heavy-jowled congressmen walked beside tourists in porkpie hats. Matrons in mink coats strolled next to college kids toting picnic lunches. The parade of humanity took on the aura of a bizarre carnival. And the aroma from the roasting chestnuts being sold by sidewalk vendors gave the air a Christmasy tang.

As they neared the Capitol Plaza, they could see thousands of people standing there, waiting excitedly for the ceremonies to begin. The Inaugural platform itself was situated on the steps of the Capitol's East Portico, backed by eight white Corinthian columns matching those of the Capitol itself. The columns seemed to glitter in the now brilliant sunshine as the flags whipped in the cold wind.

The Danforth seats were excellent, as befitted a presidential assistant, but it was still a neck-craning process to see the faces around the podium. The platform was now filling up with the great and the near-great. Elizabeth caught a quick view of a beaming Joe Kennedy, looking very much the part of the national patriarch. The other Kennedys, arrayed around him, jut-jawed and outdoorsy-looking, reminded Elizabeth of a proud family who might be attending a kid brother's graduation from a riding academy. Elizabeth looked over at Eisenhower, wrapped in his muffler, pink-cheeked and jowly, seeming to sag in his chair like an aged balloon slowly being deflated. Sprinkled around the stands were the faces of the new Kennedy men, lean, hungry-eyed, fiercely resolute. Their well-groomed wives, Elizabeth thought, looked far less self-confident, indeed almost apprehensive, as if they were wondering what sort of arena they were being tossed into. Carta felt Elizabeth's hand crawl into his as Marian Anderson started singing "The Star-Spangled Banner" in her rich, velvety voice.

Despite the meticulous planning, the ceremony kept bogging down in awkward moments. Eden broke into giggles when, as Cardinal Cushing was delivering what seemed like an interminable invocation, smoke started pouring in a steady stream from the lectern as if the Devil himself were delivering an instant rebuttal. Aides swarmed about the lectern, searching out the short-circuited wires, while the Cardinal stood in elegant repose, quite unruffled by it all. Then Gustavo, seated next to

Elizabeth, her arm hooked in his, feeling slightly cold and cramped, saw Robert Frost's white head appear at the distant lectern. His stomach churned with embarrassment for the great poet, for although he looked like a figure from Mount Rushmore, he couldn't manage to struggle through his notes in the wind and the glare. The sea of faces beneath him crackled with subdued laughter as first the Vice-President, Lyndon Johnson, then the President-elect himself tried to coach him through.

Elizabeth stirred, and there was an electric tension in the whole mob as they saw Kennedy rise and, looking young and suntanned in his dark suit, take the oath of office, his lips moving, his voice echoing an instant later from the loudspeakers. Gustavo had heard the voice before, during the campaign, but he could not help reacting to its tone, its compelling confidence. As Kennedy began his address, it seemed to Gustavo Carta that the excitement of the last two days coalesced in the figure of this square-jawed young man, as though all light and energy flowed into him, into his youth, his gestures, his handsome face. He looked around at the rows and rows of people, acres of heads and shoulders, black hats and brown mufflers, stitches of yellow and white amid a mosaic of gray, all listening to that voice echoing and ringing in the magnification of the loudspeakers, steam drifting from lips, smoke rising above hats, all in intense concentration, listening, an occasional cough, a scattering of applause building into a crescendo, enthusiasm, excitement, expectation. It seized him, caught him in its vortex, and he had that strange feeling that he was swept up in a moment, living through it, experiencing it, feeling the iron-cold air, the wintry sun, the frosty bite of the wind, and looking at the distant figure of a vital young man who as he now raised his hand, flashbulbs popping below him, would become a photograph in a history book, indelible. So enraptured by his own reactions that he hardly heard the words Kennedy spoke, Carta turned to Elizabeth and saw a glistening of tears in the corners of her eyes. She gave him a faint smile, not of joy, nor of sadness, but moved, deeply moved by what she was witnessing. He looked back at the figure of Kennedy, flanked by rows of dark suits, muted grays and browns of dresses and hats, small at this distance, but radiating an energy that affected him, moved him too, and he heard echoing from the loudspeaker system: ". . . to those nations who would make themselves our adversary . . . we offer not a pledge, but a request . . . that both sides begin anew a quest for peace . . . before the dark powers of destruction engulf all humanity in planned or accidental self-destruction . . ." Carta felt a twinge of alarm, his mind skimming over the image of a bearded Fidel listening intently to those phrases. Were they aimed at Cuba? Was Kennedy backing off his campaign pledges of support for the Cuban exiles and trying to make a peace with Fidel? What was it he said, both sides begin anew the quest for peace? Disturbed, Carta tried to grasp the nuances of the statement, his mind not hearing the new words being intoned, struggling to fasten on the importance of what the new President had just said in relation to Cuba and his own circumstances, and he realized as he had the night before at the parties, amid all the gaily dressed men and women, the excitement and enthusiasm, that these people were blind to him, to the realities of Cuba; oceans removed from the concerns he and all Cubans in exile had. Really, Gustavo, you must see the broader picture, what is Cuba compared with our concerns over Russia, Europe, the Middle East, Africa, the Far East, Laos and Vietnam, you see? You are such a small island, insignificant really in the context of all Latin America. Castro? The United States can brush him aside any moment it chooses to do so. He's simply not a factor in world affairs.

Carta felt a sudden depression, a sadness of isolation; they had succeeded in making him feel his own impotence, his insignificance in the panorama of world power and politics. What the hell was Cuba to these people? A tiny island that produces sugar, rum, whores and the cha-cha-cha! A small people, a ridiculous people, always shouting and waving their arms in impotent gestures of outrage. He smarted under his realization of the viewpoint these Americans held of his country and his people. They were so smugly superior, yet so pervasively powerful they could dismiss all that he and others had risked their lives for, with no more concern than as if they refused dessert after gorging themselves at dinner.

His dark mood lingered through the rest of the speech, leaving him broodingly silent as they walked back along the crowded streets in the chill winter sun to the limousine. Elizabeth recognized his pensiveness and hugged his arm, chatting cheerily with the Danforths, who walked briskly along, linked arm in arm in their winter coats, ears and noses pink from the cold, their eyes bright with excitement.

BOCA DE JARACO, CUBA, JANUARY 20, 1961

David came down the stairs and found that someone had cleared away the empty bottles and cleaned the ashes out of the fireplace. The tile floor had been mopped, and their clothes were folded neatly on one of the boxes. The block of ice had been replaced. Set neatly around the edges of the ice, beneath a wet gunnysack, he saw the little gold caps of bottled beer. He lifted one out and found the opener, and then went

214

out the door onto the veranda. The stones were hot under his bare feet. He went to the wall and sat down in the shade. Opening the beer, feeling the bottle cold in his hand, he glanced around. The sunlight glittered on the water. When he looked at the sand, it was so bright it hurt his eyes. But the air smelled fresh and cool. The trade wind stirred against his shoulders, cooling him. It seemed unreal that he was here again.

"Good morning!"

Following the sound of her voice, he saw her above him on the balcony. She had on Camilo's khaki shirt, and the angle of his vision gave him a view through the rusted iron grille. He saw her white-skinned legs and thighs, her shoulders and face, leaning over the rail, her black hair stirring in the breeze. He tried to focus on her face. Her hair was cut short like a boy's, and the wind blew it.

"How did you sleep?"

"I think I'm still drunk."

"Go back to bed. Camilo's sleeping."

"What time is it?"

She reacted to his stare by placing a hand over the shirttail to hold it in place against her legs. "It's only ten-fifteen," she said. "Why don't you go back to bed? You should sleep."

"I think I'll go for a swim. Want to go?"

"I'll wait for Camilo." She seemed very shy and he saw the wind tugging at the shirttail, flapping it against her hand, and he saw she was naked. He wondered if they had made love during the night. David sensed that she read his thought, for she stepped back slightly from the iron grille, still holding the shirt in place with her hand.

David looked down at the stones of the veranda and pretended to adjust his glasses.

"Would you like me to make you some coffee?" he heard her say to him. "There is some in one of the boxes."

"No, thanks. I think I'll swim first."

He walked down the stone steps, the sand hot and gritty under his feet, and then ran down to the beach. The sand was burning hot in the sun. At the edge of the water, in the cool of the wet sand, he took off his pants, carefully wrapped his glasses in them and set them down where the surf could not reach, and then waded into the cold water. The shallow surf came boiling toward him and slapped over his ankles, and he felt the tug around his knees as it went out again. Ahead, the next breaker was rising. He waded out into it and let it bump against him, lifting him slightly. The water felt cold. He heard it crash on the beach behind him. He looked back over his shoulder and saw her still standing on the balcony watching him. From here she looked very small. He saw her wave her hand. He felt suddenly happy. He waved back to her and turned to dive.

He stroked under the water with his eyes closed. He looked up and saw the bottle-green surface bright from the sun and swam up, breaking into the fresh air. He blew out his breath and treaded water, looking around. The white beach went off in either direction, east and west, for a quarter of a mile and then disappeared in clusters of green coconut palms. To his right he saw the reef. It went out from the eastern point for two miles. He remembered it from the times he had been swimming here as a boy. He and Camilo used to race to it. The reef had always been an agonizing challenge for David because Camilo had been a stronger swimmer even though he was younger, and it humiliated him when he lost.

He swam toward it automatically, pushing himself against the imaginary competition of his brother. The water warmed as he swam. The swells came at him gently, lifting him like a cork and then lowering him into the trough. He stopped once to catch his breath, his muscles aching from the effort, and looked back to see the house, across the clear, sparkling water, looking smaller in the cluster of palm trees.

What's this all about? he thought. Why did he bring me out here? Why here, to this house? Why now?

When the swell lifted him this time he saw a naked Camilo coming from the house. David waved and shouted to him. Camilo dived into the surge of the surf. He vanished. David turned to look at the reef. He had a half mile left to swim. He did not want to spoil it now by competing with his brother, so he began swimming. The residual lethargy of the night's heavy drinking lifted from him and he felt his strength return with a rush of joy. The last hundred yards he put his face down in the water and forced his muscles to work.

His knee bumped the sandy bottom and he stopped, breathing hard, and staggered to his feet, water dripping from his hair into his eyes. He saw the splash of Camilo swimming toward him, with his face down in the water, his long powerful arms working steadily, his rhythm smooth and undiminished. David sat down in the ankle-deep water that was warm as a bath. The sun was hot on his wet shoulders. He felt a tickling along his legs and looked down to see tiny fish darting at the hairs. He moved his legs. The fish darted away. Over the distant green jungle hills he saw a cluster of vultures circling. At this distance they looked like flies. His shoulders and upper arms were drying quickly in the hot sun. The water lapped gently against him, so clear he could pick out the individual grains of white sand and the tiny bits of white shells, magnified by the water, and he saw the tiny pompano working at the floating hairs above his wrist and felt them touch, as gently as flowers, then dart away in a tiny glitter of silver.

Camilo came very fast and then lifted his dripping head out of the water and stood up, sloshing along the reef toward him, smiling, very tall and lean and brown in the sun. His shoulders were large and powerful and his chest muscles were as fully developed as a weight lifter's. There was not an ounce of fat on him. He was rubbing the salt water out of his beard when he came to David, casting his shadow across him.

"I thought you were going to wait for me so we could race."

"I figured I'd beat you anyway. So I decided not to spoil your morning. How do you feel?"

"Incredible!"

Camilo sat down beside him in the water, leaned his head back, closing his eyes against the glare of the sun. "I heard you talking to Pepita. I kept thinking about how it would be to swim out here with you. My God, my head hurts. Yours?"

"Better now."

"Ah, here comes Pepita. Can you see that far?"

"I've got one good eye. I can see fine."

She looked very tiny in the open water. As he watched, she stopped swimming and tossed her head. He could see the faint splashes from the water coming off her hair. Then she turned and began to swim again, very slowly, deliberately.

"You never saw Alicia, did you?"

"Only photographs."

"Pepita is much like her, Davy. Her voice is the same. The way she walks. The way she smiles. Alicia." Camilo drew a deep breath and let it out very slowly. "She is in love with me and that makes many complications . . ."

"Are you in love with her?"

Camilo lowered his eyes and shifted his feet in the water, his face expressing a deep sadness, a flaring of hopelessness that unnerved David. "I could be," he said gently. "I am not sure my feeling for her is not the revival of something that died with Alicia . . ." The expression changed, as quickly as it had appeared. Camilo lifted his chin and wiped his beard with his dripping hand, staring off at the swimming girl. "Before I left Mexico with Fidel, I had a bad quarrel with Alicia. She took the baby and flew back to Havana to stay with Mother and Father. All the time we were in the Sierra, I wrote to her as often as I could. She never answered. She died with the quarrel still between us. I have never loved a woman the way I did Alicia. She was not only beautiful, but brave. I have had a hard time forgiving her for dying."

"Pepita said Batista's police killed her . . . is that true?"

Camilo turned his head. He was watching Pepita swimming toward them again. "Yes . . . it's true."

David saw her head in the water about fifty yards away now. She was treading water and looking toward them. "Cam, I didn't tell you, but I was followed by a car when we left the hotel last night. The driver lost it, but it was touch and go for a while. He said something about it being the secret police. I don't know how important it is to you, but I thought I should mention it. Are you in trouble?"

"Yes."

"Is it because of what you did for Father?"

Camilo opened his eyes and nodded. His eyes closed again. David waited for him to speak. After a silence, he said, "How are they?"

"Mother and Father? They're all right. You know that someone tried to kill him last Monday."

Camilo did not stir or open his eyes.

"They drove by the house in two cars, the way I got the story. A lot of shots were fired. Mother was in the living room with a bunch of bigwigs from Miami. . . ."

Camilo turned his head, his intense blue eyes looking straight at David.

David went on, "No one was hurt, but it shook them up pretty good."

Camilo listened in silence. "Did any of the shots come close to Mother?"

"I don't think so. She was pretty reluctant to give the details. All she said was that she was scared to death they'd killed Gustavo."

He heard Camilo sigh. "Why can't he leave politics to younger men?"

"I don't think Gustavo thinks of himself as being very old. What is he this year, forty-nine, fifty?"

"He's too old. The world's changed and he doesn't know it. It takes young men now. You know how old Fidel is? Thirty-two. We're all young. How old is Kennedy? Forty-one, two? Papa's crazy to be involved in this thing. He had his time, against Machado. He should stay out of it."

"From what Amato tells me, he's in it up to his ass."

"Our father is the most dangerous type of old man because he thinks he is young. He thinks he's a reformer, that he stands for the poor man. He has no understanding of social change. He thinks you will set things straight by taking a little bit from this rich man and giving a little bit to that poor one. That is not the way you change society. It is not a matter of giving a little and taking a little. Cuba needs a whole new social order, not a little giving and taking."

218

"You know I'm not political, Cam. But aren't there people in Cuba who respect Father?"

Camilo glowered. "Too many. Too many people for his own good."

"You think someone will make another attempt on his life?"

"Possibly. He has many enemies. It makes it dangerous for both of them. He's made it very dangerous for me now." Camilo looked off and gestured. "Ah, here comes Pepita . . . see?"

"Before she gets here," said David, "you want to tell me why you brought me over?"

Camilo's jaw worked beneath his beard. His lips were pressed tight together. "I want you to take my daughter back to Miami."

"Elena?"

"I want you to take her back to Mother. OK?"

"Sure. But I don't understand."

"I think very soon now they will decide to kill me."

WASHINGTON, D.C., JANUARY 20, 1961

It was nine o'clock by the time they reached the Danforth home, and they were all stamping their feet and exercising their arms to shake off the frost. The maid served a light supper, and Danforth opened a bottle of champagne.

After supper, however, Elizabeth announced that she was exhausted and intended to go right to bed, and Eden said she wasn't even sure she could make it up the stairs.

Carta looked over at Danforth and noticed that his face seemed aglow with energy and exhilaration.

"Are you good for a nightcap, Gustavo?" Danforth asked, and Carta, though bone-tired, tried to muster up some enthusiasm and assented as cheerfully as possible. They strolled into the oak-paneled den and Charles took out the Courvoisier.

"Well, you and I have seen a lot of history today, my friend," Danforth said as he picked out two delicately contoured brandy snifters.

"I overheard a young couple talking on the street. The girl was cold and plaintive and was saying to her boy friend, 'I don't know why we're here.' So he answered, 'We're here so we can tell our grandchildren.' "

Danforth smiled and handed a snifter to his guest. "Do you remember Carlyle's old bromide, Gustavo? 'The history of the world is but the biography of great men.' I think today we saw the coming to power of a man who can show us what Carlyle meant."

219

"I devoutly hope you're right. I hate to sound fatalistic, but sometimes it seems as if events determine their own ebb and flow. There are forces which we can't begin to comprehend. And the public leaders end up posturing and making pronouncements. They just stand around and watch."

"Kennedy won't stand around and watch, Gustavo. I can promise you that."

"Well, I'll drink to that," Carta said, clinking glasses with his host. They both sipped their drinks, the warm glow slowly settling down into their stomachs.

Charles paced the floor as he began to talk, waving his glass for emphasis. His handsome face seemed flushed, the even features animated by his excitement. He brushed a strand of dark hair from his forehead. Watching Danforth, Carta was struck by the fine-boned elegance he projected. Like a well-bred racehorse.

"Gustavo, I just can't seem to contain my enthusiasm about what is happening in this country. I have a hunch that the times are turning for the better, that for the first time in three decades we have our finest minds at the helm, men with ideals and toughness and style. When is the last time you can remember that anyone in Washington had any style? It's like someone just opened up a musty attic and let in the fresh air."

Carta swirled the brandy in his snifter, his eyes transfixed by the amber glow. Charles observed his pensive mood.

"You think I'm getting carried away, don't you—that I'll awaken tomorrow having recovered from my Inaugural orgasm and be thoroughly ashamed of myself?"

"No, Charles, I don't think you're being carried away. But there's still something about today—I can't put my finger on it. It's been almost too perfect, too pretty. You hit it when you asked me whether I could remember anyone in Washington who had style. Maybe we're all too worried about style and façade. Elizabeth and I saw men from the National Park Service spraying green paint on the grass around the Lincoln Memorial so it would look like spring. Hell, it's winter, Charles, why should the grass look green?"

Danforth looked at Carta thoughtfully. "You have a legitimate point there, Gustavo, I can't dispute it. There's an annoying artifice to the Kennedy mystique—it's too studied. Jackie overdresses like hell and Jack works on his macho image, even though he's got such a bad back he can't even stand up straight much of the time. All that is true. But what's important is that there's substance beneath all that glitter."

"It's hard to see substance when the glitter becomes blinding."

"If I may say so, I think you're overreacting, my friend. I'm not criticizing you—I'd feel the same way in your shoes. These have been difficult times for you; Fidel Castro has seen to that. Perhaps that is coloring your thinking."

"Charles, while this week everyone's talking about the Kennedys and Uri Gagarin and the space race and Laos, two or three months from now it will be Fidel Castro's name that will be on everyone's lips."

Charles settled into an antique Morris chair across from Carta and propped his feet on a stool. "I don't know about your theory. Fidel has a lot of heavies to compete with—Lumumba, Khrushchev, you name it. But let me tell you something, Gustavo, I'm as worried about the Cuban mess as you are. It scares the shit out of me."

"Don't indulge me, Charles. With all the things on your mind . . ."

"What worries me most, Gustavo, is the attitude of game-playing about Cuba. The Eisenhower people had that attitude, and I hate to say this but so do the Kennedy people. It's as if everyone thinks, 'Here's this little toy of a country, you can't take it very seriously.' "

"Cuba has always been America's playground, its whorehouse. Why shouldn't you regard it as a toy?"

"During the campaign, do you remember when Jack Kennedy said we should fully support the exiles in their fight against Castro, and Nixon denounced Kennedy's position as irresponsible and warlike? And yet Nixon knew that the CIA had already started training Cuban exiles in Guatemala to attack Cuba."

"That's gamesmanship. It's also very cynical."

"Jack Kennedy felt he could safely advocate his position because officially he wasn't supposed to know about the CIA training bases. And Nixon was afraid to take an even stronger stance because as early as 1959 he had gone to Eisenhower and demanded sending in the Marines. Ike got very angry and turned him down. Nixon, as you know, had some very good friends on the Batista side."

"And I suppose that Kennedy knew about that too."

"Damned right."

"And now Kennedy wants to back down from his campaign rhetoric?"

"No, Gustavo, he doesn't want to back down, but it's a dilemma for him. It is no longer a matter of infiltrating a few guerrillas. It is now an outright invasion. War. The CIA has given Kennedy more than he bargained for. Suddenly the whole country has its ass on the line."

"You're starting a war you can't win. In the eyes of the world, not to mention the eyes of the Cuban people, you are going to find yourself— if you follow this CIA invasion plan—waging a war of conquest. Yes, conquest. This has to be a war of liberation. Even if you win, you are

221

bound to create deep resentment in Cuba and throughout Latin America. I find it hard to believe that is the impression you wish to make."

"Of course it isn't."

"Then you realize the extent of the problem . . ."

"The problem is clear, Gustavo. The solution is what seems obscure."

"The solution, in my opinion, Charles, is to abandon this one-thrust invasion, discard it for what it is—ill-conceived."

"Even if I agreed with you, those troops are in Guatemala. What kind of strategy would replace them?"

Gustavo brightened. The weariness of the day fell from his features, and he became animated. "Give support to the guerrilla units already operating inside Cuba—to the underground. Give the people of Cuba a chance. It won't take much to convince them of Castro's duplicity, his betrayal of the revolution. But they have to be convinced by Cubans, working within my country itself. With the support of the United States, even modest support, weapons, ammunition, explosives, radios, the Cuban underground can effectively defeat Castro."

"The CIA's argument is that the underground has been heavily infiltrated by Castro's agents. It's unreliable."

"Yes." Carta nodded. "That's why they've purposely misdirected supplies and let air drops fall into enemy hands. They ignored radio messages from our people. Why? They want control. They want to make this operation in Cuba exactly like the one they mounted in Guatemala in 1954. If they don't have control, they can't take credit. Hmm?"

"But to purposely botch supply drops. Really, Gustavo."

"Listen," Carta said, "we constantly are supplying our people in Cuba —constantly! And our means are extremely limited. We have underground cells from Havana to Santiago. We have guerrillas in Oriente, in Pinar del Río, in the Escambray. We manage to get supplies to them. If we, working hand to mouth, can succeed, why can't the CIA?"

"And you believe there is a great deal of dissatisfaction with Fidel— within the country itself?"

"Yes, and it's the key to defeating Fidel. If that dissatisfaction can be exploited, Fidel is finished. He is robbing our people of their most precious possession—freedom. Cubans will see that—many do now. There is much resistance. But you must understand one thing, Charles . . ."

"Which is?"

"All that I have outlined to you must be linked to a sound political program of reform, of social justice, of democracy. Free of all imperialistic and economic ties. It must, in short, be *our* revolution, without Fidel. You cannot turn the clock back in Cuba. The time of colonial philosophy is behind us."

"You think that's what we are trying to achieve, Gustavo? A return to the Platt Amendment, gunboat diplomacy, American economic domination of Cuba?"

"Doesn't it smack of that? Look at the officers in your CIA brigade in Guatemala, Charles. Who are they? I'll tell you—Batista reactionaries, in the main. And the Revolutionary Front, the Frente, you've set up in Miami? Well-meaning but ineffective men who are dupes of your CIA agents. Have you any idea of the fiefdoms your people have set up for themselves in Miami and Guatemala? Do you really know what's happening?"

"Quite frankly, I don't. But I wish to find out. The CIA chaps have put together their package, Gustavo. And presented it to us, neatly. They claim it's the tool, the one tool, available to effect our policy toward Castro."

"You find it hard to reject out of hand?"

"Yes." Danforth suddenly looked troubled and quite weary. The day's pressures were beginning to take their toll, and so was the Courvoisier. "Look, Gustavo, I want your help. You have to understand the way government works, the limitations of my position. I cannot simply toss out this plan—it has gained too much momentum. But I can work within it to alter its course and change its direction. That's why I want you to join the show, Gustavo. Become a leader of the Frente. With you working from the inside and me working within the Administration, we can swing things toward the moderates. That is very much what the President wants to do."

Carta looked intently at Danforth, then turned away, shaking his head. "I can't do it, Charles. I have my own friends and allies, men who risked their lives because they believe in our revolution. We have our own plan to overthrow the Communists—it is a plan that can work, it is not the plan of some CIA bureaucrat sitting in Washington who doesn't understand the realities. To do what you suggest would mean their betrayal."

"Betrayal? Don't be melodramatic."

"You don't understand my country, Charles. In Cuba, betrayal is a way of life. Time after time leaders have come to power promising great things to the people, only to turn against them. I don't want the Cuban people to think they're fighting for their freedom only to be delivered once again into the hands of another tyrant. The CIA people understand all this. That is why they regard me as their enemy, as a dangerous radical."

"But that's absurd. You're hardly a radical. I know the CIA people—they're intelligent men, well educated . . ."

"There are two CIA's, Charles. There's the Washington CIA with all the Harvard and Princeton men with their old-school ties and their good clubs and their good manners. And then there are the men in the field —the men who have been on the front lines in Laos and Manila and Guatemala and Berlin. They are a different sort. They do as they wish and take their orders from no man."

"I find that hard to believe. I am sorry."

"Tomorrow you will go to your office and Mr. Kennedy goes to his office and you will find out how things are in the world. Tomorrow you will be on the front lines, Charles, no longer in your academic cocoon."

"I think that's rather unkind, Gustavo." The two men exchanged glances for a moment. "You are an old and dear friend. Elizabeth through the years has been like a sister to me. I would not allow my friends to be used as pawns in a game. I want to help you, not cause you to betray your friends."

Carta's face seemed flushed. He rose from his chair, as did Danforth. "You must forgive me," Carta said softly. "I have said some rude things tonight. Perhaps it is too late and I have had too much brandy."

Danforth and Carta embraced each other, then stood apart, each looking a bit uncomfortable.

"You have suffered a great deal these past months—it was wrong of me to push you," Danforth said.

"Wasn't it Maugham who said, 'Suffering does not ennoble, it only embitters'? He knew whereof he spoke."

Danforth gave a wan smile. "You have never been a bitter man, Gustavo. You have been a fiercely independent man, and I've admired that. But I worry about fiercely independent men in times like these. Think about it, Gustavo. Think about history. It's always been the independent men, the middle-of-the roaders, the men of honor who got their balls caught in the wringer in times of crisis and revolution. They always get crushed between the crazy ones on the right and the crazy ones on the left. It's the extremists who survive those times, not the honorable ones. Remember our friend Robert Hale Merriman?"

"Yes. Very well."

"He was like you, Gustavo, a decent-minded middle-of-the-roader, a lone wolf. He led the American battalion in the Spanish Civil War. We went to his goodbye party, remember? It was goodbye, all right. They shot him in the back. He was too good for them. There have been a lot of Robert Hale Merrimans in history."

Carta's eyes studied his friend for a moment. "I'll take your advice to heart," he said, his voice flat with exhaustion. "But right now I think I'd better go to bed."

224

"Sleep well, my friend," Danforth said.

Carta turned and walked slowly toward the stairs. Danforth looked after him, then started switching off the lights.

CHAPTER TWENTY

Havana, January 22, 1961

A double line of Catholic schoolgirls in their navy-blue uniforms moved across the four-century-old cobblestones of the cathedral square. In the dim light, their faces were scrubbed clean and shiny. They made no sounds other than their shoes scuffing on the cobbles as they moved, flanked by nuns in their black flowing robes and hoods. The San Cristóbal Cathedral doors were opened, revealing the candlelit interior. Pepita came up the steps. The girls passed in ranks of twos. Her gaze fell on one little girl who was whispering rapidly in Spanish to her taller companion. Pepita recognized her immediately. Her little upturned nose and protruding lips were a child's, but her eyes were Camilo's, pale blue, quick. And the shape of her face and the slender neck were Alicia's. The child glanced at her and stopped whispering, afraid of being reprimanded. But Pepita smiled and took Elena's hand and went into the cathedral.

"Sister, what are you doing here?"

"Shhh."

An organ began playing as they entered the vaulted interior. Gaudily painted saints stood in their candlelit alcoves, the flickering lights of dozens of candles at their feet, the altar gleamed in gold, and the famous statue of Saint Christopher carrying the Child looked down at them. The line of girls moved ahead, peeling off into the pews, which were decorated here and there by the heads of old women in black shawls. Each child genuflected ahead of her before moving to her seat. Pepita led Elena aside into an empty row and kept moving across toward the alcove exit. She heard a stirring behind her.

As she reached the curtained exit, Pepita looked back over her shoulder and saw two men in civilian suits pushing and shoving their way through the children.

"What is it?" Elena asked.

"Come, we must be quick."

Pepita led the child across the plaza onto Mercaderas Street, where a car waited. The black door opened as they approached, walking rapidly.

Elena released her hand and ran to the bearded man seated in the car, throwing her arms around his neck. "Papa, Papa, Papa!" she cried.

Camilo's blue eyes looked up at Pepita, who opened the front door.

"It went well," she said, and got in beside the driver.

Camilo lifted his daughter into his arms and pulled her into the back seat and shut the door. The car moved with a lurch into traffic.

"Where are we going?" the child asked, glancing at the strange blond man seated on her left.

Her father's arm encircled her shoulders and held her against his chest. "You are going to Miami, my darling," he told her. He lowered his head to hers and gestured. "You don't know this man, do you?"

Elena looked at the strange man with her wide blue eyes and shook her head. "This is your Uncle David. My brother. Remember I told you about him? I told you he was coming to Havana to see us?"

She nodded, her eyes fixed on David, her chin lowered in an expression of shyness.

"Don't be shy," her father told her. "Say hello to your uncle."

"I am pleased to meet you, Uncle David," she said in Spanish, and timidly held out her hand.

David took the little hand in his. "Enchanted, Elena," he replied in Spanish. "Do you speak English?"

"Oh, yes," she said and looked at her father brightly. "Is he really my uncle?"

"Of course."

She turned back to David and smiled, pleased and shy.

"Give him a kiss hello."

Elena blushed and looked at David with her chin lowered, as though weighing the thought. Deciding against it, she shook her head. David and Camilo both laughed.

"It's all right, Elena," David said.

She turned away quickly to Camilo. "He doesn't look like you."

"See his eyes. See?"

She watched David's face in the flickering lights from the traffic.

"What color are they?"

"Blue." She smiled in the childish delight of discovery and giggled.

Amused, David glanced out the window. The taxi turned onto the Prado at Parque Central. José Martí's marble statue showed through the laurel leaves. He turned back to see Elena's face leaning against her

226

father's chest, his arm around her shoulders. Camilo lifted his gaze to David, a twisting of private agony behind his eyes.

"Your Uncle David is going to take you to Miami, Elena," he said.

Elena looked up at him, puzzled. "Aren't you coming, Papa?"

"Not this time."

At the sound of her words Pepita turned and looked back at David, her face shadowed beneath the nun's hood she wore. David kept his gaze on her. He did not want to look at the child.

"Why do I have to go to Miami?"

"Because I have told you that you must go," Camilo said to her, gently.

"But I don't want to." Her voice broke, and David knew she was near tears. Pepita turned away.

"I know you don't," said Camilo. "But it is necessary."

"Papa?" Her voice was small and broken, and she was crying now. "Mama wouldn't want me to go to Miami and leave you all alone."

David saw tears on her cheeks as she hugged against Camilo. His brother glanced at him, helplessly, and then looked down at his daughter and touched her face with his fingertips. She turned her body and put her arm around his neck and hugged him tightly. Again Camilo gave David that furtive, desperate glance.

"Why do I have to go?"

Camilo let out his breath. "Listen to me very carefully, *carida*. Your father has many things he must do now. The revolution is at a critical time, you understand? We may have war soon. You know what I mean?" Still crying, Elena lifted her face to look at him. "There will be much danger. Men will be killed. Planes will come to drop bombs here. I want you to be safe with your grandmother in Miami."

"Won't our planes drop bombs on Miami?"

Camilo looked at David. "No, there will be no bombs in Miami."

"Why?"

"Cuba has no bombing planes, you see?"

"What about all my friends at school? Will Blanca be killed by the bombs?"

"No, I don't think so. Blanca will be safe."

"Then why won't I be?"

Her logic was difficult to deal with. Camilo smiled at her. "I must know in my heart when I am doing my duty here that you are safe. I must know it."

"Why?"

"Because I love you."

Elena's face melted and tears welled again, glistening in her eyes. "I . . . love you, too, Papa."

She hugged him. Camilo closed his eyes. His lips trembled as he held his child in his arms. "You must be very brave, Elena, and obey your Uncle David and your grandmother. Will you do that for me? Will you?"

Her head nodded.

The ride to the airport took less than half an hour in the traffic. When the car eased to a stop in front of the terminal, Camilo told Elena to wait inside the car for a moment and got out with David. Paco unloaded two bags from the trunk, and David was surprised to see his battered blue flight bag, which had been picked up at the hotel for him in advance. Paco carried both his bag and Elena's leather valise into the terminal and handed them to the porter. Camilo took David's arm and led him to the back of the car.

"I will say goodbye to her alone," he said. Then, holding David's arm, he hesitated, looking down at his boots. "If anything happens to me, I want you to promise you will look after her." He lifted his gaze, his blue eyes holding David's. "Will you?"

"Of course."

"One other thing. If it goes badly for me here in Havana, I will try to get out."

"Good."

"But in that event, Miami will be a dangerous place for me. You understand?" He watched David's nod of agreement, then continued. "I'll try to get in touch with you. Only you. No one else must know, even Mother. All right?"

"When?"

"Four, maybe five weeks. Will you be gone? To Peru?"

Looking at his brother's grim face, David realized he was being presented an agonizing decision.

"If you come to Florida, and I'm not there, what happens to you?"

Camilo's crooked smile answered him.

"I'll be there," David said.

"You are sure? This expedition is important to you . . ."

"I'll be there."

Camilo embraced him silently. David put his arms around his brother, feeling the softness of his beard against his cheek and the strong muscles of his back and shoulders and within his soul the weight of what he had just committed himself to. He pressed Camilo tightly against him, and then they separated.

"I love you, David. You are one hell of a brother." Camilo turned aside and got into the back of the car with his daughter.

David felt a sudden void. Hollow, saddened, he walked around the car and saw Pepita standing a few yards away, looking at him. He went up to her and took her hands.

"I would like to kiss you."

"And I you, David."

He kissed her cheek, feeling her grasp tighten against his.

The door of the car opened and Elena stepped out gravely. She looked back at her father's face, dimly lighted in the back of the taxi. He nodded to her and she turned to David and took his hand. She looked back once as they went to the glass door of the terminal.

In the twilight they drove back to Havana along Rancho Boyeros road. Camilo waited in the car at the edge of the field until he saw the airliner take off, make its turn and head north, the lights becoming tiny sparks blinking in the evening sky. He watched it go out of sight.

He had set it all in motion.

He felt his apprehension begin to lessen, the sense of failure leaving him. Now it was possible. He was in control. Seeing David and saying goodbye to Elena had stirred up the past he thought had long been put to rest. But Elena and David were gone now, off to Miami. It had all gone according to plan, and Camilo felt a satisfaction in that. Now there was so much still to do.

When they turned onto the Malecón it was suddenly night. Only moments before, the city had basked in the sun's incandescence. It had always been like that, Camilo thought. Cuba's blazing sun seemed to divide its universe between pervasive tones of light and dark. At the brilliance of high noon, the island shimmered against the sea; even the trees and the houses seemed bleached into the sun-drenched landscape. Then suddenly all life was engulfed by clotted shadows, and the horizon receded into an indigo sea.

He sensed all that within himself as well: that interplay of light and darkness; the exhilaration that came with the brilliance of noon, only to recede into blackness. Camilo loved the sun and dreaded the shadows.

He turned suddenly, as though awakening from a sleep, and looked at Pepita, huddled in the dimness of the back seat. Her eyes and skin glowed from the frame of her cowl. "Do you want to go back to the convent, or stay with me?"

"With you," she said quietly.

Camilo said to Paco, "Drop her at the apartment in Vedado."

"Aren't you going to be there, Camilo?"

"Later," he told her. "I have to see someone."

When they had let her out of the car in front of the stucco apartment

229

building and watched her go inside, Camilo turned to Paco and said, "Let's go."

"Where to, Comandante?"

"Cojimar. I want to see Fidel."

As they drove, Camilo fell silent again. Sitting there beside Paco, he began to think of the men he had known whose fleeting friendship he had shared—men who, like the cars, went darting quickly by him in the night. They were dead now, caught in the relentless wake of the revolution. He thought of Candido with his stern pockmarked face, who had taught him everything he knew about weapons and who had worshiped Fidel. He thought of Yañes, with his clean-shaven face and military bearing, who had saved Fidel's life after the attack on Moncada by refusing to poison him in prison at Santiago, and who had been the best of them. He had been shot a week ago at La Cabaña. And Morgan, the American, who was so tough and brave with them in the mountains, shot, too, at La Cabaña. Of Cienfuegos, who liked to drink and play with the girls too much, but who rivaled Fidel in the hearts of all Cubans; charming, smiling, don't-give-a-damn Cienfuegos, supposedly missing in a flight to nowhere. Frank País, who led the revolt in Santiago and saved their ass when they were in the mountains, murdered after his brother was shot. Huber Matos, making the mistake of resigning from the rebel army and inciting Fidel's wrath, imprisoned now on the Isle of Pines, a living death. He felt sick remembering them all. It was a long list—men who had been close to Fidel, his comrades in arms, dead or in prison.

He knew he would fear death when the instant came, but he did not now, any more than he feared sleep. Yet the thought awed him. "Paco," he said softly, "you ever think about dying?"

The black man turned his face to him and nodded gravely. "Certainly, Camilo, hasn't every man?"

"Does it worry you?"

Paco shrugged his heavy shoulders, holding his hands on the wheel, watching the tunnel entrance looming up in front of them, and then they were into its white-tiled gleaming interior, flashing along, and he thought a moment before he replied. "Sometimes. But then, what were we to begin with?"

"Nothing," Camilo said.

Paco flashed a smile. "My father used to say, 'I don't mind dying, I just don't want to be there when it happens.' "

Camilo laughed ruefully. "It doesn't work that way very often, does it?"

230

BOOK IV

CHAPTER TWENTY-ONE

*T*he houses of Santa Marta, on the northeast coast of Colombia, lie white in the tropical glare. The bay glints in the stillness of midday. On the Ranch of San Pedro stands a Spanish hacienda, tile roof, veranda, white in the sun. It is so hot you can hear the earth tick. Inside, the barefoot blacks move silently along the corridors to the open door of Don Joaquín de Mier's bedroom, where Simón Bolívar lies dying. It is the seventeenth of December, 1830.

The Liberator is forty-seven. His sunken chest, his creased gaunt face, furrowed by fatigue and disappointments, attest to his final hours. Yet his large dark eyes still glitter with the spirit that for twenty years electrified Latin America. In the crowded room, blacks, whites, men and women, stifle their sobs. His voice is weak as he dictates his last words to a notary:

"You have been witness of my efforts to implant liberty where tyranny once reigned. My enemies took advantage of your credulity and desecrated that which I hold most sacred—my love of liberty."

From Peru to Venezuela, in every land where he had beaten the Spaniards and won freedom, anarchy was spreading. The generals who had supported him had turned on Bolívar, wanting to keep for themselves the spoils of victory. He alone had fought these bloody, vicious wars not seeking personal enrichment. Twenty years he had struggled. Many times he had failed.

"We have no other weapons," he had once written, "than our arms, our breasts, our horses, our lances. The weak need a long struggle to win; the strong can destroy an empire with one battle. . . ."

With clear insight, Bolívar appraised the Latin-American wars of independence that had started in 1810:

> The American colonies now fighting for their emancipation will, in the end, be successful. It is overambitious to think of forming the whole New World into a single nation with a single power linking its parts to each other and into a whole. It would seem that with their common origin, language, customs, and religion, it should be possible to organize a government that would confederate the various states comprising it; but this cannot be. Climatic differences, geographical differences, conflicting interests, contradictions of character divide America. How beautiful if the Isthmus of Panama could be for us what that of Corinth was for the Greeks! Perhaps someday we shall have the good fortune to set up there an eminent Congress made up of the representatives of all the Republics. . . .

Now, betrayed, he lay in the heat of Santa Marta, feeling life ebbing from his frail body. Beside him was Manuela Sáenz, the woman who had loved him and shared his fortunes to the end. She had saved his life when a group of assassins burst into his bedroom in Bogotá to kill him. They claimed he was a dictator.

His quivering voice continued his last testament: "My persecutors have brought me to the doors of the tomb—I forgive them. If my death helps bring an end to strife and consolidates union, I shall go down to my grave in Peace."

Bolívar turned his head to look out at the sun on the waters of the bay. Beyond, he could see the blue line of the Caribbean Sea. Out there lay Jamaica, Hispaniola, Puerto Rico, and Cuba. He had wanted to see them all free of foreign domination. He died looking at that water.

When the explosion finally arrived, the flashpoint came principally over issues of Latin pride. The Spanish governors had become increasingly contemptuous in their treatment of the Creoles. Cuban deputies were denied seats in the Spanish Cortés—a slight the Cubans were never to forget. Administrations had grown steadily harsher through the 1800s and taxes more burdensome. And the Cubans more and more began to think of themselves in terms of their own identity as a nation, not as mere colonials.

When war ultimately broke out in 1868, it was organized and directed by radical Creole landowners from Oriente province who combined with a group of lawyers and professionals. But while the organizers were wealthy, the people who did the fighting were peasants, including many blacks and Chinese. The leader of the rebellion was Carlos Manuel de Céspedes, a wealthy lawyer and landowner who started his war carrying a gold-handled tortoiseshell cane. A lawyer, he was also a poet whose romantic verse extolled the beauty of his native Bayamo. His first act was to free the slaves on his plantation at Yara, which happened to be the site where the Indian martyr Hatuey had been burned at the stake. In front of his own mansion, Céspedes issued the Grito de Yara (Cry of Yara): "Independence or death!" It was to be the battle cry for Cuban freedom.

The next day, Céspedes attacked the Spanish garrison in the village of Yara with fewer than forty men, mostly his former black slaves. The Spanish soldiers mowed them down. With his survivors, Céspedes rode off in retreat. They came to a small clearing in the woods and halted. Céspedes counted his men. Only twelve had survived.

"It does not matter," he said. "Twelve men with me are enough to free Cuba."

Meeting in the village of Guáimara during April, 1869, the revolutionary government drew up a constitution for Cuba, electing Céspedes as President. It also formed a House of Representatives, which had control over the presidential power. At the same time, Céspedes made several attempts to obtain United States recognition.

President Ulysses S. Grant, yielding to pressure from business groups which still had hopes of buying Cuba from Spain, quoted U.S. neutrality laws, refused to recognize the revolutionary government, and announced that America would not intervene in Cuba. To the exile groups working in New York and Florida it was a devastating blow. Spanish espionage agents had a free hand to work against them. Shipments of arms were blocked during the long ten years of war.

Against their ragged troops, armed mostly with machetes, was the might of Spain's half-million-man military force, well disciplined, equipped with up-to-date weapons from artillery to breech-loading rifles and rapid-fire Gatling guns, and reinforced steadily from the homeland. The odds against the Cubans were almost insurmountable.

With Céspedes at the head of the civilian leadership, the rebel military campaign was placed in the hands of Máximo Gómez, a quiet-spoken man with a heavy moustache and gentle eyes. He was a master of guerrilla warfare. He organized his poorly armed Cubans into small units that were highly mobile, quick to harass the ponderous Spanish divisions.

From out of the peasant ranks arose a guerrilla leader, Antonio Maceo. A mulatto originally from Costa Rica, he was a magnificent physical specimen, weighing 210 pounds. He rode with such skill the Cubans came to call him "the Centaur." The machete was his weapon. The Spaniards came to fear and hate him.

The war was a bitter struggle in which battles of consequence rarely crystallized. By 1871, the Spaniards had driven the rebels back into the mountains of Oriente province, on the southeastern tip of the island. It was Céspedes' strategy to destroy

235

Cuba's sugar crop so that the war would become "an unbearable economic burden for Spain." Maceo flashed through the cane, rallying black slaves and burning thousands of acres in devastating raids.

The Spaniards retaliated by bringing in a young officer, Valeriano Weyler, a man so skilled at killing and so ruthless he became known as "the Butcher." Weyler's orders were clear. The Spanish knew how to deal with guerrillas. Every Cuban above the age of fifteen who was found away from his home was shot on the spot. Every house that was not occupied and flying the white flag was burned to the ground.

As the struggle wore on, neither side could gain advantage over the other. Internal dissension flared among the rebel leaders. Conservative Cubans who supported the rebels were suspicious of Maceo, fearing he would set up a black republic as Toussaint had in Haiti. Officers in the rebel army were jealous of Gómez because he was Dominican, not Cuban. Céspedes was driven from office by political bickering.

Disheartened, Gómez finally resigned his command in 1876, writing in his war journal: "I retired this day with a heart broken by so many deceptions."

Like Céspedes, Perucho Figueredo was a rich, wellborn Creole romantic from Bayamo. He loved Cuba and longed for its freedom. He sat at his piano composing melodies that would be on everyone's lips. Among his compositions was a martial tune which the Creoles titled "Perucho's March." It was heard hummed and whistled everywhere in Cuba. Even the Spanish governor sang his baby to sleep with it.

On Figueredo's plantation, Las Mangas, he organized and drilled a division of fighting men. People worked night and day in a warehouse turned into a war plant, making bullets and powder. One morning, he mounted his horse and rode into Bayamo, passing out copies of the Cry of Yara in broad daylight. Before the Spanish governor knew what was happening, the entire town was filled with excitement, and Perucho was riding back to his plantation to organize the attack. In his hacienda, men and women were sewing a flag. It was the same flag Narciso López had carried. All of them, men and women, blacks and whites, touched it solemnly and swore to give their lives for it.

Figueredo declared his slaves free. The Africans went mad with joy. The Cuban army moved out toward Bayamo, the ranks swelling every foot of the way, and all whistling "Perucho's March." Bayamo was surrounded. The fighting was brief but fierce. After the battle, church bells began ringing. Standing in the town square, Perucho Figueredo shouted, "Long live Free Cuba!" and thousands of voices began to hum his song.

As Perucho mounted his horse, with his daughter Candelaria, just sixteen, at his side, the crowd roared at him, "Write the words, write the words!" The jammed square fell silent. He sat scribbling the improvised stanzas on the pommel of his saddle, while his horse pranced nervously. Then he lifted his head and looked around at the silent mob. They waited in reverence. His dry thin voice, wavering with emotion, rose above their heads as he sang:

> "*Bayamese,* rush to arms!
> Your country looks on in pride.
> Fear not a glorious death—
> Who dies for his country lives. . . ."

Cuba had its national anthem.

In Oriente one morning in 1874, Céspedes ordered his horse, Telemaco, saddled. He intended to ride to the village of San Lorenzo to give some children lessons in reading and writing.

Political bickering among the rebel leaders had forced Céspedes to abandon his command and take refuge in the hills. He rode out like a gentleman in his velvet waistcoat, a revolver in his belt.

But someone had betrayed him. Spanish soldiers waited in ambush. As he rode near, they opened fire.

Dismounting, Céspedes, the lawyer who had started the war with his gold-handled cane and his cry for independence, worked his way along the edge of a ravine, firing back at the pursuing Spaniards with his six-shooter.

He had once told friends, "My revolver has six shots—five for the Spaniards and one for myself."

One Spanish soldier, Brigido Verdecia, sweating up through the brush, managed to get his sights on the Cuban rebel. He fired. Céspedes fell into the ravine.

When the Spanish soldiers reached Céspedes' body, he still had the revolver clutched in his hand. Opening it, they discovered one bullet in the chamber.

Ten bitter years of sporadic warfare had resolved nothing. Two hundred and sixty thousand lives had been lost.

In 1878, a Spanish general, Martínez Campos, persuaded rebel leaders to meet in the war-devastated village of Zanjón, near Camagüey, to discuss peace terms. His strategy was simple: He would buy out those revolutionary leaders he had been unable to defeat. By the end of the "negotiations" some ten million dollars had been paid out in bribes by the Spaniards. It was a betrayal of the revolution; not the first nor the last in Cuban history. The Spanish agreed to changes in the island's laws and administration, a phasing out of slavery and the admission of Cuban delegates to Spain's Cortés. Dutifully, the Cuban rebel leaders signed the pact.

Only Máximo Gómez refused. With his remaining troops he withdrew into the Sierra Maestra, where he waged a losing guerrilla campaign, finally going into exile in the United States, setting up headquarters in New York.

Though slavery was indeed abolished over the following eight years, the Spaniards, who had bought their peace with hard cash, chose to ignore their other promises. Crushing taxes were newly imposed; the delegates to the Cortés were mostly Spaniards, not Cubans; military rule prevailed, harsh and oppressive. The dictatorship continued, "as usual."

The war had been lost. But in the homes of Cuban exiles in Key West, Tampa, New York, Mexico, Guatemala, Bogotá, Caracas and Santo Domingo, hope was kept alive. In each center the Cubans formed political clubs, published newspapers and solicited funds for the cause. Wherever there were Cubans, there was a hotbed of plots against the Spanish government. In Key West, the U.S. collector of customs was so moved he dug in his pocket and donated a hundred dollars. He was promptly fired.

Cuban volunteers who joined the Spanish Army were treated with scorn by everyone, especially the girls and the students, who whistled and greeted them with mocking smiles. One young Cuban volunteer received a note from three of his fellow students asking, "Do you know how apostasy was punished in olden times?" Castration, one of the weapons of the Spanish Inquisition, was clearly implied, and the young soldier took the note to the Spanish authorities. He demanded satisfaction. The Spaniards, not amused, quickly responded by arresting the three Cuban students. The author was sentenced to six years at hard labor in the stone quarries.

He was a frail boy of fifteen, with a pale thin face, broad forehead and shining eyes. His name was José Martí.

Hardened criminals were broken in that military prison. They pounded at rock in the fierce tropical sun from first light to darkness, day in and day out, until the weeks blurred into years. The Spanish guards were vicious, punishment was swift and severe. Food was meager, discipline harsh and absolute. Few survived the experience.

Martí spent his first days in physical agony. His pale skin burned in the sun. His muscles ached so that he could hardly move. Yet he suffered with his fellow prisoners without complaint. There was something about this thin boy that commanded respect. The inmates liked him.

One day the guards came for Martí and led him away. A Spanish official who knew the family and had influence in high circles had procured the boy's release. He was exiled to Spain. Aboard the ship, young Martí watched the green hills of Cuba disappear on the horizon with tears in his eyes.

In Spain, Martí enrolled in the University of Zaragoza and received a degree in law and philosophy. He spent a great deal of his time in the sidewalk cafés, on street corners, wherever he could find two Spaniards willing to argue; his theme

238

was freedom. He spoke at Masonic meetings, he wrote articles for newspapers, published a report condemning political imprisonment in Cuba. Despite his youth, he was a gifted orator, unable to resist the fascination of hearing his own voice. He was applauded and treated with respect wherever he appeared. He had a dynamic quality about him. He seemed the last romantic.

They called him "the Apostle."

In 1881, Martí appeared in New York and joined Máximo Gómez. He supported himself by writing poetry and articles for various publications in North and South America. He also wrote a book of children's poems, which delighted generations of Latin Americans. Charles A. Dana, editor of the New York Sun, was so impressed with Martí he gave him carte blanche to write anything he saw fit for the paper, "in any language." Dana flew the Cuban rebel flag from the Sun's flagstaff.

Martí was tireless. He traveled to Mexico, to Guatemala, to Tampa and Key West, and wherever he spoke he lifted the hearts of Cuban exiles. He managed to collect enough funds to assemble three ships loaded with arms in New York harbor. But the intrigues of Cuban politics had not changed, even for a man like Martí. Someone talked. The United States government seized the ships in the harbor just before they sailed.

Now, with the police on his trail, Martí became a fugitive. But he managed to elude capture. He slipped like a ghost through the cities, always in touch with the exiles, encouraging them, reviving the flagging spirits of the military leaders. Penny by penny, he supported the revolution. In Cuba, word spread, "The Apostle is coming."

He thought of himself as a son of America. A disciple of Bolívar, he looked to his own country but never lost sight of the continent. He believed the time would come when all the republics of Latin America would be united, like the United States, in one great union. "The spiritual union," he wrote, "is indispensable to the salvation and happiness of the peoples of America."

He saw Cuba as a new and independent nation based on the close cooperation of all social classes, not on "the struggle of one class against another." It would be "a nation based on law, order and the hard work of its inhabitants." He advocated land reform, not by taking land away from large landholders, but by redistributing vast lands owned by the government.

"The greatness of nations," he wrote, "is dependent on the economic independence of its citizens. It is necessary that everyone possess a piece of land."

Despite his occasional forays into radical rhetoric, Martí was a firm believer in individual initiative and private property. He admired the United States, but felt that it placed too much emphasis on material wealth and self-interest. "Cubans admire this nation, the greatest ever built by freedom, but they cannot believe that excess individualism and reverence for wealth are preparing the United States to be the typical nation of liberty."

239

He was wary of economic domination by any foreign power. He urged Cuba to sell its products to many different countries. "Whoever says economic union," he wrote, "says political union. The people who buy, command; the people who sell obey." And appraising the shadow of the United States, he warned:

"Once the United States is in Cuba, who will get it out?"

Martí, with Gómez and Maceo, organized and supplied the Cuban rebels on the island with patience, skill and extreme efficiency. Their revolutionary propaganda fell on rich soil. In 1894 the Blaine reciprocity agreement that favored the entry of Cuban sugar into the United States market was repealed. It was a disaster for the island's economy. Cuba's planters, caught between both U.S. and Spanish economic protection, faced ruin. Work became scarce, and thousands could not feed their families as unemployment mounted. Restless, unhappy, and growing more desperate each day, the Cubans looked for salvation. When Martí, Gómez and Maceo called for the revolution on February 24, 1895, the long-suffering people of Cuba welcomed it.

The meeting of the triumvirate on Cuban soil on the night of April 11, 1895, was a scene of high drama.

Maceo was already in Oriente, directing guerrilla fighters in raids on the Spaniards. On two occasions, the Cuban patriots had bought a schooner in Santo Domingo and fitted it out for the expedition. But both times the crews deserted when they learned the hazards of the trip. Finally, the two leaders, one old and rugged, the other young and frail, managed to bribe the captain of a German tramp freighter to drop them off Playitas, near the eastern tip of Cuba.

It was dark, and a storm had come up. Wind blew in gusts. Rain pelted them as they climbed into the small boat bobbing in the swell beside the steel hull.

Ahead lay the dark shape of the Cuban shore. They caught glimpses of it in the flashes of lightning. Waves tossed the boat. Once they broached, and the force of the wave carried off the rudder. Gómez, his white hair plastered on his head, steered with an oar. Martí and four companions rowed with the desperation and energy fear puts in a man.

After hours of frantic rowing, they neared the beach. The surf thundered as they were swept onto the sand. The boat broke up in the combers. The bone-weary and soaked Cubans waded ashore at Playitas. They were a few miles west of Baracoa, where Velásquez and Cortés had landed in 1511 to conquer Cuba.

Maceo embraced his bedraggled companions. All three were deeply moved. They expressed mutual devotion. Maceo turned over his command to Gómez.

With deep affection, Gómez turned to the thin, pale young man beside him. With a touch of humor, he made José Martí, the poet-philosopher, a major general. He didn't look much like a general. In his wrinkled clothes, he seemed more like an aging schoolboy who had just been plucked from drowning in the sea.

240

But Martí was feverishly happy. "My one desire is to die here, without a word, beside the last tree, the humblest soldier. . . ."

At last free Cuba was about to be born, before his eyes.

Martí set out into the heavily wooded mountains of Oriente with his soldiers. He waded rivers. He slept in the damp nights on the ground. He moved along the narrow paths through the green trees in the mottled shade and sun. He felt the sting of mosquitoes.

On April 19, 1895, a Cuban guide betrayed him. The Spanish ambushed Martí's guerrillas in a field near the village of Dos Ríos in Oriente. Small arms crackled from the trees. Men fell all around him. The heat was terrific; it made the line of trees where the Spanish were firing shimmy and waver before his eyes. Something had to be done.

Martí called for his men and charged across the field. Behind him came the waves of Cubans, their machetes gleaming in the sun, their voices raised in one long shrieking roar.

In the vanguard, Martí was struck by a fusillade of bullets and he fell in the grass, dying, wrapped in the bloody red remnant of his clothes. He was forty-two.

Maceo became the central flame of the holocaust that swept Cuba during the years of 1895 and 1896. After Martí's death, command of the rebel forces had fallen to him and Gómez.

Their strategy, which had been thwarted during the Ten Years' War, was to invade Cuba's western provinces. In repeated and brilliant attacks, the Cubans defeated the Spanish troops wherever they met. But losses were heavy.

At one point, during his bitter but successful campaign against superior Spanish forces in Piñar del Río, Maceo led his men into battle on horseback, carrying some twenty-five wounds on his body with no more distress "than if they had been insect bites."

He was the incarnation of personal battle, striking boldly and quickly rather than working out blueprinted maneuvers. He kept tight discipline in his encampments, constantly thinking ahead in the minds of the enemy, trying to devise new plans of attack. He enjoyed outsmarting and outmaneuvering the Spanish generals. He inflicted a terrible toll.

By mid-1896 the Spaniards were in retreat and the Cubans seemed on the verge of victory throughout the island.

Then on December 7, 1896, in a minor battle, Maceo was shot from his horse. The Titan of Bronze was dead.

*Frederic Remington, the famous American artist, wired William Randolph Hearst from Cuba: "*EVERYTHING IS QUIET. STOP. THERE IS NO TROUBLE HERE. STOP. THERE WILL BE NO WAR. STOP.*"*

241

Hearst's reply from the New York Journal: "YOU FURNISH PICTURES, AND I'LL FURNISH THE WAR. STOP."

The revolution in Cuba had not turned out, as Martí had hoped, to be a fast and decisive struggle. After his death in 1895 it dragged on for three more years, growing more intense and brutal.

When Maceo was killed, the tide shifted in favor of the Spaniards. Their commanding general, Weyler, was tough, ruthless and intelligent. He had learned his trade in North Africa fighting the Moroccans. He had experienced this kind of warfare and knew all the traps as well as the techniques.

He faced now only the old man, Gómez, who was in his seventy-second year. It would soon be over. The old man could not endure. But Gómez held on. Weyler could never quite catch him. He could never quite defeat him. Exasperation and frustration had its effect on Weyler, who reasoned that the rebels drew their support from the population, both rural and urban. Deny this support and Gómez' ragged army would fall apart.

Hundreds of thousands were rounded up by Spanish troops and put into concentration camps. Villages were fortified into garrisons. The countryside was cleared of inhabitants. They were herded into the fortified compounds. Weyler's plan was the classic tactic of a powerful orthodox army engaged in guerrilla warfare. It was effective.

Hundreds of Cuban men, women and children died each day of hunger and fever in the concentration camps. Conditions were unbelievably bad. Witnesses reported that you could hear the cries and moans of the people in the pens from miles away. The stench of the places was staggering. The American consul in Havana informed Washington that there were 400,000 people shut up in these living graveyards. More than half the population of Havana's province was behind barbed wire.

Into this appalling scene strode the swashbuckling Richard Harding Davis in his pith helmet and tailored khakis. Davis was more than a newspaper correspondent. He was a hero. Tall, handsome, with a profile that would have made him a motion picture star in another generation, Davis had a haughty, arrogant manner that made him unpopular with his fellow reporters. But he also had an uncanny ability to get a story and write it. His report on Weyler's inhuman concentration camps filled the entire front page of the New York Journal. It inflamed public opinion in the United States to a bright hot heat. Which was just what William Randolph Hearst wanted. He was in a circulation war with Joseph Pulitzer's World and he intended to win it.

Neither side in the war wanted United States intervention. Gómez and his Cuban rebels held strong positions in Oriente, and their guerrilla campaign was draining the Spaniards effectively, wearing away at Spain's manpower and treasure. Much cane had been devastated. It was only a matter of time, Gómez reasoned, before the enemy would assess the cost and want to find a way out.

From the viewpoint of the Cuban patriots, although their people were suffering terribly under Weyler's tactics, they felt they would eventually win. The Cubans sensed that the appearance of American troops on Cuban soil would not lead to a free and independent country, which they had spilled so much of their blood to achieve, but to a change of masters.

As for the Spaniards, they knew how bad off they were and feared greatly so powerful an enemy as the United States. War with the Americans would threaten the last bastions of their tarnished golden era. Decadent, corrupt, Spain was ripe for attack.

This fact had not escaped the attention of the politicians and the business barons of the United States. One Samuel Janny of 6 Wall Street led the resurgence of the lobby to buy Cuba from Spain, and the sentiment, undercover for the moment, to take the island by force, if necessary.

With a nervous eye on the Americans, who publicly grew more indignant each day over the injustices and suffering that Weyler had imposed on the Cubans, the Spanish government recalled its tough-minded commander and offered the Cuban rebels a large share of self-government, with their own constitution and legislature.

But Gómez and his Cuban compatriots had experienced Spanish promises before, to their regret. They rejected the offer. They demanded complete independence.

At that moment ambitious eyes were fastened on Cuba.

"God Himself," said President McKinley, had favored him, "with a Divine Revelation to take over the Philippines." He was speaking to the American Congress on December 6, 1897. As to Cuba: "We have the desire to see the Cubans prosperous and contented, protected in their right to reap the benefit of the inexhaustible treasures of their country."

Those "inexhaustible treasures" had been attracting Wall Street attention for some time now. In 1895 the American Sugar Refining Company had cornered ninety-eight percent of the industry's market. Many of its cane fields had been burned by the Cuban rebels. McKinley's "Divine Revelation" seemed to be coming from the vicinity of Wall Street, not heaven.

On the twenty-fifth of January, 1898, the white steel hull of the United States battleship Maine slid past Morro Castle and into Havana harbor. The American sailors lined the decks, peering out at the tile roofs of the city. To their eyes it looked exotic and exciting. There is a photograph taken that day which depicts the ship with its two tall masts, fore and aft, its two funnels amidships, flanked by curved steel cranes, the cluttered look of its superstructure, the white bow raising *a slight wave in the flat surface as it passed the old masonry lighthouse on the rock at the harbor entrance. In view is a solitary Cuban in a rowboat looking languidly out at the warship. It is the before shot.*

The after shot, taken on February 16, reveals a twisted mass of steel and a single mast, with a broad crow's nest, jutting out of the surface of the bay, amid a tangle of ropes and cables. A small, empty rowboat is moored beside the wreckage. The two photographs have one thing in common—in both, the American flag is snapping smartly in the breeze.

"$50,000 REWARD—WHO DESTROYED THE MAINE—$50,000 REWARD"

That was Hearst's banner line in the New York Journal *on February 17, 1898. It got quite a lot of attention.*

To this day it is still a mystery as to what caused the explosion that rocked Havana harbor that night of February 15. According to the survivors, "The explosion occurred at 9:40 P.M., and split the Maine *in two, throwing one Marine who was sleeping on the superstructure forty feet in the air and into the water. The explosion was an absolute mystery to everyone. It occurred in the forward magazine."*

A Spanish board of inquiry decided that the blast had been caused by an internal accident. The U.S. Naval Board of Inquiry reported on March 28: "The Maine *was destroyed by the explosion of a submarine mine." Both boards were reflecting what their governments desperately wanted to hear. Thirteen years later, after another inconclusive investigation, the hull was towed out of the harbor and sunk in deep water.*

Mr. Hearst got to keep his fifty-thousand-dollar reward. He also got his war.

On the outskirts of Tampa, Florida, there was a flat sandy plain dotted with open woods of stunted pine. The city itself sat on a shallow peninsula of Tampa Bay, connected to the port by a single-track railway. The railway and the flat were the property of Morton F. Plant, Esquire. Into this sandy spit of land, in the intense heat, came the American army that was to fight in Cuba. The absorbent soil made a good site for the camp, but the sun and the humidity were unbearable for most of the men who were brought from the higher, cooler Western plains. They had been issued red woolen underwear and wool uniforms that Teddy Roosevelt described as "better fit for Montana in autumn."

The First Missouri Volunteers had no shoes and no socks. Many other volunteer units had no uniforms at all. There were few tents and fewer blankets. One crack regiment, the Thirty-second Michigan, arrived without any rifles.

The First Volunteer Cavalry, made up of cowboys, Indians, Southerners, Texas Rangers, bear hunters and gamblers, reached Tampa to find that their saddles had been shipped on one freighter, their blankets on another. There was no water supply at the camp. Mr. Plant obligingly furnished it from his water company in

244

Tampa at two cents a gallon. Lemonade provided by Mr. Plant was five cents a glass. Everything was in short supply—tents, blankets, rifles, ammunition. Freight cars loaded with supplies were scattered all over Florida. The railroad let them sit on sidings. There they would stay. Mr. Plant, who had the contract for the Army's transportation business, also owned the railroad to Tampa. It seemed more businesslike and reasonable to concentrate efforts on transporting tourists, sightseers, sweethearts and wives—all paying premium prices—to the area to watch the show. They flocked in. Of course, Mr. Plant also owned Tampa's biggest and best hotel. Business was terrific.

Back in New York, Mr. Hearst's business wasn't too bad, either. He sold a record 1.3 million copies of the Journal *in one day.*

The Spanish-American War was declared by the U.S. Congress on the nineteenth of April, 1898. Spain simply did not want to fight a war with the United States. By the seventeenth of July American troops, after having encircled Santiago, entered the city, and the Spanish surrendered.

In Cuba, the rebel army of 53,000 had been ignored totally by the brash, tough Americans. Outside of supplying a few guides with local knowledge to the Yankees, they stood by forgotten and ignored while the blue-clad Americans, sweating and swearing in the jungle underbrush, swarmed up San Juan Hill and took the Spanish forts at El Caney. "The insurgents," wrote the Army's historian, "were of little real value to the Americans." Some 4,200 Cubans, under General García, stood on the hills and watched the Spanish fleet steam out of Santiago's harbor and make a desperate dash up the west coast, and saw the American ships move in, guns blazing, and sink them all. As Bolívar had pointed out, the strong nations could end it with one battle.

But when the Americans marched into the streets of Santiago and lowered the Spanish flag, it was not the Cuban flag that was raised in the square; it was the Stars and Stripes. The Cubans, who had fought these Spaniards since 1868, suffering more than a quarter million killed, were not allowed to take part in the ceremonies.

It was evident to José Martí's followers that their war for freedom had failed.

The aftermath of the Spanish-American War had profound and far-reaching effect on the future of the United States.

Historian Gregory Mason summed it up:

> This war which we had started with professions of altruism for oppressed brown-skinned peoples, found us conducting a more efficient slaughter of Filipinos than Spain had ever conducted. It found us annexing behind legal phraseology, the rich island of Puerto Rico. It even found us considering the advice of our more avaricious imperialists that we annex Cuba itself. . . .
>
> The outstanding change which the war marked on the character of the United

States, was the country's definite step from the ranks of the self sufficient and anti-imperialistic nations, into the group of colony-grabbing powers.

After the surrender of the Spanish in 1898, the United States was faced with a dilemma insofar as Cuba was concerned. During the heated debate over the joint resolution that stated America's aims in the war with Spain, four Democratic senators from the Senate Foreign Relations Committee proposed the inclusion of a paragraph which recognized the "Republic of Cuba as the true and lawful government of that island." It was rejected. Senator Henry M. Teller of Colorado then offered a compromise which promised that when the United States had restored order in Cuba, the island would be turned over to the Cubans.

Now, with peace at hand, the Americans were reluctant to let Cuba slip out of their hands. Yet they were committed to a moral position which was difficult to abandon.

A lanky senator from Connecticut found the ideal solution. His name was Orville H. Platt.

Introduced on February 25, 1901, the Platt Amendment stipulated, among other things, that the government of Cuba would consent automatically to any U.S. intervention in order to "preserve Cuban independence" or to maintain a regime adequate to protect "life, property and individual liberty."

Meeting in Havana, the Cuban delegates to the constitutional convention were told that the United States would not lift military rule unless the Platt Amendment became part of Cuba's new constitution. With great reluctance and by a vote of sixteen to eleven, it was adopted by the convention on June 12, 1901.

In a letter to Theodore Roosevelt, written from Havana October 28, 1901, the American military governor General Leonard Wood put it even more clearly: "There is, of course, little or no real independence left to Cuba under the Platt Amendment . . . it is quite apparent that she is absolutely in our hands."

The Cubans, after a century of struggle, could count their dead and assess the misery their people had suffered, and realize that it all had been for nothing. Cuba had simply exchanged Spanish domination for that of the United States.

CHAPTER TWENTY-TWO

MIAMI, JANUARY 22, 1961

The Carta mansion that Sunday night was ablaze with light. Red-jacketed attendants parked cars for arriving guests, who were resplen-

246

dent in evening clothes and glittering jewelry. Inside the house, waiters circulated with cocktails. It took two tables to display the massive buffet. Gustavo Carta, attired in a dark-blue evening jacket, greeted guests in the main entry hall. Elizabeth looked flawlessly regal in a flowing white gown and long white gloves as she stood beside him. As they moved past, the guests exchanged pleasantries with the two of them, but Elizabeth felt an undercurrent of tension. Everyone knew, of course, about the earlier attempt on Carta's life, and some of the guests expressed encouragement and admiration for their carrying on with their activities despite the danger. Yet it was clear there was uneasiness about the possibility of a recurrence. Many of those invited had sent their regrets, and Elizabeth knew that fear was one reason. Four security guards had been posted outside, and three police cars were stationed at a tactful distance from the entrance to the driveway, but these security measures, Elizabeth sensed, only underscored the guests' edginess rather than assuaged it.

Robin arrived alone, nervous and ill at ease as she greeted her parents-in-law. Carta kissed her formally on the cheek and Elizabeth embraced her, suppressing her distaste for Robin's shiny pink taffeta dress, a dress she had seen several times before. Oh well, Elizabeth told herself, Robin had many good qualities.

"Sorry I'm late," Robin blurted. "I had a paper to write. I'm afraid I lost track of time."

"We're glad you could come," Elizabeth said patiently.

"I'm sorry David couldn't make it," Carta told her. Elizabeth looked at him quickly. Carta smiled. "But it's good to see the professor away from her books."

"I'm not a professor yet," Robin said. "One more year of classes and then I have my doctoral dissertation to write."

"It's time we had a scholar among the women in the family," Elizabeth said.

Robin smiled, then moved quickly through the house and out onto the lawn area, pushing through the crowds of guests. As she walked across the lawn she helped herself to a glass of white wine which a waiter offered her. She looked at the faces of the other guests. There was no one she recognized. But then she hadn't expected to see anyone she knew. Her friends were mostly people connected with the university. None of them had the social rank to be invited to one of the Cartas' fund raisers. Indeed, Robin herself had not wanted to come. She had pleaded overwork, but Elizabeth had been insistent. With David away in Havana, Robin should not simply bury herself in her books, Elizabeth had said. And so, despite her better instincts, Robin now found herself surrounded by the social elite of Miami and feeling very uncomfortable about it.

Her discomfort was increased by worry. Robin had not heard from David since his departure. She had expected a phone call, even though she knew phone communications were unpredictable between Miami and Havana. With Gustavo and Elizabeth at the Inauguration and David in Havana, Robin had found herself feeling suddenly alone and vulnerable. She had always been a little awed by the wealth and the strong-mindedness of the Carta clan. Now she had become increasingly cognizant of the aura of danger that surrounded them as well. It was all very disquieting.

Robin wandered toward the swimming pool. A wooden platform had been erected, and ten musicians, attired in black tie and tails, were setting themselves up. She watched them taking out their instruments and arranging their music on the stands. Robin remembered now that Elizabeth had told her there would be a chamber-music recital by several leading members of the Havana Symphony Orchestra who had recently escaped to Miami. Their performance, Elizabeth hoped, would remind the Miami establishment of the problems facing the exiles and encourage them to contribute to the Cuban Relief Society.

Robin was engrossed in sipping her wine and watching the musicians prepare themselves when one of the waiters approached her. He stared at her for a moment, then called out a greeting. Robin's mouth dropped open and she tipped her wineglass so that it spilled on her dress.

"What are you doing here?" she said. "Is this your idea of a joke?"

"Hey, I'm working my way through college," Michael Danielson said with a sly grin. "I don't have a rich Cuban sugar-daddy to pay my way."

Robin shot a furtive glance to see if anyone was watching them. "You could have spared me this."

"I really apologize, Rob," Michael said. "The job came up. I took it without even thinking for a second that it was your father-in-law, honest. Parties like this come up all the time. It's just another night's work."

Robin stared at him, assessing his mirthful eyes.

"Forgive me?"

"Yes, I forgive you, damn it."

"Look, they'll only be serving here another few minutes. Then I can leave. Why don't you split and drive over to my place? OK?"

Robin turned away. "We'll see," she said, walking away. She glanced quickly toward the house again. Neither Elizabeth nor Gustavo was in evidence. She took a napkin and patted at the moist stain on her dress. Michael had startled her. It was outrageously inconsiderate for him to take a job at the Carta house—she didn't believe for a minute that he had done it without realizing. It was stupid and thoughtless.

But she knew she would drive to his place later. She knew she had to.

The musicians had been playing for twenty minutes when Elizabeth noticed Gustavo's absence. He had looked preoccupied all evening, and his face had seemed drawn. Elizabeth looked around at the guests. They appeared to be enjoying the music. She got up as inconspicuously as possible and made her way toward the house.

She found Carta in his study, standing at the window, staring out onto the lawn. He turned as she entered.

"You have an uncanny second sense," Carta said. "I was just debating whether to come and get you."

Elizabeth smiled. "I was worried about you, Gustavo." But she saw that his eyes were bright as if he'd just received a gift.

"David called a few minutes ago," he said. "He's at the airport. He's got Elena with him."

Elizabeth caught her breath. "Elena!"

"He said Camilo is well. Camilo asked David to bring Elena to Miami to stay with us."

"I'm so relieved," Elizabeth said, her voice suddenly tentative.

Carta held her and looked sternly into her eyes. "So am I," he said. "Elizabeth, I don't like secrets between us. If I had thought David was in any danger, I would have prevented his trip. But I didn't, did I?"

"I didn't think you knew," Elizabeth said sheepishly.

"You know better," he said, amused with her. "Eh?"

Elizabeth responded with a nod.

Carta took her hand. "Simply because my son feels I am politically his enemy doesn't mean I don't love him just as much as you do."

"If I say I am sorry, can we proceed to being happy about Elena?"

"Why not?" His face cracked into a broad smile. "She will put a little fun into this old barn! It will be a tonic for both of us."

"Did David say he had trouble getting her out?"

"No. No trouble."

"And is he coming here tonight?"

"Within the hour."

Elizabeth's eyes were brimming with tears. "I've got to prepare her room. I should get out her old toys and things." She noticed that her husband was lost in his own thoughts. "What are you thinking about, Gustavo?"

"About her father."

Elizabeth walked over to the desk and stood before him. The sounds of the chamber music could be heard in the background. "If Camilo sent his child away with David he must be expecting things to get difficult for him," she said.

"That's one possibility."

"Either that or he himself expects to defect soon. That could be! Camilo could be coming home, too, couldn't he?" Tears glistened on her cheeks.

Carta took out his handkerchief and patted her face tenderly. "Don't leap to conclusions, darling. It does no good to pump yourself up with expectations and then be disappointed."

"I know, Gustavo. But I've felt for a long time Camilo would be coming home. It's silly, and I can't explain it."

Carta looked at her gravely. "It's foolish to try to anticipate Camilo's actions, Elizabeth. You know that as well as I. There is no predicting Camilo."

"Do you know, Gustavo, when he came to me that day in Havana—the day he said we would have to leave Cuba—I was furious with him. I denounced him in front of his men. But I have had such deep regrets about that—it's tormented me. I think I misjudged him. I think now that he was genuinely trying to protect us, that he was acting within the restrictions set down for him, trying to save his own position while still helping us."

"I don't know," Carta said thoughtfully.

"And later when you stayed behind, I felt Camilo was quietly shielding you all that time—shielding you from your enemies. He was doing it in his own way, behind the scenes. Camilo has been loyal, Gustavo. I know he has!"

Carta put his hand on her arm. "Don't get your hopes up, Elizabeth. Nothing is simple in these times. Why don't you prepare Elena's room? I will go and see to our guests."

Elizabeth leaned over and kissed him. "Oh, Gustavo . . ."

"Yes," he said, smiling. "I know."

He could see that the musicians had finished playing. The guests were applauding the performance. He should be getting outside. There were social amenities to attend to.

He turned and started toward the door, but his eyes caught the desk drawer and he walked over to it and brought out an old photograph of Camilo. He stared into his son's deep-set eyes. He stood there, riveted, and suddenly he felt a deep longing. A longing for his son. A longing for Cuba.

250

An idea was gnawing at his mind, and it startled and disturbed him. His life, Carta reflected, seemed to be governed by a cruel irony. The son he loved so deeply, the country he loved so deeply, each flawed in the same way. Each possessing such energy and beauty, a promise of greatness. Yet always in the background the looming shadow of violence and betrayal.

Carta opened the door and started toward his guests. If Elizabeth was convinced that Camilo was protecting him, Carta did not share her conviction. He had heard stories. Rumors. Havana was always rife with rumors.

Who knows? he thought wearily. Maybe Elizabeth is right. Maybe my son is indeed coming home. Maybe.

But he still wondered why.

Shortly after the music began, Robin noticed her mother-in-law moving out of her chair. She waited till Elizabeth disappeared before she got up, hurried through the house and gave her ticket to the car-park. Twenty minutes later she pulled up in front of Michael's garage apartment in Coconut Grove and hurried up the stairs. She paused for a moment to gather herself. Running into Michael at that party had shocked her. The notion of her in-laws finding out about her affair with a nineteen-year-old college sophomore left her limp. If she had any brains, she told herself, she would go home and get to work on her studies. And yet here she was, waiting at his door, feeling strangely helpless to do otherwise.

Michael opened the door and beamed. He was dressed in worn blue jeans which were stained with white paint and had a hole in the knee. He wore no shirt or shoes. He kissed her on the lips, the sort of quick, perfunctory kiss exchanged by long-term lovers.

"Hi, Robin," he said cheerfully, but she did not reply, walking past him into his small apartment. He patted her on her fanny as she went past. "You'd never guess where I was tonight."

She sank into a battered bamboo sofa that was covered with worn red plush cushions. "I don't know why the hell I'm here. I should be home working."

"You're here because of my wonderful refreshments," Michael said. "I can offer you some coffee, but the milk is sour, or some Gallo that tastes like vinegar, or a beer."

"I hate beer," Robin said.

Michael pulled a bottle from the refrigerator, gave her a quick smile and plunked himself down on the floor in front of her.

"What's that?" Robin asked.

251

"Champagne. I stole it from the party. Figured it was all in the family."

Robin studied Michael as he tried to wrestle the cork with his thumbs. He looks like a street urchin out of Charles Dickens, she thought, with his shirt off, his ribs jutting through his skinny hairless chest, his shaggy black hair shaking with the exertion. Watching him, she tried to analyze again, for the thousandth time, what impulse drew her to him. His face still bore the sort of prettiness that goes with early adolescence. His features were too sculpted, his hands too delicate, his manner too vulnerable. Michael clearly didn't come together as a grown man, and yet she adored him.

She and Michael had first met six months earlier when she was a teaching assistant. He started hanging around her like a homeless puppy. She ignored him, but that didn't help. She told him that she was married, that she was ten years older than he, but he didn't listen. He started writing romantic poems to her and buying gifts; his attentions were unrelenting. After two months of it, they saw an old Bette Davis tear-jerker together. She had looked over at Michael in the middle of the movie and seen the tears rolling down his cheeks. She had laughed at him, but he was not embarrassed. He said he wanted to be a poet and he didn't care whether anyone saw him laughing or crying, and she realized that in five years of marriage she had rarely seen David laugh and had never seen him cry. That night she went home with Michael and they became lovers.

The cork came off with a pop and Michael poured the champagne into two coffee-stained mugs.

"Stop," Robin protested. "It'll ruin the taste."

"I don't have wineglasses, remember?"

"At least you could let me rinse them out so we wouldn't be tasting coffee," she responded, but he was already clinking mugs and announcing a toast.

"To the Carta clan for the champagne and to Miami for bringing us together and to you because you're beautiful." Michael guzzled down his champagne in five exuberant gulps, then grimaced and said, "You were right, it tastes of coffee."

Robin smiled.

Michael poured more champagne for them both, then lifted his mug again. "And, I forgot, here's to your husband for leaving for three months."

"Oh, shut up," Robin said. "Besides, he hasn't left yet."

"Shit," Michael said.

"He's in Havana on some secret mission."

252

"I didn't think he was the type for secret missions."

"It's something in the family. He wouldn't tell me."

But Michael was suddenly scrambling to his feet, oblivious of what she was saying. "Wait a minute—there's something else I swiped from the party," he said, disappearing into the kitchen again.

Robin looked around the room and mused how Michael managed to combine neatness and sloppiness. As usual, there were items of clothing strewn on the floor—a sock here, a T-shirt there. Dirty dishes were stacked in the kitchen along with some opened cans. Yet there was a pervasive orderliness to the place, as there was to Michael's character. He had constructed enormous bookshelves out of wood and bricks, and his hundreds of books were placed so that he knew where each was located. His desk was always neat, his papers carefully arrayed. Michael loved the French Impressionist painters, and the walls of the living room were emblazoned with Cézanne and Monet and Pissarro. He also enjoyed Mozart and Beethoven and Brahms, and his records were carefully stacked next to the old record player. Robin admired Michael for caring about these things and for trying to surround himself with beauty. David never seemed to care what was around him—she hated herself for making invidious comparisons.

Michael appeared with a dish containing four big shrimps skewered with fancy toothpicks. "I should have nabbed the caviar, but it was gone by the time I got there," he said, offering the shrimps to Robin.

She realized that she was hungry, and took the shrimps eagerly. "You're a scrounge," she said through her full mouth. He was refilling their mugs with champagne.

"Fringe benefits of being a waiter. By the way, did I tell you I figured out what I'm going to do my term paper about?"

"What?"

"I'm going to go through the great Victorian novels and finish all the big love scenes."

"What does that mean?" she said, washing down the shrimps with more champagne.

"I'm going to rewrite them as the novelists would have done if they hadn't had to worry about censorship and all that Victorian shit."

"I still don't know what you mean."

"Take Dickens. When you read him you realize he really must have been a salty old buzzard. But he always worried about the newspapers that ran his stuff. He was afraid of doing his thing."

"Go on."

"What do you mean, go on? Are you going to play or aren't you?"

"Play? I didn't know it was a game!"

"It's a game to help get me ready for the paper, see?"

"What are the rules?" Robin asked, drinking her second mug of champagne.

"Well, one person picks a scene and explains how it ended in the novel. Then the second person guesses how it really would have ended."

"I see. But who knows how it really would have ended?"

"I know, because I've figured it out. And if the second person guesses wrong, then he or she has to act it out."

Robin grinned. "Sounds like the game could get very gamey."

She watched as Michael got to his feet. She always loved his games. He seemed to have a limitless imagination for inventing new forms of play —word games, literary games, card games. Everything became a game with Michael—getting dressed, washing, eating. It was all play. And it made her laugh.

"OK, I'll go first," Michael was saying as he stood in front of her. "I'm going to start with Dickens' *Great Expectations*. You remember it pretty well, don't you?"

"Yes," Robin said.

"OK, remember how Pip really has fallen for Estella, but she rejects his advances and teases the hell out of him. One day during tea, she finally lets him hold her hand. He kisses it. Then she invites him to kiss her cheek, but just as Pip leans over to make contact she glides away and leaves him standing there in frustration."

"That was pretty cruel."

"You know how Dickens really wanted to write it?"

"Show me." Robin grinned.

"Delighted to. Are you ready?"

"Ready as I'll ever be. . . ."

"When Estella ducked down and slid away from him, this is what Pip would have done. He would have grabbed her by the hair," said Michael, grabbing Robin's hair. "And he would have yanked her to the floor," he said, pulling her roughly onto the carpet, where Robin lay in a heap. "He would have hoisted her rump into the air," Michael said, pulling up her dress. "And old Pip would have had at her." And Michael started spanking Robin, his hand pounding against her. Robin giggled and tried to roll away, but Michael had a strong grip on her and continued walloping her backside, admiring, as he did so, the contours of her buttocks as they reddened under his assault.

"OK, OK, you've made your point," Robin squealed as she finally extricated herself from his grip.

Michael relented. They sat facing each other, breathing hard.

"You bastard," Robin said, her face red.

"You loved it, admit it."

"Darned right I did."

"Good."

"But now it's my turn."

"I'm ready," he said, reaching for his mug of champagne.

Robin was thining, her eyes racing across the titles on his bookshelves. She brightened. "OK, I'm going with Henry Fielding."

"Good choice."

"In *Tom Jones,* do you remember when Tom saves Mrs. Waters from a rapist on the road? She is very attracted to him and invites him to dinner. All during dinner she is giving him lecherous looks, but he's too busy eating to notice. Then she drops her handkerchief and Tom finally catches on."

"I remember all that."

"Fielding gets very vague after that."

"He sure does."

"Let me show you how he wanted to end it. Stand up and close your eyes."

"Why should I close my eyes?" Michael asked, getting to his feet.

"Shut up."

Michael stood in front of her, his eyes closed. With a quick, deft movement, Robin unsnapped his jeans and yanked them over his flanks. She looked at him for a moment, standing there with his pants down around his ankles, a look of sublime expectation on his face. She saw his penis bob in anticipation. And then she started.

Michael gave a yelp of surprise and his eyes popped open. He saw her bent over, gnawing away at his kneecap.

"What the hell are you doing down there?"

"I'm giving you a knee job."

"A what?"

"Everybody knew Fielding had a fetish for kneecaps," Robin explained blithely. "I figure Mrs. Waters would have given Tom a good old-fashioned knee job."

Michael stared incredulously at her, then burst into laughter. "OK, goddamn it, you win the game."

She grabbed his ankle suddenly and tugged it and he tumbled to the floor. She sat down on his chest, pinning him, and smiled at him. She leaned forward and kissed his lips.

"You're crazy, you know that?" Michael said.

She peered into his face. "If I wasn't crazy I wouldn't be here." And she kissed him again.

David sipped on the beer, savoring its cool bite, and closed his eyes against the soft night breeze. Seated on the upstairs screened-in porch, he tilted back the old straw chair and propped his feet on the wooden railing. It was probably about one o'clock, he figured. He had wanted to come home and go to sleep, but his emotions were too scrambled, his nerves on edge. Too much had happened too fast. He was beyond sleep.

He had taken Elena to his parents' house earlier. Their reunion had been tearful. The child had lived with them several years before and loved them deeply. Elizabeth was like a mother to her. And Elena was the daughter Elizabeth had always wanted. There was something very touching about seeing Gustavo and Elizabeth standing in the hallway of their old mansion amid the debris of their party and exchanging hugs and kisses with this small child, who was so sleepy-eyed she hardly knew where she was.

David had excused himself after a few minutes. The moment, he felt, belonged to them. Moreover, he felt uneasy about all that Camilo had confided in him. Unlike his brother, David had never been talented at keeping secrets. Elizabeth especially had a way of getting things out of him. Camilo had been specific about not wanting them to know about the possibility of his imminent return to Miami. He had to honor that trust. So he pleaded weariness and departed. As he left he felt Elena's eyes on him. He saw her staring, as if he embodied a flickering memory of Camilo. He knew she wondered if she would ever see her father again. Elizabeth too wanted him to assure her Camilo would return to the family. He was too tired to offer reassurances. He was tired of reassuring others. He needed some reassurances of his own.

David stretched and breathed in the scented night air. He flicked away a mosquito that landed on his nose. Christ, he thought, where the hell is Robin? He had desperately hoped she would be at home. He wanted to kiss her, to tell her that he had missed her, to explain that he would not be leaving on the expedition. But she wasn't there for him. Perhaps she was studying with a friend. Perhaps. Who knew with Robin? When they had first been married he thought he had access to her every thought and understood her every emotion. Another one of those wondrous illusions, he thought. The illusions that go with passion. That go with falling in love. How strangely ephemeral they are, like bubbles in a bath. Maybe they'd get you through a year, maybe two. And then they would simply melt away, leaving you stranded, feeling somewhat stupid, wondering whether there was reality to any of it in the first place.

256

Perhaps if he waited up for a while Robin would come home. They would talk, make love. David would like that. He wondered how she would react to the news. Amato's warnings gnawed away at the edge of his mind. Maybe she'd be disappointed he was canceling his trip. Perhaps she was banking on his departure so she could have her freedom again.

David also dreaded facing Dr. Barnes. How could he explain his sudden change of plans? Dr. Barnes, the head of the Marine Lab, knew how ardent David had been about the expedition, knew how important it was to his career. David couldn't simply say it was a family emergency. That sounded too vague. Yet he couldn't explain about Camilo. No, David would have to think up a better story. His colleagues would also resent him for suddenly dropping out. They were counting on him. What would he tell them?

He knew his decision was the right one. If Camilo were to arrive in Miami the danger would be great. Camilo would have enemies on all sides. The Castro people would be looking for him and so would the CIA. Understanding all that now, David could not simply pull up and leave all that behind. He couldn't do that to Camilo. Not now. Not after what had happened in Havana.

I have to be here and take care of him, he thought. But I can choose the time to tell Dr. Barnes. What if Camilo shows up here next week, or the week after? That would mean I could still make the trip to Peru. The best idea is to wait. Don't say anything to them until the last minute.

David got up groggily and went downstairs for another beer. He almost missed a step and had to catch himself to avoid falling. Christ, he was tired. He wished Robin would come home. Why did he spend so much time waiting? Waiting for the expedition to start. Waiting for Robin to come home. And now, waiting for Camilo.

CHAPTER TWENTY-THREE

MIAMI, FEBRUARY 14, 1961

Elizabeth lunched with Elena that afternoon in the sunny breakfast room off the kitchen. They had spent the morning shopping in downtown Miami, buying dresses and jeans and skirts at the big Burdine's department store. Underwear and stockings were purchased at a little shop off Flagler that Elizabeth liked. They had arrived back at the house just before noon, burdened with packages that were left in Elena's bedroom. Elena put on her new green swimsuit that had the likeness of a dolphin sewed on the hip.

It made Elizabeth happy having her again. Elena had been shy when she first arrived, but after the first week she began bubbling with energy. She was curious about everything. She bombarded Elizabeth with questions faster than Elizabeth could find answers. Elizabeth was exhausted. She had gotten used to being alone. Normally she filled her day with chores that served to absorb her interest as well as her time. This energetic little girl made her readjust her routine and relearn all the devices and all the artifices by which one instructed and entertained a five-year-old.

What she found most disconcerting in those first few weeks with Elena was her striking resemblance to Camilo. She saw him in the little way the child moved her mouth, in all her gestures, in the eager excitement in her blue eyes when something delighted her, and she saw him in her quick charming smile. Occasionally, Elizabeth could catch glimpses of Alicia in the child's face, in a look, or the way she would turn her head. But mostly she saw her son. The Carta look. How she ached to be close to Camilo again, to see and to touch him.

"Why are you looking at me like that, Elizabeth?" Elena wiped her mouth with a napkin. "Is something wrong?"

It made Elizabeth feel awkward to be called Grandmother. They had agreed Elena would use her first name. "It makes us friends," she'd told her. So the child had taken delight in their little intimacy and obliged. She stared now, her head cocked. "You look so sad, Elizabeth. Why?"

"I'm not sad, darling, just thinking."

"About what? Can I have your pickle? I love pickles."

"Certainly."

"My papa looks sad, too. Did I tell you? I think he's worried a lot."

"About what, darling?"

"I don't know. He's just like you. When I ask why, he doesn't answer."

Gustavo came into the room, beaming. He had been in conference with some stranger in the library, and now he appeared in his shirt sleeves, a half-smoked cigar in his mouth. He looked excited and pleased.

Elizabeth asked, "Is your guest gone?"

"No," said Gustavo. "He's still there. I asked Alfaro to call me when you got home." He knelt beside Elena. She looked at him over her shoulder, shyly. "How was the shopping?"

258

Elena hunched her head in her shoulders, a little shy smile on her face. She glanced quickly at Elizabeth and then back at her grandfather. "Fine," she said quietly.

Gustavo laughed. "You aren't afraid of me, are you?"

Elena shook her head.

"Good. You remember when you used to swim with me in the pool at the *finca?*"

She nodded, still maintaining that same vague smile.

"You used to like to stand on my shoulders and dive, remember?"

Elena giggled.

"Is that your new swimming suit? Can I see it?"

Elena got down off the chair and turned around slowly, so he could see the new suit on her.

Gustavo's eyes widened. "Ah, you're a future bathing beauty—*magnifico!*"

"It's got a dolphin on it, see?" Elena showed him the dolphin. "Isn't he funny?"

Elizabeth sat watching them together. Her husband's face had lost its weariness. His expression had lightened the moment he began talking to Elena. The desire for family, the warmth and love of children, seemed to radiate from him. She realized the depth of their loneliness and isolation.

"Well, this afternoon," Gustavo was saying to Elena, "we can have a swim together, eh?"

Gustavo hugged the child and excused himself to go back to the library.

Elena sat back down in the chair and finished her Coke, sucking on the melted ice cubes. Then she looked up at Elizabeth and said, "He's nice, my *abuelo*. Why does Papa say he's a bad man?"

"Did he say that?"

"He said that my *abuelo* was rich and that all rich men were bad men."

"Your grandfather is not a bad man, darling. He and your father disagree on certain things, and that has made for bad feelings between them."

"But why?"

Elizabeth sighed. It was so difficult to explain. Explaining it to a child, it didn't really make much sense. "It's politics, darling . . ."

"But he's my father's papa, isn't he?"

"Yes, he's your father's papa."

"I love my papa. Why doesn't he love his papa?"

"He does, my darling. It's just hard to explain. Someday you'll understand."

"When is someday?"

"When you're older."

"I hope I get older fast," she said. "Papa keeps saying someday this, someday that—someday we're going to be together all the time. Someday. It never comes. I wait and I wait and it never comes."

"It will, darling," said Elizabeth. She felt as though she were about to cry.

THE EVERGLADES

As they drove through the barbed-wire gate into the camp, Carta saw the moon rising over the horizon, the delicate black silhouettes of scrub pine and palms showing in the dark swamp plain. There were a number of changes in the camp. He saw three new barracks buildings under construction to his left. Floodlights had been set up, and men in their camouflaged fatigues were milling about amid the steady staccato of hammers. The fresh lumber showed in the brilliant light. He counted a dozen men at work hammering sheets of corrugated tin onto the roofs. Beyond the command shack, he saw the tall spire of the new radio tower. Two squads of men, their pants legs wet, were marching past the barracks, the lights of the windows glowing on their sweating faces. The whole area seemed alive with activity.

The electric light from inside the command shack glowed through the screen door onto the steps. As Carta went up the steps he heard the steady crunch of marching feet behind him and the rapping of hammers. It gave a lift to his heart. He was not prepared for what greeted him.

"We put two infiltration teams ashore last night in Pinar del Río," Tipton began the briefing. "We had radio contact with them at 0500 hours. Oddly enough, things went rather smoothly for a change. They made contact with Hernando's men in the Sierra Cristal mountains. They are short of food and ammunition, but the arrival of our men perked that up a bit. The militia is applying pressure in the area, but in general, reports are encouraging."

Tipton lifted his brows and wiped the sweat from his chin. It was stifling in the headquarters shack, even though the sun had gone down two hours earlier. There were just three of them gathered around the table—Carta, Rodríguez and Tipton. Tipton wanted it that way. He alone knew what was to be discussed at the briefing. The fewer people, the better. Tipton had informed the other officers that there were to be no interruptions. Not this time.

"Now for the not-too-good news."

Rodríguez leaned forward and fixed Carta's eyes with his own. "As you know, our third infiltration team was to be landed last night in Matanzas. They were to be met by Juanito and infiltrated. Five men attempted the landing. Without success."

"What happened?"

"Nothing. When they reached the coast, they flashed the light signal to shore. No reply. They waited two hours and tried again. Nothing. So, they returned here."

"From here on in it gets black," said Tipton, sipping his coffee. "We learned from Masetti this morning that Juanito had been taken and shot. Castro's militia mined the beach where we were to land—they knew exactly where we were coming."

"How? Juanito?"

"No. They had a tip from a source in Havana."

"Our friends," said Rodríguez, using the euphemism the Cubans gave the CIA. "Pure and simple."

"Impossible," Carta exclaimed.

Tipton raised his hands like a traffic cop. "You haven't got it all yet. Tell him, Rod."

"Two things. First—Castro's intelligence has broken our code, using a new Russian computer. That's openers. Secondly, they are jamming our radio, so that we can only transmit very early in the day—up to seven o'clock. Since they now seem capable of breaking any code we use, we dare use the radio only with caution. Hence, our reports from Masetti are more sketchy and difficult."

"Now for the real ball buster." Tipton leaned forward, planting his elbows on the table. "The Monroe County sheriff raided our base at Shark Key at three this afternoon. Alfredo and six of his men were arrested. Three tons of equipment and munitions were confiscated."

Carta sighed. "Our friends again?"

"Seems so."

"What happened to the boats?"

Rodríguez shook his head. He raised his hand and held up three fingers.

Carta gasped. "All three?"

"Confiscated. By Dobbs, Pelham's man. Our lawyer, Mr. Kaufman in Key West, informs us that you are very likely to face a federal grand jury, Gustavo—in Miami, based on this happy little incident at Shark Key." He turned his head. "Shit!" he spat.

"We expect them to move against this camp at any time," said Rodríguez. "I've issued orders that there's to be no shooting. I don't like it. But I figured if they indict you, let it be for violation of the Neutrality Act, not murder."

Carta sat staring at their downcast faces, feeling the sick emptiness of disaster. He said nothing for a long moment. Outside, the hammering echoed across the yard. Someone called a name and there was a shouted answer. A jeep started up with a roar. His breath came out from between his clenched teeth in a rush. "How long do you think we have?" he asked.

"Who knows?" Tipton shrugged. "Mr. Kaufman didn't say. But he said it would certainly come, and soon. And now that you've had a chance to absorb that lovely news, let me tell you about Victorio's plight in the Escambray. Castro's in the process of assembling fifty thousand militia in Las Villas province to attack Victorio's guerrillas. It looks very bad. Very bad indeed. We've been getting anguished radio messages all week from him, pleading for our help."

"We don't have anything to send him, Gustavo," said Rodríguez. He seemed near tears. "Even if we did, they've taken our boats. We don't have a way to get to Cuba."

As he listened, Gustavo Carta realized that he could not afford the luxury of being angry, or bitter. He had underestimated Pelham's power, and it had been a bad mistake. He was discovering rapidly what the score was. The CIA strikes swiftly at people who do not submit to its control. That was certain. They wanted control over him, over his people, both here and in Cuba, and if they couldn't get it they'd wipe them all out. That was their policy. The troops in Guatemala were the only force the CIA wanted. It had made sure of its control.

He put his hand out to pick up the mug Tipton had set on the table in front of him, and saw that his fingers were trembling. He sipped the hot black coffee and looked at them. "What about our people in Oriente?"

"Intact," said Tipton. "Getting a bit anxious for us to do something. They too are under pressure."

"Major Mahío?"

"No change."

"Masetti in Havana?"

"Anxious."

"Then we are still the principal anti-Castro movement within Cuba."

Tipton looked annoyed. "Look, Gustavo, it's obvious what's happening. They're isolating us. They're destroying us piecemeal. Another month and this camp will be out of business. Our people in Cuba will wither on the vine. The handwriting's on the wall, Gustavo."

262

Carta sat holding the coffee mug. He stared at the map of Oriente province on the wall, and the thought of it, all he had planned, was just an irony. It isn't that bad, he thought. It can't be.

He said, "I want to start our operation before they have a chance to use that bunch in Guatemala."

Tipton exploded. "Our operation? Damn it, Gustavo, we don't have an operation! We're fucked!"

Looking at his flushed face, Carta knew it was the disappointment that made him lose control. He'd never seen Tipton this way before. He seemed defeated. So did Rodríguez, who said nothing, but sat there with that funereal look on his face, trying to avoid his eyes.

He tapped the bottom of the mug on the table, staring at it. "We'll do it with what we have. There are still three shrimp boats. We'll use them. We have ammunition and arms here in the camp. We'll use those. Send them to Victorio, if we must. But we won't let them beat us."

Tipton shook his head and looked at Rodríguez helplessly, then back at Carta. "You don't understand, Gustavo. They have beaten us. We have to admit it."

"I can't," Carta said curtly, grinding his teeth. "You understand, Tip? I can't."

MIAMI, FEBRUARY 15, 1961

Elizabeth sat in front of the telephone and stared at it tentatively, then rose to her feet and paced across the bedroom, trying to ward off the feeling of disquiet. She was not eager to make the phone call. Something in her said it was the wrong thing to do, and yet the necessary thing to do. Further, she did not like the idea of bothering Charles Danforth at a time like this. Charles's life was a turmoil of last-minute crises. But what were her options? The situation, she knew, had become critical. She had to call him now. He would understand. He had always understood.

If only Charles could have seen Gustavo the night before, when he returned from the meeting at the camp, he would understand why she was calling. She'd been reading in bed when he arrived home. Even as he entered their room she noticed immediately how his normally erect posture seemed to sag. His face bore heavy lines of fatigue. He was uncommunicative about the details of the meeting; it was late and she didn't want to prod him. Clearly, the situation was deteriorating. Gustavo was such a proud man, a man accustomed to not thinking about money. Yet she knew that their financial situation had become critical.

263

That had become clear from scattered bits of overheard conversation, and her own secret visit to the bank that morning had confirmed her suspicions. He had done his best to conceal it from her, but she knew now they were near the end of his resources.

As for Charles, he would understand. He always understood.

Thank God for Charles Danforth, she thought.

As she thought of Charles, it occurred to Elizabeth how difficult it was to conceive of some people as ever having been young, as ever having been childlishly impulsive and bubbling with uncontrolled energy. She could remember Charles Danforth as a small child in short pants, a little kid with red cheeks and intense eyes, who even then functioned under some sort of inner discipline and constraint. Try as she might, she could not recall one childish tantrum when he had screamed or beaten his fists and been out of control. Indeed, she could not even recall him looking dirty or mud-stained. And, though Elizabeth had thought of her own adolescence as having been one prolonged state of embarrassment, she could not recall Charles as ever having been embarrassed.

Only once, perhaps. That was the time when, at age fifteen, she was visiting the Danforths' big white shingled home on Martha's Vineyard while her mother was doing the circuit of horse shows in Kentucky. It was her first day at the house, and, after swimming at South Beach, braving the tall breakers, fighting the fierce undertow, Elizabeth, covered with sand, had ducked into the bathshed to shower before entering the main house. She had been standing under the steaming shower for several minutes, holding her face under the stinging needles of water, when she felt a sudden cold draft. She turned toward the door, rubbing the water from her eyes, to see Charles Danforth, then fourteen, standing there naked and wide-eyed, holding his trunks in his hand, his face scarlet.

"I'm terribly sorry," Charles said. "It's just, I always shower now . . . not used to visitors. Sorry, really I am." He slammed the door, and then he quickly reopened it again! Elizabeth now looked at him in disbelief as he stood there, studying her body with almost clinical fascination, compulsively intrigued with the ripening teenage figure of his first cousin. Elizabeth was annoyed and even humiliated by his intrusion and tried desperately to cover herself with her hands. But as she saw Charles becoming aroused, a look of utter helplessness on his face, she could not resist the temptation to laugh and she let her hands fall to her side. She remembered his penis, how odd it looked, and how comical, jutting from his tuft of pubic hair like a fat pink crayon. Charles seemed startled, but then his eyes met hers, his expression not that of an embarrassed schoolboy but rather one of masculine defiance. Tumescent but unchastened, he closed the shower door slowly, and she heard him stomping out of the shed.

The incident had never been mentioned again till they were both in college, Charles at Harvard and Elizabeth at Duke. By then they had long since developed an intense bond, deeply relished each other's company and shared the most intimate secrets. And when either one was in trouble, whether the cause was a lover or a parent or bad grades, one would seek out the other for counsel and compassion.

At Charles's wedding, just before he started down the aisle, Charles had looked around furtively and moved over to Elizabeth and whispered, in a phony Charles Boyer accent, "It's you I should be marrying, *ma chérie*. My first love, my last friend."

And Elizabeth had whispered back, mustering up her best long-suffering Bette Davis imitation, "You are right, my love. At least I can carry with me the knowledge that I witnessed your first pubic erection."

"How true," Charles said, as he started down the aisle.

You're being very stupid this morning, she thought. Why are you sitting here daydreaming? You can't avoid making this call. You absolutely must.

She dialed the operator, gave her the number of the White House and Charles's name, making it person-to-person. She waited with her eyes closed, taking slow, deep breaths to calm her anxiety.

Elizabeth heard Charles's voice coming over the line clear and confident. "How are you, love?"

"All right, Charley. Are you keeping Camelot glued together?"

"Camelot has a way of becoming unglued on an hourly basis. As a matter of fact, I may have to break this off in a few moments. I'm meeting with Curtis Le May—can't keep all those shiny buttons and combat ribbons standing around."

"I'm calling about a very unglamorous subject, Charles. I hate to disturb you about it, especially when I know you're under so much pressure. I just wondered, things are getting a little tight here. Did you have a chance to look into the trust-fund thing we discussed?"

"I've talked to the lawyers. It's going to be hard to swing. It could mean revising a lot of documents and covenants. It could take months."

"But the money belongs to all of us, Charles. There are only six of us."

"There's no way you can use your portion of the trust as collateral for a personal loan. You've got to face that, Liz. I'm sorry, dear."

"There's got to be a way."

"Why the sudden panic, Liz? It's not like you."

"I've been putting my personal funds into our joint checking account,

265

slipping it in so Gustavo wouldn't notice. This morning I put in the last ten thousand from my savings, and I found out we had an overdraft of twenty-five thousand. We're flat broke, Charley."

There was a short pause on the other end of the line. "There's got to be something Gustavo can do . . ."

"All the bankers have been slamming doors in his face. It's just torment to see him knocking his head against the wall while I have two million dollars sitting in this damn trust fund at Morgan Guaranty."

"Look, I've got a bunch of people in the office." Danforth's voice suddenly sounded tired to her. "Let me give it some thought, and then I'll talk to the damned bankers directly."

"Perhaps you could loan me something as collateral . . ." It was then that Elizabeth looked up to see a shadow in the doorway. She stopped talking as Carta took a step into the room. "Goodbye, Charles. Thank you." She hung up the phone.

Carta walked over to her slowly, then sat down on the edge of the bed. His face looked bleached, his expression was one of shock.

"How long has this been going on?"

Elizabeth turned and walked over to the French windows, which were open. Trying to gain her composure, she peered through the screens down at the swimming pool, where Carlota was standing watching Elena swim. The child swam with her face in the water, taking rapid, splashing strokes. Elizabeth stood there, her back to her husband, afraid to look at him.

"How long?!" His voice resonated with anger.

"I thought you had left the house," Elizabeth said.

Carta was upon her now. He grasped her shoulders, spinning her around, Elizabeth's hair swirling about her face. "Answer me!"

"All right, Gustavo, what is it you want to know?"

"How much of your money has been put into my ventures?"

"Does it really matter?"

"It matters a great deal to me."

She still was silent.

"How much!?" he roared at her.

Elizabeth flinched. "I don't know exactly. A great deal of money. A very great amount. There—does that make you happy? Does the amount really matter?"

"It matters to me." His voice carried a deep hurt.

"You are all that matters to me," Elizabeth said.

"You rob me of my pride, woman!"

Elizabeth saw Carta's facial muscles twitch, as if in reaction to some inner spasm of emotion. She brought her hand to his face, touching his

266

cheek softly. Carta shook off her hand, took a step backward, in control once again.

"You will call Charles Danforth back," he said. "You will call him and you will call your banker friends and you will tell them all that I do not want their charity, nor do I need that of my wife."

He walked quickly from the room.

Forty minutes later, Elizabeth parked her Jaguar in front of the Dallas Park Hotel in downtown Miami and went into the quiet bar. She saw Amato seated alone. He turned as she came toward him, grizzled face breaking into a smile. He kissed her cheek and hugged her warmly.

"You know," he said, "I forget how damned beautiful you are."

"Is that a compliment, Sal?" she replied, seating herself on the bar stool.

"You bet. What will you have?"

Paul, the bartender, a slender, quiet man in his shirt sleeves, came over and greeted her. She ordered a gimlet.

Amato folded his big hands on the bar and looked at her steadily with his oddly triangular eyes. She looked at him now affectionately.

"Did you know that Camilo sent Elena to us?" she asked.

"Yes. I saw him in Havana."

"Sal, is he bitter toward us?"

Amato shook his big head. "You think if he was bitter, he'd send you his daughter?"

"I didn't know . . . I had hoped, of course." She looked quickly into his eyes. "What's behind it, do you know? David was quite vague about it all."

Amato shrugged. "I don't know. You know how it is in Havana now —they're sure they'll be invaded. That bunch in Guatemala isn't a soccer team, you know?"

"Is Camilo in any danger?"

"They're all in danger. How would you feel if you knew the United States was out to get you? There's a lot of politics—people maneuvering for position. Camilo has his enemies. I think he tends to exaggerate his personal danger a bit, but then you never know. Cuba is Cuba. And the Communists don't like him much."

"What about Fidel?"

"Fidel thinks the sun rises and sets on your son, Mrs. Carta."

"Is there a chance . . . Camilo might . . ."

"Defect?" Amato laughed in his throat. "Your guess is as good as mine, Liz. But if I were him, I'd think twice. He's got more enemies in Miami than in Havana. I think if he came here someone would kill him."

"But what if it becomes unsafe for him in Havana?"

"Then he's got one helluva problem."

"Poor Camilo." She sipped the lime drink thoughtfully. "Poor darling."

"We're all poor darlings," Amato said, and smiled ironically. "What's your problem of the moment, poor darling?"

Elizabeth touched his hand. "Money."

"You've got whatever you need."

"You know if Gustavo ever found out you loaned us money, it'd be my neck."

"I'd like to be his friend. Always have . . ." Amato shrugged his thick shoulders. "Hey, I guess we can't have everything. How do you want to work this?"

"Is there any way it can be done without his realizing the source?"

"Sure. What bank did you say he'd asked for a loan at?"

"The First Miami."

Amato smiled. "No problem. I'll take care of everything. He may be a bit surprised, but he won't know where it came from. And, listen, if you need any more, just pick up the phone and call. I'm here."

Elizabeth regarded him, feeling very grateful, and said, "Sal, I don't know what my life would have been without you. I truly don't." She squeezed his fingers. "I love you, you know?"

"Hey," said Amato, "you think you've got an exclusive on that one, Liz? I've loved you longer than anybody."

Carta looked out on the waters of Biscayne Bay from the window of his Buick as it glided along the narrow causeway. His overriding emotion was one of desperate humiliation. The idea of his wife soliciting financial help among her family was almost unbearable to ponder. Yet even his own actions, hovering in the hallway, straining to overhear Elizabeth's conversations, made him cringe with embarrassment. Elizabeth had seemed deeply hurt over being discovered—but perhaps she was merely being condescending to his hurt, and that made it all the worse.

Elizabeth, he thought, had always been a woman of great emotional resources and an inner life which, despite the deep love which they felt for each other, remained largely inaccessible to him. There was always something going on within her, something clouded in mystery, something which at once added to her sexuality and yet, as now, aroused his ire.

And that, Carta thought, was why there had been such a sickening ache in the pit of his stomach as he grasped at Elizabeth in the bedroom and demanded imperiously that she rescind her requests for help—the underlying humiliation was that Elizabeth was right and Carta was wrong. She was right to be on her knees looking for help. They needed help. And he had grabbed her and talked of pride. She was talking about survival and he pontificated about pride!

Carta groaned and ran his hand through his hair. The time had come to face reality. Pride was a luxury that had now priced itself out of the market.

Carta's head was throbbing as he walked through the canopied entrance of the Biscayne Yacht Club, strode quickly across the lobby and paused at the door of the cocktail lounge. The atmosphere of the lounge was not one to assuage a headache. All of the glass-topped tables were occupied, cigar smoke hung heavily in the air and waiters scurried to fill drink orders. The noise from the cocktail-hour revelers was clangorous, reverberating off the walls of the small room, which were painted in broad green and white stripes. Carta found himself almost cringing against the onslaught of noise, but he forced his eyes to probe the smoky haze. His gaze came to rest on a trim, conservatively dressed man sitting alone at a corner table. The man nodded to him. Carta moved toward his table. As he passed, several men called to him or gesticulated a greeting. Carta returned their greetings but kept moving.

When he reached the table, the man rose and extended his hand stiffly. "I'm Ellis Kern, Mr. Carta," he said, sitting quickly as if to emphasize that his greeting, while respectful, could not be construed as deferential.

A waiter now darted toward the table, nodded to Carta and helped seat him.

"May I take your order?" the waiter asked.

"Scotch and soda, please, Rinaldo," Carta said.

"Another iced tea," Kern said. The waiter retreated.

"It is a pleasure to meet you," Kern said. "I've heard a lot about you over the years."

"And it is a pleasure to meet you, Mr. Kern, but you are at an advantage because I know absolutely nothing about you. Jack Kleinman at the First Miami Bank tells me I should meet you because you are, as he said, someone with important business contacts. And then you call, so here we are."

The waiter brought the drinks, and Kern sipped his iced tea. "I am a business consultant. My clients include many very big companies, including some of those who had substantial holdings in Cuba."

"And how do you feel I can help you?"

"On the contrary, Carta. We would like to help you."

"I see," Carta said, sipping his scotch and shooting a skeptical glance at Kern.

"Mr. Kleinman has told me of your difficulties in capitalizing some of your new ventures. We believe we can assist you in this area. My clients respect your business acumen. We do not have to be as conservative as the banks."

Looking at Kern now, Carta sensed that they were not really having a conversation but rather enacting a preplanned scenario, and that Kern was enunciating things that had been carefully written for him or by him. There was something too smooth about his delivery, too premeditated about his responses. Sitting there in his gray suit and white shirt and conservative blue tie, amid a room filled with vividly gesticulating men attired in plaid jackets and colorful sports shirts, Kern seemed curiously robotlike, a visitor from another planet or at least another society. Carta's temptation was to stop the charade, to say to Kern, "OK, who the hell are you and why are you taking up my time? Are you another CIA emissary and, if so, why don't you tell me what you want from me and stop playing games?" And yet, if Kern had a scenario to play out, Carta was curious where it led.

"I appreciate your interest in my financial problems," Carta said. "But I am not sure whether any of my ventures, as you describe them, would be of the magnitude to interest your corporate clients. After all, I am not exactly in a league with United Fruit and ITT."

"Let me be more specific. We have been made aware of your proposals for reestablishing the Cuban tobacco industry in the Canary Islands. That is a project my clients find intriguing."

"And I find it intriguing that you know about it. I've discussed it with, at most, four or five people, but they did not include Jack Kleinman."

"I try to do my homework," Kern said.

"There are many problems involved . . ."

"Cuban tobacco is coveted the world over. From what I know of Castro, he probably regards cigars as a symbol of corrupt capitalism, even though he smokes them all day. He will turn the tobacco-growing areas into tomato fields for the workers."

"That is exactly what he is doing," Carta said.

"I am told that you have taken some seedlings from the Vuelta and have planted them in Costa Rica. That's an interesting idea but a modest one. We are prepared to back you on a much broader scheme. We will take your seedlings and also tobacco from Brazil and the Dominican Republic. We will manufacture the cigars, not in some decrepit factory in Tampa, where costs are high and labor is indifferent, but in the

Canary Islands of Spain, which has an ideal climate and labor force for this sort of industry."

Carta looked at Kern and could not suppress a smile. He had indeed done his homework. The Canary Islands had been a secret dream. He had remembered stories his father had told him about the obscure Spanish archipelago that nestled off the northwest of Africa. The islands, which themselves had rudimentary tobacco and sugar industries, resembled Cuba in many ways.

Carta drained his scotch and signaled the waiter for another round.

"Well, Mr. Kern, you seem to have all of the answers. So why don't I let you ask the questions?"

"The main question is financial. My group is prepared to put up one million dollars to start the venture. We are also prepared to talk to the banks about the remainder of the capital."

"You are talking about a lot of money."

"My clients are accustomed to talking about a lot of money."

"And my role . . . ?"

"We would, of course, want you to run the show."

Carta sampled his new drink. Kern stirred his iced tea.

"Just like that?"

"Just like that!" Kern said.

"And am I ever to learn who my mysterious partners are?"

"Of course. But these are strange times, difficult times. For the time being, my clients would like all the dealings to flow through me. I will be, in effect, your board of directors."

The two men sat silently for a few moments. Finally Kern took out his card and handed it across the table to Carta. "If you wish to reach me, Mr. Carta . . ."

"One more thing, Mr. Kern. What are the strings?"

"Strings?"

"Strings. Look at it from my point of view. You are a man who is encountering certain financial setbacks. You are in a foreign country where the banks distrust you. Suddenly a total stranger asks to meet you in a bar, unfolds all of your most secret plans and aspirations, offers to put up one million dollars and collateralize millions more—would you not be curious about the strings?"

"You are missing the point, Carta. We are not total strangers. We have a very important interest in common. We are all interested in a free Cuba. There is much that my clients can do to help bring that about. There is also much that you can do. We must each work in our separate ways to eradicate the Communist threat."

"That is all very vague."

Kern started to get to his feet. "You have my card. Think over what we have discussed today. If you wish to pursue it, give me a call and we shall meet again."

Carta rose. He and Kern shook hands, then Kern headed toward the door. Carta sat down again and stared thoughtfully into his scotch.

Carta paused to see his wife. She was standing pensively at the far side of the pool in the shallow end watching Elena swim toward her. The breeze freshened and rippled the surface of the water. Her sun-browned figure and her swimsuit distorted by the water seemed to absorb the sunlight. In his mind there emerged a vision of that instant twenty-eight years ago, when out of a crowd of faces he first saw her. He stood up from the table, the familiar figure of Danforth looking at him in amusement, his glass tinkling with ice, the music still in his ears, the musicians in their white jackets stirring to leave the bandstand under the trees. She wore a floppy straw hat and a silk dress with colored flowers. Her brown legs appeared out of the scattering crowd. She walked toward them with that undulating stride that stirred and shaped and reshaped the silk about her body; one hand raised with a crooked elbow to hold the white straw hat in place, her auburn hair trembling around her face. She beamed and blushed slightly when she saw him staring. He could not recall the tall young male who bowed from the waist in mock humility and then vanished; only Danforth standing, tall, slender, elegant in whites with that superior expression on his face and his amused blue eyes; gesturing with his hands as he spoke the introductions. God, how blue her eyes were! She nodded merrily at him and smiled. To Gustavo there was a radiance about her that set her apart from everyone else in that garden, as though his eyes had focused, cameralike, upon her, and all else had blurred in the background.

As he felt the afternoon wind on his face now, the image of her fading, dissolving into the labyrinth of his memory, he reflected upon the lingering ache that that moment had produced in him. What luck he'd had! What if he had not attended the Danforths' garden party that May afternoon in Virginia? He had almost not gone! He wanted to go to the New York Yankee baseball game that afternoon. What was a garden party to a game like that? The great Babe Ruth! He was to play that day. Moments of baseball history one could spend a lifetime reflecting on and telling one's friends about, and one's children. But he had relented at the personal invitation from young Danforth. God, if he hadn't! What would his life have been? He shuddered when he thought about what he would have missed. The image of her lying on the sheets, breasts, belly, naked thighs, opened to him, her face glowing, smiling up at him as her urgent soft Southern voice whispered unspeakably exciting things to him. God in heaven, that he had been denied such a woman!

"Excuse me, señor, your guest is getting impatient." He looked up into Salazar's Indian face with its intelligent eyes. "He was asking about you . . ."

"Yes, of course. Sorry."

"There are two others just arrived, Cantillo and Alfonso. I brought them coffee in the anteroom, señor."

"Yes, yes." Carta sighed. "Tell them I'll be there in a moment."

He walked out onto the patio.

"That's it, darling, kick your feet!" She was shouting encouragement to Elena, who splashed furiously as she swam. "That's it, kick, kick, kick!"

Elena came up to her in the shallow end and grasped her hand and laughed.

Gustavo caught her eye.

"Did you see me, Grandfather? Did you see me swim? Watch me. Grandfather, watch me!" She put her face down in the water and went to thrashing furiously.

Gustavo held Elizabeth's eyes. "I want to apologize," he said.

"You don't have to, you know? I understand."

"I am sorry. I acted very stupidly. Accepted?"

"Of course."

"I think our financial problems have been taken care of . . . I think I'm going to be able to work something out."

Her expression brightened. "Really? How?"

"I think through Jack Kleinman at the bank. I'll give you the details later." He smiled.

Elena came up at the edge of the pool rubbing the water from her eyes and coughing. "Did you see me, Grandfather?"

"Yes, you are a wonderful swimmer, Elena!"

"Why don't you come and swim with us?"

He looked at her loving eyes. He smiled. "I'll get rid of these people and be right back."

"He's going to swim with us, Elizabeth!"

"Yes, darling." Elizabeth held his gaze. "It's wonderful news, Gustavo."

"Isn't it?" He started to turn away. "Wait for me, Elena. I won't be long."

273

Elizabeth watched him go back into the library.

"Aren't you happy he's coming to swim with us?"

She took Elena's hand. "Yes, my darling, very happy. . . ."

CHAPTER TWENTY-FOUR

D r. Barnes removed his spectacles and stared at David incredulously. "David, you realize this is madness?"

"I know it must seem strange to you, the suddenness and all." David uncrossed his legs and leaned forward in the chair. "Needless to say, I've given it a great deal of thought."

"But, man, where's the logic? Think of your career. An opportunity like this comes once in a lifetime. And you're throwing it all away. For what?"

"I have my reasons, sir."

"They must be damned compelling, I must say."

"Most compelling."

David looked at the man across the desk. He was thickset, with a ruddy face and a bulbous nose, and with tufts of gray hair above his little ears. His florid face bore a continual kindly expression, and his brown eyes looked back at David now with genuine concern.

"Have you thought about your doctoral thesis? I mean, David, this is a personal disaster for you. Set aside the inconvenience of getting a man to replace you on the expedition—that I can certainly do, we have enough candidates. It's you I'm thinking of."

"I appreciate that, Dr. Barnes." David let out his breath. He wanted this interview to be concluded. He had dreaded it all day.

"I'm not one to pry into another's personal life, David. Lord knows, we've all got our problems at home, with the hours we work. But is it something that I may be of help with—your marriage perhaps? If I stopped for a visit with Robin . . . ?"

"No, sir. It's a family matter . . . not my marriage."

"I see." Dr. Barnes pursed his lips and pressed his hands into a spire.

"I realize my behavior must seem bizarre to you. Also my inability to explain my actions." David leaned forward again. "It really comes down to a question of honor. I know that sounds abstract and even pompous,

274

but that's really what it's all about. Everything in me, every part of me, wants to go on this expedition. And yet there's a trust I can't betray."

"Then good luck to you."

Dr. Barnes was frowning as they shook hands and David moved quickly into the hall.

He thought about Camilo all the way home. When he came into the empty house, with its normal chaotic litter, he poured himself a gin on the rocks and sat down on the screened porch to await Robin's arrival. He thought about that time when they were boys at the estate outside Havana and had found a baby osprey that had fallen from its nest in the big laurel tree behind the horse barn. It had been nothing more than a puff of white feathers with dark eyes and a beak when Camilo picked it up in the grass. They kept it in a bamboo cage that René produced from the attic, and there had been a fight about whose room it would stay in. As always, David gave in and let Camilo have it in his room. Camilo was enormously pleased. He was fascinated by the little fish hawk. He sat for hours in front of the cage and gazed at it, as though he were in some kind of secret communication with it. Camilo fed it by hand, cutting little pieces of sardines with his knife and poking them through the bamboo bars of the cage. "See?" he would say, his blue eyes bright with joy. "He likes me, David. See? Look at him eat. That means he's not afraid of me."

Camilo began letting the little hawk, which was growing rapidly, out of the cage to flutter and hop about his room. It was a handsome bird, even at this age, with a milk-white breast and fierce eyes that glittered out of a mask of black feathers in the white head. Camilo adored it. One afternoon, David came down the hall and barely noticed that Shadow, their big gray tomcat, was curled up in the sun at the top of the stairs. He heard Camilo's laughter from his room, went to the door and opened it. The little osprey was fluttering in the air. Camilo stood across the room, laughing. "Look, David, he can fly!" he shouted.

Just then, the osprey fluttered toward David. Startled, he stepped aside. It went with a rush out into the hall and dropped onto the tile floor. "Get him, Davy!" Camilo yelled.

But as David turned, he saw the osprey flapping its delicate wings, starting to rise off the tiles. Shadow flashed through the air. There was a burst of feathers. And there was the big cat running down the hill with the osprey in its jaws.

Camilo had been heartbroken. He carried the tattered little body into his room and locked the door. When David tried to get him to let him in, he told him to go away. David felt responsible.

275

"Don't fret yourself, darling," his mother had said. "It's just one of those accidents. It happened. Nothing to be done about it now. It really wasn't your fault."

But he always felt guilty when he remembered the incident. A week afterward, Camilo seemed to have forgotten the whole thing. But David hadn't.

Sitting there now, on the screened porch of his house in Miami, watching the light go out of the trees and the color change in the water down at the yacht harbor, sipping on the bitter-tasting gin, seventeen years later, he was thinking to himself, rather oddly, that what he'd done today maybe made up for what he owed his brother. Why is it, he wondered, that I've always felt I owed him something?

David sat there long after the street lights came on, long after the evening traffic subsided, thinking about Camilo. He didn't realize until he looked at his watch that it was after nine o'clock and Robin hadn't appeared.

★

They had arranged to meet at Chez Denise, a small French bistro near Coral Gables. Pelham had eaten there before, usually alone, and had responded to both its cuisine and its privacy. The décor consisted of checked tablecloths and some travel posters of the French countryside. The sauces were predictable but reliable. The waitresses always greeted Pelham warmly but never sought to engage him in conversation, and Pelham liked that too.

He had set the meeting for eight-thirty. He arrived on time, as always, and asked for a table at the rear. Sipping a martini, he glanced around the room nervously. Only two tables were still occupied. An elderly couple sat at one table and two pudgy middle-aged women at the other. He had been very uneasy about this encounter and was glad there was no one in the restaurant who looked familiar.

He checked his watch. It was eight-forty-five. Where the hell was the boy? His tension suddenly surged again. Maybe he wouldn't show. Christ, Pelham thought, it had been twenty years since he'd been stood up. And to be stood up by a mere kid!

Pelham checked his watch again. It was not just the kid—he was also annoyed with MR/CASTLE. Before he had driven to Chez Denise they'd had their second phone conversation of the week, and MR/CASTLE sounded remote, even suspicious. Pelham gave him the explicit instructions that he and Vermillion had worked out. The instructions were complicated—not as complicated as MR/CASTLE complained they were, but complicated nonetheless. The mission was of the utmost importance, Pelham told him. So was the timing. It all had to go smoothly. Everything depended on it.

MR/CASTLE was an old pro, and Pelham had total confidence that he could make the necessary arrangements. He was irritated when the agent asked a lot of questions. MR/CASTLE demanded answers, but Pelham told him he had been instructed not to discuss details. All in due time, he said. After all, it was the agent's job to do as he was told, not to ask questions or make complaints. He had been handsomely remunerated for his assignments. Remunerated beyond the wildest expectations of the average mortal. MR/CASTLE had a pivotal role to play in the plans of the next eight weeks. Pelham couldn't help fretting that if he was starting to balk already his attitude later on might really cause problems. He would have to arrange for a meeting and have a talk with him. MR/CASTLE had always hated meetings. Indeed, through all their years of contact, they had never met face to face. They had always communicated by phone or letter. But these affectations would have to be dropped now. It was too late in the game to cater to frivolous affectations.

The waitress came over, and Pelham ordered a second drink. He was surprised about Michael. He struck Pelham as the kind of boy who would be punctual. Maybe he'd totally misread him. He'd give him till nine o'clock and then he'd simply order dinner without him.

He had first met Michael at the Hamlet in Coconut Grove. It was a bustling, frenetic watering hole for young people, noisy and informal. The place reminded Pelham a little bit of Greenwich Village, with its boys and girls in sandals and jeans, the girls with their hair long, and many of the young men with beards. Pelham liked to drop by the Hamlet for a beer on those nights when his loneliness closed in on him. Sitting alone, he would watch the attractive youngsters drinking and talking and playing darts. They provided a welcome relief from the heavy-jowled Cuban politicians and furtive CIA bureaucrats who customarily dominated his days.

He had first noticed Michael reading alone at a corner table one night. As Pelham passed him on the way to the men's room, he had been amused to notice that the young man was reading Aristophanes. The idea of a student in Miami, this remote outpost of civilization, reading Greek literature struck him as being both absurd and reassuring. On his way back to the bar, Pelham had tried to glance over Michael's shoulder to check whether perhaps a Mickey Spillane novel was tucked inside the covers of the book; but, no, it was undeniably Aristophanes.

Pelham had glanced over at Michael from time to time during the course of the evening. There was a curiously ascetic quality to the boy,

277

with his gaunt, fine-boned features and pale, white skin. He marveled at the boy's ability to concentrate on his reading amid the relentless din.

At one point, Michael suddenly looked up from his book and stared across the room, his eyes connecting with Pelham's. The eye contact continued for a long and awkward moment until Michael rose and walked over to the dart board. And Pelham found himself drifting over to him, picking up two darts and challenging him to a game.

Later, Michael joined Pelham at the bar and talked effusively about the play he was reading, *The Birds,* and about the other Greek poets and philosophers he wanted to study. Impressed by the boy's enthusiasm, Pelham mentioned that Greek literature had been his minor in college and had remained one of his favorite diversions. They had been talking for forty-five minutes when Pelham heard himself suggesting dinner to the boy and the boy accepting eagerly. And then they had parted.

Pelham checked his watch again. Christ, he thought, what had induced him to invite the boy to dinner? It was one thing to meet a pleasant kid at a bar, but why spend an entire evening with him? Yet there was something about Michael that had captured his attention. Perhaps it was simply his admiration for the boy's willingness to sit alone in a crowded restaurant while all the others clustered together. Perhaps it was his look of almost fragile vulnerability. Or perhaps it was his physical beauty—lean-shanked, graceful in his movements. Pelham found himself distressed by this last possibility; the idea of responding to a male's physical presence ran counter to all his basic impulses. It was something he disapproved of. Women represented beauty; men represented power.

Suddenly Michael appeared at the door, his eyes darting about the room. He was dressed in a checkered sports shirt and tight jeans. His wavy dark hair reached down his collar. Michael spotted Pelham and made his way quickly across the room. As he reached the table he extended his hand, and his face broke into a broad smile.

"Sorry I'm late," he said, sliding into his chair. "I was studying—lost track of time."

"It's all right," Pelham replied coolly. "That has happened to me many times."

They sat looking at each other awkwardly for a moment in a pall of embarrassed silence.

"Do you think we could order some wine?"

"Of course," Pelham replied, summoning the waitress, a thin, hawk-faced woman who had waited on Pelham several times before. As she came over, Pelham felt her eyes registering surprise at his companion.

But why should that make a damn bit of difference, he told himself, as he selected a twelve-dollar bottle of good French Burgundy.

"Would you like to order the rest of your dinner?" the waitress asked. "The kitchen is closing in ten minutes."

"I'm starving anyway," Michael said, his eyes avidly searching the menu. Pelham watched him with curiosity. Would Michael resort to the proverbial cheeseburger and fries?

"I'd like the snails, maybe an endive salad and the filet of sole almandine—no, make that meunière."

Pelham smiled. Whatever this boy may be, he is not predictable, he thought. "I'll have exactly the same," Pelham told the waitress.

The waitress brought the wine and they both sampled it and agreed it was a good year, and suddenly the barriers and the constraints disappeared. Michael spoke expansively about his classes and interests. He was a junior at the University of Miami, an English major, and his ambition, which he stated without embarrassment, was to become a poet. Pelham could not recall the last time he had encountered anyone ingenuous, or indeed innocent, enough to admit to an ambition other than law school or the civil service—he wanted to be a poet!

They were into their second glass of wine and had finished the snails when Michael started talking about the more intimate details of his life. He had few, if any, friends at school, he related. His only girl friend was an older student at school. They enjoyed each other's company, but he sensed her ambivalence toward their relationship.

Pelham listened sympathetically. As a college student, he had endured a brief and passionate affair with an older woman. "I learned a great deal about technique, but also about remorse," Pelham said.

Michael sipped his wine thoughtfully and then leaned forward across the table. "I lied to you before, Mr. Pelham," he said. "I want to apologize about that."

"How did you lie?"

"About why I was late. I was with my girl friend. We were making love, and that's why I was late. It sounds coarse to put it that way, but I wanted to tell the truth. I hope you won't be angry with me."

Pelham saw Michael's brown eyes staring at him ruefully, earnestly. "I'm glad you told the truth."

The waitress was serving the sole now, and Pelham welcomed the lull in the conversation. He told himself he should be relieved by Michael's confession. Pelham had been uneasy over the possibility that Michael could be a homosexual; now that fear was put to rest. Yet he felt a twinge of annoyance. Was it because of the boy's coarseness? Or was it jealousy?

Michael's soft voice broke into Pelham's thoughts. "Do you have a wife and kids?"

"Why do you ask?"

"I'm just curious. I've been talking too much anyway—I've said enough dumb things this evening."

Pelham found himself disarmed again. "Yes, I have a wife, but we are separated. In my line of work I travel a great deal. Three years ago I'm afraid the whole thing became too much of a strain on both of us."

"Did you have any kids?"

"A daughter," Pelham said, and then lapsed into silence.

But Michael pressed on. He reached over for the wine and refilled their glasses. "Do you like living alone?"

Again, the utter directness of the question caused Pelham to recoil. "I don't care for it very much at all," Pelham said, his tone measured. "Living alone is just something you have to do. So you learn to relish your privacy and cope with your loneliness."

"I shared a place last year with a guy, but it was awful. Everywhere I went I found his smelly socks and filled-up ashtrays. I have to give up my little place that I have now."

"Why do you have to give it up?"

"I've run out of bread. My father died five years ago and left me a small trust fund to get me through college. But the money just covered my first three years, and my mother is broke—she's got arthritis and can't work anymore."

"How will you stay in college?"

"I'll have to get a job, I suppose. There goes my time for writing poetry." Michael shook his head and stared ruefully at his plate. "Oh, well. I suppose there's nothing new about that. Just another starving poet." He looked at Pelham, who smiled sympathetically. "Who wrote, 'Poverty is the mother of the arts'?" Michael asked.

Pelham pondered for a moment. "I believe that was Aeschylus."

"Close. It was Theocritus."

"Very good, Michael. Let me try one. . . . OK, who wrote, 'Honorable poverty is better than dishonorable wealth'?"

"That was Euripides, I think."

"Superb. You're right."

They ordered coffee and chatted some more about Miami, which Michael detested as much as Pelham. Then Pelham signaled for the bill and paid it.

"I really appreciate all of this—the dinner, the company," Michael said.

"It's nothing."

"No, seriously. It really means a lot to me. You can go an awful long time down here without really meeting someone—you know, serious. Someone who understands poetry and listens to Mozart."

"You like Mozart, Michael?"

"Desperately."

Pelham shook his head. "I have all of Mozart . . . everything ever recorded."

Michael was wide-eyed. "No kidding?"

"No kidding. Someday if you wish, you could drop by and listen to anything you like. I'm just renting my house, but it's got an excellent stereo system."

"Can I do it tonight?"

Pelham looked startled, then glanced at his watch. He looked into the earnest young face. Then he shook his head and started to rise from the table. "OK, Michael. We'll put on some Mozart."

As Pelham drove through the darkened streets, he tried again to struggle with his conflicting feelings toward this strangely pushy boy. Accustomed by disposition and training to regard people skeptically, Pelham was annoyed with himself for confiding in the boy. He had been interrogated by some of the shrewdest operators around, yet found this bony, precocious youngster to be a far more effective questioner. What did the boy want from him? And what did he want from the boy? Was it really as simple as it seemed—two people starved for civility, yearning for companionship? Yes, Pelham thought, for once things might be simpler than they seemed rather than more complex. It was indeed as simple as that. It was a matter of reciprocal need.

The strains of chamber music resounded through the house. Michael had pushed open the glass doors and was looking out at the pool when Pelham joined him.

"Do you like it?" Pelham asked.

Michael was still wide-eyed. "Enormously."

"I meant the music."

"I like the swimming pool and the music, both. It's Mozart's Clarinet Quintet, isn't it?"

Pelham nodded his assent, then seated himself on the sofa and picked up his pipe, which he started to light. Michael sat across from him. They listened to the music in silence.

"You have such good taste—I really admire you," Michael blurted suddenly. "I don't admire many people. I admire you."

Pelham flushed but continued to puff his pipe. "You're very good to have around, Michael," he said softly. "Good for the morale."

281

"What's the building over there beyond the pool?" Michael pointed to a small house that huddled in a maze of ferns and hammock.

"That's just a shed. The landlord calls it a guest house. There's a little bathroom in it, but it's minuscule."

Michael fixed his gaze on Pelham. "I hope you don't think I'm too aggressive. I hate aggressive people. It's just that, well, I'd like very much to live in that guest house."

Pelham took out the pipe and started to speak, but Michael cut him short. "I wouldn't just leach off you, don't get me wrong. I'd do any chores you want. I can cook, you know. And I'd even contribute toward the rent—couldn't afford much . . ."

"No, Michael. Absolutely not!"

"Is it that you think I'd steal things from you?" Michael asked in a small voice.

"It's just impossible. Impossible." Pelham's own voice was shaking with emotion, and the sound of it shocked him. He rose quickly and started to leave the room. "I've got to open my mail and do some odds and ends. Feel free to stay as long as you like and enjoy the music."

Pelham walked into his bedroom and took off his jacket. He noticed that his hands were shaking as he hung the jacket in the closet. The whole thing was absurd. It could never work. What about the mission? What about the middle-of-the-night crises, the phone calls from Washington, the hysterical Cubans invading his home at three o'clock in the morning? How would he explain them to Michael, and how would he explain Michael to them? It was impossible. But Pelham had handled it badly. Surely, he had deeply offended the boy, Pelham thought. He was obviously an impulsive, highly vulnerable young man who possibly looked upon him as some sort of father figure. He might have inflicted a real psychological hurt on the boy by rejecting him as angrily as he did —he didn't intend to seem angry, but it must have come across that way to Michael. He must return to the boy and make amends.

Pelham entered the bathroom and ran some cold water over his face, dabbing it dry with a towel. When he reentered the living room there was no sign of Michael. He looked in the kitchen but saw no one. Pelham had become nervous now as he walked into his den and flicked on the light. Again no one. Could the boy have fled in humiliation? Pelham was moving hurriedly into the courtyard toward the pool. "Michael?" he called. No answer.

He was almost at the edge of the darkened pool before he heard the small splashing sounds and saw Michael's pale body sliding beneath the surface of the pool, swimming gracefully underwater.

Collapsing into a chaise lounge, Pelham took a deep breath of the humid night air. The sounds of Mozart came booming over the speakers. Pelham put his head back and stared at the clear night sky. He felt a bit foolish now over his alarm, over becoming so goddamn panicky about a kid he barely knew. Perhaps it was the wine, Pelham thought. Two martinis and all that wine and he had been overtired to start with.

Michael's voice startled him. He looked down to see the boy seated at the edge of a chair perhaps two feet from his own, water dripping from his sleek pale skin. "I took a swim—I hope you don't mind."

"I don't mind."

Pelham stared at the boy. His black hair was plastered down around his face, almost covering his forehead. His naked body seemed incredibly thin, almost fragile, his shoulders narrow like a girl's. His arms and legs, slim and virtually hairless, glistened in the shadowy light. Pelham could see ribs protruding through the sides of his body. He saw the boy's belly, heaving from the swim. Between his legs he saw the dark outline of pubic hair and his penis, thin and vulnerable. Pelham once again felt his own stomach clench in panic. He was struggling for control—control over what? Control over desire, Pelham acknowledged to himself. He desired the boy. He had never before desired another male, not since puberty certainly, but now he desperately desired this slender child with glistening limbs who was staring at him with those patient brown eyes.

Pelham sucked in his breath. "For God's sake, Michael, get a towel."

"I'm not cold."

"Get one anyway." Pelham's voice seemed more shrill than he meant it to sound.

He felt Michael's clammy wet hand clasping his. He looked down at the two hands together.

"Please let me live with you," Michael said, his voice almost a whisper. "I'll do anything. Anything you want."

Pelham tried to reply, but his words congealed in his throat. He felt his hand being lifted and looked down to see Michael placing it on his long, wet leg, several inches above the knee. The boy's skin felt slick with moisture, but it pulsated with warmth. Michael was moving his leg slightly now, sliding it toward Pelham. Pelham stared over at it, noticing that the boy's legs had parted and that his penis had stiffened. It stood there in the darkness utterly smooth and straight, and Pelham looked down at his trousers and saw himself bulging at the crotch.

"I want you to do something for me, Michael, are you listening?"

"I am."

"If you care for me at all, as you say you do . . ."

"I care."

"Then I want you to get up and put your clothes on right away and leave the house, just as quickly as you possibly can. I want you to do that, do you understand?"

"Are you angry with me?"

"I am not angry. I am terribly confused and I want to be absolutely alone. So please go, right away. Now."

Pelham removed his hand from Michael's knee, and he saw the boy stand up and gather up his things. Pelham closed his eyes and kept them closed.

"Will I see you again?"

"Yes. I want to see you again."

"I will be at the Hamlet tomorrow night around ten."

"Good night, Michael."

He heard the boy walking away and listened as the front door slammed. He remained by the pool for a long time, his eyes focused on the black sky.

It was past midnight. Robin sat in the living room at the desk, working. She moved three of the books from a stack and slid out a folded sheet of paper. She pulled open a drawer where she kept her notes, and started to dig down into them to find a manila envelope. When she pulled the envelope out, unfastened the metal clasp and started to deposit the folded sheet with the others inside, she hesitated, unfolding the paper. She read the first words: "Robin, my darling: Nothing I cared in the lamb white days, that . . ." She smiled tenderly and refolded the sheet and dropped it into the envelope, refastened the clasp, and put the envelope under the books and the papers in the drawer.

You're crazy, she thought. Absolutely, insanely, madly crazy!

CHAPTER TWENTY-FIVE

FORT LAUDERDALE, FLORIDA, FEBRUARY 23, 1961

"Step on it!" Tipton said to Rodríguez. "Let's get out of here."

Rodríguez was driving the Ford. He looked bewildered, but he stepped on the gas and moved past where the whole circus of blue-and-red police lights were flashing in the dark around the two trucks. A sheriff's deputy was waving traffic past the roadblock with an anxious, annoyed swing of his flashlight.

"They were set up waiting for us," said Rodríguez.

Tipton felt sick. He saw the two truck drivers standing in the red light of the flares, talking with a cluster of uniformed policemen and two plainclothes officers. One driver looked down at his boots as he spoke.

"What can we do, Tip?"

"Nothing."

"But those arms? All that money?"

"It's gone," Tipton said.

He sighed and watched the road coming up at him in the darkness. Traffic was slow-moving both ways.

"I guess we better call Gustavo."

"Yes. Stop at the next off ramp. We'll look for a phone."

Tipton swore under his breath. It had all gone so well. The purchase of arms. The arrival of the freighter in Fort Lauderdale. He had stood in the lights of the dock, an hour before, feeling better than he had in months. He watched the heavy crates, marked as farm machinery, being lifted by the winch out of the hold of the ship, the forklifts moving back and forth to the trucks with the pallets of heavy boxes, and he thought with uncharacteristic elation that they had beaten the bastards who had tried in every way they could to ruin them. Here was enough to keep the underground groups supplied for weeks. Enough to start the war. Afterward, he had taken Rodríguez out for hamburgers. He had never been more hungry in his life. He ate three, with cheese, and washed them down with beer, all the time thinking about those trucks moving south on the toll road toward Miami. Now, after having passed the roadblock, having seen the swarm of police, he knew it had all been too good to last.

"Here's the off ramp," Rodríguez said. "God, Tip, what did they do that to us for?"

"They're out to ruin us," Tipton told him. "We knew that. We took the risk and lost. Forget it."

"I can't forget it," Rodríguez said. "I can't forget. We're bankrupt. How can I forget it? I want to kill someone."

Tipton nodded. "There's a petrol station ahead. They've got a phone."

He was sitting there in the car, as they turned into the lighted gas station, dreading making that call to Gustavo Carta. How could he tell him it was all balls? How could he tell that man they were finished?

★

Elizabeth found herself unable to reply.

She got up from the chair across from his desk and went to the liquor cabinet. She was wearing her blue silk nightgown and was barefoot. The tiles beyond the Oriental rug felt cold under her feet. "Would you like a drink, Gustavo?"

"Yes, why not?" his heavy voice replied. All of his spirit seemed to have drained out of him.

"What can we do? How can we fight back?" she asked. She poured the scotch into two tumblers, without ice, and walked back to his desk. The little desk clock announced it was now 3:30 A.M. Awakened because she had not heard him come to bed, she had opened the door upstairs and seen the light in his study. She'd found him, deep in thought, seated behind the desk, the single lamp shadowing his big frame. His posture at the desk, his chin cupped in his hand, had arrested her at the doorway. In the darkness of the library, the lamplight on his forehead, chin and nose, he reminded her of a painting she had seen in the Louvre in Paris, years ago, of a man seated before a burning candle, staring at the flame as though the secret of life was about to be revealed from its radiant light.

When he told her of what had transpired, she was speechless.

Taking the tumbler she offered, Carta gave her a tender smile and said, "Well, Elizabeth, I don't know. Tipton said it—we can't fight the United States government *and* Castro. But I've been sitting here for the last three hours, telling myself I should quit—abandon everything, let them do what they want in Cuba. Yet I can't bring myself to do it."

"Of course you can't. You wouldn't be Gustavo Carta if you could."

Carta looked at her warmly, the sadness in the corners of his eyes. "What do you suggest?"

"I suggest that you forget it for the next two days."

"Forget it? How does one forget? I'm likely to be arrested. Indicted."

"They haven't moved yet, Gustavo."

Gustavo shrugged. "What's to prevent it?"

"I shall."

"What?"

Elizabeth took a sip of scotch, feeling it warm her, and she shuddered. She looked up at her husband and smiled.

CHAPTER TWENTY-SIX

They were bullshitting him and they weren't even good at it. Kern knew going in that they'd be inept; he had warned Pelham, but Pelham didn't seem to care. And now, sitting across the table from them in the cocktail lounge, Kern struggled to mask his contempt.

"When we took on this job we were assured there'd be plenty of time," Bruno Costanza was saying. "This is not the sort of situation where you want to have pressure." He was the younger of the two, early forties, beefy, yet a rather handsome man, impeccably tailored in a tan blazer and beige slacks.

"There's a time frame in every business situation," Kern replied in his dry, controlled voice.

"We're used to business situations," Victor Vitelli said. "But you have to admit this one is special. We have special problems to deal with. We need more time to deal with them."

Kern studied Vitelli's thin, strangely ascetic face with its sullen gray eyes. Despite his benign appearance, Kern disliked Vitelli even more than he disliked Vitelli's younger partner. The lean white-haired Vitelli was a whiner and a conniver, Kern felt. He resented the fact that Vitelli affected the mannerisms of a respectable business executive. Costanza was rougher, more feral, but at least he talked straight now and then.

"When we made our deal six weeks ago the understanding was you'd come up with a plan," Kern said insistently. "As far as I can tell you have nothing."

"We've been examining the possibilities," Bruno Costanza replied, glancing quickly around the surrounding tables. At three o'clock in the morning, the room was empty except for a table of twelve conventioneers seated near the bar. "The individual we're talking about here is a very strange character, with weird habits. He never sleeps in the same place two nights in a row. He never seems to sleep at the same time of the day or night. The security around the sonofabitch is much better than it looks from the outside."

Vitelli leaned across the table toward Kern and spoke in a quiet, confiding tone. "This is our first job for the United States government. We

287

want to do well. We're trying to go about it in a scientific way, looking at every possible angle. We're even looking at different types of poisons."

"Poisons?" Kern exclaimed. "Who do you think you're killing—some medieval archduke?"

"Look, Kern, we can't shoot the cocksucker—it would be a suicide mission," Costanza cut in. "We've tried automobile accidents, but you can never predict where he's going and when he's going to be there."

Kern felt his temples throbbing. It would be all too easy to lose his temper with these vermin. It would be sinking to their level. "Let me cut through all this," he said, his tone sharp. "The government people asked me to retain your services because you're professionals. In the next ten days I want to know precisely how you're going to kill Castro and when. I don't want to hear copouts or idle speculation, I want the blueprint, is that clear?"

He stared irritably at the two men in front of him. He disliked being seen in public with these men and he hated the Fontainebleau Hotel as well. His skin always crawled as he walked through the lobby, squinting his eyes against the brilliant reflections of the antiqued mirrors with their gold-leaf ornamentation, the plastic glitter of the furnishings and the ludicrous crystal chandeliers. Only a hotel of such overwhelming vulgarity could name its cocktail lounge the Boom Boom Room, Kern thought. Only the Fontainebleau. But Pelham had insisted that he meet with these two, and Costanza and Vitelli both said they held all their Miami meetings in the Boom Boom Room.

The waiter appeared and Costanza ordered another scotch. Vitelli was drinking Seven-Up, and Kern ordered iced tea.

"Look, Kern, there's no reason for anyone to get upset," Vitelli said in the soft, obsequious tone Kern found so cloying. "You paid us one hundred fifty thousand. Bruno and I intend to deliver. We'd even do it for nothing. As far as we're concerned, getting rid of this guy is an act of patriotism. We may not be Standard Oil or United Fruit, but me and Bruno don't like dealing with Commies. We still have a couple of casinos over there. We got a stake in this thing. Besides, it's something to tell our grandchildren."

"Then get on with it," Kern snapped, rising to leave.

Costanza glared at him. "What's your angle in all this, Kern?"

"Angle? I have no angle."

"I hear stories. I hear you're tight with a very wealthy individual who wants to own all the casinos in Havana after Castro is knocked out. That true?"

"I'm just doing a job for my government," Kern replied blandly.

288

Vitelli rose, his hand extended. "Then we've got a lot in common," he said.

Kern winced as he turned quickly and left the room.

He had set out to be an accountant. It seemed to him to be a prudent, secure profession. Ellis Kern acquired an abiding respect for prudence and security during the Great Depression. His father had been a good family man and a good Catholic, but he hadn't been prudent. When times turned bad he was squashed like a bug. He operated a thriving real-estate business in Queens, New York, but had allowed himself to get carried away on the euphoric wave of stock speculation in the late 1920s. Kern remembered his father tucking him into bed one night—a bed he shared with a younger brother—and telling him how lucky he was to be the firstborn son of a millionaire. Within six months his father had lost everything, and his wife and six children were subsisting on scraps of food contributed by compassionate neighbors. Kern remembered his mother going to church every morning, seeking divine guidance to ease the shame of her sudden poverty, then coming home to take in the neighbors' washing and sewing. He remembered his father returning home with liquor on his breath after a day of job hunting. Kern also remembered seeing men who looked like his father selling apples on the corner. He had nightmares about seeing his father among them someday.

The family crisis was resolved a year later when, thanks to the intervention of an uncle, Kern's father managed to secure a job as assistant manager of an A & P grocery store in Bloomington, Indiana. Kern and his brothers and sisters were pulled out of their various public and parochial schools, and they all gratefully trekked West. Kern missed his old neighborhood and friends, but the family was eating three square meals again, and his mother, who had aged twenty years during the previous two, seemed to regain her equanimity. Kern noticed that a growing pall of bitterness had settled upon his father, however. He went to the store faithfully every morning, but he had become an angry, disappointed man. He remembered his father lecturing him on how a Jew-loving radical like Franklin Delano Roosevelt was incapable of solving the problems of the country. Kern's father admired the teachings of Father Coughlin. His hero was Henry Ford.

They were driving to the store together in the family Ford in April, 1939, when his father suddenly moaned and sagged in his seat, his head striking the steering wheel. The heart attack proved fatal. He was fifty-one, and Kern felt it was almost an act of mercy.

After his father's death, the manager of the A & P, out of sympathy, gave young Kern a job clerking in the store. Though his support was vital to feed his younger brothers and sisters, Kern hated the work. He could see his long, drab life stretching out in front of him—working in the grocery store, marrying, having children. Though he dreaded the fanaticism that he had seen overtaking his father, he found himself sliding into the same channel of bitterness.

It was the war that saved him. He enlisted eagerly in the Army. By exaggerating his experience in the grocery business, Kern negotiated his way into the Quartermaster Corps. Over the next five years, he rose to the rank of captain and helped preside over the disposition of hundreds of millions of dollars in supplies and war matériel. He also learned a great deal about the inner workings of a vast bureaucracy. There was something about his Irish-Catholic mind that instinctively grasped the intricacies of maneuvering and manipulating within a big organization.

His rank and officer's uniform also gave him access to a different class of women. He remembered his mother's sense of shame over their poverty. He wanted to find a wife who had never known shame.

It was in 1944, while on leave in New York, that he met Mildred Goltz through a mutual friend. Her family, who were German Catholics, had lived in New York for four generations and had established a secure niche in the investment banking business. The family's Teutonic diligence had helped it weather the Depression years. Mildred was a tall, serious girl with a generously endowed bosom and a dignified bearing. There was something too broad about the caste of her face—her jaw was too jutting, her forehead too wide—that prevented her from being described as attractive. But she had gone to the best parochial schools and colleges and had a good sense of herself. And she also had money —not a great amount of it, because the Goltz family was a vast one, but enough to give Kern an added sense of security. Mildred's money sparked Kern's desire to have children; it also rekindled his ambition.

After the war Kern used the GI Bill to get his degree in accounting at Indiana University. Then he looked for a job; he wanted to find another big organization, like the military, that could offer security as well as opportunity.

He joined the Federal Bureau of Investigation in 1949, and he liked it from the start. He found within its ranks many men from backgrounds similar to his. He admired what the bureau stood for. He felt J. Edgar Hoover was possibly, along with General Douglas MacArthur, the outstanding American of his generation. Most of all, he relished the sense of status the bureau gave him. Whenever he had returned home before, he was still regarded in his home town as a grocery clerk. It was like a stain on his past. Now he was suddenly the FBI man, fighting crime and battling subversives.

His transfer to the New York bureau, Kern felt, exemplified the bureau's faith in his future. It also afforded him the chance to go back to his old neighborhood and look up old pals. Most of them were struggling to support large families on blue-collar wages. They venerated Kern's success in the world.

Kern's transfer to Havana was the break he had been angling for. It was an important assignment. It was exotic. It was almost like being in the Foreign Service, and Kern, having spent the entire war in the U.S., longed for a change of scene. Kern even liked the nomenclature of his new job. He would be what the FBI called a "legat," which stood for "legal attaché." Legats occupied a little-known nook of the FBI structure. Though the bureau's operations were thought to be mainly confined to the U.S., the FBI, under J. Edgar Hoover, had quietly managed to construct a network of foreign operatives in fifteen cities around the world, ranging in size and importance from Paris and Buenos Aires to Ottawa and Bern. The legats functioned as a combination of investigator, diplomat, gumshoe and public-relations man. They were customarily attached to the local embassies, but were free to operate totally outside normal diplomatic channels. They reported only to FBI headquarters in Washington. Indeed, the only telltale indication of their true affiliation was a big photograph of J. Edgar Hoover that was always implanted on the wall.

Though Kern reveled in his new role as a legat, Mildred was far from happy. She worried about the effect on their two daughters. Kern tried to assuage her fears by explaining that Havana had good parochial schools and that the warm climate might prove beneficial.

From the outset, Kern found Havana full of surprises. An unpassionate man, he found himself responding to its romantic setting. He loved the warm, sunny days, the pretty young girls, the carefree spirit. He also admired the way the country was governed. Fulgencio Batista was a strong, purposeful man, and he ran his country with a brisk efficiency. He did not coddle the radicals, as Kern's own government did. Further, Kern approved of the way the American government viewed its role in Cuba. Cuba was a bountiful resource for American capitalism. The Cubans benefited in jobs and tourist dollars, and U.S. businessmen benefited from their know-how and their capital investment.

Kern spent a great deal of his time in Havana cultivating American business leaders. He got to know the men at United Fruit, Coca-Cola, Richfield Oil and Procter and Gamble. He dined with sugar men and tobacco men. He represented himself as having been a successful accountant in the U.S. before entering the FBI, and they respected his business acumen. Kern was useful to them. He made it his business to know his way around the Cuban bureaucracy. He knew which officials could make something happen, and how much it would cost to accomplish it. In Cuba everything and everyone had a price, but the prices, Kern felt, were not unreasonable and he enjoyed his role as the knowledgeable middle man. And the American businessmen were duly appreciative of his counsel. They showed their appreciation with gifts and dinner parties; one company even gave him a new Chrysler.

The only thing Kern found disquieting was the regime's uneasy alliance with crime. He rationalized it in his mind. It was a matter of know-how, he told himself. The Mafia understood the gambling business. They were useful to the regime. Still, Kern felt that Batista was wrong in not appointing a knowledgeable American businessman—a man like himself—as a sort of czar over the gambling industry and tossing the Mafia out. He even saw to it that this proposal was tactfully presented to Batista through the proper channels, and he had been told that it was being given thoughtful examination.

It was in January of 1956 that Frank Conlan, the top FBI "attaché" in Havana, suffered a heart attack and was hospitalized in Miami. Kern became the acting senior FBI man in Havana and assumed added responsibilities. He was to make regular reports to the home office not only about underworld figures but also about the growing threat of radical guerrilla activity against Batista. A young rebel lawyer named Fidel Castro was coming into prominence and had gone into exile in Mexico, and Kern was determined to be known as the man in Havana who knew more about him than anyone else. He felt that the Foreign Service officers and even the American ambassador were ineffectual as sources of information. Kern understood Communism. He could better interpret its threat.

But Kern's formidable ambitions—specifically his designs on the top spot in Havana—were not winning him friends within the sedate FBI bureaucracy. Some of the agents felt he was a social climber and an opportunist. They felt he was trying to climb too far too fast.

In March of 1957 Kern was notified that Hoover's top aide in the FBI hierarchy had scheduled a visit to Havana. It was part vacation—the man had been suffering from a prolonged bout with the flu—and in part his visit reflected the chief's growing concern about the threat of Castroism. A senior FBI agent at headquarters named Coffey alerted Kern to the importance of the visit and suggested that Kern give him the full red-carpet treatment. Hoover's aide, Coffey confided, was a bachelor and would surely enjoy some female companionship.

This request was not new to Kern. He had often arranged for prostitutes for visiting dignitaries. For a hundred dollars it was possible to obtain the professional services of some truly beautiful women. Kern had even auditioned several himself to be sure of their credentials.

Kern felt, however, that a top FBI official deserved something better. At a party thrown by a local business executive, he had recently met a beautiful Scandinavian actress named Inga Dolborg. Kern had read about Inga. She had received a certain degree of notoriety lately as the newest Scandinavian sex goddess. Her photographs adorned the pages of one of the most popular men's "flesh" magazines.

Conversing with her, however, Kern found her to be a rather sensible and candid girl. She had responded to Kern's fatherly attentions at the party and confided her intimate problems to him over lunch the next day. She had been engaged to Rod Dixon, the American movie actor, but the two had had a terrible blowup two days earlier at a society party in Palm Beach. Inga had fled to Havana, wanting to get far away from Dixon and his Palm Beach crowd. She was all alone in Havana and sought Kern's advice as to how she could busy herself.

Staring at this beautiful young specimen, Kern found himself fantasizing as to what it would be like having an affair with her. But he quickly put that out of his mind in favor of more practical considerations. If only he could arrange a meeting between Inga and the top aide to Hoover; surely, any confirmed bachelor would be enormously grateful to anyone who could introduce him to a girl with such a lovely face and spectacular bosom.

He broached the idea to Inga, who thought it over and then assented. She was having certain problems with the immigration agency over work permits in the U.S., she said. Perhaps this official, if he took a liking to her, could help clear away the red tape.

Kern met the Hoover aide at the airport. He was a gray-haired dignified-looking man with a shy yet abrasively authoritarian manner. Kern saw to it that he was settled comfortably in his hotel suite and then said casually that there was a famous celebrity visiting Havana who had wanted to meet him. The FBI aide wearily replied that he would be glad to meet anyone whom Kern suggested but that he had come mainly to rest. This, Kern felt, was the green light for Inga.

Kern was sitting in bed reading that night when he received a call from Inga. She had just left the Hoover aide, she said, and it had been a disaster.

"What happened?" Kern demanded, slamming his book shut.

"I don't understand it," Inga said, her voice breaking. "I knocked at the door and introduced myself. He looked at me as if I had leprosy. I said I was the visitor Mr. Kern had mentioned. He frowned and asked if this was some sort of upset."

"Setup," Kern corrected. "Men who have been in the FBI too long always think they're being set up."

"That man is a homosexual," Inga said.

"Nonsense," snapped Kern.

"I could tell in the way he talked. He was so flustered. He didn't respond to me at all. I tried to be friendly. He just went pale and told me to leave immediately."

Kern's mind flashed back to the advice he'd received from Coffey, the aide in Washington. Coffey, he now recalled, had seemed antagonistic to Kern several times in the past. It was Kern who had been set up, he now realized, and the realization made him sick to his stomach. His enemies in Washington had deliberately done this to embarrass him, to destroy his chances for promotion.

"Go home and go to bed," Kern snapped at Inga, hanging up the phone abruptly.

His wife, Mildred, looked over at him. "Is anything wrong, dear?" she asked.

"I think I have been played for a fool," Kern said, his face ashen.

Two weeks later Kern received official word that he was being transferred to the Butte, Montana, office. Butte had long been renowned in FBI circles as the ultimate Siberia for FBI men who had fallen from favor with the hierarchy in Washington. Kern flew to Washington and submitted his resignation. He did not intend to go to Butte. It was as unthinkable as clerking in a grocery store. Kern had other plans in mind.

"Those men are scum," Kern said into the phone. "They took the money we paid them and haven't done a damned thing. They don't even begin to have the capability to execute their mission."

Kern had promised Pelham to give him a call after meeting Costanza and Vitelli at the Boom Boom Room.

"Did you tell them you wanted a specific plan in ten days?" Pelham asked.

"Yes, I told them. I don't know if it made much of an impression. The old guy, Vitelli, talks like he's president of ITT. He thinks he's such a shrewd operator."

"We'll see what they come up with," Pelham said.

"As I told you before, I think it's a mistake doing business with these Mafia low-life," Kern said. "They talk a big game but they're always playing both sides of the street."

"I don't care what side of the street they play," Pelham replied.

"But they won't get the job done!"

"Getting the job done is my concern," Pelham said briskly.

Kern was about to reply, but caught himself. He knew Pelham to be a shrewd and devious man. Kern's years in the FBI had taught him not to push his superiors against the wall and not to ask the wrong questions. Yet he bridled at Pelham's abruptness. After all, he wasn't just another bureaucrat anymore. He had a big role to play in this operation, important people to answer to. People at high levels of industry. He resented being pushed into a corner, not knowing the whole picture. Still, one had to be careful with Pelham. His manner was always taut, controlled, but Kern sensed in him an inner turmoil. He had known someone like Pelham in the FBI once. He had seemed to have everything under control, but one day he just snapped, and he ended up in a mental hospital. Pelham was not someone who could be pushed too far.

"I'll leave it all in your hands," Kern said tactfully. "I just wanted to register my skepticism."

"I appreciate your input, Ellis," Pelham said, and he clicked off.

Kern stared at the phone for a few moments. The whole situation irked him, all of it. The Cuban operation was such a solid idea. Everyone had so much to gain from its success, especially Kern. But it wouldn't work if they got too cute, too tricky.

The trouble with the Ivy-League CIA types like Pelham and his boss, Vermillion, was that they didn't have any street smarts. They all came from good families and privileged circumstances, but they lived, Kern felt, in too rarefied an atmosphere. They were like hothouse plants suddenly transplanted to the outside world. They could propound their theories and formulate their grand schemes, but they had no idea what was going on in the streets, in the alleys, in the gutters. Yet that was where the battles were won or lost, not in the classrooms, not in the fancy men's clubs. Kern had learned that much. But the others—they didn't understand. They could ruin it all.

CHAPTER TWENTY-SEVEN

Charles Danforth opened the door with his key. It was a little past seven o'clock, the earliest he had been home in weeks. But he was responding to a call he had received at the White House from his wife, Eden.

"Elizabeth is here, darling," she told him. "I think you had better come home as soon as possible and hear what she has to say."

"Is it that important?" he replied.

"I happen to think it is," Eden had said, that edge in her voice—the edge he had heard before; the outraged journalist who was onto a scandal and was trying to sound restrained yet threatening at the same time, so you would understand that if you didn't talk, you had trouble. "But I want her to tell it to you, just as she has me," Eden continued. "Will you come?"

"Of course. I have a meeting with the President in five minutes. Won't take long. I'll leave immediately after, all right?"

"Splendid. See you soon."

He had thought about Eden's call all during the ten-minute conference he had with President Kennedy. The President had read an economic-policy memo that Danforth had submitted. They discussed briefly Danforth's case for lower interest rates. The President said that he'd had a similar suggestion from Galbraith recently and that he liked the proposal very much. He asked Danforth to have breakfast with him in the morning, because he had several matters, including Cuba, which he wished to discuss with him. They walked out of the Oval Office together and Danforth left him in the hallway on his way to meet some guests in one of the reception rooms. As he turned down the stairs, Danforth glanced back and noticed the President pausing outside the door to the reception room, his hand on the small of his back, his shoulders arched in a stretching gesture to relieve the pain. His face looked tired. But he plunged abruptly into the doorway, a smile fixed on his face. Danforth heard laughter and voices as he went down the stairs.

Now, entering his house, Danforth had a strange sense of anticipation. Whatever Elizabeth's reason for coming unannounced to Washington, he knew she must be motivated by urgency. In all the years of his government service, when a word here and there in the right places to which he had easy access could have made some moment in her life considerably easier, she had never once asked his intervention. Family matters, yes. They were allies in dealing with the bankers and the other family members, a solid coalition. But in his professional career, never.

"They're upstairs in your bedroom," the maid told him as he shed his topcoat and handed her the briefcase. "Would you like a drink or something, Mr. Danforth?"

An hour later, Danforth sat in the easy chair across from the bed, staring into the melting ice cubes in the bottom of his glass. Eden was sitting at the dressing table, wearing a gray sweater and tan slacks, holding one knee in her hands and watching him indignantly. Elizabeth was sprawled on the bed, in a robe, appraising his reaction with the steady gaze of her blue eyes. She reached for her glass on the nightstand.

"And so you see, Charles, the story you're getting here is not what is happening out there in the trenches."

"Yes," he said with a sigh. "I confess, Liz, I feel a bit more sympathetic with poor old General Gough at Ypres. Hmmmm?" He shook his head. "It seems incredible, you understand. What we've been getting . . . it's not what you've been telling me, certainly."

"What I've told you is quite true, Charles. Furthermore, let me add something. Gustavo went to a meeting last night which was supposed to unify all the Cuban liberation organizations in Miami. He'd been steadfast against it, yet he went—I suppose out of deference to you and the talk you had when we came up to the Inauguration."

"That I appreciate, Elizabeth."

"Were you aware of this meeting?"

"I'd been informed of it, yes."

"Were you told that the Central Intelligence Agency man presented a list of eighteen names, of which he said ten were to be included in any coalition front, regardless? Hmmmm? Charles, among those ten names were several of the most right-wing and, I may add, corrupt individuals in the long history of corrupters that Cuba has suffered. Shall I tell you who they were?"

"I can guess," said Danforth. He stood and paced across the carpet and, turning, looked down at Eden. She stared at him, pursing her lips in a silent reaction. "Do we get dinner tonight?" he asked.

"If you're not too sick to your stomach from all this to eat," Eden replied. "As for myself—I'm close."

"Yes," said Danforth. "I understand that."

"What can you do about this, Charles? Anything?" Eden continued staring straight at him. "Or does it get swept under the carpet of the New Frontier, along with the other gatherings of fresh dust?"

"It's too early to be cynical, darling," said Danforth.

"I was brought up cynical," said Eden. "Came from my mother's breast, I suppose."

"Let's eat. I want to think awhile. You hungry, Liz?"

"Famished," Elizabeth said. "All this talk has given me an appetite. But first I want a shower, then another drink—and then food."

Eden sprang to her feet energetically. "You've got it. I'll see to the cook while you shower, Liz. Charley, another drink?"

"I'll come down," Danforth told her.

Eden smiled teasingly. "Oh, I thought you were going to stay up here and watch Liz take her shower!"

"I've done that once," Danforth said, blushing and glancing from Eden to Elizabeth and back to Eden. The women laughed.

"Charles, you amaze me," said Eden. "At your age and stage of development—my God, you can still blush. Look at him, Liz. He's positively pink."

"Hey, drop my complexion problems, will you?"

"I rather admire a man who can blush," said Elizabeth. "Don't you, Eden?"

"Absolutely."

Elizabeth got up from the bed and crossed to Danforth, kissing his lips lightly. Her eyes were bright with mischief. "You're perfectly welcome to look over the body, if you wish, Charles. I'm afraid there have been some changes since fourteen—and not all improvements."

"Go ahead, darling," said Eden. "Complete your education while I make us drinks." She waved and went out.

Danforth looked at Elizabeth and made a brief chuckle in his throat. Then his face became serious. "I want you to know I appreciate your coming, Elizabeth. It's been enlightening."

"I thought perhaps it would be," Elizabeth said. "Now I'm off to the shower." She started out into the hall to go to her room. But she glanced back at Danforth. Half turning, she fixed him with her eyes and said, "I must tell you, Charles—if those bastards continue to harass my husband I won't stand still for it."

"I take that as a jest, Elizabeth?"

"I didn't intend it in jest."

"A threat, perhaps?"

"Exactly." And she was gone.

Left alone, Danforth rattled the thin slivers of ice in the bottom of his

298

glass. He was suddenly quite weary. He needed to get some sleep. He wanted to get to bed early. Tomorrow he would have to be clearheaded. He had a lot to speak to the President about at breakfast.

MIAMI, FEBRUARY 28, 1961

Returning to Miami from Washington that Tuesday afternoon, Elizabeth found her granddaughter in the spare upstairs bedroom that had been converted into a studio and classroom. Her tutor, Mrs. Gloria Sánchez, a plump Cuban woman in her forties who had been a graduate in education from the University of Michigan, was conjugating English verbs. Elena sat in her red shorts and white T-shirt frowning at the difficult logic involved in sorting out the tenses. Opening the door quietly, Elizabeth watched the lesson a few moments and nodded to Mrs. Sánchez, then softly shut the door again and went downstairs. She could hear her husband in conversation in the library.

"I think it would be all right to go in," Salazar told her. "He's in conference with Tipton and Rod."

Tapping at the door, Elizabeth entered. The three men stood as she came into the room. Gustavo, in shirt sleeves, tie askew, came from behind his desk to greet her with a kiss.

"Please sit down," she said to Tipton and Rodríguez. "I just wanted to tell you that I'm back."

"How did it go?" Carta asked her.

"Quite well, I think. Have you any further word on the grand jury?"

"They're in session now. I suppose we shall hear something late today or tomorrow. I've called Mr. Miller, our attorney, and alerted him. Kaufman in Key West has managed to get Alfredo and his men out on bail."

"And the boats?"

"Being held as evidence."

"By federal authorities?"

"Yes. They've referred the case up here to the Miami office of the federal attorney. How are you going to like being married to a criminal?" Gustavo grinned. "What does that make you, a moll?"

"That's a very old-fashioned word, my dear," Elizabeth said gently. "Don't worry, if it takes fifty years, I'll get you out."

"Now, there's a comfort, Gustavo," said Tipton, smiling.

After she had gone, Carta opened the humidor on his desk and offered cigars to Tipton and Rodríguez. Leaning back with his freshly lit cigar, Tipton blew a smoke ring and watched it float lazily in the air before he blew out a cloud of smoke and destroyed its symmetry.

"That's a smashing lady, Gustavo," he said. "Have you ever reflected on the fact that you're one of the lucky men of the world to have such a woman?"

"It has occurred to me," Carta told him, his voice deliberately dry. "There is some possibility, you understand, that this trip of hers could make a difference."

"Never doubted it," said Tipton, and he looked at Rodríguez, who was puffing silently on his cigar. "Can you imagine, Rod, when history is written, it shall say that the turning point in the revolt against Fidel came not in the form of thousands of guns, but in the form of a handsome woman named Elizabeth Carta?"

Rodríguez smiled. "You'd have to know her to believe it."

At 10:45 P.M. Carta and Tipton were playing chess in the library when the telephone rang. They had started their Tuesday-night games weeks earlier, resuming a rivalry begun years ago in Havana. In the process, they had discovered they had changed very little during the years. Like most Cubans, Carta still played with enthusiastic zeal, impulsive and inspired. But Tipton, patient and methodical, had won more than half their matches.

The only interruption this evening had been Elena, wearing her nightgown and robe, ready for bed. Elizabeth and Carta made a fuss over her, making little teasing jokes to elicit giggles from the child. With her clear skin and blue eyes, all framed by a mass of shiny black hair, Elena appeared to Tipton like a miniature feminine version of her father. He remarked about it to Gustavo after she had been carried upstairs by Elizabeth.

Carta smiled warmly and said, "Every time I look at her, it gives me a strange feeling, Tip. Camilo looked very much like that when he was her age. When he'd come down to the library to say good night, he'd crawl up into my lap, put his arms around me and say, 'Papa—why can't I sleep with you and Momma?' " Carta's smile broadened. "They capture your heart at that age. You love them so much, you forgive all they do later."

"I wish now I'd had children with Teresa," said Tipton.

"I think, when all the smoke and fire of life blows away, and we see it for what it is, clearly, we'll make the shocking discovery that what it all boiled down to is children. Raising them, perpetuating the family."

"Ah, but what about the parents?" said Elizabeth, sweeping into the room, her face flushed from her play with Elena. "What about their relationship? Isn't that important, too? What happens to the lovers after the children are grown and gone? What do they have of value from their lives, besides having made their contribution to the world's population?"

Carta caught Elizabeth's eyes. He smiled at her. "Either love or alimony," he said. "That's what they have. If they've been lucky, love is the thing that lasts between them. What it was all built on. Out of that thing we call love come children."

"No," said Elizabeth. "I refuse to believe that what two people feel for each other is simply part of a biological process. Maybe Southerners are all hopeless romantics."

"Aren't you forgetting the classic test, Elizabeth?" asked Tipton. "You know the one I mean? The husband and child topple out of the boat. The mother can only save one. Which does she choose? Which would you save?"

Elizabeth made a gesture with her hand and started across the room to turn on a lamp in the corner. "I shan't get into that argument," she said. "I think the truth is, one wouldn't know—not until faced with the decision. Until you actually come face to face with it."

Carta looked amused. His eyes swept the chessboard. "I seem to be faced with a situation here," he said. He picked up one of the pawns, and both men returned their attention to the game.

Two hours later the telephone rang.

Since Carta was involved in his next move and Elizabeth was fetching coffee, it was Tipton who answered the phone.

"It's for you, Gustavo," he said. "It's the White House."

Carta nodded and crossed to his desk to pick up the extension.

"Hello?" Carta said.

"Is this Gustavo Carta?" a female voice asked.

"It is."

"Charles Danforth is calling you. One moment and I'll put him on."

"Gustavo?" It was Danforth's brisk, precise New England voice all right.

"How are you, Charles?"

"I was just leaving for home, but I wanted to call you first. I've got some good news."

Carta felt moisture on his palms. "I could use some good news," he responded in as normal a tone as he could muster.

"Since my discussion last night with Elizabeth, I've been exploring some of the realities of this situation. Rather interesting. I think we've

301

got a better grasp on what's happening down there now. I can't get into specifics on the phone with you, Gustavo—we have no way of knowing whether your phone is tapped, do we?"

"No, we don't."

"All right. What I can tell you is that I've just had a conversation with Justice. That business of the federal grand jury? Don't worry about it, Gustavo. It was a mistake."

"That, my friend, is good news."

"Secondly," Danforth's voice said, "I've discussed these matters at some length with a man named Vermillion. Do you know him?"

"Yes, I met him last fall in Washington."

"Yes, yes. I recall that. We had an informative chat, Vermillion and I. Actually, Gustavo, I came down on him with both feet. He's gotten the word in no uncertain terms. And, Gustavo, he has communicated it directly to the local man in charge there. I believe his name is Pullman."

"Pelham."

"Yes. He should be on his way over to your place by now. I just wanted to call you first. I know of your suspicions about these things, so I wanted to assure you that what Pullman tells you reflects White House policy."

"Thank you very much, Charles. That is wonderful to hear."

"Then give my love to Elizabeth, all right?"

"Fine."

"I'll be on my way home, then, before Eden files for divorce. See you soon." The connection clicked off.

Carta walked over to the chessboard and stared at the pieces in silence.

Driving through the near-empty streets, Pelham found himself hurtling past a parked police car and realized he was driving far too fast. He braked and glanced back into his rear-view mirror. The cop was not pursuing him; perhaps he'd been dozing. He told himself he must take it slow.

There were several things causing him impatience. He had been having a beer with Michael at the Hamlet when the phone call from Vermillion had come in, a call diverted to the bar by his answering service. The public phone at the Hamlet lacked privacy, and, given the background noise, Pelham simply listened to what Vermillion had told him, much of it phrased in a circumlocutious code.

"You understand, Pel," Vermillion had said. "We want this subject kept at home. Under no circumstances is he to be allowed access to the cooky jar. Clear?"

"Very clear, sir," Pelham had replied.

"One would expect that we could toss a cooky to him now and then, Pel. Keep him happy. It's the jar itself we wish to preserve. It belongs to us."

"I understand."

Pelham looked tired, his face drawn, as he stood in the doorway. Carta ushered him into the library.

"The hours are getting a little long on the job," Pelham said wearily.

"Sorry if I'm the cause of your overtime," Carta said.

Pelham stared at Tipton.

"Oh, you two have not met. This is Major Ian Tipton, Kirby Pelham." The two shook hands.

"Ah, yes, Tipton. I've heard of you. British Army, am I correct?"

"Retired," Tipton added crisply.

"Of course."

Pelham looked over at Carta, then at Tipton. "Ian is my top aide, Pel," Carta said. "I'm sure whatever you have to tell me can be said in front of him."

"That's your decision," Pelham said, seating himself.

"Let me get you some coffee," Carta said.

"No, thank you, Gustavo. I'd be awake all night."

Carta took a chair across from Pelham and sat there waiting. Pelham was taking his sweet time, Carta thought. The old trick of prolonging the suspense as long as possible. He exchanged a quick glance with Tipton, who clearly had deduced the same thing.

"I've come to talk to you in strictest confidence about matters of strategy," he said at last. "It is understood that nothing said here tonight should be repeated outside of this room."

"Understood," Carta said.

"There have been some high-level meetings in Washington about the Cuban operation," Pelham said briskly. "The central points are these. One, any military operations against Cuba will be under Cuban control, strictly."

Pelham's gray eyes blinked behind his glasses as he watched the looks of surprise coming from Carta and Tipton. "Second," he said in the same dry, flat tone, "top priority shall be given to aiding your underground organization in Cuba."

"I'd given up believing in miracles, along with Santa Claus," said Tipton, unable to disguise the amazement in his voice. "Did I hear you right, Pelham?"

"You heard me correctly, Major Tipton. Whatever you people need, we'll provide it. You are to have the full cooperation of the CIA, as well as other branches of the United States government, including the Navy, if you need it."

"Is there more?" asked Carta.

"Yes, all former Batista officers in the brigade in Guatemala will be removed from the training camps."

Tipton let out his breath in a low whistle. Carta merely stared at Pelham, trying to discern a trace of emotion in his eyes. He saw none. Pelham stared back at him, the lamplight glinting on the edges of his glasses.

Carta cleared his throat. "What do you expect of us?"

"Yes, Pelham, give us the bill," said Tipton. "You certainly expect something in return, don't you?"

Ignoring Tipton, Pelham addressed himself directly to Carta. "You know Dr. José Miró Cardona, do you not?"

"Of course," said Carta.

"What do you think of him?"

"I have respect for him. He's a moderate."

"And Varona?"

"Head of the Frente?" Carta collected his thoughts a moment. "In my opinion, he's an honorable gentleman—who wishes to return Cuba to the glories of the Batista days, without Batista, of course."

"We're asking you to explore—explore, mind you—the possibility of forming a new provisional government, with Dr. Cardona as the leader. You will be his chief deputy. You, of course, will be charged with the control and leadership of all insurgent forces operating within Cuba."

"And your brigade in Guatemala?"

"On the first of April, the brigade will launch its amphibious assault on Cuba. The invasion site is under review and will be selected shortly."

"Who will command it?" Carta asked.

"A Cuban officer to be selected by the provisional government. Perhaps someone like this man of yours. What's his name? Rodríguez?"

Again Tipton exhaled sharply, as though he had been hit a blow in the stomach. He gaped at Gustavo.

Carta remained placid, but behind his eyes his mind was working rapidly. It seemed incredible. Danforth had certainly come down with both feet—or was it the President himself who had brought Vermillion to the carpet? No matter. The results were astonishing. Carta shifted in his chair, crossing his legs, letting a moment pass before he spoke. "Let me ask you, Pel, how is the Guatemala brigade to be used?"

"That question will be reviewed shortly, in light of whatever strategy you people decide."

"By 'you people' you mean the provisional government?"

"The new provisional government, yes."

"Cubans?"

"Cubans."

"I am, Pel, quite frankly—astounded."

Pelham's thin lips formed a cool smile. "I thought perhaps you might be. I suppose I should congratulate you, Gustavo—you've won."

"So it seems," said Carta. "At least the initial battle. We must now take on Fidel."

He followed Pelham to the door. They shook hands.

When Carta returned to the library, he found Tipton pacing back and forth, a worried look on his face.

"I don't trust him," Tipton said. "What do you make of all of that?"

Carta went to his desk and took out the cigars. He offered them to Tipton, who helped himself.

"I'd say there are two possibilities, Tip. Possibility number one is that our friend Charles Danforth has somehow managed to shake them up over at Central Intelligence. That being the case, I'd say things look brighter than they ever have."

"You said there were two possibilities?"

"The second possibility is that this is a very elegant, gentlemanly way to keep us in limbo. We've been given some vague words of encouragement and a pat on the head and told not to get in the way."

"In which case we're like a telephone caller who has just been put on hold."

"Exactly."

Tipton bit off the end of a cigar and lit it. He stared thoughtfully at the yellow smoke curling toward the ceiling. "And which of those possibilities, in your candid and always jaded opinion, Gustavo, do you think is the right one?"

"Let me answer this way. I prefer to believe in the first possibility. I prefer that because I believe in Danforth. And perhaps because I still believe, for reasons I cannot comprehend, in common sense and common decency. Besides, I find the implications of the second possibility to be rather horrifying."

"All right, even if I agree with you—it's number one—how do we go about proving it to ourselves?"

Carta chuckled to himself. "You're worse than I am, Tip. Paranoia seems to be a communicable disease. Shall we check all this out, Tip?"

"Quite. You've got an idea?"

"Certainly."

At dinner Robin seemed curiously detached as she consumed the fried cabbage-and-sausage patties—a dish she coveted but one which usually gave David a stomachache. The conversation was sparse, for she kept reading her thick text all the time, occasionally glancing up at his face across the table.

"Why are you staring, David?" she asked him, looking up from her book.

"I like what I see. Isn't it permitted for a husband to stare at his wife?"

Her smile was noncommittal and she lowered her eyes back to the page she had been reading. "It's permitted, but it makes me nervous when I'm trying to concentrate."

"It's supposed to," he replied, but she said nothing.

After dinner, she took the dishes into the kitchen and stacked them in the sink, while David sat at the cleared table and smoked, watching her move back and forth. The undulation of her small rounded buttocks beneath the yellow skirt sent through him a pang of lust. She washed the dishes, an unusual feat for her to perform, he noted, and then came back to the living room and sat down at the desk with her text and began to read again, taking notes, referring to other books. Once she looked up at him and cocked her head. "Why don't you read, or something? You haven't worked on your thesis this week, have you?"

"I don't feel like it tonight," David replied, stubbing out his third cigaret in the ashtray. "I had other plans for this evening."

But she ignored his intimation and went back to scribbling notes, turning the page in front of her, her eyes devouring the words. David went to the porch. A dull resentment began to gather at the back of his mind. He found himself drifting obsessively to the subjects that had been occupying him lately—his sense of frustration with his wife, his sense of futility with his job. Both of these irritants had come together a couple of days earlier when David informed Robin that his conversations with the people at Scripps were growing more serious, that the possibility might arise of a job opening in San Diego. Instead of registering enthusiasm and support, Robin had become whiningly plaintive and had repeated her complaints again and again. She had too many friends in Miami to pull up stakes so suddenly; her studies would suffer if she had to transfer to another university. The whole thing was messing up her life.

"Sit and talk awhile, Rob."

"I'd love to, but I'm really tired. My brain is mush."

"You're beginning to sound like me." He smiled at her, trying to make light of it. "Are you really that tired?"

"Really."

It was a familiar tone, David thought. A tone of making excuses.

"I can hardly hold my eyes open." She yawned again. Turning aside, she said, "Good night."

He heard her go up the stairs and saw the bedroom light flick on. David went back into the kitchen and opened the refrigerator and took the half-filled bottle of vodka out of the freezer. The bottle was frosted and stuck to his fingers. He poured the syrupy liquid over ice in a glass, recapped the bottle and put it back into the freezer. Freezing vodka was a trick they'd learned at sea, where the rule was they were allowed one martini a night while they were diving. His friend Angus had come up with the idea, chattering away in his Australian accent, "If we put the bloody fucking vodka down in the freezer, supercold temperature, it'll thicken up a bit, you see. Drinking it ought to be like sipping nitro, eh?"

When he walked back to the porch and sat down, he lifted his glass. "To you, Angus," he said aloud. "I wish the hell I was with you."

He missed the Australian and he missed the Italian, Cesare, too. They were his only friends in Miami. He had never been one to make a lot of friends.

He sat sipping the vodka and ice, a pang of envy in him, thinking about what Angus and Cesare would be doing now aboard the *Cachalot*. It was only nine o'clock off Peru now. They'd probably be sitting around the table in the galley, drinking black coffee, arguing and telling stories of the day's adventures. He longed to be with them, but Camilo had seen to that.

HAVANA, MARCH 2, 1961

Camilo left Pepita at El Templete restaurant. He went to the jeep, where Paco was waiting. As he got into the front seat, he looked back and saw her sitting at the table. She looked very small and vulnerable sitting alone at the table with its white cloth. Camilo waved. She lifted her hand. Paco started the jeep and turned onto the Malecón. Traffic was heavy.

"What time is Maceo expecting you?" Paco asked.

"We have time. You know the hotel?"

"The Trotcha? Sure."

They drove out through the traffic to Vedado and pulled up in front of the unpretentious old hotel, where Maceo kept a room. It had once been a very famous French-style hotel in Havana, but it had fallen on bad times. There was a wonderful old garden, shut off from the street by a high wall. He found Maceo walking in the garden, smoking a cigar. A girl with him. She wore a militia uniform and had a pretty face and a thick bosom.

"Ah, Camilo," Maceo said. They embraced. He introduced the girl as María. "We were discussing agrarian reform." Maceo smiled at her. "She has some very interesting theories about utilizing small farms. Very interesting."

"I'll be in my room," she said, smiling back at him, her eyes bright. "If you like, when you have finished, knock."

She went out of the garden, swaying her hips. Camilo saw her big breasts under the khaki shirt. They bounced as she walked. At the door she glanced back at them over her shoulder and smiled again and then went inside.

Maceo made a growling sound in his throat. "Mmmmmm-uhm! I am going to do a little chopping with the machete this evening." He offered Camilo a cigar. Then he lit it with his lighter and snapped the cap closed. "How are things?"

"I want a boat," Camilo told him quietly.

Maceo's grin faded. His eyes grew serious. He drew in his breath, then exhaled. "I see. . . . You know I am against this, Camilo."

"Will you order me to not go?"

"I cannot. You know it. I am against it in principle. I am against it in general. But?" He shrugged. "Do you know Vega?"

"The one who went to Miami last year? Yes."

"I have had a very interesting communication from him recently. There is a man in touch with Vega who says he has some very valuable information on a certain CIA assassin, whose code name seems to be Castle. Interested?"

"Of course."

"You should be. We are including it in your assignment."

"What do we know about him?"

"Nothing. We only know his target."

"Fidel?"

"Who else?" Maceo lifted his hands in a gesture. "They hope to kill Fidel at the precise moment of invasion. You see? See how they think?"

"It is a separate problem," Camilo said.

"Yes. We've discussed your primary target at great length. My colleagues and I all agree that he represents a very legitimate threat. He could be an effective leader for the counterrevolution, the man that people would rally to. That's what makes us feel he must be eliminated. But I am still against you doing it."

308

"That is a decision that must rest with me. The man humiliates me. Because he is my father, he is my humiliation."

Maceo looked sullen.

"Besides, whom else would you send?" Camilo said with a sardonic grin.

"Camilo, you are the best there is! I know it. But I have been your friend since we were boys. A long time. I love you, *compadre*. I shall not like it, having you in this. What will I do without my Camilo?"

"Discuss agrarian reform with that María upstairs. Perhaps she has some unique methods of plowing that we have not seen, huh?"

"Possibly. I am always willing to learn, *compadre*."

"He suspects nothing," said Camilo. "He is chasing a girl. A very pretty, plump girl."

Paco's black face broke into a wide grin. "Then we go?"

"When the time is ripe, Paco. When the time is ripe."

"Let it be soon," Paco said. "I am tired of this revolution. Too many Communists."

CHAPTER TWENTY-EIGHT

By 1920 what had happened to Cuba was apparent in the streets of Havana. The dignified lethargy of Spain had given way to the business-first ethic. Office buildings that looked transported from New York loomed beside the crumbling Spanish Colonial churches. A constant procession of Fords, the mufflers wide open and barking, flowed along the Malecón and the Prado into the narrow cobblestone streets built for horse-drawn carriages. Crowds as hustling and business-bent as those on Wall Street hurried through narrow callejones *that seemed, with their baroque Spanish stone façades and massive wood-and-metal doors, to be harking to the days of Ponce de León and the buccaneers of the Spanish Main. Billboards were as numerous in Havana and her suburbs as in New York. Huge electric signs flashed the virtues of products and shops far into warm tropical nights. Sidewalk cafés lined the Prado where patrons could look out at the old Spanish laurel trees and the traffic. Beyond the walls of old Havana into the newer residential suburbs the streets grew wider, the buildings more modern. The Old Colón market was as dark and unsanitary as the days when a Creole mistress* sent her slave to do the day's shopping. Its long lines of stalls filled with cackling chickens and the stench of freshly killed meat that hung fly-blown in the carnicerías, the rows of vegetable and fruit stands, mingled with bins of modern machine-made clothes, racks of shoes, and piles of canned goods; loaves of bread baked in the European fashion were enclosed in sanitary paper wrappings, Yankee style. The Cuban soldiers with their campaign hats and webbed belts looked the exact replicas of the U.S. troops of the era. The streets at night were as brightly lit as any United States city. Ferryboats as modern as those that crossed the Hudson River plied between the waterfront and Casablanca across the harbor. But these steam-driven craft still had as competition the heavy old Havana rowboats, equipped with awnings against the tropical sun, and manned by oarsmen as weathered and strong-armed as the gondoliers of Venice. Amid the mechanical roar of the Fords flashing along the Malecón came the occasional horse and carriage with its liveried footman, clip-clopping on the pavement.

Havana was a far different city from what it had been twenty years ago when the Spanish flag was lowered. Its best streets then were lanes of mud, the cobblestones mired so deep in the filth of centuries that uncovering them had resembled a mining operation. The city's garbage dump along the waterfront had been replaced with the paved Malecón and a sea wall. The hovels that had lined the Prado had been torn down. The massive walls of the new Presidential Palace, adorned with every manner of artistic scroll, were nearing completion. Yellow fever, which had terrified the city since the days of Velásquez, had been eradicated by Cuba's Dr. Carlos Juan Finlay and Dr. Walter Reed of the United States. The population of the city had trebled. The outlying country villages of thatched huts had been transformed into thriving suburbs; Vedado, which had been an area of a few scattered farmers when the Treaty of Paris was signed, now had become a rich residential section where sugar millionaires and politicians competed with each other in the erection of private palaces.

The mixture of Spanish and North American cultures carried over into the politics of the island, where the democratic and the autocratic commingled in a vast system of corruption, intrigue and graft that had aspects of Boss Tweed's Tammany Hall and the despotism of the Spanish captains general.

Graft in Cuba was known as chivo. During Spanish rule the governors looked upon the island as a legitimate source of quick wealth. Royal grants were bestowed upon favorites; titles and government positions were created as a means of securing all the graft possible. The few years of American rule simply added a new dimension, making the vote the ingredient of political power rather than royal whim. The Cubans' system of cliques and political machines differed from those of the United States only in that they were set in a tropical island. The thugs who shot at each other differed little from the gangsters in Chicago and New York. The crooked politicians who siphoned vast sums off public-works contracts had much in common with all the corrupt officials who handed out political jobs to

310

their friends in all the cities of the United States. The greedy Cuban businessman had J. P. Morgan and John D. Rockefeller for models as well as the Basque entrepreneurs who had controlled the island economy for centuries. Chivo or graft, it was the same system, only translated into Cuban. It reigned supreme on the island in 1920.

Cuba's national lottery provided an unfailing source of revenue and a splendid means of rewarding political henchmen. Thirty thousand tickets were sold in the average lottery, at twenty dollars each. The government took $180,000 off the top. The remaining $420,000 was offered in prizes. Each twenty-dollar ticket was broken down into a hundred pieces, at a peseta each, for the small gamblers. But the pieces were never sold at that price. From one end of the island to the other, the district billeteros demanded at least thirty dollars a ticket. The corruption filtered to the lowest level.

Concessions and government permits were other prime sources of chivo. The Cubans accepted it as a way of life. In Havana, each morning six men who had the concession to clean the rubbish that floated in the harbor went down to the dock, rowed across the harbor and back, and hurried away to their other jobs without having touched the flotsam. They collected money each month from the government. During a hurricane, the sea wall along the Malecón crumbled in sections. The millionaire Spanish contractor had saved on cement. He put some of the money into his own pocket. He paid out the rest in bribes to Cuban inspectors.

As one contemporary Cuban writer put it:

> The Cuban has a habit of beating himself on the chest and shouting about his honor at the very moment when both he and his hearers know he is lying. We cultivate falsehood with a facility which becomes prodigious . . . Our dominating nervous temperament has contributed to make us irritable, sometimes insufferable. We have more sensations than ideas, more imagination than understanding. We are better path followers than originators; we prefer to triumph by astuteness rather than by reason; we are prodigal, and for that reason the thirst for riches is our dominant characteristic. The rascality of our priests, largely from Spain, has made the average Cuban, if not an atheist, at least a skeptic and indifferent to religious matters.

The Catholic Church in Cuba was not above chivo. The Spanish priests demanded fabulous sums for marrying, or baptizing, and were frequently advising the guajiros and laboring classes who could not afford the prices to go without.

José Martí had written: "The enemies of a people's freedom are not so much the foreigners who oppress them as the timidity and vanity of its own sons."

President Theodore Roosevelt sent William Howard Taft to Havana early in 1906 to try to reconcile differences between the revolting Liberal Party under José

Miguel Gómez and Conservative Party President Tomás Estrada Palma. Well-meaning and conscientious, Palma was Cuba's first elected President. He faced a Congress beset with factional hostilities. When he tried to take office for a second term, the Liberals revolted, claiming that the election was fraudulent. Palma had no army to protect his government—the Americans had disbanded it—so he turned to the Platt Amendment. When Taft's efforts proved futile, Palma resigned and went into poverty-stricken retirement in Bayamo, a broken man. The Cuban legislature adjourned without naming a successor.

Taft turned power over to Charles E. Magoon, a former U.S. governor of the Canal Zone. Magoon brought in American troops to reoccupy the island and proclaimed a provisional government "to restore order and hold new elections."

The second U.S. occupation of Cuba lasted more than two years. In a message to Congress, Roosevelt declared that while the U.S. had no desire to annex Cuba, it was "absolutely out of the question that the island should continue independent if the insurrectionary habit becomes confirmed." The message to the Cubans was extremely clear.

By spring of 1912, riots on the island were approaching the proportions of civil war. José Miguel Gómez, the Liberal Party leader, had been in power since 1909, and the corruption of his regime had led to revolt. In a bitterly contested presidential campaign the Conservative candidate was elected, with eight U.S. warships standing by. General Mario García Menocal took office. He quickly announced his intention "to cement friendly relations with the United States." With its financial interests thus protected, the U.S. withdrew.

In 1917, President Menocal ran for a second term, after an administration that was called in the streets of Havana "Cuba's Great Disappointment." But this was the era of the island's "Dance of the Millions," when fortunes in sugar were to be had for the taking. Prosperity aided Menocal's cause.

His opponent was the Liberal candidate, Alfredo Zayas, who had been Vice-President under Gómez. The election was close. Both sides claimed victory. But before the Cuban Supreme Court could decide the outcome, ex-President Gómez and his followers went into armed revolt in Oriente province, burning cane fields. Gómez was warned that the United States would not recognize any government founded on violence, and four hundred U.S. Marines were landed at Santiago.

Menocal entered his second term.

In November, 1921, an election took place and ended without result. Both sides charged fraud. Coupled with this critical situation was a financial crisis caused by the catastrophic drop in the price of sugar. President Woodrow Wilson sent Major General Enoch Crowder to Havana aboard the battleship Minnesota to intervene in Cuba once again.

Crowder was no stranger to Cuban politics. A military man, he had been sent to Havana in 1919 to rewrite Cuba's electoral laws. Now he had come to straighten out Cuba's election mess.

Crowder acted swiftly and decisively, and with full authority. He named Zayas as the winner. The new President was inaugurated on May 20. At Crowder's suggestion, the new President asked the U.S. general to remain in Cuba "in an advisory capacity." Crowder went so far as to impose his own cabinet on Zayas. At first the Cuban President cooperated. But, capitalizing on the growing resentment against U.S. interference in the island's affairs, Zayas negotiated a loan of fifty million dollars with J. P. Morgan's bank and disbanded Crowder's cabinet. The U.S. government frowned.

Zayas managed to retrieve his country's credit, avert U.S. intervention and, through negotiation, secure title to the Isle of Pines, off Cuba's southwest coast, after two decades' delay imposed by the Platt Amendment. Yet his administration was so corrupt it overshadowed these achievements. The habaneros made a joke of Zayas. He had erected a magnificent bronze statue to himself in front of the Presidential Palace. But the sculptor placed Zayas' left hand in a position which made it look as though he was patting his trouser pocket; his right hand gestured toward the palace. The street joke had it that Zayas was forever saying, "There, caballeros, is where I got the money to fill my pockets."

After more than twenty years of United States economic and political domination, Cubans began to rekindle their desire for independence. They felt that their revolution had been frustrated by the Yankees. In 1924 the end result of foreign domination was about to take a most sinister form. In trying to sow the seeds of their own democracy and economic laissez-faire in the Cuban climate, the Americans succeeded only in fostering a corrupt dictatorship.

His enemies called him "the tropical Mussolini." In Cuba he was known as "the President of a thousand murders." It was probably a conservative estimate. For Gerardo Machado was to Cuban politics what the mako shark was to the blue waters of the Gulf, a natural product. But at least that great shark had the nobility of being motivated by hunger. The ruthlessness of Machado seemed rooted in avarice, stupidity and greed.

Machado was heavy, thick in the waist. He had a fat-jowled neck that framed a badly pockmarked face. His eyes were dark, almost hidden beneath fleshy lids. A pair of circular horn-rimmed glasses gave him an owlish expression. He combed his white hair straight back from his forehead, and it tended to pop out at the back of his head like a tuft of feathers. He was fond of white suits and Panama hats and made many people nervous by keeping his hands in his pockets whenever he appeared in public. The reason was not what was presumed: Machado had lost the ends of the index and middle fingers on his right hand and was very self-conscious about it. He also liked making people nervous.

Born in Manajanado, Santa Clara, in Las Villas province, on September 29, 1871, Machado was the son of a cattle thief. He studied in the elementary schools of Santa Clara. As a young man he was physically powerful. He worked in a *butcher shop for a time. During the practice of his trade he chopped off his fingertips.*

He was twenty-four when José Martí resumed Cuba's rebellion against the Spaniards. Machado joined the mambisas, *as the rebels were called, and fought with a cool bravery that led to his rapid rise in the ranks of the Cuban Army. He was made a captain in 1895. By the end of the war he held the rank of general. He made a striking figure with his powerful frame and full handlebar moustache.*

After the war, he became closely associated with José Miguel Gómez, and with him formed the Liberal Party, one of two main political organizations in Cuba during the first years of the Republic. Gómez was appointed governor of Las Villas province under the American military administration. Machado was elected mayor of Santa Clara. One of his first acts was to burn down the Audiencia, which housed the only copies of his father's criminal record. Machado clearly understood the uses of power.

When Gómez became President in 1909, Machado moved through a series of posts, including that of inspector of the tough Guardia Rural. At each step, Machado learned more. Eventually he became Minister of the Interior. He got to be an expert at collecting chivo. *When a section of the Central Highway was built through Las Villas province, Machado and Gómez sold lands they had purchased cheaply for the route. They also let the contracts and collected kickbacks. He made friends with the owners of the U.S.-owned Electric Bond and Share Company, which held a monopoly on the island's electrical supply. A shady American entrepreneur named Henry Catlin became company president. Machado was named vice-president. As Minister of the Interior, he allowed Catlin to charge the then outrageously high price of fifteen cents a kilowatt hour in Havana, and up to twenty-two cents in the rural areas. Machado was learning.*

At a time when Adolf Hitler was living in a two-room apartment on the top floor of 41 Thierschstrasse in Munich dictating feverishly the first draft of Volume One of Mein Kampf, *a thick-waisted ex-butcher in Havana with two fingers missing from his right hand was putting together one of the tightest little dictatorships in the world. It was a classic fascist organization, and it had deep roots within Cuban society.*

The upper classes, grown prosperous on sugar and dazzled by the tight-knit relationship to the American market, wanted more than anything to maintain the status quo, which the U.S. and British interests encouraged with vigor. The Cuban Army, which had been formed in 1909, wanted to flex its muscles. The vast government bureaucracy with thousands on the payroll—in a time when jobs were hard to get—wanted to keep what they had. The members of the Cuban Congress, the provincial governors and the municipal councils were knee-deep in graft and wanted to keep their pieces of the action. The merchants and the businessmen all needed stability to maintain their prosperity. During the "Dance

314

of the Millions" less than a decade before, the laborers, the wage earners and even the fishermen were rich. They were all ready to trade any idea they may have had of political freedom for material gain.

"Cuban society is disintegrating," wrote scholar Fernando Ortiz in 1924. "Cuba is rushing headlong into barbarism."

Machado knew his politics intimately. Extroverted, a good orator, he had been schooled under Gómez in the nuances of threat, bribe, violence and graft. He knew how to manipulate the American and British financial interests. He knew what everyone wanted. He welded it all together, carefully and patiently, during his first two years in office. He purged the army officers who opposed him, bringing the others in line with threats and bribes. He beefed up the police and formed a secret-police network called the porristas. *He appointed army officers to more and more civil posts, gradually bonding the seams of his fascist society. He used fear and greed and self-interest to manipulate the politicians. He inaugurated public-works programs that gained him a strong following.*

Early in 1928, Machado made his move to secure dictatorial power. He announced that his economic program could not be completed within his four-year term and that only he could carry it out. Before a packed constitutional convention in April he pushed through his decision to reelect himself. The delegates granted him a new six-year term of office and abolished the vice-presidency. Machado was dictator of Cuba.

To satisfy his vanity and cloak himself in some kind of political legality, Machado held an election in November in which he was the only candidate. His political machine turned out the votes. His new term was to run from May 20, 1929, to May 20, 1935.

The reaction of the United States government was clear-cut approval. Machado had subordinated the island's judiciary and its Congress, created a single-party political system by gaining control of all three party organizations, eliminated all opposition, closed antigovernment newspapers, expelled labor leaders, bribed and threatened, assassinated and tortured, and turned his country into a tight little police state. President Calvin Coolidge said it was fine with him and invited Machado to the White House for the Pan American Conference.

Machado's trip to Washington was billed by his propagandists as "a triumphal visit." When his ship sailed back into Havana the Malecón was jammed with crowds of cheering Cubans. His henchmen had turned out the entire cadre of public employees and ordered all schoolchildren to appear for the parade carrying flowers to throw in his path.

However, in the week prior to his arrival small groups of young men and women, intelligent-looking, well dressed, had appeared at the schools around Havana, urging the younger children not to take part in the welcoming ceremonies for Machado. He was, they said, a dictator. It would be better if the order to appear was disobeyed. Many stayed home. The young men and women were

315

students from the University of Havana. Machado had not yet firmly suppressed that faction of his society. He had not expected that he would have to. They were only children.

The country was soon plunged into an economic crisis touched off by the Wall Street crash of 1929 and the Great Depression that was now gripping the United States. Sugar dropped to a low of one half cent a pound and hovered there, bringing financial ruin. Machado's carefully welded political support had simply crumbled.

The number of children attending school in Cuba had fallen from seventy-five out of every thousand in 1900 to only twelve in 1932. Though millions of dollars were appropriated for school construction, no schools were built. Prostitution was sharply on the increase. Open "cribs" flourished in the middle of Havana. Slums were spreading. Wages were declining year by year.

The steady disintegration of its island neighbor did not go unnoticed in the United States. With Cuba's economy on its knees, the investment opportunities for American bargain-hunters proved enticing. The worse things became, the bigger the U.S. stake.

Between 1923 and 1933, for example, the share of the Cuban sugar industry controlled by American companies soared from thirty-five percent to eighty percent. Americans controlled sixty percent of total landholdings in Cuba by 1933, compared with only seventeen percent a decade earlier. To protect this investment, the State Department assumed the official position of looking down its nose at Machado's corruption while at the same time countenancing loans and subsidies to his regime and permitting huge arms shipments from U.S. ports.

Cuba was rapidly becoming one enormous slum. Public employees had not been paid for months and were edging toward riot. Unemployment and discontent ranged through all levels of the society, from the business community to the laborers. The University of Havana students, hard hit by Machado's secret police, were nonetheless organized into underground cliques that were carrying out assassinations and exploding bombs all over Havana. Sabotage was rife in the factories and the big industries. A rumor spread in Havana that Machado had resigned from office. People spilled into the streets, heading in a mass toward the Presidential Palace. Police and soldiers blocked the way and opened fire. The mob was scattered, but hatred for the Machado regime reached a high pitch. The whole island seemed to be in a suicidal mood. A general strike was called by Cuba's unions, which had been forced to go underground when Machado's secret police began shooting down labor leaders in the streets. The strike was supported by workers throughout the island. Taking advantage of the chaos and confusion, the Cuban Communist Party assumed command. But its leader, César Vilar, went to make a deal with Machado, gaining concessions for his party in return for calling off the strike. Vilar had misjudged his influence. The Cubans ignored his back-to-work order. His pact with Machado discredited the Communists for genera-

316

tions. It was clearly betrayal. From New York to Miami anti-Machado exile groups were actively supplying arms to the underground rebels.

Into this mounting chaos President Franklin Roosevelt sent Undersecretary of State Sumner Welles to try to divert the violent reaction to Machado "toward a peaceful solution." Tall, urbane and supremely confident, Welles coolly assessed the deteriorating situation in Cuba and formulated a plan to combat it. He was closely connected with Machado's highest officials. He had little trouble persuading them to deliver a coup d'état in the form of a request for Machado to resign. Welles assured Machado that if he left the country and went into exile in Miami his family would be well treated and his property protected. The commander of Machado's army, General Alberto Herrera, would take over the Cuban government for a few hours until Welles's hand-picked successor, Carlos Manuel de Céspedes, could be named President. Céspedes was the son of the Cuban poet-patriot who had touched off the Ten Years' War with his Cry of Yara in Oriente in 1868. Machado began packing his bags.

On the night of August 12, 1933, Gerardo Machado, in his wrinkled white suit, climbed aboard a plane on the outskirts of Havana with his family and carloads of luggage containing millions in cash. The Cuban dictator seemed in a tense mood, one moment grave, the next smiling and passing small bits of nervous humor with his pilots and bodyguards. When the plane roared off the ground and climbed into the clear tropical night, Machado looked back at the lights of Havana spread out before him. His wife was crying. It was the last time he was to see the city, or Cuba.

Behind him, Machado left a Cuba in total disarray.

Thousands swarmed into the streets of Havana. Hysterical mobs seized Machado's minor henchmen and assassins and dragged them through the streets. All through the island mobs hunted down the members of the secret police and murdered them. Eighteen were killed and more than a hundred wounded on that day, which became known as "Bloody Saturday." Machado's police chief committed suicide, but the enraged crowds dragged his body to the university and hung it from a post. The mansions of Machado supporters in Vedado and Miramar were sacked. Cheering and shouting wildly, the looters tossed whole libraries of books into the streets. Machado's name was expunged from signs, cornerstones and plaques all over the island. Two bronze panels describing his achievements were cut from the main doors of the Capitol, which he had built.

After the violent mobs had spent their fury, armed students started methodically going through the confidential files in Havana's police headquarters, looking for names of assassins and informers. The killing continued steadily; few of Machado's killers ever reached a court. While this violence raged in Cuba, Machado and his family were quietly being passed through U.S. customs in Miami. He retired in exile in a mansion that his stolen millions had bought, pampered and closely guarded until he died on March 29, 1939. On that day, across the

Atlantic, Adolf Hitler was preparing to invade Poland and touch off World War II. Machado's death was little noted.

Sumner Welles was a prudent and pragmatic man. He quickly perceived that the country was on the brink of anarchy. A new generation of leaders was emerging—young men and women who would not bend either to American influence or to Machado's tyranny. It was a whole new generation of Cubans who felt they had their own destinies and the destiny of their country in their hands.

Welles listened to the strongly anti-American tenor of this rebellious "Generation of the 1930s" and the cries for social justice, echoed by many exiles returning from the United States who had listened carefully to Roosevelt's New Deal. He became concerned. He had a major revolution on his hands. The situation was delicate in the extreme.

Welles's choice for a replacement of Machado, Carlos Manuel de Céspedes, did not reflect the prevailing spirit of the Cubans, who had fought for and now demanded their own new deal.

With Welles's blessing, Céspedes annulled Machado's repressive laws and restored the 1901 constitution, which had been literally dictated by the Americans. Céspedes' actions were honorable, but the times militated against him. Cuba's downward spiral had picked up too much momentum. Every sector of the nation seemed to boil with unrest.

One important sector was the Army. Part of Céspedes' austerity program called for a reduction in pay for the Army and a limitation on promotions. One of those who recoiled against these measures was an obscure sergeant-stenographer named Fulgencio Batista. Tough, thick-skinned, Batista was, in every sense, a man of the people. He was an exotic mixture of Spanish, Negro, Indian and Chinese blood. Orphaned at thirteen, Batista had gone to work as a youth in the cane fields and dreaded the prospect of a life as a common laborer. The only escape was the Army. Equipped with an agile mind, Batista fitted in well with the Cuban military bureaucracy. He studied stenography and served as court stenographer during the trials of student rebels. The trials taught him a great deal about the tactics of rebellion and power.

Now, with the lower ranks of the Army seething with unrest, Batista decided to put his theories to work. He set about organizing his fellow enlisted men into a tight-knit unit. The enlisted men then proceeded to arrest their own officers. It was a bold move—in effect, a group of sergeants had pulled off a coup d'état! *With the enlisted men in control of the Army, the nation's political leaders now had to consult with Batista in an effort to shore up their regime.*

On September 4, 1933, Sumner Welles's symbolic President, Céspedes, disappeared into the void of history. An uneasy alliance was forged between the two most volatile segments in Cuban society, the students and the Army. The man

318

named to serve as provisional leader of the new regime was a professor from the University of Havana's Medical School with no previous political experience, Dr. Ramón Grau San Martín.

Grau was determined not to become the victim of inaction like his predecessors. He purged all Machado followers from government positions, guaranteed the university freedom from government control, and promulgated a series of liberal social and political laws while at the same time sharply curtailing the growing influence of the Communists.

He also made one critical tactical error, however. He did not curry the favor of Sumner Welles, who, though an appointee of Roosevelt, had more conservative notions about the way Cuba should be governed. For one thing, Welles looked askance at Grau's demand for abrogation of the venerable Platt Amendment. Grau also committed the heresy of seizing two American-owned sugar mills which had long been shut down because of labor disputes.

In addition, Welles was personally affronted when Grau summoned the young rebel Antonio Guiteras Holmes and named him combined Minister of War, the Interior and the Navy. Guiteras had delivered a speech in which he questioned Welles's motives for ousting Machado and for choosing an ineffectual successor. Further, upon taking office, Guiteras proclaimed: "No movement in Cuba can be revolutionary unless it is also anti-imperialist. One can serve either imperialism or the people—their interests are incompatible."

Among Guiteras' first actions was to announce a "temporary" seizure of the American-owned Cuban Electric Company and to enact an immediate reduction in electric rates.

Sumner Welles grew more and more displeased with the way things were going. He declared a personal and private war on the Grau government as well as on the upstart Sergeant Batista. His first move came on September 5, after the sergeants' revolt. U.S. warships entered Havana harbor.

The impression Welles had hoped for did not materialize. A large segment of Havana's population appeared along the Malecón, jamming the streets. The shouts from the quay echoed out across the water where the gray-hulled warships were moored. "Get out! You have no business here! Go back to your own country!" It was the full-dress rehearsal of the "Yankee go home!" cry that was to sweep the world thirty years later. A Cuban in the crowd drew a revolver and fired a shot at one of the battleships. The bullet plopped into the water far from its target, but Havana's newspapers gave it a big play the next day.

It seemed for a tense few days that the U.S. Marines on board the warships were about to make another landing. But Roosevelt rejected the proposal. Welles, however, seeking to find a better solution to his problem than either the Grau-Guiteras government or Batista's military group, set about engineering a new coup. He summoned the Cuban army officers Batista had deposed to the Hotel Nacional, where he had a suite. He began holding conferences, also attended by *his military attaché. The officers, meanwhile, started building sandbag fortifications around the hotel and bringing in carloads of weapons and ammunition. A sensitive man, Welles began to realize after a few weeks that he was in an increasingly untenable position personally. He moved out of the hotel.*

Batista, meanwhile, had been given the rank of colonel and was placed in command of all Cuba's armed forces. Seemingly unambitious politically, the thin, amiable ex-sergeant went to work reorganizing the Army, drawing on his fellow noncommissioned officers to fill the ranks of lieutenants, captains and majors. He was a first-rate organizer. He set up military control throughout Cuba to fill the vacuum left by the disappearance of Machado's politicians and his civil police.

On October 2 he ordered an attack on the Hotel Nacional, where the deposed army officers had refused to quit their fortifications. The big old hotel stood exposed to assault on all sides. Batista's khaki-clad soldiers, well armed, and supported by gunboats in the harbor, surrounded the hotel and opened fire. Once again, the staccato popping of small-arms fire echoed in the Havana streets. At the same time, a terrorist group calling itself the ABC revolted in support of Welles and the ex-officers fighting in the hotel. The uprising centered in Havana. ABC terrorists attacked barracks and fortifications. Snipers fired from rooftops at the soldiers in the streets. Two days later, nearly a thousand lives had been lost. But Batista prevailed.

Welles next proclaimed his decision to withhold U.S. recognition from the Grau government on the grounds that it had failed to restore true unity to the country. As evidence, Welles pointed to a rash of Communist demonstrations and terrorist acts by a dissident band of army officers (whom he had encouraged).

Grau's hopes rose momentarily with the announcement by President Roosevelt that he was replacing Welles with a new envoy named Jefferson Caffrey. Upon arriving in Havana, however, Caffrey quickly demonstrated that, if anything, he was less sympathetic to Grau than was his predecessor. The Grau regime, Caffrey said, was supported only by the "ignorant masses who have been misled by utopian promises."

There was only one leader capable of maintaining order and protecting U.S. economic interests in Cuba, Caffrey said. That man was Fulgencio Batista. He alone "represented true authority."

Grau and his supporters were stunned. Never before had the U.S. intervened so blatantly in Cuba's internal politics. And never before had it so openly expressed the doctrine that a totalitarian regime was more "reliable" than a democratic one.

But Caffrey moved swiftly now. On January 15, 1934, Grau was propelled from office and Batista was installed as the new leader. Official U.S. recognition, which was withheld from the liberal regime, was promptly accorded to Batista, who quickly cemented his position. He rounded up the followers of dissident leaders. It was the Machado pattern all over again: arrests, torture, executions.

320

The United States's role as a power broker in Cuba had now been established. Its envoys had succeeded in selecting a new leader and a new regime. They had also succeeded, however, in engendering a wave of anti-American bitterness among Cuba's middle classes. The price of intervention would prove to be dear.

CHAPTER TWENTY-NINE

MONROE COUNTY, FLORIDA, MARCH 15, 1961

At 11:15 A.M., federal agents in Key West returned without comment the three motorboats confiscated the end of February in the raid on Gustavo Carta's base at Shark Key.

An hour later, two truckloads of munitions were released to Carta's agents in Fort Lauderdale. It clearly was a triumphant day for Carta. He and his staff wasted no time in planning and mounting an operation. Raúl Masetti, in Havana, was pressing for a more rapid increase in the distribution of arms and equipment. The urgency had become critical. In Las Villas province nearly fifty thousand of Castro's militia had begun a final assault on the guerrillas operating in the Escambray Mountains. If he succeeded in wiping out the guerrilla units, Castro would be able to turn his full attention to any landing in southern Oriente, the core of Carta's plan.

"If we are to have any chance of success," Carta told Tipton and Rodríguez, "we must move now, fast."

Late that afternoon, after a phone call to Pelham and a long conversation with a man named Dobbs, Carta watched one and a half tons of weapons, ammunition and explosives being unloaded from a U-Haul truck and reloaded by his men onto three shrimp boats at the dock at Jew Fish. Alfredo, the boatman, was in a frenzy of activity. "I don't believe this, *jefe*," the fisherman said. "And I see it with my own eyes."

The plan was to land the weapons at a small bay north of Trinidad, in Las Villas province, on Cuba's west coast. Because of his British passport, Tipton was dispatched on the afternoon plane to Havana to coordinate the landings with Masetti and the Escambray guerrillas. The guerrillas were to provide a screen of fifty men, blocking the roads to the small bay, named Bahía Pargo, while the arms were being unloaded from the

321

boats. If all went well, Masetti's morning radio message would be received with the code words "Sea bird." Carta would then order the boats to depart, with sealed orders as to the rendezvous points and times.

It was a bold plan, because the slow shrimp boats would be vulnerable from the moment they entered Cuban waters. They planned to use the cover of darkness to make the actual landings. But it would be risky.

"I am requesting officially," Carta told Dobbs, "that the United States Navy at Key West fly cover for these three boats—the mission is critical."

Dobbs's face had been immobile as he listened. When Carta had finished, he simply nodded. "No problem, Dr. Carta, you got it."

The next day, as they watched Alfredo sail, Tipton turned to Carta and said, "I suppose we can do nothing now but sweat."

For five days, they did sweat.

"I have asked God for many things in my life," Carta told Elizabeth as they got into bed that fifth night. "Tonight, I am begging for the lives of those men."

At 4:30 A.M. the telephone at the bedside rang. Elizabeth came awake instantly. Carta was across the room, hurrying toward the phone. She let it ring until he picked up the receiver.

"Gustavo," came Tipton's calm voice, "Alfredo's back."

"Thank God." Carta sighed. "I'll be right there."

"Not without me," Elizabeth told him as he hung up. "I wouldn't miss this for the world."

They drove in Elizabeth's Jaguar down the Dixie Highway, south of Miami, and turned off onto the back road near Dade City into the swamps. Half an hour later they came out of the tunnel of mangroves into the flat white clearing at the boatyard. Three shrimp boats were moored in the river. There was a jeep parked at the dock. Rodríguez, in his camouflage fatigues, stood outside the shack in a cluster of men. Carta saw Alfredo and Tipton move from a second group toward them. Elizabeth braked the car, the white coral dust blowing over them, and they got out.

Alfredo's creased face, darkened even more by the tropical sun, was beaming. "*Jefe*, you wouldn't have believed it. It was beautiful! Those jets were there wooshing over us all the time. Man, I never saw anything so beautiful in my life!"

"Any trouble from Fidel's patrol boats?"

"Twice they started to come at us. But those big birds up there—I mean, they were scary, and I knew they were on my side—they came in low over that water, like this!" Alfredo demonstrated with his hand shaped like an airplane, making a roaring sound in his throat. He looked at Carta, his brown face split with a toothy grin. "Woooooosh!" He laughed. "You should have seen those Castro people turn tail! It was terrific! Terrific!"

Carta's eyes met those of Tipton and Rodríguez.

"I guess that answers our questions, eh?" said Tipton.

"Tip, I want you to make one more trip to Havana," Carta told him. "I want to set up a meeting at sea with Masetti, Victorio from Escambray, Andrés from Sierra Maestra—I want it as soon as possible. We can work out the details this morning at the house. When we strike, I want it to be well coordinated, no misunderstandings. OK?"

For the first time in weeks, Carta saw smiles on the faces of his two aides.

"What about this proposal for a coalition?" Rodríguez asked him. "Are we going along with it?"

"I haven't decided," Carta told him. "I first want to talk to Masetti and the others, to get their feelings—I am not the sole member of this party, you know?"

Later, in the car as they turned back into the heavy commuter traffic that jammed the Dixie Highway, Elizabeth glanced at Carta. "Well, Charles has kept his part of the bargain . . . hasn't he?"

"Yes," Carta agreed thoughtfully. "I keep looking for the hitch—but there doesn't seem to be one. Amazing. Can you imagine? United States Navy jets flying cover for our boats?" He laughed joyfully. "I can hardly believe it's true."

BARACOA, CUBA, APRIL 1, 1961

The meeting at sea off Capo Verde, Cuba, between the underground and guerrilla leaders of the Partido Revolucionario Cubano and Gustavo Carta took place at 2300 hours. Two small boats carried the leaders from Cayo Güin to the side of a small coastal freighter, the *Bahama Star,* and then moved off a hundred yards in either direction to stand by in the heavy seas that were running. Squall lines moved steadily across the dark sky that night, with occasional flashes of lightning and the distant rumble of thunder. Waves of eight to ten feet lifted the two small boats in the swell and then lowered them into the troughs. The two Cuban fishermen who piloted the boats remained alert at the wheels, their eyes fixed on the black smudge of the freighter, awaiting the flashlight signal to pick up their passengers. Twice they were drenched with rain that came hissing across the water like the sound of millions of snakes in the dark. Soaked to the skin, cold and trembling with anxiety, the two fishermen waited, watching the hull of the freighter rise and fall into view. They both knew that what was happening aboard that ship out there in the dark held great portent for their Cuba, and though the danger of participating in this event was extreme, now and later, they gave it no importance. José Martí had said it for them, for all Cubans: "to die for your country is to live."

Aboard the *Bahama Star,* the heavy seas made movement below troublesome. The single electric light cast long shadows over the galley where they convened. Occasionally, the light would dim to an amber glow, like candlelight, the figures of the seated men becoming dark phantom shapes around the table, like monks at prayer in a dungeon. The air was humid and close and stank of stale food and rancid cooking oil. On the shelves above the stove and the sink, pots and pans rattled and clanked as the old freighter hove to in the beam sea, swayed and groaned with each wave.

Gustavo Carta, in a denim shirt, sat at the head of the mess table. On his right was Raúl Masetti, seasick despite the Dramamine pills Carta had given him. There were deep shadows under his eyes. He kept his mouth tightly shut. Yet when he had something to say, he spoke in a clear, forceful lawyer's voice.

On Carta's left sat young Victorio, wearing a khaki field jacket darkened with water from the rain and the sea, his handsome girlish features set in a stoic calm, his cat-green eyes fastened on Carta, like a student in class listening to his professor. Victorio had been a music student in Havana and had fought in the Escambray as a guerrilla leader against Batista. His position at the moment was the most critical of all. His people were under direct attack by Castro's militia in overwhelming numbers. He had told Carta and the others that his people would not be able to hold out longer than a week at the most. "Unless the pressure is relieved by a new front," he told them, "we are finished. As I sit here, my men are being hunted down and killed. Our situation is desperate. We are short of food, ammunition and medical supplies. Desperately short."

He said this dramatically, gesturing with his hands. "Without a strong front in the Escambray, we are lost," he said. "I beg you, Señor Carta, to strike quickly. Or I sit here before you already a dead man."

Next to Victorio, Andrés, the Sierra Maestra leader, sat with the light directly behind his head, like a halo, his hawk's face tight and fierce-looking in the shadow. He had removed his hat and revealed that he was almost bald. He sat watching Carta with a critical gaze. He wore a camouflage field jacket with a rain hood and smoked a long thin cigar. From where Carta sat, it looked as though Andrés were smoldering.

324

When it came his time to speak, Andrés's voice was so faint, the others had to lean forward to hear him clearly against the metal groan of the ship and the clatter of the cooking utensils. Once, a clap of thunder buried his voice and he had to repeat his words, which he did with reluctance. He seemed very shy in their presence and reluctant to speak. He had been a small farmer, raising vegetables in a truck garden at his place in Oriente, selling them in Santiago, and working as a cane-cutter in the harvest months. He had joined Fidel Castro's Twenty-sixth of July guerrillas shortly after the rebel leader made his disastrous landing in Oriente in 1956. Quiet-spoken, with a *campesino*'s natural shyness, he remained in the background politically, but gained a formidable reputation as a fighting man during the series of skirmishes with Batista's soldiers. Now, in his quiet tone, his words halting, he described his situation in the Sierra as increasingly untenable. But his forces were intact, nine hundred men, well armed, and anxious for combat. "We do not wish to fight skirmishes that bring us nothing but retaliation from Fidel," he said. "We wish to fight with a plan which will give us a meaningful victory."

Across from Andrés sat Major Mahío, chubby, round-faced, bristling with whiskers. His head was covered with an olive-green billed cap of the rebel army. Mahío sat erect, his jaw thrust out, hands on his knees as though he were about to leap up from the bench and begin shouting. The cigar that stuck from the corner of his lips added to his posture of militant belligerency. He would, he told them, muster four hundred men for the attack on Baracoa. Once the new rebel government was declared, he said, the Castro militia would be significantly weakened by defections. But their great weapon, he said, was suspicion. "Whom will Castro trust? His own troops will be unreliable. The militia? Who will say with certainty where each man's real loyalty lies? If we declare for the revolution, without Fidel, without dictatorship, without Communists, and make the people believe it, we shall defeat him, and quickly. Most Cubans have no sympathy for the Communists. But we love our revolution."

"Exactly," said Carta. He glanced at Tipton and Rodríguez, who stood in the corner, against the bunks, with two rebel army lieutenants. They had accompanied Mahío. "Rod, you want to detail the operation for us?"

"Yes, sir," said Rodríguez, moving to the table, with the maps in his hand.

Major Mahío interrupted with a gesture. "One more very important factor," he told them, glancing from face to face. "I am in close contact with officers at the naval base of Baracoa. The whole Navy is in a state of rebellion against Castro. Not just here, but throughout the entire country. The shooting of Roberto Escalante has angered many. It is my opinion that the Navy will come over to us as soon as we have secured Baracoa."

Tipton moved out of the shadow into the brilliance of the electric light. "What about the torpedo boats at the base?" he asked.

"They all are ready to defect."

"Good," said Carta briskly. "I want those boats in on the attack." He turned his head. "Rod?"

Rodríguez lit a cigar and spread the map on the table so that all could see. Looking from one to the other, he said, "Our D-Day is ten April. Nine days from now. At 0300 hours, we shall move in toward shore, arriving at Point A no later than 0350 hours. That is, as you see, just off the reef at the village of Cayo Güin, about three miles north of Baracoa. We will have a company of men, about a hundred and thirty-five, of whom fifty will make up the assault team. The others will be engaged in unloading supplies and ammunition in this little bay here. There is a *bohío* there, you know it?" The others nodded. "Andrés will provide us with a screen for the landing. Fifty men. They will block the road from this point and this, north and south. They are to be in position no later than 0400 hours. We'll be ashore at 0410 hours. Clear?"

There was a mumble of assent from the men. Tipton, looking over their heads, caught Gustavo Carta's eye. He smiled.

It had been Tipton's brainchild, this attack. For a guerrilla operation it could not have been more perfect. At 0500 hours, tenth April, Major Mahío, with four hundred men, was to launch his attack on Baracoa from the village of Maisí, on the south. Simultaneously, Andrés with eight hundred men would attack from the mountains in the west. Carta's fifty-man combat team, joined by a hundred of Andrés's guerrillas from the Cuchillas de Toars mountains, would strike from the north at Cayo Güin.

"As soon as our people in the naval base hear gunfire, they shall take command of the base. The torpedo boats will be refueled at sea after Baracoa is secured. When they hear our guns, they will block the harbor entrance, coordinated with our ground attacks. Andrés, what about our people in Baracoa itself?"

Andrés leaned forward on his elbows. "We have an underground in the village—maybe fifty men. I'll send them against the radio station as soon as they hear the attack start. *Bueno?*"

They looked to Carta, who nodded, chewing on his unlit cigar.

Rodríguez let out his breath. He was excited and trying to keep control of his voice. "Now for the broader operation. We must have Baracoa secured at 0600 hours. The key to holding all of southern Oriente is here." His finger ran northwest up the island to the edge of the Sierra Maestra. "At Contra Maestro, these two bridges. Cut them, and Castro is unable to send troops to Santiago."

"That will be my responsibility," said Tipton, moving in beside Rodríguez, leaning over his shoulder. "Raúl Masetti's underground at Bayamo and Holquin will provide me with a hundred men. We'll attack the bridges at 0400 hours, ten April, from the north."

"You want people from the south?" said Andrés, looking up, the light gleaming on his bald spot. "I have reliable people at Palma Soriano, south of the brigades. Maybe thirty men. I can get them equipment and arms, easy."

"Good," said Tipton. "Have them in position to attack at precisely 0400 hours. Can you do that?"

Andrés shrugged. *"Cómo no?"*

"What of us in the north, in the Escambray?" asked Victorio. He turned to Carta.

"You will hold," said Carta. "The same as for the people in the Sierra Cristal, in Pinar del Río. As soon as we have secured here, in the south, we shall begin supplying you with men and arms. Castro will be forced to divert his militia which is attacking you now, and deal with us. That means he will have to fight on two major fronts. But that will not be the end of his troubles." Carta turned to Masetti, who was just then wiping his mouth with a handkerchief. "Raúl?"

Raúl Masetti lifted his long Spanish face and cleared his throat. "I apologize for my illness," he said. "I never was much of a seaman." He smiled faintly. "Let me tell you what my underground has planned."

All eyes shifted to him.

Masetti's long, thin forefinger touched the map of Cuba at the northwest tip. "Beginning in Pinar del Río, on tenth April, there shall be sabotage at the docks in Mariel. In the city of Pinar del Río we assault the police station. In Havana, we shall begin sabotage on the same morning. The department store El Encanto will be blown up. There will be no civilians inside. My underground people now poised outside the city, will move in for targets all that day and night. We will try to cause enough problems to hold Castro's militia in place during your attack on Baracoa. That applies to you, Victorio, also. Any way you can freeze the militia would be helpful."

Victorio blinked his long lashes and nodded. "We can do it."

"Then," Masetti continued, moving his long finger southeast down the island. "At Cienfuegos, Trinidad, Sancti Spíritus, Ciego de Ávila, Camagüey, Guáimaro, Bayamo, and finally Santiago itself, we shall mount a steady campaign of sabotage. Gustavo will give a call to arms

327

for all Cubans to rally to our side. We shall mount a general campaign to attract support. All aimed at stripping Castro of his forces, as well as his martyrdom. In the end, Havana shall fall. I am confident."

They all fell silent, studying the maps, puffing their cigars, smoke billowing into the light. The freighter creaked and groaned, swaying heavily in the sea.

Victorio was the first to react. He looked at Carta, his teeth showing in his smile. "I like it, Gustavo."

"So do I," Carta said to him in his deep, throaty voice. He looked away to the faces of the others. "Let us hope that it will mean the end of the revolution that Céspedes started for us a century ago."

"And that of José Martí," said Mahío.

"Amen," said Rodríguez.

Carta nodded. "It's been a long legacy, my friends."

There was a general murmur of agreement. Major Mahío leaned to-ward Carta, pressing against Masetti. "Gustavo, what of this bunch in Guatemala we've heard so much about? How do they figure in this?"

"That is the next question I wish to pose to you," said Carta. He looked at the faces of his guerrilla leaders.

"The Kennedy Administration has offered us a deal, gentlemen. They have relented in their policy of opposition to our cause. They have not only restored to us our confiscated ships and munitions, but they have pledged supplies and full tactical support once our operation com-mences. In addition, they promise the full support of their eleven hundred troops in Guatemala, equipped with tanks, artillery, planes."

"What do they want in return, Gustavo?" Raúl asked.

"In return they demand the following: First, that I join a coalition front which will be declared the provisional government of Cuba. This regime will include all political factions, including, no doubt, some Ba-tista people. Second, they ask that we withhold any military action until their Guatemala brigade is ready to strike, that our operations are fully in synch with theirs."

"And when will they make their attack?"

"We are told that the brigade will launch a full-scale amphibious land-ing, supported by air strikes, by mid-April. But this operation has been delayed repeatedly and probably will be again."

Masetti frowned. "A military force like that could be a problem after we defeat Fidel," he said. "How do you feel, Gustavo?"

"I believe it is possible to neutralize the brigade politically, and to make it useful militarily in this manner. If we join this Council, Rodrí-guez will be named military liaison between the Council and the brigade.

328

Thus, he could effectively be in command of the brigade. Under those circumstances, it would be very advantageous to us, you see?" Carta pointed at the map, at the west-central coast of Cuba. "Using the Guatemala troops, we could effect an amphibious landing here—at Trinidad."

Victorio stiffened. "Ah, I see!" he said with excitement. "Of course, landing at Trinidad, you could relieve and reinforce the Escambray immediately. What a front we'd have against Castro then, eh? *Magnífico*, Gustavo! Brilliant!" His green eyes flashed as he looked around at the others. "You see it? It is brilliant! A thousand well-armed men land at Trinidad and drive east into the Escambray! We've cut Cuba in half!"

Carta looked amused at his sudden enthusiasm. "That is what we have in mind. But I want to hear your opinions. Remember, however, this military group was organized and financed by the Americans. It could be a powerful instrument in their hands. We shall have to deal with it once Fidel is beaten."

"I am for it," said Victorio, grinning and looking around at the others. "It's brilliant."

"Raúl?"

"I worry, Gustavo. Even with Rod in command of these troops, we've had so much trouble with our friends from the CIA. What assurances do we have that this brigade won't put Navarro in power once they're in Havana?"

"None," said Carta. "Except perhaps the word of one of President Kennedy's advisers. That's all."

"This adviser of Kennedy's—do you trust him, Gustavo?"

"He's not Cuban," Carta said. They all smiled.

Masetti said, "We have at our command, at the moment, only fifteen hundred reliable men. After victory we will be scattered throughout the island. This CIA brigade smacks of a dangerous political force to me, Gustavo. I am against joining this front in Miami."

"Mahío?"

Major Mahío took his cigar from his mouth and looked at the slick chewed end. "I too am against it, Gustavo. Too dangerous. We know here what we deal with—each other. It could come to pass that some of us will be enemies after the revolution. But at least now we are friends. We have a common interest. Politically, this other brigade, what is it? Who will really command it? I vote we stay out of their politics."

"Andrés?"

Andrés stubbed his thin cigar in the ashtray and shrugged. "No matter how we decide, we shall still have this brigade to deal with, won't we?

What is to prevent them from landing the moment we take Oriente? Better we have Rod in command, I say. At least we'll know what way that group will go. I say yes, Gustavo."

Carta sighed and leaned back.

"Look, Gustavo," Raúl Masetti said. "You are the one who is in the best position to evaluate this situation. We are in Cuba, you are in the United States. I say we leave this decision to you. You can decide what to do as you see events unfold."

The men around the table murmured their agreement. Major Mahío too nodded effusively.

"If you want to go along with them, you have our blessing," Mahío said. "If you feel our overall plan cannot succeed without their help, so be it. You are our leader, Gustavo. The final decision must be yours."

Again the men murmured their assent.

"The one thing is time," Raúl said. "We must make our move quickly. We cannot let the Americans delay us too long with their promises."

"Very well," Carta said. "I shall reserve my final decision until I get back to Maimi, but it's my present disposition to go along with the deal. I think it is our best chance—with all its risks. Our best chance."

The men around the table nodded soberly.

Ten minutes later Carta stood on the slippery deck of the *Bahama Star,* rain pelting hard against his face in the wind, and watched the small boats pull away from the starboard side. Beside him were Tipton and Rodríguez, bundled against the rain and the wind. He did not envy Masetti that ride back in the heavy seas, nor the long drive back to Havana. He caught a glimpse of him in the stern of the boat just as it turned into the sea. He waved. He wondered if he'd ever see him again.

CHAPTER THIRTY

He had been meeting Michael a couple of times a week at the Hamlet. They would usually get together in the late evening and talk for an hour or so, then go their separate ways. They talked about literature and music, and sometimes Michael would carry on about personal problems. The incident at Pelham's swimming pool was never mentioned again after their faltering, aborted conversation that had been interrupted by the Vermillion telephone call.

That phone call, together with other things that Pelham had alluded to, had fortified Michael's intuitive suspicion that Pelham was indeed a man of substance, albeit a very guarded one. Michael was impressed by the depth of his knowledge and the breadth of his experience, but it was the aura of mystery that particularly fascinated him. Pelham was consistently vague about the nature of his business, other than to say he was in printed circuits; he was also vague about his position within that business. From his home and clothes, Michael judged that it must be an important position, perhaps even the president of the company. But he could never pin Pelham down, and he had decided to be carefully circumspect about trying. What he did know about Pelham sufficed: that he had education, breeding, money and a desire for privacy that was matched by what Michael instinctively felt was a very deep loneliness.

Given this determination to be cautious, Michael had never revived his suggestion of moving into Pelham's guest house, though he often complained about his lack of money. Pelham always paid for drinks. Once he even gave Michael thirty-five dollars to cover a repair bill on his creaking old Renault—a bill which Michael said he couldn't possibly have afforded to pay. Michael had accepted the money gratefully.

"I hate to pour money into that old car," he said. "It's throwing good money after bad. What I'd really like to do is to junk the damn thing and get myself a motorcycle."

"Motorcycles are death traps," Pelham snapped. "I can't understand for the life of me why they're getting so popular. One mistake and you're a dead man."

Michael shook his head emphatically. "No, no, you're missing the point. The thing about bikes is the sense of freedom. Sitting over that big engine, the wind blasting against you, your bike snaking between all those cars that have to plod along in their lanes. It's the greatest. And then at night, barreling along at sixty, feeling that hot wind . . ."

"What entices you is not the freedom but the danger," Pelham cut in. "There are enough dangers in the world without courting them."

"It's like poetry—it's not something you can rationally defend, it's just something you feel."

Pelham felt his anger rising. "You're talking childishly," he scolded, surprising even himself at the severity of his tone. "When we talk about poetry we are talking about art. It's nonsense to compare your foolish appetite for a dangerous destructive toy with art."

"Hey, don't get mad at me, I didn't mean anything," Michael said, his voice trembling. "It's all academic anyway. I don't have the money for a motorcycle. I'll never have the money for the damn thing, so don't let it anger you."

"I'm not angry," Pelham lied.

"Yes you are—I got you pissed off. I'm sorry."

Walking to his car, Pelham was rankled for losing his temper with the boy. It was strange, he thought, that he found it so difficult to exercise the same iron restraint with Michael that he imposed toward everyone else in his life. But motorcycles were a special sore point. It was one of the things that he and his daughter, Andrea, or Andy, as he had always called her, had quarreled bitterly about shortly before her death. Motorcycles definitely touched a sensitive nerve.

Andy! Pelham had managed to eradicate her from his thoughts for several weeks now. She had been an obsession with him for so long. Only recently had he begun to place those events in their proper perspective, to let her slowly recede into the recesses of his memory.

But his bitterness about Andy kept surfacing at unexpected times. Or it might even be a word casually mentioned, such as Michael's sudden reference to motorcycles.

He had always trusted and admired his daughter as a stable and intelligent child. That was what really hurt so much. People had said she was her father's daughter. After she reached the age of twelve, Pelham had been able to spend less and less time with her. His career had begun to progress and he had received a succession of prized but distant posts—places like London and Manila. He found himself increasingly estranged from his family. Pelham's growing tensions with his wife also seemed to prey upon Andy and fuel her teenage rebelliousness. But her grades remained good, and Pelham had been enormously proud of her for gaining admission to Bryn Mawr, the small, highly selective Quaker girls' college near Philadelphia. Pelham entertained high hopes that the college's soothing Quaker influence and conservative traditions would bring her a new sense of equanimity.

His hopes were quickly demolished. Several weeks into her freshman year she had taken up with a young beatnik who was an undergraduate at the University of Pennsylvania. Pelham visited her at the college during his last Thanksgiving leave and was shocked to see her roar up with her boy friend on a motorcycle, both of them dressed sloppily in blue jeans. Pelham had angrily disapproved of the boy, who was Jewish, and whose manners were primitive, but what offended him most of all was that Andy's appearance had somehow coarsened. The gentle, almost demure traits of her childhood had been supplanted by a new set of blunt-spoken crude mannerisms which, in Pelham's mind, failed to reflect her own breeding and background.

332

The Thanksgiving dinner, which Pelham had so eagerly looked forward to, was disastrous. They went to a nearby inn, and the dining room was filled with attractive families and holiday cheer. But the conversation of the three of them was strained from the outset. They argued about the motorcycle. They argued about what Pelham considered to be their improper attire for Thanksgiving dinner. And then they even argued about politics. Andy had fallen under the influence of her boy friend and had affected positions Pelham believed to be brazenly radical. It was all a pose. She and her boy friend felt that J. Edgar Hoover was trying to turn the country into a police state. They asserted that the U.S. was conducting imperialist policies in Southeast Asia. The boy even charged that the CIA was about to launch a secret invasion in Cuba. Pelham felt he was being deliberately baited. It took all his restraint not to rise to the battle. Instead, he kept trying to shift the topic, questioning them about their courses and instructors. But their responses were unenthusiastic.

The fresh-faced young waitress was just serving the turkey when Andy suddenly turned to her father with what he felt was an almost clinical gaze. "You work for the Central Intelligence Agency, don't you, Daddy?"

Pelham felt his scalp twinge. That had been one subject that his family had never discussed. He looked at his daughter, stunned.

"Answer me," she said insistently.

"We are here to enjoy Thanksgiving dinner together," Pelham said, an edge in his voice. "Not to harangue each other about politics."

"I'm not talking about politics. I'm talking about what my daddy does for a living."

Pelham did not reply. He looked at the waitress's smooth, bland face. He remembered when Andy had looked like that—short brown hair, calm, agreeable eyes. What had happened? When would his Andy return?

"Answer me!" Andy's eyes peered at him with a fierce intensity; her face had reddened with anger.

"Yes, I work for the CIA." His words were cold, clipped.

"But all these years—all the time I was growing up—you never told me that, did you?"

"That's the policy of the agency. It was a question of cover . . ."

"You kept telling me little lies about consulting for private industry or doing a job for the State Department. Just a fabric of lies."

"It's not that I wanted to, Andy. What we're discussing here is the secrecy of a key agency of the United States government. We are not talking about something that we can adjust for our convenience within our own family!"

333

But she was losing control now, and her boy friend was egging her on. "All the terrible things I read about the CIA—all the things going back to germ warfare in Korea, to overthrowing progressive regimes in the Philippines and Guatemala—you were involved in all those ugly things, weren't you, Daddy?"

"This is not the time or place," Pelham flared, shooting a murderous glance at the boy friend. Pelham started forcing down his food, but then he noticed tears on his daughter's face.

"I just want to say I am ashamed and disgusted," she said, struggling to get her words past her trembling lips. "I'm humiliated that I was so dumb and trusting. All those years you were doing those terrible things and I believed in you, like a dumb cow . . ." She broke off her sentence and ran from the table. Her boy friend put down his drumstick and gave Pelham a helpless, almost apologetic look, then went after her. Pelham was left sitting at the table alone, picking at his dry turkey and feeling thoroughly confused and miserable. They never returned to the table.

A week later, his wife called to say that Andy had discussed the Thanksgiving Day fight with her and that she was still distraught about it.

"I knew I should have been there," she said. "This whole thing wouldn't have happened."

"We'd agreed it would be much better if I took Thanksgiving with her and you took Christmas. Besides, there's nothing you could have said . . ."

"I would have made you explain to the child that you weren't involved in any of the things that upset her."

"But I *was* involved in them. It would have made matters worse."

His wife was silent on the other end of the phone.

"It's the damn boy friend who's behind this," Pelham said bitterly. "He's messing up her mind with leftist rot."

"They've broken off, so you don't have to worry about him anymore. Andy is taking that very hard, too. She really sounded terrible on the phone."

"It's just a phase. Freshmanitis. They all go through it. She's a solid, substantial girl, and these traumas will pass," Pelham replied, terminating the conversation.

He made a mental note to phone Andy, but he got caught up in a new crisis and let it slip for two days. It was three o'clock in the morning when his wife called again.

"She's dead," she said simply, her voice numb with grief. "She swallowed a bottleful of Nembutal. They tried to save her, but they never had a chance."

334

Pelham told himself he would be strong. He had serious responsibilities to cope with. His career was on the line. Issues of national importance were at stake. He flew to Pennsylvania and arranged for Andy's funeral. He stopped off to console her mother and see her home safely. Then he returned to Miami to get on with the business at hand. Two days after returning to Miami he was sitting in a meeting when he suddenly felt a rising swell of nausea. He left the room quickly and fled to the washroom. He started heaving, but nothing came up. He tried again. It was then he realized that he was weeping. The sound of his own sobs shocked him as they echoed off the white tile walls; the utterly lonely, desolate sound of his own despair made him weep even harder.

That afternoon he phoned his doctor and checked himself into a local private hospital. He took a private room and saw no one and took no phone calls. For three days he lay in bed, watching the soap operas on his grainy TV set and staring at the bleak, antiseptic walls of his room. The morning of the fourth day he checked out and returned to work. He told his colleagues that it had been the flu and that it had passed now. But he knew it would never really pass. It would be like a wound that would never heal, but that he could choose to disregard if he were strong enough. And he told himself he had to be strong enough, otherwise it would defeat him.

CHAPTER THIRTY-ONE

MIAMI, APRIL 4, 1961

The two days following his meeting with Michael had not gone well for Pelham. He sensed that events surrounding the Cuban operation were rushing toward a climax, but also that things had become disorderly, and this offended his fastidious nature.

What had him deeply concerned at the moment was the disappearance from Miami of Gustavo Carta. He had called the house twice to set up meetings between Carta and the other Cuban leaders in Miami, only to be told by his wife that he was out of town for a few days. When he had asked where Gustavo had gone, she'd replied to visit friends in Toronto. Toronto? What the hell would Carta be doing in Canada? It was a ruse, Pelham decided. He had more likely gone to Cuba. And if so, Pelham had real trouble on his hands. His instructions were to keep Carta out of the "cooky jar" at all costs. If he got ashore now and declared a new government, this mess would really come apart. Damn Danforth—if they'd kept out of this, Pelham would have had Carta completely neutralized by now. He'd been ready to throw in the towel when that call came from Vermillion. Pelham knew he'd had Carta on the ropes. Just a few more days and he would have finished him off.

Now, after all this meddling, it was likely the man was in Cuba, ready to declare to the world a new rebel regime. It would be extremely embarrassing to all concerned. Pelham had ordered a close monitoring of all broadcasts out of Cuba. He awaited the word with dread.

But it had come, unexpectedly at 9:20 P.M., in the form of a phone call from Dobbs, who was in Key West. "I thought you ought to know," Dobbs's voice said on the phone. "Your bad boy has come home. He was aboard the *Bahama Star*. It docked here five minutes ago. Any instructions?"

Pelham felt a wave of relief. "None. Keep him under surveillance. I want to know every move he makes. But don't interfere with him."

"Well, right at the moment he's sitting in the Pierhouse bar having a scotch with two of his honchos. I'll keep an eye on him."

After he hung up, Pelham found himself wondering what that had all been about. Where had Carta gone? What had he been up to? There were a lot of questions to be answered. He picked up the phone again. "Get me Vermillion," he told the operator.

That night, Carta and Tipton arrived home from Key West. Both were tired. Their faces and hair had that wind- and sun-burned look that comes from being at sea in the tropics. The meetings had gone well. On the way into Key West they had received a radio message aboard the *Bahama Star* from the Everglades camp, which reported: "The birds are back in the nest." All had returned safely to their various positions in Cuba. That relieved them both. They had dropped Rodríguez at the gas station to take the jeep back to camp. They were all excited about the prospect of the operations to come. Rodríguez had embraced them both. "We're going to win," he said to them. "For the first time, I believe we really are going to go back to Cuba." They had driven off, last seeing him opening the garage door. Now, feeling too keyed up to sleep as the Buick pulled into the drive of Carta's lighted mansion, Gustavo insisted the Englishman stop for a drink before going home.

They got out of the big car and went up the steps, returning the silent greeting of the two men on guard outside the door. As they entered, there were two more seated in the entrance hall. They started to get up,

336

but Carta waved them down and led Tipton into the house. Walking into the main hallway, they heard Elizabeth's high-pitched laugh coming from the living room. It occurred to Carta that he had not heard Elizabeth laugh for quite a while.

"Sounds like you have guests," Tipton said. "I'll wait for you in the library."

"I wasn't expecting anyone . . ." Carta said as Tipton cleaved off to his right. Carta entered the living room and drew up short, his face breaking into an expression of surprise.

Charles Danforth was seated across from Elizabeth on the sofa, each holding a scotch and engaged in animated conversation. He looked distinguished in his dark-blue pin-striped suit. Carta noticed streaks of gray in his brown hair, which he had let grow longer since they had last seen each other. He and Elizabeth, Carta thought, looked cut from the same cloth. Seated there together, their facial tones burnished in the yellowish light, they looked as if they were sitting for an official portrait—an ambassador and his wife; perhaps even the Secretary of State. Seeing them together, and yet himself not being seen, observing the ease and intimacy of their conversation, the patrician cast of their mannerisms, Carta felt an instinctual twinge he could not identify. These people are not of my world, he told himself. They belong together, not with me. How did our lives become so intertwined?

It was Charles who noticed him standing there and who broke his mood, calling out to him, rising to his feet, his hand extended. "By God, Gustavo, what are you standing there for? It's so damned good to see you. I hope you don't mind my crashing in on you like this."

Carta came forward and shook his hand. Elizabeth, as if sensing his distance, kissed him on the cheek and put her arm around his waist.

"This was all very impromptu," Elizabeth said, wanting to quash any conspiracy suspicions on Carta's part. "Charley was in Venezuela yesterday, and he just stopped over in Miami for a couple of hours before going back to Washington."

"I had a meeting with President Betancourt," Danforth said, as he walked back toward the sofa. "Very impressive fellow. He said he was an old friend of yours, Gustavo. He sends you his warmest regards."

"He's a great man," Carta said, moving over to the bar and pouring himself a scotch. "A truly fine man."

"He's got a vitality and straightforward honesty that you don't find in many Latin heads of state," Danforth said. "Did you know the backs of his hands still carry scorch marks from the assassination attempt last year? The story is that Trujillo sent some boys over to blow him up during a parade. As Betancourt's car drove by, there was a tremendous

337

explosion from a car parked along the parade route. Betancourt put his hands over his face to escape the flames. He was unhurt except for his hands."

"Trujillo is such a vicious bastard," Elizabeth said. "We met him once in Paris, remember, Gustavo? I thought he looked slimy, pale, like something that crawled out from under a log. Does Betancourt make him that uncomfortable, Charles?"

"Democratic leaders always make the Trujillos and Castros uncomfortable," Carta said, seating himself in a chair across from Elizabeth and Danforth. "And, as you know, in Latin America, tradition dictates that if someone makes you uncomfortable, you assassinate him."

"Betancourt represents a new wave of leadership," Danforth said. "The President wanted me to do a little reconnaissance mission and quietly feel him out about the Alliance for Progress. We've got to get a handle on a new policy toward Latin America—it's come time to put the Good Neighbor Policy and that sort of thing back in the barn."

"What's his take on Castro?" Elizabeth asked.

"The encouraging thing is that Betancourt, like Paz Estenssoro in Bolivia and Haya de la Torre in Peru, is turning against Castro. The democratic left in Latin America is beginning to realize that Castro doesn't stand for social revolution, he just represents the inroads of Soviet power."

Carta nodded his assent. "The people of Latin America are not fooled by Castro, nor are the people of Cuba. If only we could give them a chance to do something about it . . ."

Danforth's eyes locked with Carta's. "We're going to give them a chance. Damned soon." A pall of silence descended on the room.

Elizabeth's glance darted quickly from Danforth to Carta. "Do you have time for a bite to eat, Charles?" she asked. "We can offer you some positively delicious cracked crab. Unless my memory betrays me, that's one of your favorites."

Danforth checked his watch. "I have half an hour before I have to leave for my plane. I couldn't do justice to dinner. I'm sorry. Besides, there's something I want to talk to Gustavo about."

Elizabeth got up quickly. "Then I'll leave you two and have Carlota bring something on a tray just in case you weaken." She kissed Danforth and they embraced warmly.

"See you soon, my sweet," he said softly.

"I hope so," she replied, walking briskly from the room.

Gustavo replenished Danforth's scotch as well as his own. "And when was the last time we were together? The Inauguration? It seems like a couple of years ago."

"It's been ten weeks," Danforth said. "I feel as if I've gone through a world war since then."

"I'm afraid I was very rude that night," Carta said. "I was an ungracious guest. I've been meaning to apologize."

"Nonsense. I was sounding off with my New Frontier idealism. I must have come on like a college sophomore. We were going to take the world by storm."

Carlota entered with a silver tray containing cracked crab and a small salad. Danforth thanked her.

"And are you?"

"Am I what?"

"Taking the world by storm?"

"No, Gustavo, we are not. We're doing pretty damned well in some areas. But every time you look around something's sneaking up on you. The space race. Laos. The goddamn recession. Africa. You name it, we got it."

"And the President, is he up to it?"

"You know, I really think he is. And this isn't another pre-Inaugural spiel—this is the battle-hardened Charles Danforth speaking to you now. He's tough as hell. And pragmatic. Open to criticism. But what I like most about him, Gustavo, is that he seeks out and listens to advice. When an expert tells him something, he heeds it. I think he can cut it."

"That's encouraging, it really is."

Danforth was attacking the crab. Carta took out a cigar and fidgeted with it, not lighting it while his guest was eating.

"You know, Gustavo, what you said that night of the Inauguration—you were absolutely on the nose. I haven't forgotten."

"What was that?"

"You said that with all the problems facing Kennedy, with all the crises poking their way into the headlines, the one man who would come back to haunt us was Fidel Castro. When you said it, I thought to myself, Poor Gustavo Carta, he is obsessed with Castro. It is natural that he would feel that way. But you were right, Gustavo. I should have known it myself. There were early briefings—hints of trouble ahead. But so much was breaking around me I kept putting it out of my mind." Danforth put aside his tray and leaned forward intently. "You should have been there when the CIA boys first sold it to us, Gustavo. It was a beautiful job. Allen Dulles and Richard Bissell were there, looking like two scholarly headmasters from Groton or Exeter. Jack Kennedy was obviously impressed by them. There's this little clandestine operation going on, they said blandly. Just a few exiles being trained. The CIA would land them in Cuba, the local populace would join forces and suddenly, poof,

Castro would blow away. Just like Arbenz in Guatemala in 1954. It would all be clean and safe and sanitized. No one would even know the United States government was involved."

Carta chuckled. "You'll excuse me, Charles, but I find it amusing."

"It would border on the comic opera, if it wasn't such a damned serious business," Danforth agreed. "Something like an elephant trying to hide behind a tulip."

Both men chuckled. Carta clinked the ice in his scotch, then said, "You understand the problem, Charles—it's a matter of levels, as I see it. In Washington it appears one thing, but from here it is quite another. Your CIA people here in Miami—they lack any apparent background to evaluate what is happening in Cuba. This man Pelham I've known for years. He doesn't even speak Spanish! What he knows about Cubans, Cuban politics or Cuban history would hardly fill your pocket. He's clever, cunning, intelligent, but woefully naïve."

"I partially agree," said Danforth. "However, I feel we are making strides in altering the direction of our policy, don't you agree?"

"When I have your navy jets flying cover for my boats going to Cuba, I'm forced to." Carta smiled.

"Obviously, Gustavo, we felt after all that had gone on here we needed to earn your trust. We'll continue to exert every effort to do that, believe me."

"I appreciate that, Charles."

"What I need from you now, Gustavo, is information."

"For example?"

"For example: I know you've spent the last few days out of the country. I presume you were in Cuba, correct?"

"How did you know that?"

Danforth laughed. "No, not Elizabeth. Our people here. They may be naïve, Gustavo, but in some areas they are quite efficient. Listen, let me be candid with you—we have no idea what your plans are. We know something is in the wind, but what? That we must know. We don't want to be pulling at opposite ends of the rope. You understand me? We must coordiante our plans, and now! You must agree, Gustavo, that our common interests are at stake."

Carta fell silent a moment, a thoughtful expression on his sunburned face. Then he looked at Danforth. "Can I trust you, Charles?"

"Good heavens, Gustavo, if not me, who? You have to trust someone, don't you?"

Gustavo nodded. "Come over to the desk," he said, and got up from the chair. At the desk he turned on the lamp, drew a map from the top drawer and spread it out under the light. He pointed at the map. "You

340

see, Charles, here at the southern tip of Cuba—this village, Baracoa?"
he began.

Twenty minutes later, Carta folded the map, placed it in the drawer
and snapped off the desk lamp. He turned to Danforth, who stood with
his hands shoved in the pockets of his coat. His face looked so serious
and thoughtful Carta did not speak, but crossed back to the easy chair
and sat down. Danforth followed a moment later.

"Well," asked Carta, "what do you think, Charles?"

Danforth went to the window and looked out at the green glow of the
lighted swimming pool in the patio. "You plan to attack on April tenth?"

"Yes."

"Hmmm," Danforth said, his mind working. "How long could you
postpone this operation, if I asked you to do it?"

"I have a dread of postponing operations," Carta told him. "You postpone them and they fall apart."

Danforth wheeled and paced back toward him, speaking as he moved,
a brightness edging into his mood. "Listen, Gustavo, I think your plan is
brilliant. No question. Look at it from our point of view—it solves the
problem of United States involvement. To the world, it is what it is: a
Cuban operation, run by Cubans, for Cuba. Splendid. Secondly, it would
solve what we've come to call our disposal problem. That is, what
to do with the brigade in Guatemala. If it could, as you pointed out,
attack in the Trinidad area and relieve the guerrillas in the Escambray,
while you attack in Oriente, declare the new government and appeal
for aid from the Organization of American States . . ." His voice trailed
off.

"The idea," said Carta, his enthusiasm mounting, "is to make Castro
fight us on two strong fronts—then a campaign of mounting sabotage,
and a call for a general uprising throughout the country."

"Yes, yes" said Danforth, his mind elsewhere. "But you see, Gustavo,
what this does? It makes a new unified council, representing all factions,
even more important politically! Besides your organization in Cuba,
there are many others, correct?"

"Yes, that's correct."

"Look at the advantage of having all those organizations fighting together, with a coordinated plan—your plan! It would increase the effec-
tiveness, how much?"

"Twenty, thirty percent, possibly."

"Then it seems to me imperative that you take your place in the
coalition. Imperative, Gustavo. This can only work if there is a unified
front, politically and militarily. Do you see that? The logic?"

"I can see certain advantages, yes . . ."

"Without you it doesn't make sense. But with you it means there's a good possibility Castro will fall quickly. Isn't that our common goal?"

"It is, but . . ."

"But what?"

Carta's fingers twisted the corner of his moustache, his eyes inward. "I want to give it more thought, Charles."

"I can foresee many of your objections," said Danforth, getting to his feet and standing over Carta. "But let me leave you with this thought: You must trust me, Gustavo. You must."

Carta lifted his eyes and met Danforth's steady gaze.

"You must," Danforth repeated. Then he turned aside, stretched his arms and groaned wearily. "Look, Gustavo, I've a plane waiting to take me back to Washington." He turned back to face Carta. "I have a meeting with the President at ten-thirty tomorrow morning. I want you to call me at ten and give me your decision on this. Will you?"

"If I must."

"You must. I want you not only to join the team but to lead it. It'll be your show, Gustavo. We'll give you any help you need. But the show will be yours. I promise you. Look, how can I make you feel more secure? You want this man you mentioned—what was his name?"

"Rodríguez?"

"Yes, Rodríguez—if you want him to command the troops in Guatemala, just ask. We'll back him all the way. Will that satisfy you?"

"It would go a long way in that direction."

"Then think about it, Gustavo. Give me your answer in the morning." Danforth glanced at his watch. "I must be going."

"I'll see you to the door."

Danforth took several long strides toward the door, Carta behind him. A limousine was waiting. The chauffeur opened the door briskly. Danforth started to get in, then suddenly wheeled around to confront Carta, who was framed in his doorway.

"We're going to win your country back, Gustavo." He flashed a "V" sign, smiled and climbed into the car.

When Carta returned to the living room he called out to Elizabeth, but she did not respond. Climbing the stairs, he checked their bedroom and again called her name, but there was no answer. Moving to the window, Carta looked across the back yard and pool area. In the pool light he discerned Elizabeth's solitary figure sitting on a lounge chair. Carta went back down the stairs and poked his head into the anteroom. Tipton was seated in one of the big leather chairs and had fallen fast asleep. Carta closed the door softly and walked down to the pool.

Elizabeth looked up and smiled when she saw him approaching. He

342

seated himself in a chaise lounge next to hers. The lawn had been cut late that afternoon, and the fragrance of the newly mowed grass hung in the warm humid night air. A gentle breeze rippled the pool.

"Did you have a nice talk with Charles, dear?"

"The thing about your pal Charles Danforth is that I envy him and I'm glad I'm old enough to be able to admit it to myself," Carta said, his tone reflective.

"Why do you say that?"

"I envy him because he's so goddamn sure of himself. He's like all those Kennedy people—they all believe in themselves and in their leader."

"But why does that bother you?"

"Because I'm sitting here feeling like a helpless schoolboy, wavering from one position to another, hearing a dozen inner voices telling me different things and not knowing which voice to listen to."

"We've been so close to it for so long, dear. Maybe we have just been seeing the trees, and someone like Charles can see the forest."

"Which is a polite way of saying that I've lost my perspective."

"It can happen to the best of us."

"Could it not also be true that Cousin Charles perceives such a cosmic stretch of forest that he has not taken the time to understand what the individual trees are telling him?"

Elizabeth glanced away and was silent. They sat there together, but their minds were drifting far apart.

"Why so quiet?" Carta said finally.

Elizabeth smiled wearily. "I don't know, Gustavo. I've gotten wary lately about telling you what I think, because I detect your suspicion. You think I'm in league with Charles—that we scheme together and try to manipulate you. I could see that in your face when you stood in the doorway this evening."

Carta looked at her playfully. "It's true—the moment I saw you and Charles together, the first thing that occurred to me was, 'What are those two hatching up now?' "

"No, seriously, I want to help you, Gustavo. I want to help you so desperately. I see what is happening to you. You've always been a strong individualist, Gustavo. But you can't do what you want to do alone. You have to believe in someone."

"In other words, believe in Charles."

"Yes, believe in Charles, but don't you see? Charles also believes in you. He wants to help you. He believes you can bring a sense of unity. He sees you as Cuba's Betancourt. You see?"

"I wish I shared his confidence."

Elizabeth moved from her chair and seated herself on the edge of Carta's. She put her hand under his shirt and massaged his chest gently. "Darling, we're going to win. Charles and the President want a new, democratic Cuba. And they want you to be the leader."

Carta shook his head dubiously. "Somehow my mind goes back to high-school English—are you playing Lady Macbeth?"

"Don't be facetious, Gustavo. This is your chance—don't you see? You know in your heart you could lead. You know the people want you to lead." She leaned over and kissed him on the lips.

He held her close to him, stroking her back, running his hand over her hips. "I love you," he said softly.

"I love you, too."

"It's all become so complicated, Elizabeth. So unbelievably complicated. I feel like a ship moving through uncharted waters. I know there are treacherous reefs ahead. I just don't know where the hell they are."

Elizabeth looked into his eyes. "Charles wouldn't lead us astray, Gustavo. You don't believe he would, do you?"

Carta shook his head. She kissed him again, a soft brush of lips against his forehead. Carta sighed. "All right. I'll give it a try."

She smiled at him. "A wise decision, Mr. Presidente."

"Oh, it's 'Mr. Presidente' suddenly, is it?"

"It'll be a matter of weeks, that's all." She stood up and unzipped her dress, quickly discarding her bra and panties, standing before him.

"What the hell are you doing?" Carta asked.

"I'm going to swim, Mr. Presidente, and you're coming with me." She started working on his belt and trousers.

He resisted. "What about the servants?"

"To hell with the servants."

Carta undressed quickly and gave her a sharp but affectionate slap on her backside. She laughed and pushed him into the pool. Then she dived in after him.

CHAPTER THIRTY-TWO

WASHINGTON, D.C., APRIL 7, 1961

The vast corridors of the Pentagon had always made Charles Danforth very uneasy. Whenever he found himself there, which was as seldom as possible, he always walked briskly, looking neither left nor right, avoiding the glances of the androidal bureaucrats who traversed its halls, their faces bluish in the fluorescent glare, the hushed shuffling of their feet echoing with their voices. Danforth had always harbored the nightmarish suspicion that these people never went home at night; that instead, when their work was done, they walked calmly, along with their piles of memoranda, into some vast shredder, only to be recycled the following morning.

Yet Danforth realized how seductively orderly and self-contained the Pentagon must seem to its denizens—how easy it would be to surrender oneself to it. There was no problem that could not be solved by its small army of systems analysts and tacticians and programmers. In the outside world one had a name and a personality. Inside the Pentagon one needed only a number and a clearance. No matter what one's rank and accomplishments in the world outside, the clearance was the only measure of worth inside the fortress. It was a shrewd mechanism, Danforth thought—a system designed by the military-bureaucratic mind to erase the inefficiency and inconvenience posed by human individuality. It obviously worked.

Danforth flashed his clearance now as he stood before a desk occupied by a black Marine sergeant. The sergeant's brown face nodded him through a glass door. As Danforth started down yet another corridor, he passed a four-star general, a cluster of chattering secretaries and a janitor riding an electric cart; all their faces seemed pale, shadowless in the fluorescent light.

There was a wonderful egalitarianism to these corridors, he reflected, as he continued walking briskly. The top brass mingled with the ubiquitous clerks, sharing the same cafeterias and newsstands. The janitors and the electricians rode the carts while the admirals and the generals dogged it on foot. And yet, once they all got tucked away into their offices, the egalitarian illusion quickly faded. This place belonged to the men with the medals and the shiny buttons, and they would never let you forget it.

Another checkpoint loomed ahead now, and Danforth produced his credentials to be scanned by a sergeant burlier than the first one. This time, however, the doors he was directed through led to an enormous white-walled conference room dominated by a large oval table. Around the table were arrayed thirty chairs, and each chair was positioned in front of a sort of miniconsole embracing a telephone, dictation equipment and compartments for paper and pens. The room was filled with men in military uniforms and dark suits, in the process of settling themselves, their briefcases and their papers in their designated places.

An aide greeted Danforth and indicated his position along the conference table. As he lowered himself into the deep-cushioned swivel chair, Danforth became aware of a hushed murmur in the room. Aides scampered around the table, keeping up a steady drumfire of "Yes, sir" and "Good morning, sir." The senior officials present were exchanging perfunctory greetings. Danforth nodded to several of them. His eyes scanned the other occupants of the room. At the head of the table, in an Oxford-gray suit, sat Vermillion, tall and severe, peering down through rimless glasses, his hands methodically shuffling through a stack of papers. Adjacent to him was Pelham, crisply alert, looking like a student who had crammed for a tough exam and now was serenely confident over his success. Then came a long line of generals and admirals, mostly gray-haired senior officers. They presented a rank of square jaws, close-cropped heads, cleanly shaven faces, confident expressions, the overhead light reflecting off the clusters of brass and silver stars on their shoulders. Finally, toward Danforth's side of the table sat the civilians, clad in dark-blue suits, a row of serious, pale faces, their eyes intent, their manner restless. Danforth recognized a few of the military men and most of the civilians: they were the top Kennedy appointees in the Departments of Defense and State, intermixed with some senior civil servants. The career government people generally looked older than the Kennedy appointees, and also considerably calmer. The Kennedy men fidgeted with their pens and papers and, it seemed to Danforth, were trying manfully but unsuccessfully to conceal their discomfort. Danforth identified with their dilemma. In the safe confines of the Sans Souci it was always tempting to parody the military establishment, their brisk mannerisms and rigid postures. But when they were arrayed before you, their uniforms presenting an intimidating rainbow of combat ribbons, gleaming buttons and stars, there was no escaping the sharp thrust of institutional authority, the phalanx of power they embodied. Sitting there, it seemed as if the civilians were somehow extraneous to the proceedings. Theirs was an evanescent presence. The military was there to stay.

Vermillion now looked up from his papers and tapped his gold pen gently against the table. "Gentlemen, as you know, the President has called a meeting tomorrow morning for a final review of the Cuban operation. Mr. Danforth and I thought it would be constructive if we assembled today to discuss agenda and format and clarify any procedural issues that may be raised."

Whatever inhibitions the Kennedy men might feel, none was apparent in Vermillion's manner. It was clear to Danforth that Vermillion was totally at home with the military; indeed, there was something persuasively dominating about this gangly, bespectacled, almost pedantic-looking man, as if he were saying, "You generals may be good at implementing policy, but I alone have the knowledge to formulate it."

"I take it tomorrow's meeting will be attended only by the President and by those of us around the table." The speaker, a four-star general whose jet-black hair and erect posture belied his heavily creased face, turned his eyes toward Danforth.

"That is correct, General," Vermillion replied.

"And possibly Senator Fulbright, I believe," Danforth added.

His addendum was greeted with a pall of silence.

"Then I gather it will be intended as a debate," an Air Force general said.

"The President has high regard for the Senator's foreign-policy views," Danforth said.

"But Fulbright is antagonistic toward the Cuban operation," the four-star general said, his chin tightening against his collar.

"To my knowledge, Senator Fulbright has not formally expressed his views on the operation," Danforth said. "The President intends to go around the table tomorrow and hear everyone's position, including that of Senator Fulbright."

"I think Fulbright might feel a little lonely tomorrow," a senior civilian from the Department of Defense said. "We've all given the operation careful review, and we're behind it one hundred percent."

"The Joint Chiefs concur," the Air Force General said. "And so does the National Security Council."

Danforth cut in quickly. "There are certain facets of the invasion plan that have been subject to last-minute tactical review. I refer to such questions as landing sites, air strikes, assessments of internal support. I think it would be constructive if Mr. Vermillion brought us up to date on these questions."

Vermillion nodded. He saw what Danforth was doing. Danforth did not want the meeting to turn into a ringing endorsement of the project. He wanted to ward off the sense of unanimity.

Vermillion got to his feet and punched some buttons on his console. Suddenly the entire wall of the conference room lit up with a brilliant display of illuminated reconnaissance photos of the landing sites, maps showing the target areas of the air strikes, diagrams illustrating alternative routes that the assault forces would take on their path to Havana.

As Danforth watched Vermillion's presentation, he marveled at his mastery of military jargon and tactics. Vermillion was not only laying out the detailed invasion plan, but he was making it sound as if the Joint Chiefs of Staff had authored it. Yet, as Danforth translated Vermillion's jargon and analyzed his logic, he found himself increasingly perplexed at the way this hard-edged audience of military men was blandly accepting what seemed to him to be a series of questionable assumptions. Castro's air force, Vermillion was saying, was "entirely disorganized and obsolete," consisting of fifteen B-26s, ten ancient Sea Furies and four T-33 jet trainers. Relying on the element of surprise, he said, the initial air strike by the brigade's air force would cripple Castro's air capability. But what if the raid were not a success? Danforth wondered. The brigade's aircraft were really no more modern than Castro's. What if the invasion ships, already on the seas by this time, were devastated by Castro's pilots? Danforth looked at the two Air Force officials across the table; they seemed untroubled by Vermillion's assumptions. Could Danforth be missing some point of military subtlety?

Once ashore, Vermillion was saying, pointing to another monitor, the fifteen hundred invasion troops would be joined by a force of twenty-five hundred men actively belonging to Cuban resistance organizations, and by twenty thousand more who were "known sympathizers." Moreover, once the liberators had established their positions, they could surely count on the support, "at the very least," of one quarter of the Cuban people. Where did Vermillion acquire this astoundingly precise data? Danforth wondered. Yet no questions were asked. The looks around the table were serene, accepting, as if universal truths were being uttered from on high.

Vermillion was talking now about "fall-back" positions, explaining that in the "unlikely event" that his forces were unable to gain a strong foothold on the beaches, they would simply "melt away" into the mountains. But as Danforth's eyes studied the maps, it seemed to him that the Escambray mountains lay some eighty miles from the invasion site, the Bay of Pigs, across a menacing-looking landscape of swamps and jungles. Would this "melt-away" thesis be quite as practical as the CIA represented?

"Included among the memoranda," Vermillion was continuing, "you will find, gentlemen, a detail drawn up by Mr. Danforth and evaluated by our tactical people in reference to the proposed indigenous operation at Baracoa, on the southern tip of Cuba. I presume you've all had the opportunity to read and evaluate this material, and our objections as well."

"Yes," a tall army officer said. "We were curious as to the negative response to this operation."

Vermillion glanced at Danforth and back at the general. "We are reevaluating it at the moment. We think it has some tactical merit. However, we are negative as to its political implications. Our preliminary

348

evaluation, and mind you this has very recently been submitted to us, is that it would tend to destabilize the political environment in Cuba after the fall of Castro. Quite possibly, gentlemen, it could leave us with a divided Cuba, similar to Korea. Hence the possibility of continued civil war on the island, which we feel would be detrimental to the interests of the United States, as well, of course, as to the Cubans."

Again Vermillion glanced at Danforth. The look was intended to put a period on the discussion. Feeling that it would serve no useful purpose to continue a debate at this time, Danforth shrugged. He had already argued his position with Vermillion at length, supporting Carta's plan of operation. It had come late and was to the CIA personnel a new dimension to their already elaborate plans. He expected opposition, but felt he could see it through, fight his battles when the proper time came. The proper time was in the presence of the President. Not now.

Vermillion concluded his presentation, returned to his seat at the head of the table and solicited questions.

After several moments of silence, the squat, baldheaded State Department official leaned forward and began to speak. "It is the position of the State Department that the integrity of Operation Pluto be sustained as a Cuban struggle against a Cuban regime. For that reason, we are opposed to any air strikes against Castro until the invasion force has secured its beachhead and constructed its own airstrip within Cuba."

"That is totally out of the question," Vermillion countered. "The invasion fleet would be open to constant air attack."

"That proposal makes no goddamn military sense at all," the Air Force general said, his face reddening.

The State Department official looked somewhat chastened by this assault. "The President has emphasized from the start that this country should keep a low visibility in this operation," he said defensively. "It is my job to be concerned about the diplomatic as well as the military consequences. We must consider the OAS charter, our hemispheric treaties, our posture at the UN. We must also consider the response of the Soviet Union . . ."

"We didn't intervene in Hungary, and they won't intervene in Cuba," another four-star army general intoned in a gravely Southern-accented voice.

"Then we shall leave that for the President to decide," Danforth interjected. "These diverse positions must be enunciated tomorrow."

"This is primarily a military operation, and the State Department clearly must defer to military considerations in the event of—" the State Department man was saying.

"We can get into this with the President," Danforth said quickly, infuriated that this weak-willed diplomat was already retreating even before the President had had a chance to hear his views.

A portly, heavy-jowled admiral at the end of the table signaled his desire to be recognized. "I feel impelled to state for the record that Naval Intelligence is at variance with the CIA on several issues." Eyes were now focused on the admiral, who leaned forward intently across a stack of official reports.

Balding, gray, forty pounds overweight, he was a benign-looking figure who seemed grandfatherly in contrast to the trim and erect younger officers. "I don't know how much of this you want to bring out in the open in front of the President tomorrow, but we might as well hash it out now."

"Please delineate your areas of disagreement," Danforth said.

"As you know, gentlemen, the military planning for the invasion was conducted at the Fleet Intelligence Center at CINCLANT headquarters at Norfolk, Virginia, so our Navy people have had the opportunity to talk over their differences with the CIA. One reason for basing at CINCLANT was that this was always conceived as an amphibious operation and the CIA people wanted input from the Navy."

"The areas of disagreement?" Danforth prodded.

The admiral ran his hand through his thin white hair. "All right, here we go," he said blandly, consulting some papers in front of him. His manner, Danforth thought, was like that of a marketing manager matter-of-factly running down a list of sales prospects. There was no hint that he was dealing with men's lives and with strategies that would have international repercussions. "Number one, our Fleet Intelligence officers believe the CIA is exaggerating anti-Castro feeling at this time inside the country," the admiral said, starting down his list. "Number two, we believe a prerequisite for a successful amphibious landing must be continuous air support during the actual invasion, not just one or two preliminary strikes. Number three, our assessment of the landing sites is that the Bay of Pigs is inadequate. The reefs are too hazardous, that's the first problem. And a landing force could be trapped in the swamps even by a single properly deployed platoon equipped with automatic weapons. Under the circumstances, we challenge the validity of a night landing."

Danforth and Vermillion both started talking at the same time. Vermillion continued talking until Danforth tapped his pen on the table insistently, indicating that he did not intend to relinquish the floor.

Danforth snapped to attention.

"This is the first occasion I've had to hear the Navy's assessment of this situation," he said. "Why have these points been kept so quiet?" Danforth was aware of the temperature rising in the room. Nervously, many of the men around the table had lit cigarets.

The admiral started to respond, but the four-star general cut him off. "I wish to point out that these points were all reviewed by the Joint Chiefs," he said. "We gave due consideration to the naval intelligence reports and to those of the CIA, and it was our determination that the CIA knows more about intelligence gathering than the Navy."

"It is my feeling the Navy's report should not be discussed at tomorrow's meeting, since it has been reviewed and rejected at the appropriate level," Vermillion stated.

Eyes now turned to the rotund admiral, who sat straight in his chair, unintimidated by this onslaught. "My colleagues and I disagree. We feel strongly about our analysis of the situation and would like to bring it to the attention of the President. We feel some grave errors have been included in the planning of this operation."

Danforth nodded. "Your views shall have a full hearing at tomorrow's meeting."

"We have spent a great deal of time talking about what we in this room will or will not say tomorrow," the Air Force general said. "I would like to ask Mr. Danforth what the President is prepared to say."

"Please clarify your question," Danforth said.

"Will he give us the final green light?"

"The President has supported this operation since taking office."

"But he hasn't really said, 'OK, fellas, let 'er rip!' He hasn't said that. He has reserved his right to pull the plug."

Danforth stared at the general. "What exactly is your question?"

"My question is, when will he give us the goddamn green light? The real one! Will he give it tomorrow?"

"No," Danforth replied sharply.

"Then when will he give it? Surely the President understands the time frame in which we are operating. This thing cannot be allowed to drift."

"The President understands."

Vermillion strained forward in his chair. "Castro's military preparedness is increasing daily. Furthermore, it is our estimation that the morale of the exile troops now in training will seriously deteriorate unless Operation Pluto is mounted within the next week. We'll simply lose credibility with these men."

Danforth nodded affirmatively. "As I said, the White House is cognizant of these pressures. A final response from the President will be forthcoming Friday. This is our commitment."

351

The men around the table seemed buoyed by this reassurance.

"Thank you, gentlemen," Vermillion said. "I think this has been a very productive meeting. We shall see you all tomorrow."

Sipping a scotch at the club bar, Pelham studied his surroundings approvingly. The room's oak-paneled walls were adorned with large oils depicting fox hunts and other equestrian rituals. The entire room bespoke wealth and power; so did the club which housed it. As a young man attending Georgetown, Pelham had always yearned to join the prominent lawyers, businessmen and government leaders who comprised its elite membership. He had never made it.

He had gone to the club an hour earlier as the guest of Richard Vermillion, who had invited him for a drink following the Pentagon meeting. They'd had a pleasant talk—Vermillion was in one of his rare expansive moods following what he considered to be a triumphant session. Then he had rushed off to a staff meeting. Pelham, who had another forty-five minutes to kill before leaving for the airport to catch his plane back to Miami, decided to stay on by himself and have another round.

As he studied the room, he noticed that the bar was beginning to fill up now. He could recognize a few of the members: a syndicated columnist, a senator. It did not bother him that none recognized him. After this week, after events had run their course, he would no longer be an anonymous government employee charging drinks to his host's membership number. Clubs like this would be courting him, soliciting his patronage. Pelham had grown weary of the forced anonymity of the CIA, weary of the paltry government checks and pension allocations. It was time to make a name for himself and to branch out into something more rewarding. Yes, it was definitely time.

He was holding his scotch to his lips when he saw Charles Danforth stride into the room and survey the faces. Not finding whomever he was looking for, Danforth came over to the bar and took the vacant seat next to Pelham.

"Kirby Pelham."

Danforth shook the extended hand and smiled cordially.

Pelham could imagine Danforth forming the inevitable question in his mind: What's this middle-level bureaucrat doing in *my* club? Pelham decided to compound his confusion by offering to buy him a drink. It seemed like a delicious opportunity to play the benefactor.

Danforth checked the room once again. "That would be very nice," he said. "I may have to excuse myself when the Senator arrives, of course . . ."

"Of course," Pelham said, signaling the bartender.

The drinks arrived, and Pelham and Danforth exchanged small talk for a few moments, trading anecdotes about some of the military brass who had attended the meeting. Pelham was surprised to find Danforth rather witty and gracious. He had expected him to be more the pedantic type and was pleased by his self-effacing sense of humor.

Then the conversation shifted to the meeting planned for the following day, and Danforth suddenly turned serious. "I don't envy the President this week. I wouldn't like to be in his shoes. There are some tough decisions to be made."

Pelham nodded his agreement, and then a mischievous thought overtook him. Perhaps it was the drink, perhaps the strange irony of their encounter. "I don't really think I agree with you, Charles," Pelham heard himself saying.

Danforth looked puzzled. "What's that again?"

Pelham leaned forward. "I don't think the President is especially on the spot this week. I don't think we need feel sorry for him."

Danforth cocked an eyebrow. "What do you mean?"

Pelham saw his opportunity. He had started it and now he was going to finish it. "Well, when you really analyze it, Charles, Jack Kennedy doesn't really make much of a difference, does he?" He saw Danforth start to recoil, but he pushed ahead. "No, really. Think about it. Jack and Jackie sit up there at the White House, like royalty. The King and Queen of America."

"I don't think I know what you're getting at, Pelham." Danforth was growing visibly impatient now.

"Who really runs the country, Charles? I mean, really runs it. The professionals run it, that's who. It's always been that way. The Kennedys come and go, but policy is set and executed, not by the people in the White House, but by the professionals."

Danforth was looking at him clinically now, cradling his scotch. It was as if he had decided to sit back and be entertained.

"It's been the same dating back to Metternich and Talleyrand," Pelham continued. "It never made any difference who was titular ruler. Didn't then and doesn't now. It's the men sitting around that table at the Pentagon today who make the difference. The people running the machinery of government. The hand on the throttle. The true custodians of power."

"Then you don't think it makes much difference what the President decides about the Cuban situation? Do I understand you correctly?"

Pelham nodded nonchalantly. "The President can call meetings to consider his options, but he really doesn't have any. He's committed and doesn't even know it. The die is cast."

Danforth had been staring at Pelham soberly, but suddenly he was on his feet signaling an elderly gentleman across the room. Probably the Senator, Pelham concluded.

"You must excuse me," Danforth explained hastily. He started to move off, then turned suddenly and stared at Pelham. "By the way, Pelham, I enjoyed your theories," he said, taking a stride or two, smiling graciously to an elderly man at a nearby table. Then suddenly Pelham saw him coming back, stopping so that his face was only a few inches from his. "You know, Pelham, six weeks ago if I heard someone say those things I would have said you don't know what you're talking about."

Pelham gave him a smile. "Of course—you people always do. It's a matter of education, isn't it?"

Danforth's face was flushed, a large vein showing down the middle of his forehead. "OK, now I'm educated. I know you're right. And I still say, go fuck yourself!"

Then he was off across the room.

CHAPTER THIRTY-THREE

Someone once asked Comandante Juan Almeida whether men of destiny like Fidel Castro have charmed lives or astonishing luck. Almeida replied with a gleam of amusement in his eyes, "No! No suerte, testículos!" ("No! Not luck, balls!")

A neighbor remembered Fidel Castro as a wild, unruly youngster, out of control. A girl who knew him said he seemed as a boy like "a volcano ready to explode." One story he tells about himself as a child has it that when his father refused to spend the money to send him to school, Fidel exploded and threatened to burn the family house to the ground. His outburst so impressed his parents with the possibility he might that they relented.

Reckless, erratic, the young Fidel could at times be coldly brutal, at others warm, compassionate and even romantic. But he was always a loner. He had a tendency to keep his emotions to himself, except for anger, which he expressed loudly and fiercely in his high-pitched, hoarse voice that could dominate all others in a room; and eventually would dominate his country.

When the Spaniards surrendered to the American forces in Santiago in 1898, one of the soldiers who decided not to return to his native Lugo, in Galicia, was a tough, physically hardened young man named Ángel Castro. He took a job on the railroad of the new United Fruit Company plantation at Mayari, about twenty miles inland from the Bay of Nipe, on the northeast coast of Oriente. Uneducated but bold, Ángel Castro could work "like a horse," and he was shrewd. By the time Fidel was born, on August 13, 1926, Ángel owned 23,300 acres of sugar plantation. He was a proud, irascible husband and father who had a peasant's love of the earth.

He married a schoolteacher as his first wife and had two children by her, Pedro Emilio and Lidia. When an attractive Creole girl came to work at the finca as a cook, Ángel took her as his woman. Lina Ruz and Ángel had five children, Ramón, Fidel, Juana, Emma and Raúl, all illegitimate. He later married Lina, his first wife having died, so that the children could be baptized, confirmed and legitimate to enter Catholic schools.

Fidel was never very close to his father. When he was a youngster they often quarreled. Once, in 1940, he tried to organize a strike of the finca sugar workers against him. All of Ángel's children were restless and rebellious, hard to handle. The oldest son, Pedro, openly broke with him. But Fidel was very close to his brother Raúl, who was four years younger. When Ángel died in 1956, the news was sent to Mexico City, where Castro was preparing for his invasion of Cuba. He never mentioned it to his close associates.

"The important thing about Fidel's character," Raúl Castro once was quoted as saying, "is that he will not accept defeat."

The people of Oriente are a different breed from the others of Cuba. Even in the intense heat they are energetic, tending to move around a lot restlessly, talking, gesturing, when the average Cuban would be looking for a shady place to sweat out the heat and humidity of the afternoon. Even as a young boy, Fidel was like that.

After attending well-to-do Catholic schools in Santiago, Fidel entered the fashionable Colegio Belén in Havana. He was a bright student, a natural leader and a great athlete. At the age of eighteen, he entered the University of Havana to study law. He had an extremely retentive memory and read voraciously. His marks were high.

But at that time the campus was in a state of open warfare between rival political gangs. Fidel went to classes carrying a revolver.

He was once ambushed in the streets of Havana with a fellow student, Justo Fuentes. They had a daily program on a local Havana radio station and apparently said something that offended one of the rival student gangs. Young Fuentes was killed in the shooting. Castro escaped.

In 1947, Fidel joined a group of Latin-American revolutionaries who planned to land a force of a thousand armed men in the Dominican Republic to overthrow dictator General Rafael Trujillo. Among them was Juan Bosch, the Dominican rebel leader.

355

They gathered at Cayo Confites, a small sandy key off Camagüey on Cuba's east coast. But someone talked. Trujillo brought pressure through the United States to halt the invasion. Cuban police and Coast Guard moved in on the three expedition boats. Fidel jumped overboard and swam ashore with his submachine gun strapped to his back. Although the water was infested with sharks, Castro made the long swim unmolested and escaped.

The following year, he joined a Cuban student delegation to the Conference of Latin-American University Associations, held in Bogotá, Colombia. A madman assassinated Jorge Gaitán, a Colombian Liberal Party leader, during a demonstration on the eighth of April. The assassin was caught on the spot by the mob and lynched. A riot followed. Three thousand were killed in the looting and gunfire that raged for three days. Castro took part in the riot. The Cubans were found to be stockpiling weapons in their hotel rooms. They were asked to leave the country. Castro walked away from the violence untouched.

Returning to Cuba, Castro veered into new directions, but none panned out successfully. He completed his law degree at the University of Havana, but disliked the law and vowed never to practice. He ran for political office, but the election was disrupted by a Batista coup d'état. He became enmeshed in a Romeo-and-Juliet love affair. She was the daughter of a former official in the Batista government, who vehemently disapproved of the union. They were married nonetheless on October 12, 1948, in the Roman Catholic church in Banes, Oriente province. In 1949 a son, Fidelito, was born. Shortly thereafter their marriage fell apart.

Fidel Castro believed he had a destiny to fulfill. When Batista again took over the Cuban government in a coup d'état in the early morning of March 10, 1952, Castro, then twenty-six, began to think revolution. Despite the appearance that his acts seemed rash, he was a man who thought carefully before he made a move. His calculations during the next year and four months were to test his personal courage to its limit and bring about the deaths of sixty-seven of his comrades.

Castro had scribbled in the margin of one of José Martí's books: "I prefer to die riddled with bullets rather than live humiliated."

To understand that he meant it is to understand all that was to come.

It was just getting light the morning of August 1, 1953. On the outskirts of Mampriva Farm at the foot of the Sierra Maestra mountains in Oriente, Lieutenant Pedro Sarría led his patrol of soldiers toward a small palm-thatched hut that loomed ahead in the humid morning twilight. Sarría was fifty-three, tall, black-skinned, and intelligent. He lived his life by what he called his "ethic." That morning he was on patrol by accident. He had replaced another lieutenant who had become ill with influenza. As he walked toward the hut the silence was broken *only by the whisper of boots on the ground and the occasional cries of the morning birds in the trees.*

Lieutenant Sarría was under orders to kill any rebels found armed. An informer had told the Army that Fidel Castro and some of his men had taken refuge near the Gran Piedra, and this morning patrols were out everywhere, searching for them.

Seven days before, on July 26, almost to the hour, eighteen cars had rolled out of a farm near Siboney and headed for the heart of Santiago. There were 131 men in the cars, and Fidel Castro. It was 4:45 A.M. Before getting into the cars, they had all stood holding their weapons in the darkness and sung the national anthem, "La Bayamesa" (Perucho's March), ". . . to die for the fatherland is to live!" Fidel Castro then spoke, invoking the memory of José Martí and the War of Independence. "We shall win," he said. For sixteen months they had planned and trained. Fidel had hand-picked each man. His brother Raúl, fresh from a Communist Youth conference in Europe, had joined him. It seemed to all of them that nothing else mattered but that they had joined Fidel Castro and that he was going to make a revolution. At twenty-seven, the charisma of Fidel had begun to turn people's heads.

The plan was to make two simultaneous attacks. The main force, under Castro, was to assault the Moncada barracks in Santiago. There were 402 Batista soldiers in the military compound, and Castro was outnumbered better than three to one. Everything depended upon surprise. Another group of twenty-nine men was to simultaneously attack the small garrison at Bayamo, to the northwest along the Cauto River.

As Raúl Castro and nineteen men took positions in the windows of the fourth floor of the Palace of Justice, having surprised and disarmed the guards, a second group occupied the Civic Hospital. From the rear windows they commanded the back of the barracks across the Central Highway. Fidel was driving in the second car up to the gate in the barracks wall at Post Three. The first car had surprised the guards at the gate, disarmed them, and sped on inside. Up to that point the attack had gone as planned.

But just then, down Trinidad Street, past the gate came an army car. Two soldiers in the front seat, armed with submachine guns, noticed the commotion around Gate Three. They had been out on patrol because there had been a big festival in Santiago that night and they were expecting trouble. Puzzled by what seemed to be a disturbance at the gate, the two soldiers stopped their car and looked back. At that same moment, an army sergeant whose suspicions had also been aroused came along the street on foot, drawing his automatic pistol. Fidel's men, in the third car, seeing the sergeant reach for his gun, fired at him. Fidel swung his car in front of the patrol vehicle and crashed into the curb. As he jumped out with his men, the firing started. In a matter of seconds it was over.

357

But the barracks were alerted. Machine guns began firing. Soldiers took up positions, rubbing sleep from their eyes. All surprise was lost.

In Bayamo, at the same hour, the attack on the Céspedes Garrison also failed. After the first wave had gone over the fence and into the grounds, a second wave of Fidel's men were waiting to scale the fence. One of them saw a Rural Guard standing at the stables. Without orders, he fired at the man. The shot alerted the garrison. A machine gun on the roof of the building began firing. After half an hour of fighting, the attackers fled in disorder.

In Santiago, Fidel Castro managed to escape by car. His hope had been to duplicate Guiteras' feat in taking the garrison at San Luis twenty years earlier. With weapons from Moncada he would have armed the uprising against Batista. As he sped away from the gunfire, all this had crumbled in defeat. The main group of his force, armed with the best and heaviest weapons, had not even showed up for the fight. They had taken a wrong turn and were driving around hopelessly lost in Santiago's streets.

When he reached the farm near Siboney, Fidel found about forty survivors. He faced his disheartened men and gave them the alternatives: they could follow him into the mountains or go back to Santiago and try to escape from there. Eighteen decided to go into the mountains with him to carry on a guerrilla campaign. For a week, Fidel and his small group wandered in the wooded hills, suffering from hunger and thirst. Meanwhile, in Santiago and Bayamo the tally totaled eight dead and eight wounded for the rebels; nineteen Batista soldiers had been killed, twenty-two wounded. General Martín Tamayo, on written orders from an angry Batista, began torturing and murdering rebel prisoners. Fifty-nine were killed. Thirty-two rebel prisoners were spared, largely through the efforts of Santiago Bishop Pérez Serantes and the public outcry that arose from the citizens of Santiago when word of the atrocities spread. About sixty rebels escaped. Raúl Castro was picked up on the streets by a patrol and jailed.

On the sixth day in the mountains, Fidel realized that the condition of his eighteen men was deteriorating rapidly. Their physical endurance had reached its limit. He decided they should make their way out of the mountains in small groups. His plan was to reach the mouth of the Bay of Santiago and cross it in order to reach the Sierra Maestra and carry on the guerrilla war. He kept two men with him.

After walking miles in the darkness, Fidel and his companions came upon a bohío, a small palm-thatched hut. They were dazed with lack of sleep and hunger. In weary exhaustion, they went inside and flopped on the ground, sleeping with their weapons at their sides. They were in deep sleep when the soldiers burst in, rifles ready to fire. The three sat up quickly, staring with puffy eyes at the muzzles of the guns. Fidel was an instant away from death. The soldiers were extremely nervous and about to fire.

At that moment, Lieutenant Sarría entered the hut. He recognized Fidel. It *would have meant a promotion, perhaps a decoration, a bonus even, if he had let his men shoot. But Sarría was a different kind of man. He abhorred the killing of prisoners. He had already saved two young rebels from being murdered. He took the three young men prisoners, treated them politely, and instead of taking them to Moncada barracks, where the killings were in progress, he insisted on putting them in the safety of the civil prison. His superiors were outraged.*

Lieutenant Sarría was court-martialed. He went into exile in the United States.

Fidel Castro, after a secret trial, was sentenced to fifteen years in the prison on the Isle of Pines. During his trial he gave a two-hour oration in his own defense, which he later rewrote into a propaganda document entitled "History Will Absolve Me," circulated after he came to power in 1959. His brother Raúl and twenty-seven others were sent to the same Isle of Pines prison.

The attack on the Moncada barracks had been a mad adventure that ended in complete failure. Yet Fidel responded, "The second phase of the revolution is about to begin."

His aide Celia Sánchez said years later, "The Cuban Revolution was born at Moncada."

The fact that Fidel Castro had not been killed in the fighting, or executed at the moment of his arrest, or later in his cell, was to many of his followers a miracle.

Suerte *or* testículos? *He had both.*

On the night of November 24, 1956, it was blowing a gale across the Gulf of Mexico. The Mexican Marine had ordered small-craft warnings posted outside the port of Tuxpan on the Yucatán coast. The seas were heavy and ugly.

In the gusty darkness, a sixty-two-foot yacht moved out of the mouth of the river and into the big swell. It was an old boat, white-hulled, twin-engined, and badly in need of repairs. Its radio could only receive. The tanks would hold only twelve hundred gallons of fuel, not enough to make the trip across the Gulf to the coast of Oriente, where it was headed. Another two thousand gallons in tins had been strapped down on deck. Not more than fourteen men could fit aboard in reasonable discomfort. Fidel Castro had boarded with eighty-two men, plus food, weapons, ammunition and equipment.

Among those on board was a short, thin Argentine doctor, Ernesto Guevara. He had been in Guatemala when the CIA-backed coup had toppled the leftist government of Jacobo Arbenz. He had joined Castro a few weeks after he appeared in Mexico City. He was a dedicated revolutionary. He suffered from asthma, which was to plague him in the years to come but not diminish his spirit. It was a habit of the Argentinians to call "Che" (Hey) to everyone, where the Cubans would get your attention by saying "Oye." So he had begun to be known by a nickname, "Che." Also present were Raúl Castro and Camilo Cienfuegos, a charming, good-humored young man who would turn out to be a crack guerrilla leader.

359

At the wheel was the pilot, former Navy Lieutenant Roberto Roque, an extraordinary seaman. He had to be. The overloaded boat wallowed and yawed in the seas, making it a monster to steer, let alone keep it on course. The waves were steep and high and topped with whitecaps. The yacht, named rather appropriately the Granma, considering its age, plowed to the crests and then fell, slamming into the troughs with a bang that jarred it from stem to stern. Sea water broke over the bow and drenched the cabin. Food was ruined. Everyone was seasick. The old bilge pumps stopped working. The crammed and miserable Fidelistas, their faces gray and pale with seasickness, had to bail water continuously to keep the yacht afloat.

That it was madness to move out of the safety of port in that bad weather in any kind of a boat, let alone an overloaded yacht that was in need of repairs, didn't seem to matter to Fidel Castro. He was determined to make a landing in Oriente before Frank País pulled off an uprising in Santiago on November 30. His excuse was that his landing would pull Batista's troops away from Santiago. Chances are good that he did not want País to steal his thunder. Fidel had to be first.

The crossing took six days. All aboard were miserable. The storm blew the Granma off course. The downcast Fidel could only listen to the radio reports of the fighting in Santiago, which lasted until December 2, 1956. By then the Granma was off the Oriente coastline, ten miles north of Cabo Cruz.

As the morning light came into the sky, Fidel decided to head straight for shore. No one was sure exactly where they were. Roque turned the bow toward the dark line of mangrove swamp showing ahead. Abruptly, there was a grinding crunch. They had run aground at Playa de los Colorados, on the southwestern tip of Cuba.

It would be dangerous getting ashore. Struggling through water up to their necks, the eighty-two men set out. The bottom was slippery. Their feet snarled in the mangrove roots. Weapons, ammunition, food had to be abandoned. It took five hours to reach dry land. Soaked and shivering, Fidel Castro wiped the mud from his face and started talking about getting up to the Sierra. He seemed cheerful. To his bedraggled men he spoke with urgency, because the grounded yacht would certainly give them away. Soon Batista air patrols would pass overhead.

It took them three days to work their way eight miles inland to a cane field near an area called Alegría de Pío. There they were ambushed by Batista soldiers. Planes appeared and began to strafe and bomb. The cane field caught fire. Smoke turned the sun red. Castro's men, exhausted, thirsty, scattered in panic. Volleys of rifle shots ripped through the cane.

"The fate of the small and scattered groups who tried to get away from that unlucky spot was varied," wrote one survivor. "Some were ambushed in the gulleys lined with soldiers; many were captured and immediately killed; other more fortunate ones landed in prison."

A peasant guide they had allowed to go free the night before had betrayed them to the Batista Guardia Rural. Che Guevara was badly wounded. But a stonemason, Juan Almeida, remained cool and clearheaded, leading Guevara and others out of the smoke and the gunfire to the relative safety of the woods. A peasant truck driver, Crescencio Pérez, an uncle of one of the group, rounded up as many as he could find, including Fidel Castro, and guided them to a nearby farmhouse owned by his brother. When Fidel got to the house he found twelve survivors. It eventually swelled to more than twenty. Like Céspedes' twelve, Castro's group became a legend.

It is not known how many were killed in the cane-field ambush. Twenty-two were taken prisoner. A few others escaped. Castro was reported dead.

"He embraced us," reported one survivor at the farmhouse. "He was very happy. He told us not to despair. This was only the beginning. He told us we had already won the war."

"Now," Fidel said, "we can begin the campaign."

Oriente's Sierra Maestra range is the wildest area of Cuba. One hundred miles of rugged peaks, east to west, about thirty miles in width, and covered with thick hammock and dense forests, it is a constant vista of green. The mountains are often shrouded in mist. Rainfall is heavy. Pico Turquino, the highest peak, looms 6,496 feet into the sky. The peasants are few, mostly charcoal makers, extremely poor and suspicious of armed men. They had reason to be. The mountain trails were patrolled by the Guardia Rural, a tough, disciplined and ruthless force of police. It was into these mountains Castro fled with his ragged band of followers. For two years, 1957 and 1958, they fought an almost continuous guerrilla war. The first few months were bleak. The Sierra horseflies tormented the men in the bush, leaving bites that infected quickly. Mosquitoes were a constant torment.

In their first month, Batista sent them what in black humor was to be called a "Christmas present." He had twenty-two young men killed in Oriente province. Several were hanged in the trees along the highway outside Holguin just before Christmas Day. On January 17 they fought a skirmish at a small army garrison at the mouth of the Plata River and won. "Our first victory," wrote Guevara. Another followed at Arroyo del Infierno five days later. Seven Batista soldiers were killed without loss to the rebels.

Fidel, according to his companions, had an uncanny ability to detect danger. Repeatedly, as they moved through the rough jungle trails, he would stop, listen, then divert the column in another direction. "Always," said one of the guerrillas, "we learned there were soldiers in ambush ahead."

In late January, fighter planes roared over their jungle camp. Bullets whispered through the leaves, chopping them to shreds and sending them over the scattering guerrillas "like green snow." It was learned later that they had a traitor in their ranks. The peasant Eurimio Guerra had pinpointed the encampment for Batista's planes. "Morale," wrote Guevara, "was low." One follower recalled coming upon Castro sitting by the campfire at night reading Hitler's Mein Kampf. Books on Marx and Lenin lay nearby.

One cold night in February, Eurimio Guerra complained that he had no blanket. He asked Fidel to lend him one. The rebel commander laughed and said that if he lent one of his blankets they'd both be cold. Why not share? Guerra crawled in with Fidel. The night was not only chilly but damp. Guerra had been offered a lot of money and military rank if he would assassinate Fidel. As he crawled under the blanket, next to the warmth of Castro's body, Guerra held his .45 automatic in his hand. He stayed awake all that night trying to make up his mind to do it. Che Guevara described it: "Throughout the night, a great part of the Revolution depended on the thoughts of courage, fear, scruples, ambition, power, and money, running through the mind of a traitor." Guerra also had two grenades which the Batista agents had given him to cover his escape. Snuggled next to the would-be assassin, Castro slept soundly until first light. His luck held. Guerra was too afraid to act.

Earl E. T. Smith, the American ambassador, flew back to Havana from Washington on December 12, 1958, in a bad mood. He had a most distasteful task to perform. As a protégé of John Hay Whitney, who had the largest block of stock in the Freeport Sulphur Company, which owned Cuba's nickel mines, Smith had steadfastly supported the Cuban dictator and American financial interests. He had grown fond of Batista and saw much of him socially.

Havana was gloomy as the Christmas season approached. Tourist trade had dropped to nothing, because of the revolution. Streets were deserted. Pimps stood smoking cigarets on the street corners in front of the bodegas while prostitutes roamed in pairs along the vacant sidewalks. Police cars glided past, the officers in their denim-blue uniforms keeping a careful eye on every corner. The casinos in the big hotels had few customers at the roulette wheels and the crap tables.

For Batista's forces in the country to the southeast, things looked especially bleak.

The Castro brothers had Santiago encircled. Che Guevara and Camilo Cienfuegos had broken out of Oriente in two columns and were fighting a pitched battle for Santa Clara. Student guerrillas were attacking outposts in the Escambray mountains of Las Villas province and harassing Batista's troops from bases in the mountains of Pinar del Río to the west of Havana. Urban sabotage and attacks were frequent in Havana itself.

As a last-ditch effort, Batista was outfitting an armored train to relieve Santa Clara. But his soldiers were unreliable. Some fought quite bravely, but others simply surrendered or deserted. Castro had undermined their morale by releasing all prisoners unharmed after treating them with respect and kindness. Why fight? they asked one another.

On December 17, Smith went to Batista's office. The President was cordial, his broad face somewhat lined with fatigue, but his eyes were bright.

Smith later recalled: "I did not tell Batista he ought to get out. I would not put it so bluntly as that. I spent two hours and twenty-five minutes trying to tactfully explain that the Department believed he had lost effective control. To avoid further bloodshed, did he not think it might be in the best interests of all concerned if he retired? This had to be done without giving the impression that I was intervening."

Batista listened. But he was still buying time; he would wait to see the outcome in Santa Clara.

He still had some fifty thousand troops, equipped with modern American weapons, artillery, bazookas and machine guns, and his Air Force was still intact, bombing and strafing the rebels and the captured villages at will. He felt he still had a chance. Against him Castro could not have had much more than three thousand men in the field; he simply made it seem as if he had more.

On December 29, as Batista's armored train rolled into Santa Clara, Guevara's guerrillas used tractors to rip out the tracks in front of and behind the train. Then he derailed it with dynamite. It caught fire. The khaki-clad soldiers poured out of the smoldering wreck and surrendered, laughing and talking with the rebels, exchanging cigarets and jokes.

At 9 P.M. on December 31, Batista was notified that Santa Clara had fallen into rebel hands. At 10 P.M. he received a long-distance call from Santiago. His commander there informed him the city could not be held. All of Oriente had fallen to Castro. Batista hung up the telephone. He ordered his bags packed.

In the early-morning darkness of January 1, 1959, a small crowd gathered at Camp Columbia, the big military base in Havana. They boarded several planes. Among them was the short, thin, jut-jawed figure of Fulgencio Batista. He had millions of dollars stashed in Europe and Miami. He took his family and some friends. His plane lifted off the ground exactly at 3 A.M. Behind him, thousands of his loyalists were left to their fate.

In Washington, the lights were burning late at the Pentagon. Admiral Arleigh Burke, CIA Director Allen Dulles and Undersecretary of State Robert Murphy were trying to find a solution to the Cuban problem. They agreed that Castro was not the man they wanted in power. But who? They did not resolve it. Actually, there was no way they could.

"This time it is Cuba's good fortune that the revolution will really take power," Fidel Castro said to the joyous multitudes gathered in Santiago. The great throng roared its approval. Castro was proclaiming the independence of Cuba in Santiago, Oriente province, the city where it would have been proclaimed in 1898 had not the American troops invaded and shoved the Cuban rebel forces aside. The past was very close to Cubans. Fidel Castro was closing the link.

He had been drinking his morning coffee when the news came that Batista had fled to the Dominican Republic. He had not expected Batista to quit. Now he was suspicious and worried about what the Americans would do.

In Havana, Batista had named Carlos Manuel Piedra, a Supreme Court judge, as the Provisional President. On that morning Piedra was trying to carry out the duties as though he were really in charge, but no one paid much attention to him. There was something else in the wind. Ambassador Smith was trying to work out "a solution." Two days earlier the CIA had paid $100,000 to the warden of the prison on the Isle of Pines to release Colonel Ramón Barquín, a hero of an army revolt against Batista that had failed in 1956. Smith and his delegation in Havana were awaiting Colonel Barquín's arrival. It was hoped he could form a military junta that would prevent Castro from filling the vacuum left by Batista's sudden departure.

Castro countered in his speech in Santiago, calling for a general strike. "Revolution, yes!" he shouted. "Military coup, no!" He further declared Santiago de Cuba the provisional capital and named Manuel Urrutia, a liberal Santiago judge, as Provisional President. He then ordered Che Guevara and Camilo Cienfuegos to lead their bearded columns into Havana as fast as they could move. It was a masterful stroke.

With Ambassador Smith thus checkmated, Fidel Castro began a slow, triumphant journey toward Havana, letting the excitement build in the city. Cuba simply exploded with joy. It took eight days for Castro to travel the five hundred miles to the capital. Thousands lined the road. He stopped often to make speeches, his high, hoarse voice pouring out words of hope and triumph. Wearing his olive-drab fatigues, gesturing, speaking sometimes for five or six hours, Castro centered the attention of his country on his singular figure. The bearded faces of his men, his own beatific expression, created an aura that invoked in thousands of Cubans the image of Christ and his disciples, an impression that was largely encouraged.

In Havana, meanwhile, thousands filled the streets in an explosion of emotion and euphoria. There were shots fired and a few sustained gun battles between diehard Batista supporters and rebels. But generally the feeling in the air was one of great relief and pure, unadulterated joy! Exaltation reigned among the mobs. Guns were everywhere. The whole country seemed on an emotional binge. The revolution had finally triumphed. People stood on the street corners cheering each other and waving their arms. Others ran in groups waving Cuban flags and Twenty-Sixth-of-July banners. It was a New Year's celebration to end all New Year's celebrations. Fidel Castro's name was on everyone's lips.

Colonel Barquín, meanwhile, arrived in Havana on January 1, before any of the rebel leaders. He set up headquarters at Camp Columbia. But the twenty-sixth of July cadres in the streets of Havana did not listen to his orders. He tried without success to contact Fidel Castro. Finally he was informed that Che Guevara was to take over La Cabaña Fortress and that Camp Columbia was to be turned over to Camilo Cienfuegos. The columns of bearded rebels were moving into the streets of Havana, surrounded by the delirious crowds. Colonel Barquín greeted Che and Camilo with warmth and courtesy. He yielded his tenuous position with grace and quietly went into exile.

Cuba now belonged to Fidel Castro. He alone had its destiny in his hands.

In April, 1959, Fidel Castro came to Washington for an unofficial visit. He delivered a speech before the American Society of Newspaper Editors which was warmly received. If he secretly expected anyone in the Eisenhower Administration to extend cordiality toward him, he kept it to himself. He went out to restaurants, chatting with bystanders, giving press interviews. He knew he was making a good impression, and that seemed to please him. He had become the new Cuban Premier in February, officially. He was clearly having a good time.

His public and private utterances were following a moderate line. He told newspaper editors that he wanted a free press in Cuba. When a member of the Senate Foreign Relations Committee asked him to describe his "connection to Communism," he replied, "None."

In Havana, the Communists who controlled the daily newspaper Hoy *imposed a complete blackout on Castro's visit. Not one word of what he said was printed. Although* Revolución, *the new organ of the twenty-sixth of July, published extensive coverage of his ten-day tour, the editors were under great pressure, cutting, distorting, rewriting the copy.*

In Moscow, the Russians were troubled by Castro's moderate statements. He was talking like a nationalist. In confronting the United States, he seemed to be offering an olive branch. At a reception in the Cuban Embassy, Castro seemed to purposely avoid the Russian ambassador, Menshikov. In public and private conversation, Castro kept sounding more like José Martí than like a Soviet pawn. He kept stressing Cuban independence and sovereignty. "We are neither capitalists nor Communists," he said. "We are humanists." He was opposed "to capitalism without bread—Communist bread without freedom." He invited foreign investments in Cuban industry, but not in Cuban agriculture. He did not ask for U.S. aid, but for a better commercial treaty. He wanted to sell more sugar and raise tariffs on imported U.S. goods to encourage the growth of Cuban industry. He did plan agrarian reform, but there were no plans for further expropriation of foreign property.

His remarks seemed to confuse the Americans as much as the Russians. President Eisenhower decided to take a golfing vacation. He went out of town. Vice-President Nixon was left to deal with this enigmatic visitor.

The meeting between Nixon and Castro had been initiated by a couple of congressmen who thought it might be diplomatically productive. Both Castro and Nixon appeared to be pragmatists, they reasoned. They might hit it off.

They were terribly wrong.

The two men met in the Vice-President's office in the Capitol building. There were no interpreters present. No written record was kept. The minute they emerged, one thing became clear: The meeting had been a disaster.

"The s.o.b. kept scowling at me all the time," Castro said. "He kept telling me what to do and what not to do." As he started describing the meeting to aides, Castro's once-cheerful mood seemed to blacken. He even mentioned the possibility of an American-backed attack on Cuba—a subject he had not before raised during his Washington trip.

Indeed, the more Castro reflected upon the meeting, the more alarmed he became. That night Castro startled aides at the Cuban Embassy by suddenly issuing orders that arms and food be stockpiled in the Sierra Maestra mountains in the event he and his high command would have to take refuge there again. His friends and colleagues were stunned and appalled. What could have been discussed with Nixon? What threats could have been made?

If Castro seemed suddenly militant, so was Nixon. Returning to his office, he dictated a memorandum asserting that Castro, despite his then protestations, was either a member of the Communist Party or was "hopelessly naïve" about Communism. He predicted that relations between the U.S. and Cuba would deteriorate drastically.

It was a self-fulfilling prophecy. A year later, on March 17, 1960, the Eisenhower Administration authorized establishment of a training camp in Guatemala to train guerrillas for an attack on Cuba. Eisenhower also acceded to another request by his Vice-President—a rather unorthodox one. He appointed Nixon to be the "action officer" supervising the entire Cuban project.

It was to be Nixon's ball game. The die was cast.

Anastas Ivanovich Mikoyan, the Russian Deputy Premier, appeared in Havana in February, 1960, to open a Soviet exposition. Unlike Nixon, he was warm and friendly. He made a deal to buy Cuban sugar. He shook hands with Castro. Said Che Guevara after Mikoyan left for Moscow: "There has been talk of reducing our sugar quota [by the U.S.] or suspending it entirely. The sooner the better. For Cuba, it is a symbol of colonialism. We shall be better off without imperialist yokes."

The leadership of Fidel Castro's government was brash, young, inexperienced. Detaching its country from the domination of the United States was its primary goal.

In Cuba itself, Castro's power was all-pervading. He had done what no other Cuban government had during the centuries of domination by Spain and the U.S.—he had created an honest government. The regime was making many *mistakes, but to the Cuban people they were honest mistakes. Castro spent hours on television trying to explain, step by step, what his government was out to accomplish and how. He once started a long speech by saying, "This speech is going to be boring." But Cubans sat next to the TV sets and struggled to understand the long columns of bewildering statistics Castro laid before them. He was their leader and sharing with them the experience of self-government. No one had ever done that before. He formed "defense committees," block organizations of vigilantes whose job it was to spy on their neighbors. He redistributed land. He built schools and hospitals in the rural areas. He set as a national goal the eradication of illiteracy.*

Meanwhile, subtle changes were taking place within the Castro regime. Hardline Communists were moving into key positions of power. Che Guevara's allies were sliding into the top ranks of the rebel army. More and more Cubans, especially the middle class, started packing their possessions and moving to voluntary exile in Miami.

The one-on-one verbal skirmishes with the United States led in June to a direct confrontation—not over sugar, but over oil.

Oil was the only energy source used in Cuba. Its whole economy ran on it. Standard Oil Company, Texaco and Royal Dutch Shell had built refineries there to process crude from their own fields in Venezuela. The Cubans felt that the prices charged were too high. Russian oil was available on the market at lower prices. Since 1955, Russia had expanded its oil production dramatically; now it was dangling oil before Castro's eyes like a carrot. He went for it. The Cuban government demanded that the American and British refineries process Soviet crude. At first, the companies agreed. But Washington brought pressure to bear. If Castro couldn't get oil, his government would surely collapse. On June 7, 1960, the Cuban government was informed that the oil companies refused to refine the Russian crude.

On June 29, Castro took over the refineries. Cuba was now totally dependent upon Russian oil to survive.

On July 6, President Eisenhower retaliated. He suspended Cuba's sugar quota.

Wrote a disheartened U.S. Ambassador Bonsal: "With this action, I contend the United States turned its back on thirty years of statesmanship in the Latin American field."

"Once the United States is in Cuba," José Martí had asked, "who will get it out?" In 1960, the answer was Fidel Castro. The link was broken.

On December 19, 1960, it was announced in Moscow by Nikita Khrushchev and Che Guevara that a Soviet-Cuban trade pact on a larger scale than the one signed with Mikoyan had been approved.

Soviet purchases of Cuban sugar were increased under the agreement from one million to 2.7 million tons annually. The U.S.S.R. also agreed to build an iron and steel mill in Cuba and to send technicians to the island to search for minerals.

367

Besides sugar, Cuba agreed to supply the Soviet Union with other products. The next day, Castro announced that the Soviet bloc had also agreed to buy four million tons of Cuban sugar annually. Only twenty percent of the purchase price was to be paid in hard cash. The rest would be in Russian manufactured goods. Cuba was also granted a $100 million loan for twelve years at 2.5 percent interest.

Communist Russia undertook to supplant the United States in the Cuban economy.

"Whoever says economic union," José Martí had warned, "says political union. The people who buy, command; the people who sell, obey."

After centuries of domination by Spain, then more than half a century of domination by the United States, Cuba had now traded independence for a new master, Soviet Russia. The Cuban Revolution was yet to be won by some future generation.

CHAPTER THIRTY-FOUR

HAVANA, APRIL 10, 1961

Camilo lay on the bed with his head cupped in his hands, listening to the noise of the traffic on the street outside. Pepita stood at the hot plate by the tile sink, waiting for the coffee to boil. She wore a plain brown skirt and a white blouse and was barefoot. The sunlight slanted into the window and lit her face as she turned to smile at him.

"Camilo, you should take your boots off before you get on the bed."

"You sound like my mother."

"And your father and sister and brother too! How would you like that? Hmmmm?"

He yawned and stretched his arms. He looked at the paint peeling off the high ceiling. It was a single-room apartment, with a bed, a dresser, a sink and a hot plate. There were two high windows, with a small balcony that looked down onto the street. There were iron bars on the windows. He had rented it a year ago to have a place to go when he didn't want to go out to Vedado, or as a place where he might hide temporarily if he needed to. "How's the coffee?"

"Ready in a minute."

He could smell coffee in the air. He loved the aroma. He heard the clatter of her taking down saucers. "How did it all go last night?" she asked.

"I got the boat."

She turned, clasping her hands in front of her, excited. "Camilo, you didn't? Tell me. I must know. Are you going?"

She came to the bed and sat beside him, touching his chest with her fingertips.

"We're going," he said, his eyes closed. He opened them and smiled at her.

She looked dumbfounded. "I don't understand."

"You and me and Paco and maybe Sabino. We're going to take the boat across."

"Are you serious, Camilo?"

"You want to go?"

"I want to go with you, wherever you go. But . . . I . . . I never thought it possible . . ."

He grabbed her hand and pulled her down to him and kissed her. He looked into her eyes. "You love me, Pepita?"

"More than my life."

"You wish to be with me in Miami? With my family? With my mother and my father and my brother?"

She swallowed hard, not believing it was true. "Yes."

"What about your mother, won't you miss her?"

"Very much. I am very sad about leaving my mother."

"Bring her too."

"She's too old. She wouldn't go."

"But you will?"

"Oh, yes, Camilo. Yes." She kissed his lips, his bearded cheeks, his neck, his throat and then his lips again, and looked steadily into his blue eyes. "I can't believe it," she whispered. "When?"

"Soon. The timing has to be correct. I don't want them to suspect anything. Maybe a week, maybe two, three. I don't know yet. I can't arouse suspicion."

Pepita snuggled against his chest, staring off into the darkness of the room. "Will it be dangerous?"

"Very. From now until we leave, very dangerous."

"And in Miami?"

"The same."

"But you'll have your father there, and David, to protect you. All his people. From what I hear, your father has many people with him."

"Yes, he has many. I intend to join him."

"And fight against Fidel?"

"It had to come. You know how many of his old comrades, real revolutionaries, he's had shot?"

"I know . . . I know . . ."

"You know, I counted the other day. Damn near every one who was with him in the beginning in Mexico is gone, except Raúl and Che. Almost every one. We must be very cautious. Display nothing. Say nothing. It is a very dangerous time for us."

She hugged him against her, feeling his warmth. "But it's going to be all right, isn't it? Isn't it?"

He hesitated and then ran his fingers through her short-cut black hair. "Let it grow when we get to Miami, eh? Let it grow out long."

"It's in fashion, this kind of hair."

"I like it long."

"Like Alicia's?"

"I didn't say that, Pepita, *cara.*"

"Do you think of her?"

"Some of the time."

"You loved her very much, I know."

"Yes. But now I have you."

"Tell me something."

"What? What something can I tell you?"

"Was she . . . was she better than I . . . in bed, I mean?"

He sat up and held her arms, staring at her. "What a question!"

"Will you answer, Camilo?"

"She was different. She had nothing to do with you. You have nothing to do with her. In bed, you are a glory, woman."

He drew her to him and pressed his lips against hers. Then he whispered, "In Miami, we make baby, all right?"

"Don't say things like that if you don't mean them. Be sincere with me, Camilo."

"But I mean it. I have a daughter. But I am the last Carta. I need a son. No, I need many sons. Will you give me sons?"

"As many as you want!" She bit his lip. Kissed him. Buried her face against his bearded cheek. "As many as you are man enough to make!" She pulled away from his face suddenly.

"What's the matter?"

"The coffee, smell it?"

He smelled the slightly burned coffee aroma in the air. She jumped from the bed and rushed to the tiny aluminum pot and pulled the plug. Steam hissed in the air. "I don't think it's ruined. You want to try it?"

When Pelham arrived at the Hamlet at nine-forty-five, having missed dinner, he started eating peanuts, and suddenly it was ten-fifteen and he was into his fourth martini. By the time Michael arrived, full of his usual melodramatic apologies for his tardiness, Pelham was feeling light-headed and dizzy.

"It was the damn car again," Michael said. "It wouldn't start." He ordered a beer and then opened his canvas satchel and took out a handsomely wrapped gift, placing it before Pelham.

"What's this?"

"It's for you. A surprise."

Pelham flushed. "It's not my birthday and it's not Christmas."

"It's just something I saw in a store and I thought of you and wanted you to have it."

"You shouldn't do things like that, Michael. You don't have the money . . ."

"Open it. Please."

Pelham started to unwrap the present; his hands, he realized, were not functioning too well under the influence of the alcohol. Tearing off the paper, he found himself holding a copy of Plato's *Republic*. It was a very old edition, but its elegant fine leather binding was in remarkably good condition. Indeed, the volume had a wonderful musty, leathery aroma.

"It's almost a hundred years old," Michael said. "And it's in Greek."

"It's beautiful," Pelham said softly.

"I saw it in a bookstore. They had just bought the library of an old book collector who had died. They hadn't even sorted out the books yet. When I saw this lying there I knew I wanted you to have it."

Pelham looked at Michael's eager young eyes beaming at him, then down at the exquisite volume. Suddenly he felt his own eyes brimming with moisture and he looked away and tried to pull himself together. It's foolish to get sentimental over something like this, he told himself. Yet the thought was such a touching one, and the choice was truly admirable. The boy, with all his problems, had a core of civility that Pelham deeply responded to. He was a boy who was reaching out to him, who needed him, yet Pelham had fallen into his old habit of pulling away.

"I'm truly touched," Pelham said finally. "It was a lovely thing to do."

"I'm thrilled you like it." The bartender served his beer. "I'm going to celebrate. Another one for my friend here."

"No, I think I've had plenty . . ."

"Come on. Have a round with me."

They fell into an animated conversation. Michael had gotten an A on a history exam and he was exultant. Also he had started reading Chaucer and was delighted by the intricacies of Middle English as well as the ribald vigor of the writing.

Pelham found the boy's high spirits contagious; he felt the heavy weight of his own depression beginning to lift. He didn't even notice when Michael ordered yet another round.

"I'm drunk," Pelham blurted.

Michael stopped his conversation and gazed at him with curiosity. "What?" he said, noticing that Pelham was holding himself very rigid as if to conceal his imminent collapse.

"I'm drunk. I think if I so much as move a muscle I'll fall off this stool and land flat on my face."

"Can I give you a hand?"

"I would be very grateful. Perhaps if you could help me get outside, the air would help . . ." Pelham heard his words slurring. It was all terribly disconcerting. As Michael helped him off the stool, Pelham's eyes darted around the room to see if anyone was noticing. But the place had emptied out considerably and no one was paying any special attention.

Once outside, however, Pelham didn't feel any better. The dizziness was still there and it was exacerbated now by a sudden overwhelming sleepiness. He was aware of being helped into his own car, but as the car pulled away he slumped into a deep sleep. The next thing he knew, he felt the car jolt to a stop and he was being helped up his front walk and Michael was fishing in his pocket for a key.

"I've got it here," Pelham mumbled, managing somehow to retrieve the key from what seemed to be the vast recesses of his trouser pocket.

Walking seemed to be a terribly awkward procedure; he could manage his legs all right, but his sense of balance had deserted him. It seemed that walls and furniture were constantly swaying in his direction, but he felt Michael's firm hand on his shoulder, deftly guiding him down the hall and into his bedroom.

". . . haven't been drunk in twenty years," Pelham kept mumbling, his words coming together in clumps. Michael was helping him remove his shoes. "I'm all right, Michael . . . feeling better now," Pelham mumbled, but then he plummeted onto his bed, lying on his back, staring helplessly at the ceiling. It was not that he felt nauseous or even uncomfortable. He almost felt splendid, as a matter of fact; the whole experience seemed so bizarre to him, so outlandish, that it was more funny than upsetting, especially now that he felt safely home again. Pelham began

372

to giggle, and Michael, looking at him with amusement, began to laugh, too.

"It's nice to see you laughing for a change," Michael said. "You have seemed so troubled lately."

". . . not troubled now . . ." Pelham gurgled, and then suddenly his eyes clamped shut.

When Pelham awakened he was aware of the pervasive coolness of the sheets, the softness of the pillow. He was naked, lying beneath the covers, but could not recall how he had gotten there. It was still night, and a lamp was burning atop his dresser, but the bright reading lamps above his bed were turned off. The house was silent. Pelham tried to sit up, but he felt dizzy and settled back awkwardly. He wondered what time it was. It couldn't be near dawn, he thought, because if it were morning he would have a splitting headache from the alcohol. His eyes fluttered now, and then opened wide as he saw Michael standing before him. In the dimness of the room, with only a single light glowing behind him, the boy took on an aura of beauty and innocence. Pelham was keenly aware of the fineness of his features—the high cheekbones, the delicate lips, the sculpted nose. Everything about him was slender—his arms, his waist, his legs. He was clearly a boy of breeding, Pelham thought. His mind flashed back to the schoolboys at Exeter, with their chiseled, patrician features and handsome eyes and boyish faces. Exeter! He hadn't thought about school for years—the musty smell of the old classrooms, the shouts and laughter of camaraderie emanating from the dormitory, the dank, austere chapel, the aroma of socks and sweat and liniment in the locker room, the stark white landscape in winter and the sudden, sensuous bursting forth of spring in all its verdant splendor. God, he wished he were back at Exeter.

"I could call a cab, but I don't have the money."

Michael was talking to him, but Pelham couldn't understand what he was saying.

"I said I don't have my car. I don't know how to get home. I would borrow your car, but I know you have to be at the office early."

"Yes . . . office . . . early."

Pelham couldn't comprehend all of what Michael was saying, but he knew he didn't want the boy to leave. He liked to have him there, and it would be lonely if he were to go.

"Stay," Pelham said. "I want you to stay."

"Where shall I sleep?"

"Sleep here," Pelham heard himself saying.

373

"Here?"

"Please."

"You want me to sleep here. In this room?"

"Yes, I would like that . . ."

Pelham could see Michael standing above him, motionless, as if lost in thought. He saw his soft brown eyes staring at him, felt the gaze. Then he saw him pull off his shirt and kick off his shoes. He whipped off his trousers, and Pelham saw his white underpants tight against his groin. Michael was naked and Pelham saw his lean flanks moving toward the lamp, his buttocks slim and white like those of a beautiful young girl. And then the room was dark.

A moment later Pelham felt the sheet and the blanket being lifted as Michael's body moved under the covers beside him in the double bed. They lay there silently together in the blackness, breathing the soft night air. Pelham felt a stirring within him, but the sensation seemed somehow disconnected, removed from himself, as if belonging to another body apart from his own. But the stirring was there nonetheless, and Pelham felt impelled to respond to it. He reached out with his arm and it came to rest against the warm, taut flesh of Michael's chest. He heard Michael's breathing now, heard it quicken as he caressed his chest and belly. Again, Pelham felt a strange detachment from his motions, as if it were someone else maneuvering his limbs, some other spirit guiding his actions.

"I thought you hated me," he heard the boy whisper in the dark.

"I don't hate you," Pelham heard himself whisper.

There was a pause. Then: "I still want to live in your guest house."

"I know."

"And I still want you to buy me a motorcycle."

"I will."

Then he felt the boy rustling the bedclothes as he moved against him. His body felt bony and sinewy, but his skin was soft and seemed to radiate a soothing warmth. Pelham felt the boy's head nestle against his shoulder, and his hair felt soft and fine against his skin. Pelham's hand moved down the delicate slope of his back and settled against the gentle curve of his buttocks. He felt Michael stir and move more tightly against him, the warmth of his body arousing him further. The boy's hand was sliding gently down his stomach now, gliding toward his groin, circling it playfully, then tracing a finger against Pelham's stiffening penis. Pelham heard himself groan as the boy's motions quickened. Pelham turned over on his side and his eyes tried to penetrate the darkness, but everything seemed distant and gauzy. His hands were sliding over Mi-

374

chael's body now, across his bony ribs, caressing the soft fleshiness of his hips. The boy responded to the touch, rubbing himself against him, and now his body was moving upward and Pelham could perceive his white flesh above him. It all seemed surreal to him now. He tried to focus his eyes, but the room was spinning. He felt as if he were on a ride in an amusement park, spinning out of control. And now he felt a shape move against his lips, narrow and taut. His lips parted and he tasted a drop of salty moisture on his tongue, but the shape was pressing into his mouth and his lips parted further to receive it. Pelham felt a momentary panic as this choking object moved into him, but then his lips and tongue began to react to the sensuality of its warmth and the shape of its crests and ridges. "Please," he heard the boy say. "Please." And he received still more of it, relishing its salty, animal taste, his hands reaching now and grasping the soft buttocks that pressed against his chest. And then a veil of darkness pressed down on him and he felt a pervasive numbness and it became dark and cold.

"What are you doing, David?"

She had awakened from a dreamless sleep, feeling him between her legs, his tongue wet against her, and, in that groggy disoriented instant of first awakening, she had imagined she was in bed with Michael, and had responded, letting the soft touching sensation excite her. She had pressed eagerly against the touch of his tongue, letting the waves of sensation grow more and more intense, the need more urgent, before she was fully awake and realized it was not Michael, but David.

"Just relax," his voice said out of the dark. His head started to lower again and she grabbed his face.

"David, please, I'm too tired for this,"

"Come on, Rob, it's all right. Just lie back . . ."

"I want to get some sleep. Please, David, don't." She squirmed away from him.

David sat up again. She realized his feelings were hurt, but she couldn't help it. She did not want him. She lay silent until he got off the bed and stood in the dark. She could smell the vodka on his breath, the alcoholic scent making her stomach turn. He turned and went into the bathroom. She saw the light go on under the door.

"You've got to get away from here," she said aloud to herself.

Still groggy from her sleep, she swung out of the bed and went to the closet. She pulled on her white duck trousers and reached for a sweat-shirt, slipping it over her head quickly. She swore under her breath when the shoestring broke on her tennis shoes. She heard the water turn off in the bathroom with a sudden chatter of pipes. Reaching for her purse, she glanced over her shoulder. The door was still closed. She wanted to be out of here by the time he came from the bathroom.

CHAPTER THIRTY-FIVE

Miami, April 11, 1961

Pelham woke with a start. A shaft of sunlight was coming through a slit in the curtain. He felt hot and clammy. As he lifted his head he felt the ache, as if a hammer had struck him behind his ear. He was aware of a foul taste in his mouth. He forced himself to his feet and lurched toward the bathroom, his head throbbing. He tossed cold water on himself, then straightened out and stared into the mirror. His face looked yellowish, with dark lines under his eyes. He felt a sudden clamp of pain in his stomach and an onrush of nausea. He told himself he was not going to be sick and he bent over the sink, and, again, immersed his face in cold water. When he straightened up, he felt better and he went over to the toilet and urinated.

He tried to reconstruct the events of the previous night, but they seemed scrambled and disjointed. He remembered drinking. He remembered being helped into his car, but he couldn't remember driving.

And then he thought of Michael. He hurried back into his bedroom and saw him then, or, rather, parts of him. He saw a clump of dark hair protruding above the sheet. He saw an ankle and a foot sticking out from below.

And then he felt rage. It was like a sudden surge from some alien force over which he could exercise no control. He felt his brain contort under its coercive drive.

Pelham grabbed the boy's ankle and yanked it with all his strength. His body came shooting off the bed as if propelled by a cannon. The naked form lay crumpled on the floor, curling up in self-protection. Pelham's foot lashed out and embedded itself on the boy's upper leg, leaving an ugly red welt. The boy cried out. Pelham reached down and took hold of his hair, pulling him to his feet.

Michael stood cowering before him now, still groggy from sleep, his eyes frightened like a deer caught in the sudden glare of headlights on a dark road.

"What the hell are you doing here?" Pelham was screaming.

"You wanted me . . ." Michael started to reply, but his words were choked off by a quick blow from Pelham's fist, which glanced off his cheekbone.

"I said what are you doing here?" the voice repeated. Then Pelham lashed out again, this time catching him on the lips. Michael keeled over backward, his head thumping against the dresser, and he landed in a heap on the floor. Blood spurted from his lip and he rubbed his head groggily.

Pelham stood over him now, screaming at him. "You miserable little bastard! What are you trying to do to me, eh? Are you trying to destroy me?" And Pelham kicked him again, his foot this time landing with a heavy thud on the boy's scrotum. Michael coiled up in agony on the floor. "Maybe you're even one of them? Trying to get something on me, right?"

And Pelham was upon him again, dragging him to his feet. The boy backed away, his hands clamped protectively over his genitals as Pelham lashed at him with his fists, striking him with blow after blow. Pelham's hair was askew and his gray eyes shone with hate and rage. Michael was crying, trying to run, but Pelham wrestled him to the floor, beating on his head with his fists.

Suddenly the boy lay still. Pelham stared at him and rose slowly to his feet, his chest heaving. Then he turned and ran into the bathroom. He vomited, then splashed water on his face, then vomited again. His chest was still heaving from the exertion. He had to get a grip on himself, Pelham thought. He had to get himself under control. His knuckles ached from the force of the blows.

The boy lay in a pile on the floor. There were scarlet bruises over his body. He looked as if he'd been hit by a train.

Pelham felt a twinge of panic. What if the kid was dead? He took his hands and felt his pulse. It was OK. He rubbed a washcloth gently over Michael's face now, sopping up the blood dripping from his eye and lip. The boy moaned softly. His eyes flickered open.

Pelham suddenly felt totally in control of himself again, even detached from the situation. It was almost as if he had just arrived on the scene and could take stock in a cool, calculating manner. An indiscretion had been committed. The boy must be patched up and dispensed with as quickly as possible. What had happened was totally comprehensible; things like this occurred from time to time under stress of wartime conditions. They had to be dealt with quickly and rationally.

Pelham helped Michael hobble to the bathroom. The bruised, bewildered boy sat on the toilet while Pelham cleaned his wounds and applied medication.

"Do you have any broken bones?"

Michael looked at him in total disbelief. The man who moments before had beaten him into unconsciousness was now talking to him in the detached, aloof tone of a doctor.

"No," Michael said in a small voice, still choked with panic.

"You must get dressed now. I will drive you to your apartment. If you require a doctor, I will call one for you."

Michael started to get up, but slumped to the floor. Pelham dragged him into the bedroom and gathered his clothes in front of him.

"Now get dressed," he said sharply.

"My balls hurt so bad," Michael whimpered as he cringed on the floor. "What the hell did you do to me, you son of a bitch?"

"Shut up and get dressed."

Michael slowly, painfully began to pull on his clothes. "You didn't need to belt me around. And kick me, for Christ's sake. Only a maniac starts kicking someone, especially—"

"If anyone asks, you got into a fight in a bar. Is that clear?"

"Son of a bitch," Michael mumbled as he continued dressing.

They did not exchange any further words. When Pelham pulled up in front of the boy's house, Michael simply opened the door, got out and started limping toward his front door. He did not look back.

CHAPTER THIRTY-SIX

MIAMI, APRIL 11, 1961

All that day Robin tried desperately to quell her feelings of anguish about the previous night. She went to her morning classes, wearing a fresh new print dress she'd bought secretly at Burdine's department store the week before, tormenting herself with what she knew to be an impossible dilemma. She had been incapable of making love with her husband. She was in love—yes, in love!—with Michael Danielson, a boy ten years younger than herself. Impossible! How could such a thing happen?

She had further compounded her dilemma by running to her lover. It shocked her when she reflected on it. She had gone down to the car and started driving, thinking perhaps she would get a motel room for the night and go back in the morning after David went to work. When she came out of her thoughts, she found herself on Michael's street. She automatically turned into his drive, went up the garage stairs and knocked on the door. No answer. The door was locked. Walking back to the car, she considered going home. But then the memory of her revulsion at waking to find David making love to her strengthened her resolve.

She had spent the night in a cheap motel on Tigertail. When she got back to the house in the morning, she dressed quickly, picked up her books, and drove to school.

During the psychology lecture she sat in a stupor, realizing that her life had stumbled into a critical moment. A decision had to be made, but she couldn't make it.

There was no future with Michael, really. How could there be? But it was so flattering, so good for her self-esteem, to know that this incredible young man loved her; she couldn't let go.

"Look," he'd said to her once, "I don't feel all that wonderful about fooling around with someone else's wife, you understand? If he finds out and gets sore—if he wants to fight or something—I'll just get out of the way, out of your life, OK? Who needs that kind of destructive thing anyway?"

The instant he said it, she'd felt an urgent need to maintain her hold on him. She couldn't let go. Last night with David had been too much. What she had done to him was wrong. It couldn't go on this way. It just couldn't. She felt too confused. Too suspended. The anxiety of it all was ruining her.

When she went out to the quad in the bright sun, seeing students hurrying here and there across the compound between the modernistic buildings, she felt eager with anticipation. Michael would be there.

She sat down in their secret place. She knew that when she saw him all her doubts would go away—and for those few moments she would feel complete. She would tell him about what had happened last night with David. She had to do that. She would ask his advice and they would talk it through to some logical solution. She was confident he would help her. Looking across the compound, she scanned all the faces and shapes of the people she could see, trying to detect Michael's slender dark-haired figure. He wasn't in sight. He must have been delayed getting out of class, she thought. He'll be along.

An hour later she realized he wasn't coming. She felt sharply disappointed, then hurt. Slowly she roused herself and went off toward her class, glancing right and left at the crowd, still hoping he might appear.

That morning at ten-thirty, Pelham was in a budget meeting with five aides when his secretary brought in a note. It said: "A Michael is holding. Says it's urgent. Says he's an old friend."

Pelham looked quickly around his crowded office. It would look peculiar to ask everyone to adjourn while he took the call.

"Get his number. Tell him I'll call him back in a minute," he whispered.

A short while later Pelham excused himself from the meeting and hurried down the hall into an empty office. He dialed the number his secretary had given him. He heard Michael's voice on the other end of the line.

"What is it you want?" Pelham said.

"You busted me up pretty good," Michael said. "I have a split lip, lacerations all over my body. And a cracked rib."

"Mail the doctor's bill to my home."

"It's caused me a great deal of embarrassment with my friends. And I missed some classes. I'm hurting pretty bad."

"Sorry to hear that."

There was a pause on the other end of the line. "That was a completely unprovoked attack," Michael said. "A couple of friends of mine saw how beat up I was and said I should press charges."

"I wouldn't listen to the advice of your friends, Michael."

"Well, I don't know. I have a pretty good case."

"Listen, young man," said Pelham, his voice edged with a threat. "Let me give you some advice. You have no idea what you're dealing with."

"What are you trying to say?"

"I think you know what I mean."

"Is that a threat? Are you threatening me?"

"I don't threaten people, Michael. But I detect a certain tone of fear in your voice right now. One is always wise to heed one's instincts."

"I'm not afraid of you, Mr. Pelham."

"You have no reason to be afraid of me, personally. None whatsoever."

"You mean you'll get somebody else to . . ."

"Michael, you have a wonderfully agile mind. Use it. Now, what is it you want from me? What is it you were trying to say before I interrupted?"

Another pause. "Just that I could press charges. That's what anyone

380

else would do in my place. It's just that we were once friends, you know?"

"I repeat, what is it you're trying to say? Are you asking me for money?"

"Yes, I guess that's what I mean. I think it would only be fair. I mean, you've got a lot of money, and I have nothing."

"How much do you want, Michael?" Pelham's voice was ice cold.

"You're not even sorry for what you did, are you?"

"I don't care to discuss it. How much do you want?"

"I mean, there was nothing I did to provoke that! Not to kick me around like that. Even kick me in the balls, Christ! If you're that up-tight—"

"I don't know what you're talking about."

"You should really see a shrink. You can't even stand it if another human being touches you, can you?"

"If it's money you are looking for, come by my house at seven o'clock tonight. Understand? You will get your money."

"At seven o'clock?"

"That's right."

"You won't try to beat me up some more? I'm hurt pretty bad already."

"I promise you I will not lay a hand on you."

"You won't. But how about somebody else? You were making that pretty clear a moment ago."

"What I was trying to impress upon you, Michael, was this: I'm willing to pay you for your medical expenses and whatever embarrassment you've suffered. Understand? But only this once. No more. I don't want to hear from you again. Clear? It might be advisable for you to explore other areas of the country. Start a new life elsewhere, so to speak. Do I make myself clear, young man?"

"I don't know. What if I want to stay in Miami?"

"That's up to you, Michael."

There was a long pause. Then Michael's voice said, "If I come to your place tonight, nothing will happen to me, right?"

"Seven o'clock."

"All right. You promise I won't get hurt?"

"Seven o'clock." Pelham hung up the phone and checked his watch. There was a lot that he had to do.

Michael checked his watch. It was seven on the nose. He might as well get it over with. He got out of the car and walked slowly up the front walk. As he approached the front door he felt his stomach going queasy on him. Oh, sweet Jesus, please don't let him beat me up again. Don't let him kill me.

He rang the bell. There was no answer. He waited, then rang again. He peeked in a side window, but the curtain obscured the view.

He waited at the front door for a couple of minutes before he decided to ring one more time. When there was no response, he felt furious with himself for having been fooled into coming out. It was degrading enough begging for money, but not even to have the courtesy to answer the door! That miserable son of a bitch! He kicked the door as hard as he could. To his surprise, the door opened.

That's very strange, he thought. A man like Pelham wasn't the sort who would leave his door unlocked. He remembered seeing at least one dead-bolt on the door, perhaps two. Something was very strange.

He pushed the door all the way open and called Pelham's name. There was no answer. Perhaps the crazy bastard had been murdered, he thought. The idea gave him a brief feeling of elation. Or maybe he committed suicide! Men with sex hangups are prone to suicide. He walked cautiously into the front hallway when a thought suddenly hit him. Maybe he was being set up! If Pelham was found with his throat cut or his wrists slashed and his, Michael's, fingerprints were all over the place, it would look very bad for him. What story could he possibly give the police? No one was aware they had been friendly. Maybe the bartender at the Hamlet would remember serving them, but he was so dense it was doubtful that he ever noticed anything.

He was treading cautiously into the house, peering nervously, expecting to find a body strewn across the floor, blood everywhere. He imagined how sickening Pelham would look, his dead eyes staring at him, blood and tissue oozing from the gashes.

It was too much. He was just about to turn and run when something strange caught his eye. The sofa that sat at the end of the living room had disappeared. There was nothing in its place. He took several steps forward. The whole living room was empty, stripped bare!

He ran into the bedroom. That was empty, too! Not so much as a lamp—absolutely bare. It was incredible!

He walked slowly back into the living room. He was in a daze. It was as if Pelham had never existed at all. The whole thing was a figment of his imagination! Except how about his busted rib and his torn eye and his aching balls? They weren't a figment of his imagination.

It was then that he noticed it. A small white envelope sat on the beige wall-to-wall carpet right in the middle of the living room. It was the only object left in the house. He walked toward the envelope, approaching it cautiously as if it were a bomb. Bending over to examine it, he noticed that something was typed on the envelope. It was a name. It was his name!

He picked it up quickly and tore it open. Inside the envelope was a piece of typewriter paper, but there were other papers wadded inside that. As he opened the folded paper, a wad of bills fell to the floor. He bent to retrieve them, feeling a charge of excitement. The bills were hundreds! He counted twenty of them. Two thousand dollars! Oh, Christ, he thought, that's a helluva lot of money!

He remembered the piece of paper. A single sentence was typed on the page. It said: "Buy a motorcycle if you wish. Best." There was no signature.

He turned and ran outside. He ran so fast he almost tripped over the front doorstep, struggling to keep his balance. He ran down the front path, forgetting his aches and pains, and jumped into his Renault. He shot a quick look at the house as he pulled away. He had left the front door swinging open. Screw the front door, he thought as he gunned the car as fast as it could go. Screw the door, screw Pelham, screw the old Renault. He would go out and buy himself a new motorcycle.

*

In the gathering twilight, David sat on the dock and let his feet rest on the gunwale of the skiff. He felt the anger easing out of him. It had been the right idea to get out of the house. He lowered his head into his hands and ran his fingers through his hair, which was still damp with sweat. Jesus, he thought. Jesus.

It was humiliating, all of it. He heard a sound and looked back at the house. The light was still on in the bedroom upstairs. He could see it through the screen. Then he heard the car. The headlights appeared, suddenly silhouetting the branches of the trees, blazing brilliantly as the car came to the foot of the drive. It was her Chevrolet. It turned onto South Bayshore Drive, heading north toward town, and he heard the engine rev up as she shifted gears. He watched it go out of sight down the street.

David felt everything go out of him.

He had come home from the lab early, anxious to talk things out, and felt relieved to find her car parked in its usual spot. She had run out of the house the night before and been gone all night. Why? David asked himself. What the hell did I do? The time had come when they had to be honest with each other, get all their problems out in the open and then figure out what was to be done. It could be worked out. But where has she been all night? he asked himself. That was what made him hurt inside.

He had found her upstairs, on the screen porch, curled up on the couch, a blanket pulled up around her neck. Her eyes were open and she stared blankly into the night.

He'd kissed her cheek and said hello, gently. She did not move or acknowledge his presence, but continued staring.

"May I ask where you were last night?"

She did not reply, nor even stir.

David sat down on the bed and put his hand on her shoulder. "Robin, what's wrong? What did I do?"

"Nothing," she said quietly.

"I must have done something wrong. You just don't get out of bed and run off for no reason at all! Was it because I tried to make love with you? Was it that horrible for you?"

Robin did not reply.

"Jesus, Rob, you make me feel like . . . dirt!"

"How do you think you make me feel?"

"I don't know. You tell me." She did not answer. David felt his temper flaring. "God damn it, Robin, talk to me!"

He grabbed her shoulder and tried to turn her to face him. She resisted, avoiding his eyes.

"Don't hurt me, David," she said, her body taut.

"I'm not going to hurt you, I want to talk to you! I want to find out what's wrong! Where did you go? Rob? Answer me, please?"

"I haven't anything to say." She pulled the blanket tighter about her throat. "Please leave me alone, David."

"I expect an answer, Robin."

Robin opened her eyes and looked up at him. "Go away," she said sullenly and turned her head into the pillow, closing her eyes again.

He grabbed the blanket and jerked it off her. Robin sat up, startled, tugging the hem of her white nightgown over her thighs, staring at him fiercely.

"Why don't you hit me? That'll make you feel better, won't it?"

"I don't want to hit you. I want you to tell me what you did last night!"

"What good would it do?"

He struggled to control the intensity of his anger. He modulated his voice, trying to sound conciliatory. "OK. Can we start over?"

Without answering, Robin flopped back against the pillow and turned over on her side.

"Robin?"

384

No answer.

"Answer me!"

"Will you please stop? I want to get some sleep."

Anger hit him again like an electric shock. Blindly he grabbed the shoulder strap of her nightgown. Turning her body, he ripped it. She glared up at him, her face flushed, her green eyes flashing with outrage as she slapped at his head with her hands. In a fury, David felt the blows against his cheeks and ears, and he grabbed her wrists and held them, his face a few inches from hers. They glared at each other. She tried to squirm out from under him, her two pointed breasts jiggling with the effort, her teeth gritted. She couldn't move. She relaxed suddenly, her whole body limp.

"All right . . . all right," she whispered hoarsely, her breath coming between her teeth. "All right, I said! You can let me go now, David . . ." He stared into her eyes, into her hatred and anger. "I know you're strong. Now let . . . me . . . go!" She burst into movement, twisting and turning her body, trying to kick at him, trying to drive a knee into his groin. David shifted his body and held her, struggling, under him. "You bastard! You bastard!"

Again she surrendered, her body going limp, her bare breasts heaving with the effort to get her breath. She avoided his stare, turning her head aside, her hair tangled on the pillow, copper strands falling over her forehead. After a moment, she looked at him out of the corner of her eye. "Are you going to hold me here all night?"

On impulse, David released her and sat back. The right side of his face stung, and he touched his cheek, feeling the raw spot where she had scratched him. She lay before him, naked to the waist, her pink nipples erect in her emotion, heaving, staring at him with glittering eyes.

"I'm sorry," he said quietly. He got off the bed and went into the bathroom without looking back at her. In the mirror, when he turned on the light, he saw the two-inch-long red scrape on his cheek. He washed his face in the basin, splashing the cold water around his neck and over his hair. He looked again at his pale, dripping face. He felt nauseated.

When he came back into the bedroom she was dressed and putting on her sneakers. Sitting on the end of the bed, her attention on the shoe-lace, she did not look up at him.

"Where are you going?"

She gave him a sullen look, finished the knot and stood up. "Out."

"Where?"

"What business is that of yours?"

"I'm your husband, remember?"

"My mistake," she said and started to go past him. He grabbed her arm.

"Robin, you just can't go wandering out into the night!"

"Why can't I? Don't tell me you're going to stop me? Crawl back into your shell, David. It's where you belong. Don't try to pretend you're a big macho bastard. You aren't. You're a snail! Crawl inside that shell and leave me alone!"

She tried to pull free. He held her. She looked at him, furious again, and slapped his face, stinging sharply. "Let me go! Let me go!" She hit him again and again, sharp, fierce blows that made his eyes water.

"I said let go!"

He felt the whack of her hand jarring against the side of his head. In a blind rage, he reacted. His right hand flashed, backhanding her across the jaw. He felt the blow hit and saw her stiffen and flop back onto the bed, her feet flying into the air.

He stood over her, looking down into her pale face, panting for breath, his shirt torn where she had grabbed him. He saw her whole body trembling, her neck arched. Then she turned on her side and began to sob.

Now, seated at the edge of the dock, with both feet resting on the gunwale of the skiff, he felt sick with shame. He shouldn't have hit her. He had never done anything like that before. Ever. The awful slap of his hand against her jaw resounded in his ears. He shook his head, as if to clear it from his mind, and stared down at the water.

★

It was almost midnight when Robin arrived at Michael's garage apartment. She had driven aimlessly for a while, her mind whirling with conflicting emotions. It occurred to her to sleep at her friend Eleanor's, but Eleanor, who was also in the doctoral program in psychology, would want to talk about her problems. Robin didn't feel like a long heart-to-heart chat tonight. She considered the possibility of simply checking back into the motel where she had stayed the night before.

But she knew what it was she wanted. She wanted to go to Michael, to crawl into his bed. If only he'd be home this time!

Robin was at the foot of Michael's stairs before she noticed that his car was gone, and her heart sank. Maybe he was out on a date? Was Michael seeing someone else? Perhaps he had fallen in love. That would be the end of a perfect evening—finding Michael in bed with someone else!

There was no turning back now. Robin climbed the stairs and peered into the apartment. It was dark. She listened for sounds of lovemaking.

But there was only the distant siren of a police car. She knocked softly. Michael never locked the door when he was home. She turned the knob and it opened. Relieved, she walked in.

She stood just inside the door until her eyes became acclimated to the darkness. Then she walked softly toward his bedroom and peeked in. She could make out Michael's sleeping form curled in a pile of tangled sheets. He was mumbling in his sleep, as if in the midst of a nightmare. She quickly slipped off her clothes and slid into bed with him.

She ran her hand through his hair. To her shock, Michael let out a quick, terror-stricken cry and sat bolt upright, as if an electric shock had penetrated his body. "Who is it? Who's there?" His voice sounded terrified.

"It's me. Robin. For God's sake, Michael."

Michael turned on the bedside lamp and stared at her, saucer-eyed. When he recognized her, the look of alarm on his face melted, but it was Robin now who was shaken.

"What's happened to you, Michael?" she said, as her eyes traced across his battered face down the heavy adhesive tape over his ribs. "What in God's name . . ." Michael's eyes averted hers. "What happened to you?"

The air around David was oppressive. The chair creaked as he shifted his right foot from his knee to the floor and leaned forward, a mosquito zinging his ear. He turned and swiped with his hand. Missed. As he lifted his eye from his empty palm he caught another lightning flare on the horizon. Big storm, he thought. It'll rain like hell here tomorrow.

Well? He looked at his empty glass. He saw the tattered green lime.

He got up and walked through the dark house to the kitchen and turned on the light. A brown cockroach the size of his thumb skittered up the wall over the sink. He smashed it with the heel of his right hand and watched it plop into the sink. It made him feel better. He opened the refrigerator door, took out the gin bottle and poured the drink. If he got drunk enough he would sleep.

He went to sit in the dark in front of the fireplace. The chair smelled of mildew. Everything in this fucking town smells like it's rotting, he thought. He switched on the lamp and squinted against the light. He saw the shadows of the moths and the mosquitoes on the ceiling. Where the hell had she gone? God damn it! He looked around the room. There were the books on the shelves. He had tried reading. It wasn't any good. He couldn't keep his mind on it.

Outside he heard the wind freshen, a rustling of leaves, coolness on the side of his face. He sipped his drink and looked into the living room. Beyond the lamp, he saw the desk.

Work, he thought, that's it. Get your mind to work on something. Forget it. Forget she even exists. Concentrate on something. Don't worry about her.

He went into the living room and sat down at the desk and reached over to turn on the lamp.

"Are you ready?"

"Mmmm-huh!"

Robin felt him move beside her, felt his hand on her arm, and she opened her legs and felt his warm skin as he put one knee across her right leg and then the other and she opened her eyes to see his silhouette above her, the slender shoulders, the shaggy hair, the thin trunk of his body, poised before her. She was extremely excited. She wanted him. She felt his fingers touching, penetrating, withdrawing, knowing herself how ready she was, aching for him. She felt the bed shift as he moved, slowly, ever so slowly. Then she felt the firm knob of his penis part her vulva, felt it slide, just the tip, into her. He knelt between her wide-open thighs, poised, holding the tip of his penis just inside her, waiting, waiting, waiting.

Her books and papers were scattered everywhere, covering the top of the desk. He carefully stacked her books and then straightened the papers into a neat pile and set them to one side, pleased with himself that he was being so practical. He glanced at the notes she had written in ink on the top sheet. ". . . at puberty a normal boy has already acquired a conscious knowledge of the vagina, but what he fears in women is something uncanny, unfamiliar, and mysterious. . . ."

"You think so, do you?" he said aloud and chuckled to himself. He felt giddy. He reached down and opened the drawer where he kept his notes and the thesis manuscript. Lifting it out, he set it on the place he had cleared on the desk. Three hundred and twenty-six pages, he said to himself. It makes an impressive stack of paper—all his knowledge, all his effort in research and writing could be reduced to that two-inch stack of typewritten sheets. Not so impressive, he thought.

He turned the manuscript in his hands and took off the last page he had written. It passed through his mind that he had written those words when Robin was sitting across the room reading. He glanced at the chair by the fireplace and then back at the sheet in his hand. He read his last sentence, which was unfinished: ". . . the major nerves branch repeatedly after leaving the central nervous system to distribute their numerous nerve fibers . . ."

It was stifling hot, like a Turkish bath. Then a cool breath of air came from the open window beside the desk and he heard the rain. It started with a pattering on the leaves and then it came with a rush of wind in the trees that grew louder and louder and then the air felt cool and pleasant. There was a crack overhead like the trunk of a tree splitting and then the rumbling boom of thunder that trembled the floor under his feet; then the fresh sound of heavy rain. He looked out the window and saw it streaking brightly in the light that went out through the screen. Lightning made an acetylene-blue flash in the trees so that he saw the glistening wet leaves and the tree trunks light up for an instant.

He took a sheet of paper and threaded it into the typewriter roller, clicking it into place. It was an old Royal typewriter they had bought when they were first married, and they had made a joke about it being older than both of them. Yet it worked well. Using his two fingers he typed out: "32& . . ." and crossed it out and retyped "@37 . . ." and crossed it out. Shit. He always had trouble hitting the right keys when he'd been drinking. He tried again and got it right and then turned the page up and began to write: "There are no synapses in the course of most of the . . ." The type faded to blank impressions on the page. Damn! The ribbon.

He took a sip of gin and opened the left-hand top drawer in the desk where she kept the new ribbons. It was full of papers and envelopes, old letters and paperback textbooks. He lifted them out. No ribbon. As he was putting the stack back in the drawer, he noticed the manila envelope marked "Michael." He stared at it a moment. Michael?

"Michael, God, Michael!"

She felt his tongue touching her spine, wet and flicking as it moved down her back. He paused. She waited, every nerve taut with anticipation. Oh, God!

Terrific! His tongue touched and she drew in her breath. It felt so good. He moved lower, licking gently, like the touch of a butterfly, and then she felt the moist warmth flickering on her anus. She drew in her breath. Again. "Please, please . . ." Again and then the steady, hard, rhythmic touch as she felt him spread the cheeks of her buttocks open wide; then the coolness, the wet cooling as he stopped. "Please, don't stop . . . God, don't stop . . . oh, Michael. Michael!"

Feeling a twinge of guilt, as though he'd looked into a window and seen something shameful, David opened the envelope. The first sheet was written in black ink. He read:

389

Poem to Robin, Miami, Winter, 1961

Under the parabola of a star
a child turning into a man,
I looked into her eyes too long.
The star fell in my hand, it sang
in the closed fist: Robin, behold
a gift designed to kill.
Now in my dial of glass appears
the man who is going to die.
He smiles, and moves about in ways
his Robin knows, habits of his.
Her hands touch his face: I cry
Now. Robin, like a familiar, hears.

The ache in his stomach growing, filling his chest with sharp pain,
David put down the sheet and took another and read:

Robin, my darling:
Nothing I cared in the lamb white days, that
she would take me
Up the seagull thronged sky by the shadow of
her hand
In the moon that is always rising
Nor that riding to sleep
I should hear her sigh
And wake to find her forever fled from my childless
bed
Oh, as I was easy in the mercy
of her thighs
She held me warm as moist fire, green
and dying
And I sang in her arms like the sea.
                              Michael, January 21, 1961

He flipped through the other sheets. There were ten of them. All
poems, written in pencil and pen in the strange hand. He set them down
under the lamp's glare and stared at them. His hands trembled as he
lifted the second poem again and looked at the date and reread the
lines.

She felt him inside her, felt herself close down on him, holding him.
And then he began to move, slowly, sliding from her, coming back,
slowly, easing in and out. She felt as though nothing else in the world
existed at that moment. Nothing. She felt the flexing warmth of his

thigh muscles and the grasp of his hands on her arms. She reached out and slid her fingers over the soft, warm skin of his hips and felt the flesh of his buttocks, pulling him toward her. But he would not yield, would not change the slow, steady, easing in and out that was driving her crazy. "Harder," she said between clenched teeth, her eyes tightly closed. "Michael . . . for God's sake, pound me, I love it! I love it when you pound me!"

She felt his muscles move beneath her fingers and the weight of him lifting, his penis withdrawing, just the knob of the tip holding, then penetrating, barely an inch, withdrawing, then penetrating again. "Oh, Michael, please don't tease me . . . I'm going to come, baby, please, please, please . . ."

For a long time David sat with a sinking heart, staring out at the rain falling heavily in the light. The drops were bright as they slanted into the window. Leaves appeared, dripping shiny, and swaying from his view with the wind. Little specks of rain clung to the wire mesh of the screen, reflecting the lamplight. He reached over and turned it out. The sound of the wind and the rain seemed a far way off from him. He was in a trance, reliving the dreadful moment when he read the first words, words that were beyond his ability to conjure or write. Questions rushed, one upon another, without answers. He did not want to believe it. What an idiot he'd been. All the time he struggled to talk to her, make love to her, she was thinking of *his* poems, thinking of *him*. He had never even had a chance.

Slowly he lifted another of the poems and read:

> Take of me what is now not my own,
> my love, my beauty, and my poem—
> the pain is mine and mine alone.

Michael? Michael who? Who the fuck is Michael? David ran his fingers through his hair and turned aside, numbed by the thought.

"Michael?" he said aloud.

He looked again at the poems. Something nagged at his memory. He looked up at the bookshelf, his eyes searching for *The Oxford Book of English Verse*. It was there somewhere. The last one, hadn't he read that before? It all sounded vaguely familiar to him. Then he spotted the white jacket. He stood and reached for it.

She grasped his shoulders in her arms and held his sweating flesh tightly. As he pressed his lips against hers, she felt the cylindrical thickness slide slowly away, leaving her suddenly empty—she felt him poise above her in the dark.

"Oh, God, Michael. Don't toy with me. Not again."

"But I like to toy with you." His voice sounded strangely distant.

"Not now."

She felt his hand press hard on her thigh, tugging her, rolling her over on her stomach. She felt his hands under her pelvis, hoisting her into the air.

She resisted him. "I said no, Michael."

She felt his penis touching her again, rubbing softly against her. It came as a sudden shock of pain. She gasped, tried to pull away. But he clasped her firmly and drove deeper. It felt as if he were splitting her in two. She let out a little scream. "Stop, please, Michael." But he didn't stop, and she realized now what the pain was, that he was penetrating her where no one had penetrated before. She felt a rush of animalistic lust flash through her as the pain intensified, that solid yet pliable male protuberance forcing her anus wider, stretching it like a fist, filling her with its girth and heat. It was an exciting new sensation for her, a filthy violation. She tried to relax her muscles to move with him. God, what had happened to her? How could she do this? Oh, good! Then she felt his fingers slide across her thighs and penetrate her and she pressed against that stiff fleshy wand inside her, harder and harder. His breath panted harshly in her ear, growing hoarse and shrill. And it began to sting in an excruciating blend of pain and ecstacy, beyond self-control. She whimpered softly, losing herself, losing all her pride and modesty, abandoning it in the lusting for climax that had begun to grip her nerves. "Oh, stop," she hissed, between her clenched teeth. "Please, stop . . ."

CHAPTER THIRTY-SEVEN

MIAMI, APRIL 11, 1961

A few heads turned as an azure-blue Bentley drove up in front of Joe's. Amato stepped out, then held the door for Valerie Cooper. He exchanged a few words with Al Baker, his burly driver, and then they walked into the restaurant.

As they opened the door, Valerie recoiled at the boisterous confusion that met them. Dishes clanked, chairs scraped, voices blared in a pizzicato of jumbled noise; all assaulting their senses amid the wonderful mélange of cooking fish and hot bread. It was eight-fifteen and the entrance to the restaurant was clogged with people waiting for tables, wall to wall. The bar was tightly packed.

"How nice," Valerie said, glancing around. "A quiet little place to have an intimate dinner."

"Great for eating, bad for talk," Amato said.

Her eyes surveyed the room. It reminded her of a men's club: burnished wood, brass, broad tables, white tablecloths, bustling waiters in white jackets. Amato was pushing a path through the crowd toward the maître d', who was fending off solicitous diners. "Quite a mob scene, eh?"

"It makes Twenty-One look positively funereal. What kind of a crowd comes here?"

"Your usual mixture. Judges and crooks." He shoved past a garishly dressed couple, the woman draped in neon-green. "Also lots of tourists." Amato winked.

As they pushed their way, several men glanced admiringly at Valerie. Looking over her shoulder, she saw a short man with a thick belly reach out his hand to pinch her. But just as she was about to flinch, she saw his eyes appraise Amato. He withdrew his hand and turned away. It didn't phase her. Few things did. Long-limbed and leggy, Valerie was not beautiful in the actressy sense. Her mouth was a touch too wide, her forehead too tall. Brown-tinted glasses perched on her nose. But her jaunty confidence and impeccable sense of style lent her an aura of beauty; she knew it and wore it well. She was dressed tonight in a smart yellow-sashed tunic and brown slacks.

The maître d' spotted Amato and greeted him effusively. They were led to a nearby table, where a waiter immediately descended on them, soliciting their cocktail order. Several of those waiting in line for a table glared at Amato, but he didn't seem to notice.

"Do you know those people over there?" Valerie asked. "They're looking at us."

Amato looked in the direction she indicated. "Yeah, that's a little twit named Kern; used to be an FBI man," he said in his rough, growly voice. "His wife has a lot of money."

She saw her beside Kern, a large woman in a black dress, her dark hair pulled severely away from her broad matronly face. She towered two inches above him.

"I knew it."

"Knew what?"

"If I asked you about someone, you'd know who they were. You can do it in New York, in London, in Rome. You have either a photographic memory or a vivid imagination."

Amato gave her a crooked smile. They'd met in New York nine months earlier at a party thrown by a theatrical producer. He'd noticed her and thought she looked "like a class act," as he chose to put it. He was a little put off when he learned she worked as a reporter on the staff of *Look* magazine. Reporters had always made him nervous. What also made him uneasy was her Brearley-Vassar education. But if these things put him off, they also intrigued him. He was accustomed to women being intimidated by him. He relished the fact that he was a bit intimidated by her.

They hit it off from the start. She loved to travel and enjoyed the lofty and often eclectic social circles in which he moved. And he loved to watch her charm people, and challenge them. He needled her about her "fancy-ass education" and reportorial zeal. She needled him about the mystery with which he cloaked his work and about his rough manners. They discovered a mutual weakness for chocolate mousse and sidewalk cafés and race tracks. He found their lovemaking irresistible, her long legs entangled around him, her lips pressed to his, the way she moved with him, the intensity of her response. Valerie was an adventure, and Amato loved adventures.

Their cocktails had just been served when Valerie nudged him. "Here comes your friend, the FBI twit," she said.

Kern was quickly upon them, hand extended, his thin lips curled in a tentative smile. He wore a light tan suit and a black tie, his gray hair carefully combed around his shiny pate.

"Good to see you, Sal," Kern said.

Amato took his hand, but did not rise to greet him. Kern eyed Valerie, expecting an introduction, which Amato did not offer.

"I'm Valerie Cooper," she said and shook his hand.

"A pleasure to meet you." Kern's eyes fixed on her. "Don't I know the name?"

"She's a journalist."

"Perhaps I've seen your byline. Do you write about politics?"

"Yes, sometimes. I did a piece on—"

"I know, you did the one on Adlai Stevenson in *Look* this week, didn't you?"

Valerie brightened. "You're a careful reader, Mr. Kern." Out of the corner of her eye she saw Amato glaring at her for being so friendly.

394

Kern's eyes flicked toward Amato. "Several people have been asking about you lately, Sal."

"Really?"

"You're out of touch too much of the time. That's bad for business."

Amato peered at Kern's strangely vacant eyes. "Thanks for the advice," he said, sarcasm heavy in his voice. "I appreciate it."

"Why don't you give me a call one of these days? Perhaps I can throw some business your way."

Amato was stone-faced. "I'd be grateful, Kern. The only thing is, I don't know if my present clients would appreciate my taking on any of your people. You know how it is—everyone's wary of the criminal element."

"The criminal element?" Kern's eyebrows were raised. "I represent companies like United Fruit and ITT."

"That's what I mean," Amato said with a sardonic smile.

Kern smiled lamely, then nodded to Valerie. "You'll have to excuse us," he said. "Sal and I go back a long way. We enjoy kidding each other."

"Who's kidding?"

"Nice meeting you," Kern said to Valerie as he started backing away. "See you soon, Sal. I suppose you'll be going to Havana any day now, won't you?"

Amato's smile froze on his face. "I wasn't planning to."

Kern shrugged. "Oh, I see. Well, nice bumping into you." And he disappeared into the melee of waiting diners.

Valerie saw that Amato's face had hardened.

"Your FBI friend really gets to you, doesn't he?"

Amato took a stiff drink of vodka, and his face relaxed a bit. "Yeah, I suppose he does."

"I have an intuitive feeling there's an interesting background story here. Am I going to hear it?"

"You're going to play reporter tonight?"

Valerie put her hand on his muscular forearm. "I'm going to try."

"Kern thinks he got fired from the FBI because he procured a hooker for a top aide of J. Edgar Hoover who turned out to be a fag. Actually, they knew in Washington he was taking payoffs in Havana. They had the goods on him."

"He looks the type."

"When he lost his FBI job he was pretty shattered. Batista's people put him on retainer. It seems Batista was getting increasingly worried about someone named Castro. He was stockpiling a considerable quantity of weapons and ammunition in Mexico. Kern's assignment was to keep him from getting any more."

"I gather he didn't succeed."

"He did at first. Fidel was in pretty bad shape around that time. He was in exile in Mexico City, preparing to make a landing in Cuba. There was a police raid on a house where he stored all of his weapons. They got everything. Kern took credit for the raid."

"But Castro got new weapons? How?"

Amato's dark eyes stared at her. He did not reply.

Valerie nodded. "Ah, so that's how you and Fidel became acquainted."

"I didn't say anything."

"And then he returned to Cuba and went into the mountains? I've always heard people speculate how he got his hands on all those guns and explosives. Do you know him really well, Sal?"

"Well enough."

"I hate to mix my professional and personal lives, but do you think—"

"No."

"Now you're just being mean."

"How?"

"You didn't let me finish what I was going to say."

"You didn't have to. And I don't have to remind you of our old rule."

She smiled. "I know. Off the record. I would really like to interview him, Sal. You know, one of those long talk sessions, maybe four or five days. I could make a book out of it."

Amato said nothing.

"Please?"

"You want to hear the rest of the Kern story?"

"Yes. But will you think about it?"

"I'll think about it."

"I'm very good. You can tell him that. And I'm honest."

Amato just stared at her. She broke into a grin. "Off the record. And meanwhile, back with the adventures of Mr. Kern."

Amato drained his martini, and his face broke into a broad smile. "Because Castro ended up better armed than before, Kern got fired by Batista for fucking up," Amato said. "Isn't that a shame?"

"A terrible shame." Valerie laughed. "An absolutely horrible shame. No wonder he has such an abiding affection for you."

The maître d' appeared at the table again. "Everything all right, Mr. Amato?"

"Wilson, I'd like you to meet Valerie Cooper, a good friend of mine. This is her first visit."

Wilson beamed and handed her a menu, then withdrew it again. "I think we should give her the full treatment, don't you, Mr. Amato?"

Amato nodded. "The full treatment."

"Then we'll forget the menus."

"Right. By the way, Wilson, how long a wait you calling for a table now?"

"Forty-five minutes to an hour."

"Do me a favor. Drop somebody and put Kern right out there in the middle, see? Where those guys are clearing off that big table."

"He likes a table in the corner."

"Did I ask?"

"No, sir. Of course."

"Put him out there where we can all see him. Tell him it's compliments of Sal Amato. Bring me the check."

"Very well, sir."

After he had gone, Valerie turned to him and wagged her finger. "You're a bad man, Sal . . . bad."

"So what are you complaining about?"

"The boring conversation."

"Any other complaints?"

Valerie's eyes glinted mischievously. "Well, your ego's a little on the big side."

"I didn't think it was my big ego that scared you. I thought it was my big something else."

Valerie let out a hoot of laughter. "Your big something else doesn't scare me one bit. Is this going to be one of our crude nights?"

"Goddamn right."

Valerie laughed. Something by the bar caught her attention. It was the presence of a tall, powerfully built Cuban who had just entered and crossed to say something to Kern at the bar. She saw Kern's face light up. Valerie nudged Amato. "Look at your friend. He's actually animated. Must be good news."

Amato turned to look over at Kern and frowned.

"What's the matter, Sal?" she asked him.

"That guy. His name is Martín. He was a police sergeant under Batista. Bad *hombre*."

They watched the two of them leave the bar and push through the crowd at the entrance and go out the door. Valerie turned back to Amato and made a little shudder of her shoulders. "He looked creepy enough."

"He's plenty creepy," Amato said, and lifted his drink. "Let's drink against him."

"Against him?"

"Like you drink against catching a bad cold."

She smiled and touched her glass to his. "Against him," she said.

"Against all those bastards," said Amato.

CHAPTER THIRTY-EIGHT

MIAMI, APRIL 12, 1961

David fumbled for the ringing telephone. He knocked a specimen bottle off the desk. He heard it splat as it broke on the floor. Formaldehyde fumes wafted in the air.

"Hello?"

"David?"

The hollow echo on the line told him it was long distance. The voice exploded in David's head. "Cam! Where the hell are you?"

"I'm in the Keys. I came in by boat tonight. Now listen to me, *chico.* I'm at the Sugarloaf Key. You know it?"

"Sure."

"I've got trouble. I want you to get down here as soon as you can. I'll tell you where to go. You got a pencil?"

David sat down in the chair. The smell of the formaldehyde was overpowering. He turned on the desk lamp and saw the shattered glass and the pool of liquid gleaming at his feet. He searched quickly for a pencil and found one in the drawer. "Got it," he said into the receiver.

"Listen, *chico,* you know the Esso station?"

"Yeah."

"Quarter-mile south, you come to a road on the east side of the highway. It's a dirt road. You'll be taking a left there. The name of the road is Cutter Creek, but there's no sign. You recognize it because of two big pines on either side . . ."

On the tin roof the rain sounded like the pattering of tiny footsteps. Pepita lay awake listening to it. She did not know what had awakened her. Perhaps it was a thunderclap. She sat up in the dark. After the long hours at sea, she still felt an undulating motion, as though she had been drugged. The air was humid and a chill went down her back as she slid out of the warm sleeping bag to sit up against the wall. She looked around in the dark. The interior of the old shack smelled of rancid oil, like an unused garage. She lifted her hand close to her face and could not make it out. The windows were shuttered. She heard the wind change the pattering rain to a staccato on the tin roof.

With her left hand she felt the sleeping bag next to her where Camilo slept. She had no idea how long they had been asleep. Her fingers touched the cloth. She could hear his steady breathing now. He was asleep. She knew now she had loved him from the first moment she saw him. She remembered her sister's wedding in the big church in Havana, how handsome Camilo had seemed that day, and how ashamed she had been at the thoughts the sight of him in his dark wedding clothes had inspired in her; yet she could not help loving him, her sister's husband. All through the ceremony, standing with the other bridesmaids in her pink gown and her crown of white flowers, watching the two of them at the altar, she could not resist imagining that it was she, Pepita, who knelt there beside him receiving the priest's blessing. At the wedding feast in the garden of her parents' home, he had danced with her, his movements quick and graceful as he led her across the floor, his blue eyes piercing, probing into her, making her a little afraid of him because she could not understand the meaning of his look.

Now in her mind she remembered standing beneath the palm trees beside the house, looking up at the light in the windows of their room on the second floor, hearing the band start playing a cha-cha-cha, the guests applauding and cheering, aching with envy, seeing the lights go out, trying to picture in her mind what was happening now up there in that room, as though it were happening to her.

She had envied her sister beyond all reason that night. The thought of her sister's whole future with a man like Camilo filled her with anguish, wishing it could be she.

But now, sitting in the dark in this strange place, touching him, she felt a lifting in her heart. The future with him was hers. There would be danger in Miami, but no less than in Havana. They would find a small house. She would make it their home. She would buy furniture and cooking utensils and linen—oh, the joy of making their bed, their very own bed, for the first time! She felt a bright thrill go through her. She had him. She had Camilo Carta for her very own. A warm feeling of love filled her breast and she turned her head in the dark, not seeing, but knowing he was there, feeling the power of him in the night.

"Camilo?" she whispered.

There was no response.

Just then, she heard footsteps outside on the porch. She was startled.

Then she remembered Sabino. That would be Sabino. He would be wanting to come in out of the rain. Poor Sabino. He had been seasick all the time crossing. She had tried to comfort him as he hung over the storm rail retching violently with nothing left in his stomach. Poor Sabino. He was such a baby. As tall and as strong-looking as Camilo, she thought, and still a little boy. Even when they came ashore, he continued to be sick. Camilo had given him all the Dramamine, the last of it. But he had sat on the dock looking pale and sick, his eyes showing how he hurt. How goes it, comrade? she had said to him. It is nothing, he had replied. Nothing serious. I am still sick from the sea. He had insisted on taking first watch. She heard the door click. They must have been asleep for four hours. Sabino was coming in.

The door opened and she smelled the fresh wind with the scent of rain in it and she saw a figure silhouetted in the shape of the door. In the dim light she could see the wet shiny gleam on his cap. He had a shotgun in his hand.

"Sabino?" she called softly.

BOOK V

CHAPTER THIRTY-NINE

David drove out of the rain south of Homestead just as it was getting light. Occasionally, he caught glimpses of the flat green expanses of the Everglades, the ponds of water bright as mirrors. Here and there, among the foliage, he saw a white heron. The big cumulus clouds were white and gray over the water, moving ponderously to the southeast. There was a steady wind that made it hard to keep the Volkswagen on the road.

He passed a fishing camp and saw three men standing on the dock beside a boat. They're late getting out, he thought. Maybe they were trying to decide whether to go out at all in this wind. There would be a big sea running out in the Stream with the storm. But the norther was passing and the fishing would probably be pretty good by tonight. One of the men, wearing a faded red cap, turned and watched him go by.

When the sun came up he crossed Jew Fish Creek and went into the

Keys. He drove through Key Largo, where the workingmen were getting out onto the road, and then in less than an hour he was on the Seven Mile Bridge, passing Bahía Honda. Ahead he could see the green trees of Big Pine Key. The traffic was thinning out now, and he drove past the Big Pine Inn, which was closed. There was a beer truck parked outside. He drove onto the bridge to Middle Torch Key, and soon he saw the Esso station ahead and knew he would find the road he wanted just beyond it. His weariness had given way to a numbness. He lit a cigaret. He wished there were someone to talk to. He flicked on the radio and twisted the dial past several stations. He listened briefly to the clatter of a news program, then turned it off. The din irritated him.

He would be seeing Camilo soon. It seemed too good to be true.

When Robin arose and looked out the window she saw it was raining. She peered up at the sky. It was slate gray. It looked the kind of rain that could last all day, she thought, and that possibility buoyed her spirits. She had always loved rainy days as a child in Boston. She had loved splashing through the streets, leaping among the puddles, then coming into a warm house, taking off her shoes and sitting by the fire. She had always liked Miami's weather, but the steady diet of one bright sunny day after another tended to become monotonous. She loved the sunshine, but why did it have to be damned inevitable?

She dressed quickly and put a kerchief over her hair and told Michael she was going for a walk. She would also stop at the grocery store and refurbish his supply of coffee, milk, sugar and a few other staples. Michael grunted and rolled over in bed.

Once outside, Robin lifted her face to receive the fine wind-blown rain. She closed her eyes and took several steps. The rain felt good on her face. She would take a good brisk walk. She would come back and make Michael a big breakfast. She would systematically avoid thinking of David or her studies or any of her other responsibilities. She had spent all of her life thinking about her damned responsibilities. She hated the word.

It was then she noticed the automobile. The coffee-colored Jaguar had been parked across the street from Michael's apartment when she first came outside—she vaguely remembered seeing it. Now it was slowly turning around to head in her direction. Robin glanced over her shoulder. The car seemed familiar. She had seen it before, but she could not recall where or when. Perhaps it belonged to a neighbor. She increased her pace. So did the car. She looked over her shoulder again, uneasy now. Could someone be following her? It was bizarre. She shuddered and walked still faster, again looking over her shoulder. Because of the

404

rain against the windshield she could not see who was driving the Jaguar; she could only make out a figure behind the wheel. Her eyes scanned the streets, the frame houses, the palm trees, lawns; no one in sight on a rainy morning. Typical! A little rain and everyone hides.

The Jaguar accelerated now and pulled up beside her.

She heard the voice then. "Robin."

It was a familiar voice, but, in her panic, Robin couldn't seem to connect it to a name or a face. She started to run, but the Jaguar kept apace.

"Robin, please stop," the voice said.

Robin peered through the open window on the passenger side and felt a sudden shock of recognition: It was Elizabeth at the wheel. She was calling to her. How could Elizabeth have known she was here? Did she know about Michael? Her first instinct was to run, but she realized this would be foolish. She stopped and reached over to open the door of the Jaguar and clambered in.

Elizabeth said nothing. The car moved smoothly down the street.

The two women drove for several blocks before either of them spoke. Robin took the kerchief from her head and dabbed the moisture from her face, struggling at the same time to control the panic that surged through her.

"Where are you taking me?" Robin asked.

Elizabeth did not answer.

"May I ask how you happened to be parked on that particular street on this particular morning?"

"Don't ask foolish questions, Robin."

"I don't think it's a foolish question. Forgive me, Elizabeth, but I'm just a naïve little girl from Boston. I'm not as accustomed to all these intrigues as you seem to be." Robin looked over at her. Elizabeth's face was calm and composed. She was smartly attired in a blue-and-gray patterned silk dress. She looked for all the world like a woman who might be driving to the country club for lunch—not someone who had just tracked down her missing daughter-in-law to the home of her lover.

"I might describe you in many ways, but one of them is not 'naïve,'" Elizabeth said, a sharpness in her tone.

"No, seriously—what did you do? Hire a private detective to find me?"

"Of course." She said it simply, unaffectedly—almost nonchalantly. As if that was what everyone would do under similar circumstances.

Robin shook her head. "I don't believe this is happening to me."

"Neither do I." Elizabeth braked and turned the corner. "Are you in love with this young man?"

"I don't want to discuss it."

"Fine. Then we can make this brief. My son means a great deal to me. I don't wish to see him hurt any more than he has already been. Do I make my point clear?"

Robin looked at her silently, her lips tight.

Elizabeth said, "If you want to go with another man, then do so. But have the decency to divorce David."

"It isn't that simple."

"I am sure it doesn't seem so. But it is. Think of it this way. You're either David's wife or you're not. I won't let you have any other choice."

"By that, I presume you mean you'll go to David . . ."

Elizabeth did not reply. She eased the car to a stop in front of the grocery store in the Grove. "Was this where you were going?"

Robin looked at her. "Yes." Opening the door, she got out into the rain. She looked at Elizabeth again. "If I go back to David, what will you do?"

"Forget that I have seen you this morning."

"Yes, of course, that's what you would do, isn't it. All right, Elizabeth, thank you for the ride." She shut the door.

Through the windshield, Elizabeth watched her walk into the store and go out of sight.

The shack looked like an old army barracks that someone had dismantled and then reassembled out on the peninsula. They had built a screen porch around the house, and the screen had rusted out in places and hung stiffly, swaying in the wind, with gaping holes.

The screen door was askew, its hinges creaking as the wind blew it. He saw the ruins of a shed down near the pier. The tin had partially blown off the roof, and one side had caved in. The open space of the clearing around the shack was sandy and there were three palms growing down by the pier where the sailboat was moored. The ground was littered with dead brown fronds and old coconuts, dried and turned gray in the sand.

David walked slowly up to the steps and looked into the screen porch. There was sand blown on the bare planks of the flooring. The door to the inside of the shack was closed.

"Camilo!" he shouted. "Hello! Camilo!"

The wind was swaying the masts of the boat as he turned and walked down the path toward the dock. The sand was packed hard and there were no footprints. Then he saw the ketch. It was an old boat. The hull was painted green and the cabin was gray. There were four fresh bullet holes in the cabin. The hatch was open and the body of a Negro was sprawled in it, holding it open.

David dropped down and stepped aboard. He saw an oil drum lashed

406

to the top of the cabin, with two bullet holes in it. The oil ran down the port side of the cabin and into the cockpit. Everything was soaked in it. The smell of diesel oil was overpowering. He turned and looked at the kinky black hair of the dead Negro. His face was gray and his eyes were partially open. Flies swarmed on his back where the bullets had ripped him along the spine. Whoever had shot him, David thought, got him from inside the cabin. He must have tried to run for it, or just turned his back as he was going out the hatch. He saw three splintered holes, the broken wood showing white in the hatch, and flecks of blood splashed on the gray paint and dried. The wind caught the hatch door and swung it against the body.

David moved closer to get a better look at the dead man's face. He knelt down on the deck until he could see it. The Negro's face was misshapen. He saw a fly crawl into the nostril. The face was the color of clay in the sunlight. His mouth was open and David saw a row of gold teeth.

It was not until he tried to stand up, catching a whiff of the dead smell, which had been overpowered by the diesel oil, and felt the wind blowing his hair, that he realized it was Paco, Camilo's driver from Havana. He continued to look at the dead face for a long moment, afraid to turn around.

When he stepped off the boat and stood on the concrete sea wall, David stared in a daze at the fishing shack with its rusted tin roof. The torn places in the screen stuck out like ragged fans, wavering stiffly as the wind blew. He could hear the faint creaking of the hinges on the broken door and then, abruptly, he heard it slam and he saw it open again in the wind and then slam. He kept expecting something to happen. But nothing did.

The wind was blowing against his back as he walked toward the shack. The screen door slammed again. He grabbed it with his hand. He stood holding it firmly for a moment, feeling the wind tug at it. Then he stepped inside.

The sand crunching under his shoes like granulated sugar, he walked to the double door and hesitated. The door panels were painted gray. The paint had blistered and peeled, and the plywood was wrinkled like skin that has been in the water too long. He looked down at the white porcelain doorknob. He took it in his hand and turned it. The door opened toward him. From inside came the smell of rancid oil.

He swung it open wide to let in as much light as possible. He saw a stovepipe hole in the wall across the long room. He could see it in the light from the open door. He leaned inside and felt along the edge of

407

the second door until he found the latch and pulled it. The door swung creaking on its hinges. The light widened.

He saw the shuttered windows, four of them, along the far wall, and the bare wood floors. The walls were painted a cream color and the place where the stove had been was discolored by grease. He looked to his right. The darkness in the corner obscured his view, but he could see something huddled there. When he saw it, he felt his heart constrict.

He did not cross directly to the corner, but went to the window and worked open the rusted latch on the shutter and pulled it off, letting in the sunlight. Then he turned to look.

The inflated face of the dead woman had a shiny look in the light. She wore khaki army fatigues. The khaki cloth was torn, and the remains of her left breast, with just the nipple hanging clear of the dried blood, showed pale white through the tattered cloth. Someone had used a sawed-off shotgun. Two blasts, one in the chest and the other in the belly. The bloated, plastic-looking entrails showed below her waist. She was lying on her side. He looked at the bloated face. Pepita!

The other body was crumpled in the corner. He saw a lot of dried blood splashed on the wall, and the torn patches where the buckshot had ripped splinters in the boards. David went toward it and stopped a few feet from Pepita, getting the smell now. It was that scent of raw flesh. He forced back the bile that tasted in his mouth. He had to make sure about the other one.

Leaning across Pepita, he grabbed the edge of the man's sleeve and pulled him over. The head flopped. Or what was left of the head. The face was gone. David saw the half-shell of the blasted skull. Only parts of the bearded lower jaw remained. There were pieces of skull and brains and teeth. He'd been shot full on.

He must have put his hand up when he saw the gunman, because half the palm and all the fingers of his right hand were gone, except for the thumb, which dangled by a tendon. David saw the length of his legs and the width of his shoulders.

David's stomach lurched and he pulled himself away and retched. After a moment, he lifted his head, the taste of vomit in his mouth, and wiped his lips. When he turned and looked back over his shoulder at the broken bodies, he realized in a stupor he had not been mistaken. Camilo. He started to cry.

Just then, he heard the distinct crunch of sand under a footstep. A shadow fell across the door. His heart beating, David whirled. There were two of them. They had the light behind them, so he could not make out their faces.

CHAPTER FORTY

"**M**aybe it's prophetic," Enrique Navarro said to Gustavo Carta as they came out of the hotel entrance and saw the sun making faint whisps of steam rise from the pavement. "We go inside, it's raining—we come out, sunshine!"

"Let's hope so, Enrique," said Carta.

"Listen," Navarro said. "We have differences. OK. But we have the same goals. I tell you alone, Gustavo, I have reservations about our friends from Washington, like you do. I am not in favor of Yankee imperialism. I am against Yankee economic domination of Cuba, believe me. I say nothing now, because I want to beat Fidel. You understand? When we have beaten him, then you will probably find many of our views similar. I speak to you frankly, Gustavo, and in strictest confidence."

"Of course," said Carta.

"We are Cubans," Navarro said.

"Yes, we are Cubans."

Navarro looked up at Carta fondly. "Let's not be enemies. Let us work together to destroy the Communists. After..." Navarro shrugged. "After, we will work out the politics, eh?"

"That's our purpose," said Carta guardedly. "As you say ..."

Twisting his face in a show of emotion, Navarro looked up at Carta. "When next we see each other, Gustavo, we shall be in Havana. God be with you."

Navarro embraced him and then got into the car that was waiting and drove off. Carta went to the Buick, nodded to Salazar, who held the door open, and got into the front seat.

During the ride home, Carta reflected on the meeting. Events had been moving swiftly for him these last few days. The meeting, which had been presided over by Dr. Miró Cardona, had produced a semblance of unity. Although Carta thought of the coalition as something of a shotgun marriage politically, it now existed. He would honor his word to Danforth. He wanted to avoid open warfare between the rebel factions. And he needed the brigade to invade at Trinidad. The reports from the Escambray, which he received each day from the radio in the Everglades, were not encouraging. He thought of young Victorio with his long lashes and girlish face. He hoped he was still alive now. Time was running out.

The Revolutionary Council itself had proved Carta's worst fears. Debate had lasted a long while, and the longer it lasted, the more heated it became. Voices were raised in clamorous shouts, and the more the members shouted, the less clear the issues became. Carta's sense of being an outsider, awkward, ill at ease, grew even more acute as he listened to the propositions, the plans, the shouts and the objections. For nearly two hours the debate raged. Near the end of it, Carta began to discern a clear pattern; a political agreement was actually emerging.

It would serve its purpose as far as Danforth and the Kennedy people were concerned. The Council would issue its pronunciamentos, taking responsibility for the invasion, proclaiming its democratic program for the world to see. Instead of a cacophony of rebel groups, each struggling for attention, there would now be one voice, one cause. It would attract a lot of media attention and thus take the CIA and the Kennedy Administration off the hook. It would now be a Cuban war, not a Kennedy war.

This is what Danforth wanted, he knew. Carta had kept his end of the bargain and in so doing had stalled his own operation for two weeks. It had cost him lives and supplies—a cost that curdled his stomach when he thought about it. It was now the second week in April; they had effectively been locked in a holding pattern since the murder of Escalante nearly three months ago.

But perhaps it would all be worthwhile. If it was a shotgun wedding, at least it might hold together long enough for them to win their victory. Once they were all back in Havana they would work out their own coalition. In the euphoria of victory, there would be a mood of compromise.

The debate at the Council meeting, muted though it was, had pointed up all the incipient problems. Navarro and his CIA-backed group were quick to support a pledge that, once Castro was banished, all the property and corporations expropriated by his regime would be returned to their original owners. But when Carta and his supporters insisted that foreign-owned utilities, such as power, telephone and transportation, be nationalized rather than be returned to the ownership of foreign corporations, the Navarro faction wanted no part of it.

Similarly, the Navarro group were quick to condemn all Castro policies; the Carta group supported educational reform and land redistribution. There were dark looks of suspicion across the table.

"I think we shall ask this Council for the right to reserve a separate position on these key points," Carta said, attempting to break the deadlock, and others nodded reluctant agreement around the table. It was going to be a hard day.

Carta determined to keep his patience. This was something he had promised Danforth he would do. He would see it through.

When debate turned to the appointment of a military delegate to the camps in Guatemala, Carta proposed Rodríguez and presented his qualifications to the room, which had grown strangely silent. Rodríguez had won his battlefield commission with the American Army in Korea, had defected from Castro, had spent years in prison on the Isle of Pines, had served Carta effectively as chief of staff.

Varona, the leader of the old Frente, responded politely that Rodríguez was indeed highly qualified, but he wished to nominate a man who was better known to all the delegates. He then proposed Navarro. The motion was passed amid a flurry of booming yeas as Carta smoldered. Danforth had promised him that Rodríguez would have the position.

At that moment, Carta seriously considered walking out of the meeting, but the urgent appeals from the other members for "Unity, Gustavo. We must have unity here!" forced him to reconsider and then, finally, relent. "In the interest of unity," he told them gruffly, "I shall remain a member of this Council."

Dr. Miró Cardona then issued an order, as head of the Council, for a general mobilization. He read his written statement which was to be released to the news media that afternoon:

"To arms, Cubans! We must conquer or we shall die choked by slavery. In the name of God we assure you all that after the victory we will have peace, human solidarity, general well-being and absolute respect for the dignity of Cubans without exception. Duty calls us to war against the executioners of our Cuban brethren. Cubans! To Victory! For Democracy! For the Constitution! For Liberty!"

His emotional words were met with applause and cheers.

Salazar turned the Buick into the gate at Carta's house, pulling Carta from his thoughts. This had been a morning of compromise, he told himself as he sought to shake off his mood of depression. There is never much satisfaction to be gleaned from compromise. Yet governments are run on compromise. And wars are won.

If only this war could be won.

411

Carta emerged from the French doors of his living room to find his garden swarming with workmen. Several were toting stacks of collapsible tables and chairs from a truck parked in the driveway onto the lawn. Others were hauling in portable food warmers and cartons containing plates and glassware.

Carta caught sight of Elizabeth. She was conferring with a gaunt, nervous man with flowing gray hair who punctuated his remarks with animated gesticulations, using his hands and arms to describe the delicacies that were to be brought before the guests. It was a muggy morning after the rain, and he was already swabbing his forehead with a handkerchief, gesturing with his other hand like a frantic referee at a soccer match. Carta also saw Elena standing amid the scurrying workmen, oblivious to the feverish activity around her, playing calmly with a blue yo-yo.

Elizabeth noticed Carta surveying the preparations and hurried to his side, the gray-haired man on her heels. "You look absolutely wonderful," she said as she straightened out his gray silk tie and ran her hands across the broad lapels of his dark-blue suit.

Carta was staring at the gray-haired man.

"Oh, this is Pierre," Elizabeth said. "He's put together the luncheon for me."

Pierre extended his thin hand, which Carta shook.

"It will be an exquisite lunch, monsieur," Pierre blurted. "There will be a quiche, some sautéed crab Marguery, a little chicken Tetrazzini—"

"I'm sure it will be fine," Carta cut in.

"I'll be back with you in a moment, Pierre," Elizabeth said, taking Carta by the arm and walking him away from the workmen. When they had gone a few yards away, Elizabeth turned and kissed him lightly on the lips. "How did it go this morning, darling? I hope well."

"Not as well as I expected, but better than I had hoped," he said, smiling. "They appointed Navarro as military representative to the brigade."

A little furrow appeared in Elizabeth's forehead. "But didn't Charles . . . ?"

"Promise it to Rodríguez? Yes."

"What does it mean?"

"It can mean several things," said Gustavo, the smile fading.

She smiled at him and tugged at the handkerchief peeking out of his jacket. "You look very statesmanlike this morning. That's the way I like you to look."

They started walking back toward the house. Carta could see Gutiér-

412

rez, the bodyguard, conferring with Pierre near the French doors. Gutiérrez cast a worried look over the scurrying intruders.

As Carta neared the French doors leading to the living room, he heard Elena's piping voice calling to him. He turned in the direction of the voice and saw her running toward him, her arms outstretched, the blue yo-yo clasped tightly in one hand. "Grandpa, Grandpa," she was calling. "Come see my yo-yo. I want to show you."

Carta smiled as she came toward him, her eyes wide with excitement, her feet racing across the grass. She was still about twenty feet away from him when Carta's eyes focused on the thick black extension cord that the workmen had just hooked up to the aluminum food warmers. He started to call out a warning to her when the child's foot struck the cord and her small body tumbled, her arms outstretched to cushion her fall, the yo-yo flying.

"Easy there. Are you all right, Elena?" Carta bent quickly to help the child. As he leaned, he felt a sudden force tear across his back, as of a blast of wind. Simultaneously the air around him exploded with a deafening impact. From the corner of his eye, he could see the body of the gray-haired caterer hurtling through the air like a puppet abruptly cut loose from its guide strings. It crashed through the French doors leading to the living room, splintering the glass into millions of flying shards that shattered on the tile in a violent hail. Carta covered Elena with his body.

He now felt crushing weight hit him. He heard Gutiérrez' alarmed voice whispering to him, "Señor, señor." Carta realized now that Gutiérrez had spreadeagled himself over both of them, protecting their bodies with his own.

Struggling to recover from the momentary shock, Carta quickly began to assimilate the rush of events. There had been a rifle shot. He had heard the ominous crack. Despite Gutiérrez' weight, Carta could feel the full sensations of his own body. He had not been hit. It had been close. The bullet intended for him had hit the caterer, who had been standing behind him. He heard Elena's whimper and felt her body stir under him. She was terrified but unhurt.

An eerie silence settled over the garden. Suddenly the scene exploded in frightened cries and the sound of pounding feet. Gutiérrez slid off Carta, who grasped Elena in his arms, both men kneeling now, surveying the scene cautiously. "Please get inside, señor," Gutiérrez said, his eyes darting back and forth over the yard. The catering crew was running in full panic toward their truck, some of them tripping over the metal chairs that were strewn on the ground. Carta noticed Salazar, the second guard, racing across the lawn, his gun drawn, heading toward a cluster of palms at the far end of the property.

Carta's eyes were searching for Elizabeth, but she was suddenly at his side now, clasping Elena. "Come inside, Gustavo," she said in a tense whisper. "Come, Elena."

They darted into the house. The French doors, Carta noticed, had been shattered. Just inside the door, his head propped awkwardly against the side of an end table, lay the body of Pierre, the caterer. Blood was seeping from glass cuts on his face and a massive wound in his chest. His eyes were open; his expression in death was one of total astonishment.

"It must have been a powerful rifle to blow him through the door like that," Carta said as he covered the body with his jacket.

Elizabeth buried Elena's face in her dress.

"The firing was from the trees, señor," Gutiérrez said as he moved inside.

"How about the wall?" Elizabeth asked. "It's supposed to be electrified." Her arms were still wrapped tightly around Elena's small body.

"It was the caterer," Gutiérrez said helplessly. "That is what we were arguing about. He insisted we turn off the current for a few minutes. There would have been an overload—we had to switch to his generator."

"Then someone knew just when to get over the wall. Someone who knew about the party," Carta said.

"They must have had us under careful surveillance," Gutiérrez said.

"What kind of maniac?" Elizabeth said.

"We must call the police," Carta said. He picked up the phone and started dialing.

"He was very good with a rifle," Gutiérrez said. "And very sure of himself. He fired only once."

Elizabeth looked at him intently. "Are you sure? Only once?"

They heard shouts from across the lawn. It was the gardener, a big Negro in denims, holding his straw hat in one hand, pointing as he ran. "It came from over there," he yelled as he ran. He was pointing to the window of the house next door. Carta and Elizabeth stared in confusion at where he pointed. The white stucco of the Sherman house showed through the leaves of the banyan trees a hundred yards away.

Gutiérrez moved beside Carta. "He could be right," he said, his eyes trying to measure the angle of the bullet. "I will check." He started cautiously toward the Sherman house.

Carta's jaw was set firmly. His eyes glared with anger. His voice was a quiet growl. "I will call Tipton. We will have to have more men here now." He put his arms around his wife. "Are you all right, Elizabeth?"

He could feel a shudder pass through her body as he touched her, but then he felt her straightening her shoulders as if steeling herself against a new peril.

Elizabeth went over to Elena, who was sitting on the edge of the stairs. Her face was pale but she had stopped crying.

Elizabeth took Elena's hand and started leading the child upstairs. Carta looked after them and started to follow, slowly.

"We are not frightened, are we, darling?" Elizabeth said to Elena.

The child looked up at her and clasped her hand more tightly. "No, Elizabeth, we are not frightened," she repeated in a soft, timid voice.

CHAPTER FORTY-ONE

MIAMI, APRIL 12, 1961

Pelham was indignant. Adele, his corpulent, slow-moving secretary whose Georgia accent had never ceased grating on him, had mixed up some correspondence, sending one confidential report to Vermillion's office that was intended for CINCLANT (Commander in Chief Atlantic), and the CINCLANT report to Vermillion. The CINCLANT office at Norfolk, Virginia, was where a top-level CIA team was planning the military strategy for the invasion, using the Fleet Intelligence Center as cover. The Navy had become increasingly testy about housing the CIA operatives, and to Pelham the task of sending the necessary apologetic Telexes to clear up the matter was an acute embarrassment. He found himself standing over Adele's desk, shouting into her chubby, bovine face, his anger out of control; then he caught himself and retreated quickly to his office, disgusted with his own display. Losing control, Pelham sensed, was more outrageous than Adele's error—control was self-mastery, the mark of a gentleman. He sat slumped behind his desk, breathing deeply and dabbing perspiration from his forehead.

It was all finally getting to him, Pelham thought. He was sick of Miami, sick of the mission, sick of the heat, sick of the goddamn Cubans and

415

their intrigues and incivilities. He found himself thinking about Michael. He missed the boy; the notion appalled him, but it was there nonetheless.

What distressed him the most was the sense that he was losing control —control over both himself and his mission. Just two months earlier the whole scheme had seemed so surgically clean and precise in his mind. It had direction and it had a leader—Pelham. Now there were too many levels of authority. The decision-making machinery had become too cumbersome. It was no longer Pelham's show. It was everybody's show. And, for the first time since he had arrived in Miami, the idea had begun to take hold in Pelham's mind that the whole thing was possibly not going to work.

The constant delays in the invasion date epitomized his frustrations. D-Day had originally been proposed for April 5. At the end of March the President had postponed it to April 10. Then that date was abruptly canceled and no new one had been set. Also disturbing to him were the rumors that Kennedy was objecting to the "noise level" of the planned air strikes and asking that they be scaled down drastically. Politics, he felt, were rapidly diminishing their chances for a military victory.

With each new vacillation, Pelham felt the chances for success had faded significantly. Fidel Castro knew what was coming. It gave him more time to solidify his position. A further postponement, in Pelham's eyes, could prove fatal to the morale of the brigade and to the unity of the Cubans.

The door to Pelham's office opened suddenly and Dobbs walked in, unshaven and disheveled-looking in baggy corduroy trousers and stained fatigue jacket. It was typical of Dobbs, Pelham thought, that he alone would not pay him the courtesy of knocking before barging in. He had asked him several times, but Dobbs was not the knocking type. Pelham, who was crisply attired in a seersucker jacket and tan slacks, regarded Dobbs's outfit with visible disgust.

"I take it you're modeling your combat clothes in anticipation of D-Day," he snapped.

"I don't spend my time jawboning with Cuban politicians—I'm out in the field," Dobbs growled as he slumped into a chair. "What do you think the old man wants?"

"All I know is that we received a Telex from Vermillion advising us to stand by for an eleven-A.M. conference call. I assume he wants to know the outcome of the 'jawboning,' as you put it."

Dobbs shook his head wearily. "I've been in this business a few years and I've learned to trust the seat of my pants. And right now the seat of my pants tells me that we've reached the point where we better stop the

416

talking and start the shooting or we'll jawbone this whole goddamn operation right into the shithouse."

"The agency apparently thinks it has more sophisticated criteria at its disposal than the one on which you are presently seated."

Dobbs lit a cigaret and was about to reply when Pelham's intercom buzzed.

Pelham picked up the phone. "It's Vermillion," he said to Dobbs, who reached for the other extension. They both waited for the familiar voice of their superior to come on the line.

"Gentlemen, our new date is April seventeenth." Vermillion's voice sounded strong and confident. "The President authorized it last night."

"But do you feel that date is going to be firm?" Pelham said.

"This date is firm."

Elated, Pelham looked over at Dobbs, who had a sardonic grin on his face. He had heard about "firm" dates before.

"You both have a lot to do and you better start doing it. Tonight I want you to cut the orders to start moving the brigade from Trax down to Trampoline. I've already ordered the ships out of New Orleans. They're on their way to Puerto Cabezas. . . ."

Dobbs's sardonic grin had vanished. There was a startled expression on his face. Pelham knew what Dobbs was thinking: Oh, Christ, this is really it! He means what he says!

"What about the landing craft?" Dobbs said in a husky, uncertain voice.

"They're on those ships." Vermillion's tone left no doubt that he considered it a stupid question. "And I want the B-26s on their way to Nicaragua by 0300 this morning. Understood?"

"I've set it up so the pilots will open their sealed orders after they're in the air," Pelham said. He was struggling to keep the excitement out of his voice. Pelham admired the calm decisiveness of Vermillion's manner, in sharp contrast to Dobbs's obvious confusion.

"The maps and detailed tactical plans for the briefing are on their way by Air Force jet to Trax," Vermillion said. "I want one of you there to supervise the briefing."

"I'll be there," Dobbs snapped.

"You know all the ancillary plans, gentlemen," Vermillion added. "As I said before, you two have a lot to do. I want to emphasize how vital it is that things move along smoothly now. Congress and the White House will be very sensitive to any signs of discord or confusion."

"Understood," Pelham said.

"We want to underscore the theme of unity. I want the Revolutionary Council in New York by tonight. Get them where the media can see

them. The feeling in Washington now is that the Cuban exiles are unified in support of the operation. I want to emphasize that further."

"There are some press releases coming out of the Council this morning," Pelham said. "A unified statement of their political aims and a call
to arms by Dr. Cardona. Quite dramatic, actually."

"Excellent, Pel. I've had our people in New York make arrangements
to put them up at the Lexington. You know it?"

"Quite well, sir."

"There will be specific instructions in the courier pouch with regard
to how you shall proceed with Carta. He's got support here, close to the
President. I don't want him clouding the issues at the wrong moment.
Your task is outlined in detail. I want those orders carried out to the
letter. Clear?"

"Yes, sir," said Pelham.

"Any other questions?"

Dobbs's face grew troubled. "You had any word on whether we're
going to back up the landing?"

"The President is maintaining his position that our forces will not
become engaged. However, gentlemen, I can tell you the Navy will have
a task force, including the carrier *Essex,* standing by off the landing site,
with Marines aboard. Do you get my drift?"

Dobbs winked at Pelham.

"About the landing site, the Cubans in the Revolutionary Council still
think it's Trinidad," Pelham said. "Should we tell them about the Bay of
Pigs?"

"Tell them nothing," Vermillion responded. "As far as they are concerned we are hitting Trinidad on April twenty-first. That's the date we
can give them."

"Carta too?"

"Carta especially. We're on the homestretch now, gentlemen," Vermillion said.

The connection clicked off.

An hour later Pelham was handed a sealed pouch that had been
hand-carried by courier from Washington. He read it hurriedly. It contained the details of the plan, which was now under the code name
"Operation Pluto." He scanned it with increasing excitement. Then he
sat down and reread the passages and various cables, which were directed to his eyes alone, until he had a complete grasp of the entire
situation. He marveled at its scope. It was extraordinary. The CIA, when
it got all things together, was an incredible instrument, he thought.

418

He turned back to one section—an analysis of the role of "dissident exile groups." His eyes studied the words carefully.

IN HIGH QUARTERS HERE IT IS THE CLEAR-CUT CONCLUSION THAT IF [CARTA] CONTINUES UN-CHECKED THE INEVITABLE RESULT WILL AT BEST BE CHAOS AND AT WORST PAVE THE WAY CONTINUED COMMUNIST PRESENCE IN CUBA SANS FIDEL WITH DISASTROUS CONSEQUENCES POSSIBLE CIVIL WAR INDIGENOUS CUBA CONTRARY TO THE INTERESTS OF THE US AND THE FREE WORLD GENERALLY. CONSEQUENTLY WE CONCLUDE THAT THE CARTA FACTION MUST BE NEUTRALIZED AND PRIME OBJECTIVE AND THAT UNDER EXISTING CONDITIONS THIS SHOULD BE HIGH PRIORITY OF OUR COVERT ACTION. (CIA CABLE. VERMILLION TO STATION OFFICER PELHAM. EYES ONLY.)

Now he stood up from his desk, placing the sheets carefully back in the envelope, sealed it and went to the wall safe, where he dialed the combination, swung open the heavy little door and placed the envelope inside. Pelham was satisfied. All of his fears, all of his doubts, all worry about the operation getting out of control, had evaporated from his mind. He knew what he had to accomplish. He went back to his desk and made two quick phone calls.

He was just going out the door when his telephone rang again. Swearing under his breath, he went back to his desk. "Hello? Pelham here."

The operator came on. "Mr. Pelham, you've a call from Washington. It's urgent. One moment."

He waited as he listened to the operator say, "White House? Yes, I have Mr. Pelham on the line," then click off. He waited on hold for an interminable minute. Then the operator's voice clicked on: "Here's your party, Mr. Pelham."

It was Vermillion's voice again. "Pel, I'm here with Danforth. He's on the other phone. What's going on down there?"

"Going on, sir?"

"The attempt on Carta's life this morning."

Pelham decided, after a flash of mental calculation, to play it through. "I'm afraid I wasn't aware . . ."

Danforth's voice came on the line. He sounded annoyed. "It happened at ten o'clock, after he returned from the Council meeting. Luckily, the assassin missed. Now, this is the second attempt to kill Carta. I don't want a third."

Vermillion's voice cut in. "I've explained to Danforth our plan to have

419

Carta go to Trax to coordinate his operation with the invasion. He thinks we should accelerate it. Get him over to Guatemala for his own safety."

"I see. Of course."

"Can that be arranged?"

"I think so, sir."

Vermillion said, "Assure him that we'll have him back to Key West in time for his operation to begin."

"To join his men," Danforth added.

"Certainly. I'll get right on it."

"Excellent, Pel. You accompany Carta, will you? See that everything goes smoothly. I'll arrange for you to get back to New Orleans tomorrow afternoon. I want you in Washington for the meeting tomorrow night."

"Yes, sir,"

Danforth said, "I'll call Carta myself and prepare him for this. He's too damned valuable to us to lose him now."

"Of course, sir," Pelham replied. "We have no intention of losing him."

The connection clicked off.

*

The jai-alai match was already in progress when Pelham arrived at the *frontón*. He could hear the noise of the crowd as he veered off the main corridor leading to the stands and walked down a narrow unmarked hallway. His steps echoed in the silent passageway. He stopped at a door marked "Private—No Admittance," then pushed it open and walked in. In the dim light from the entryway he could see a man seated behind a desk. He was a big man, but his facial features were not discernible in the shadows. As Pelham let the door close, the room was plunged into darkness.

"You'll find a chair to your left."

Pelham's eyes had begun to accustom themselves to the darkness. He touched the back of the chair and seated himself. In light that came from the crack under the door he could see the shape of the man's head and shoulders on the other side of the desk.

"This is something of an occasion, Mr. Castle," Pelham said. "We're finally face to face."

"I thought about that, flying here today. I was thinking I never would have gotten messed up in that Iranian caper of yours if I'd known I'd still be in business with you ten years later."

"You should have no regrets. You've benefited handsomely from our business understanding. Very handsomely. That's one reason I wanted you involved in this project."

420

"So I owe this thing to you? Christ!"

"It was my idea, yes. An idea that was enthusiastically accepted by my superiors."

"Fuck."

His conversational manner had always fascinated Pelham. His deep, gravelly voice could growl out vulgar epithets one moment, as he was doing now, and then speak in rather cultivated language the next. Pelham wondered what he looked like—perhaps he looked like Frank Costello, perhaps like Dean Acheson. That would be ironic, Pelham mused.

"You should have no regrets."

"Let's get this over with," the man said. "I met Dr. Shirer last night."

"Excellent," said Pelham. "I am authorized to tell you we have now advanced to the implementation phase."

"You mean you guys are really going through with this thing?"

"I've been authorized to give you any assistance you may require. You understand about the lethal agent?"

"I know it isn't for someone to get his polio shot up to date."

"Dr. Shirer was instructed to check you out on its use. Did he?"

"He did. You want a cigar?"

"Let's drop the levity. I don't find it amusing. You said in our last conversation that you would be in intimate contact with Castro, or could be, on any given date, is that correct?"

"Yes. But now I need precise dates."

"I was about to be specific. D-Day is April seventeenth, 0300 hours. There will be air strikes on the fifteenth and sixteenth. You should make your appointment accordingly. We want him neutralized by the morning of the seventeenth, understood?"

"Clearly."

"We have set up several cutouts to screen you."

"How many?"

"Several."

"Give me some examples."

"A two-man team will be landed near Havana on the fifteenth. They're marksmen. They'll be your back-up. It is possible the air strikes will provoke movement and exposure by Castro. They'll act on a target-of-opportunity basis."

"What else?"

"There are two other Cubans, both in Havana. We've arranged it with the gentlemen of the Mafia on a contract basis."

"Who did that?"

"Ellis Kern."

"You know they're conning the hell out of you?"

"We don't care. We are banking on you. We've invested a lot of money in you over the years. Now we're looking for a return on our investment."

"You make me feel like a debenture."

"We'll give you all the support you need. You tell me what you want, I'll see that you get it."

"How about transportation? You guys have cut off commercial travel to Havana."

"When you've finalized your plans, let me know. It will be arranged through one of Kern's corporate clients. I think it would be best if you don't leave from New York or Florida. We'll have to pick a place in the Bahamas. Will that work for you?"

"Certainly. I'll let you know what time, the date, how many passengers to expect."

"Passengers? Are you proposing to take someone with you?"

"A cutout, maybe."

"This is a sensitive area. I don't like the inclusion of a third party."

"Then get somebody else."

"Don't put me on a spot like that!" Pelham said furiously. "You know there is no one else."

"Try your Mafia pals. They've had a lot of practice at this shit."

Pelham heard the man stir. He heard the scrape of his chair on the cement floor. He felt a moment of panic seize him. "Wait, try to see it from my point of view, will you? The pressure to get this accomplished is coming from extremely high authority. Your role will be decisive. Any deviation can be extremely dangerous."

The man rose in the darkness. Pelham appraised him with a mounting tightness in his chest. He fought to control himself. He straightened his back and cleared his throat. "Sit down, please . . ."

"I'm leaving."

Pelham began to tremble. "What if I withdrew my objection to this third party?"

"I might sit down." The voice carried a tone of mocking amusement that annoyed Pelham greatly. Yet he had gained control. He felt it.

He tried to match the man's tone. "I'd like you to sit down."

He saw movement in the dark and heard the chair scrape again and saw the man sit behind the desk.

"You don't mind if I ask why you think you need this cutout?"

"I'm the one who has to figure how to get in and out with a whole skin."

"Very well. Anything else? Did you get the blueprints?"

422

"I got them. It's a clever piece of bait. I congratulate you, Pelham."

"Thank you. We expected Fidel to be interested."

"He thinks he can get the Russians to manufacture it for him."

"They probably would." Pelham strained his eyes in the dark to see the man's face. He could not make out the features clearly. "Is there anything else?" He waited for the man to respond. "Well, I guess that takes care of it." He heard the drumming of the man's fingers on the top of the desk.

"I've been waiting for you to mention Camilo Carta. You know he is in Miami?"

"I think your information is a little out of date. Kern informed me fifteen minutes before I left to join you that Camilo's body was found in an abandoned fishing camp at Sugarloaf Key this morning."

Pelham could see in the dark that the big man behind the desk was shaking his head slowly.

"The dead man wasn't Camilo Carta. It was a man named Sabino."

"You care to explain that?"

"All right. Your man Kern has a link with a G-2 officer in Havana named Major Ángel Maceo, through an ex-fighter named Paco Sánchez. Paco acted as Camilo's bodyguard and driver. You want to hear it all, Pelham?"

"Surely."

"Ángel Maceo laid it all out for Kern's man, Paco. He knew he was a leak. He knew it would get back to you people."

"What would get back?"

"That the Cubans were sending the young Carta to kill his father."

"What has that to do with us?"

"Don't fuck with me, Pelham. You know what I'm talking about. Maceo sold Kern a bill of goods. He knew if a man like Camilo suddenly showed up in this country, you'd hear about it. He wanted to eliminate your interference. You hear me? He knew Carta was a problem to you. He banked on your people letting the kid get to the old man. Which you did. You fell for it, because you guys don't understand how clever Cubans can be."

"That is impossible," Pelham said, exhaling his breath in bewilderment. "I find it hard to—"

"Listen, Pelham, he had no intention of killing his father, for Christ's sake. Think. What happened this morning at the Carta place? How many shots were fired? That had to be Camilo's work. And he's good at it. Why didn't he finish the job? He had the opportunity. And he had the weapon. Think it through. You've been stung. He went through with the charade to get you off his back. You know why?"

423

Pelham felt his heart beating faster. "You tell me."

"His real target is me."

★

"I hope this is important," Ellis Kern said peevishly. "I don't like meeting in saloons."

Pelham looked across the narrow table at Kern, who was nervously patting down some errant strands of hair across his bald top. "I don't call meetings unless they are important," Pelham told him. "As to this saloon, I wanted to be absolutely sure we're in a safe house."

Kern started to ask a question, then thought better of it. He looked around the bar. The stools all had tattered seats, and the rungs were worn smooth. He saw two whores at the end of the bar. The blond one looked over at him and smiled. He turned away and took a sip of his beer.

"All right, sorry, Pel. It's Wednesday, my day to pick up the kids at school. I get upset when I have to interrupt a family situation for business. You know how it is."

Pelham fixed an almost clinical gaze on Kern. What a curiously disciplined man he must be, Pelham thought, to compartmentalize his life the way he has done. Ever since he had first known him, Kern had been a stickler for family obligations, driving his two daughters to parochial school every morning, never missing mass on Sunday, escorting his wife to dinner at the country club every Sunday night. Yet he had seen Kern leave church after his daughter's confirmation and thirty seconds later be blandly discussing business with a paid assassin.

Kern clearly regarded himself as a "good man," Pelham reasoned. They had always been the most dangerous types—the pious ones.

"Let me fill you in on our problem," Pelham said. In a way he relished how uncomfortable he was about to make Kern. "You heard what happened at the Carta house this morning?"

"I tried to call you about it. You were out."

"I'm afraid, Ellis, you've been guilty of a rather bad miscalculation."

"Don't worry, he'll try again."

"No, you're wrong. He won't. Because you're going to find him and kill him."

In the gathering darkness Michael geared down and slowed the bike and turned into the narrow dirt road that went through the trees to the back of the old house. He stopped in the gloom under the mango tree and shut off the engine. Bracing them with one booted foot, he turned to look at her over his shoulder. Robin held tightly to his chest, her

424

cheek against the muscle of his shoulder. His jacket felt smooth and smelled of leather. She stared at the bushes along the fence beyond the tree. The darkness seemed to rise from all directions. In the silence, sharp after the roaring engine stopped, she heard the traffic on the street behind them, a horn honking. She did not want to let go of him.

"Hey, Rob?"

"What?"

"I've been thinking of something. An idea I've had. I haven't told you about it."

"I must go."

"I want you to stay with me, Rob. I've been thinking we could make a run together. A long, happy run, just you and me. You could get your stuff together and we'll take the bike and head out for Los Angeles."

She stared at him, incredulously.

"You ever been to LA? Hollywood? Those places?"

She shook her head.

Michael stared down bashfully at the handlebars, rubbing them as he talked. "I don't want you going back to him."

Robin avoided his eyes. She released him, got off the bike and walked under the mango tree. For a moment she did not turn to look at him, afraid to speak. She heard him snap the kick stand and then his footsteps crunching in the leaves behind her. When he touched her shoulders with his hands she felt her breath stop. His hands went away. When she turned he was standing, slump-shouldered, his black hair shaggy and falling on his forehead, and he stared up through the leaves at the nocturnal blue sky as though seeing it for the first time. His face was still bruised from the beating he'd had, but the swelling in his nose gave him a rugged, handsome look he'd not had before. He made a vague, awkward gesture with his delicate hand. His eyes swept to her, quickly, and held her gaze.

"You don't want to go with me, huh?"

"You know I do. But I can't."

Michael made a gesture as though rousing himself from deep thought and looked at her out of the corner of his eye, a faint smile on his lips. "You, ah . . ." he began. He let out his breath. His head lowered and she looked at his profile, her heart aching. Again his eyes lifted to hers. "You want to go with him, huh?"

"I have to."

"You have to, or you want to? You're going back to him because you can't give up that safe, comfortable world of yours, aren't you?"

"Michael, I will always love you. You'll always be a part of my life."

"See ya," he said softly.

425

"Goodbye, Michael." Her throat felt as though she were choking.

He turned aside quickly and walked back to the motorcycle in the twilight, his hips swaggering in that walk of his that had so arrested her attention when they first met. She saw him throw a leg over the bike and then kick the stand back into place. He sat for a long moment, staring at her. There was accusation and hurt and affection in his expression. Her instinct was to go to him, get on the motorcycle and take him in her arms and let happen whatever was going to happen.

Without saying anything, she turned away and walked the drive toward the big dark house. She did not look back. She crossed under the palm trees and opened the screen door. She heard the motorcycle start up. It roared loudly, then revved down to a puttering under the trees. She turned and looked back to make out his shape, a darker shape under the wide-spreading foliage of the tree.

Then with a roar the Harley came toward her and flashed past and vanished behind the corner of the house. He did not look at her.

Robin went into the house, letting the screen door slam behind her. The hallway was dark. In the musty air, she smelled the faint pungent aroma of formaldehyde. The irritating scent grew stronger as she approached the living room. Stopping at the entry, she looked around the living room. The windows were luminous rectangles. The smell of formaldehyde hung in the sultry air. The desk lamp was still lit. She saw the gleam of broken glass on the floor beside the desk. There were manuscript papers scattered everywhere on the floor, apparently blown about by the wind.

She felt numb and dazed. The knowledge that she had lost Michael left a physical feeling in her throat and chest, like the ache of homesickness. She had cut him off. She leaned against the door trim, feeling the varnished wood against her cheek. Her face felt hot. Tears blurred her vision. Her whole being ached. She put her hands to her face.

It was then she heard the movement behind her and turned, startled, to see the man standing there.

Michael got as far as the drugstore in the Grove and then wheeled the Harley around the corner to the right, retracing his path to the back entrance to Robin's place. He knew the impression he'd made gunning out of the yard. She must have had a heart attack when he did it, he thought. He felt pleased with himself. A car passed and honked as he slowed, looking for the entrance in the trees. The headlamp picked up the slope in the curbing and he swung in under the trees. He cut the engine and got off.

As he walked toward the back of the old house, he saw the glow of the lamp from the living room in the leaves of the banyan tree across the drive. It was thin light that made shadows on the gray pillared roots under the tree. There was no Volkswagen parked by the back porch, so he felt secure that she was in the house alone. Probably crying her heart out, he thought. He felt breathless and uneasy.

He walked in the darkness along the drive, under the trees to the house. The night insects were buzzing and chirping in the shrubs. He would surprise her. He would ease into the house quietly and come up behind her and kiss her on the neck. He wanted to take her in that house, in their bed if possible. He'd take her and really fuck her. Yes. That's what he'd do. He'd leave a well-used broad for her old man to deal with if that was the way she wanted it. The thought excited him. He smiled to himself as he came out from under the trees and stood in the cul-de-sac looking at the great dark shape of the house.

It suddenly struck him that a car was coming up the driveway. He saw the headlights brighten the trees.

It must be David! He lurched behind the corner of the screen porch. The headlights glared as the car turned and stopped. He heard the screen door open and slam. He lifted his head to look through the screen.

In the headlights, he saw Robin. She was being led by two burly men. He could not make out their faces, only their shapes and silhouettes. For an instant, he caught a glimpse of Robin's terrified eyes. Her mouth was gagged. Both hands were tied behind her back. She was being half-dragged to the car by the two men.

Michael's face felt suddenly hot. An abyss opened before him.

Jesus! he thought. That bastard Pelham. He's after me. He's having me followed. And they got Robin! Christ, I thought all that was behind me! He never gives up.

Michael abandoned all thoughts of her; there was nothing to do now but save himself.

He waited until the car turned out of the drive and went off, leaving him in the darkness.

What the hell will I do? he wondered, desperately. I can't go back to my place. Too risky.

He felt the wad of money in his pocket. There was two hundred bucks. What else did he need!

He eased out from behind the screened porch and stood for an instant, still as a hunter, watching to see if they'd left someone behind.

He ran back through the darkness toward where he'd left the motor-cycle. He stumbled and fell in the dark, scraping his hand. It stung terribly. He did not like being hurt. He got to his feet and found the

427

Harley. He felt better as he stepped over onto the seat and felt its metal power between his legs. He fumbled to fit the key into the ignition. For a moment, it wouldn't go. He grew frantic and jammed it in. He was breathing hard. He kicked the motor to life and revved it. He felt better, calmer.

He knew what would happen. In a little while they would become aware of his whole relationship with Robin. She would tell them everything. They'd be coming for him at his place. That fruit bastard Pelham. Why the hell had he ever gone along with him? Well, they'd never find me in Los Angeles, Michael thought. He said if I got out of town he'd leave me alone. "Boy!" The word blew out of Michael's mouth.

Shall I take a chance for my stuff? he thought. He turned the motorcycle out onto the street and cruised easily for a while in the traffic, trying to decide what to do. The pounding of his heart gave rhythm to his fear and excitement.

Poor Robin, he thought. I wonder what they'll do to her?

CHAPTER FORTY-TWO

HELVETIA PLANTATION, GUATEMALA, APRIL 12, 1961

In the twilight the Chevy continued to climb. The jungle thickened densely on both sides of the road. When he looked to his left, Carta could see down a precipice that seemed to fall a thousand feet. It was like peering into a waterless lake. As he watched, he saw the blinking red and green lights of the Piper that had flown them from Retalhuleu soaring below them, the engine noise high-pitched and angry as it climbed into the early-evening darkness. He watched until he saw the lights dissolve into the clouds. The window was open beside him, but there was not a breath of wind. The air smelled of wet earth and green foliage, tainted by the perpetual scent of mildew and rotten leaves. The road was churned mud and the Chevy lurched, tires spinning, weaving uneasily toward the sheer drop at the edge of the road, as though on ice.

Pelham sat stiffly beside him, holding with one hand the edge of the seat and with the other the door handle, as though poised to leap out at the slightest provocation. His face was pale and sweating, his glasses partially fogged in the humidity. A strand of hair fell across his forehead, and his eyes kept darting past Carta to the edge of the road.

"Are you all right, Pelham?" Carta asked him.

"Yes, of course. We're almost there."

"Are we meeting tonight with the brigade staff?"

"No, in the morning," Pelham said. He kept glancing out at the edge of the road. "It's been delayed so all the combat officers can be there. They want to know your battle plans in exact detail, so there'll be less chance of error in coordinating with your people from Baracoa."

"Yes, I understand." Carta took delight in his companion's discomfort. Though he too was a little concerned about the car as it fishtailed on the mud-slick road, he relished the sweltering tropical heat, the strange bird sounds from the overhanging trees, the splashes of reds and yellows and whites amid the dense green wall of leaves that confronted him at every curve. The pungent aroma of moist vegetation carried its own special sensuality, as did the vast and mysterious presence of the jungle itself, with its haunting shadows and its vivid silence. It awoke in him recollections of Oriente, dispelling the gloom and depression he had felt just before landing at Retalhuleu.

He turned to Pelham's sweating face. The man's eyes were fastened on the curve ahead, his mouth bowed into the shape of someone sucking a straw.

"I'd forgotten how steep it is," Pelham said.

As the Chevy continued to climb, the jungle seemed to thin out and the earth began to look redder in the twilight, more volcanic. The car shuddered and rattled ceaselessly now. The road became rougher. Soon a scattering of shacks began to appear along the side of the road. Clusters of Indian children peered at the car through the encroaching darkness.

"We're at the outskirts of the Helvetia plantation," Pelham said. "It shouldn't be too long now."

Through the broken clouds, a bright piece of moon illuminated the landscape. Carta caught a glint of the River Nil winding far below. It was growing cooler. Pelham, who had been slumped in his seat, his face flushed, had suddenly begun to revive.

A high barbed-wire fence and a guardhouse loomed ahead. Two carbine-bearing soldiers waved the Chevy to a halt. After the driver identified himself and his passengers, the car was signaled into the campground. Rows of barracks were visible. Then a larger building, probably the mess hall, and several smaller structures. Trees, dark in the thin moonlight, flanked the cleared ground. And in the distance he saw the mountain peaks cut off sharply by clouds.

He noticed lights in the windows of only two of the barracks buildings. The others looked dark, deserted. The whole area had a recently abandoned air about it.

The Chevy pulled up in front of a small wooden structure. Above the door, Carta could make out a small sign that said simply, "Headquarters 2506 Brigade." The Cuban driver, who had remained silent during the entire journey, sprang out to open the rear doors for his passengers.

As Carta stepped out, he took a deep breath. The familiar aromas of the jungle were gone now. He was immediately aware of the dust that seems to pervade every military base.

"We might as well go inside," Pelham said, and he began to lead the way into the headquarters building.

Carta's ears were assaulted by the sudden roar of a rapidly approaching helicopter. Startled, he looked skyward to see the craft, its light flashing, seemingly headed directly toward the spot where they were standing.

"That will be Colonel Jack," Pelham shouted over the roar. "He likes dramatic entrances."

The helicopter was setting down now in a small dimly lit clearing about twenty yards from the headquarters. The instant the craft hit the ground in a haze of dust, the door popped open and a man leaped out. The rotary blades were still whirling.

"That's our Marine," Pelham said as Colonel Jack strode up to them in the darkness. He was a pink-faced, compactly built man with an extremely large forehead and a jutting jaw. He looked dapper in a neatly pressed gray jumpsuit with a red bandanna tucked around his neck. As he walked, his thick chest seemed to protrude, a chest decorated with three rows of combat ribbons. It must take a considerable ego, Carta thought, to wear combat ribbons on one's custom-made fatigues in a remote jungle outpost.

Colonel Jack said in a rather high-pitched voice, "Welcome to Trax."

The plantation house was painted white and had a wide porch decorated with white lattice. Colonel Jack, immaculately attired now in a crisp white Marine uniform replete with medals, greeted Carta heartily and led him through the entryway. As he walked, Carta's eyes assimilated fleeting images of shiny tiled floors, expensive mahogany chairs and tables, elegantly patterned quilts hanging on the walls. He was startled by the opulence—a home befitting a banana-republic potentate rather than a Marine officer. The only military trappings in evidence adorned a wall of the hallway, a wall filled with military mementos:

photographs of Colonel Jack posing in full combat regalia on a beach in the South Pacific; Colonel Jack accepting a citation from a four-star general; Colonel Jack on horseback in a military parade; standing in front of a unit of paratroopers. Displayed in the living room was an impressive collection of Indian crafts and Haitian masks.

The first face Carta recognized inside the vast living room was that of Pelham, looking refreshed. They were quickly joined by Colonel Jack's two aides. They wore light-colored sports shirts and slacks and had the taut, arrogant look Carta associated with paid mercenaries.

The dinner consisted of roast chicken and canned carrots and peas. Colonel Jack, who had poured himself two scotches before dinner, had two more with each of the courses and, as dinner progressed, became increasingly animated and jovial, salting his conversation with Marine battle stories about the South Pacific. Pelham made several tentative efforts to guide the conversation into other channels, but the more Colonel Jack drank, the more determined he seemed to relive the Second World War, campaign by campaign and whorehouse by whorehouse. His two aides, introduced as Fred and Mike, listened attentively and laughed at all the appropriate places as though they had never heard the stories before, though it was clear to Carta that this was a familiar routine.

After the main course was cleared away, a servant brought a bottle of Courvoisier and filled everyone's glass. Colonel Jack got to his feet unsteadily and held his glass in the air.

"We've been stuck in this shit hole for six months now, and, Jesus, we've done our job, so let's drink to victory, gentlemen." He raised his tumbler even higher, his face flushed. "To victory."

Glasses were clinked around the table, and all the men drank. Carta glanced over at Pelham, who was regarding Colonel Jack with visible apprehension.

"Let me tell you something, Carta," Colonel Jack said. "These Cuban boys are good soldiers. They're going to hit those beaches and beat the living shit out of old Fidel. I feel sorry for that poor bugger—I mean, I'll bet he's sitting somewhere tonight thinking about us. He knows he's lost the war. He knows it."

"You should meet Fidel someday, Colonel," Carta said to him. "The thought of defeat has never and will never enter his head."

Colonel Jack leaned on his elbows, folded his red hands and peered at Carta from under his bushy gray brows. "You've met Fidel Castro? Talked to him?"

"Many times. He's a charming man—"

A burst of air exploded from the colonel's lips. "Charming? What the hell kind of word is that for a fucking Commie dictator? Isn't this man your enemy?"

"Yes. But that does not change the truth of his character. He is charming."

Colonel Jack glanced in disgust at his aide. "Shit. Charming." He looked back at Carta, blinking. "I'll tell you, that son of a bitch is going to look charming to me when I see him dangling from the business end of a bayonet, by Christ!" He roared with laughter, glancing at his aides for approval.

Two orderlies in white coats started serving the dessert course—an exotic-looking mixture of tropical fruits floating in a liqueur. Carta took no special notice of the orderlies until one placed a fresh napkin in his lap. "Please, señor," he said softly in Carta's ear. The voice, Carta felt, seemed to carry a note of urgency. As Colonel Jack continued talking, Carta glanced at the servant, who paused briefly at the door to the kitchen and was staring in his direction. With a shock of recognition, he realized it was Pepín, his former houseboy who had resigned to join the brigade in early February. His alarmed look prevented Carta from reacting. After a brief moment of eye contact, Pepín disappeared into the kitchen.

Colonel Jack was replenishing the Courvoisier now and holding forth about the landing sites. "We finally got confirmation last night," he said, waving his cigar. "We're going into Playa Larga, Playa Girón and another beach east of Girón. All of them are beaches in the Bay of Pigs. There'll also be a small diversionary force landing in Oriente—maybe one hundred fifty commandos, that's all. They're going to be wearing Castro uniforms." He chortled. "That should confuse the shit out of them."

Carta felt a sudden jolt. That was the landing site!

Girón. The Zapata Swamps. The Bay of Pigs! Not Trinidad as he'd been told.

His mind raced with images drawn from his past: the green marshes, the boggy wetlands, the reefs outside the wide mouth of the bay that narrowed as you went farther east, inland. He had fished along the reefs. It was remote, all right. The last site for a major landing of troops he'd ever have picked. No one who'd been there would consider it. He tried to stem his alarm, reassuring himself that the Americans were experienced in these kinds of military affairs. Certainly, experts had looked into it. Certainly, they'd charted the reefs, and discovered military advantages of which he was not aware. He calculated the distance from Girón to the Escambray as about eighty miles. The attack site would be a long way from relieving the pressure on Victorio. And this diversionary force? Was that his group? There had been no mention of Castro uniforms! What was that? If these facts had been kept from him, what other surprises were in store? Was the invasion date really April 21, as he'd been told, or was that false, too? He felt paralyzed. Sweat broke out on his face. He wiped his mouth with his napkin and heard Pelham saying:

"Dr. Carta was not aware of the new site selected for the landing, Colonel . . . I think . . ."

The broad grin widened on the ruddy face. "Hell, it don't make no difference. Those troops of mine'll be in Havana in a week, you watch. By God, nothing'll even slow the bastards down! Right, Mike?"

"That's right, sir," Mike said, smiling.

"Shit," Colonel Jack said. "We should have been on the beaches two weeks ago! My men are getting skittish as hell." He shot a furtive look at Pelham, then turned back to Carta. "I'll let you in on a little secret, Carta, but let's keep it in this room, all right?"

Carta nodded.

Colonel Jack leaned across the table toward him. "Two weeks ago I issued orders to the four top Cuban officers in the brigade that if there were any further delays they were to put me under arrest and proceed with the invasion immediately."

He looked around the room for effect. Fred and Mike beamed proudly. Pelham was squinting at Colonel Jack through disapproving eyes. Colonel Jack detected Pelham's glance, but was undeterred.

"There's no fucking way anybody in Washington or Moscow or any-place else is going to call off our little party. No way," Colonel Jack said, and sat back in his chair, puffing his cigar.

"Your determination is to be commended," Carta said. "I wouldn't like to be your commanding officer, Colonel, but that's beside the point."

Colonel Jack beamed. "Determination wins wars," he said expansively. "Washington doesn't know how to win wars anymore. They let bureau-crats fart around. Bureaucrats don't understand war."

"Our troops are convinced they're going to win," Mike interjected. "I've never seen men with a better attitude."

"Hell, why bullshit around?" Colonel Jack was glaring at Pelham. "I mean, what the fuck's the difference?" He pointed a finger at Carta. "Your people are good, don't get me wrong. They'll fight. Fight like hell, because we've trained 'em. But they have confidence up their ass, and do you know why? Because they know the U.S. Marines are backing them up all the way. All the fucking way!"

433

"As you know, no commitments have been made," Pelham said quickly. "No commitments and no promises."

"Hell, why bullshit?" Colonel Jack was still glaring at Pelham. "Of course the Marines will save their ass if things go bad."

"Would they?" Carta asked.

"You're damned right they would."

Pelham frowned and remained silent.

Colonel Jack took another drink of brandy. "There's no way John Fitzgerald Kennedy could afford to let this operation go down the tube. No way. Hell, I've still got buddies in the Pentagon. They know the score."

"But if your armed forces are used, Colonel," Carta said, glancing at Pelham, "wouldn't that mean U.S. domination of Cuba after Castro falls?"

"Hell," Colonel Jack said with a wave of his dead cigar, "Cuba's ours anyway, ain't it? We should've made a possession out of it after we took it from Spain, in the first place. Right, Pelham?"

"Colonel, I don't think you realize how sensitive a matter this—"

"Oh, fuck that fucking diplomatic bullshit," the Colonel said to him. "This is the operating end of this business, mister. This is where the guns are."

Colonel Jack relit the cigar, puffing swiftly until it glowed into a bright coal. He clicked the lighter shut and resumed his posture of elbows on the table, fingers clutching the cigar as he pointed at Carta. "Let me tell you, Carta, the aircraft carrier *Essex* will be out there, and a whole damn combat-ready battalion of Marines, just itching to kill some hostiles. You ever seen a Marine battalion in action? It's one helluva killing machine, I'll clue you. One helluva killing machine."

"It's been a long day," Pelham started, looking at Carta helplessly. "I think—"

"You know what we're going to do for your people, Carta? We're going to clean up that little mess you got there. We're going to clean out every fucking red son of a bitch in Cuba. Put 'em against the wall and pop their brains out. Clean. Know what I mean? Clean. You won't have to worry about the Commies again. Ever." He winked and made a level gesture with his right hand. "What the hell's the matter with you, Pelham?" he slurred. "Hell, that's a good man there. Five'll get you ten he already knows about Operation Forty-one. Right, Carta?"

"You've had too much to drink, Colonel. I suggest your aides see you to bed." Pelham's words flew like shrapnel. He gestured to the two aides. Both young men stood erect and moved to the colonel's side.

"Hell, leave me alone. I can take myself to bed, goddamn it." Colonel

Jack glared at Pelham. "What the hell's eating you, mister?" Unsteadily, he stood up. There was a spot of spilled brandy on his white trousers. He frowned, putting his fingers between his eyes. "Ahh, maybe I have had a touch too much brandy, boys." He blinked his eyes, straightened, lifted his brows and focused his eyes on Carta, who also stood up now. "You'll excuse me, sir?"

"Of course," Carta said hoarsely. He could not believe the things he had heard at this table tonight. He needed to get away to think it all through.

CHAPTER FORTY-THREE

DADE CITY, FLORIDA, APRIL 12, 1961

Edmundo Gaitán came softly into the dark bedroom, and when he reached out to touch the sleeping man on the cot he saw that his eyes were open and staring at him, as though measuring him for intent.

"I'm sorry, Comandante," he said softly. "It is necessary to wake you. There are cars approaching this house."

The cold blue eyes in the angular, clean-shaven face seemed to appraise him cautiously, but without alarm.

Camilo had slept in his clothes, and as he lifted himself from the pillow Edmundo saw the automatic pistol. He sat on the edge of the cot and placed his face in his hands, then ran his fingers through his dark hair slowly. He sighed.

"All right." He stood his full height from the cot, yawned and stretched his long arms. Then he scratched his chest and nodded. "All right."

The young man watched, fascinated, as Camilo leaned down, picked up the automatic pistol and shoved it into the holster on his belt behind his hip. He grabbed his coat from the chair and slung it over one arm. Edmundo had seen many photographs of this man in the newspapers and the magazines in Havana, but never before had he been in his presence. He felt a certain awe.

"We go?" Camilo said to him.

For a moment Edmundo hesitated. "Of . . . of course," he stammered, and turned to lead the way through the door and down the hall.

435

When they came out of the house into the starlit darkness, Edmundo's eyes automatically scanned the flat tomato fields that stretched off in all four directions from the yard. The frogs were chirping down by the well. Nothing. Looking off down the road, he said, "See the lights?"

They could faintly perceive the glow of headlights coming slowly along the road in the dust, about two miles away.

"Is there another way out of here, Edmundo?"

"No. Only that road. The others dead-end in the tomato fields."

"Which way is the highway?"

Edmundo pointed. "Three miles, that way."

"One can walk in the fields?"

"Yes."

Camilo walked to the back of the black Ford sedan, dug in his pocket and took out a key to unlock the trunk. As he lifted the lid a small light went on and Edmundo saw two sawed-off shotguns, paper boxes of ammunition and a Czech submachine gun with its long curved forty-round clip already inserted in the breech. Beside it were four extra clips, the brass casings of the bullets showing.

Camilo looked at him. "You ever use one of these?"

"*Sí*, Comandante."

"How do you feel?"

"I'll be all right, Comandante."

"Who's down at the gate?"

"Roberto and Luis."

"If you need them, take them with you."

Camilo stared at the young man in the darkness, then grasped his arm with his hand, holding it a moment. "Much luck."

"Thank you, Comandante. Luck to you also."

Running across the open field, Camilo heard the thump of the shotgun in the sultry night air. He was sweating and short of breath from running on the plowed ground. He stopped and looked back.

He saw the headlights in the distance. There was a staccato rattle of small arms from the road, then a silence and then the sudden rattle of an automatic weapon. It sounded like fireworks from this distance.

He stood for a moment to catch his breath, the muscles of his thighs twitching from the effort. The sweat felt sticky and unpleasant beneath his clothes. He wiped his forehead. The gunfire increased to a crescendo and then fell off to an occasional popping.

He's making a hell of a fight of it, Camilo thought.

Turning his back, he walked quickly along the row of tomatoes in the

436

dark. Ahead, in the far distance, he saw the lights of cars moving along the highway.

Someone must have talked, he thought. Someone always talks.

For more than an hour Camilo had been walking in the dark. Once he had stumbled into a ditch and found himself in water up to his waist. Not wanting to get out onto the highway, he had kept it to his right and followed it, moving across the plowed fields until his legs ached. His wet clothes clung to him, and the night air was filled with mosquitoes. Ahead, he saw the lights of a house. He walked toward it, all the time hearing the hum of the cars moving along the highway in the distance.

A dog began barking as he approached the house, so he circled around it. A door opened and a man yelled something angrily at the dog and then went back into the house. There was a pickup truck in the yard, but he did not dare approach it. He cursed his luck.

A dry buzzing in the darkness ahead, not more than two paces away, made him freeze. Rattlesnake! These fields were probably alive with them in the night. There was only the dim glow of passing headlights to see by, and he could not make out where the snake was exactly. He waited until the buzzing stopped. It was just off to the left there. It must have crawled away.

He took a step. Then another. Nothing. To hell with it, he thought. If I step on one, I step on one. He started to walk again. But the dry hissing began again, closer now. He held himself rigid. Maybe there was more than one? He thought he saw a faint movement on the ground. He waited, holding his breath.

It stopped. He laughed to himself. Wait until he told Maceo. It was a great joke. Camilo Carta, trapped in a field in Florida by a rattlesnake. He chuckled to himself at the thought.

After waiting for a moment, he moved, this time to his right, toward the highway.

He crossed the field, wary of every step, angry at himself for being afraid of snakes. Yet he was trembling when he touched the barbed wire of the fence and climbed over it, dropping into the ditch that ran along the edge of the two-lane paved highway. A truck passed with a rumbling roar and a blast of air. Then two cars. Another truck, bigger this time, the loud rasp of the diesel engine, the whine of the big tires. He could see the rear of the trailer, covered with mud and dust, the yellow lights on the top edges, growing smaller and smaller down the road. Then, to the left, about a quarter of a mile away, he saw the sudden glow of a blue light that flashed. He saw it pull out onto the highway and move off fast after the truck.

Camilo stood for a long moment watching the flashing blue light, a tiny speck now far off in the dark, close rapidly on the truck, which veered to the side of the road. The blue light kept on flickering like a beacon.

Ten minutes later he came up the embankment and stepped into the brilliance of the flashing blue light that stood like an inverted glass jar on top of the patrol car, the reflector spinning inside. The big truck was just pulling back onto the highway with a roar of its mufflers. Camilo watched the patrolman behind the wheel. He was writing something on a clipboard, a flashlight held under his chin.

He walked to the passenger door and pulled it open. The officer, who was young, with a solid, square-jawed face, wearing one of those blue campaign hats, turned to him. Camilo lifted the automatic pistol and placed the muzzle against the bridge of the officer's nose. The flashlight thumped onto the floorboard.

"What the hell?" the young officer said with a tone of indignation. "What the hell?"

"Take your gun very carefully by the grip and lift it out . . ."

Camilo watched the man's right hand as it moved cautiously. The officer held the revolver in his fingertips until Camilo took it from him and tossed it out the open door. "Now," Camilo said, "you have the key to this shotgun?"

The young officer nodded.

Camilo held out his left hand. The officer, his eyes frightened, unbuttoned his left shirt pocket and lifted out the key. "Unlock it."

"I'll have to lean over."

He leaned forward and Camilo took the pistol from the bridge of his nose and placed it in his ear. The young man glanced at him sideways. He twisted the key, and the shackle came off the sawed-off shotgun that stood in the center of the dash. Camilo put a little pressure on the muzzle of the pistol and the officer leaned back. "Is it loaded?"

"Yes."

"Splendid."

"You know, you'll get a long jolt for this," the officer said, trying hard to sound firm. "Why don't you just give me your gun and we'll see what we can work out? You don't want to kill anybody. Just hand over the gun. No harm, OK, fella? You really don't want to kill anybody, do you?"

Camilo put the muzzle of the revolver against the young man's temple,

438

a quarter inch from his ear. He whispered very softly, "You're wrong. I want very badly to kill you right now."

He saw the man stiffen.

"And," said Camilo pleasantly, "if you don't start the car, turn off the light on top and drive me to Miami immediately, I shall blow half your face away. You got me?"

"Yes, sir."

The officer's hand turned the key, and the car started.

"May I put it in gear?"

"Yes."

He put it in gear and glanced in the rear-view mirror.

"The light."

"Sorry."

He flicked off the light. The blue flashing ceased. He glanced at Camilo and then again in the rear-view mirror. "Now?"

"Now."

They pulled out onto the highway. Camilo leaned back, holding the pistol. The officer, his face in profile, lit by the dash glow, said, "What is all this? What are you after?"

"You really want to know?"

"Sure."

"I'm a Castro spy. I'm here to kill some people for my government."

The young policeman glanced at him and shook his head. "Come on, do I look stupid?"

"Yes," Camilo said quietly. "You look stupid."

The young officer glanced at him again.

"Keep your eyes on the road," Camilo said. He carefully lifted the sawed-off shotgun from the rack and placed it across his lap, the muzzle pointed at the officer. He cocked it. Then he slid the barrel across the young man's thighs and placed the muzzle against the bulge between his legs.

The officer started to perspire. His face glistened in the glare of the oncoming headlights. "Hey," he said, "that's not funny, y'know? I got . . . a wife and kids."

Camilo just met his gaze with a cold stare. He said nothing.

★

Michael let the Harley roll. His eyes were hooded now and his cheeks drawn tight. Behind him he felt the bulk of his sleeping bag in which he had rolled all his possessions.

He had gone to the garage apartment and waited outside for fifteen minutes, watching. Nothing had stirred. He'd taken the stairs three at a

439

time. There was a note on the door from his landlord reminding him that he was three weeks overdue on his rent. He laughed to himself and crumpled the note and left it on the floor. He'd taken very little time and wasted no effort in gathering up the clothes he wanted, his extra pair of boots, his shaving gear, stacks of manuscripts. He was back down the stairs and on the Harley in less than ten minutes.

He'd given the old place a final glance and then let out the clutch and felt the metal bulk of the motorcycle surge forward under him.

Never in his life had he felt so good.

He was on his way to California. New territory, new adventures. He was going to be OK.

After he got to Mobile, Alabama, perhaps he would stop and call his folks in Cincinnati. His folks! He laughed to himself how that fruit Pelham had bought his story about his penniless, arthritic mother. His actual mother was a big woman, almost six feet tall, hard as nails. His father was scared to death of her. But Pelham had bought it, as suspicious as he was.

Yes, he was pretty good at making up stories. Maybe when he got to Los Angeles he should try to do some writing and put his fertile imagination to use. That could be interesting.

He watched the taillights of the truck ahead of him and started to swing the bike around it, accelerating and feeling a joy in the surge of response from the bike.

The taillights all suddenly brightened.

What the hell? Michael thought. You stupid fuck-head, what are you stopping out here for?

He swung the motorcycle to the left lane and glanced at the gray side of the truck as he flashed past. He wanted to give the driver a piece of his mind. As he swept past, seeing the face of the driver dimly outlined in his cab, he waved his hand and shouted, "Ass hole!"

He turned his head, gripping the handles, and saw the huge shape of the freight train moving across the road directly in front of him. "What the fuck . . . ?"

440

CHAPTER FORTY-FOUR

Kern saw the porch light blink on as he drove into the yard. Two jeeps and a green Chevrolet were parked in front of the single-story house, which had a large screen porch and a tin roof. It had once been a farmhouse, and its builder had put it together in a series of boxlike additions, all centered on a big kitchen where the hands gathered to eat. There was an old barn beyond the house and a tin-roofed shed with no walls where the farm vehicles had been kept. Kern had been pleased with the place the moment he'd set eyes on it. It was ideal for his purposes. The old frame building had been erected in the 1920s during one of the Florida booms. The owner had abandoned it after his crops had failed, and it had sat deserted until the outbreak of World War II, when a religious cult bought it and tried to work the land as a commune to avoid being drafted. They had installed indoor plumbing and jury-rigged electrical wiring, which operated from a diesel generator in the shed. The last owner before Kern was Dade County, which had taken the place over for back taxes. It had been up for auction several times, but the location was too remote and too swampy to find buyers.

Kern braked the big car behind the jeeps and opened the door to see Martín's big frame emerging like the silhouette of a great bear out of the rectangle of light that was the kitchen door.

"*Hola,* Ellis," Martín's deep Cuban-accented voice resonated in the dark.

Kern pushed shut the door of the Cadillac. Martín, who loomed above him in the night, had been with Kern in the Havana days, a tough police sergeant who had been feared by everyone. He was the kind of man that Kern found useful, yet trusted with great reservation.

"How'd it go, Martín?" Kern said. He could hear the steady chirping night sounds from the swamp.

"No problem."

They walked slowly toward the porch, side by side.

"Have you talked with them?"

"Not yet. We waited for you. I brought the interrogation team from the camp, in the event their services would be needed."

441

"Good."

David was seated at the end of a long harvest table. He was squinting his eyes behind his glasses. They had kept him all day in a dark stuffy room in the back. He'd had to deal with the anguish over his brother's death. Yet to him Camilo was one of those people who would never die. He would always expect to see him again. He had cried alone. He could not help that. His remorse had overwhelmed him. He just didn't care anymore. Why the hell did they have to do that to Camilo? It seemed he was in a dark void, until they had come for him and brought him here into the kitchen. Now the brilliance of the overhead light bulb blinded him. It lit up the sweating faces of the five tough-looking Cubans who guarded him in silence. The table was covered with oilcloth, and the light glared brightly on the slick surface. David turned his head as he heard the screen door slam. He saw the tall, thick-chested Cuban they called Martín. Behind him was a short man in a tan business suit. The light reflected off the man's glasses. He looked to David like a lawyer, or a bank executive. He had a mild-mannered air about him, almost meek.

The man came toward him and smiled faintly with his thin lips. "Good evening, Mr. Carta." His voice was measured.

David decided he was the one in charge. He stood.

"May I ask what this is all about, sir?" David said, struggling to keep his voice calm. "I think there has been a mistake."

Kern lifted his hand in the gesture of a patient umpire about to correct a wrong decision. "Yes, I know," he said with a certainty that inspired confidence in David. "I know, Mr. Carta. I trust you've not been too badly treated?"

David gestured toward the squat, powerful-looking Cuban across from him, whose battered face looked as though he had spent too many years of his life face down on a canvas floor. "That thug . . ." he started to say, but again the man's hand lifted.

"Don't be alarmed," said Kern. "Sit down, please."

David sat in the cane-back chair and looked up into the faces of the man with glasses and the big Cuban. He read the big man as dangerous. His face was surly, his eyes hardly visible beneath the heavy brows. David tried to control his mounting panic. "What is it you want with me. Mr. . . . ?"

"My name is not important to you," the man said in that precise banker's tone of his. "What is important at the moment is you."

"What do you want?"

"It's quite simple, young man. We wish to ask you some questions. If your answers are satisfactory, then you shall be released at once. You won't see us again. Understood?"

442

"What do you want to know?"

"You are the brother of Camilo Carta, are you not?"

"Yes."

"Last night you received a telephone call from Camilo giving you certain instructions."

"How did you know that?"

Kern gave David a cold smile.

David looked around at the faces of the other men in the room. Their eyes all looked at him in the same distracted manner. No one seemed the least interested in whether he lived or died. "Just who are you?" David said. He swallowed hard, but there was no saliva in his mouth. It was as dry as paste. He cleared his throat. "Are you police of some kind?"

"You might say that," said the man mildly. "We represent, as you say, the right side in this matter. Now, where is your brother Camilo hiding?"

The angle of the overhead light accented the thin lips in the man's face. David stared at him a moment, not knowing how to answer. He looked from the banker's face to that of the big Cuban with the thick nose, his skin oily in the light. Then again David looked around at the other faces. He saw the short man with a face like a boxer, the nose flat and wide, his brows thick with scar tissue, his mouth thick and brutal. He sat flexing his right hand and staring back at David. To his left he saw a thin young man who looked like a student, his sharp cheekbones casting deep shadows, dressed in a clean white shirt and a summer sports coat. Three other Cubans sat at the end of the table. Two of them wore olive-green military fatigues. One was quite tall, angular, with a black Pancho Villa moustache. To his left David saw a round-faced little man who looked like a well-fed undertaker. The third man was enormous. He wore a too-tight blue suit and sat sweating heavily, his breath wheezing between his blubbery lips, so that he looked, with his thick-lens glasses, like a fish expiring out of water. He must have weighed three hundred pounds, David thought. A heavy black suitcase had been placed on the table in front of the fat man.

"Did you hear me? Where is Camilo hiding?"

"I don't . . ."

Kern's pale fingers lifted in a gesture of caution. "Please, think about what you are going to say. We shall get at the truth here this evening, believe me. It will be considerably less complicated for all of us if you answer honestly and at once. Now, again, where is Camilo hiding?"

David let out his breath and shook his head slightly.

"You don't understand. My brother's dead."

"We have good reason to believe otherwise."

443

"But I saw his body!" David pointed at Martín. "So did he! He was there. He's the bastard that killed him!"

Kern shook his head and smiled. "Won't do. You know that was not Camilo's body you saw."

"The hell it wasn't!" David said. "He killed him."

Kern gestured with his right hand. Martín moved aside and looked at David sharply, then went to the door that led to a hallway and disappeared, ducking under the doorframe. David saw that all the others seemed to be holding their breath, intent on something other than himself. In the silence, David heard insects hitting the window screen. He heard, from somewhere in the house, the big man's heavy footsteps, then a pause. A door opened. The man in front of him cleared his throat. David looked at him.

"Look, if I knew anything, I'd tell you. Why shouldn't I?"

"I'm sure you have your reasons," Kern said softly.

David heard voices, muffled, coming from one of the back rooms. He thought he recognized the tone of a woman's voice. He looked at Kern's blinking eyes questioningly. Kern's expression did not change.

He heard the footsteps coming down the hallway. The door beyond the table opened and he saw the big Cuban's oily face appear in the light. Behind him was Robin.

David shot to his feet, his chair falling with a crash behind him.

"David!"

She rushed to him and clasped him in her arms. He felt her body against him and smelled her hair, her hands holding his shoulders, his whole sense of reality spinning.

"Are you all right, Rob?"

She lifted her face to him, her eyes wide with anxiety. "What's this all about? Who are these people?"

It was all too clear to David what their position was with these men. They thought he knew something and he didn't. His mind raced with possibilities. "They want some information," he said. He felt her trembling under his hands.

"What about?"

Kern leaned toward her, and spoke in his quiet tone. "The whereabouts of your brother-in-law, Mrs. Carta. It's quite simple."

Robin looked back at David. "He's in Havana . . ."

"I'm afraid he's here, Mrs. Carta. But your husband is reluctant to tell us where. We thought perhaps you could persuade him."

"Do you know, David?"

David looked from her terrified eyes to Kern's cool stare. "Yes. He's dead."

444

"Now, David, you know better. Before we must resort to any unpleasantness, I'll ask you again—where is your brother?"

He heard the scraping of chairs and the shuffle of feet on the gritty linoleum floor and out of the corner of his eye saw three men at the end of the table stand up. The fat Cuban took something out of his pocket and handed it to his companion. They were all looking at him. David kept his attention centered on Kern's stare.

"Where is your brother?" he repeated.

"If he isn't dead, I swear to you, I don't know where he is!"

"A pity."

"You want me to lie to you?"

"You are lying."

Kern gestured. David felt his arms being grasped, and he turned his head to see the flat-nosed face of the ex-boxer close to his own. He smelled his sour breath. His arm was twisted sharply and painfully behind his back, forcing him to bend forward. He heard Robin shriek. He tried to get his head up, the pain of his pinned arm became sharp. He looked at the buttons on the man's gray nylon jacket and then twisted his head to see the big Cuban standing on the far side of the table, behind Robin. He was holding her struggling body with his two big hands. He had her at the elbows, pulling her backward across the table. She tried to kick the tall Cuban who was reaching for her legs.

"Leave her alone!" David shouted.

The boxer did something to David's wrist behind his back that hurt sharply. He gritted his teeth and grunted, "You bastard . . ."

Kern leaned down to him. "Where is your brother?"

"I . . ." David panted. "I told you, he's dead!" The pain eased and he looked sideways up at Kern. "What are you going to do? For God's sake, don't hurt her. She doesn't know anything."

"But you do."

"I don't. I swear to you, I don't!"

Kern's face went away. David heard the sticky screech of adhesive tape being stripped from a roll. He felt the hard grasp of the hands holding him.

They moved very fast and efficiently. His hands were pinned to his side. The adhesive tape was wrapped quickly around him, and then across his chest. The back of the chair pressed the middle of his shoulder blades, painfully. The tape went up and around his neck, so that his head was forced erect. He felt the tape go around his wrists, which were being held behind the chair. He watched the Cuban with the broken face tape his ankles to the chair.

He saw Robin. She stared at him, her copper hair tousled, the strands

445

falling across her face, which was red with the straining now. She looked at David like a child who was about to be spanked. The tall Cuban held her legs. She had on the white duck pants and blue sweatshirt she had left in. He saw her trying to twist her body.

"What are you going to do?" Robin screamed. "Please don't hurt me, please. . . . Oh, David, if you know, tell them, please, please?"

The lean Cuban turned and, raising his hand, slapped her face sharply. Robin gasped.

There was a pause, as though each man in the room had become frozen in place. They were all looking at Robin, who lifted her chin, her eyes dazed, filling with tears. Her lips were swelling from the blow.

"You bastard!" David shouted. He tried to lunge at the man and realized his helplessness. "You dirty bastard!" he shouted. "Why don't you hit me?"

In the light on the long kitchen table, the Cuban with the rolls of fat under his chin unsnapped the locks on the black suitcase. David saw what appeared to be some electrical testing device, with dials indicating volts and amps, and two gleaming metal electrodes that looked like needles fitted at the ends of two long black cords. The fat Cuban snapped a switch, and he heard a faint hum. He looked around. Kern's face came close to David's. He could smell the Lavoris on Kern's breath.

"Have you ever seen a device like this?"

David felt the muscles convulse along his back. He was surprised to find himself trembling. He could not take his eyes off Robin.

"It's ingenious, you see," Kern told him. "It was developed for inter-rogation purposes. Essentially, it's an electrical mechanism designed to deliver a painful shock to the body when these electrodes are applied." Kern lifted the wires, letting the two needlepoints of the electrodes dangle over his hand. David watched them turn in the light, winking with a metallic gleam. "In its cruder form it is called a telephone. Per-haps you've heard of it?"

David's lips were dry and he licked them, but his tongue was dry, too.

Kern placed the electrodes back on the control panel. "We've refined it considerably," he continued in the curiously detached tone of a college professor explaining a scientific precept to his class. "This model is con-siderably more effective and useful than in its earlier versions, as you shall presently observe." He turned his cool eyes to David again. "Ap-plied to the genitals, the pain is unbearable. Beyond imagination."

"Look," David said, unable to control the quiver in his voice. "You can do what you want to me. I don't know where he is . . . I swear to God,

446

Camilo's dead! That's all I know. No matter what you do to me, that's all I can tell you!"

"We're not going to do anything to you, Mr. Carta," Kern said finally. "You are the one who must answer our questions."

Robin watched their leering faces, sick with loathing and terror. Just then, the fat Cuban turned and she saw his eyes, enormous and white, like a bloated fish, his cupid lips pursed. Sweat glistened on his fat cheeks. He stank of sweat and rum. As he leaned over her, he smiled, his eyes blinking at her from behind the thick lenses. His labored breathing made a faint whistling through his nostrils.

She felt his hand grasp the waistband of her pants, lifting her slightly, so that the tape around her arms and ankles hurt.

She glared at him until she saw the knife, a quick flash of light on steel. Her head and neck were taped so that she could not lower her chin. Her eyes looked down over her nose to see his thick, hairy hand holding the front of her pants. She saw the knife flash again. She felt it slicing the cloth and she sank back into the chair. She felt the coolness of being exposed suddenly to the air. Her flesh crawled, sprouting goose bumps. The stench of the man was too much for her. She wanted to retch. She could feel him slicing open the cloth on her thighs with deft strokes of the knife. His bulk and shadow dominated her view. His thick glasses with the bulging eyes appeared suddenly in her view and she watched his expression change from leering to admiration. He smiled and nodded at her and then stood, holding the bits of cut cloth in his hand, and said something she did not hear in Spanish to the man who stood near David.

She felt their eyes on her, staring at her. She cringed. She tried to close her legs, but they were securely fastened to the chair so that her knees were spread wide, leaving her open and exposed, terrifyingly vulnerable. It was at this moment she touched the limit of her fear.

She heard a low rumble of male voices. She could not look at David now. He was helpless. He could do nothing for her now. Nothing. He could not save her, she thought. God, what's going to happen to me?

She closed her eyes, trembling.

In the darkness, she heard the man's quiet, infuriating voice. "Where is your brother, Mr. Carta?"

Kern removed his glasses and took a handkerchief from his pocket and carefully wiped the lenses.

Without his glasses, his face took on a different cast—harsher, even wolf-like. His myopic eyes looked curiously lifeless. Kern seemed to be deliberating. David saw him lift the glasses to the light, checking them for marks, then hook them carefully to one ear, then the other. He turned toward David.

"Where is your brother?"

"Oh, please, please don't!" Robin's shriek filled the room. "Oh, no, Oh, no! Please, please, no!"

David saw the fat man move from the table, holding the electrodes, the long thin cords making a faint scraping as they uncoiled and slid across the table, unwinding, snakelike from their coils in the briefcase.

"Don't hurt her, please," he said to the man. "Please . . ."

"Your brother," Kern said in the same remote tone, "where is he?"

David saw the fat man lean over Robin. She tried to cringe away from him, her mouth half open, her eyes watching him with panic. "Oh, no, no, no!"

Her mouth flew open wide, her eyes suddenly showing white, her head flapping from side to side in its bindings. David saw the needle tips of the electrodes, tiny silver gleams in the light, squeezing her nipple. The pink knob of flesh bulged, the breast trembling, her whole body trying to flop against the stress of the adhesive that held her. She screamed. Her scream was one long sustained shriek of agony. Her whole body convulsed. The wrinkled nipple swelled red, squeezed tightly between the gleaming points of the electrodes. Her breast kept jiggling spastically.

Then the fat man stepped back, robotlike, his head half turned to Kern. His sweating face bore no expression. Robin's head fell foward against the bonds, her whole body twitching. Her mouth hung open. A trickle of saliva dribbled from her lips onto her breast, gleaming wetly in the light. She groaned.

"Where is your brother?"

MIAMI, APRIL 12, 1961

Camilo heard the knock. As he opened his eyes, he did not know where he was. Then the musty smell of the hotel room came to him. He blinked his eyes to clear them. The glow of the neon sign outside the window cast everything in the little room in a red tint. He heard the soft knock again.

He sat up. Slipping the pistol from under the pillow, he crossed to the door. He stood to one side, against the wall.

"Yes?"

448

"It's Vega."

He reached out and unlatched the night lock and then the dead bolt.

"The door is open," he said and stepped back. He crouched on his haunches, holding the automatic pistol, cocked and ready, in both hands. He heard a click in the door and then saw the gleam of yellow light from the hallway.

He heard Vega's voice say softly, in Spanish, "I enter now, OK?"

The light widened. Vega stepped inside and closed the door behind him. The taut look to his hollow cheeks was all Camilo needed to see to know the tension the man was under.

"Where are you?"

"Here." Camilo emerged from the darkness into the neon glow.

Vega looked relieved. "I am pleased you are alive, Comandante. It has been a terrible day. Terrible. When I heard your voice on the telephone I was greatly relieved. How did you get here?"

"The Florida police gave me a ride."

"Police?"

"Don't worry. He won't talk."

Vega threw the dead bolt and latched the night chain. He let out his breath and crossed to the cot and sat down. He sat looking up at Camilo, who stood to one side of the window, the red luminescence of the neon brightening his profile.

"Well?"

"I came to tell you they are looking for you everywhere. Six of our men have been taken. Four have been killed. You are in great danger, Comandante."

"How did they know I was alive?"

"We think they had information."

"But that could only come from Havana . . ."

"Yes, you were right. Paco."

"*Coño*," Camilo swore in the dark. "What do you say?"

Vega looked at him miserably. "Perhaps it would be better for you to return to Havana. I have a boat . . ."

"What about my mission?"

"I'll take care of it."

Camilo turned away and looked out the window. The street below was quiet and deserted. He saw a black-and-white cat walking under the street light. The cat started across the street and he watched it disappear between two buildings. "I have no wish to leave," he said.

Vega did not say anything.

"What is your opinion of this man who says he wants to give us information?"

"As I told you, he is convinced the counterrevolution will fail and that Kennedy will then seek to negotiate peace with Fidel. What this man asks are certain concessions for a very wealthy man he represents. Gambling concessions in Havana. He believes Fidel will try to rebuild tourism. That gambling will flourish. This very wealthy American wants a monopoly on the casinos."

"Is he loco?"

Vega shook his head. "I don't know, Comandante. He could be legitimate. He certainly has the information. But he is very ambitious. I fear him."

"But you're sure he knows?"

"Absolutely."

"You can take me to him?"

"Whenever you like. He says he will give the information to you alone. I don't like it, Comandante. He knows they're after you. What's to prevent him from betraying you?"

"Nothing."

"I don't like it." Vega stiffened. "He's dangerous, this man."

"Where does this informant live?"

"Not far. You want me to take you there now?"

"No, there is something I wish you to check out first."

"Whatever you wish."

Camilo stared off thoughtfully. "It will be interesting. He wants so much. Maybe he really has something to trade for it."

THE EVERGLADES, APRIL 13, 1961

Coming out of the kitchen into the morning air, Ellis Kern felt a sense of relief. He let the screen door slam behind him and started walking toward his white Cadillac. He heard the door open again and the mumble of voices and the thumping of shoes on the plank floor of the porch. He turned to see Martín's hulking figure followed by the fat man carrying the suitcase. He looked like a hardware salesman. He walked off to the Chevrolet parked to the right. The fat man dug in his pocket for keys and opened the lid of the trunk. He swung the big suitcase. Martín came up to Kern.

"What do you want me to do with them?"

"Make it look like an auto accident. You have his car, don't you?"

Martín gestured. "Over in the shed."

450

"I'd suggest you use gasoline. A fire goes a long way toward destroying evidence."

Kern opened the door of the Cadillac. The morning air was wet and cool, and he took a deep breath. It was a pleasure to be out of the stuffy kitchen with its smell of vomit and sweat and burned hair. There was something in the tension and fear that went with it. It made him feel as he did now, depressed, as though he had just slept with a prostitute. Especially on those rare occasions like this one when it was all futile, when nothing was learned. Kern got into the soft seat behind the wheel and started the engine.

Martín put one hand on the top of the car and leaned in the window. "Have you heard anything about the invasion?"

"Only that it is going to be soon."

Martín's big face broke into a grin. "We are still included, eh?"

"Don't worry, Martín. When they go to Cuba, you'll go. I promise you."

"That's good enough for me. I dream at night of going back to Cuba. It is my obsession."

Kern looked at him. "The time will come, Martín. The time will come. Now we have much work to do, my friend."

"As you say . . ."

"I want to have Camilo Carta by this time tomorrow. And I'd like him to be alive. Understand?"

"We'll get him. Where can he hide?"

Kern put the Cadillac in gear and drove out of the yard, passing the man at the gate, who looked cold and cramped, his collar turned up, hands shoved into his pockets. Kern waved at him. The man took his hand from his pocket and waved.

Martín stood watching the taillights going off down the dark road.

David heard cars driving out of the yard. He counted two and the jeep. There was no telling how many were left in the house. His eyes were becoming accustomed to the darkness of the tiny room. There was only one window, which was covered with heavy wire mesh. A dim glow from the yard lights shone through. He sat on the floor, which was covered with worn linoleum, and looked at his hands. He kept clenching them into fists in a helpless rage. He could not shake the images of Robin from his mind, nor the hollow feeling he had from the humiliation.

But what could he have done? Bound like a pig for slaughter, what could he do?

451

You could have done something, he told himself. For once, done something! What are you waiting for? Camilo or Amato to protect you? David felt miserably ashamed.

He stood and looked around the room again. Keep your head clear, he thought. There is always a way.

He walked to the door, counting the paces. Two and one half, wall to wall, he figured. All right, what next?

The room could not be more than ten feet by ten feet. Probably an old bedroom, he thought. He felt the door with his hands, carefully. It was solid. He ran his fingers along the doorframe, his fingers touching the wiring that was nailed to the edge of the trim boards. He felt the old-fashioned light switch and then ran his fingers again along the cord that went up the doorframe, across the top, up the molding on the wall to the molding along the ceiling. They must have built the house before they had electricity, he thought. They jury-rigged the wiring. He turned the light-switch knob and heard it click. Nothing happened. There was a light cord in the center of the room, but no bulb. He could see the cord dangling from the ceiling against the luminous window. He followed the wire from the switch to the baseboard and along the baseboard to the plug that had been tacked to the wall.

He sat down. His fingers were trembling. The frustration and the anger were almost too much to bear.

He knew their situation was hopeless. There was no power on earth that could save them now. A numbness began to settle over him.

He had no idea how long he had been in the room when he heard footsteps outside in the hallway. He heard male voices and the door unlock.

The door opened, revealing two Cubans in khaki fatigues. They were holding Robin between them. She had a wool army blanket wrapped around her shoulders. Her skin was colorless. Her hair, golden red in the light, fell in tangled strings around her shoulders. As they led her into the room David saw her bare feet taking short, painful steps. She was staring at him without recognition, the dull, lifeless stare of a catatonic.

The short Cuban with the round face smiled at David. The guard in the doorway was the one who looked like a young student, moustached, standing with a sawed-off shotgun. The two Cubans went out and shut the door.

David turned to Robin. She stood as they had left her, without moving. Only her hands trembled, holding the blanket around her naked shoulders.

452

"Robin?" She did not look at him, nor answer. "Baby?"

He took her gently in his arms, feeling her shudder beneath the blanket. "Oh, God, what have they done?"

She put her hand on his arm, and then slowly sank to the floor. David knelt with her. She lowered her face into her hands. David pressed her head against his chest, holding her, a tightness in his throat.

Robin did not move. She sat on her knees, the blanket pulled tightly about her, staring at nothing in the semidarkness.

"You . . ." she whispered tensely. "You won't ever tell anyone . . . what . . . they did to me, will you? Will you, David? Please? I couldn't . . . I couldn't . . ." Her voice trailed off. "Please, don't tell anyone, David, please?"

David closed her in his arms, but she did not yield to him. He felt her shivering and he released her. He stood, his legs weak and unsteady. He looked around for something, anything, to hit.

He crossed to the window and pulled aside the tattered cotton curtain and looked out through the wire-mesh screen at the mangroves beyond the yard that showed in the floodlight. He placed his hands on the windowsill and lowered his head against the screen. Something hurt his hand sharply and he jerked it away. Then he felt it again. It was the tip of a big nail protruding through the windowsill. He felt below and touched the round, thin metal shaft of the nail and then felt the head. Absently, he began to work it back and forth.

Driving back to his house in Coral Gables, Kern kept thinking about the girl. Little things about her. The way the sweat glistened on her flesh. The trembling of her muscles when they touched the electrodes to her. The look of shock when they inserted the tips of the electrodes into the crease between her spread legs. Her pubic hair the color of fox fur. He could not help wondering at the helplessness she felt when Carlos' fat fingers spread open her vaginal lips. Kern had felt a rush of excitement, which he found, even now, hard to suppress. He parked the car in the garage with that image in his mind.

As he shut the garage doors and walked across the lawn, he kept playing the scene, the way her legs tried to thrash against the bonds that held her to the chair, the way her flesh pulsated after the electrodes were lifted from the swollen genitals, red and angry-looking from the shock and heat, her copper hair wet and flashing in the light, the absolute terror in her eyes.

He had tortured women before, always with this same residual excitement. But he could not remember one as pretty as Robin Carta. He

453

found himself wondering what it would have been like if he could have stayed and fucked her after the torture. Pain and pleasure. It fascinated his imagination.

He fitted the keys into the double locks on his door, worked one and then the other, and then entered. The house smelled of dead cigaret smoke, airless and closed. The family was asleep upstairs. He flicked on the living-room lights and went to the sliding glass doors and opened them, glancing out at the swimming pool and the patio garden, smelling the fresh morning air. He took a deep breath to ease the tension in his chest.

Again, the image of the girl came to his mind, the white naked figure strapped to the chair, her legs spread open, the copper tuft between her white thighs. There was no question she had affected him. He felt a pleasant tightness in his groin.

Turning back to the living room, he touched himself, the pleasant sensation growing in his lower belly. I shouldn't do it, he thought. He felt a contraction of his penis, which was growing larger in his grasp, bulging through the cloth of his trousers, his fingers gently massaging until he felt himself taut. Damn, he thought to himself, I shouldn't. But the image of the girl was in his mind, indelibly, excitingly. He saw her buttocks straining, squirming against the pain, the needle points of the electrodes probing her, the flesh pink and glistening, yielding, quivering as the electricity crackled fiercely into her body. He crossed to the couch and sat down on the soft cushions. He unzipped his fly and took the thick flesh in his fingers and leaned back his head, closing his eyes.

Now in his mind he saw her clearly, her lips parting now, her eyes wide open, nostrils flaring, her pointed breasts jiggling—Jesus!

"Oh, God damn, damn, damn!" he groaned.

He felt the hand touch his shoulder and looked up with a pang of fear into the face of Camilo Carta.

"I'm embarrassed," Kern said softly, his thin lips barely moving to form the words.

Camilo's gaunt face broke into a mirthless smile. "There's worse to come," he said.

THE EVERGLADES, APRIL 13, 1961

David reached up and unhooked the curtain rod from above the window. He glanced outside. There was a faint daylight glow in the eastern sky. Already the mangroves behind the house were beginning to appear out of the gloom. He would have to hurry. He stripped the faded curtains from the rod. He glanced at Robin, who still had not moved. She sat on her knees, her eyes glazed. He placed the curtain rod on the floor beside the nail and moved to her.

"Why don't you try to lie down?" He took her shoulders in his hands.

"Please . . ." Her voice seemed far off. "Don't . . . don't touch me."

"I want to help you lie down."

"If I move, it hurts."

She lifted her shoulders to free his grasp. The blanket fell open. David gasped. Her breasts looked like distended balloons, the skin shiny and bruised. Her nipples so badly swollen they seemed about to burst. She was staring up at him. "Don't touch me," she said faintly. "Please. Leave me alone."

"God, Robin . . ."

Her breath came in quick, hard gasps between her teeth. "God, I hurt . . . I hurt!" Her look to him was filled with anguish and accusation. "Why don't you make them kill us, David? I don't want to . . ." The feverish glint in her eyes grew more intense, her whole body shaking involuntarily, her thighs twitching as she tried to sit with them spread wider, her hands fluttering to touch herself, then hesitating, moving to her breasts, hesitating, the frantic look in her face growing more and more intense until tears welled in her eyes, glistening. "For the love of God, help me!" she shrieked.

David watched her helplessly, not knowing what to do. Her hysterics continued to intensify and he was afraid the guard would come bursting in and discover the things he had already done. In desperation, he cocked his right hand and swung. He felt the impact of his fist against her jaw. Her head snapped back with a jarring crack. He saw her body hit the floor. She was trembling, like a stricken bird. For one panicky instant, he thought he had broken her neck. He leaned down and touched her. She groaned. She would be unconscious for a few moments.

Turning quickly, he ran his hands along the gritty linoleum floor until he touched the nail and then the curtain rod. His plan was desperate, but it had a chance. He had to do something. He had to. His hands shook and he was sweating as he worked the head of the nail into the hollow tubing of the curtain rod. It went in at an angle and jammed. For a moment he fought off the frustration, then placed the tip of the nail in the floor and pressed his weight onto the metal rod as much as he dared, afraid of bending it. He felt the nail give and move into the tubing. When he lifted it to the gray light by window he saw the sharp tip jutting from the end of the tubing by an inch. Perfect. He had a crude spear. He was armed.

Crossing the room from the window, David felt for the dangling electric wire that he'd pulled from the frame of the door. The wire ran from the switch on the wall to a plug that had been nailed to the baseboard. He had carefully pulled the wires from the plug. The two copper ends that had been attached to the terminals in the plug winked brightly as he lifted them and worked them into the opposite end of the hollow rod. It was crude and simple, but it might work. If only there's juice to this switch, he thought.

What he held in his hand now was a short metal spear with a nail tip. Theoretically, all he had to do was stab it into a vital area and turn the switch. The 110 volts of electricity would do the rest. Theoretically. The wire had to be hot, and there was no way to determine that without throwing the switch. But if he threw the switch, it would blow the fuse and alert the others. There was no alternative. He had to trust his luck.

He had six feet of wire attached to the curtain rod. If it stretched out too far, the wire would pull free and there would be trouble. No farther than here. Understand? he said in his mind. Got to be here.

He knelt beside Robin. He could hear her labored breathing, and then she groaned faintly and stirred. She would be coming around any second. David held her limp fingers in his for a moment. In the dark, her face seemed no more than a pale shape against the darker area of the blanket. He carefully reached down and lifted the blanket and tossed it aside. He could make out her naked body now, a pallid fleshy shape in the gray light. Then he got to his feet.

At the door, he placed his lips against the crack. "Can you hear me out there?" he said in a moderate tone. "Hello?"

Nothing.

"Hello, can you hear me? You out there in the hall? Can you hear my voice?"

He heard a footfall from the other side of the door. "What?" came the Cuban's voice. "What is it?"

"I need some help," he said in a low voice. "It's my wife—her breasts. Will you help me?"

The lock made a metallic snick in the door. David stepped back. The electric light from the hallway glared into the tiny room, revealing the dark shape of the tall young Cuban. "What's the matter?"

Startled by the light, Robin raised herself onto one elbow and stared. There was a dazed, bewildered glint in her eyes.

Light played on her swollen breasts. The tall young Cuban's face melted into a grin. His eyes swept her body. He scratched his head and

456

looked at her with a chuckle, shrugging his thin shoulders. "What do you want?" he said.

Robin just stared at him as though she was unaware of who he was or why he was there.

"I said what do you want?" the Cuban's voice said again. He stepped toward her.

From behind the door, David glanced through the crack into the hallway and saw the sawed-off shotgun beside the chair. He heard the shuffle of the tall Cuban's feet on the floor as he moved farther into the room, past the edge of the door.

"Say," he heard him speak. "You got pretty swollen, huh? How you feel, huh?"

"What?" Robin said weakly. "What?"

The young Cuban stared down at her. He had been greatly excited during her torture, and now, seeing her naked on the blanket, her shoulders and swollen breasts, her white-skinned thighs opened wide, he felt aroused. He glanced over his shoulder at the empty hall behind him. Then he looked back at her and smiled. "What you want me to do, señorita?"

He took a step toward her and reached out his hand, leaning toward her, and felt the taut flesh of her breast. She gave a sharp cry of pain. Her green eyes gleamed up at him feverishly in the light. He smiled at her.

From behind the door he heard a quick movement and knew he had stepped into a trap. But as he turned he caught only a flash of something coming at him out of the dark.

Holding the curtain rod in both hands, David lunged at him and drove the nail into his left ear with all his strength. It felt as though he had plunged it into a melon. He saw the man jolt. He wheeled and turned the switch. A spark leaped from the base of the curtain rod. The young Cuban, in shock and surprise, grabbed the rod that protruded from his ear like an antenna, his face contorted. Just then the current hit him and he went down thrashing wildly on the floor. He made no sound, just the gasping of his breath and the thumping of his legs.

The hallway light faded. Then, pitch black.

David felt for the doorjamb and went carefully into the darkness. He could hear voices coming from the kitchen. A chair scraped. A man's voice cursed loudly in Spanish. Then his fingers, moving along the wall very gently, touched the hard, cold metal of the shotgun barrel. He let out his breath in relief. He had the weapon in his hands now. He jacked a shell into the chamber. The *snick-snick* of the metal sounded loud in the cramped hallway. He could hear the voices and the movement from behind the door that led to the kitchen. He wondered how many rounds were in the shotgun. His head ached. He heard Robin whimper in the dark.

He whispered, "Get back in the far corner against the wall. Down on the floor. All right?"

"Yes."

"Go on, now." He had caught the Spanish phrases from down at the far end. This was it. They'd be coming now. He heard her move in the dark, the squeak of her bare flesh on the linoleum, then the rustle of the blanket as she went down onto the floor. "All right?" he whispered into the darkness.

"Yes . . ."

Squatting with his shoulder against the door, David waited. He knew his hands were trembling, and the sinking feeling in his stomach seemed to reach down to his bowel. He felt wobbly. A pain in his head throbbed in time with his pulse.

To his left, down the hall, the door handle squeaked in the dark. A flashlight winked and then glared full into his eyes. He pushed the butt of the shotgun against his shoulder. He fired. In the flash from the muzzle he caught a glimpse of the Cuban with the broken face. The gun made a roaring in the hall. His ears rang. He heard the heavy flop of the body. Then a shout and the scuffling of feet from the kitchen behind the dead man. A chair clattered to the floor. Footsteps, very rapid, and the screen door slammed. Then silence.

The air in the darkness around him smelled of burnt cordite. He squatted, listening to the sound of his own breathing. Then, very slowly and carefully, he eased himself across the hall until his right shoulder felt the wall. They would try to come in from behind him, he thought. Squatting here, he could cover both ends of the hallway.

His heart beating fast, he knew he was an instant away from oblivion. It yawned before him in the dark. All right, he thought. So it happens? Fuck it. Come on, you bastards, come on! With the shotgun in his hands, the weight of it, he felt an exhilarating sense of power. He realized he had never felt more alive. Yes, he was crazy now, he thought. Camilo is right. It's in our blood. I like it. I like the feel of it. Come on now, bastards. I'm here. I'm right here. Come on, kill me, fuckers! He knew it would come. A flash. A ripping force. Blackness. Eternity. You'll know it now.

Come on, he said to himself, come on, you bastards, what are you waiting for?

Then he heard it. Someone was crawling into the hallway from the kitchen. He could hear the heaviness of the man's body being drawn across the floor, and then he felt the faint vibration of the man's knee thumping softly on the wood floor as he moved.

David looked around. Nothing behind him yet. I wonder how many I can get? he thought.

Just then he saw movement in the dark at the end of the hallway by the kitchen door. He braced the pump gun against his side, cocked it and fired. It made an ear-smashing roar. Flame stabbed from the barrel. He saw the man, in that instant of light, on his hands and knees, just crossing the threshold. He heard the body hit the table in the kitchen and the thumping of feet on the floor as he flopped around out there. I must have got him in the head, David thought. The flopping continued for a long minute. Then stopped.

He had recognized the face of the tall, gaunt man who had helped torture Robin. "You son of a bitch!" He jacked the shell out of the shotgun and closed the breech with a snap. The empty clattered on the floor. All concern for himself had left him. His jaw ached from the clenching of his teeth, and his side hurt from the kick of the gun. He moved three steps down the hall and changed sides, so that his left shoulder touched the wall.

He waited, staring at the open doorway. The man he had caught on his hands and knees gave another thump from the kitchen floor and then silence. Then he thumped again. The sound carried through the wooden house. But there was no movement from the kitchen. Just then he felt a tingling at the back of his shoulders and turned quickly to see only darkness from the opposite end of the hallway.

There must be a door that leads in here, he thought. They're bound to try for it.

He waited, sweating in the dark, for something to move. Nothing. He felt the slick wetness where his hands gripped the pump gun. The steel barrel burned his fingers. The ringing in his ears annoyed him. Come on, come on! he said to himself impatiently. What the hell are you bastards waiting for?

CORAL GABLES, FLORIDA, APRIL 13, 1961

"You know I have gone to great lengths trying to find you," Kern said.

They were having coffee. Kern sat opposite him in the modest living room, looking composed once again. It was almost seven o'clock and Camilo heard from upstairs the morning sounds of a family awakening.

An alarm clock went off, two children exchanged quarrelsome words, a toilet flushed.

The living room reminded Camilo of a hotel. The furniture was spare and utilitarian. A TV set sat in the corner. Two oil paintings of seascapes hung from the wall. The only personal items were plastic-framed photographs of two young girls in frilly dresses which sat on the mantel.

"We have a bargain to strike," Kern said simply. "There's nothing very complicated about it."

It was like dealing with an attorney, Camilo thought. Only minutes earlier Kern had been masturbating and had seemed sick with embarrassment. He had excused himself and had been gone for only five minutes at most. And now he sat before him, having combed his hair and changed his shirt, looking crisply businesslike, prepared to negotiate a deal in his quiet, lawyerlike voice.

"Before a negotiation can be concluded, each side must know precisely what the other is willing to offer," Camilo said. "I don't know exactly what you are prepared to give me. Nor why you want to give it."

"I explained it all to Vega. Surely he filled you in," Kern said, sipping his coffee.

"He said you were prepared to tell me Castle's identity and where to find him. We're curious why." Camilo heard more footsteps upstairs and the slamming of doors.

"It's a question of simple expediency," Kern said blandly. "You see, Comandante, I am a different sort from the CIA people, even though we have been working together on this operation. They are caught up in a crusade. They believe they're going to win."

"And you don't?"

"I am a businessman. I have been retained to work on a business venture. From my present perspective I can now see that the venture is not panning out, so I am making contingency plans of my own."

"I take it the invasion of Cuba is the 'business venture' you refer to."

Kern nodded and poured himself some more coffee.

Camilo shook his head, as if to sharpen his perceptions. "I am sorry if I seem a bit obtuse, Mr. Kern. It's just that I have never heard an act of war referred to in these terms before."

Kern did not seem to hear. He was on his feet, his face turned toward the stairs. A tall, rather stately woman dressed in a long blue bathrobe was emerging into the living room.

"Good morning, my dear," Kern said, planting a kiss on her broad cheek. "We have an unexpected guest for breakfast this morning." He turned toward Camilo, who also rose to his feet. "Camilo Carta, I would like to introduce my wife, Mildred."

460

They shook hands somewhat stiffly. Mrs. Kern, Camilo thought, did not seem especially startled to find a visitor in her living room at such an early hour. She must be accustomed to these intrusions.

"Would you care for some eggs?" Mildred Kern asked.

"No, please don't go to any trouble—" Camilo started to say.

"No trouble," Kern interrupted. "The children have eggs every morning. We believe in starting the day with a nourishing breakfast."

Camilo shook his head. "Nothing for me, thank you. The coffee is fine."

Mrs. Kern walked toward the kitchen while Kern and Camilo seated themselves.

"I am curious," Camilo said. "What makes you so sure the invasion will fail?"

"Because of the bureaucrats and the romantics." Kern straightened in the chair, looking directly at Camilo, as though he had just confided the ultimate truth.

Camilo stared back at him. "I'm afraid I don't understand," he said.

Kern leaned forward and tapped Camilo on the knee with his forefinger. "The CIA people are bureaucrats. Bureaucrats don't win wars."

"I see."

"Jack Kennedy is the romantic."

"The romantic?"

"Yes, the romantic. He's been sold a bill of goods, but it won't take him long to figure it out. He won't have the stomach for this invasion of Cuba, you see? An invasion of Cuba—Americans shooting Cubans— doesn't fit into his idea of Camelot."

"I see." Camilo nodded as if in agreement.

Kern lifted his finger like a punctuation mark and said, "The day Castro first came to power I advocated sending in the Marines. That was the time to move. I had friends in positions of considerable influence at the time, Comandante. We couldn't get Eisenhower to move." Kern was reciting all this in a didactic tone. He might as well be analyzing the Peloponnesian Wars rather than the events that were breaking around them, Camilo thought.

Kern sipped his coffee and cleared his throat. "Now, getting back to my proposition, Comandante. I assume from your presence here this morning that your people want to make my deal."

"The deal Vega related to me is acceptable to us, Mr. Kern. However, Fidel may wish to finalize the negotiations personally, face to face. I am instructed to ask you if your client would be willing to come to Havana at some future date to meet with us."

Kern frowned.

Camilo said quickly, "Of course, that would be after the whole picture has clarified with regard to relations between our countries."

"I know," Kern said, thoughtfully. He cleared his throat, obviously having some difficulty making up his mind what to say. "Let me ask you, Comandante, is this request from Fidel himself?"

"Yes."

"And would it be an absolute condition of negotiations that my client be present?"

"Nothing is absolute. But it is Fidel's wish that the deal be consummated directly between himself and your client. It is a big commitment, Mr. Kern. Fidel likes to deal face to face."

"I see." Kern studied his visitor. "You understand it would be highly unusual for my client to agree to such a meeting. He is a man who is involved in a great many diverse enterprises. He is also a very shy man. On the other hand, considering the importance he places on this entire project, he might consent."

Two young girls were scampering down the stairs. The younger one ran straight for the kitchen, but the older, whom Camilo judged to be in her midteens, walked to Kern and gave him a morning kiss. Kern beamed and put a fatherly arm around her waist. "This is Camilo Carta, Emily," he said. "Emily Kern," he said to Camilo.

Emily smiled politely.

"Camilo is from Havana, Emily," Kern said. "Emily loves Cuba. She spent four very happy years there."

"That's right," Emily said, staring at the handsome visitor. "Did you just come from Havana?"

"Just a few days ago," Camilo replied.

"And did you ever meet Fidel Castro?"

"I know him very well."

The child's face was gleaming. "Really?"

"Run along and get your breakfast," Kern urged gently. "Camilo and I are in a business meeting. We'll be finished in a few minutes. If you have any questions about Havana, I am sure our guest would be glad to answer them."

Emily smiled and retreated toward the kitchen, from which sounds of clanking pans and dishes were emanating along with the aroma of frying bacon.

Kern leaned forward. "I take it, then, we have an agreement? It all rests on your word, Camilo."

"We would like to meet your client personally. He is welcome in Cuba. We feel your client and his organization would be a benefit to our economy. We are prepared to negotiate."

462

"Will you have Fidel send a personal note to that effect to my client?"

"I shall. Today. Will you give me your client's address?"

"Certainly." Kern dug into his back pocket and drew out his wallet. He selected a card and handed it to Camilo, who read it, frowned, and gave Kern a quizzical look. Kern smiled. "I'm sorry, it's on the back. You may not know it, but that is his own handwriting. You see, he's now residing in Nassau. In the Bahamas."

Camilo slipped the card into his shirt pocket. "I'll have the message sent from Havana this afternoon."

"You might have him include his request for a meeting on a personal basis in Havana. It might be persuasive."

"As you wish."

Kern folded his hands and let out his breath. In the kitchen, the children were arguing. Kern turned his head stiffly. "Keep it down in there!" The voices of the girls fell silent. One giggled. Kern turned back to Camilo with a thin smile. "The agent known as CASTLE is scheduled to depart for Havana on Friday at four-thirty-five A.M. He'll be met at the airstrip on South Bimini. He will arrive there a few minutes prior in a small plane. A larger one, a Beechcraft twin-engine out of Nassau, will follow him onto the strip."

"Why Bimini?" Camilo asked.

"My government has canceled all commercial air traffic to Havana."

"Who is this man Castle?"

"I don't know. All I honestly know is that the CIA has used him from time to time as a deep-cover agent, mostly in the Middle East."

"Is he in Miami now?"

"I know he flew here from Paris a few days ago to meet with the CIA's station chief. Whether he's now in town I can't say." Kern shrugged again.

"Do you know how he plans to carry out this assignment?"

"No. He has a plan of operation, I'm sure. But I've been unable to get access to the details. On the face of it, Comandante, I'd suspect he has some access to Fidel, wouldn't you?"

"Possibly." Camilo was thoughtfully silent for a moment. "I'd like to know how he plans to do it," he said finally.

"Well, I do know that if he fails, this whole Cuban operation will collapse. It all really depends on him."

"I see."

"They feel certain that with Fidel dead, your government will cave in. Operation Pluto, the landing, will push right into Havana."

"If you don't know his identity, how is it you know the details of his departure?"

"The details were run through my client, as a cover, you see? No matter how you investigate, you won't be able to trace that plane back to the CIA or the United States government."

Camilo shook his head slowly.

"Well, there you have it." Kern checked his watch. "I have to drive the children to school now," he said. "Unless you have any further questions?"

"No." Camilo shook his head. "No more questions."

He took her shoulders in his hands, trying to lift her.

"Stop it."

"Rob, we've got to get outa here."

"Stop it."

He sank down beside her. "Now listen, there's three dead guys in this house. The others ran off. But they could come back any time. If they do, they'll kill us, Rob."

"Ouch! That hurts, David."

"Listen, Rob, I'm going to carry you. It may hurt some, but it's the only way. We've got to get away from here."

"Please, don't. Stop! Stop it! Stop it!"

David stood, holding her in his arms. She felt light, thin. She struggled to free herself. Then she cried out in pain. She buried her face against his throat.

"Oh, David. I hurt so much!" she said in an outburst of tears.

David was walking down the hallway. He stepped over the body in the door and went through the kitchen, kicking open the screen with his foot. It slammed behind him as he went down the steps and across the dusty yard to where the Volkswagen sat puttering in the morning light. He'd left both doors open. He crossed to the passenger side and said to her as he began to lower, "I'm going to put you down now, Rob. Hang on to my neck."

Leaning over, David placed her in the passenger seat. He looked on her tangled copper hair and half-opened mouth. He closed the door and watched her as he walked around the front of the Volkswagen to the driver's side. She sat staring straight ahead through the windshield. He got in behind the wheel and slammed the door. He put the Volkswagen into gear and drove out of the yard. His eyes moved from the road to her haggard face.

"You're angry, aren't you?

David felt like crying.

"Say you're angry, David."

464

"All right, I'm angry. I'm fucking angry. I just killed three guys and I'm fucking angry!"

"You know what you are, David? You know . . . you liked killing those people didn't you?"

"You're damned right I did. After what they did to you!"

"Me? You cared what happened to me?"

"Yes. I cared!"

He braked, approaching the paved road. There was no traffic. Without making a stop, he turned onto the highway and gave it the gas. "We'll get you to a doctor," he said to her. "Hang on, huh?"

Glancing at her, he saw she had not changed position.

She raised her head from her hands and wiped her eyes with her knuckles, like a child.

"Why did it happen?" her voice said. It had that vague, far-away quality. "I just don't know why this happened, do you?"

"They were out to get Cam."

"But why hurt me? I didn't do anything to them, did I?"

"Robin, baby, just try to relax, huh? Take it easy. We'll be at the hospital in twenty minutes."

"I wish I'd gone with him. He wanted me to go with him." She turned her head and he saw the hurt expression in her eyes. "None of this would have happened to me, if I hadn't come back. I would have been all right, if I hadn't listened to—"

"What are you talking about?"

"I'm talking about *Michael!*" she screamed. "Don't you see? I should have gone with *Michael!*"

CHAPTER FORTY-FIVE

GUATEMALA, APRIL 13, 1961

As far as he could see there was jungle—millions of trees in the morning light. Gustavo Carta looked over his left shoulder at the helicopter pilot, a thin young man in a red baseball cap, his jaws chewing like a cow at its cud. His face was browned by the sun, clean-shaven. He wore earphones and he looked at Carta now out of the side of his eyes

465

and gave him a vague expression that was supposed to convey a sense of security. "Don't worry, we're all right," his look tried to say. But there was something uneasy in it. Carta did not feel comforted.

"I'd certainly hate to be stuck down there," he shouted.

The pilot lifted his earphones and said, "What?"

Carta pointed down at the dense jungle gliding under them a hundred and fifty feet below. He shouted, "I'd hate to crash in that stuff!"

The pilot replaced the earphones, smiled, and tossed his head in acknowledgment.

Carta could see a river now. It glistened through the trees. The mist was rising like steam.

"What river is that, do you know?" he shouted. Again the pilot went through the ritual of lifting the earphones, having Carta repeat, "That river? What's its name?"

The pilot gave him a shrug.

Leaning back in his seat, the helicopter vibrating, the whir of the blades overhead, Carta looked from horizon to horizon through the clear Plexiglas bubble. On his right were dark forested mountains; below, a mass of jungle trees cut by the river that twisted back and forth like a smoldering ribbon; on his left, beyond the profile of the pilot, were volcanic mountains. Then, ahead, he saw a thin column of blue smoke hanging in the air; the top diffused, spreading out over the trees. He caught a faint winking of what looked like campfires. The helicopter veered to the right and then turned back in a half circle, approaching the column of smoke with the sun at their backs. Carta gave the pilot a puzzled look, but the man was intent upon maneuvering the machine.

Now they were heading directly at the smoke. It seemed to rush at him rapidly, and then they were in it and he looked down into the clearing below and saw what looked like the thatched roofs of a dozen rectangular sheds in a clearing at the edge of the river.

He felt the helicopter sway and turn as they swept out over the river, banking sharply back toward the clearing, where he saw dozens of men standing in khaki fatigues. They were all looking up, watching them approach. The helicopter slowed, swayed, and began to descend directly into the clearing. It felt to Carta like going down very slowly in an elevator. The apprehension he had felt since yesterday began to mount.

He had been awake in his barrack room most of the night, trying to assess the reality of his position, trying to sort out the things Colonel Jack had blurted out in his drunken enthusiasm. Was it actually possible, Carta thought, pacing the room, that he was really not an official visitor at all, but rather a prisoner? Yesterday morning he had been seated in

466

that Miami hotel room, debating issues of historical significance to Cuba, and now he was a prisoner in a remote jungle camp in Guatemala? Impossible! Hadn't he spoken with Danforth, an assistant to the President of the United States, not twenty hours ago? A prisoner? How could they imprison him?

He had been awakened just before daylight by the presence of young Fernando Díaz in his room. The boy had been polite, quiet-spoken. It was time to leave, he told Carta. Groggy from fatigue, Carta had shaved in cold water, dressed quickly and gone out into the cool morning darkness to the jeep that awaited him. When they pulled up at the helicopter pad, there was the pilot in his red baseball cap waiting, talking with Mike, one of the crew-cut Americans who had been at dinner the night before. Mike had smiled at Carta and said that they would have to be flown separately to the staff meeting because the helicopter held only one passenger. Mr. Pelham would follow. Colonel Jack had sent his regards. And he had been rushed into the plastic bubble of this machine, strapped in, given a pat on the shoulder, and they had lifted off into the darkness.

Now fully awake, watching the red earth of the clearing at the edge of the river coming up toward him rapidly, seeing the thatched roofs of the long sheds around the compound in the trees, the men in khaki fatigues standing and watching, seeing their Cuban faces, their filthy, tangled hair and unshaven jaws, their eyes hollow and staring, the dust rising as the helicopter swayed and shuddered just above the ground, Gustavo Carta felt his fears of the night before revive. For what he was seeing now was not a military post. It was a prison. He knew it.

As soon as he stepped from the cockpit, a man came toward him, ducking his head as he came under the still-rotating blades, a short, moon-faced man in khaki fatigues, showing his gold teeth. His voice, when he spoke, holding out his hand, carried an unmistakable Middle European accent. "Good morning, Dr. Carta," he said, taking Carta's hand. "My name is Rudy. Welcome to Petén."

NEW ORLEANS, APRIL 13, 1961

Listening to the muted whine of the jet engines, feeling the smooth thrusting motion of the plane, Pelham settled back in his first-class seat and closed his eyes. He felt weary, yet there was also an edge of excitement.

"Excuse me, sir."

467

He opened his eyes to see the stewardess leaning over him. "Would you like anything?" She had lovely skin, long chestnut hair and wore no makeup. Pelham ordered a scotch. She placed it before him. "Would you like anything else?"

"Nothing, thank you." Pelham watched her move. She had a thick rump and heavy, graceless legs. Pelham thought it a shame that a girl with such a nice face should suffer such an ungainly shape.

He poured his Chivas Regal from the tiny bottle. It tasted good even at this early hour. It warmed him. Time to relax, he told himself. Now the important thing, Pelham told himself, was to put it in perspective, to keep it all under control. Everyone would be losing his head in the excitement and confusion. Pelham would have to be the steadying influence. He'd be the man who kept the ultimate objectives in clear focus.

Pelham stifled a yawn. He had not slept much. There had been that unnerving helicopter ride in the dark from Trax to Retalhuleu, and then the boring bumpy flight to New Orleans. Pelham smiled to himself, picturing Carta's face as he stepped off that helicopter and found himself in a prison camp. All his dignity, all that superior aloofness collapsing in the realization of what he really was; just another damn Cuban who tried to go against the mainstream. It amused Pelham now to consider all this. What good does your money and your social position do you now, Gustavo, old boy?

There would probably be some kind of unpleasant incident about this later, but it would be after the fact. The brigade would take Cuba, Navarro would be President, the hero of the hour—and he, Pelham, amicus curiae to the new government in Havana. Who would listen to Carta? Who would care?

With that sense of satisfaction, he turned his thoughts to New York, his destination. He looked forward to New York with keen anticipation.

Pelham felt confident, now, that he was playing a strong hand. There were times when he'd had his doubts, but now all the elements were in position. He was ready. All he needed was a little luck.

The stewardess came toward him and turned to the two men seated across the aisle and delivered their drinks. Pelham glanced at her broad rear as she bent over to set the drinks on their trays. He glanced at the crooked seam in her nylons. Her legs were as thick as a football player's, he thought. Really too bad. Such a pretty face.

He saw in his mind the pale image of Michael kneeling on the bed, his chest and arms hairless as a girl's.

Pelham groaned softly and opened his eyes and took a drink of scotch. He felt guilty, as though his fellow passengers had all been privy to his

468

thoughts. He felt disgusted with himself. He drained the glass and pushed the button for the stewardess. She appeared abruptly, her arm reaching up to punch out the call button.

"Yes, sir?"

"Another, please," he said, holding up his glass. Her eyes were hazel and they looked at him with a warmth of greeting that he could not ignore. Hello, she seemed to be saying.

She had a nice motion when she walked, her thick hips and thighs undulating beneath the brown skirt. Pelham suddenly found her attractive. He speculated whether it would be possible to arrange some kind of liaison in New York. He needed something like that; something to wipe away the ugliness he felt over the incident with that boy in Miami. It had been a mistake from the beginning, he knew that now. A terrible blunder. But it was in the past. Nothing could be done about it.

The stewardess came back carrying a fresh glass with the ice and two small Chivas bottles.

"Do you live in New York?" Pelham asked as she set the drinks down.

"Yes. I'm based in New York," she said, smiling at him. "Are you from New Orleans?"

"Miami, at the moment. I have a small electronics business there."

"How interesting."

"Not really, but it pays the bills."

"Your family lives in Miami, then?"

"No. I'm not married."

"I see."

"Are you?"

"No," she laughed softly. "We're not allowed to be married . . . I mean, and stay on this job."

"May I ask your name?"

"Ellen. Ellen Purvis. And you're Mr. Pelham, right?"

"How'd you know?"

"I read the manifest."

"Of course. How stupid of me. What do you do when you're in New York and not working? Have a beau, do you?"

"Now, there's a word I've not heard in some time, Mr. Pelham."

" 'Beau'?"

"Yes. It's a very old-fashioned word. Are you an old-fashioned man?"

"Make you curious?"

Her pretty face broke into a white smile. "Yes," she said with a cock of her head.

"Why don't you have dinner with me and find out?"

469

"Are you serious?"

"Quite."

The other stewardess poked her head out from behind the partition and gestured.

"I'll be back," Ellen Purvis said to Pelham, and she went off down the aisle to the front of the plane. As she turned, her hazel eyes glanced sideways at him.

Pelham stretched his legs. Yes, he thought to himself, that would be nice, wouldn't it?

He poured the amber-brown liquid into the plastic glass. He felt, just then, serenely confident.

CHAPTER FORTY-SIX

WASHINGTON, D.C., APRIL 14, 1961

President Kennedy walked briskly into the new State Department auditorium for his weekly press conference. The reporters arrayed before him looked harried. It would take a major story to crack the front pages the next day. That day's papers were emblazoned with the story of Major Yuri Alekseyevich Gagarin hurtling into space in his rocket to become the first man to orbit the earth. Adolf Eichmann, the Nazi chief of the Gestapo's Jewish Affairs section, had just gone on trial in Jerusalem. In Laos, the pro-Communist Pathet Lao guerrillas were plunging through the confused ranks of the retreating royalist forces backed by the United States.

The reporters' hands shot into the air. The first question dealt not with Gagarin or with Laos. It dealt with Cuba. Would the President rule out American intervention?

The President worded his reply cautiously. "The basic issue in Cuba," he said, "is not one between the United States and Cuba. It is between the Cubans themselves. And I intend to see that we adhere to that principle. This Administration's attitude is so understood and shared by the anti-Castro exiles."

There would be no intervention in Cuba by United States armed forces, the President reiterated, "under any condition."

470

Navarro took off his shirt. They were all sitting in the clearing, looking at the blackboard the CIA men had set up. All around were pine trees.

The Americans arrived, smiling, shaking hands. Navarro recognized one from the guerrilla training camp in Panama. The acetate cover was removed from the map on the blackboard. Copies of the invasion plan were passed out by the CIA men. Dobbs smiled as he gave Navarro his folder marked "Operation Pluto." He read:

"Commencing at H-Hour of D-Day, the brigade is to engage in amphibious and parachute landings, take, occupy, and defend beachheads in the areas of Cochinos Bay and Playa Girón of the Zapata Swamps in order to establish a base from which ground and air attacks against the Castro government of Cuba may be carried out."

The briefing began now, but Navarro's mind was distracted. The Bay of Pigs! He couldn't believe it. It didn't make sense. The brigade was to land and control forty miles of Cuban coastline. The bay was twelve miles in width at the entrance, tapering like a spear tip to Playa Larga, eighteen miles inland. It was surrounded by mangrove swamps. Eighty miles away were the Escambray mountains. The brigade was to land at three points in the bay. Diversionary attacks were planned by commando groups in Oriente and Pinar del Río provinces. Castro had no troops close to the main landing site. Besides, the only way to communicate from the Bay of Pigs to Havana was a single telephone fifty miles away. The brigade's air force would destroy any attempts by Castro to move troops. Planes would bomb the main road every five minutes. "Don't worry about the air, boys, it belongs to us."

All the brigade had to do was hold the forty miles of beachhead at the Bay of Pigs for seventy-two hours.

"And what do we do after that?" Navarro asked.

Dobbs stepped forward and smiled at them. "After that, we'll be there to tell you the next step," he told them. "You'll pick up five hundred guerrillas the first day, five thousand additional volunteers by the next. You'll be so strong by then, you won't want to wait for us. So I'll tell you what I want you to do." He glanced around at the faces of the Cuban officers. "Boys, I want you to put your hands out, make a left turn and head straight for Havana!"

Dobbs watched the men clamber onto the ships. He felt a swell of satisfaction. It was all going to happen. They were really going to get to Havana after all!

They were a strange assortment of men, he reflected. When he had first gotten them, many had never even fired a gun. Only 135 of the fourteen hundred in the brigade were professional soldiers. Of the rest, most were students or professional people—lawyers, doctors, businessmen. Three of the men were Catholic priests, one was a Protestant minister. Several were U.S. citizens, including a truck driver from Brooklyn. The average age was twenty-nine, though one man was as old as sixty-one. A few were kids still in their teens. Nearly all were white men; only fifty were Negroes. Many of them were real patriots. They would lay down their lives for their country. One of them had told him he was a playboy—he had joined the fight because he enjoyed playing in Havana more than anyplace else. It was reason enough to be there, Dobbs figured.

Yes, they were a strange lot. He was glad they would all be together in Havana.

CHAPTER FORTY-SEVEN

MIAMI, APRIL 14, 1961

It was light outside, but the shutters, closed and latched, blocked the sun. Terrifyingly awake, Elizabeth tried to pray. "Our Father Who art . . ."

No. She was too frightened. She had experienced this panic before. What was it? What had caused it? Something she had seen in her dream. Something she could not now bring to mind. She felt the terror in her mind, pressing against her, devouring her.

"No!" her voice rang out in the bedroom.

As though a membrane had split, she recognized the familiar surroundings. The yellow hibiscus in the brown earthen pot on the glass top of the coffee table, the blue cushions of the couch, the wing chairs with their gay blue floral print covers, the metal frames of the photographs on the mantel, like friends out of the twilight gloom of her own bedroom. She sighed to herself in relief. The sheets around her felt damp. The air was oppressive.

Throwing back the sheet, she placed her feet solidly on the floor.

For a moment she sat staring in a stupor at her bare knees, the tiny bleached hairs on the tanned skin of her thighs. She raised her eyes to stare straight in front of her, inhaling through her mouth. I wonder if anyone else has been faced with this? she thought. Surely.

But there's no comfort in that.

How can you expect comfort? she wondered. There is no comfort.

Standing, she went through the open bathroom door and entered the cold smell of tile. Lifting her nightgown, she sat on the commode. She looked down at the unpainted nails on her toes.

Generous tears welled in her eyes, flooding out the vision of her knees and the stubby shapes of her toes. She looked upward at the high, bare ceiling in the gloom, and she felt as though she were encased, the tightness, the weight, living within her and growing with each breath. She saw it now, in her mind, clear and indelible. Gustavo leaning down to Elena, the caterer, lean, gray-haired, walking away from them—and then the terrifying shot, the man's body jolting with the sound of the bullet striking flesh and being thrust as if by an invisible force through the glass door. Gustavo on the patio, face down, his body covering Elena, whose white legs protruded from beneath him. Yes, she thought, yes! That was it. Elena!

She found herself standing naked in front of the shower, the light turned on. She saw the gleam on the clean white tile. She heard the running water in the commode, not quite sure of how she got there. She realized that she had to see him, to explain her reasoning, beg his advice. She needed his help.

She could not face this alone. Not really. Not by herself. It was simply too much.

My God, she thought, I'll go insane!

Quickly, she reached out and turned the metal handles and heard the hissing splash of the shower, feeling it on her arms, warming. Then she stepped under.

When he saw she was crying, he wanted to rush to her, to hold her. But instead Amato watched helplessly, as Elizabeth dabbed at her eyes. Then, torn with his own emotions, he had gotten up and walked to the window of the yacht and stared out at the river.

It had been many years since he'd seen Elizabeth cry. She had cried when she first saw Amato after David was born. Amato had cried, too. He had told her it was a boy, a healthy nine-pounder. She smiled at him before they both started bawling. The nurse looked at them as if they were both idiotically sentimental.

Elizabeth had cried when she saw him at the airport in Miami. Despite Camilo's warning of their imminent danger, Carta had hurriedly put her on the plane for Miami and had decided to remain in Havana.

Elizabeth, feeling very desolate and alone, had not expected to see Amato at the airport. She hadn't even had time to phone him and tell him what had happened, but Amato had known and he was there to meet her. She saw him, standing to one side of the crowd. She rushed to him and they hugged each other.

All that seemed long in the past now. As he heard her sobbing, he sensed the depth of her despair. It was as if she had been fighting off the knowledge that she had long carried within her, and now she could do it no longer. The forces that had been set in motion were now reaching their inevitable climax, and Amato shared with her that sense of the helpless observer looking on with shocked disbelief at the events that were overtaking their lives.

Elizabeth had been there on the yacht when he arrived, puttering about the cabin, fixing coffee and tidying up. Amato felt a tremendous lift seeing her again. He kissed her and felt her body glide into his, felt her warmth stirring against him.

It had been several weeks since he had last been on this grand boat, which he had purchased for her at auction six years before. He knew the boat had been very special to her—her private place. She would meet him there from time to time and they would have coffee and talk. Incredibly, though many weeks or sometimes even months would intervene, it had always seemed as if they would pick up the thread of their relationship without a moment's awkwardness. There was a closeness that transcended time or events—a deeper bond than any other he had known.

She had served coffee and they talked gravely for forty-five minutes. Elizabeth had been in firm control of herself, but he could sense her inner turmoil. She said the difficult things she had to say in a calm, even voice. Amato watched her and marveled at her self-mastery. She talked about Camilo. She had it all carefully analyzed in her mind. Her reasoning was impeccable, but Amato felt himself sag as he listened to Elizabeth's cool, cultivated voice reason its way through the muddle of events toward her inexorable conclusion. There was nothing in the world Elizabeth had wanted more than to have Camilo back. The family together again. It was as though Elizabeth had willed these things to happen and because of her will they would indeed happen.

And that had frightened Elizabeth. She was a woman who understood love but who also understood tragedy. Her life had dealt both to her, and had annealed her perceptions to reality. And reality, in this case, had crystallized suddenly the morning of the assassination attempt on Carta. The bullet had been deadly accurate, but in the split second

474

before it was fired Carta had bent forward to pick up Elena, who had tumbled to the ground.

An assassin would surely have taken another shot, even though the bodies of Carta and Elena were intertwined.

And yet, whoever it was had vanished. No further bullets were fired, and then the bodyguard had leaped upon Carta, shielding his body. And everyone assumed the assassin had been frightened off, but Elizabeth knew that assassins are not frightened off that easily.

"It was Camilo, wasn't it?" she had demanded, her eyes that fierce and sparkling blue as they held him in their steady gaze. "Wasn't it?"

Amato nodded. "Yes, it was."

Her hands had fluttered in the air and she had walked to the window and stood with her back toward him, her head down. She was silent a long time.

Her head moved, rising slowly until she was erect again. She did not look around at him. He heard her voice, small and far off, saying, "At first, I couldn't believe it . . . but I knew, Sal. I knew."

"There's a lot more to it, Elizabeth," Amato said to her.

She turned to look at him, her eyes wet and red with her crying, yet they had changed expression, a hard, cold glint in them now.

"What are you talking about?"

Amato walked over to her and took both her hands in his and told her. By the time he was finished, they were sitting in the bright and streaming light that flooded into the cabin through the windows; Elizabeth sitting half in the sunlight, her hair, the side of her face, the shoulder in the white blouse that had become almost transparent so that he could see the strap of her bra against her skin, her bare arm and hand and half her thigh in the white slacks, brilliant in the sunlight, and the far side of her shaded, dim and away from him, her hand sweating as he held it. She did not move, save for the steady rise and fall of her breast as she breathed.

"Oh, Sal," she said very quietly, leaning her head against his shoulder. "My dear, dear, Sal . . ."

Amato nodded. "We best be ready." He paused for a moment and lit a cigaret. He inhaled deeply. "I just hope we're wrong, Elizabeth."

"I hope so, too," she started to say. It was then Amato noticed that her iron self-control had begun to shatter completely. She struggled for composure, but the tears had begun to flow, followed by racking sobs. He scurried into the head in search of tissues, not knowing what else to do, but there were none there, so he lamely offered her some paper napkins from the galley. He looked at her for a moment, and it was then he walked to the window and stared out at a barge that was chugging slowly through the narrow channel. Amato felt very weary now, and he also felt another emotion that he had not been aware of for a very long time. He was getting old, Amato realized, and he was also becoming afraid.

CHAPTER FORTY-EIGHT

The "Iranian caper," as MR/CASTLE chose to describe it, had been an early success of Pelham's career. When stationed in London in the 1950s, Pelham had specialized in the affairs of the turbulent Middle East. In 1953 he was summoned to Washington for a top-secret assignment. He had suspected what it was even before his briefing. He had been keeping a special eye on Iran for years. He knew it would become a powder keg.

The Shah of Iran had been placed in power by the British and he had seen his nation successively invaded by the Russians, annexed as a base for the Allies and then in effect appropriated as a fiefdom of the oil companies. Then in 1951 the erratic Dr. Mossadegh had come to power and the nation suddenly veered toward the left. Mossadegh nationalized the oil companies, exiled the Shah and seemed bent on establishing firm relations with Moscow. By 1953 the U.S. and England had lost patience; it was decreed that Mossadegh had to go. The Shah, if returned to power, would be a dependable friend of the U.S. and of the oil companies.

It was Pelham's task to organize the coup and coordinate his activities with the British Secret Service. To effect his mission, Pelham required the services of a man who could help arrange the shipments of arms the Shah would require, and who also would be prepared to deal forcefully with those individuals who might get in the way.

Pelham had been following the activities of MR/CASTLE, as he had come to be called, ever since he first started making his presence felt in the months immediately after World War II. In those days of turmoil and near-anarchy, MR/CASTLE exhibited a remarkable facility for locating caches of surplus weapons and bidding on them quickly before they could come on the market.

He did not care about the politics of his customers, whether they were left or right, established regimes or upstart rebel bands. MR/CASTLE's inventory was impressive: Garand rifles he had bought in Britain, machine guns he had found in Sweden, British Enfield rifles from the Philippines, Mausers that had been stockpiled in Taiwan, German ME-42s left by Hitler's troops in Greece; British Sten guns parachuted by the Allies into France during World War II for the underground; American Brownings stashed in Argentina. The secret arsenals were everywhere. And so were the customers—the guerrillas in Greece, Moslem rebels in Libya, the Trujillo regime in the Dominican Republic, King Faisal in the Middle East. And now the Shah.

There were several advantages, Pelham reasoned, to dealing with MR/CASTLE. Since he conducted his business with both Communist and anti-Communist factions, he could not be pinned to the U.S. or to the CIA. Further, MR/CASTLE was, at the time, an enormously ambitious man. His activities thus far had been confined to the highly volatile and competitive small-arms trade. Now he wanted to move up to bigger game—customers whose aims were grander and who had the resources to pay their bills on time. If MR/CASTLE saw the chance to break into the big time, Pelham argued, he would be more than ready and willing to implement those "special instructions" that the CIA would occasionally require of him. He would be a valuable resource for the agency—it was simply a matter of making a deal with him and then setting him up for the big moves.

Pelham's superiors in Washington readily agreed with his reasoning and with his plan. It was "green light" all the way. Now there was the question of MR/CASTLE himself.

It took Pelham three weeks just to find him. His associates in New York and Havana professed to have no knowledge of his whereabouts. When Pelham finally ran him down in Athens, MR/CASTLE declined Pelham's request for a face-to-face meeting. He made his living as "an independent," he stressed. He was not particularly eager to talk with the CIA about a long-term arrangement. He distrusted long-term arrangements.

It took several phone calls for Pelham to persuade MR/CASTLE to commence serious negotiations. Even then he shied away from a meeting, insisting on written memoranda. For three days they exchanged their memos. Pelham would dispatch a four-page letter to MR/CASTLE's hotel in the morning. He would receive a response that night. At the end of the three days Pelham returned to London and cabled Washington that he had made the deal. MR/CASTLE was now on retainer. It was time to move ahead with the Iranian plan.

Events moved quickly from there. The coup had been carefully planned and was executed with surgical precision. Mossadegh fled into exile. The Shah was back in power and was dutifully grateful to his benefactors. He was also appreciative of MR/CASTLE's talents. Having survived the trauma of invasion and exile, the Shah was now determined to assemble an arsenal that would ensure his future autonomy. Through MR/CASTLE's good offices, he initiated a grandiose buying spree that included not only guns and tanks but also sophisticated electronic gear for Savak, his secret police. And then came his Air Force—Tiger jet fighters first, then Sabres. The orders were in the millions and then hundreds of millions of dollars.

And so it had all been accomplished. The Shah had established himself as a force to reckon with. MR/CASTLE had moved into the big time. And the CIA had made itself some valuable allies. The "due bills" would be collected someday.

Despite their complex dealings, Pelham still had never even seen a photograph of MR/CASTLE over the years, although he knew that one was on secret file at the agency; nor had their paths crossed since the coup in Iran. From time to time, Pelham heard rumors in the agency that MR/CASTLE had been called upon to make an occasional arrangement. During the Guatemalan uprising in 1954, for example, it was reported that MR/CASTLE had been prevailed upon to divert a key arms shipment that had been ordered by the Árbenz regime, thus leaving that leftist government helpless before the CIA-backed forces of Castillo Armas. MR/CASTLE had performed well. But these were minor missions. The "big chit" had not as yet been collected.

MR/CASTLE's role in the Cuban operation, Pelham felt, seemed almost preordained. Mindful of his valuable contacts around the world, Castro had already enlisted his services not only for munitions but also for other key supplies. Their relationship had gone back to Castro's days in exile in Mexico City. Despite his network of friends and allies, however, MR/CASTLE had run into trouble. Castro's finances were limited. Moreover, he found himself confronted with tacit trade embargoes brought by U.S. pressures. The U.S. did not want Castro to get his supplies. Even someone of MR/CASTLE's abilities found it hard to buck the U.S.

Aware of these problems, Pelham had flown to Washington to meet with Vermillion and to propose an unorthodox idea. It was Pelham's notion that the CIA would help resolve Castro's supply problems through MR/CASTLE. The CIA would see to it that limited quantities of matériel would be made available to the Castro regime—sufficient to enhance MR/CASTLE's credibility. Once the bond of trust between Castro and MR/CASTLE had been solidified, then he would be in a position to implement what would be his most important assignment. Vermillion had concurred with Pelham's plan. He had cleared it with the White House.

The only one who was unenthusiastic was MR/CASTLE. It had taken Pelham ten arduous hours of persuasion and several less-than-gentle reminders of past favors, plus some $500,000 in cash, to bring him around. This was to be, MR/CASTLE emphasized, his final mission. The slate was to be wiped clean.

CHAPTER FORTY-NINE

KEY BISCAYNE, FLORIDA, APRIL 14, 1961

Amato finished packing shortly after midnight. He had only packed his shaving things, a clean shirt and socks and a change of underwear. He had cleaned his 44-caliber magnum and placed it in the holster that he would wear under his jacket. The weapon had been his constant companion for years now. It had served him well.

Then there was nothing to do but wait. That was always the worst part. At the moments of action, the life-and-death moments, he always found within himself a remarkable reservoir of calmness that surprised even him. It was as if he were detached from his body, viewing events from a distant perspective. Sometimes, at those moments, he felt as if he had already moved past that point in time, dwelling in some future continuum, and was now reliving the event, knowing already that he had survived it, that all had turned out well. He wondered whether other men who lived in the frequent presence of danger experienced similar sensations. And yet it was something he could never talk about. It would sound foolish, even sentimental.

The thing that had suited him for the life he had lived had been this detachment. He did not fear dying. He simply felt it was of minor importance. His death would leave only a faint ripple among the acquaintances he had, and perhaps one or two sincere regrets. His attorney in Miami had his will, with instructions to open it in the event of his death. He had left everything to Elizabeth Carta.

He felt entrapped in the whole web of intrigue that had taken over MR/CASTLE's life. His first instincts, years ago, had been to tell Pelham to fuck off. He'd been doing well enough on his own. He didn't need help from the goddamn Ivy-League CIA spooks—didn't need them at all. But he'd been naïve. He had no idea of the money they could offer, the power they could wield. Or how addictive it would get—the apartments in New York, Paris, Miami, Havana, the big accounts in the banks, the cars and women and clothes, and being greeted everywhere with deference. It all flowed from money and power, and the problem was he had always needed more; there was not enough. Why the hell hadn't he gotten out when he had a chance? You didn't get out, he told himself, because it was all too damned good. It took his breath away. It still took his breath away.

He picked up the heavy revolver and slipped it into the shoulder holster under his jacket, took the valise and the tan trench coat and walked out of the bedroom into the living room. As he did, he brooded about the plans for the coming day. It had all been brilliantly worked out, he thought. It was so simple it seemed to him to be sinister.

Two nights ago, he had gone to the Cadillac Hotel on Miami Beach and taken the elevator to the fourth floor. Room 417. The door was opened by a small, compactly built man in his early fifties. The man wore gold-rimmed glasses and had a large head sparsely covered with gray hair. Behind the glasses the man's eyes were shiny as rosin. They kept blinking steadily as though he had something in them. He identified himself as Dr. Shirer, special assistant to the deputy CIA director for scientific affairs. He said he'd flown in from Washington to check him out on the material he was to use.

Dr. Shirer had gone to his suitcase and taken out a small leather kit containing rubber gloves, two surgical masks, and a syringe. Then he had carefully extracted a small medicine bottle which had a sealed tinfoil cap. The fluid in it was faintly milky. Dr. Shirer took a cedar box of cigars from the suitcase, and a cellophane envelope containing tax stamps, both Cuban and French. He and Amato had gone into the bathroom wearing the surgical masks.

"You must memorize which of these cigars we have contaminated before we seal the box," Dr. Shirer told him. "This is extremely potent. Once it is introduced into the mouth, the course of the disease is impossible to arrest."

He had watched as each H. Upmann Number 1 cigar was carefully injected with the milky fluid from the syringe. "You see?" Dr. Shirer said to him, his eyes emotionless behind his thin glasses. "When he settles back and puts the cigar in his mouth, it will all be over. The thing for you, of course, is to leave the country as soon as possible."

"I got it," he'd said.

"Very well. Is there anything you wish to ask?"

480

"Only a technical question."

"Yes?"

"You say this agent is lethal. What is it? Poison?"

"No, a virus." Dr. Shirer cleared his throat. "It has a limitation to its effect, you understand? It must be used within the next seven to ten days."

"How will it get him?"

"As though he caught a virus indigenous to Havana. We've done all this carefully. It will take a few hours to feel its effect. Like the flu. Once under way, its course is terminal. An autopsy will reveal acute viral pneumonia. Nothing more. It's an extremely virulent microorganism," Dr. Shirer told him. "Basically, it is a virus type currently causing a flu epidemic in sections of old Havana. We've managed to develop a strain which is quite effective for our purposes."

He carefully replaced the last cigar in its silver metal container, sealed it expertly, and placed it in the last space in the box. "Please note, both top panel and bottom rows, except for the last one on your right, when you hold the box thus, have been contaminated. If you take a cigar, take this one. If he happens to pick this one, you take the one below it on the next layer."

He stared at the row of cigars that Dr. Shirer had sealed so expertly they looked untouched. They were Castro's favorite. He handed the box back to Dr. Shirer and watched him seal it with the tax stamps. An expert would have thought they had come freshly from a tobacco shop in Paris.

"Is this gentleman a close associate of yours?" the doctor asked him as he carefully placed the last stamp.

"He's a friend."

"And he trusts you." Shirer smiled thinly. "It's always your friends, isn't it?"

That was the plan. It had an incredible simplicity that amazed him. He wondered who in the labyrinth of the CIA had formulated it. They had baited the trap with a set of detailed blueprints of a mechanical cane-cutting machine. Castro had described his problem to Amato as one of "extreme urgency and difficulty to solve." They had to find a way to cut sugarcane with machinery. The professional cane-cutting labor force had dwindled as the laborers went into better-paying jobs in the vast bureaucracies that had sprung up in Cuba almost overnight. The volunteer labor which Castro had mobilized from the general population cut the cane slowly and badly. Furthermore, he had said, since the government provided the volunteers with boots, gloves, machetes, medical care, food and lodging, as well as their regular salaries, "the cost of production is higher than the price we get for sugar." So the CIA had come up with the plans, which the Hawaiian producers had been working on for ten years. They grew cane similar to Cuba, in tangled clumps. If it worked in Hawaii, it would work for Fidel.

So they had him. Fidel would be at the breakfast meeting in Havana tomorrow, without fail. It was all so simple and deadly, he thought. You take a man's habits and you find a means to use them to kill him. It made him shudder when he thought about it. How can anyone escape? One way or another, they'll find your weaknesses. Women. Liquor. Wine. Tobacco. Golf. Tennis. Or just riding in a car. Or eating. Yes, eating would be a simple way. How about brushing your teeth? Everybody's vulnerable. A little shot of Dr. Shirer's favorite juice in your toothpaste and you die with a clean smile. Shit. What a world.

He mixed a gin martini, saluted the nameless genius who had conceived the plan, and sipped the clean-tasting drink. You thought up a winner, pal, he said to the glass. It's too bad. Sometimes we just don't get to the ball park in time. He flicked on the television set and sat down on the sofa and, sipping the martini, watched the wrestling match. He grinned at the obviously staged antics of the two televised combatants as they grunted and groaned on cue and tried to look menacing. It was strange, he reflected, how the public's appetite for rage and violence was such that they would pay to see these pudgy, stumbling actors as they went through the motions of a fight. With himself, whenever it came down to the crunch, he never felt rage. If anything, he felt remorse.

He felt that remorse now. He felt it far more acutely than ever before. He waited.

Twenty minutes later he heard the buzzer. That would be his companion downstairs. He went to the foyer to let her in.

PETÉN, GUATEMALA, APRIL 14, 1961

Gustavo Carta was confronted in the uncertain firelight by a tall, thick-chested man. He wore a broad-brimmed straw hat. His copper face suggested to Carta the features he'd seen in Mayan stone carvings.

"My name is Lezo, señor," he said in Spanish. His voice was deep, soft. "I was sent to help you."

"Yes?"

"I come from my village downriver."

"Yes?"

"I was told to tell you Alfaro sent me."

482

Carta looked around. The shed was dark. He had been awake for hours, thinking, listening to the tropical rain on the thatched roof. All around him he heard the snoring of the prisoners. There were more than a hundred in the camp, poor wretches from the brigade who had defied the CIA agents back in January, when the purge hit the training camp. He heard someone at the end of the shed coughing. Out in the compound a half-dozen smudge fires were burning, filling the air with acrid smoke against the mosquitoes. He felt a touch on his arm.

"Come," the man whispered.

Carta followed him out from under the roof of the hut and squatted beside one of the fires. The rain had stopped. The red earth had turned to a thick mud that stuck to his shoes.

Looking around him, Carta could smell the latrine that had been dug off in the jungle behind the shed. It was the sort of smell you get in the filthiest, most backward peasant villages in the tropics, where no one has ever heard of sanitation facilities. The aroma of sewage permeated the jungle darkness, and combined with the damp heat it was overpowering. Around the clearing Carta saw the series of barracks buildings, lean-tos really, with thatched roofs and open sides. Despite the smoke, drifting low to the ground in the humidity, the night air whined with mosquitoes. They stung him viciously and seemed to whirl about his face in an unrelenting cloud.

Lezo pointed to where silhouettes of men were moving in the glow of the fires. He whispered, "Guards. Over there."

Carta squatted beside Lezo, feeling the steady, irritating feather touch of the mosquitoes on his face and hands.

"Alfaro will come," Lezo told him, making a whirling gesture with his hand.

"Helicopter? Here?"

"No. Downriver. You will see. We must go."

"How far?"

Lezo pointed up at the sky, indicating the position of the sun. "To-morrow we shall be there. Come."

They crossed the open area to the barracks building. The light from inside came from a kerosene lantern. It cast an elongated glow on the wet leaves that covered the ground. Carta hesitated, listening. From inside, he heard the crackling static of what sounded like a radio. He listened more closely. It was music he heard. He stood there, puzzled. Now he heard singing. It was an opera! *The Marriage of Figaro,* that was it. He was sitting here, in the middle of the goddamn jungle, listening to Mozart! The record sounded ancient and the sound crackled, but it was Mozart nonetheless.

The next thing he heard was Lezo's shout. When he turned his head, the pane of glass broke in the window beside the door. He saw the blinking flash of the gun in the dark to the right. All the time Rudy sat there, with the record player going and the soprano shrieking for a high note. Out of the corner of his eye, he saw Rudy kick himself out of the chair and go under the table.

Carta realized he hadn't moved. He was still standing, motionless, in the open doorway, silhouetted against the kerosene light. There were footsteps running out to the right and he heard the gun fire again and saw the spark from the weapon. Something ripped the air close to his head and he heard a faint *ping!* as the bullet went past him. He felt a sharp sting in his forearm and glanced down at it. He was surprised to see flecks of blood on his wrist. Tiny shards of wood were sticking from the skin, like the needles from a cactus. Then he saw where the bullet had splintered the frame of the door.

"Come!" Lezo reached out his hand, and Gustavo felt his grasp. It had all happened so fast it bewildered him. To his right he heard shouting, he saw dark shapes moving among the trees in the firelight, men running. "We must hurry," Lezo said. "This way!"

He followed, running in the darkness, holding to Lezo's hand. It was so dark when they entered the jungle he could not see the man moving in front of him. If he had not held his hand, he would have been lost. He was in total blackness.

It started to rain again as he followed Lezo along a narrow path. The dark was hot and wet under the trees. Gustavo walked, listening to the squish of his shoes in the thick mud and the steady pattering of the raindrops on the leaves around him. Occasionally a bird made a rasping cry. The air was heavy. Once, Lezo stopped, frozen motionless on the path ahead of him. Carta could see nothing. He felt the pressure of his guide's hand.

"*Muy malo,*" Lezo said. "Snake."

BIMINI, APRIL 14, 1961

Camilo saw the island ahead in the dark and eased back on the throttle, slowing the boat in the swell. They had been pounding all the way across from Miami. As he slacked off, letting it ride the waves, he felt relieved at the loss of tension. It made him nervous to be out alone at night with that much water around him. The swell had been huge when they left Government Cut and passed the sea buoy. There must have been a quarter mile between the crests. He could see them coming in the starlight like huge moving walls off the starboard quarter, lifting the little boat slowly and then very rapidly as the crest came, and then there would be the long gliding run down the back of the wave with the next one beginning to show ahead. They came like that, in big rolling swells, for the first hour until the wind came up out of the northeast. He had steered all the way. Vega was seasick below in the cabin. All the time Camilo kept repeating to himself what Amato had explained to him and David years ago after they had been caught in a bad squall east of Havana. "It's best not to be afraid of the sea," he'd said. "You must be respectful, but not be afraid." Camilo had heard Amato's voice in his mind: "Heavy seas run with the wind—you've got to face it. Keep a cool head. That's the way to get through. Face it."

Now he looked ahead at the whole length of the small island and saw the dark shapes of the casuarina trees like horsetails blowing in the wind and the wink of lights here and there on the bigger island, and he felt a lifting of his spirits.

He heard Vega come up onto the flying bridge. The wind was not so strong in the lee of the island. Vega stood in his jacket with the collar up and his hair blowing and looked at the shoreline.

"Is that Bimini?" Camilo asked him. "Or the south island?"

"That's the south island," Vega told him. "Bimini is the one you see on the other side. You want to go into the harbor?"

"I want to put in where I can walk to the airstrip."

"Go around there," Vega said. "There's a channel inside. You'll come to a small dock. The airstrip is about a mile walk down the road."

"Is there anyone in the customs shack at night?"

"No. The shack is closed at night. No problem to get inside."

He went very slowly into the harbor from the lee side, seeing Bimini's waterfront with the coconut palms and the wooden houses. The houses were all dark. The whole village seemed asleep.

Camilo glanced at the luminous dial of his wristwatch. They were early. It was twenty minutes after three. It would give him plenty of time.

Five minutes later, he eased the boat up to the dock at South Bimini and cut the engines. Vega stepped off onto the pier with the bowline in his hands and tied it to the metal cleat. Camilo came down from the bridge and tossed him the stern line. In the quiet after he had shut down the engines, Camilo could hear the hiss of the wind through the trees and the washing of the little waves against the coral. There was no other sound except for their own footsteps. He went into the cabin and picked up an aluminum suitcase and the khaki-painted entrenching tool. The metal felt cold in his hand.

When he climbed off the boat onto the pier he felt the swaying sensation of being at sea in his head, his feet solid on the dock. Vega came walking toward him.

"There's no one around the warehouse," he told him. "The road goes off there, see? You come right out at the airstrip. It's about a mile. You want me to come with you and help with the stuff?"

"No, stay with the boat. I want to know it's secure. You have a pistol?"

"Yes."

"No one is to come up this road, clear?"

He started walking in the dark. The road was unpaved and narrow going through the brush, which was higher than his head. It was a warm, sultry night, and he was damp with sweat when he came out at the end of the road and saw the open ground of the landing strip. The shack was to the left. It looked as though the runway went all the way to the edge of the water.

Carrying the weight of the metal suitcase, Camilo walked out onto the runway. There were no other buildings that he could see, but he felt exposed and vulnerable, walking on the sandy coral. There were sea gulls on the field, and they rose in a whispering panic. Looking now at the two small planes he walked past in the dark, feeling the cool breeze of the morning, he had an uneasy feeling that someone would challenge him out of the darkness. But nothing happened. When he reached the end of the runway, he stopped and opened the suitcase. From inside he took two tele-explosive mines, which were metal discs that felt heavy for their size. He carried them to a point about thirty yards from where the runway ended. It was a short strip bulldozed out of the brush. He gauged it at eight hundred feet. The twin-engine plane would need most of it to get off, he thought. He placed the mines carefully on the ground. They had been obtained from Algeria, he knew, and he felt uneasy with them. He looked at his watch. A few minutes before four o'clock. He had to hurry. The planes were due to land in half an hour. According to the schedule Kern had given him, the Beechcraft would load its passengers and depart precisely at 4:35 A.M.

He dug into the packed coral, sweating heavily as he worked. It would have been better, he thought, to have brought a pick. The surface was like cement. The tip of the shovel clanked into the coral. But bit by bit he was getting it. He felt the sting of a blister forming at the base of his right thumb. He ignored it. It popped and began to sting sharply as he finished the first hole.

He did not know whom he would kill, nor how many, only that what he would do was necessary. He had known Fidel a long time and he loved him. He loved the revolution they had made and he would give his life for it, gladly. The termination of life is not an evil, he thought. It is inevitable. We don't kill to eat, but to survive in other ways. It is better to believe in something and kill for it than to have nothing. A man without something he believes in leads a wasted life. We think it is proper that we live and die by what our minds project. What are we if we are not the expression of a thought?

There will probably be others like me afterwards, he thought. The way these things are going, there could be many like me.

You don't understand Fidel, he said to someone in his mind who didn't understand. Probably because you aren't Cuban. You don't feel manhood the way we feel it. Whatever they teach you at Harvard or wherever it is they teach you, it is different from what we learn.

If you understood, you wouldn't send these assassins you're sending to Havana. Don't you see, sooner or later, he will have to send more like me, to do things like what I am going to do today, just so he can go on calling himself a man. He'll have to do it. Just to say, *Coño, hombre,* two can play this game, eh? You scare me, I'll scare you! That's how the game is, huh? I am not going to sit here and take it while you have all the fun. Let me show you how it feels. Let me have some fun, huh? It's easy to be the one who sends the assassin. How do you like it when someone takes a shot at you, huh?

Yes, he thought, there will be others like me.

He finished the second hole and again looked at the watch which he had carefully slipped from his wrist and placed in the pocket of his windbreaker before he started digging. Eleven minutes after four. He looked up at the luminous morning sky. A few stars still glittered to the west. Far out on the eastern horizon he saw dark squall clouds over the sea. The wind had fallen off.

Kneeling, he eased the first mine into the hole, which he had dug six inches into the runway. He set the arming device. Then, using his hands, he scooped the freshly dug dirt over it and patted it down hard with the shovel. He repeated the procedure with the second mine. Then he stood, wiped the sweat from his face with his sleeve and looked around. The sea had turned a waxen gray, slick and calm, reflecting the sky. The brush around the field formed a tendriled wall. The planes would approach from the north, circle and land, then turn at the far end by the shack. They would take off again almost immediately, lifting off about ten yards from where he'd planted the two mines.

He was ready.

Walking back to the shack, the shovel in his left hand, he tried to picture in his mind the blast and the plane suddenly cartwheeling in the air and plunging into the shallow water beyond the end of the runway.

It would be a spectacular sight, he thought. I wonder if he believes in what he's doing, or whether they paid him for it. Probably both. You never get anything that is clean and uncomplicated in this kind of affair. It's the system, he thought. Everything operates on the basis of greed in the world. It was the one thing you could trust in people, their greed. The basic. Ellis Kern had betrayed MR/CASTLE because of his greed. MR/CASTLE would kill Fidel because of his greed. This was the universal law. Cuba was fighting for its life now because of the industrialists and their greed. It all boiled down to money in one way or the other. The lack of it, the need for it, the necessity for more of it.

Camilo felt clean. Like a priest. Or like the way a priest should feel all his life, if he lived austerely and without corruption. He saw himself in his own mind as a clean, untarnished sword, with a single purpose to his life, to destroy the enemies of his country.

Camilo looked up at the empty sky at the end of the runway, then turned and went into the shack, closed the door and locked it. From inside, he had a good view of the field through the window. He took the transistor out of the suitcase and placed it on the table, checked it, then sat back and waited. It was 4:26 A.M.

"Is that Bimini?" Valerie asked, pointing her finger from the rear seat. "I didn't know there were two islands."

Through the windscreen she could see the dark shapes of two small islands in the expanse of open sea. A few lights glinted from the northern island. To the east the sky was aglow with morning light. It brightened the rippled surface of the water. On the horizon she saw the clouds of a squall line taking shape out of the darkness. One cloud mass seemed to cover another. The air in which they were flying was turbulent, and the small Cessna Skylane kept staggering and taking sudden up-and-down plunges that made her heart stop. She had always been tense in small planes.

"Will the flight to Havana be this rough?" she asked.

In the co-pilot's seat, Sal Amato turned. The lines of his face broke into a smile. "Make you nervous?"

"Extremely," she told him. "But I'm too excited to worry about it." She had to raise her voice to be heard over the mechanical chatter of the engine. "Are we going to be late?"

Al Baker, who was piloting the plane, glanced back over his shoulder. "We're right on time."

She laughed nervously. "We may be on time, but I think my stomach's going to be an hour late."

488

The plane bumped and dropped suddenly, the wings staggering. Valerie let out an involuntary gasp. "Must you do that?"

Amato said, "Tighten your seat belt. It'll be rough until we land."

"It's as tight as it'll go."

He reached back and gave the web belt a tug. Valerie felt it tighten hard against her waist.

"I think you just bruised a kidney," she said. "You'll be sorry if I wet my pants."

"I thought you big-time reporters were supposed to be cool."

"It isn't every day I get to fly off to Havana to interview Fidel Castro, you know."

Al Baker was talking into the mike and leaning forward to scan the sky through the windscreen. She heard a static-covered voice come out of the speaker. Valerie did not understand what the radio voice had said, but Amato turned to look at Al Baker.

"Tell him we'll go in first."

Baker nodded and Valerie could see his lips moving as he spoke into the mike, but she could not hear his words against the sound of the engine. Amato caught her eye and smiled. The port wing of the little Cessna tilted downward as they started to circle the island. Amato pointed off to the right. Following his gesture, she saw a tiny red blinking light in the sky off to the northeast.

"Is that our plane?"

"Yeah."

"What time do we get to Havana?"

"About seven."

"But aren't we supposed to see Fidel for breakfast at seven-thirty?"

"For him it'll be dinner. He's been up all night."

"Will we be late?"

"Maybe a few minutes. He's never on time, anyway."

"What if he doesn't come?"

"Don't worry, he'll be there."

She gave him her broad smile. "You know something, Sal Amato? I'm crazy in love with you."

Amato did not answer. He was looking out the window as they circled back, the starboard wing dipping so that they were almost perpendicular to the ocean below. Valerie glanced out. She saw the two wooded islands in the vast shiny expanse of the sea below. In the harbor she saw a dozen sailboats and three white yachts. The roofs of the houses showed through the palm trees. There was a large white house on a wooded ridge, then a line of roofs on either side of a narrow road that ran along the edge of the harbor. It looked very tropical with the coconut palms above the roofs. The south island looked flat, with a dirt airstrip bull-dozed through the brush. She saw a narrow channel and a dock and the tin roof of a warehouse. There was a white boat at the end of the dock. Amato stared at it. His jaw tightened. She saw the turning of his head as they passed over, the narrowing of his eyes, the look of tension in his face. The earth was sliding rapidly beneath them. She heard the pitch of the engines change, slowing, and felt the sudden slack in speed. The wings wavered. Looking past Amato's head through the windscreen, she saw the dirt airstrip ahead, the brushy landscape rushing up at them and then passing behind.

"Will we come back this way?" she shouted at Amato. He turned his head. "Are we going to come back from Havana this way?"

At first she did not think he had heard her, and she started to repeat the question, but the expression in his eyes froze the words in her throat. Just then, she felt the bump as the wheels touched down.

Through the window, Camilo saw the two sets of landing lights in the air to his right. The Cessna was landing first. He watched it glide onto the runway and settle with a smooth flowing motion. The prop of the little blue plane revved at the end of the runway, and it came taxiing back toward the shack. He saw two heads through the windscreen as the plane went by. He wished he could see MR/CASTLE's face, but his face was blocked by a woman. There was a woman in the passenger seat in the back. She looked out the window as the plane moved out of sight behind the line of trees.

Could it really be a woman? he asked himself. Would they send a woman?

Then Camilo looked up to see the twin-engine Beechcraft in the sky. He watched the landing lights come on, brilliant gems of light on the wings of the plane, coming fast now; the size of a sea gull, a sea gull with bright landing lights, he thought and smiled. The Beechcraft was just off the end of the runway, the landing gear dangling like a bird's legs beneath the fuselage, and he watched it coming in, touching down with a puff of coral dust, sliding very fast toward him, a gleaming silver bird that came sweeping up to the end of the runway as gracefully and smoothly as anything he'd ever seen.

The Cessna pulled out of sight to the right of the shack, so he couldn't see it from his angle at the window. He watched the Beechcraft move past out of sight, too. Camilo waited, feeling his own tension. He inhaled and let out his breath. He was ready. He watched the second hand ticking. Ten. Fifteen. Twenty. Twenty-five. Thirty. They would be get-

490

ting into the Beechcraft now, he thought. He could see them, vague figures, in his mind. He pictured how they would be getting off the small plane carrying their luggage. Maybe that was wrong and they had no bags. But he saw them with the luggage in their hands, bending their heads slightly against the prop blast, getting in the silver plane now, ducking their heads into the door. Two minutes had passed. He frowned. Out of the window he could see the line of gray-green trees, the bare coral field. What was taking so long? he wondered.

Just then he saw a little dust haze blow up through the trees and the blue nose of the single-prop plane emerged from behind the windblown branches. Camilo watched it taxi to the far end of the runway, turn, rev its engine, the little fuselage trembling, dust blowing. Then he saw it start to move, slowly at first, then faster and faster, rising in the air. He watched the blinking running lights as they grew smaller in the sky.

Turning his gaze, he saw the Beechcraft reappear, barely moving, trembling, then edging forward slowly. The shriek of the engines drowned out everything. The landing lights flashed into the room as it turned. Camilo kept his eyes fastened on the plane. It taxied to the end of the runway and turned, the props blurring. It was gaining speed now rapidly, hurtling toward him. His finger felt the switch on the transistor. Wait. Wait. Wait.

He flicked the switch.

In the yellow flash and white roar of smoke he saw the little plane stagger, the nose bouncing into the air, pieces of the wings and tail fluttering off like cards in the wind. He saw the whole plane dive forward out of the dust and smoke and, cartwheeling wildly, hit the water with a WHOMP!, exploding in a luminous flash of yellow flame.

He opened the door and looked out at it. There was oil burning brightly on the surface of the water for more than a mile. Bits and pieces of things were floating on the surface. At the end of the runway, he could see the gap in the wall of brush where the wreckage had plowed into the water. What was left of it, out of sight from here, was sending up a column of black oily smoke. The air smelled of burning rubber.

CHAPTER FIFTY

*F*idel Castro was awake in the early-morning hours Saturday when word was flashed from Oriente that a flotilla of small ships had been spotted in the vicinity of Baracoa. The news came as no surprise. Castro had been expecting the invasion fleet for some time now. He had taken to sleeping through the afternoons and staying awake all night, moving to a different place every night for security reasons. And now the critical moment was finally at hand. Castro rose and went immediately to his headquarters at Camp Libertad, just outside Havana. It was time to set his plans in action.

Castro had been thinking for a long time about the strategy of the invaders. As D-Day approached, he had become more and more convinced the brigade would divide itself into small attack forces and strike at many different points. The aim would be to spread the defenders thin and also to panic the Cuban population into thinking that the so-called liberators were actually a vast army. There was also the question of honor, Castro reasoned. "The invaders would not be so foolish as to concentrate their attack," he told his aides, because of the "discredit to which they would be exposed in case of defeat—discredit to the United States and to the counterrevolution."

Acting on this premise, Castro selected what he considered to be the most probable landing sites and established posts manned by from one hundred to five hundred men at each site. He concentrated especially on access zones to the mountains, such as Trinidad. When the invasion came, he reasoned, the troops might try to head for the Escambray mountains.

Castro was also convinced that the invasion would be preceded by an air strike. Anticipating this move, he took his obsolete aircraft that were out of service for mechanical reasons and clustered them in groups of threes in the most obvious sections of his major airfields at Managua, San Antonio de los Baños, Santiago de Cuba and Ciudad Libertad, which adjoined Camp Columbia, the main base for his Air Force. He carefully dispersed and camouflaged his best planes—the operative B-26s, Sea Furies and T-33s—and concentrated his antiaircraft batteries to protect them.

Arriving at his headquarters, Castro moved quickly into action. Orders began to crackle. All troops were immediately placed on alert. Instructions were issued to *the militia to begin mass roundups of everyone suspected of underground connections. Theaters and auditoriums had been set aside to receive the suspects. On intelligence information his G-2 had received, he alerted two battalions and sent them immediately to southern Oriente, one taking up positions near Baracoa, the other digging in near Playitas. He supported them with antitank and mortar batteries.*

Castro next ordered a T-33 jet into the air to circle the area where the flotilla was sighted and report on the direction of the invasion fleet. Castro was meeting with aides only a few minutes later when he was notified that the jet had gone down in flames two or three miles off the coast. Castro had just issued the order to dispatch helicopters to search for the T-33 when the skies began to thunder with the sound of low-flying aircraft. The brigade's B-26s came in low, dropping their bombs onto the nearby airfield.

Castro seemed utterly calm as he turned to his aides. "The aggression has begun," he said simply.

That same morning, Raúl Masetti was awakened a little after six o'clock by the pounding of antiaircraft guns. He went to the balcony and looked south over Havana. The sky was clear. Then he saw the sudden puffs of antiaircraft shells exploding. They appeared gray-white in the clear blue sky above the tile roofs of the houses. He saw the faint spark-like tracers floating upward, and then he saw the two bombers, tiny and silver in the light. He watched them veer off and dive to attack, and then he saw the luminous flash of the explosion and felt the thump a moment later. It looked from here as though they were attacking Ciudad Libertad.

Raúl watched the planes with a sinking feeling in his stomach. He knew it had started. There had been rumors in the early morning that Fidel had alerted the militia. For days now there had been no radio contact with Carta's station in Florida. What had gone wrong?

An hour later Victorio and Ortega came to his door. They were both excited and worried. He led them into the kitchen, where he started his own breakfast. He poured coffee. He fried two eggs while the two of them sat there looking glumly into their coffee cups.

"I don't like it, Raúl," said Ortega. "There's something wrong."

"Your instinct is correct, my friend," said Masetti. "There is a great deal wrong. We have been betrayed by our friends in the CIA. We do not risk our people until we hear from Gustavo."

"But what could have happened to Gustavo? Why haven't we heard from him?"

"I don't know."

493

David went to the laboratory that morning. All that could be done for Robin at Mercy Hospital had been done. Two psychiatrists had seen her and they had called in a third. David did not want to be there. He did not want to listen to what they had to say after they'd talked to her. He had answered their questions in a flat voice, telling it as though it had happened to someone else. Then he went out. It was a hot spring morning. He took the causeway to Virginia Key and turned into the main gate. It was locked. The security shack was empty. Using his key he opened the gate, drove through, then closed and locked it behind him. He parked in the space reserved for him behind the lab building and went in to his desk. The lab was empty.

At his desk, David spent the morning cataloging his notes. At ten o'clock the telephone on his desk rang. He let it ring. He was afraid it might be Elizabeth, and he didn't want to talk to her about Camilo—he didn't know what to tell her. At 4 P.M. he finally called the hospital to reach Dr. Lewin.

"I've just had a long talk with my colleagues," Dr. Lewin said. "We think we should send Robin to Connecticut tomorrow. There's a small, very special clinic there where she can get the best treatment available. She's in a bad way, David. Very. She feels you and your family are responsible for the trauma she's suffered. She's quite distraught. She needs care and rest and therapy."

"I'd like to see her before she leaves."

"Of course." Dr. Lewin's voice sounded strained at the other end of the line. "Why don't you come by the hospital in the morning."

After he had hung up the telephone, David sat at his desk, staring blankly at the wall. He'd left it that Dr. Lewin would charter a plane to fly Robin to Hartford tomorrow afternoon. Dr. Lewin would accompany her. It was deemed inadvisable that David accompany them on the flight. The psychiatrist had repeated several times on the phone the phrase "She's obsessed with the fear that someone might find out what happened. She doesn't want anyone to know."

He tried to return to his work. He wrote in his notebook, ". . . at the tip of the anemone's tentacle is a trigger hair. When a fish (or diver) touches it, the stinging cells, or nematocysts, are actuated . . ." An hour later he found himself staring at the wall.

She picked up the telephone and dialed David's number. As she listened to it ringing, she realized that she had not heard from him for days now. Nor Robin. There was no answer. She puzzled about it for a moment. It was Saturday. Surely, they were home. She let the phone ring for a minute longer, hoping that they were outside and would come into the house to answer. It was urgent she reach David. Had they gone somewhere?

She would have to reach him today. That was the only thing left to do.

A loud knock at the door broke into her thoughts. Ramiro, the major domo, opened the door, his eyes bright with excitement. "Señora, have you heard the news?"

"What?"

"It has started. They bombed Havana this morning."

Elizabeth went downstairs and found the household staff gathered in the kitchen watching the black-and-white television screen. A news announcer was broadcasting details of the raids. Cuban airfields had been bombed. In Havana, Castro had declared an emergency. He had ordered the militia mobilized.

Orlando, the cook, turned his grave face to Elizabeth as she entered. "It's started, Señora," he said. "God help us all."

BOOK VI

CHAPTER FIFTY-ONE

Playa Girón, Cuba, April 17,1961

First thing, Navarro saw the beaches ablaze with light. The CIA advisers had said the beach at Girón was deserted, nothing there but unfinished tourist housing. The light filled Navarro with foreboding. Standing next to him was the Norwegian captain. The captain wore a black eye patch like a pirate and had bristling gray hair. When he first saw him Navarro thought it was a joke. Then the captain told him no one had explained the mission until they'd reached Nicaragua. He had assumed it was just another load of bananas. In Managua they had given him the choice of jail or signing on for the invasion, so he'd agreed to sign on. Staring at the lights on the beach, however, he demanded to know what the hell was going on. Navarro ignored him. He was watching the frogmen move off in their rubber boats toward shore.

Forty-five minutes later, he saw the first landing light flashing on the beach from beside a concrete pier. He did not know yet that the frogmen had found, instead of a smooth approach to the beach, a series of sharp coral reefs and jagged rocks blocking the approach. The Norwegian captain stood beside him on the bridge. "What's that?" he demanded. He pointed down the beach. Navarro saw the headlights of a jeep moving fast from the village of Girón, half a mile away. The jeep stopped and turned its headlights out toward the sea. Then he heard the crackle of small-arms fire. The frogmen had opened up with their automatic rifles. Another set of headlights was approaching, very fast. It was a truck carrying militia. The gunfire increased. He saw tracers flashing through the dark. And just then the lights went out along the beach. They stared into blackness. Gunfire sparked. Red-and-orange tracers flashed out toward them. Something whacked through the funnel overhead.

"Jesus Christ, what are they doing?" the Norwegian demanded in his thick accent. "They aren't firing real bullets at us?"

"What the hell do you think they're firing—Chicklets?" cried Navarro.

With a growing apprehension, Navarro realized the seriousness of the situation. The invasion force had been detected. His men had to disembark at once. The first eight fiber-glass boats were hoisted over the side. The rusted winches screeched so piercingly the sound echoed for miles across the water. The men started loading into the boats from three stations, aft to bow. The boats hit the water. Navarro waited tensely for the sounds of their engines. Nothing. Now he heard curses in Spanish. He strained to hear what was wrong. The outboard motors wouldn't start. None of the damned things! Loaded with troops, the eight boats floated aimlessly, their pilots desperately pulling at the lanyards, trying to get the motors running. They puttered to life, choked and died. One or two managed to get started. They headed in for the beach. The others continued to drift alongside the rusted hull of the cargo ship, the sounds of *brrrr-uuppp-pthhh! brrrr-uuuuuup-pthhh! brrrr-uppp-pthhh!* mingled with Spanish curses.

Navarro climbed down the rope ladder into the boat with Pepe. "What a hell of a mess," Pepe said to him. Something bumped against the side of their boat. When they looked up they saw a boatload of troops alongside, the figures like dark statues. "What the hell's the matter in that boat?" Pepe shouted.

"The fucking propeller dropped off the minute we got in the water," came the reply.

Pepe turned to Navarro. "Shit," he said.

Getting to shore in the small boats was a nightmare. When the lights at Girón had gone out, throwing the beach into darkness, the men knew the enemy was there waiting for them. Crowded into the little fourteen-foot boats, their faces painted black, their spotted camouflage uniforms soaked from the waves, they rode toward the beach with their eyes fastened on the shadowy buildings of the unfinished tourist center. All around them boats were striking the reefs and sinking. Men were floundering in the water. Voices shouted for help. Navarro heard the pilot say in a tense voice, "This is the place, get out . . ." The first man over the side splashed and sank over his head. Hands reached out and grabbed him, pulling him heavily back aboard. There was an angry exchange between Navarro and the pilot, who was afraid to go closer. "Go," said Navarro, pulling his .45 automatic, "or your career as a hero ends right now." Ten yards farther, they hit a reef and the boat started to sink.

The water was up to their shoulders. They waded ashore, carrying their weapons. Four men struggled with the 4.2 mortar which weighed more than six hundred pounds. What unnerved him the most was the silence. The half-finished buildings loomed in the moonless night. Soaked to the skin, he led his people across the beach toward the line of dark trees along the road behind the buildings. As he came up to the last building, he stopped short. There, like a mechanical tree against the stars, he saw the radio antenna of a microwave station. Even before he burst in the door, gun in hand, and felt the radio with his fingers, the metal hot to his touch, he knew it was all over now. The plan had been based on the inability of the Castro people to communicate with large concentrations of troops outside the beachhead.

Pepe came in the door behind him. "Well," he said, "are your ears burning? I think they're talking about us in Havana."

Fidel Castro had been expecting the invasion that morning. His excellent intelligence network throughout Latin America and the United States had kept him well informed. He had known the moment the brigade of rebels had moved out of their base in Guatemala. He had known when they were loaded in the old Liberty ships at Puerto Cabezas in Nicaragua. He was aware that landing craft carrying tanks and heavy equipment had departed from the U.S. naval base at Vieques Island in Puerto Rico to rendezvous with the five principal invasion ships. He knew that there were fifteen hundred men aboard the ships and that they were well trained and heavily armed. But he did not know what orders had been given to the U.S. naval task force maneuvering off his shores, complete with an aircraft carrier, the Essex, *and U.S. Marines. It was his major worry.*

He was sipping his morning coffee when the telephone call came confirming that the invaders were ashore at three points near the village of Girón. They were being engaged by militia composed mostly of peasants—charcoal makers who had been greatly benefited by the revolution. They were putting up stiff resistance.

501

"The site," he would say later, "was well chosen." It was, but for Castro's coun-terattack.

The Bay of Pigs cuts eighteen miles into the Cuban west coast from the Carib-bean, and is surrounded by the Ciénaga de Zapata, known as the "Great Swamp of the Caribbean." Three good paved highways had recently been built dissecting the swamp. The invaders, Castro was told now, had dropped some 175 paratroop-ers to control these three roads to the beachhead.

But he saw that the paratroopers had not been dropped far enough from the beach to effectively cut off the roads. His problem was simply to isolate the invasion site with overwhelming force and crush it in repeated and unrelenting attacks. He moved quickly to accomplish it. An understrength battalion training at the Australia sugar mill a few miles north of Girón was ordered into action. Another battalion moved in from nearby Cienfuegos. He ordered other militia units from neighboring Matanzas province in to attack positions near the beaches. In Ha-vana, artillery and tanks were loaded onto flatbed trucks and sent roaring off down the highway toward the battle.

Castro knew that the beachhead could be expanded only if he could be prevented from pouring in reinforcements from his 250,000-man army. The Cuban under-ground, which could have accomplished this with sabotage and uprisings, was strangely silent. Throughout the island, his secret police and militia moved quickly to prevent any support of the invaders. Some 100,000 suspects were arrested and imprisoned. Most were later to be released, but several known underground lead-ers were executed. Without local support, the invaders were doomed and Castro knew it. There was nothing to prevent his massive counterstroke.

CHAPTER FIFTY-TWO

MIAMI, APRIL 17, 1961

Her telephone started ringing early. Excitement was at a fever pitch. Friends she had not heard from in years, since the days in Havana, were on the line. Most were gleeful. One woman told her breathlessly that ten thousand prisoners on the Isle of Pines had been freed by the brigade landing force and were being armed to join the fighting. Her husband was among the prisoners there, and her tearful joy deeply moved Eliza-beth. Among the callers were the wives of several men under Gustavo's command in the Everglades. Their voices barely masked their alarm.

502

They had not heard from their husbands. No word whatsoever. Were they in the invasion force? Were they on the beaches? Where was Gustavo? Elizabeth tried to reassure them. She was sure they were safe. She would try to find answers for them. Yet her attempts to reach Tipton by phone had been futile. There was no answer at the camp. No answer at his apartment in North Miami.

Now one station was reporting that Castro's Navy had mutinied and joined the liberating army. The report said the mutiny had been fomented by the Cuban underground and touched off with the code word "Bounty."

Landings were reported near Cienfuegos, in Pinar del Río province, and at Baracoa in Oriente. Later news bulletins said forces were striking within ninety miles of Havana itself. Heavy fighting was reported on the Isle of Pines. As the day wore on, the bulletins poured in. The city of Santiago de Cuba, second largest on the island, was reported to have fallen. The Matanzas radio had been captured by invading forces and was broadcasting messages urging the Cuban people to rise against Castro's dictatorship. One news source claimed that more than fifty thousand troops were ashore and engaged in the fighting.

She placed a dozen calls to friends, only to be told by servants that the women had gone to church, "to pray for their sons and husbands . . ." One local news broadcast said that all Catholic churches in Miami were jammed with women praying for the men in the invasion.

It all seemed too fantastic to be true. As she listened to the radio, with Elena by her side, she heard that Raúl Castro had been captured by invading forces near Santiago, which had fallen to the liberating army earlier in the morning. Fidel Castro, the report had it, was seen in Havana, heading with his secretary and a few trusted ministers for Camp Libertad, where a four-engined plane was standing by to fly them to Moscow.

"Is that my Fidel Castro?" Elena asked. "My friend?"

"Is he your friend, darling?"

"He's nice," she said. "Papa says that he's a great man." She giggled. "He always kisses me when he sees me. His beard tickles, just like Papa's."

Later, Elizabeth received a disturbing call from Laureano, a Cuban exile leader who had formed an alliance with her husband. "Where the hell did they get all those men, Elizabeth?" he asked. "It looks like we're not even needed. Half the underground organizations in Miami are sitting around waiting to be called to fight."

"What does the CIA say?"

"They tell us to stand by, be alert, be ready—but nothing happens.

Maybe we're to be part of the occupation force. Who knows? Is Gustavo there?"

"No, he's out of town."

"Ah, he too, eh? My God, I feel like a racehorse who's been training for two years to race and they won't let me out of the stall! If you hear from Gustavo, please call me, eh?"

By noon there had still been no call from Danforth. She phoned his house in Georgetown. Eden was excited about the invasion news. "Oh, Liz, just think, we might be visiting you in Havana this summer! Aren't you excited?"

"Terribly. Is Charles home?"

"No, I think he's in his office at the White House."

But when she called the White House, she was informed by Danforth's secretary that he was not taking any calls. She would see he got Elizabeth's message. "I'm sure he'll call you as soon as possible, Mrs. Carta."

But he had not called.

A growing sense that something was wrong began to nag at Elizabeth. Why didn't Charles return her calls? Was he avoiding her? Why would he be? Before he left for Guatemala, Gustavo had told her that Pelham had given him the invasion date as the twenty-first of April. At first she had assumed it was simply a contrived cover to disguise the real invasion. But what if it wasn't? What if they had purposefully set out to deceive Gustavo? But Charles wouldn't let them do it, she thought. He wouldn't. But what if they had?

Oh, dear God, she thought. Where's Gustavo? What's happening to him?

She wished she could see him, hold him, talk to him.

Walking through the library, she went out into the bright sun on the pool patio. It glinted on the water. Elena was seated on the edge at the shallow end. When she saw Elizabeth, she dived in with a splash. Elizabeth took off her robe and sat on one of the lounge chairs, feeling the warmth of the sun on her skin. There was a breeze that kept the sun from being unbearable. Shading her eyes, she looked across the yard at the turquoise water of the bay beyond the boat dock. There were two sails on the water and a white sports fishing boat anchored about a half mile away. She saw two men in the stern, tiny at this distance, and one of them seemed to be rigging a fishing line. Then she saw Gutiérrez walking along the sea wall, looking out at the boat. He stopped and put his hands on his hips. One of the men in camouflage fatigues, a carbine slung over his shoulder, came up to Gutiérrez and stood talking with him as they watched the boat. They must have thought it was in rather close. They had become very wary since the shooting last week. She saw one of the men on the boat disappear into the cabin. The other man sat down in the fishing chair and had his line in the water. It was nothing, she thought. Just fishermen.

"Watch me, Elizabeth!" Elena called to her. "I'll swim the whole length of the pool."

She watched Elena swim for an hour. She went in the water herself once, swam two laps and then got out and dried in the sun. As they started back into the house, she glanced out at the bay. The white boat was still there.

For three nights David stayed in the house on Northwest Seventh Street. His friend Angus had given him the key when he left for Peru. It was a small house with a screen porch. He knew that Angus had rented it because two big Australian pines grew in the front yard. The needles were all over the ground. David had slept on a single bed in the back bedroom. The nights were turning warm, and he kept the windows open. All during Saturday night he had heard a baby crying in the next house. Every now and then the mother would scream at it. Once he heard her beating the child. Her voice sounded drunk. It made him sick to listen to it.

On Sunday he decided to move back to the house in Coconut Grove. He had gone to the house on Saturday morning to pick up the mail and change clothes, but walking through the rooms, seeing her things, had made him too lonely. He wasn't ready to face being there. He found himself frantically changing his clothes and hurrying out without even looking around. When he got into the Volkswagen and drove off, he could not remember in detail what he had done. He only felt the vague panic the house invoked, as though it were haunted. He had been glad to get away.

But after Saturday night at Angus' he decided he had to go home. He did not feel comfortable staying in someone else's place, and he could not bear to think about that drunken woman beating her baby. At ten o'clock Sunday morning he drove directly to Mercy Hospital and spent ten minutes with Robin. Then he drove down Bayshore to the house and parked in back.

Coming back into the house made him keenly aware of how much had changed in so little time. It was just as he had left it. As soon as he came in the door, he smelled the formaldehyde and remembered he'd broken the specimen bottle reaching for the telephone. The bottle had contained a tiny sea horse he had brought home from the lab intending to give it to Elena. He saw it in the broken glass on the floor by the desk. It looked like a small dried root.

505

He decided the best thing to do was to keep busy. So he set to work cleaning the house. He swept up the glass. His manuscript had blown off the desk and was scattered over the floor. He spent an hour picking up the pages and putting them back in order, with his notes. He secured the pages with a rubber band and put the manuscript back in the drawer. He washed the sinkful of dishes, dried them and put them away. He took off his shoes, got out the metal bucket and mopped the floors. While the floors were drying, the smell of wet wood permeating the air, he cleaned the refrigerator. He poured out the curdled milk. He washed down the inside and defrosted the freezer compartment. He cleaned the ashes out of the fireplace and carried the garbage out to the cans in back. Then he waxed the floors, sloshing the milky fluid around with the wet mop. While the floors dried, he went upstairs to the bedroom and found the clean sheets and pillowcases in the hall closet and made the bed.

When he had finished he felt a sense of satisfaction. The house was clean, neat and in order. He could not remember it being like this. He felt happy knowing everything was in place.

Twilight was always a difficult time for David. It was the cocktail hour. The time for a drink and friends and talk, and when he was alone at that hour, as now, he felt particularly lonely. He went back out to the screen porch and sat on the cot and watched the darkness grow in the trees along the drive, occasionally looking out at the yacht harbor and the bay. He smoked one cigaret after another, trying to keep from thinking about things. He wondered what Angus and the others were doing now off Peru. All the reports that were coming back indicated the project had been an enormous success. David keenly regretted not being a part of it. He disliked the position he was in. He did not like to picture their sun-browned faces, their laughter at the little stories they would tell on each other, their prideful detailing of their achievements. He would be the outsider.

It was dark when he went back into the bedroom and turned on the lamp beside the bed. He pictured Robin as he had last seen her in the hospital room, the gray dress, her copper hair in a ponytail, her pale face, her green eyes looking at him, defiant and hurt. He could not keep away from it. He started to think about her, and all of it came back and suddenly he started to cry.

After a while, he felt better. He decided to go downstairs and make a drink and get a fresh pack of cigarets. He went barefoot out into the hall and down the stairway. His bare feet squeaked as he walked on the newly waxed floor. When he turned on the light in the kitchen and started to open the refrigerator, he saw something over near the sink on the linoleum floor. It was a black scorpion. He gauged it at about three inches long. It had been crawling around in the wet wax, and the wax had dried. It was stiff as a potato chip. Smiling to himself, he reached down and picked it up. He saw it was still alive. The tip of the stinger kept pulsing up and down harmlessly. The wax gave its body a sinister shine.

"I'm glad I didn't step on you," he said. He carried the scorpion to the fireplace. He knew the old house was full of them. You couldn't keep them out. Their sting was not much worse than a hornet's, but still he did not like them much. He took one of the newspapers from where he had stacked them neatly on the hearth, rolled it up, and struck a match. He tossed the flaming paper onto the scorpion and went back to the kitchen and made himself a drink.

When he came back into the living room the paper had burned out. He saw the sparks in the fireplace. He sat down in the easy chair and looped his leg over the arm and took a drink of cold gin. It made him shudder. He probably should put some ice in it, he thought. He felt it burning in his stomach. He took another sip. It tasted smoother. He closed his eyes and sat holding the cold glass and took a deep breath.

He felt as if an enormous pressure had been lifted from his shoulders. His life, which had once been so orderly and routinized, had been torn asunder these past few months. Perhaps he would now be left alone to pick up the pieces.

He was aware now that his life was over, or rather the life he'd had here in Miami these last six years. He'd known it since this morning. She had been standing before a large mirror doing something with her hair. David had paused a moment, watching her. The sunlight lay in a long shaft on the shiny floor from the window, and she had stepped into it, moving close to the mirror, the strands of her copper hair glowing as she brushed it. She wore a sheath dress of gray linen and white high-heeled shoes, and her face seemed to David to be a little hard, brittle, as though the agonizing experiences of the last few days had burned away her childlike quality and thrust her suddenly into middle age. At last she turned toward him. There was something wrong with her eyes.

"You look tired," he said.

"I am tired," she said. Her eyes flashed a look at him. Then she went to the window and stood there looking out, her arms folded across her breasts. David waited. He felt in his pocket for the envelope that had come to the house in the Saturday morning mail. It contained a gasoline credit card that had been issued to Robin last May and a letter from the captain of the Highway Patrol, telling them that the card had been found on the body of a Michael Kevin Danielson, killed in a motorcycle accident the twelfth of April. He had not spoken to her about it on the phone and he did not relish the thought of telling her the news now. He did not know how Michael had gotten the credit card. Maybe she gave it to him. Maybe he stole it from her purse. He didn't know.

What he did know was about the poems. One was a crib from Dylan Thomas, one was paraphrased from Kathleen Raine, and the third had been originally written as a war poem by Keith Douglas. It was damning evidence. This Michael had been a phony. She had to see that. He felt it was necessary for her to face reality now. When the proper moment came, he would reveal all this to her.

"What are you thinking about, David?" she said, without turning to look at him. "Are you wondering about us?"

"As a matter of fact, yes, I am."

He saw her shoulders shake, as though she were crying, and he took a step toward her before he realized she was chuckling silently to herself. She did not turn her head. He waited, looking at the long copper hair falling down the back of the gray dress.

"Why are you laughing?" he said with a tone of amusement in his voice he had not intended, a nervous, anxious amusement. "What's funny?"

"I was coming back to you before all this happened." She looked at him over her shoulder and then turned away again. "I was leaving someone quite dear to me and coming back to you."

"Who is he?"

"A boy I met at school." She sighed and blinked her eyes at him. "His name is Michael Danielson. He's a very nice, very sensitive boy."

David remained silent, looking at her green eyes. She seemed to have no idea of how he was feeling, nor any concern. Her face looked thinner, drawn. The changes in her, the unfamiliar hospital room, the distance between them, made all that he had once felt for her seem unreal.

"I slept with him," she said, her voice firm, crisp.

David felt a morbid curiosity to hear her out, learn all the details. It was ridiculous! He saw himself ludicrously trying to act out some romantic ideal of himself. In his mind he saw all those years of pain and loneliness—trying to overcome his limp, his ruined eyesight, to become something physically he was not, something he had no need to be. And he'd gone on crippling himself to conform to an image he was not, trying to live in someone else's world, not his own, to satisfy Robin's idea of him, as he had tried to do with his mother. His blood rebelled. He felt the collapse of distorted images and illusions, and it was a relief. His mind grasped the truth of himself and he suddenly felt sealed off from her, closed on the subject of her. Robin? He didn't possess her. He never

508

had. Never could. How could he regret losing something he had never had? He was gaining himself. In that moment, he was no longer afraid of being alone. He looked forward to it.

"Well?" she said, her green eyes strangely bright, transparent, expressionless. "I did. And I loved it."

"Are you in love with him now?"

"I'm not sure. I'm only certain I'm not through seeing him."

"I see."

"Is that all you're going to say, David?"

That was all he had to say. He was out. He refused to take the bait, because he wasn't hungry for it any longer. It was over. He couldn't live in her world, yet what good would come of disillusioning her, destroying what she had and needed to have?

"What can I say?" he told her finally. "Maybe what I want is to tell you that I'm sorry."

"Sorry?" She smiled wanly. Her eyes stared at something on the floor. "Yes, so am I, David. Truly sorry. I never really wanted to hurt you." She looked up at him, her eyes intense and bright, that strange detached expression behind them, as though part of her was gone, too. "You know I'm leaving you."

"Rob, were we ever together?"

She stared at him. He'd left it at that. He'd turned away from her and walked out of the hospital room. She did not try to stop him.

He made himself another drink and came back into the living room and sat in the chair in the dark. He felt sorry about what had happened. What do you suppose she's going to do when she finds out the poor guy's dead? he thought.

He got up from the chair and went barefoot in the dark to the kitchen. I hope I don't step on your brother, he said to the scorpion he had burned in the fireplace. He opened the refrigerator, taking pleasure in seeing it clean, empty, with only the bottles of beer on the lower shelf. He took the gin bottle out of the freezer and carried it back to the comfortable chair and sat down with it in his lap. In the dark, the bottle felt like a lump of ice in his hand. He unscrewed the cap and drank it straight. It's cold, he thought. You don't need ice.

CHAPTER FIFTY-THREE

*P*resident Kennedy was angry. The pile of telegrams did not make pleasant reading. The one that particularly nettled him was signed simply "Harvard Graduate Students." It contained only eight words: "Nixon or Kennedy: Does it make any difference?" Another telegram was signed by a long list of influential liberals. The President, it said, was driving Castro into the arms of the Russians. The Bay of Pigs was barbarism.

It was a sudden drumfire of opposition. That previous night there had been protest meetings at a dozen Eastern universities. Three thousand protesters attended a Fair Play for Cuba Rally in New York City.

It was time to consolidate national leadership behind the invasion. Otherwise his entire Administration would be threatened. It was time for unity.

He began his phone calls. The list of leaders was familiar: Eisenhower, Rockefeller, Goldwater, Nixon. They were supportive, all reassuring. Only one of them offered specific advice. That was Nixon. "Find a proper legal cover," Nixon told him. "Then just go in!"

★

Once he had been a public-relations man for Wendell Willkie. He was elderly now, specializing mainly in proxy fights and corporate publicity. He had a benign presence.

When the CIA hired Lem Jones, they told him he would be public-relations consultant for a new organization called the Cuban Revolutionary Council. They didn't tell him about the war.

Now the men were on the beaches in Cuba, and the official dispatches about the battle were emanating, in the name of the Council, from Lem Jones's office at 280 Madison Avenue, New York City. The press was astonished. A CBS reporter buttonholed Jones after receiving the first bulletin. Why was a specialist in proxy fights issuing war communiqués? Jones looked at him blandly. The situation was analogous to corporate warfare, he replied. It was just another case of "insurgent elements going against entrenched management."

His bulletins were lengthy and often flowery. The first one stated:

> Before dawn today, Cuban patriots in the cities and in the hills began the battle to liberate our homeland from the despotic rule of Fidel Castro. In their unquenchable thirst for liberty, the Cuban people today seized arms to obliterate a vicious alien oppressor, fired by the vision of inevitable victory and convinced that the freedom-loving peoples of the hemisphere will make common cause with them. . . .

The press received the communiqués and dutifully reported them. Several reporters asked for direct interviews with the members of the Revolutionary Council.

Lem Jones said that would be impossible to arrange. His "clients," he said, were too busy running the war to answer questions.

His "clients," he knew, had in truth been at the Hotel Lexington in Manhattan until the previous afternoon, when they were taken by chartered airplane to the Opa-Locka airstrip outside Miami. There they were locked away in an old naval barracks. They had a radio to listen to, but no telephone. They were hermetically sealed off from the outside world.

★

He saw it very high up in the late afternoon sky, a faint, fast-moving silvery speck diving on one of their B-26s. It was drawing closer and closer to the old twin-engine bomber, and there was the faintest trail of smoke from its guns as it seemed to shimmer in the air. Then came the burst of yellow flame from the bomber and the blast, like a thump in his eardrums. The B-26 burned brightly all the way down, trailing black smoke. He thought it looked like a leaf falling. It made a white splash far out to sea. Ernesto Sosa felt sorry for the pilot, and, standing shoulder to shoulder with the others on the deck of the *Houston,* he solemnly crossed himself. He was twenty-four and had been a student of journalism at Columbia University in New York when he joined the brigade. He was anxious to get to the fighting and nervous about it, too. For some reason there had been a delay in getting them ashore. They had to stand there on deck with their weapons and their packs watching the sudden puffs of white-and-gray smoke appear in the carpet of trees and mangroves beyond the beach. They could hear the crack and the echoing bang of the explosions a moment after the smoke appeared. He could see several small boats shuttling back and forth to the beach, and he wondered why they didn't come and take them off.

Just then two Sea Fury fighter planes with their gull wings came roaring toward them, low over the water. Someone yelled and pointed. It happened so fast he couldn't believe it. One instant he saw the blue-painted fighter plane, the blur of the prop, the Plexiglas cockpit; the next, he heard a loud WHANG! of something hitting the hull and felt the shudder on the deck under his feet. Someone yelled they'd been hit. He'd seen them load the ammunition below. He was sure they'd blow up.

There was a big oil slick on the surface of the water. They watched it spread, then begin to trail out behind the stern. They were moving in to shore. Someone said that a rocket from the Castro plane had gone clean through the hull and they were sinking.

Ten minutes later they were aground. Ernesto could see the trees on the shore, about three hundred yards away. They all started over the side. Men were stripping off their camouflage fatigues and jumping. He saw a dozen rifles go over the side at once and splash in the oily water. Then a bunch of them jumped right behind. Ernesto stepped over the rail and dived. It was a long drop and it took his breath away, falling. He hit the water, went under and came up in the middle of a half-dozen men. They were panicky, thrashing their arms and yelling. He started swimming toward shore. There were more than a hundred of them in the water now. Once he looked back and saw the planes coming again, so he went underwater. When he thought his lungs would burst, he kicked his way to the surface. There was a man of forty not three feet away, with a rotund face and flabby arms. His skin was white in the sun. He was screaming in terror. Ernesto saw a thrashing around the man in the water. Then he saw the blood and in it the slick gray back of the shark.

Ernesto was one of the first to crawl up onto solid ground. He flopped under a tree and watched it all happen out there on the water as though he were watching some terrible game from a good seat. It was the worst thing he'd ever seen. The men were splashing around in the water, and the foam turned from white to pink with blood. After a while a jeep and a small truck came by. A tall officer with a sweating black face yelled at him. He got into the back of the truck. Someone handed him a rifle and a heavy bandolier of ammunition. He was still wearing his wet camouflage fatigues. There were five others from his group in the truck. They already looked dispirited and beaten. He asked the man who had given him the rifle where they were going. He just shrugged his shoulders. "They've already kicked the shit out of us. It doesn't matter where you go to die. One place is as good as another." Ernesto sat hunched up, wet and miserable in the bouncing truck, thinking that it was after one o'clock. In New York his friends were just now going back to class after lunch. He wondered if it was raining there.

CHAPTER FIFTY-FOUR

MIAMI, APRIL 17, 1961

That night Elizabeth took Elena into the master bedroom to sleep with her. She did not want to be alone. With her, Elizabeth put forth all

512

the strength of her love and it seemed to relieve, at least momentarily, the intensity of her anxiety. There had sprung up between them a tender and loving friendship. When Elena was out of the room, Elizabeth felt uneasy and hurried off to find her. They were continually exchanging their impressions. They would wash each other's hair and then spend hours brushing and setting it, chattering constantly together. Elena was an extremely affectionate child, and she would often break off her conversation to hug and kiss Elizabeth and say tender things to her.

When Elizabeth came out of the dressing room in her nightgown, her hair down, Elena was perched in the center of the big bed on her knees. She was delighted to be allowed to sleep with her grandmother and her dark eyes were bright. She clasped Elizabeth's neck in her arms and kissed her, then looked into her eyes quizzically. "Was my mother as nice as you, Elizabeth?"

"Your mother was as loving as anyone I've ever known."

"But was she like you?"

"We had things in common, why?"

"Was she as pretty?"

"Much prettier, I'm afraid."

"Did she look like my Aunt Pepita?"

"Mmm, not really. Alicia was quite different from her sister, darling. She was much better-looking, for one thing. And much more energetic. Your mother was the kind of woman who walked into a room full of people and everyone felt her presence. Oh, Elena, she was such a beauty and such a wonderful person."

"Do you think she would have liked me, Elizabeth?"

Elizabeth laughed and hugged Elena to her. "She would have adored you, my darling."

They were awake long after Elena's normal bedtime hour, both too keyed up to sleep. They listened to the radio to get the late-night news reports on the invasion. The newscaster's voice bore an edge of urgency, confirming the fall of Santiago and the general collapse of Castro's government in the face of the successful assault. It seemed unbelievable to Elizabeth. In one day, could it all have changed? Her heart quickened thinking that by the time they awoke in the morning it could all be over. What if—farfetched as it might seem—they could go back to Havana by this weekend? She tried to picture in her mind what their home looked like at this very instant, in the dark of night, deserted, the garden overgrown and unpruned. She wondered if the pool would be filled with leaves. Probably. As far as she knew, no one was living in the house. Amato had stopped once three months ago to look over it. He'd said

513

that a caretaker was staying on the property, but no one was living in the house. There would be so much work when she got back. But it thrilled her to imagine the moment she would walk in the front door again and see it.

"Wouldn't it be wonderful, darling?" she said to Elena.

"Can I live with you, like before?"

"Most certainly you can."

"I'd like that."

After she turned off the radio, Elizabeth told Elena stories about the family, about her parents and grandparents in South Carolina, anecdotes of her own childhood, how she had met Gustavo, how Alicia had been shy and frightened when Camilo first brought her to their home and what great friends they had become, how excited Alicia had been when she learned she was pregnant with Elena—weaving the fabric of their family life for her granddaughter, knowing how it would become indelible in the child's memory. Elena sat in wide-eyed fascination, interrupting with questions, giggling, squirming, laughing, clapping her little hands in delight.

It was nearly midnight when Elena finally grew sleepy and yawned. She curled up next to Elizabeth and closed her eyes. "Good night, Elizabeth," she said, yawning. "I love you."

"I love you, too, darling," Elizabeth said, turning out the lamp. For a long time she lay awake and listened to the ticking of the clock on the nightstand. The room was cast in an eerie glow from the floodlights in the yard.

She did not want to sleep. But the excitement of the day, the anxiety she'd felt so keenly at the news from Cuba, had drained her energy and left her exhausted. She yawned. Her eyes felt heavy.

Now she saw the dark forest. She saw a dirt path going off through the trees. The grass at the edge of the forest was green in the sun. She knew it was spring from the color of the grass and the slant of the sunlight. She saw Camilo and David walking ahead of her on the path. They were laughing and skipping as they went under the trees. The leaves and limbs over the path made a dark tunnel. Look, Mother, Camilo said to her, there's a hawk. She looked up and saw it overhead, circling, wings spread wide. She watched it turn in the wind and fold its wings against its body and plunge rapidly downward to disappear into the trees. Let's find it! Camilo shouted. They disappeared ahead of her into the gloomy light under the trees. It frightened her. She started walking faster along the path, but she could not see the boys. A little sunlight filtered through the thick foliage overhead and made tiny patterns of light on the sandy path. She could hear them ahead, shouting back and forth to each other, their voices ringing in the woods, but she could not seem to catch up to them. Wait for me, boys! she shouted. Wait!

All the time she kept walking with that sense of fear growing in her. The wind had come up suddenly. She heard it blowing in the tops of the trees. It made a rushing sound like the sea. Then she saw the leaves starting to fall. They had changed suddenly from green to gold. They came fluttering down in the streaks of sunlight all around her like coins. The wind blew stronger. The sound of it was an angry whistling now. The limbs of the trees swayed, and it made it seem the earth was moving. Now she saw David poised ahead of her. His face was pale and he looked frightened. Why are all the leaves falling so early, Mother? What's happening? I don't understand. She reached for him and asked, Where's your brother? Oh, he's gone after the hawk. In the sunlight the leaves glittered and blew in the wind. That is strange, she thought. Why are the leaves falling so early? It frightened her to watch it. The wind grew stronger and the leaves blew across the path, rushing past them. She felt compelled to stop them. But when she moved they only blew faster and faster, and then all the trees were bare, the branches like frantic black arms against the blue sky, and the whole forest was flooded with blinding sunlight. The path looked naked and white in the sun.

A voice that sounded close in the room called to her, "Where's Camilo?"

She woke, sure that someone had spoken to her.

CHAPTER FIFTY-FIVE

The bombardment was tearing up the road. Pepín crouched with his face against the dirt and felt the jolt and the lifting sensation when the shells hit. His ears were ringing. In the dark he could hear the *zzzz-bang!* of the incoming rounds and then feel the earth shake. The air smelled thickly of cordite. Pieces of tree limbs kept clipping off and falling on him. Then, suddenly, it lifted. Someone yelled, "Here they come again!" He eased his head up and looked down the road. He saw the lights of the trucks, and in the lights he could see the silhouettes of men. They were walking down the raised road right at them. The headlights made them perfect targets. He got his rifle up to his shoulder. He found the tip of the sight through the peephole and put it on one of the men he saw walking in front of the headlights. The rifle banged hard against his shoulder as it fired. People were shooting all around him now. He saw the column of militia melting away. The headlights shattered and went out. A truck caught fire and burned fiercely, lighting up the whole area. There was mangrove swamp on either side of the road. They couldn't come any other way. Pepín kept firing and reloading clips and firing until the barrel of his rifle smoldered. It was too hot to touch. Pretty soon he heard a tank coming, and then he saw it in the glare of the burning truck. It looked huge, prehistoric, with the great snout of a cannon jutting out of the turret. It was a Russian tank, all right. He'd seen pictures of it. Someone fired a recoilless rifle. He saw the flash and heard the *whoosh!* as the rocket went out. The Russian tank was just moving out of the firelight. He saw it stagger. Then it started to billow smoke. It stopped. The hatch opened in the turret and he saw someone start to get out. He fired at him. They were all shooting at the tank now. The crewmen came out one at a time, and they shot them all. Pepín was out of ammunition. So were the men on both his flanks. "What are we going to do?" he shouted. A man stood and made a sweeping gesture with his arm. "Fall back! Fall back!"

It went like that all through the night. They would take up positions farther back down the road. The truck would drive up and unload the ammunition cases. Then the Castro militia would appear on the road, walking right into their fire. He saw them falling on either side of the road. Two trucks vanished in flashes of green smoke. He saw a line of royal palms burning and men running out from them with their clothes on fire. The noise of the firing was ear-shattering. But they just kept coming, wave after wave. Before morning, Pepín retreated eight times, regrouped with the men of his platoon, and dug in. Each time they kept running out of ammunition and grenades.

At daylight, the attacks stopped. There was an eerie silence as the light changed and he began to see trees and the mangroves with their twisted roots in the water and the tops all freshly clipped off from the firing. Occasionally he could hear a wounded man crying somewhere out in the swamp. He was so thirsty he couldn't swallow. But there was neither food nor water and damn little ammunition now. The men around him were exhausted. Pepín could not keep his eyes open. He thought if he could just close them for a minute he'd be all right. When he closed his eyes everything went in circles. He pictured in his mind the comfort of his little room in the Carta house back in Miami. He saw the dresser and the red bullfight poster he'd hung on the wall and he wished with all his heart he was back there now. He wondered if Alfaro had gotten to Señor Carta in time. They had left early that morning and he'd never found out what happened. He pictured Carlota, the maid, and the way she moved in her black dress, the way her haunches swayed

516

under the cloth, the strain her breasts put on the blouse, and he tried to picture her naked, legs spread wide, lying on his bed in that little room, smiling at him. He had never touched her or expressed his feeling about her, but now he wished that he had. He wondered with anguish if he would ever see her again.

He woke with someone pulling on his sleeve. When he opened his eyes he could hardly believe what he saw. There was the paved road stretching off across the flat mangrove swamp. Trucks and broken tanks were smoldering here and there. But there were hundreds of bodies in their blue denim uniforms scattered everywhere along the road. Bodies and bits and pieces of equipment. It looked as though someone had unearthed a graveyard. And overhead, Pepín saw that the sky was filled with vultures. Thousands of them. They circled as thick as flies. He watched them plane down and land. In his life he'd never seen so many birds in one place. He sat in his foxhole watching. He'd never seen a bird eat a man before. Afterward, the lieutenant came along and told them the flanks had caved in and they had to retreat to the beach at Girón. As they walked along the road, incoming shells kept zinging overhead and exploding somewhere down near the beach. Pepín wondered if he was going to die today. Somehow he was so tired it didn't seem to matter. He just didn't like the thought of a bird eating him afterward.

CHAPTER FIFTY-SIX

MIAMI, APRIL 18, 1961

When Elizabeth drove into the yard she became excited at seeing David's Volkswagen parked by the screen porch. She got out of the Jaguar and went into the house. The screen wasn't latched.

"David? Hello?" she called, walking down the hallway past the stairs. The house smelled musty, faintly of insecticide and fresh floor wax. She stepped into the living room. She was surprised to see the shiny wood floors, the neatness of the big room, with its walls of books all in place, the desk that was normally cluttered now tidy, bare.

"Who is it?" David's voice drew her to the stairs. He was standing in his white shorts, his face puffy, sleepy-eyed, a cowlick of blond hair sticking straight up from the back of his head. "Mother . . . I was asleep."

He came thumping down the steps and embraced her. She felt the prickle of his unshaven cheek and smelled the sour tobacco and liquor on his breath.

"I was beginning to worry about you," she said. "I couldn't get you on the phone . . ."

"I'll make some coffee." He led her back into the living room. "Sit down. I'll be right with you."

He went into the kitchen. Elizabeth walked to the window and looked out at the yacht harbor. There was so much she had to tell him, but she did not know how, really. ·

"Have you heard the news—about the invasion?"

She turned to see him appear out of the kitchen alcove, the red tin of coffee in one hand, a spoon in the other, a look of astonishment on his face. "Invasion, you say?"

"It started yesterday morning . . ."

"Is Gustavo in it?"

"Forget the coffee, darling. Come sit down with me. There's a great deal I have to discuss with you."

David nodded. He turned and put the coffee can back in the kitchen.

They decided to put down at a small airstrip south of Miami. It was a nearly deserted landing site for private planes and crop dusters and they hoped to avoid Customs and Immigration officers. Alfaro brought the old twin-engine plane onto the runway smoothly, so expertly that Carta had trouble distinguishing the moment the wheels touched. They taxied to the end of the strip and climbed out. It was a hot, sunny day, with a northwest wind. No cars came out to meet them.

They crossed the road to a squat concrete-block structure that served as both a gas station and a café. When they went in the door Carta smelled frying sausage and bacon. The smell of cooking food made him feel faint. There were four small booths and a counter with the kitchen behind it. Two of the booths were occupied by workingmen. They looked at Carta and Alfaro when they entered and then went on talking. The two sat down at the counter and looked at the menus.

The cook and waitress was a woman in her fifties with dyed blond hair and puffy eyes. She came from the kitchen carrying platters of ham and eggs and sausage and eggs. It made Carta ache to look at them. He had not eaten now for three days. The woman came back wiping her hands on her dirty apron. "What'll it be, boys?"

"I'll take three eggs, fried, and ham," Carta told her.

"You want coffee?"

518

"Yes."

Alfaro ordered the same. The woman poured two mugs of coffee and placed them on the counter and then went behind the kitchen counter.

There were two pay phones outside the café. One had an "Out of Order" sign on it. Carta went to the other and picked up the receiver, praying that the second one was functioning. He put in some change and dialed their home number. Salazar answered. He seemed flustered and relieved to hear Carta's voice. *La señora* was out, he said. She would be back within the hour. Could she reach him someplace? Carta said he would call back.

He put in another coin and decided to try the Everglades number for Tipton. As he waited for a response, he pondered all he had to do, trying to work out an order of priority. It was several moments before he realized that the number had been ringing for an unusually long time without response. He was about to hang up when he heard the voice.

"Hello?" It was an unfamiliar voice, flat, Midwestern.

"Who is this?"

"Who is calling?" Carta felt his stomach tighten.

"Give me Major Tipton."

There was a pause at the other end of the line. "He is not available."

"What do you mean, 'not available'?"

There was another brief pause. "Who is calling?" The tone was sharper this time; Carta sensed that someone was instructing him what to say.

"This is Kirby Pelham from the Central Intelligence Agency," Carta lied. "Whom am I speaking with?"

Another short pause. "I am Sergeant Perry. Is there anything I can do for you, sir?"

"What's going on there, Perry? Where are the men?"

"They were moved out two days ago, sir."

Carta's mind was whirling with the possibilities now. Moved out? His troops? And who was Sergeant Perry? There was no such man in his outfit.

"Thank you very much, Sergeant," Carta said quickly, and he hung up. He then dialed Tipton's home number. In his urgency he missed a digit and had to dial over. It rang several times.

"Hello?" Carta found it reassuring to hear his husky voice.

"Tip, this Gustavo."

"Gustavo. Thank God you're all right."

"What's happening, Tip?"

519

"Where are you?"

"We're at a little airport south of Miami. What's happened at the camp?"

"They moved in on us two days ago. A detachment of about thirty U.S. Marines. Everybody's under arrest. They call it 'protective detention.'"

Carta felt himself grow cold.

"We thought they were coming with those trucks to escort us to Key West," Tipton said. They were driving in the heavy traffic north along the Dixie Highway, passing the blocks of stores with their eye-blurring mass of advertising signs that Carta had always considered a kind of mercantile madness. "We bloody welcomed the bastards, Gustavo," Tipton went on. "We were all goddamn excited about getting under way, you know?"

"Where did they take you?"

"Out the Tamiami Trail. They've got a farm out there. They've done some bloody rotten things to us, but this takes the prize. Marine guards, would you believe it? Shabby bastards. Protective custody, my blooming ass!"

He had never seen Tipton this angry.

"I got away last night. Swam the damn canal." Tipton went suddenly quiet and gave Carta an uneasy glance. "You're up to date on the rest of it, Gustavo? Not very good news, I'm afraid."

Carta nodded. "They wanted it to be their war after all. Wanted it that way from the start."

★

The attendant handed him the two towels, and he walked, feeling the tile warm under his bare feet, to the steam room. The heat made it hard to breathe. There were two Cubans seated in the corner, their sweating bodies obscured in the curtain of steam. He sat down on the hot tiles and leaned his head back, inhaling the stinging humid air. They were talking about the invasion of Cuba. One said that he'd read in the *Miami News* that the invaders had hit the beaches in four of Cuba's six provinces. "Why do you suppose they didn't hit Havana?" one of them asked. They were coming through the haze now, and they only glanced at him as they went out. He heard the short one saying, "I suppose because Fidel concentrated his forces around the city." The door swung shut behind them and he was alone.

Camilo sat waiting for the sweat to come now. It always took a while. There was always an intense feeling of pressure before his pores opened and the relief came. He looked at his muscular arms and ran his hand up over the heavy muscles of his shoulder, feeling the skin slick now, the muscles working beneath his fingers. He ran his hands down over the hairs of his now sweating legs, feeling the moisture and the faint tingle on his fingers. He felt no regret or remorse. It was as though something had been amputated. Why didn't he feel more?

He tore his mind from his thoughts and stood in the swirling steam, stretching his limbs, feeling the strength and the joy in his body. His skin glistened in the light, shiny cords of muscles rippling on his chest and shoulders as he moved. He bent over and touched his toes, feeling the pull of the muscles in the backs of his legs. He straightened, sucked the hot steamy air into his lungs and exhaled. He ran his fingers over his slick chest muscles and down his abdomen to the thatch of black hair below his navel, to his penis. He loved his body. Sweat dripped from his fingertips and he shook his hands at his sides.

He sat down again and picked up a towel and wiped his dripping face. It was Pepita that bothered him a little. Killing Pepita was a mistake. All right? So? You admit it was a mistake, it doesn't give her life back, does it? It seemed necessary to the mission. They were all his friends. He needed to make it look like they were all killed together. So it was a mistake. So?

At least he hadn't made the same mistake later, at the house. He could have fired the second shot. No, he couldn't. That 180-grain bullet traveling at 3,200 feet per second would have torn through an elephant from ass end to head. When he fell on Elena like that I couldn't shoot again. She is all there is left of me and Alicia.

He tossed the towel over his lap and leaned back, feeling the hard slick wet tiles against his head.

Now in his mind he saw her in the bedroom that night, the light slanting in from the garden, the music, the guests cheering, and she was standing beside the lamp, looking at him, in her wedding dress, her hands reaching around the back to unhook the snaps. He ached for her. He couldn't make himself remember the rest of it. It had gone with her.

He opened his eyes and stood, flipping the towel over his shoulders, around his neck. He opened the door. Across the locker room he saw the man behind the wire window. "Hey, *chico,* what time is it?"

"Ten o'clock, exactly."

"Thanks." He stepped out and shut the door to the steam room behind him and walked to the showers. He turned the faucet handle and stepped under the shock of cold water. His arms and legs steamed. He sucked in air.

When he came out of the shower Camilo felt refreshed. He scrubbed his wet hair with a towel and went to the locker where he had left his clothes. He was dressing when Vega came in. He seemed to be very excited. He sat down on the bench and talked while Camilo finished dressing.

"He arrived back at the house about twenty minutes ago," Vega told him. "But that's not all. We have a man in reservations at Eastern Air Lines. He reported that Carta made a reservation to fly to Washington. Flight Six forty-eight. It leaves at four-forty P.M."

"Washington?"

Vega nodded. "He doesn't plan to stay long. He's made return reservations on a midnight plane back to Miami."

"The rest I'll take care of myself." Camilo tried to control his excitement. "I'll be no further burden to you. When I see Maceo I shall tell him how well you and your people performed."

"Thank you. I appreciate that, Camilo."

They embraced. "*Hasta luego,*" Camilo said to him.

"In truth, Camilo. Listen, you be careful. They're still looking for you, you know?"

"I'll be careful. I don't know where the boat will be when I'm finished."

Vega shrugged and smiled. "I'll report it stolen tomorrow morning. It won't matter. Good luck."

He watched Vega walk out through the door. Camilo put on the lightweight windbreaker and closed the metal door of the locker and went to the mirror and combed his hair.

CHAPTER FIFTY-SEVEN

Enrique Navarro sat down on the edge of the trench they'd dug in the sand and put his head in his hands. The brigade's planes were gone. The lack of air support had ruined them. He had been on the radio all day begging for planes to hit this target and that target. Nothing came. Two of Castro's T-33 trainer jets armed with rockets had strafed them at will all during the day. Four times he'd seen B-26s approaching and excitedly, wildly, hoped they were his, but when he saw them slant down and start their bombing runs he knew it was hopeless. Ever since he'd seen the lights on the beach at Girón from the ship he had felt increasingly alarmed, and now he knew that the whole operation had grooved into the pattern of failure and tragedy and there was nothing to be done about it. So many things had ruined them. The unexpected and unexplained reefs had ruined them. The small boats with the engines that didn't work had ruined them. The sinking of the *Houston* and the *Río Escondido* with all their ammunition and supplies had ruined them. The fact that the other supply ships had been chased out to sea and scattered by Castro's planes, the two radios they'd been told didn't exist at the Bay of Pigs, and the rapid deployment of so many of Castro's militia into the battle area had ruined them. Having too few men ruined them. The whole Fifth Battalion with its recruits who wouldn't fight had ruined them. But what made him angriest was that the Americans, or the lack of them, had really ruined them. Even when they'd pulled back, their backs to the sea, ammunition almost gone, gasoline for the tanks almost gone, radio communications failing, medicines for the wounded gone, he still could not believe the Americans would abandon them like this. Surely the jets were on the way. Surely they'd land Marines. Surely the ships from the American task force just over the horizon would appear and begin shelling Castro's lines. But now, sitting there in the sand in the gathering dusk, he knew the jets would not come, nor would the Marines. It was over.

Behind him it looked like photographs of Dunkirk. Men were wading out into the water, hundreds of them. Small boats were loaded to gunwales with wet, hurt, defeated men escaping the beach in any way they could. He couldn't blame them for their panic. They'd been left to die on this beach. He'd sat and watched a dozen men in a small sailboat paddling with their hands frantically for nearly ten minutes, unaware they hadn't cut the anchor rope. The sounds of the fighting were less than a mile away in either direction. A young Negro militiaman who'd been taken prisoner an hour ago had just told him that Fidel was at Playa Larga, just up the road, directing the attacks. He could hear the bump and banging of the shells exploding. Occasionally a round would zip overhead and explode in the water behind him.

In his stupor, he did not see Pepe until he stood before him, his face almost faded out in the gathering darkness.

"I've just been on the radio to Dobbs in Nicaragua," Pepe said. "I've made one last urgent request for jets to cover our supply ships in the morning."

"You've talked to the supply ships?"

"Yes. They say if they get American air cover they will move in to the beach tomorrow and unload supplies. Also, they promise that our B-26s will hit Castro's positions."

"They promise?"

"To get the jets they are making a direct appeal to Washington. To President Kennedy. He's the only one who can grant our request."

The broken trees along the road behind the beach were now a dark shaggy wall against the pale sky. Navarro looked at the trees and smiled. "So, we are in the hands of God after all."

Pepín was exhausted and hungry and tired of it all, but most of all he was thirsty. He could not remember ever having been so thirsty. His unit had lost communication with the main force hours earlier. They had run out of ammunition and water. Pepín had been told by his commander to avoid being taken prisoner at all cost. "They will shoot you like a dog," he'd said. But when the unit of Castro militia surprised them, his captors didn't look that fierce.

"Shoot us if you wish, but give us water first," Pepín pleaded with them.

One of the captors looked at him blankly. "Why should we shoot you?" he said, offering his canteen. "You are just a mercenary."

Pepín and the others were told to line up. The militiamen looked at their captives with detached curiosity. They had never seen mercenaries before, they explained. One of them went from man to man, stripping the invaders of their watches, pens, wallets, wedding rings. If they were mercenaries, they should be made to pay. It was a very businesslike operation.

Pepín didn't mind giving it all away, except for the ring. He regretted losing his gold ring. He was thinking about the ring when he turned away and suddenly found himself confronting a tall blond woman. Pepín was stunned. He thought she was a mirage. The woman introduced herself in faltering Spanish. She said she was a magazine writer from France. There were several European journalists at the beachhead, she said.

"They took away my ring," Pepín told her, expecting sympathy.

"What do you expect?" she answered coldly. "You are nothing but a mercenary."

Pepín shook his head. "That is not so."

"Then why are you here?"

"I am here to fight Communists," Pepín replied.

The tall Frenchwoman stared at him in disgust. "You have been brainwashed," she snapped, and walked away.

524

CHAPTER FIFTY-EIGHT

Elizabeth held his hand as they hurried around the ticket counter and went down the long corridor toward the gate. Alfaro and Salazar walked behind them, Tipton and Gutiérrez led the way. The Miami air terminal was crowded. People walking past kept glancing at him. When they reached the gate, the other passengers had already gone on board. Three or four people were standing at the big glass window looking out at the plane. Alfaro took Carta's ticket to check him in.

"You better get aboard, Gustavo," Tipton told him. "I don't like you standing out here."

"Yes." Carta's eyes searched Elizabeth's. "I am going to have a great deal to say to Charles Danforth. Anything you wish to add?"

Her hand fluttered to touch his face, to hold him.

"I feel as though we're living in a nightmare," she said. She looked up into his face, her expression intense, grief-stricken. "We were wrong to trust them."

She wrapped him in her arms. She held him for an extended moment, not speaking. There was comfort, at last, being close to each other, an instant passing in time, refuge. She said, holding tightly to him, "I am so sorry. So terribly sorry about all of it." Her voice was quiet with remorse.

Carta kissed her quickly and turned, nodding to Tipton and Salazar, and went to the entrance. He hesitated, looking back at her, and then went off down the tunnel to the plane.

After he had settled in his seat, Carta looked out the window at the runway. He saw the silver engine cowlings on the wing and the ground crew in white uniforms moving back and forth. Glancing around, he saw he was almost alone in the first-class section. There was an affluent-looking woman in a brown dress across from him, and a thin man in a gray flannel suit reading something in the overhead light, his black briefcase open on his lap. The stewardess went by and smiled at him. He looked back out the window and watched a man in overalls get onto a small tractor with the empty baggage carts behind it and drive away. In his mind he kept thinking of Elizabeth. She had always been there in times like this in his life.

We get caught, somehow, in the middle of things, he thought. You try to do the very best you can, but there are always forces on either side pressing you, trying to crush you. You spend your entire life trying to keep them from smashing you. You're in that now. Caught in that vise they catch you in. But you always have a little hope to go on, to keep alive on. A bit of a chance. It's what keeps you going, that little bit of a chance, isn't it? When they've got you squeezed and it hurts, you always keep thinking, I'll get out of this somehow. It'll be all right, if only. If only what? A miracle? We can't trust in miracles, but sometimes you have things come along that seem like miracles or whatever one would call them, like that time the bankers in New York said, Don't worry, we'll stick with you. That was a miracle, in its way. When David wasn't killed that time in the car on the Malecón, that was a miracle, in its way. When you went to the party that afternoon with Danforth and you saw her, Elizabeth, standing in that silk dress and floppy hat, that was a miracle. So you have those things to sustain you.

Just then, he heard the whine of the prop engines starting up and felt the vibration in the seat.

CHAPTER FIFTY-NINE

WASHINGTON, D.C., APRIL 18, 1961

They shook hands stiffly. Danforth moved quickly to the liquor cabinet and poured them both a brandy. Carta could see his hand trembling as he poured. He was startled by the change in Danforth's appearance since their last meeting. His face looked puffy, his shoulders stooped with fatigue.

Despite his fatigue, Carta felt his adrenaline pumping. He was here; he was in the White House. The decisions affecting his men, his life, his country, were being made right here, in this very building.

When he'd called Danforth, he'd been apprehensive that he would not take the call or would duck the meeting. But after a long wait, Danforth had come on the line and, when he heard Carta's tone, urged him to come directly to the White House. And now he confronted him at last, man to man.

Carta seated himself, surprised that the office was not larger, more

526

elegant. In its clutter of papers and folders and books it resembled the office of a moderately successful small-town lawyer.

"How current are you?" Danforth asked, sipping the brandy.

"Current enough to know two things, Charles. First, that the war is being lost, even as we sit here. And second, that my men and I have been ruthlessly betrayed!"

Danforth seemed to wince. "Please try not to be histrionic, Gustavo. It is very late in the day—"

"Charles, the CIA in Miami has placed one hundred and eighty-two of my men in a detention camp in the Everglades. Among other things, I'm here to ask your help in securing their release."

Danforth's eyes became narrow, and he leaned back in his chair, contemplating the glass of brandy. "I see," he said quietly. "Detention, you say?"

"Under armed Marine guards. They were transported from our camp on Sunday, under arrest."

"Do you have any idea why?"

"I think we both know why, Charles. What's the point of carrying on a charade?"

"That was not the thrust of my question, Gustavo. I meant, do you know the reason?"

"In the practical sense, no. Your brigade wouldn't be where it is now if we had landed in Oriente as we planned."

"They sent another group, did you know that?"

"What? What group?" Carta asked.

"One under the command of a man named Díaz. They had a hundred and fifty guerrillas, dressed like Castro's troops. But they were frightened off. Never went ashore."

"I can't believe it. Charles, what happened?"

Danforth stared to one side a moment, as though considering a statement. "Let me be candid with you, Gustavo. The CIA told the President they did not trust you, nor your organization, either in Cuba or in Miami. They came on very strong. They said you or some of your people had betrayed their secrets to Castro. Simple as that."

"And you, Charles? Did you go along with this?"

"Of course not. But you understand, the CIA people are very difficult to refute in these matters. They are the experts, and the President believes in experts. Their opinions carry a great deal of weight in the crunch. More than I suspected."

Carta continued to look straight at Danforth's eyes. The man, who seemed like a stranger suddenly, smiled back at him ruefully, as though they shared a secret between them. "So, I am politically unreliable,"

Carta said softly. "My people, people who have trusted me, and whose trust was placed in your hands, are led to slaughter because you deem me politically unreliable."

"Not I. Surely, Gustavo, you don't think I share those views?"

"Did you know, Charles, that last Friday morning I was taken by subterfuge to a jungle prison camp in Guatemala, called Petén? I escaped Sunday night. I returned to Miami this morning."

"I didn't know, Gustavo. Truly, I didn't . . ."

"You didn't know I had been imprisoned, without a charge, and against my will? Charles, these illegal acts were committed in the name of your government!"

Danforth stared into his brandy glass. "I think you should know, Gustavo, that the Revolutionary Council is also under protective detention. The CIA has flown them to a base near Miami—Opa-Locka."

"And the communiqués from the Council I hear on the radio?"

"They're from a public-relations firm in New York."

"How could you allow all this to happen, Charles? How could you sit by, after all your promises and pledges? Do you have any idea what's been going on under your nose? Let me tell you what I found in Guatemala, Charles. Did you know that those men who were thought to be 'unreliable' were removed from the brigade and slammed into a concentration camp in the jungle where they were treated like animals?

"Did you know the CIA also set up assassination squads that would follow the brigade into the towns and villages and help establish civil government? Their specific mission was to murder any local leaders they deemed politically suspect. The squads are headed by former paid assassins for Batista, Charles. I will leave it to your imagination to decide what chance a moderate would have in the face of these hoodlums!"

Danforth's eyes, which had been averted from Carta's, now looked directly into his gaze. "What is the point of all this, my friend? What is it you want me to say or do? Nothing I could say would satisfy you. No explanation I could make." He made a gesture of appeal with his hand. "You say this whole thing was going on under our nose. Very well—if that's the way you want to put it. One can see only so much, stay on top of only so many critical situations. We're only human beings running this Administration, Gustavo. You are right—the situation clearly got away from us. This Administration has been in office eighty-eight days, I would remind you of that. None of us was ready for this sort of game."

Carta got up and walked over to Danforth, looming over him. "It's not a game, goddamn it!" His voice came rasping from his throat, a deep, wounded roar. "You can't simply sit there and write it off to experience, as if it were an examination at the university that you have failed. There are men—real flesh-and-blood men—dying now in Cuba. Something must be done!"

Danforth shook his head wearily and looked up at Carta. "What would you have me do, Gustavo?" His voice was almost pleading.

But they were interrupted by the shrill jangling of the telephone. Danforth rose wearily to answer it. Carta, standing there, felt a sudden surge of nausea. He hurried to the guest bathroom and soaked a towel in cold water. He held the towel against his face, feeling the coolness against his throbbing temples.

"Are you feeling ill, Gustavo?"

Danforth was standing at the open door. "You looked very pale . . ."

"I'll be all right. It was a sudden thing."

They walked back to the couch together, Carta still holding the wet towel.

"That was Vermillion," Danforth said. "The President has called a meeting in half an hour. I want you to wait here for me."

Carta stared at him.

"I can't guarantee anything," Danforth said. "But I'll talk to the President. I think I owe you that much."

"You think there's hope?"

"The President's a very complicated man. Anything can happen. We'll see."

CORAL GABLES, APRIL 18, 1961

"Have you checked it? Are you absolutely sure?" Pelham said into the telephone. "You realize how urgently important this is?"

He was in the Coral Gables office in the dark. He could see the light from the rooms down the hall where they were all standing around the maps and answering the ringing telephones. He had just broken out in a cold sweat as he listened to Kern's voice.

"I've checked and rechecked," Kern said. "I even sent a man over by plane this afternoon. Communications are lousy between here and Bimini. He came in ten minutes ago with confirmation. The plane was blown up as it left the runway Friday morning. It never reached Havana, Pel. It's in about thirty fathoms of water off the end of South Bimini. You can be assured of who's in that wreckage."

Pelham felt his stomach lurch.

"Have you any details?"

"Only what the constable was able to give my man. The explosion occurred about four-thirty-seven A.M. Friday. The assassin used two land mines. He'd planted them at the end of the runway."

"Camilo Carta?"

"It could have been."

As he hung up the telephone, Pelham's vision of collapse and failure seeped through his body. His hands trembled uncontrollably. The thing he had dreaded most and considered least these last few days had happened. He had failed. He had to call Vermillion in Washington and tell him. God!

He sat in the chair, staring into the darkness.

CHAPTER SIXTY

WASHINGTON, D.C., APRIL 18, 1961

About twenty men were gathered in the Situation Room as Danforth entered. He could sense immediately that it was going to be a long evening. The faces of the men were somber.

He recognized all of them. They were the top echelons of the Pentagon, the CIA and the Departments of State and Defense, and a handful of senior White House aides. Aides kept shuttling in and out with new dispatches, which were handed among the various clusters of men standing around the room. Several were assembled around a large illuminated map at the head of the conference table, rearranging the positions of various ships and aircraft.

There was something absurdly incongruous, Danforth thought, about these men, attired in their tuxedos and formal military whites, their medals flashing in the overhead lights, poring over the dispatches and exchanging worried stratagems. They had all come to the White House prepared to attend the annual Congressional Ball. Somewhere in the building, no doubt, their wives, coiffed and gowned, waited impatiently while their husbands dispensed with what had come to be known as the "Cuban mess."

Danforth seated himself next to a young aide who seemed to have the tallest stack of dispatches in front of him. "What's the latest?" he said.

"We have lots of news and it's all bad," the aide said, studying a handful of Telexes and typed summaries. "There are now about thirteen hundred men on the beaches, but many of them swam ashore without weapons or supplies. Castro has them pretty well pinned. He's deployed his artillery and tanks incredibly fast—it's almost like he knew we were coming. Best we can make out, he's trying to crush the beachhead with Russian tanks and heavy artillery. The troops are really catching it from the howitzers."

"How about supplies?"

"We have confirmation now that the *Houston* was hit by a rocket fired by one of Castro's Sea Furies. It ran aground on a sand spit two miles from the beach. The *Houston* carried most of the Brigade's ammo and other supplies. The *Marsopa*, the control ship for the landing, has also been sunk. So have eight smaller landing craft."

Danforth felt his stomach tighten. He had heard enough. He wanted to get away from the young aide with his infuriating dispatches. He swung his chair around and started across the room.

The tall, slightly stooped figure of Richard Vermillion stood before him. "Not very cheerful news, is it?" As usual his facial expression was noncommittal, his voice dry.

"It's a fiasco," Danforth said glumly.

"I'd like a word with you outside," Vermillion said. "There are a few items . . ."

He led the way to a quiet section of the corridor a few doors down. He turned to Danforth then. His face, Danforth thought, seemed flushed.

"We want to have another go at the President tonight. We've got to give it one more try."

Danforth shook his head. "He's been adamant about any sort of direct intervention. You're drilling a dry hole."

"But he can change his mind. And you can help persuade him." Vermillion gazed at Danforth intently. "The President is a realist. He can now see the results of his own timidity."

"Timidity is the wrong word," Danforth protested. "Judicious caution."

"Call it what you want," Vermillion cut in. "He originally committed to two air strikes to provide cover for the invasion. Then at the last moment he canceled the second one. The consequences are apparent."

"If the first attack failed to knock out Castro's Air Force, why should a second one have done any better? Castro was just waiting for it."

"I'm not going to argue military strategy with you. The point is that we need planes and we need fighting men. And we need them now."

"There are a lot of fighting men you chose to overlook," Danforth said, his voice heavy with sarcasm. "I'm talking about loyal Cubans—thousands of them."

Vermillion eyed him quizzically. "What are you talking about?"

"Gustavo Carta is in my outer office, Richard. He's told me some very distressing things. I think you know what I mean."

"Carta? That's impossible."

"He's there."

Vermillion's face took on a look of keen expectancy. "I think that's very interesting, Charles. You know, Carta might be of real help to us now. The President's bored with hearing all our arguments. It occurs to me he might respond rather warmly to Gustavo Carta. He's forceful, articulate. Yes, I think the President might be very affected if Gustavo Carta made a personal appeal for direct American military intervention. Don't you?"

Danforth's expression reflected a certain bewildered admiration. "You cynical bastard. You really intend to use him."

"Damn right," Vermillion said. "For his good as well as ours. Damned right."

The door opened with such suddenness that Carta was startled. Danforth's office had been totally quiet, sealed off from the frenetic noises of the corridor. Then suddenly, Danforth towered in the doorway and, behind him, a tall, gray-haired man with horn-rim glasses. Carta knew immediately he had met this man before, but his mind, struggling to assimilate the sudden intrusion, could not place where.

"Sorry to have locked you away like this," Danforth said. "Gustavo, this is Richard Vermillion. I believe you've met before."

Receiving Vermillion's hand, Carta recalled having shaken it before. It was the soft hand and the flaccid grip of a career diplomat.

"This is not a happy occasion on which to meet," Vermillion intoned.

"No, it is not," Carta said. He remained seated, while the others chose to stand.

"I can give you approximately five minutes at the outside," Vermillion said. "We can either waste our time reviewing past grievances or we can try to strike a little bargain."

"I haven't fared very well with CIA bargains," Carta said.

"I don't know about that. You're here in the White House while all of the other members of the Revolutionary Council are sitting in a sweat box at an airstrip in Opa-Locka. I'd say you seem to create your own rules as you go along."

Carta smiled wearily. "I'm sure you've been informed, Mr. Vermillion, that I had to escape from your concentration camp at Petén."

Danforth shifted his position uneasily. "Why don't you tell Dr. Carta what it is you have on your mind, Richard?"

Vermillion was studying Carta cautiously. "You are aware, I take it, of the problems we are encountering on the beaches, is that correct?" He turned quickly toward Danforth. "How much does he know?"

"He knows things are going badly," Danforth said.

"Then let me explain some things to you, Carta, that you do not know. Whatever happens at the Bay of Pigs, it is not the end, it is the beginning. We will go after Castro again and again. We will hammer the son of a bitch into the sea, do you understand me?"

Carta nodded, his face noncommittal.

"If this invasion fails, and it looks like it could very possibly fail, there will be a great deal of recrimination. Reckless things might be said. It is of mutual interest to keep all this to a minimum. Attacks on the CIA or on the leadership of the invasion will serve no useful purpose. They will only impede future assaults on Castro. And they will harm the prestige of the President—a President who is totally dedicated to the long-term war against Castro."

"Quite right," Danforth said.

"What is it you want of me?" Carta said quietly.

"Cooperation."

"In what?"

"You cooperate with me tonight, Carta, and I'll see to it that you will receive our cooperation tomorrow."

Carta looked from one to the other, struggling to suppress a rising anger. "The word 'credibility' keeps coming to mind, gentlemen," he said finally, his voice flat with bitternesss. "Your commitments in the past have not built up a backlog of credibility—"

"We're running out of time, Carta," Vermillion said. "Let me cut through this. I want you to see the President. I can arrange it. I think there's a good chance the President will be impressed by what you have to say. But I would urge you to limit your remarks to the question of intervention. For you to go beyond that issue would work against both your interests and ours."

Carta stroked his jaw thoughtfully and squinted up at Vermillion. "How long will it be?" Carta asked.

"What difference does it make? Do you have any other place to go?"

"That man might really help us," Vermillion said to Danforth as they walked down the corridor on the way back to the Situation Room. "I think it would be a bold stroke to have the President talk directly to one of the Cuban leaders. It would make him feel that he's really plugged in."

"How can you keep dangling the same lies in front of these people?" Danforth said, his voice trembling with anger.

"Your problem, Charles, is that all your assumptions are based on the notion that Castro has the situation under perfect control, that he has everything right under his thumb."

"I'd rate that as an increasingly safe assumption."

"Nothing is safe," Vermillion said. "Assumptions aren't safe. Not even Castro is safe."

"What are you trying to tell me, Richard?" Danforth's temper had subsided now. He was weary of the whole game.

"Just that there are some cards that haven't been played as yet. Stick around. It could be instructive."

Vermillion turned and opened the door of the Situation Room.

The room was empty now. Danforth glanced down the table at Vermillion, who was looking thoughtfully at the map. The President would be arriving shortly. He had been in a testy mood all day. He was clearly sick of the whole business. It had become like a nasty, lingering infection that steadfastly resisted any orthodox medication.

He looked down the table and noticed the coffee cups, the dirty plates, the discarded napkins and the overflowing ashtrays. The room looked awful and smelled foul. He reached over and pressed the intercom to the Communications Room. An aide appeared at the door.

"Can you get some people in here to clean up this mess?" Danforth barked. "It's a goddamn pigsty."

"Yes, sir," the aide said. He remained standing at the door.

"Well, what's the matter?"

"I was under firm instructions not to put through any calls, sir," the aide added timorously. "Is that order still operative?"

"No calls unless it's the President."

"There's a call, sir, for Mr. Vermillion. The party has been holding for fifteen minutes. He says it's very urgent."

Vermillion turned toward the aide. "Who is it?"

"It's from a Mr. Pelham, sir."

"I should take it," Vermillion said to Danforth, as he punched the blinking light on the console. "Pelham?"

"Richard, I'm afraid I've got some bad news."

"All right, Pelham, let's have it."

"It concerns Castle. I'm afraid he's been killed."

Vermillion glanced over at Danforth. "Is this a secure line?"

"Yes, it is. I'm at the office."

"Are you certain?"

Danforth was studying Vermillion's face. "What's the matter?" he asked.

He could see that Vermillion's mind was clicking away again, calculating the pros and cons of an uneasy decision.

"Charles Danforth is here with me," Vermillion said into the phone. "I'm going to ask him to pick up another extension. I want him to hear your report."

"Are you sure of that?" Pelham protested.

Danforth gave Vermillion a puzzled look and reached for the phone in front of him. "I'm on," he said.

"We are discussing a deep-cover agent named Castle," Vermillion said, in an official tone of voice that sounded as if he were reading something into the record. "Castle's mission was to terminate Fidel Castro."

"He never even left Bimini," Pelham said, his voice shrill. "The plane exploded upon takeoff."

Danforth's mind flashed back to Vermillion's earlier hyperbole which had left him perplexed. "Nothing is safe," Vermillion had said. "Not even Castro is safe." So this is what he was alluding to.

But then why was he being asked to eavesdrop on this call? Why was he being invited to overhear what amounted to another CIA embarrassment?

Vermillion was proceeding with his questioning. "I gather you think someone got him."

Again Danforth sensed that Vermillion was seeking to build up a record for posterity. There was something rhetorical about his question.

"It would appear Camilo Carta got him," Pelham said, his tone denoting an edge of bitterness. "As you know, Richard, Castle has been obsessed with the idea that Castro had learned of his mission. It seems he was right."

"Carta?" Vermillion's eyes flicked to Danforth, who returned his surprised gaze. "And the other cutouts? Is there still a possibility any of them will meet with success?"

"Our reports indicate that none of them made it. The security around Castro has been extraordinary. His movements have been totally unpredictable."

"I understand, Pelham. Thank you."

Vermillion hung up the phone abruptly.

Danforth was glaring at him. "I didn't want to hear any of this. This is none of my affair."

"It's a little late in the game to play the petulant virgin."

535

"That call—it's CIA mischief. It's no concern of the White House. You shouldn't have put me on the phone."

"Isn't that carrying the idea of plausible deniability a little far?"

"The President has no notion about any of this. Nor does any member of his staff. Is that clear?"

Vermillion held his hands up in mock self-defense. "Charles, you were at those meetings as well as I. You heard Jack and Bobby talking about Fidel Castro, talking blithely about his 'removal.' You were there—"

"I don't like your games," Danforth said. "I don't like any of it."

The hint of a wry smile was tracing across Vermillion's face. Danforth could not recall ever having seen him smile before.

"Very well," Vermillion said in a calm, almost bemused voice. "Have it your way. The Central Intelligence Agency undertook on its own authority, without the knowledge or tacit consent of the Executive Branch, to eliminate the chief of state of Cuba. There, now, does that put your mind to rest?"

But Danforth's thoughts were racing now. He rose from the table and paced across the room, then confronted Vermillion again.

"This whole business with Castle—this was the key to it all along, wasn't it?"

"The key? What is that supposed to mean?"

"Weeks ago, when I started sitting in on those planning meetings, I always wondered why you people seemed so smugly self-assured that this operation would succeed. I used to listen to all the generals and the CIA people lay out these grandiose plans. And I would think to myself, Wait a minute, it's full of holes, it's all built around a chain of specious assumptions. And I watched you sitting there, absolutely sure of yourself, sure you would bring it off. And now I realize that the reason you were so goddamn confident was that you were absolutely certain you could eliminate Castro. That's it, isn't it?"

"We had good reason to be confident," Vermillion said. "The plan had worked before. It had worked in other countries, other situations. It should have worked here."

"You never really believed an invasion could succeed without that, did you?"

"It was an important ingredient in the plan, let's put it that way."

Danforth was hovering over Vermillion now, a look of open contempt on his face. "I'm embarrassed to say that I once admired your intellectual credentials. I'm embarrassed."

Vermillion looked up at him. "Sorry I didn't score better on your exam, Professor Danforth," he replied, his voice heavy with sarcasm. "Perhaps I'll do better next term."

The door to the room opened, and the President walked in.

Danforth and Vermillion rose to their feet. Only four hours earlier, when Danforth had last seen him, the President had looked wan and disgruntled and had paced the room nervously. But Danforth had always marveled at the President's powers of recovery, and he marveled at them now. The President looked handsome and commanding in his formal evening wear, and his face seemed burnished from the sun. The only signs of inner tension, Danforth noticed, were a tightness about the mouth and the familiar flinty-eyed look which he assumed when angry or impatient.

The President nodded curtly in Vermillion's direction, then turned toward Danforth. "Well, Charley, I've read the reports. Anybody have any bright ideas?"

"The meeting just broke up, Mr. President," Danforth said. "The overwhelming consensus was in favor of some form of intervention."

The President's eyes darted from Danforth to Vermillion, then back to Danforth. "That's what I expected to hear," he said, his eyes narrowing even more. "And what is the specific proposal?"

"There are two steps to the proposal. The first step is to launch an air strike from the *Essex*. Our jets would initially go after Castro's jet trainers that have been giving us so much trouble."

"That's committing American pilots and American planes."

"That's right, sir."

"And the second step?"

"The second step would be to attack the tanks and artillery from the air. This could be done by the brigade's B-26s if they're still operative. More likely, it would have to be our jets from the *Essex*."

"I see."

"We have to break through the tightening ring of tanks and artillery," Vermillion put in.

Danforth looked for a reaction from the President. His facial expression remained frozen, except for a slight twitching of his jawbone.

Danforth again recalled the President's more animated performance earlier in the day when he was in the privacy of his office. He had paced back and forth then, berating himself for having allowed the chain of events to go this far. He was angry at not having replaced the director of the CIA . The man obviously had great ability, he said, but regarded himself not as a mere government official but as a "legendary figure." There was no dealing with "legendary figures," the President had complained. He should have named his brother Bobby head of the CIA at the outset and put in Byron White as Attorney General. Then he wouldn't have lost touch with the situation and found himself overtaken

537

by the nightmare choices that now confronted him. He had kicked the corner of his desk furiously. Never again, he swore. Never again.

But that was four hours earlier. Now the President had a firm grip on himself. He had gotten over the anger. Now there was simply the question of making the final decisions.

The President turned to Danforth again.

"All right, let's assume I buy this proposal. Let's assume we run all the diplomatic risks of direct intervention. Let's assume we commit American pilots and American aircraft. But to what end? A hundred-to-one chance of military victory, is that what it's all for?"

"The odds are not that much against us, Mr. President," Vermillion said. "It is not too late to turn the tide."

The President fixed Vermillion in a stern gaze. With all of his hostility toward the man, Danforth could not help admiring Vermillion at this moment. The entire grand design on which he had labored for so many months, on which he had staked his reputation, was crumbling before him. The tough, critical eyes of the President of the United States were burning into him. But he was standing up to him, unflinchingly, not running for cover as the typical bureaucrat would do. Perhaps it was fanaticism, perhaps toughness. In any case, Danforth admired the man.

"All right, suppose we don't send the jets," the President was saying now. "Suppose the battle is lost."

"That would be unthinkable, in my opinion, sir," Vermillion said. "There's the question of American prestige."

"Let's examine that. Everyone likes to talk glibly about American prestige. What do they mean? Are they talking about the shadow of power or the substance of power? I am interested only in the substance of power."

"There are political dangers in trying to draw that distinction."

"Yes, well, I'm not worried about those dangers. I'm not going to make a reckless decision just to avoid getting kicked in the can for a couple of weeks. I'm willing to get kicked around—that won't affect the main business at hand. Not in the long term."

"Let's set aside the question of prestige," Danforth said. "I think it's too late in the day to argue about abstractions. There are men dying on the beaches. We should talk about saving those men."

The President nodded. "I agree with you, Charley." He checked his watch. "They'll be waiting for me at the reception. Walk me over there, gentlemen. We can talk as we go."

The President had already turned toward the door when Vermillion moved in front of him. "If I may suggest, Mr. President, there's a man

I would like you to meet. Perhaps he could walk over with us. His name is Carta. He is vice-chairman of the Cuban Revolutionary Council."

The President looked at Danforth. "Carta? Isn't he the one we talked about, Charley?"

"That's correct, sir. He is waiting in an office down the hall."

"The Council members are in a terrible state, Mr. President," Vermillion said. "It would be an enormous help if you could at least shake hands . . ."

"Go get him," the President said.

To Carta, the events of the last few days had been acquiring an increasingly surreal quality. And now here he was, striding briskly at the side of the President of the United States through the stately corridors of the West Wing of the White House. He felt like a pawn being maneuvered across a vast chessboard, but the maneuvers had lost all semblance of sanity and reason—the game had lost its reality. He looked at what he had to do now with a certain repugnance, but to his mind it carried no disgrace and there was no loss of pride. It all boiled down to a question of being pragmatic and realistic, and he faced it now with humility.

He was aware of the kaleidoscopic images of many faces peering at them as they walked, staring out from offices and along the hallways. There was an excited hush as they drew close to each cluster of people, broken occasionally by a voice calling encouragement from the sidelines: "Good luck, Mr. President . . . We're behind you, Mr. President." He noticed Kennedy, nodding here, smiling there, acknowledging those encountered along the way, yet at the same time pressing ahead with the conversation, honing in on the arguments, summoning up his own ideas.

The President seemed taller than Carta had expected, and also more imposing—indeed, more presidential. There was a natural grace and dignity to the man, and also an aura of authority. It was not merely the authority of high office but also of high intelligence. Carta sensed the toughness of the man, but it was a Brahmin toughness.

"I am on my way to a party, as you may know, Mr. Carta," the President said as they strode along. "I am not in a party mood. This business weighs heavily."

"I sympathize with your concern, Mr. President," Carta replied. "But in all candor, what is needed now is your help, not your compassion."

Vermillion, walking at the President's side, looked over at Carta approvingly.

"My advisers all advocate direct intervention, Mr. Carta. American pilots, American jets. Mr. Vermillion here believes that is the only course. My dilemma," the President continued, "is that I have pledged that there will be no such intervention, and I have repeated that pledge on several occasions. When this whole business was brought to me, it was a choice of whether to give support to a group of Cubans who wanted to free their homeland from oppression or whether, in effect, to oppose their efforts. I didn't sign on for an American invasion, I signed on for a Cuban invasion."

"You were misled from the outset, Mr. President, and so was I."

"Time is short," Vermillion interrupted. "We should not let ourselves get caught up in side issues."

"I believe Mr. Carta is trying to tell me something. What are you trying to tell me?"

Carta glanced quickly at the President, who was staring straight ahead, his pace unabated.

"You don't believe the invasion was intended to liberate Cuba at all, do you, Mr. Carta?"

"No, I don't. I believe that the purpose of the invasion was to restore not only a dictatorship to Cuba, but to return my country to the status of a satellite of the United States."

The President nodded.

"This is my eighty-ninth day in office, Mr. Carta," the President said. "My Administration wasn't prepared for a situation like this. Nor was I. I realize that's no help to you or to your countrymen, but I have learned a great deal this week."

"Yes, but it's not too late. If on this eighty-ninth day you would only listen, there is still so much that you personally could do to save . . ."

Suddenly the President stopped walking, and Carta realized they were at the entrance to an enormous room. The doors were being opened, and from the corner of his eye Carta could see several hundred people standing around the ornately decorated room. The loud murmur of their conversation assaulted his ears. There were suddenly people all around them, and the President, Vermillion and Danforth had been pressed into a tight little knot amid the surge of bodies.

"This invasion should have been a moment of triumph," the President was saying, "and instead it's something to survive, do you know what I mean? The question of survival is important for the men on the beaches, but it is also important for my Administration."

The President turned toward Vermillion. "You want jets from the *Essex,* is that correct?"

"At the minimum, sir. Jets and troops."

The President weighed his words for a moment and then turned toward Danforth. "Charley, I will authorize a flight of six jets—they will be unmarked jets, is that clear? They can take off from the *Essex* over the Bay of Pigs one hour after dawn tomorrow. Their mission will be to cover the B-26 attack on Castro's tanks. They are not to seek air combat or ground targets. Their mission is to defend the brigade planes from air attack if the B-26s are fired upon. Are those instructions perfectly clear, Charley?"

Danforth nodded emphatically. "Perfectly clear."

And suddenly everyone was talking and moving at once.

"That is impractical, Mr. President. It is too little . . ." a stunned Vermillion started to say, amid the confusion and the crush of bodies around them. "It is insufficient . . ."

But Kennedy had suddenly vanished from where he was standing. Carta tried to see above the swarm of heads, and now he spotted him. The President was standing with his wife, Jackie, and a spotlight was on them both, and they seemed to glow amid the crowd as if radiating a magical aura of regal elegance. The President was smiling at his wife, who was draped in a sleeveless floor-length pink-and-white sheath. An enormous diamond clip in her gold-brown hair glistened in the overhead lights. And suddenly they were dancing, whirling across the floor, beaming graciously at the guests, who were now applauding.

Carta looked over at Danforth, who was watching, entranced. Vermillion stood shell-shocked, his mouth slightly ajar, his eyes clouded over.

"Did I hear him right?" Carta shouted over the din.

"You heard him right," Vermillion said, snapping back to reality. "We've been had, my friend. We've been had."

"You've got your intervention," Danforth said.

"Cut the shit," Vermillion snarled. "Six jets an hour after dawn operating with those restrictions! It's hypocrisy, that's what it is. The men will never hold out till then. The President can now tell his critics he offered intervention when he knows damned well it was too little, too late."

"This is the wrong place for this conversation, gentlemen," Danforth said, noticing two members of the press moving in among them. "Come on home with me," he said to Carta. "Stay the night."

"Good night, Charles," Carta said simply.

"What's that?"

"I'm going home," Carta siad.

He started pushing through the throng, but felt a hand on his arm. He turned to see it was Danforth's hand and Danforth was trying to tell him something, but he could not hear; the noise of the orchestra and of the applause had become deafening now, and all Carta could see was Danforth's moving lips and the look on his face—a look of sorrow and compassion. They remained standing there for a moment, and then Danforth let go of his arm and Carta started pushing through the swarming bodies, past the gowns and the tuxedos toward the door. As Carta got to the entrance to the room, the applause began to subside, and the orchestra played on.

Carta recognized the song they were playing now. The name of the song was "Mister Wonderful."

CHAPTER SIXTY-ONE

MIAMI, APRIL 18, 1961

David went to sleep early, and when he woke in the night the pillow smelled of Robin's scent. He thought it had all been a bad dream. He reached for her in the bed next to him and felt the gin bottle and then he knew he had not dreamed it. He switched on the lamp at the side of the bed and got up, feeling dizzy from the gin, and went into the bathroom and drank out of the faucet. He was dying of thirst.

Splashing water on his face, he realized he had not eaten anything and he was very hungry. He should eat, he thought. He went down the stairs, stopping at the bottom, his hand on the smooth wood of the newel post. What the hell is that? He smelled cigar smoke. The night air in the house was cool, and there was a little breeze blowing through the open windows. But he could not mistake it. Cigar smoke.

He felt a tingling down the back of his neck. He reached around the corner into the living room, feeling the wall with his fingers, trying to get the light switch.

"Don't turn on the light, Davy."

He saw the glow of the cigar. "Cam?"

"Yeah. Leave the light. I don't know if someone's watching this place."

The wave had them both now, tugging them into the current. She felt his arms around her neck. Don't, Camilo! Don't, darling! Let go! Let go! And they were under. She couldn't get her breath. The water stung sharply in her lungs, choking her. He held her tighter and tighter. She opened her eyes, and, through the translucent green of the water, she saw his face close to hers, his hair floating upward wildly, like seaweed. He was smiling!

542

The plane was crowded. Gustavo Carta entered the cabin and showed his ticket to the brunette stewardess. The passengers were crowded all the way to the back. A thick-waisted man in a three-piece black suit stood in the first-class section taking off his coat while a stewardess waited beside him with a hanger. Carta took his seat next to the window. He'd bought the *Washington Post,* but he did not want to read about the invasion. He knew that the stories were wrong. He wanted to forget it. He folded the paper and slipped it into the pocket of the seat in front of him. People were still coming aboard and moving down the aisle. He heard a baby crying somewhere in the back.

Leaning his head back against the soft cushioned seat, he closed his eyes. He saw it all very clearly and very coldly. What he did know was he had lost. It made him sick to think about it. Well, he was out of it. All obligation was gone. His anger had passed. But what had replaced it was worse, he thought. He was against them. He should have known that he had to be against them from the very beginning. He should never have left Havana. He should have gone into the mountains in Oriente with Andrés. It had all been a mistake on his part, and now they were all paying for it. Well, he'd be against them. No matter what, he would go back to Cuba. He would go back and start rebuilding again, because he was against them.

An image of Camilo flashed across his mind. He had not thought of him in some time now, yet deep within his thoughts his son was always present. I wonder if he is in the fighting, he thought. Yes, he would be. We are alike, my son and I. How I wish we had been friends, always. How I wish now I could see him and hold him the way I did when he was a little boy and tell him how much I love him. I cannot, though; even if I did see him now, could hold him, it is not permitted when they become men. I would, though, he thought. I would do it anyway. He smiled to himself. Yes, what a real pleasure that would be. I wonder what he would do. How he feels, really. He is my son and there must be, somewhere in him, that love for his father. We all have it. No matter how badly it turns out between us. It is remarkable how one's own son can keep himself so veiled—veiled from himself, from those who love him. There are so many forces at work in that boy. Let him survive all of this. Let him live. Perhaps he is fighting even now in Havana, fighting for the revolution he believes in. He can't help what he is. None of us can, really. We are our own truths.

Someone moved into the seat beside him. He did not want to talk with anyone. He looked out the window. He saw the lights on the paved ramp and two big jets parked at the gates with ground crews and machinery moving around them. He felt the person in the seat beside him shift his weight. He felt a shoulder against his arm, and he turned to look.

"Hello, Gustavo," Sal Amato said to him.

The red taillights of the taxi turned the corner and went out of sight. Valerie watched the empty street. There were parked cars in the lights. A yellow cat came out of the shadows and glided to the steps of the brownstone house opposite her apartment. She felt let down, empty, as though drained of all energy and emotion, and she was lonely. For three days she had been with him. It was their longest sustained period together since they had met, and now she missed him. It had also been the most terrifying three days of her life. As she reflected upon it, walking back to the living room to pick up the wineglasses and put them in the kitchen sink, she realized how truly close to death she had been. They had almost been killed! From the moment they landed in Bimini, until now, it had been sustained terror for her. She kept recalling how Sal had looked as he told her to remain in the little plane, how he had sprinted across to the twin-engine craft that landed behind them, shouting at the other pilots, waving his hand, and then had come back, his hair blown wildly about his head by the props, and climbed back in beside Al Baker and told them, "Get off the ground, quick. We're in trouble," and then how they had taken off, and looked back to see the sudden burst of smoke and the flaming pieces of the other plane splashing into the blue water behind them, and Sal saying, "We were lucky." But how did you know? she'd asked him afterward. And Amato had told her, "That boat belongs to a guy named Vega, a Cuban lawyer. I fished on it once." He was a reticent, secretive man, Sal Amato, and she thought now she would probably never know the whole truth of what she had experienced, probably she really didn't want to know. It was too much for her. She knew only that their trip had overtones of things she did not want to think of as reality. She did not want to live in a world which was so threatening, so violent. Amato had only told her, "The whole trip, the whole damn thing, was stupid, and I knew it. I was dumb to even start out. I'm sorry, Val. Maybe someday I'll tell you why, and make it up to you." What had he meant? Had he been using her? Perhaps, she thought. But she loved him. It didn't matter. He was the most intriguing and exciting man she had ever known. Now, as she heard the tink of the glasses against the sink, she wanted him with her. She wanted to be with him, always. If she ever saw him again, she decided, she would tell him so. She turned out the kitchen light and walked down the hall toward the empty bedroom.

544

They walked down the drive from the house and crossed the street to the yacht harbor. "The skiff's over there," Camilo said, pointing at the end of the pier. "I put the boat on the other side of the island."

The electric lights from the dock reflected on the water. David looked out at the sailboats while Camilo climbed down into the skiff and picked up the oars.

"Come on, Davy."

He stepped numbly into the unsteady skiff and sat in the bow. Camilo started rowing. Each stroke of the oars produced a trail of glowing phosphorus, like stars in the dark water. Camilo rowed smoothly, bending forward, dipping the oars with a faint splash and then straining back, the boat thrusting forward easily. Ahead David saw the trees on the small island that blocked off the harbor. Camilo swung the bow around the end of the island, and they moved out into the bay. As they came around the tip of the island he saw the boat ahead in the dark. Beyond were the lights of Key Biscayne off across the bay.

David stood and grabbed the side of the boat to keep them from bumping. He took the bowline and climbed into the stern. Camilo came behind him, swinging his body like a gymnast onto the deck.

"You want a beer, Davy? There's some on the ice in the bait box."

"Sure."

Camilo opened the bait box, and David saw the beer cans in the water. The ice had melted, but the water was cold. "Let's go inside."

It was pitch dark in the cabin. "Feel with your hand along here," Camilo's voice said to him. He saw his shadowy figure as he stepped in front of the port window and then went on into the darkness. "There's a table, see?"

David felt the edge of the table and slid into the seat. As his eyes became accustomed to the dark he saw Camilo materialize across from him. A match flared as he lit the stub of the cigar, his shaven face bright in the glow, and then he held the match to light David's cigaret. Camilo's fingers were steady holding the match. He blew it out. They sat smoking in the dark and drank the beer from the cans.

"What the hell have you been doing?" David said, his voice measured.

"Trying to stay alive."

"For a while there I thought you hadn't made it."

"Why?"

"Because of what was waiting for me when I got to that fishing camp at Sugarloaf."

"Yes. Were they all dead?"

"Don't you know?" David struggled for control.

"I heard the shooting. I was walking back along the road when I heard the shots. I'd just talked to you on the phone."

"What did you do?"

"I kept going to the camp. I ran all the way. But when I got there, I saw four or five men with guns. So I went into the water and swam across to the key on the other side. They never knew I was there. Did you really think they'd killed me?"

"You should have seen that body. It looked a lot like you."

"And Pepita?" Camilo's voice sounded strained, and David saw him shift his position. "You saw her?"

"Yes."

"*Coño,*" Camilo swore, his voice breaking. David saw his hand go up to his face. "Those bastards . . ."

"Fidel's?"

"No. One was a man named Martín. He was a police sergeant under Batista. He was out to get me before I got one of his men."

"What?"

"I was sent from Havana to kill an assassin hired by the CIA to eliminate Fidel."

"Jesus, Cam . . ."

"I got him, too."

"Jesus."

"I killed him Friday morning at Bimini." Camilo's voice sounded taut, angry. "But that's the end of it. I'm through with all that, Davy. I killed him and that's the end of my obligation."

"Obligation?"

"They wanted me to kill Father too. I let them think I was going to do it, so I could get away from Havana, but that one on Bimini finished it. I don't owe them anything now. I'm out of it."

"What are you going to do now?"

"I want to go home. I want to see my parents and my daughter."

David felt Camilo's hand touch his arm on the table. "I am sorry about what happened to you and Robin. It makes me sick to think it was all because of me. Shit, Davy, I didn't want anything bad to happen to you. You believe me?"

"You're my brother. Why the hell wouldn't I believe you?"

"I don't know. Things get mixed up sometimes."

"Not between us. All right?"

"Yes."

David leaned his back against the cushioned seat and looked around.

He felt his emotion well up. He cleared his throat. "I wonder what you get for boat stealing these days?"

"Don't worry," Camilo said, sipping his beer. "I stole it way up at Fort Lauderdale. They won't be looking for it down here." He shook his head. "With the shit that's going on we'd be smart just to keep it and head out to sea."

"Never come back . . ."

"Yes. Just keep going always."

"It's nice to think about, isn't it?"

"We could have a hell of a good time, just the two of us, bumming around, picking up girls, a little work here and there, when we needed money. No one to worry about but ourselves. Nothing to think about but fishing each day. How would you like that life, huh?"

"I'd love it, Cam."

"So would I. I don't know how it is to live without worrying."

"It'd be nice to find out."

"Wouldn't it?"

Looking at his brother in the dark, feeling how much he loved him, David felt a sharp constriction in his chest. "I am sure as hell glad to see you, Cam," he said. "I missed you."

"I missed you, Davy. All these years, I've missed the hell out of you. I made so many damn mistakes, Davy. I wish to hell I could go back and change it. Every time I think of Pepita, I get sick inside. Why did they have to do that to her? She didn't do any harm to them." Camilo's voice broke again. "They could have let her go."

"Maybe it's best not to talk about it, OK?"

"I keep trying to put her out of my mind, but I can't."

David heard Camilo move from across the table and then he felt him sit next to him and he felt the touch of his arm around his shoulder.

"Listen, *chico,* we both have remorse. We both have lost our women. But there is nothing we can do about it, you know? Nothing. It's done."

"Yeah."

"We got to get animal happy," Camilo said. "You know what I am saying? Like a dog is happy when you pet it? Just happy. We've got to, *chico,* all right?"

"Sure, all right, Cam. Plenty all right."

"We're like a couple old women," Camilo said, sniffing. "Christ what a lot of shit. . . . Davy, you know what I want? I want to go home. I want to be with you and with Mother and with my father. I want to go home, Davy. You know?"

David turned away and wiped his eyes.

"Let's go home, huh?" Camilo said.

When David looked at Camilo in the dark, he saw him wiping his own eyes with the knuckles of his fist. "Yeah, let's," David said.

CHAPTER SIXTY-TWO

Moving outside into the warm night air, Elizabeth walked to the edge of the swimming pool and felt the evening breeze off the water. She took a deep, shuddering breath to ease her tension. It was after midnight now and the events of this day had almost overwhelmed her. She walked around the pool onto the terrace and turned on the underwater lights. The water glowed green, and the flickering reflections played on the walls of the house. Across the bay, she saw car lights on the causeway to Key Biscayne. To her left, Miami Beach gave off a diffused radiance in the night sky. The sound of footsteps on the terrace made her flinch, and she looked nervously over her shoulder. It was Alfaro's familiar figure coming toward her from the library doors.

"Sorry to disturb you, señora . . ."

"What is it?"

"It is your son, señora."

Elizabeth felt a jolt of terror. "Camilo?"

Alfaro looked puzzled and shook his head. "David."

"Of course. David."

"He is on the telephone."

Elizabeth nodded, and started into the house. She picked up the extension in the living room.

"Yes, darling?"

"Mother, I know it's late. I hope I didn't wake you?"

"No, David, I'm up waiting for your father to get home from Washington. He's due any minute. Why? Is there something wrong?"

"No, nothing wrong, really. I thought I'd come over, if you don't mind. I'm going to bring a friend."

"A friend?"

"There's somebody with me who wants to see you."

"Oh, David . . ." She was trembling. She tried to find her voice, which, with the sudden realization, had deserted her. She cleared her throat.

He assumes the phone is tapped, she reasoned. How do I know it isn't? How do I know someone isn't listening? You must be very careful now.

She heard David's voice saying, "You recall our talk yesterday?"

"Yes, I do."

"Our conclusions may have been wrong, Mother."

Elizabeth stifled the sudden involuntary cry that sprang to her throat. She took a moment to control her emotions. "Are you sure, David?"

"No."

Gutiérrez hurried out of the side entrance to the Carta house and onto the street. He checked quickly around him. The street was deserted. The Carta house was dark upstairs except for the faint light in Elena's window.

He started walking quickly, his shoes clicking against the pavement.

Halfway down the street, he darted into a driveway. The Buick glinted in the dim moonlight. He unlocked it, started the engine and pulled onto the street, heading in the opposite direction from the Carta house. He drove fast, his hands tight against the wheel.

Gutiérrez pulled a piece of chewing gum from his pocket and started chewing it nervously. He checked the rear-view mirror to see if he was being followed. There was nothing there.

The Carta house had been under surveillance these past few days, and it had made him very jittery. The ordinary passerby would never notice anything unusual, but Gutiérrez was an old pro at this sort of thing. Nothing evaded his cautious eye.

He could tell that the van parked next door most of that day was not really a TV-repair truck as its sign indicated. The coveralls worn by the man who kept climbing in and out of the van were much too new and clean. The Cuban repairman himself seemed too clean-cut and held himself too straight.

And there had been too much traffic on the street in recent days—too many casual visitors driving by, too many repairmen. It was all too obvious, a foolish game. He wondered why everyone didn't dispense with all the elaborate guises and simply stand there in the street and stare, waiting for something to happen.

Something *was* going to happen; that Gutiérrez could feel. The house seemed to him like a tinder box. It was simply a question of waiting for the spark. His instincts told him it would not be a long wait.

He drove roughly a mile and then pulled the car to the curb on the corner of Tigertail Road, as he had been instructed to do. He was relieved that it was not a dark corner. A street light shone brightly. If it was to be a trap, at least he had a chance to see, a chance to react.

In the rear-view mirror he saw another car moving swiftly down the street toward him. The car, a black Cadillac, pulled quickly to the curb. Gutiérrez felt his heart pounding and reached reflexively for his revolver. A man was getting out of the back seat of the Cadillac and coming toward him. He was a big man, who wore a familiar dark-green sports jacket. Gutiérrez almost bolted out of his seat: it was Carta! He recognized the steel-rimmed glasses Carta usually wore in the evening. But now the man's face flashed through the street light and he felt a twinge of panic and confusion.

He looked over his shoulder as the man opened the back door. "Good evening, Gutiérrez," the man said as he seated himself. "When we get to the house I want you to pull the car into the driveway. I will give you further instructions as we go."

"Yes, señor," Gutiérrez said. "I understand."

And he had indeed begun to understand.

Elizabeth had put on a clean blouse and brushed her hair, tying it in a chignon in back with a tortoiseshell clip Gustavo had given her as a present when they first started dating. Her face, despite the strain, looked fresher and prettier than it had in weeks. She licked her lips and sprayed cologne behind her ears. She heard the car drive in. Her heart began beating rapidly.

Elizabeth went down the stairs, and found herself walking toward the library. She went to his desk and looked at the big leather chair behind it. The room gave her a sense of strength. There was a lingering aroma of leather and cigar smoke, and the faint smell of mildewed books. She looked at the framed photograph on his desk, the black-and-white images of David and Camilo, arm in arm, their naked chests, their frozen smiles, their eyes looking lifelessly back at her from behind the glass. She let her gaze dwell on the blurred background, the stern of the boat, the horizon line of the water. She remembered taking the picture with her camera that day, just after the two Cuban Coast Guardsmen had come aboard from their small boat and checked their papers. It all seemed so long ago.

She could sense the conflicts within her, an almost visceral force pulling at her, telling her not to do what she was about to do, not to destroy what she and Gustavo had created, had built their lives and dreams upon.

Sitting alone in the library, Elizabeth listened to the rumbling of the boat motors down at the dock, then saw the signal from Gutiérrez' flashlight. She peered into the back yard. In a few moments she saw them, two figures, standing at the edge of the dock, staring up at the house.

550

She could see the white boat in the dock lights behind them. As they started across the lawn, Elizabeth recognized their familiar movements: David with his heavy-shouldered rolling stride, and Camilo lithe and catlike.

I don't think I'm going to be very good at this, she said to herself. She put one hand in the other to keep from trembling.

She saw them stepping into the floodlight now, their figures brightening, and she saw his face, clean-shaven, gaunt and handsome. Oh, my God, Camilo!

Put your mind elsewhere! Think about Elena. How? Think about Gustavo. Think about him, god damn you! Think about him! That's it. Keep thinking about him. Think about him that night you told him you were going to have his child and he pushed you on the bed, and afterward the men singing out there in the garden. Think, god damn you, think!

Camilo saw her first and stopped. His expression, Elizabeth thought, was one of incredulity. David looked at his mother, then at Camilo. Elizabeth felt her heart beating rapidly. Despite all she knew, despite it all, the sight of him filled her with unbearable joy. How often had she enacted this moment in her mind, savoring every look and gesture, and now here they were, confronting each other—how different from the way she had imagined it would be.

Camilo moved quickly to her now, and Elizabeth felt his arms about her, felt herself pressed against him. She felt his warm skin against her face as he kissed her. Camilo released her, and it was David who was holding her, kissing her on the cheek. Elizabeth felt everything turn over inside her. Then Camilo's handsome face broke in a grin.

"It seems incredible to be here."

Elizabeth started to speak. Tears swarmed into her eyes. "I'm sorry. I'm crying stupidly because I am so happy, Cam."

She felt his arms around her again, heard his laugh and felt him lift her, and they turned around and he let her feet touch the floor again, all the time holding her tightly to him.

"Why do people have to cry when they're happy?" he said, but she heard the catch in his voice. "Oh, God, Mother, I am so happy to be home."

She looked searchingly into Camilo's face. She had remembered him as being more boyish, softer somehow. Perhaps it was the dark toughness of his skin—the coloration of one who has lived off the land. Or perhaps it was simply that a mother always remembers her son as a boy, not as a man.

"You look wonderful, Camilo," she said. She sniffed. "Please forgive me, darling. I can't seem to stop this stupid crying."

Huddled in the warmth of her sons, Elizabeth felt enraptured. It was a moment of rare bliss for her. And she seized it. In this moment of reality, she felt their touch, the warmth of their bodies, the smell of them, the rough-skinned feel of their male faces against hers, the tingle of their hair against her cheeks, the solid pressing of their bodies that sent a joyful chill down her spine. Oh, if she could just hold them like this always! But what does it matter? I've had this, she told herself. I've had this. Just for now.

Camilo beamed. "And Elena?"

"She's asleep."

Camilo glanced around the empty room. "May I go wake her, Mother? I am desperate to see my daughter."

"Of course."

As they came to the door, Camilo stopped and looked at his mother.

"You think she'll be as excited as I am?"

"Don't be nervous."

"I can't help it."

"Come on, darling."

She opened the door. The room was dark except for the night light by the bed. She saw Elena's dark hair in a tangled mass, the sheet pulled up over her shoulder, her face profiled on the pillow. Camilo hesitated beside her.

"You know how much she looks like her mother?" he whispered. "Every time I see her, it breaks my heart."

Elizabeth gave his arm a reassuring squeeze and released him. She watched Camilo move quietly to the bed, silhouetted in the dim glow of the night lamp, looking down at his daughter. He reached down and took her hand. She saw it lying limply in his fingertips. And for a brief moment, Elizabeth saw her son's face melt into a look of serenity.

Sitting in the library, realizing that he could go on drinking gin all night and it wouldn't affect him, David heard Gustavo coming down the stairs. He felt the blood rush to his face, and he involuntarily moved, standing from the leather chair. He felt something tighten in his chest. He put down the glass and walked to the entrance and looked out at the living room. He saw Carta coming across the room, wearing his familiar green jacket, looking around as though searching for something. His face, drawn from fatigue, bore an expression of almost touching gentleness. When he saw David, his features altered, shaping into a puzzled yet genuine smile of pleasure.

"David!" Carta came walking toward him. They embraced.

Moving back into the library, Carta stopped and looked at him. David saw the dark eyes focus on him. He felt a warmth pass between them, a sense of regret that they had not known each other all these years. This man had been good to him. He had been the only father he had ever known. The other, Chapman, was only an illusion, devoid of reality and all faults. Gustavo was real, and in that moment of eye contact David had a flash memory of that day at their home when Camilo had blurted out at the swimming pool that he was a bastard, and how gentle and loving this man, Gustavo, had been to him. He felt, in this instant, the same closeness he had had and lost that day so long ago. It warmed him. David lowered his eyes and nodded, unable to say anything.

Carta went to the desk. He took a case from his pocket, opened it, and carefully fitted the earpieces of the steel-rimmed glasses over his ears. He turned, looking at David over the edge of the rims. "Will you promise me something, David?"

"Yes, sir."

"I want you to promise me—" Carta began.

David saw the disbelief come into his eyes and spread to the expression on his face. He heard the footsteps behind him now and turned toward the door. There, holding Elena sleepy-eyed in his arms, was Camilo. Behind him was Elizabeth. He saw her face in a strained smile, looking from her husband to her son and back to her husband anxiously.

Camilo's eyes were fastened upon his father. Elizabeth stepped up beside him and took Elena.

Camilo glanced at her and then looked back at his father, and this time he moved. David felt the thick feeling in his chest and throat as he watched them fall into each other's arms, Camilo two inches taller than his father, their faces buried against each other, head to head, their arms locked, the lines in their faces changing shape as though they both were in great pain. But then he saw the tears in Carta's eyes. He held Camilo to him, and David saw that his lips trembled and his eyes brimmed with tears that gleamed in the light and he kept shaking his head, holding his son, who was sobbing openly now so that David could hear it and see his brother's shoulders shaking under his shirt, and he heard his gasping for breath as he cried, aloud, and David could not bear it. He looked away at his mother. She had buried her face against Elena, who was petting the back of her head and saying to her, sweetly, "Don't cry, Elizabeth, don't cry. It's all right."

David lit a cigaret in the dark, cupping his shaky hands around the match. The light flared a bright spot on his glasses. He felt a little shaky, as though he had to sit down. He looked at the pool light that cast swaying prisms onto the stucco walls of the house. Camilo had taken Elena upstairs to bed. Elizabeth had stayed with Gustavo in the library. David had walked out to the pool in the sultry night air. He sat in one of the lounge chairs and stretched out his legs.

It could be all right, he thought. Maybe it'll be all right after all.

He heard his mother's footsteps walking across the stone and then the faint creak of the pool chair as she sat beside him. He sensed that his mother, in her silence, needed to be left to the privacy of her own emotions. He too was grateful for the moment. The night air was damp and warm. He could smell jasmine from the garden. They were all together again. He had played his part, had done what was expected of him.

He looked now at the glowing stub of his cigaret, sitting beside his mother, waiting for Camilo to come downstairs from Elena's room. He stubbed the cigaret in the ashtray and glanced over at her. She was sitting back in the chaise lounge, her eyes closed.

"What's going to happen?"

"I don't know."

"It seemed to be all right, didn't it?"

"Yes."

Camilo sat at Elena's bedside in the darkened room, watching her, listening to her soft breathing, marveling at the extraordinary stillness of her sleep. It was as if a child had access to a special reservoir of inner peace. Elena could simply close her eyes and surrender to it. Camilo wondered when he had last shared that special access. He could not seem to let go and leave her.

Elena's long eyelashes fluttered momentarily. The child sleepily asked him to tell her a story in Spanish. It was a story he had told her many times, but she enjoyed its repetition. It was about how Elena had gotten lost as a small child in a department store in Mexico City. She had been with Camilo and her mother, and she had simply wandered off. After a half hour of frantic searching, they had finally found her, serenely inspecting the stuffed animals in the toy department, as if she hadn't even noticed her parents' absence.

Camilo had never understood why Elena loved hearing the story so much—perhaps because it involved her mother.

Or perhaps because it had a happy ending—her mother and her father united with her, her family at her side. As it turned out, it would be among the last times the three of them had been together. Maybe Elena sensed that as well.

Knowing the child's fondness for the story, Camilo had embroidered it over the years. The search for her through the store had become more frantic. Store clerks had been mobilized. The police had been notified. Their ultimate reunion had become more emotional. They had bought her several of the stuffed animals as a reward for not having wandered into the street.

The way it really happened, Camilo recalled, was that Alicia had panicked. She had screamed at the child in anger, had spanked her there in the store, and Elena had cried. But in the new version of the story the reunion was a blissful one, full of hugs and kisses and rewards. Elena clearly preferred the story that way. For that matter, so did Camilo.

After he finished the story, Elena asked several questions. She asked why he hadn't written her as he had promised. He told her that he had been terribly busy, that things were very difficult for him. He would do better in the future if they were ever apart.

Then she had looked at him and asked him why he was so sad. The question shocked him. He had worked so hard to construct his casual guise.

He laughed. "Sad? I'm not sad, my dearest! I'm happy to be with you again. How could I be sad? We just had someday, didn't we?"

"Yes, but . . ." She looked at him, her blue eyes edged with doubt. "Papito, I'm afraid."

"Of what?"

"I don't know. I just am. Will you stay with me tonight? Will you come and sleep with me?"

He had hugged her tightly, surprised at the way he felt. "Of course I will."

Elena said nothing for a few moments. She just looked at him, her eyes serious, assessing her father's gaze.

"Why did Mama die?"

Camilo sucked in his breath. "It was an accident. She was killed in an accident."

"Is Elizabeth going to die?"

Camilo gazed fondly at his child. "I've told you before, Elena, all things that are born in this world eventually must die. It is the law of nature, you see?"

"I don't want you to die, Papito."

"Of course you don't. But, my dearest Elena, we've talked about this before, haven't we? What were we before we were born?"

"Nothing," she repeated, by rote, her voice quiet.

"Good. And when we die, we are again . . . ?"

"Nothing."

"You see?"

"Yes. Do you love me, Papito?"

"Oh, yes, yes . . ."

"Did my mother love me?"

"She adored you, Elena."

Elena smiled. "Elizabeth loves me."

"Yes, yes."

She yawned. "When are you coming to bed, Papito?"

"Soon, my dearest, soon."

And then she simply closed her eyes. He watched her as she slept, trying to comprehend the depths from which a child, his child, could summon up her intuitions. It reminded him of the kind of sixth sense in animals when danger is about to strike—a deer's sudden frightened look an instant before the trigger is to be pulled.

He looked down at the tiny green glowing numerals on his wrist. It was almost four o'clock now. He had to leave her. He had to let her go. He had to do it, now. He leaned close to her warmth that smelled of clean linen and touched the flesh of her cheeks with his lips. She would be all that remained of them, all that was left of them both. His heart ached. He felt it. He had long thought it was gone from him forever, but now it hurt inside him. He wrenched his face from hers.

He tiptoed from the room, taking care to close the door as quietly as possible. A stillness had settled over the house; it was an almost eerie silence, Camilo thought. He walked to the top of the stairs and looked down. The living room was deserted. As he knelt his eyes searched the shadows that the lamp by the couch cast across the big room. His fingers worked quickly, stripping the tape that held the pistol fast to the shaved calf of his leg. After a moment he stood and slid the .22 automatic into his belt at his side, covering it with the windbreaker. The metal felt cold against his flesh.

Camilo felt his muscles tighten as he walked quietly down the stairs and through the living room. He was strangely taut, yet utterly calm. He looked at his hands. They were steady.

It was 4:03 A.M.

Carta looked out the library doors and saw Camilo coming down the stairs and across the living room. The room had only a single pool of light from the lamp on the table beside the couch, and he saw Camilo's figure emerge into it, suddenly seeing his face and his whole body, clearly, the tan windbreaker, the white sports shirt, the long legs in the

556

dark slacks, moving now, toward him. He looked at his son's face, handsome, olive-skinned, the light moving across his features.

Look at him! he thought, look at him! How lucky he is to be young. How beautiful he is!

The worst was when his brother screamed. It wasn't the way a woman screams, high and shrill. He had screamed like some kind of animal, an indescribable cry of outrage and pain and terrible surprise. It was the sound he'd made. David could still hear it when he shut his eyes. When he thought later about what he'd seen, he would, at certain indelible points in his memory, recall images: the quick glint of light in the panes of glass; the piercing gleam in the irises of his brother's eyes. At other moments, he would see it all distanced from him, receded into a lonely tableau, the body of Camilo splayed out on the bloody tiles at the edge of the swimming pool in the dancing prisms of light, like a figure in a pagan rite.

He'd been sitting there in the darkness beside the pool with his mother when he heard Camilo's footsteps in the living room and then saw him passing the lamp that brightened his moving figure. And then the light was behind him so that he saw him all in shadow, looming suddenly tall and angular in the open space where the doors had been.

His mother had stirred then. She swung her legs off the lounge and stood. David saw Camilo's profile as he looked across the pool at the entrance to the library. David saw the silhouette just inside the library door. As the figure moved he saw the light brighten the green jacket.

David looked quickly to Camilo.

His face suddenly pale, Camilo took a tentative step toward the library, then stood, coiled. Elizabeth was somehow at David's side, and he felt her holding her breath and suddenly realized his own heart was pounding with the expectation and now, suddenly, with the fear. And when David's eyes again caught Camilo it had all become a kaleidoscope of isolated impressions that he saw but chose not to see, and he wondered later, had he closed his eyes?

He saw the gleam of metal, that much he remembered. Camilo was holding a gun, looking at the library door. Through it came the jacket, the glint of eyeglasses, his father's solitary figure, stepping onto the patio. Camilo started to move, still holding the gun, and then he saw it spark, BANG!, ringing in his ears, and he saw Camilo's hand lurch, and when he looked to his right he saw the shadows on the wall swaying, then Camilo hesitating, putting his other hand on the gun, pointing down at the figure, who now was thrashing like an animal that had been knocked down in the ferns. And the next thing, he saw a big flash and heard the CRACK!, an echo smashing off the walls, and he saw Camilo's body jolt, fragments flying off the back of his jacket. He flopped forward on the tiles, down on his knees, and David saw that Camilo had the pistol still in both hands down between his legs, his whole body quivering. He realized Camilo was trying with

557

all his strength and will to lift the gun. Struggling with something too heavy for him, head down, he stared at it, a look of terrible concentration on his face.

David was conscious only of Elizabeth now, Elizabeth pressing upon him, holding him, conscious of the trembling of her body, conscious of her silence.

David saw the rustle from the ferns and looked to see Amato crouched there, the green jacket flapping in the glow from the pool, his eyes like flints as he looked at Camilo a few feet away. It seemed to David they were frozen there, in fear and shock, like two men underwater, under tons of pressure, trying to make their limbs function in the kind of slow motion that immense weight produces; and then he saw Camilo lifting his body, bringing his hands up, the gun glinting metallic in the light, lifting, lifting, arms outstretched.

"Camilo!" *he heard Gustavo screaming.* "Camilo!"

And then he saw Gustavo struggling at the entrance to the library, restrained by Alfaro's big arms, his eyes white and frantic. "My God, Camilo!"

"No, Gustavo! No! NO! Leave him alone!" *His mother's voice, high-pitched, shrieking.* "Leave him alone!"

Her footsteps running on the stones, and David saw her rush away from him. He started after her. He saw Gustavo break from Alfaro's grasp and now Camilo pointing the revolver at his father.

"God damn you, *get away, Gustavo!*" Amato howled.

And then David heard the ear-splitting CRACK! of Amato's big revolver, and he saw the grimace on Camilo's face; and then again the BANG! from the big revolver in Amato's hand, the flash lighting in a blink the image of Camilo falling backward, and the terrible scream, his voice resounding and echoing.

David saw the gaping mouth just an instant before Camilo toppled onto his forehead, like a Moslem at prayer, and groaned, his legs drawing up, and then the spastic kicking out.

Amato let down the revolver, kneeling at Camilo's side, holding him.

David stopped, every muscle had become paralyzed, his mother standing motionless in front of him. He saw Gustavo staring at Camilo, his mouth agape, that look of hurt and terrible surprise in his eyes.

Then David saw the frothy blood on Camilo's teeth, his lips pale. As he watched, Camilo's eyes, tightly compressed in an expression of pain, opened and he saw a sudden glint of recognition in the frantic stare, the blue irises transparent, the lids fluttering suddenly, staring fiercely at Amato and then at his father and then up at her, at his mother, his body trembling as though being wrenched from her, his eyes fastened on her, frantic: "*Mother!*"

I loved Camilo, you know that. I loved him as few women have their children. But he wasn't Camilo. He was someone Camilo had become, don't you see?

558

I remember a long time ago when we were in Oriente and Camilo came out of the woods with a hawk he'd shot. He said, "Look at his beak. See his talons? See? Even his wings are like sabers. You should have seen his eyes, Mother. When I came to where he fell, he was still alive and he looked at me fiercely like he wanted to attack me! It was his spirit I saw in his eyes! And then he was dead. And his eyes are like they are now. Where did it go? Wasn't that his spirit I saw?" And he put his fingers under the brown feathers on the chest and plucked out a fluffy white feather, which he released so that it just hung there, floating in the air. "You see, Mother, it's weightless, like a perfect machine, perfectly designed." And I remember Gustavo shaking his head when Camilo showed him. "He's a perfect predator," Gustavo said. Camilo repeated, fascinated, "A perfect predator." And Gustavo was saying, "Yes, and we are so imperfect."

Perhaps it was the genes we presented him. Gustavo and I used to talk about it facetiously. It was too exotic a mixture—the conquistador and the Southern aristocrat, the passionate Gallego and the paroxysmal Southerner, commingled, intermixed. Sometimes I felt I could actually see it all beneath the surface, behind his blue eyes.

He was perfect.

But we killed him.

You see, we had to.

There was Salazar running toward them with a blanket, covering the body, Camilo's face the color of clay. In the stench of raw blood and urine and the bitter smell of cordite, it became to David a distant tableau, remote, inaccessible, divorced from him. Small figures in the distance. Carta and Alfaro there, facing his mother. Elizabeth, her face calm, almost serene in a kind of finality, an acceptance of it all. He could see only the back of Amato's head, his wide shoulders in the green jacket, his left arm hanging at his side, the hand from which blood still dripped, closed tightly in a fist. David had a dreadful sense that they had been through all this before, had stood like this before at the end. Death was ugly. The shock of death was uglier. The instant shock of death withered him inside. David could see, through his own stupor, Salazar carefully covering the lifeless form; his brother's limp form. Camilo's mouth wide, eyes vacant, mouth gaping, as if at the moment of death he had tried to communicate some final word. The blood was sliding slowly, darkly, from under Camilo, running thickly off the tiles into the pool, spreading in dark clouds in the crystal water.

On the night of Wednesday, the nineteenth of April, 1961, a few ham radio operators in the Southern United States heard a faint voice calling out amid the static.

"This is Cuba calling," the voice said. "Where is help? Where will it come from? This is Cuba calling the free world."

The faint voice paused, then started again.

"This is Cuba calling. . . . We need help in Cuba. . . ."

Then the voice stopped.